DIANA PALMER

LENORA WORTH
LOREE LOUGH

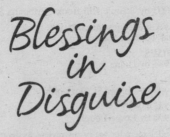

Blessings in Disguise

Steeple Hill™

Published by Steeple Hill Books™

STEEPLE HILL BOOKS

Steeple Hill™

RECYCLED PAPER

ISBN 0-373-87239-9

BLESSINGS IN DISGUISE

Copyright © 2003 by Steeple Hill Books, Fribourg, Switzerland

The publisher acknowledges the copyright holders of the individual works as follows:

BLIND PROMISES
Copyright © 1984 by Diana Palmer

LOGAN'S CHILD
Copyright © 1998 by Lenora H. Nazworth

SUDDENLY DADDY
Copyright © 1998 by Loree Lough

Visit us at www.steeplehill.com

Printed in U.S.A.

CONTENTS

DIANA PALMER

has a gift for telling heartwarming tales with charm and humor. With over forty million copies of her books in print, Diana Palmer is one of North America's most beloved authors and is considered one of the top ten romance authors in America.

Diana's hobbies and interests include gardening, archaeology, anthropology, iguanas, astronomy and music. She has been married to James Kyle for over twenty-five years, and they have one son.

BLIND PROMISES
Diana Palmer

Chapter One

Dana came to with Mrs. Pibbs standing over her, taking her pulse. For just a moment she was back in her student nurse's class six years earlier, watching Mrs. Pibbs give pointers on nursing procedure. But when she felt the stabs of pain in her head and the bruises on her slender body, she realized that she wasn't in class. She was a patient in Ashton General Hospital.

Her face felt tight when she tried to speak, and her head throbbed abominably. "Mother...?" she managed weakly.

Mrs. Pibbs sighed, laying the long, fingered young hand down on the crisp white sheet. "I'm sorry, my dear," she said gently.

Tears ran down the Nordic face, misting the soft brown eyes in their frame of tousled platinum-blond hair. She'd known before she asked the question. Her last memory was of her mother's unnatural position in the metallic tangle of the front seat. But she'd hoped...

"Your father is here," Mrs. Pibbs said.

Dana's hurt eyes flashed. "No," she said stiffly.

The older woman looked shocked. "You don't want to see Mr. Steele?"

Dana's eyes closed. After what her mother had confessed just before the wreck, she never wanted to see him again. "I don't feel up to it," she said tightly.

"You aren't critically injured, Nurse," Mrs. Pibbs reminded her in that tutor voice. "Just some bruises and a few deep lacerations; not even a broken bone. We're observing you because of a concussion and shock more than for any great injury."

"I know. Please, Mrs. Pibbs, I'm so tired," she pleaded.

The plump woman's hard face melted a little at the look. For all her facade of stone, she was a marshmallow inside. "All right," she agreed finally. "I'll tell him you aren't up to it. Shall I ask him anything?"

Dana blinked her eyes. "The funeral arrangements.... Is my Aunt Helen taking care of those, or must I...?"

"Your aunt and I spoke briefly this morning. Everything is being taken care of," came the quiet reply. "It's to be tomorrow. Your aunt will be by later to explain."

Dana nodded, closing her eyes wearily. It seemed like a nightmare. If only she could wake up!

"I'll tell Mr. Steele you're indisposed," Mrs. Pibbs added formally, and left Dana alone.

Dana turned her face to the wall. She couldn't bear even the sight of her father, the sound of his name. Poor little Mandy, poor little Mandy, who hadn't the weapons to survive all alone after twenty-five years of being provided for. It was inevitable that she'd break eventually. For the first few weeks after the divorce was final, Dana had been on the lookout for it to happen.

But it hadn't, not even when Jack Steele announced his marriage to one of the women he worked with, a blond, motherly woman whom Dana had only seen once.

Mandy had held on, working at a florist's shop, doing well, apparently happy and with everything to live for. Until Jack had been married three months. And then, last night, Mandy had called Dana, crying hysterically, and begged for a talk.

Dana had gone, as she always went when Mandy called, and found her mother drinking heavily.

"Let's go out to supper," Mandy had begged, her pale brown eyes watery with hot tears, her wrinkled face showing its age. "I can't bear being alone anymore. Let's go out to supper and talk. I thought you might want to come back home and live with me again."

Dana had been as floored by the state her mother was in as she was by the request. She didn't want to live at home again; she wanted her independence. But there had to be some kind way to tell Mandy that, and she was searching for it when they went out to the car.

"I'll drive," Mandy had insisted. "I'm fine, dear, really I am. Just a couple of martinis, you know, nothing heavy. Get in, get in."

At that point Dana should have insisted on driving, but she'd been upset by her mother's sudden request that she move back in and she'd climbed obediently into the front seat.

"It will be lovely having you home again," Mandy cooed as she drove them toward a nearby restaurant.

"But, Mother—" Dana began.

"Your father said you wouldn't, but I knew he was lying," Mandy had continued, unabashed. Tears had suddenly sprung from her eyes, and her hands on the wheel had trembled. "He said you were glad we'd divorced, so you could spend more time with him without...without having to see me at the same time. He said you hated me."

Dana remembered catching her breath and staring blankly at her mother. "I didn't!" she burst out. "I never said such a thing!"

The thin old mouth began to tremble. "He made me go along with the divorce, you know. He made me...."

"Dad?" she'd queried, shocked. It hardly sounded like him, but Mandy wouldn't lie to her, surely.

"There have been other women since we married, Dana," she'd continued hotly. "He only married me because you were on the way. And he tried to get rid of you as soon as he found out..."

Dana had been devastated. She opened her mouth to speak, but her mother wouldn't let her get a word in.

"I called you tonight because I'd decided that...that I was going to kill myself." Mandy had laughed hysterically, and her hands on the wheel had jerked; the car had accelerated. "But then I got to thinking that I needn't do that; I needn't be alone. You could come home and stay with me. You don't need to stay in that apartment alone."

"But I'm not alone, I have a roommate," Dana had tried to reason with her.

"We'll have such fun," Mandy continued wildly. She turned her head to look at Dana. "He never wanted you, but I did. You were my baby, my little girl...."

"Mama, look out!" Dana had seen the truck, but Mandy hadn't. Before she could get her fogged mind to function, the truck was on top of them. Then there was only the sound of crunching metal, splintering glass....

Dana felt hot tears run down her cheeks. She wept bitterly. Not only had she lost her mother, but now she understood why there had been arguments all the time, why her parents had been so hostile toward each other. It even explained why her father hadn't come near her since the divorce. He'd only married Mandy because he'd had to. He hadn't wanted Dana, not ever. No wonder he had always been away from home. No wonder he'd never tried to build any kind of relationship with his daughter. He'd hated her because she'd forced him to marry a woman he didn't love—had never loved.

Suddenly Mrs. Pibbs walked into the room, and Dana dabbed at the tears with a corner of the sheet.

"Your father's gone," she told the young nurse, wincing at the deep lacerations on the once spotless complexion. There would be scars, although Mrs. Pibbs had determined that she wasn't going to tell Dana about that just yet; Dana had had quite enough for one day.

Dana licked her dry lips. "Thank you, Mrs. Pibbs."

"Headache?"

She managed a wan smile. "A really murderous one. Could I have something, do you think?"

"As soon as Dr. Willis makes his rounds." She checked her wristwatch. "And that will be in a very few minutes."

Dana became aware of the discomfort in her face and felt the bandages on one cheek. She started. "My face...!"

"You should heal very well," Mrs. Pibbs said firmly.

"It was inevitable, with all that broken glass. It isn't so bad, my dear. You're alive. You're very lucky that you were wearing your seat belt."

Dana's lower lip trembled. "Mrs. Pibbs, my mother… Was it quick?"

The older woman sighed. "It was instantaneous, the ambulance attendants told us. Now, you rest. Don't dwell on it, just rest. The memory will fade, the cuts will fade. It only needs time." Her eyes were sad for a moment. "Dana, I lost my mother when I was fifteen. I remember very well how it hurt. I still miss her, but grief does pass. It has to."

"If only I'd insisted on driving…!" Dana burst out, the tears returning. "It's all my fault!"

"No, my dear, it isn't. The truck that hit your mother's car ran a stop sign. Even if you had been driving, it would have been unavoidable." She moved forward and uncharacteristically brushed the wild blond hair away from Dana's bruised face. "The driver of the truck was only scratched. Isn't it the way of things?" she added with a sad smile.

Dana bit her lip. "Yes," she murmured.

"Jenny said she'd see you later, by the way," the older nurse added. "And Miss Ena asked about you."

Dana couldn't repress a tiny smile, even through her grief. Miss Ena had undergone a gall bladder operation days before, and was the bane of the nursing staff. But strangely, she'd taken a liking to Dana and would do anything the young nurse asked.

"Tell her, please, that I'll be back on duty Friday night," Dana said gently. "If that's all right with you."

"That depends on how well you are by then," was

the stern reply. "We'll wait to see about the funeral until Dr. Willis has seen you. You have to be prepared: He may very well refuse to let you go."

Dana's eyes blurred again with hot tears. "But I must!"

"You must get well," Mrs. Pibbs replied. "I'll see you later, Nurse. I'm very busy, but I wanted to check on you. Dr. Willis will be around shortly." She paused at the door, her eyes frankly concerned as she watched the blond head settle back on the pillow. Something was wrong there, very wrong. Dana's father had said as much when he was told that she refused to see him. But he wasn't going to insist, he told Mrs. Pibbs. Dana would work it out herself.

But would she? Mrs. Pibbs wondered.

Dr. Willis stopped by thirty minutes later, and Dana was shuttled off shortly afterward to X Ray. For the rest of the day, tests were run and results were correlated, and by night the tearful young nurse was given the verdict.

"No funeral," Dr. Willis said with faint apology as he made his night rounds. "I'm sorry, Dana, but a concussion isn't something you play around with. Your head took a brutal knock: I can't risk letting you up so soon."

"Then can they postpone the funeral...?" Dana asked hopefully.

He shook his head. "Your aunt is in no condition to put it off," he said bluntly. And he should know: Her Aunt Helen was his patient too. "Mandy was her only living relative, except for you. She's pretty devastated. No, Dana, the sooner it's over, the better."

"But I want to go," Dana wailed bitterly.

"I know that. And I understand why," he said gently. "But you know that the body is only the shell. The substance, the spark, that was her soul is already with God. It would be like looking at an empty glass."

The words were oddly comforting and they made sense. But they didn't ease the hurt.

Dr. Willis took her pulse and examined her eyes. "Shall I call Dick and have him come by and talk to you?" he asked when he finished, naming her minister.

She nodded. "Yes, please. It would be…a great help right now. Aunt Helen—is she coming to see me?"

He shook his head. "Not tonight. I've had to sedate her. The shock, for both of you, has been bad. Where's Jack? I'd have thought he'd be with you."

"My father has a family to think about," she said bitterly.

He stared at her. "You're his family too."

"Tell *him*," she said curtly, staring back. "Because he hasn't even phoned me since the divorce. Since I left home. Since I went into nurse's training! Never!"

"I see."

"No, you don't." She looked down at the white hospital sheet. "I'm very sorry, Dr. Willis; I know you're only trying to help. But this is something I have to work out by myself."

He nodded. "If I can help, I will. I've known your family for a long time."

She smiled at him. "Yes. Thank you."

"We'll keep you for two or three days, depending on how you progress," he said gently. "I wish I could give you something for the grief. But only God can do that."

* * *

Aunt Helen came by the next morning, dressed in a wildly expensive blue suit with a peekaboo hat and looking as neat as a pin. She looked a lot like Mandy, but she was taller and thinner. And much more emotional.

"Oh, darling," she wailed, throwing herself on Dana in a haze of expensive perfume and a chiffon scarf. "Oh, darling, how horrible for us both. Poor Mandy!"

Dana, just beginning to get herself back together, lost control again and wept. "I know," she whispered. "Aunt Helen, she was so unhappy, so miserable."

"I know. I told her she never should have married that man. I warned her, but she wouldn't listen!" Aunt Helen drew away with a tearful sigh. Her brown eyes were wet with tears. "I knew the minute she told me about the divorce that she wouldn't be with us much longer. She wasn't strong enough to live alone, you know."

"Yes, I know," Dana groaned. She dabbed at her eyes with a tissue. "It all happened so quickly; she was drinking...."

"They told me everything. But, darling, why did you let her drive? Didn't you realize what might happen?"

Dana felt her face stiffen. "Yes, but..."

"Of all the stupid things to do, and you might have just taken the keys from her in the first place." The brown eyes so like her mother's were accusing. "Why in the world did you let her drive, Dana?"

Dana couldn't even manage a reply. She reached blindly for the buzzer and pushed it. A minute later, a nurse came to the door.

"Will you show my aunt the way out, please,

Nurse?'' Dana asked tightly, not looking at Aunt Helen, who was obviously shocked.

The nurse knew what was going on from one look at her patient's drawn face.

''I'm sorry, but Miss Steele can't be upset; she has a concussion,'' the nurse said firmly. ''Will you come with me, please?''

As if she'd just realized what she was saying, Helen's face was suddenly white and repentant. ''Darling, I'm sorry....''

But Dana closed her eyes and wouldn't look or listen. The nightmare wasn't ever going to end, it seemed, and she wondered vaguely if everyone blamed her for her mother's death. She turned her face into the pillows and cried like a child.

Her minister visited that night, after the funeral was over, and Dana poured out her heart to him.

''And it's my fault; even Aunt Helen said it's my fault,'' she confessed.

''It's no one's fault, Dana,'' he said, smiling quietly. A gentle man, he made her feel at once comforted and secure. ''When a life is taken, it's only because God has decided that He has more need of that life than those attached to it here on earth. People don't die for no reason, Dana, or because it's anyone's fault. God decided the moment of death, not any one of us.''

''But everyone thinks it's my fault. I should have stopped her—I should have tried!''

''And if you had, there would have been something else,'' he said quietly. ''I strongly believe that things happen as God means them to.''

''I can't see anything,'' she confessed wearily, ''except that my mother is gone, and now I have no one. Even Aunt Helen hates me.''

"Your aunt was literally in tears over what she said to you this morning,'' he corrected. ''She wanted to come back and apologize, but she was afraid you wouldn't let her into the room. She was upset; you know how Helen is.''

''What am I going to do?'' Dana asked him, dabbing at fresh tears.

''You're going to go on with your life,'' he said simply. ''That life belongs to God, you know. Your profession is one of service. Isn't that the best way to spend your grief, by lessening the pain for others?''

She felt warm inside at the thought, because nursing was so much more to her than a profession. It was a way of life: healing the sick, helping the injured, comforting the bereaved. Yes, she thought, and smiled. Yes, that was how she'd cope.

But it was easier said than done, unfortunately. In the days and weeks that followed, forgetting was impossible.

After the first week, time seemed to fly. Dana made the rounds on her ward, pausing to see Miss Ena, who was being difficult again. The thin old lady had demanded her injection a full hour early, but Dana only smiled and fluffed up the pillows with her usual efficiency.

''Now, Miss Ena,'' she said with a quiet smile, ''you know I'm not going to ignore Dr. Sanders's order, and you shouldn't ask me to. Suppose I have one of the volunteers come and read to you until it's time. Would that help?''

Miss Ena's sour face brightened just a little. "Well, I suppose it would," she said reluctantly. She shifted her thin body against the pillows with a sigh. "Yes," she said in a softer tone. "Thank you, it would help."

"I know hospitals are hard on people who are used to gardening and walking the woods and pruning shrubbery," Dana confessed, laying a hand on the thin shoulder. "But in a very little while, you'll be back on your feet and doing what you please. Just keep that in mind. Believe me, it will help the time pass much more quickly."

Miss Ena smiled faintly. "I'm not used to being laid up," she confessed. "I don't mean to be disagreeable. It's only that I hate feeling helpless."

"I know," Dana said quietly. "No one likes it." She fluffed the pillows again. "How about some television now? There's a special country music awards program on," she added, knowing the elderly woman's fondness for that kind of music.

The old woman's face brightened. "That would be nice," she said after a minute.

Dana flicked on the switch and adjusted the channel, hiding a smile from Miss Ena.

Several weeks later Dana was called into Mrs. Pibbs's office, and Dana knew without asking what the reason was.

"I'd like to forget this, Nurse," she said, lifting the letter of resignation that Dana had placed on her desk early that morning as she came on duty. "Nursing has been your life. Surely you don't mean to throw away all those years of training?"

Dana's eyes were troubled. "I need time," she said quietly. "Time to get over Mother's death, time to sort out my priorities, to get myself back together again. I...I can't bear familiar surroundings right now."

Mrs. Pibbs leaned back with a sigh. "I understand." She pursed her lips and frowned. "If it's a change of scene that you need, I may have a suggestion for you. A friend of mine is looking for a private-duty nurse for her son. He lives in some godforsaken place near the Atlantic Coast. He's blind."

"I hadn't thought about doing private duty," Dana murmured.

"You will have to support yourself," Mrs. Pibbs reminded her. "Although the salary will be good, I must warn you that it won't be all tranquility. I understand that Lorraine's son has a black temper. He was an executive, you know, very high-powered, and an athlete to boot. He's been relegated to the position of a figurehead with his electronics company."

"The blindness, is it permanent?"

"I don't know. Lorraine is rather desperate, however," she added with a tiny smile. "He's not an easy man to nurse."

Mrs. Pibbs had made it into a challenge, and right now Dana needed that.

"Perhaps," she murmured, "it would be just what I need."

Mrs. Pibbs nodded smugly. "It might be just what Gannon needs too."

Dana looked up. "Is that his name?"

"Yes. Gannon van der Vere. He's Dutch."

Immediately Dana pictured a small man with a mustache, very blond, as memory formed the one Dutchman she'd ever had any contact with—Mr. van Ryker, who'd once been a patient at the hospital. She smiled, softening already. Perhaps he could teach her Dutch while she helped him adjust to his blindness. And in helping him, perhaps she could forget her own anguish.

That night she was combing her long platinum-blond hair when Jenny came whirling in, hairpins flying as she rushed to get out of her nurse's uniform and into a dress.

"Not going out tonight?" Jenny asked from the bathroom.

"Nowhere to go," Dana replied, smiling into the mirror. "I'm having a quiet night."

"You always have quiet nights. Why don't you come out with Gerald and me?"

"No, thanks, I'd rather catch up on my sleep. I've been called out on cases twice in the past three days. How did that little girl do—the one with pneumonia that Dr. Hames admitted?"

"She's responding. I think she'll do." Jenny came back out in a green-and-white-striped dress with matching green pumps. "Say, what's the rumor about you quitting?" she asked. Jenny had never been one to listen to gossip without going to the object of it to get at the truth. It was the thing about her that Dana admired most.

"It's true," she said reluctantly, because she liked her roommate and would miss her. "I'm waiting to hear about a job Mrs. Pibbs knows of, but I have officially resigned as of next Monday."

"Oh, Dana," Jenny moaned.

"I'll write," she promised. "And so will you. It won't be forever."

"It's your mother's death, isn't it?" Jenny asked softly. "Yes, I imagine it's rough to be where you're constantly reminded of her. And with the situation between you and your family..."

Dana's eyes clouded. She turned away. "I'll be fine," she managed. "Have a good time tonight," she added on a bright note.

Jenny sighed as she picked up her purse. "Can I smuggle you something when I come in? A filet mignon, a silk dressing gown, a Rolls, a man...?"

Dana laughed. "How about two hours' extra sleep to put in my pocket for when old Dr. Grimms calls me down to help him dress a stab wound and tells me his entire medical background before he sends me away?"

"I'll see what I can do," Jenny promised. "Good night."

"Good night."

Chapter Two

Mrs. Pibbs was waiting for Dana in her office the next morning after she'd listened to the report and was on her way to catch up on some paperwork.

"I've just talked to Lorraine," Mrs. Pibbs said with a faint smile. "She's delighted that you're going to come."

"I'm so glad," Dana replied. "Has she told Mr. van der Vere?"

"Only that a nurse is expected, I understand," the older woman replied. "It's better not to give the enemy too much information about troop movements."

Dana blinked. That old Army nurse's background popped up every so often in Mrs. Pibbs, and she tried not to giggle when it did. Surely that was a strange choice of words for a new patient. And what a very strange way to describe her impending arrival at the van der Vere home.

"Troop movements?" she asked.

"Just an expression," Mrs. Pibbs said uncomfortably. "Get on with your duties, Nurse."

Dana stared after her. A pity she didn't have time to

think about that unusual description, but the doctors were due to make rounds shortly and there wasn't a minute to spare.

The week went by quickly, and before she knew it, the stitches were out of her face and she was on her way to Savannah by bus. She liked to travel cross country, preferring the sightseeing that way to airplane flights, during which she could see little more than clouds. It was early spring and the landscape was just beginning to turn green across the flat land, and she could still gaze at the architecture in each small town the bus went through. It was one of her hobbies, and she never tired of it.

The styles ranged from Greek revival to Victorian to Gothic and even Williamsburg. There were split-levels, ranch-style homes, modern, ultramodern, and apartment houses. Each design seemed to have its own personality, and Dana couldn't help but wonder about the people who lived in the houses they passed—what their lives were like.

Halfway across the state, she finally succumbed to drowsiness and fell asleep in her seat by the window. The driver was announcing Savannah when she woke up.

She took a cab out to the van der Vere summer house. The driver followed the directions Mrs. Pibbs had given Dana, and Dana's eyes took in the jagged boulders of a new development along the beach until they drove farther and turned into a driveway lined with palms and shade trees and what looked like flowering shrubs; it was the season for them to bloom.

The house was fairly large, built of gray stone and overlooking the Atlantic, so ethereal that it might have been an illusion. Dana loved it at first sight. *It's beau-*

tiful, she thought, *with flowers blooming all around it and the greenery profuse.*

She paid the driver and went up the cobblestone path to the door, pausing before she rang the doorbell. Well, she told herself, it was now or never. Self-consciously she tugged a lock of her loosened hair over her cheek to help conceal the scar. Bangs already hid the one on her forehead. But the worst scars were those inside, out of sight....

The door opened and a small dark woman with green eyes stood smiling at her.

"You're Dana Steele?" she asked softly. "Come in, do. I'm Lorraine van der Vere; I'm so glad to meet you. Was it a long trip—were you comfortable?" she added in a rush, moving aside to let the taller woman inside.

Dana compared her own gray suit with the woman's obviously expensive emerald pantsuit and felt shabby by comparison. It was the best she had, of course, but hardly couture. If what Mrs. van der Vere was wearing was any indication, the family was quite wealthy.

"I brought my uniform, of course," Dana said quickly. "I don't want you to think..."

"Don't be silly, my dear," Lorraine said kindly. "Would you like to go upstairs and freshen up before I, uh, introduce you to my son?"

Dana was about to reply when there was a crash and a thud, followed by muffled words in a deep, harsh voice. Probably a servant had dropped something in the kitchen, Dana thought, but Mrs. van der Vere looked suddenly uncomfortable.

"Here, I'll show you to your room," she said quickly, guiding Dana to the staircase with its mahogany banister and woodwork. "Come with me, dear."

As if I had any choice, Dana thought with muzzled

amusement. Mrs. van der Vere acted as if she were running from wolves.

The room she was given was done in shades of beige and brown, with creamy curtains and a soft quilted coverlet in a "chocolate and spice" pattern. The carpet was thick, and Dana wanted to kick off her shoes and walk through it barefoot. She took her time getting into her spotless, starched uniform. She'd wanted to put her hair up, to look more professional, but she couldn't cope with the pity in Mrs. van der Vere's eyes if those scars were allowed to show. She left off her makeup—after all, her poor patient couldn't see her anyway—adjusted her cap and went downstairs.

Mrs. van der Vere came out of the living room, hands outstretched. "My, don't you look professional," she said. "We'll have to spend some time together, my dear, once you've gotten into the routine and adjusted to Gannon." She looked briefly uncomfortable and bit her dainty lower lip. "Dana, if I may call you Dana, you…won't…that is, you're used to difficult patients, aren't you?" she asked finally.

Dana smiled. "Yes, Mrs. van der Vere…"

"Call me Lorraine, dear. We're going to be allies, you know."

"Lorraine," she corrected. "I was a floor nurse at Ashton General, you know. I think I can cope with Mr. van der Vere."

"Most people do, until they've met him" was the worried reply, accompanied by a wan smile. "Well"— she straightened—"shall we get it over with?"

Dana followed behind her, half puzzled. Surely the little Dutchman couldn't be that much of a horror. She wondered if he'd have an accent. His mother didn't seem to….

Lorraine knocked tentatively at the door of the room next to the living room.

"Gannon?" she called hesitantly.

"Well, come in or go away! Do you need an engraved invitation?" came a deep, lightly accented voice from behind the huge mahogany door.

Lorraine opened the door and stood aside to let Dana enter the room first.

"Here's your new nurse, darling: Miss Dana Steele. Dana, this is my stepson, Gannon."

Dana barely heard her. She was trying to adjust to the fact that the small, mustached Dutchman she had been told was to be her patient was actually the man she saw in front of her.

"Well?" the huge man at the desk asked harshly, his unseeing gray eyes staring straight ahead. "Is she mute, Mother? Or just weighing the advantages of silence?"

Dana found her voice and moved forward, her footsteps alerting the tall blond man to her approach. He stood up, towering over her, his shaggy mane of hair falling roguishly over his broad forehead.

"How do you do, Mr. van der Vere?" Dana asked with more confidence than she felt.

"I'm blind—how do you think I do, Miss Steele?" he demanded harshly, his deep voice cold and cutting, his unseeing wintery eyes glaring at her. "I trip over the furniture, I turn over glasses, and I hate being led around like a child! Did my stepmother tell you that you're the fifth?" he added with a bitter laugh.

"Fifth what?" she asked, holding on to her nerve.

"Nurse, of course," he replied impatiently. "I've gone through that many in a month. How long do you expect to last?"

"As long as I need to, Mr. van der Vere," she replied calmly.

He cocked his head, as if straining to hear her. "Not afraid of me, miss?" he prodded.

She shifted her shoulders. "Actually, sir, I'm quite fond of wild animals," she said with a straight face, while Lorraine gaped at her.

A faint movement in the broad face caught her attention. "Are you presuming to call me a wild animal?" he retorted.

"Oh, no, sir," Dana assured him. "I wouldn't flatter you on such short acquaintance."

He threw back his head and laughed. "Nervy, aren't you?" he murmured. "You'll need that nerve if you stay here long." He turned away and found the corner of the desk, easing himself back into his chair.

"Well, I'll leave you two to…get acquainted," Lorraine said, seizing her opportunity. She backed out the door with an apologetic smile at Dana, and closed it behind her.

"Would you like to get acquainted with me, Miss Nurse?" Gannon van der Vere asked arrogantly.

"Oh, definitely sir. I do consider it an advantage to get to know the enemy."

He chuckled. "Is that how you see me?"

"That's obviously how you want to be seen," she told him. "You don't like being nursed, do you? You'd much rather sit behind that great desk and brood about being blind."

The smile faded and his gray eyes glittered sightlessly toward the source of her voice. "I beg your pardon?"

"Have you been out of this house since the accident?" she asked. "Have you bothered to learn braille, or to walk with a cane? Have you seen about getting a seeing-eye dog?''

''I don't need crutches!'' he shot back. ''I'm a man, not a child. I won't be fussed over!''

''But you must see that the only recourse you've given your stepmother is to find help for you…'' she said, attempting reason. ''…if you won't even make the effort to help yourself.''

He lifted his nose in what Dana immediately recognized as the prelude to an outburst of pure venom.

''Perhaps I would if I could be left alone long enough,'' he replied in a voice so cold it dripped icicles. ''I've been 'helped' out of my mind. The last nurse my stepmother brought here had the audacity to suggest that I might benefit from a psychiatrist. She left in the middle of the night.''

''I can see you now, flinging her out the front steps in her bedclothes,'' Dana retorted, unperturbed.

''Impertinent little creature, aren't you?'' he growled.

''If you treat your employees this way, Mr. van der Vere, I'm amazed that you still have any,'' she said calmly. ''Now, what would you like for dinner and I'll show you how to start feeding yourself. I assume you don't like being spoon-fed…?''

He muttered something harsh and banged his fist down on the desk. ''I'm not hungry!''

''In that case I'll tell the cook not to bother preparing anything for you,'' she said cheerfully. ''When you need me, do call.''

She started out the door, trying not to hear what he was saying to her back.

''Sticks and stones, Mr. van der Vere,'' she reminded him sweetly as she opened the door.

He growled something in another language and followed it with a slam of something on the big wooden desk. Dana smiled secretly as she closed the door behind her. Challenge, was that what had been said about this job? It would certainly be that, she affirmed silently.

Chapter Three

Lorraine was waiting for her in the hall, wringing her hands. Her small face was heavily lined with apprehension.

"Now, dear," she began nervously, "he's not at all as horrible as he seems, and I don't mind raising your salary…!"

Dana laughed heartily. "Oh, that won't be necessary. You couldn't pay me to leave now. It would be like retreating, and a good nurse never retreats under fire."

The older woman was visibly relieved. "Oh" was all she managed to say.

"But I can certainly understand why my predecessors were in such a rush to get out the door," she added with a grin. "He does have a magnificent temper, doesn't he?"

Lorraine sighed. "Yes, he does. Blindness isn't easy for a man like my stepson, you know. He is—was—so athletic. He especially liked water-skiing and snow skiing and aerobatics in his plane…."

The other woman was painting a picture of a man

who had enjoyed a reckless life-style, as if he hadn't considered life precious enough to safe-guard.

She frowned. "Dangerous sports."

"Very obviously," Lorraine said quietly. "He's been that way since his wife died in the automobile wreck. He was driving, you see. It was many years ago, but he's never been the Gannon he was when I married his father."

"How old was he when you married?" she asked quietly, sensing a kindred spirit.

"He was ten." She sighed, smiling. "His mother died when he was born, and his father went to his own grave loving her. I was a substitute. He cared for me," she said quickly. "But not in the same way he cared for Gannon's mother." She turned away, as if her own memories were painful. "Is your room all right, my dear?"

"It's lovely. I'll enjoy it very much while I'm here. Mrs. van der Vere, exactly what is the problem with your stepson's eyes? Mrs. Pibbs was rather vague, and I'd like to know."

"That's the problem," Lorraine said as she led the way into her small sitting room and took a chair overlooking the rocky coastline. "There is no medical reason for his blindness. They call it—what's that word?— idiopathic. Gannon's doctor said that it could very well be hysterical blindness, brought about by the sudden shock of expecting to be stabbed in the eyes by those ragged wooden beams at the shore. The woman who was driving the speedboat lost control," she explained. "Gannon was slung toward a dock with splintered boards. How it missed his eyes was truly a miracle, but he didn't expect it to miss, you see. He was twisted and his head smashed into the dock. When he came to in the hospital, he was blind.''

''And he doesn't like the idea of admitting that it could be hysterical paralysis of the optic nerve,'' Dana concluded, pursing her lips. ''That's quite understandable, of course. Was there any emotional trauma in his life at about the same time?''

''Not that I know of,'' the smaller woman commented. ''Of course, Gannon is a very private person.''

Dana nodded. ''Does he go out at all?''

''Socially, you mean? No,'' she said sadly. ''He stays in the living room and harasses his vice-presidents over the phone.''

''His vice-presidents?''

''At the electronics firm he owns, my dear. They manufacture all sorts of communications equipment—interfaces for computers, buffers, monitors, that kind of thing.'' She shrugged and smiled apologetically. ''I don't pretend to understand; it's far too technical for me. But the company's introduced some revolutionary new system components, and apparently my stepson is something of an electronics genius. I'm very proud of him. But I have to admit, I have no idea exactly what he does.''

''I don't know anything about computers,'' Dana murmured. She smiled secretly. ''But if I asked, he might be tempted to educate me. It might even break the ice.''

''Be careful that you don't fall in,'' Lorraine cautioned. ''Gannon doesn't particularly like women right now. He was almost engaged when the accident happened. The woman walked out on him.'' She grimaced. ''Perhaps some of that was guilt. She was driving the speedboat, you see.''

Dana pondered that for the rest of the day. Poor lonely man: *His* life hadn't been any picnic so far, either. She smiled, just thinking about the challenge Gannon was going to present.

After letting him simmer all day, Dana took Gannon's dinner tray in herself.

He was sitting in a deep armchair by the open window that led onto the balcony. Outside, the waves were crashing slowly against the shore.

He lifted his shaggy blond head when he heard the door open and close. "Mother?" he called shortly.

"Hardly," Dana replied. She put the tray on the big desk, watching him stiffen at the sound of her voice.

"You again? I thought you'd gone home, Nurse."

"And leave you all alone, Mr. van der Vere?" she exclaimed. "How cowardly!"

He lifted his chin aggressively. "I don't need another nurse. I don't want another nurse. I just want to be left alone."

"Loneliness—take it from me—is bad for the soul," she said matter-of-factly. "It shrivels it up like a prune. Why don't you walk along the beach and listen to the waves and the sea gulls? Are you afraid of sea gulls, Mr. van der Vere? Do you have a feather phobia or something?"

He was trying not to laugh, but he lost. It rolled out of him like deep thunder, but he quickly stifled it. "Impertinent Miss Steele," he muttered. "Your name suits you. Are you cold and hard?"

"Pure marshmallow," she corrected, removing the lids from the dinnerware. "Just take a whiff of this delicious food. Steak and mashed potatoes and gravy, homemade rolls and buttered asparagus."

"All my favorites," he murmured. "What did you

do, bribe Mrs. Wells to fix it? She hates the smell of asparagus.''

"So she told me," she said with a smile. "But it was her night off. I cooked it."

"You cook?" he asked curtly.

"I used to live alone. I'd starve to death if I didn't. Now, if you can't manage by yourself, I'll be glad to spoon-feed you...."

He said something unpleasant, but he got to his feet and stumbled toward the desk.

She walked around it and caught his hand. He tried to free himself but she held firm, determined not to let him dominate her.

"I'm offering to help you," she said quietly, staring up at his scowling face. "That's all. One human being to another. I'd do the same for man, woman, or child, and I think you would for me if our situations were reversed."

He looked shocked for a minute, but he stopped struggling. He let her guide him to his chair behind the desk. But before he sat down, his big hands caught her thin shoulders for a minute and moved upward to her neck and her face and hair. He nodded then and let go of her to drop into the big chair, which barely contained him.

"I thought you'd be small," he said after a minute, groping for the cup of hot black coffee she'd placed within his reach.

"In fact, I'm above average height," she returned. The feel of his warm, strong hands had made her feel odd, and she wasn't sure she liked it.

"Compared to me, miss, you're small," he said firmly. "What color is your hair, your eyes?"

"I have blond hair," she said. "And brown eyes."

"An unusual combination." He picked up his fork and managed to turn over the coffee with one sudden movement. A torrent of words poured out of him.

"Stop that," Dana said sharply. "I'll walk right out the door if you continue to use such language around me."

"I must remember to search my mind for better words if it will get you out of my hair," he said with malicious enjoyment. "Are you such a prude, little Nurse?"

"No, sir, I am not," she assured him. "But I was always told that a repertoire of rude language disguised a pitiful lack of vocabulary. And I believe it."

He appeared to be taken aback by the comment. "I'm a man, Miss Steele, not a monk. The occasional word does slip out."

"I've never understood why men consider it a mark of masculinity to use shocking language," she replied. "I don't consider it so. Not that, nor getting drunk, nor driving recklessly...."

"You should have joined a nunnery, miss," he observed. "Because you are obviously not prepared to function in the real world."

"I find the real world incredibly brutal, Mr. van der Vere," she said quietly. "People slaughtering other people, abusing little children, finding new ways to kill, making heroes of villains, using sensationalism as a substitute for good drama in motion pictures.... Am I boring you? I don't find cruelty in the least pleasurable. If that makes me unrealistic, then I suppose that I am one."

"It amazes me that you can stand the company of poor weak mortals, Nurse, when you are so obviously superior to the rest of us," he said, leaning back in his chair.

She felt the shock go all the way to her toes. "Superior?" she echoed.

"You do feel superior?" he mocked. "Have you never made a mistake, I wonder? Have you never been tempted by love or desire, greed or ambition?"

She flushed wildly and finished mopping up the coffee. "I'm hardly a beauty contest candidate," she said curtly. "And even if I were, men frankly don't interest me at all."

He raised a curious eyebrow. "Venom from the little nun? Someone has hurt you badly."

"I'm not here to be mentally dissected," she said, regaining her lost composure. "I'll get you another cup of coffee."

"And I thought you didn't run from the enemy," he mused as she left him.

But she didn't answer. She couldn't.

The new environment and sparring with her patient had kept Dana's mind occupied during the day, but the night brought memories. And the memories brought a gnawing ache. It was hard to believe that Mandy was gone. Sweet little Mandy, who could be maddening and endearing all at once.

She sat by the darkened window of her room and stared blankly down to where the whitecaps were visible even at night. Why did people have to die? she asked silently. Why did it all have to end so suddenly? All her life her mother had been there when she needed someone to talk to, to confide in, to be advised by.

The divorce had been no surprise when it came. The only unexpected thing was that it had taken so many years for her parents to admit that the marriage was a failure. Dana's earliest memories were of arguments that seemed to last for days, interspersed with frozen silences. Fortunately she had had grandparents who kept her each summer, and their small farm became a refuge for the young girl who felt neither wanted nor loved by her parents. Even now, with her mother dead, nothing had changed between Dana and her father. She sighed bitterly. Perhaps it would have been different if she'd been the son her father really wanted. Or perhaps it wouldn't have been.

She got up and dressed for bed. One thing was for certain, she thought as tears welled up in her eyes and spilled over: She was an orphan now. She might as well give them both up, because it was perfectly obvious that her father had no place for her in his life anymore. Her father's remarriage hadn't been such a trauma, because they hardly communicated in the first place. But to lose her mother so soon afterward, with the shock of Mandy's confession that she was going to end it all because of her husband's remarriage, was more than she could bear. There had been no time to adjust to either change in her life. No time at all.

She put out the light and crawled between the covers. *Oh, Mandy.* She wept silently. *Mandy, why did you have to go and leave me alone? Now I have no one!*

Tears soaked the pillow. She wept for the mother she didn't have anymore; for the father she'd never had. For the future, all bleak and painful and empty. But there was no one to hold her while she cried.

The next morning Gannon was sitting on the balcony when she carried in his breakfast. The wind was ruffling his blond hair, lifting it, teasing it, and she wondered suddenly how many women had done that. He had wonderful hair, thick and pale and slightly wavy.

"Breakfast," she called cheerfully, placing the tray on the table beside his chair at the edge of the balcony. The outdoor furniture was white wrought iron, and it fit the isolation and the rustic charm of the place.

Gannon half turned, and his pale gray eyes stared blankly toward her. His shirt, worn with tan slacks, had in its multicolored pattern a shade of gray that exactly matched his pale eyes.

"Must you sound so disgustingly cheerful?" he asked curtly, scowling. "It's just past dawn, I haven't had my coffee and right now I hate the whole world."

"And a cup of coffee will help you love it?" She laughed softly. "My, my, you're easy to please."

"Don't get cute, Joan of Arc," he returned harshly. He propped his long legs on another chair and sighed heavily. "Put some cream and sugar in that coffee. And how about a sweet roll?"

"How about that," she murmured, casting an amused glance at his dark face. "I brought you bacon and eggs. More civilized. More protein."

"I want a sweet roll."

"I want a house on the Riviera and a Labrador retriever named Johnston, but we don't always get what we want, do we?" she asked, and placed the plate in front of him, rattling the utensils against it loudly.

His chiseled lips pursed angrily. "Who's the boss here, honey, you or me?"

"I am, of course, and don't call me honey. Would you like me to direct you around the plate?" she asked politely.

"Go ahead. I won't promise to listen," he added darkly. He leaned forward, easing toward the coffee cup, and picked it up while she told him what was located where on his plate.

"Why can't I call you honey?" he asked when she started to go back into the house.

She stopped, staring down at him. "Well, because it isn't professional," she said finally.

He laughed mirthlessly. "No, it isn't. But if you're blond, I imagine your hair looks like honey, doesn't it? Or is it pale?"

"It's quite pale," she said involuntarily.

"Long?"

"Yes, but I keep it put up."

"Afraid some man might mistake loosened hair for loosened morals, Joan?" he mocked.

"Don't make fun of morality, if you please," she said starchily. "Some of us are old-fashioned enough to take offense."

With that she marched back into the house, while he made a sound like muffled laughter.

That afternoon he told her he wanted to walk along the beach, a pronouncement so profound that his stepmother caught her breath when she overheard it. Dana only grinned as she took his arm to lead him down the steps to the water. She was just beginning to enjoy this job.

"What changed your mind?" she asked as she guided him along the beach by his sleeve.

"I decided that I might as well take advantage of your expertise before you desert me," he said.

She glanced up at him curiously. "Why would I desert you?"

"I might not give you the choice." He stuck his free hand in his pocket and the muscles in his arm clenched.

"I'm not an easy man. I don't take to blindness, and my temper isn't good at its best."

"How long have you had this problem?" she asked, doing her impression of a Viennese psychiatrist.

He chuckled at the mock accent. "My temper isn't my problem. It's the way people react to it."

"Oh, you mean those embarrassing things they do, like diving under heavy furniture and running for the hills when you walk through the door?"

"Such a sweet voice to be so sarcastic," he chided. His hand suddenly slid down and caught hers, holding it even when she instinctively jerked back. "No, no, Nurse; you're suppose to be guiding me, aren't you? Soft little hand, and strong for one so small."

"Yours is enormous," she replied. The feel of those strong, warm fingers was doing something odd to her breathing, to her balance. She wanted to pull free, but he was strong.

"A legacy from my Dutch father," he told her. "He was a big man."

"You aren't exactly a dwarf yourself," she mused.

He chuckled softly at that comment. "I stand six foot three in my socks."

"Did you ever play basketball?" she asked conversationally.

"No. I hated it. I didn't care for group sports so much, you see. I liked to ski, and I liked fast cars. Racing. I went to Europe every year for the Grand Prix. Until this year," he added coldly. "I will never go again, now."

"You have to stop thinking of your blindness as permanent," she said quietly.

"Has my mother handed you that fairy tale, too, about the blindness being hysterical?" he demanded.

He stopped to face her, his hands moving up to find her upper arms. "Do I seem to you to be prone to hysterics, Nurse?"

"It has nothing to do with that, Mr. van der Vere, as I'm sure your doctor explained to you. It was simply a great shock to the optic nerve...."

"I am blind," he said, each word cutting and deliberate. "That is not hysteria; it is a fact. I am blind!"

"Yes, temporarily." She stood passively in his bruising grasp, watching his scowling face intently, determined not to show fear. She sensed that he might like that, making her afraid. "It isn't unheard of for the brain to play tricks on us, you know. You saw the splinters coming straight for your eyes, and you were knocked unconscious. It's possible that your..."

"It is not possible," he said curtly, and his grip increased until she gasped. "The blindness occurred because I hit my head. The doctors simply have not found the problem. They invent this hysterical paralysis to spare their own egos!"

It wasn't possible to reason with a brick wall, she told herself. "Mr. van der Vere, you're hurting me," she said quietly.

All at once, his hands relaxed, although they still held her. He smoothed the soft flesh of her arms through the thin sleeves of her white uniform. "I'm sorry, I didn't mean to do that. Do you bruise easily, Miss Steele, despite your metallic name?"

"Yes, sir, I do," she admitted. He was standing quite close, and the warmth of his body and its clean scent were making her feel weak in the knees. She was looking straight up at him, and she liked the strength of his face, with its formidable nose and jutting brow and glittering gray eyes.

For just an instant his hands smoothed slowly, sensuously, up and down her arms. His breath quickened. "How old are you?" he asked suddenly.

"I'm twenty-four," she said breathlessly.

"Do you know how old I am?" he asked.

She shook her head before she realized that he couldn't see the motion. "No."

"I'm thirty-seven. Nearly thirteen years your senior."

"Don't let that worry you, sir; I've had geriatrics training," she managed to say pertly.

The hard lines in his face relaxed. He smiled, genuinely, for the first time since she'd been around him. It changed his whole face, and she began to realize the kind of charm such a man might be able to affect.

"Have you, Saint Joan?" he murmured. He chuckled. "Have you ever been married?"

"No, sir," she said, aware of the primness of her own soft voice.

His head tilted up and an eyebrow arched. "No opportunities?" he murmured.

She flushed. "As you accused me, Mr. van der Vere, I'm rather prudish in my outlook. I don't feel superior, I just don't believe in shallow relationships. That isn't a popular viewpoint these days."

"In other words you said no and the word got around, is that what you mean, miss?" he asked quietly.

It was so near the truth that she gaped up at him. "Well, yes," she blurted out.

He only nodded. "Virtue is a lonely companion, is it not?" he murmured. He let go of her arms, and before she realized what he was doing, he framed her face with his big, warm hands. "I want to know the shape of your face. Don't panic," he said.

But she didn't want him to feel that long, ugly scar down her cheek, and she drew away as if he'd struck her sharply.

His face hardened. "Is it so intimate, the touch of hands on a face?" he asked curtly. "Pardon me, then, if I offend you."

"I'm not offended," she said stiffly, standing apart from him on legs that threatened to buckle. His touch had affected her in an odd way. "I just don't like being touched, Mr. van der Vere."

His heavy brows arched up. "Indeed? May I suggest, miss, that you have more inhibitions than would be considered normal for a woman of your years?"

She stiffened even more. "May I suggest that I'd rather have my inhibitions than your ill temper?"

He made a rough sound and turned away. "At any rate you flatter yourself if you think there was more than curiosity in that appraisal. I can hardly lose my head over a figure I can't even see."

The flat statement cruelly reminded them of his blindness. She felt angry with herself for denying him the shape of her face, but she hadn't wanted him to feel the scar. It had made her less than perfect and much more sensitive than usual to her lack of looks.

He started along the beach, faltering. "Are you coming, Nurse, or would you like to see me fall flat on my face in the surf?" he asked sharply.

"Don't try to make me feel guilty, Mr. van der Vere," she said, taking his arm. "I won't apologize for being myself."

"Did I ask you to?" He sighed heavily. "I hate being blind."

"Yes, I know."

"Do you?" His voice was harsh with sarcasm. "But

then, you think I'm having hysterics, don't you, Nurse, so why the sympathy in your voice?''

"You won't try to understand what the term means, will you?" she shot back. "Would you rather enjoy your temporary affliction, Mr. van der Vere? Does it please you to hurt other people out of your own refusal to help yourself?"

He seemed to grow taller, and his face became rigid, like stone. "If you were a man..." he began hotly.

"If I were a man, I'd be an archaeologist," she said pleasantly, "out digging up old bones. I wouldn't be a nurse, so I wouldn't be here, and you'd have no one to yell at then, would you?"

He said a rough word under his breath and his chiseled lips made a thin line. At his sides his powerful hands clenched convulsively.

"Would you like to go swimming with me, Miss Steele?" he said after a minute.

"No, sir, I would not. And shame on you for what you're thinking. The shark would only get indigestion."

He seemed to be muffling a laugh, but he couldn't stop the sound from his throat. It was a delightful sound, full of rich humor and love of life. It was like music to Dana's ears.

"Lead me home, if you please," he chuckled. "The sea is too tempting, I confess."

"It's for your own good that I prod you, sir," she said as they walked along the beach. "Self-pity is self-defeating, you know."

"Was I feeling sorry for myself?" he mused. He stumbled, cursed and pulled himself erect. "Stop leading me into rocks."

"That was a piece of driftwood, and if you'd pick

up your feet instead of shuffling along, disturbing sand crabs, you wouldn't trip,'' she returned with a grin.

''Witch,'' he accused.

''No wonder you wanted to get me in the water,'' she mumbled. ''You wanted to find out if I'd float, right?''

He shook his head. ''I think I've met my match,'' he murmured. ''Tell me something, miss. If you and the doctors are wrong, and the blindness is not hysterical, what then? Do you move in to lead me around for the rest of my life?''

She was convinced that the doctors wouldn't have made such a mistake, not with the battery of tests that had been done. But she was weary of arguing the point.

''If they're wrong,'' she said, stressing the first word, ''then you learn to live with it. There are fantastic developments in computer science that deal with blindness—as I'm sure you know from your involvement in that field.''

''Yes, I know,'' he said quietly. ''In fact, one of my engineers developed a braille system that allows the blind access to other blind people through their computers.''

''You see? It isn't a closed door you're facing. And will you consider one other thing?''

''What?''

''That God gives us obstacles for reasons?''

''God,'' he said, ''did not make me blind. I did that all by myself, so why should I expect Him to help me?''

''Why shouldn't you?'' she countered. ''I suspect you're not a religious man.''

''You suspect correctly.''

''What are you doing about it?'' she asked. ''What do you do to justify your existence?''

"I work for myself," he said gruffly.

"And for financial gain."

"Of course. What other reason is there?" he grumbled. "I am not a philanthropist."

"Obviously."

He shifted restlessly. "Don't try to toss a mantle of guilt over me. I give to charity."

"What do you give of yourself?"

He stopped dead. "I beg your pardon?"

"What do you give of yourself? Money is vulgar."

"So speaks one without it," he returned coldly. "It never ceases to amaze me that the people who complain the most about the way wealth is distributed are usually the very people who lack it."

"Touché," she agreed pleasantly, looking up at his windblown hair, his hard face. "I've been poor most of my life, Mr. van der Vere. I'd like to have an expensive dress once in a while, and I have a deep love for luxurious perfume. But I've lived very well without those things. The difference is that I live a life of service for God. My pleasure comes from the giving of myself."

He looked uncomfortable. "Then why did you give it up to come here?" he asked suspiciously. "I'm sure you're getting paid much more here than you make working in your hospital," he added sarcastically.

She glanced away from him, flushing. "That's true. But the money wasn't the reason I came."

"Then, what was?"

She straightened. "Personal reasons, Mr. van der Vere, that have nothing to do with you. Shall we go?"

"Refusing the challenge?" he prodded. "Very well, lead me back into the house. I wouldn't want the wind to dislodge your halo."

She wanted nothing more at that moment than to

shake him. But that wouldn't accomplish anything. At least she'd nudged him out of his self-pity, a minor victory. Perhaps there would be others.

She walked alongside him, feeling oddly elated. She wanted to take the pins out of her long hair and let it blow free. She wanted to take off her sensible white nurse's shoes and run barefoot along the damp beach, like a child enjoying nature's beauty. Her eyes lifted to the somber man at her side. She was beginning to see a purpose in her presence there; it went much deeper than the nursing of a blind man.

Chapter Four

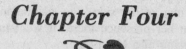

The next weeks were trying. Gannon van der Vere seemed to go out of his way to find fault with Dana. Nothing she did pleased him, and all the ground she seemed to have gained in the first few days abruptly slid back into the sea.

He sat behind his desk and stayed on the phone almost constantly. He refused to go out of the room except to sleep. He was irritable and unapproachable, and when Dana tried to talk to him, he found an excuse not to listen. The doctor's visit only irritated him further, and after his examination he retreated into his bedroom and wouldn't even come out to eat.

"Dr. Shane just restated his own opinion to Gannon." Lorraine sighed wearily as she and Dana sat down to supper by themselves. "It made him furious, of course. He won't accept that the condition isn't due to something surgically correctible."

"He's a stubborn man," Dana commented.

"Worse than stubborn. Just like his late father." She smiled. "He was quite a man, my husband. A little mellower than Gannon, but of course he was older."

"Perhaps he'll come to admit it eventually," Dana suggested. "In the meanwhile, having people around would help him tremendously. Doesn't he have friends?"

"He had plenty of them, when he could see," his stepmother said angrily. "And girl friends by the score. People who loved for him to spend money on them. Now..." She shrugged her delicate shoulders. "This place is like the end of the earth for that kind of person, Dana. They don't like peace and solitude. They like bright lights and activity and, frankly, drugs and alcohol."

"Did he?" she asked, because she wanted to know.

"Gannon?" she laughed. "No, he was never the type to need crutches of any kind. His late wife was the party-goer. Of course, I don't think she indulged. But all their friends do."

"No children?"

"They didn't want children," Lorraine said with a sigh. "Their lives were so full, you see."

Full. Dana doubted that, somehow, but she was too polite to state her convictions. She was getting a vivid picture of Gannon's life before the blindness, and it was an unpleasant one. She felt sorrier for him than ever.

Dana especially loved the beach at night, and when she could sneak away for a few minutes, she liked to walk along the shore and watch the whitecaps roll against the damp sand. Lorraine never minded her brief absences, but when Gannon discovered what she was doing, he made a point of seeking her out one Friday evening on the beach.

"Nurse!" he bellowed, pausing on the last step that led down from the house, his hand clenched on the railing.

She rushed back toward him, her loosened hair flying, afraid he'd tumble down in his anger.

"I'm here," she said breathlessly. "There's no need to yell."

"May I ask what you're doing down here?" he grumbled, staring in her general direction.

She studied his ferocious scowl while his hair and her soft green dress blew wildly in the cool ocean breeze. "I'm walking on the beach, Mr. van der Vere," she said calmly.

"On my time," he agreed.

"Excuse me, sir, I thought I had ten minutes a day to myself," she said with polite sarcasm.

"A live-in nurse is supposed to be within call every minute," he snapped.

"I was," she pointed out. "Didn't I come running?"

He drew in a sharp breath. "The beach is dangerous at night," he said after a minute, as if it annoyed him that he'd had to show any concern for her. "There are transients down the beach who like to party. You're not sophisticated enough to cope with drunken men, Miss Steele. Will you come in the house, please."

The concern touched her. Only her mother and Jenny had ever shown any for her over the years.

"Lost your tongue?" he growled after a minute.

She shrugged. "I'm not used to people worrying about me," she said finally.

He seemed to hesitate, his hand curling slowly around the banister. "Your parents do, surely?"

The question cut in a new way. She averted her gaze to the sea and tried not to cry; tears were so close to the surface these days, the grief was so raw and unfamiliar. "My mother died in a wreck a few months ago," she said softly.

"I'm sorry," he said quietly. "Your father?"

"We have very little contact," she admitted. "It's my fault as much as his. I'm not good at relationships, you see. I'm wary of letting people get close."

"Even family?" he burst out. "My God, are you fearful of contamination?"

He made her sound odd, and she didn't like it. "Fearful of being hurt, if you must know," she shot back, her eyes blazing. "I'd rather be alone than cut to ribbons emotionally, and what business is my personal life to you?"

His heavy blond brows shot straight up. "Claws," he murmured, and a corner of his mouth curved. "Well, well, you land on your feet, don't you, for all your repressed virtue."

She stared at the sand. "You irritate me," she bit off.

"We're even, because you irritate me as well. Now, will you come in, before I yield to temptation and toss you into the surf to cool you off?"

She drew in an angry breath and started past him, but his hand shot out at the sound of her steps on the stone and she was dragged against his powerful body.

Her tiny gasp was audible even above the thunderous surf, and she was aware of every cell that came in contact with him. He smelled of expensive cologne and soap, and the hand around her waist was big and very warm. His breath was on her forehead, his chest was rising and falling with a curious heaviness and her knees threatened to collapse.

He felt her hair blow against his face as it bent, and he brushed at long, silky strands of it with his free hand. "Such soft hair," he remarked quietly. "Blond?"

She swallowed. "Yes, sir." Why was her voice quavering like that? What was happening to her?

His hand brushed her shoulder and moved down her back to her shoulder blades. He drew her close with aching tenderness until her cheek was pressed against his warm, broad chest over his silky blue shirt.

She could feel the strength of him under her hand, the hard beat of his heart. It had been a long time since any man had held her, but never had it made her feel like this. She was vulnerable all at once, womanly, feminine in a totally new way.

"You smell of wildflowers," he said, his voice deep and quiet in the semidarkness. "And your thinness frightens me. You aren't hardy; you're very fragile."

She tried to breathe normally. "I'm not fragile," she protested weakly. Her hands pressed palm down over the warm muscles of his chest, half in protest. "Mr. van der Vere…"

"Isn't it ethical, little moralist?" he mused. "I thought comfort was your stock-in-trade."

"Comfort?"

His cheek nuzzled against hers. "I've been alone a long time," he said in a low whisper. "Without touching, or being touched. Sometimes just the scent of a woman is enough to drive me half mad.…"

She jerked away from him all at once, frightened of the sensuality she could hear in his voice, feel in his warm hands on her back. She put herself a safe distance away and tried to stop shaking.

"It's getting cold out here," she murmured.

"Ice cold," he said harshly. "Little Nun, why don't you join a convent?"

"I'm not on offer as a woman, Mr. van der Vere!" she burst out, furious at his casual approach. "I'm a nurse; it's my job, it's why I'm here! If you're thinking of adding anything personal to my duties, you'd better start running ads fast: I quit!''

"Wait!''

She froze a step above him, listening as he felt for the banister and started up the steps behind her, stopping when he felt her body was just ahead of him.

"All right, I'm sorry,'' he said shortly. "I only meant to tease, not to run you off. I'm…getting used to you. Don't leave me.''

The stiff pride got through to her when nothing else would have. She turned around and looked at his set features with softening eyes. It must indeed be hard for such a man, used to such a life-style, to endure the loneliness of this isolated beach house. Could she blame him for reacting to the first young woman he'd been near in months?

She drew in a slow breath. "I won't leave you,'' she said quietly. "But you've got to stop making dead sets at me if I stay. I won't be treated like a temporary amusement, especially by a patient. I take my nursing seriously: It isn't a game to me; neither is it an opportunity for a little holiday romancing on the side.''

"You speak bluntly,'' he replied. "May I?''

"Yes, sir.''

"I have been without a woman for many months, and I'm not suited to the life of a hermit.'' His shoulders lifted and fell. "I had no intention—have no intention,'' he rephrased, "of treating you like an amusement. I simply wanted a woman in my arms, for a moment. I wanted to feel like a man again.'' He shifted restlessly. "Lead me up, will you? I'm tired.''

He seemed to slump, and tears burned her eyes. She hadn't thought of how barren his emotional life would be because of the blindness, and she felt cold at her harsh rejection of him. She'd misunderstood; now she felt guilty.

"I'm sorry I snapped," she said, taking him by the arm. "I...I didn't understand. I'm a little afraid of men, I think. My fear makes me overreact."

"Afraid?" he asked curiously.

"I've led a sheltered life," she confessed. "I don't even know how to protect myself. Men are very strong...."

"You make me sound like a potential mugger," he ground out. "I wouldn't attack you!"

"How reassuring; I was worried to death about that," she said with a teasing laugh.

All his bad humor disappeared at once. "I'll bet you were," he muttered. He found her hand and clasped it in his, and she felt a strange little shock of pleasure at the warm strength of it. "Nothing personal, Nurse; I only need to be led and I can hold on to you more easily like this. All right?"

She looked down at his brown hand holding hers. "All right," she said meekly. It wasn't professional of course. But it was...practical.

He was easier after that, more approachable, regaling her with stories of his travels while she took him walking and driving in the car and tried to ease him out of his cold shell. Some of the tales he recounted were frankly shocking, and she began to wonder at the wildness of the life he'd lead.

"What about your own life?" he asked while they were drinking coffee at a local restaurant. Their table overlooked the ocean, and Dana picked at her apple pie while her eyes drank in the blueness of the water, the whiteness of the beach, dotted with swimmers in their colorful bathing suits.

"Hmmmm?" she murmured dreamily.

He made an impatient sound. "Are you worshipping the view again? Lorraine said you watch the ocean as if you're afraid it may vanish any second."

"I love it," she said sheepishly. "We don't have oceans around Ashton, you know. Just open land and a lot of farms and cattle."

"How big is Ashton?"

"About five thousand people," she told him. "It isn't far south of Atlanta, but it's mostly rural. I grew up there. I know most everybody else who did too."

"Is that one of those towns where the sidewalk draws in at six and everything closes for the night?"

"Very nearly. We don't even have a bowling alley. Although," she added, "we do have a theater and a skating rink."

"How exciting," he mused. "No bars?"

"We're in a dry county," she replied.

"You don't drink, I gather."

She sighed, watching the ocean again. "Mr. van der Vere, I never have. I'm sure my life is duller than dishwater compared to yours."

He lifted his coffee to his chiseled mouth, frowning slightly. "My world was an endless round of parties, cruises, business conventions, casinos and first-class travel. It was never dull."

She tried to imagine a life-style so hectic, and failed. "Were you happy?"

He blinked, staring in her direction. "Happy?"

"I can look it up in the dictionary and read you the definitions, if you like," she murmured.

"I was busy," he corrected, idly caressing the coffee cup. "Occupied. Entertained. But happy?" He laughed shortly. "What is happiness, Nurse? Tell me."

"Being at peace inside yourself, liking yourself and the whole world all at once," she said simply. "Going about your work with your whole heart and loving what you do."

"You're talking about a feeling," he said, "not the trappings that go with it."

"Exactly. I could be just as happy working in a sewing plant or digging in a garden as I am nursing, if it fulfilled me," she told him.

"I imagine a family could provide you with the same sense of purpose," he remarked. "Have you not wanted a husband and children?"

She toyed with her pie and laid down the fork to pick up her coffee. "Mr. van der Vere," she said after a minute, "I'm a very plain woman. I have rigid views on life and the living of it. I don't have casual affairs, I work hard and I keep to myself. It's very unlikely that I'm ever going to find a man dumb enough to marry me."

He sat up straight. "You spend so much time running yourself down, Miss Steele," he said after a minute, scowling toward her. "Is it deliberate, calculated to keep people at arm's length?"

She laughed. "I suppose so. I like my life, why change it?"

"Yet, you seem determined to change mine," he reminded her.

"That's different. Yours needs changing," she said pertly. "You were about to go into permanent hibernation, and frankly, Mr. van der Vere, you're not the best companion in the world to hibernate with. You'd have driven yourself crazy."

He burst out laughing, his voice deep and amused,

the sound of it like silver bells in the darkness. "And you're sacrificing yourself to tend me, no doubt."

"Of course," she returned, joining in the game. "Think of all the other people in the world I could inflict myself on!"

He seemed about to say something, then thought better of it. He finished his coffee in one swallow. "I wish I could see you," he said surprisingly. "I wonder if you really are as plain as you like to pretend."

She thought about the scar on her cheek and lifted her eyes to his broad, hard face. "Yes," she said softly. "I am."

His mouth broke into a smile. "Beauty is only skin deep, they say, miss."

"Yes, sir," she sighed, "but ugly goes all the way to the bone, doesn't it?"

He laughed loudly, and the sound was infectious. She laughed with him, wondering at the easy comradeship of their developing relationship. He was like another man, and she felt herself changing. Despite her neat nurse's uniform, which seemed to be drawing its share of curious stares, the woman inside it was being drawn inexplicably closer to the big blond man across from her.

They passed a wreck on the way back to the beach house. Dana paled as she watched ambulance attendants drag an unconscious form from the tangle of metal and glass, but she didn't make a big thing of it. The rest of the way back she talked about the scenery and described houses and beach property to him. But inside she was reliving every minute of the wreck that had killed her mother.

That night it was inevitable that the nightmare would come. She saw the truck coming toward her, felt the impact, saw the unearthly position of her mother's body....

Someone was shaking her roughly; a deep voice was cursing as her eyes flew open. She shook her head, breathing raggedly, and found Gannon and Lorraine standing by the bed. Gannon was wearing a dark robe over his pajamas, and Lorraine was clutching a delicate pink negligee around her, her face troubled.

"We heard you scream, dear. Are you all right?" Lorraine asked, concerned.

Dana sat up, trying to calm her wild heartbeat. Her eyes were full of tears, and she felt sick all over. "It was just...just a nightmare. I'm sorry I disturbed you both."

"It's all right," Lorraine said. "We were worried. Will you be...?"

"I'll sit with her for a moment," Gannon said curtly, ramming his hands into his pockets. "Would you have the maid fix some coffee and bring it up?"

"I'll do it myself," Lorraine said, turning. "I could use a cup, too. Back in a minute."

"You don't have to stay with me...." Dana said tautly.

He felt his way to the chair by the bed and sank into it. His blond hair was tousled, his face was grim, his blind eyes bloodshot, as if he hadn't slept at all. His pajama top and robe had fallen open over a mat of blond hair that seemed to cover his broad chest, and he looked impossibly masculine in her bedroom. He made her nervous.

Oddly enough, he seemed to be concerned about her. He looked toward her, his eyes troubled. "I won't leave you, Dana," he said quietly, and the sound of her given name on his lips disturbed and flattered her.

She pushed back her long hair with a ragged sigh and dabbed at the tears with a corner of the sheet. "I should get up," she murmured, tossing back the covers to reach for her robe at the foot of the bed. It was blue terrycloth, and old, but it made her feel more secure with a man in the room—even a sightless one.

"Self-conscious?" he asked gently. "You aren't used to men seeing you in your nightclothes, are you? Not that I can see...." he growled. "Are you all right? What happened?"

"I had a nightmare, that's all," she said, and the mattress sprung up as she got to her feet and tied the robe securely.

He stood up at the same time, colliding with her. She gasped and clung to him to keep her balance, and the magic of his warmth and strength made her knees even weaker.

"Dana?" he whispered, bending.

Incredibly, he found her knees and back and lifted her completely off the floor in his arms, holding her to his chest.

"Mr....van der Vere..." she protested.

"My name is Gannon," he breathed, searching blindly for her mouth. "Say it...."

"Gannon..."

His lips took his name from hers, and she felt their warm, soft pressure against her own with a leap of her heart. She stiffened, but when the pressure continued with the same tenderness, she let her taut muscles relax.

"That's it," he whispered. "I'm not going to hurt you. I only want to comfort you a little, that's all. Please, don't deny me the one altruistic gesture of my life."

She watched his face as he kissed her again, softly,

with the same undemanding pressure as before. His mouth was warm and hard, and she liked the feel of it rubbing against her own. She liked the minty sigh of his breath on her lips and the smell of him and the strength of his arms holding her.

She let her arms slide around his neck and her mouth tentatively moved against his, a tiny movement like a tremor. He stiffened; his arms tightened. Then his brows began to knot and his face hardened. All at once his mouth burrowed between her lips and the kiss became complete.

She gasped and pushed at his shoulders, and he drew back immediately, breathing hard.

"Predictable, wasn't it, little one?" he whispered with a wry smile. "I'm sorry, I didn't mean to take liberties. I really did mean to comfort you and nothing more."

"It's all right, I understand," she said shakily. She watched his face with awe. She hadn't dreamed that a kiss could be so...frighteningly affecting.

"Perhaps we'd better have our coffee in more sedate surroundings after all," he murmured dryly as he set her back on her feet. "You're a temptation, miss, and you have a very sweet young mouth that I could learn to like all too well. I don't want to see you rush wildly away because I lost my head in the darkness."

She dragged her robe closer. "As you said," she replied, "it was the darkness. And my fear."

He touched her sleeve. "The wreck we saw this afternoon—it brought back unpleasant memories?"

"Yes, sir." She pushed back her hair. "Hadn't we better go? Your stepmother will have a pot of coffee by now, I expect."

"Yes, I expect so." He let her take his arm and lead

him out of the room. ''And I thought I was the patient,'' he teased softly. ''Perhaps we were both mistaken.''

She made a tiny sound and smiled as they joined Lorraine in the dining room.

Chapter Five

A minor crisis in Gannon's company kept him occupied on the phone for hours the next day, and an unexpected visitor arrived just as the cook was putting dinner on the table.

"Dirk!" Lorraine cried, smiling. She jumped up from the table and darted toward a tall, dark man while Dana tried to figure out who the newcomer was.

He was as dark as Gannon was fair, and not nearly as big. He had an easy smile and his face was that of a man who laughed a lot. The only Dirk whom Dana had heard mentioned during her stay at the beach house was Gannon's brother, but of course this couldn't possibly be him...could it?

"And who is this?" Dirk asked, when Lorraine stopped hugging him, nodding past her to where Dana sat neatly in her nurse's uniform at the long table.

"Gannon's nurse, Dana Steele. Dana," Lorraine said with a gay smile, "this is my other stepson, Dirk van der Vere."

"I'm very pleased to meet you," Dana said politely. He grinned, and she realized suddenly that he wasn't much older than she was. And where Gannon's Dutch accent was detectable, Dirk spoke English without the trace of an accent.

"The pleasure is all mine," he corrected. "Am I in time for dinner? Great, I'm starved."

"What brings you down here?" Lorraine asked.

"Gannon. He's in the study, as usual, I take it?" he continued, ramming his hands into the pockets of his gray suit. He sighed. "We've got a strike on our hands, and it's all my fault."

"Is it, or is Gannon just blaming you?" Lorraine murmured with a tiny smile.

He chuckled. "Know him pretty well, don't you? No, I suppose if he'd been in my shoes, he'd have averted it. That's true enough." He shrugged. "I wasn't in a position to promise too much until I could talk to Gannon."

"Can you iron it out?"

"That's what he had me fly down here to find out. Two of the union people wanted to come with me, but Gannon wouldn't allow it: He didn't want them to see him…like this."

"If only he weren't so sensitive about it," his stepmother sighed.

"Amen." He turned to Dana. "Making any progress?"

She laughed. "Not too much, but at least I've coaxed him out of the house a few times."

"It's just that we can't mention his blindness," Lorraine added. "He won't even listen when the doctor discusses the reason for it."

"Maybe he wants to be blind. Have you ever thought of that?" Dirk asked soberly. "No, hear me out," he continued, when the older woman would have interrupted. "You know how hard he was pushing himself before the accident. And there was Layn hanging on to him like a leech, dragging him around the world with her…. He was going twenty-three out of every twenty-four hours, and it was telling on him. Maybe his body did it to him to save itself."

"Layn," Lorraine said bitterly. "Where is she now, do you know?"

"Hanging around with a rich sheikh, I hear," Dirk said coldly. "Where I hope she stays. You do realize that if Gannon regained his sight, she'd be back here like a shot?"

"Surely he wouldn't take her back," the elderly woman said.

Dirk laughed. "Are you kidding? You've seen Layn; what sighted man could resist her?"

Lorraine sighed wearily. "I suppose you're right."

Dana was sitting quietly, listening. Layn must have been the woman who had walked out on him when he was blinded. According to what they were saying, he must have cared for her very much. She stared into her plate. Against a woman like that, what chance would a plain woman have with a man like Gannon van der Vere? She blinked. Why should she have such an odd thought? She didn't care about him, so what did it matter about the woman from his past?

She became aware suddenly that Dirk was watching her, but when she looked up, he grinned.

"Deep in thought, Miss Steele?" he asked. "How in the world did Gannon manage to find such an attractive nurse? This is a pretty dull place."

She flushed at the unexpected compliment. She'd thought the scar down her cheek would detract from what slight beauty she possessed, but Dirk hadn't seemed to notice it. "You're very kind," she murmured, "but I love it here."

"Dana isn't like Layn, my dear," Lorraine said with a gentle smile. "She's managed to get your brother out of the house, out of his shell. He's even allowing me to have a small party next month for his birthday—just intimate friends, you understand, but isn't it a big step in the right direction?"

Dirk chuckled. "Yes, indeed. Miss Steele must be a miracle worker of sorts," he added, winking at her. "Well, let me go and face the dragon. Then perhaps we can sit down to a peaceful meal."

He wandered off toward the study. The door opened and closed, and there was a loud discussion behind it.

Lorraine laughed softly as Dana's head lifted curiously.

"Nothing to worry about, Dana," she said. "They argue constantly, especially when it comes to company policies. Gannon would like to expand the business; Dirk is cautious. Gannon believes in the generous approach to labor negotiations; Dirk is conservative. They're very different."

"I suppose most brothers are," came the quiet reply. "I've always hated being an only child. I used to hope for a brother or sister when I was little."

"Your parents couldn't have other children?"

Dana shifted uncomfortably. "No," she said simply, letting it go at that.

"I'd better have the maid get a room ready for Dirk. No doubt he'll be here at least overnight. I never expect quick solutions when my stepsons start discussing company politics." She patted Dana on the shoulder and left the room.

It was another hour before the men joined them at

the table, and Dana was starving. The beef and scalloped potatoes had been kept warm, and now fresh rolls and asparagus with hollandaise sauce was being brought in by the cook.

"That smells like asparagus," Gannon remarked as he slid cautiously into his chair at the head of the table. He looked out of humor, but Dana noted that he wasn't scowling as fiercely as usual.

"It is," Lorraine said. "Everything settled?"

Dirk only laughed. "If you believe that, I've got some oceanfront property in Arizona I'd like to talk to you about."

"In the middle of the Painted Desert, no doubt," Dana murmured, tongue in cheek.

Dirk's eyebrows lifted. "However did you guess?"

Gannon was listening to their conversation, and his face darkened. "How long are you staying, Dirk?" he asked curtly.

"Oh, a couple of days, I suppose—now that you've phoned Dobbs and gotten the union off my back," the younger man added wryly.

Gannon made a gruff sound and waited for Dana to fill his plate and tell him what was where. The others watched the small ritual with careful amusement. It was so new for them to have Gannon docile.

Her eyes ran over his hard face like silk, liking its rough contours, the broad forehead and jutting brow over his gray eyes. He was a handsome man. Dana could almost picture him in evening clothes; he'd stand out anywhere.

Dirk, watching, smiled at the look on her face. "Dana, how would you like to drive up to Savannah with me tomorrow and see the city?"

She jerked her eyes up, astonished at the unexpected

invitation. She wasn't the only one, because Gannon's eyes darkened menacingly.

"I can't spare her," Gannon said shortly.

"She's been here for several weeks, dear," Lorraine reminded him, "without a single day off. Don't you think she deserves a little recreation?"

Gannon's jaw tautened. "She's been out driving with me, hasn't she? Walking?"

"Really, Mrs. van der Vere, it's all right..." Dana began softly.

"No, it isn't," Dirk broke in. "She isn't slave labor."

Gannon made a rough sound. "All right, take her with you," he said harshly. "If she thinks she needs a day away from me, I can't stop her."

He was making her feel guilty, and she didn't like it.

"She does need a day away from here," Lorraine seconded. "She's young, Gannon; it must be terrible to be shut away from the world like this."

"But it isn't...!" Dana tried to say, but Gannon's deep voice drowned her words.

"Go, then," he said bitterly. "I don't need you, Miss Steele, and that's a fact. I never have." He tossed his napkin aside and almost knocked over his chair, getting to his feet. "Excuse me, I've lost my appetite."

Dana was painfully aware of the two pairs of eyes watching her, but she was too disheartened to put her thoughts into words. She felt as if she'd betrayed the big Dutchman, and it wasn't a feeling she liked. Perhaps she was getting too close to him and a day away would do her good. After all, this job was temporary. He might regain his sight any day and she'd return to Ashton.

That thought disturbed her very much. She went walking on the beach at dusk, dragging her feet in the sand, her eyes troubled as they sought the horizon across the ocean. Her disorderly mind kept going back to that warm, slow kiss they'd shared the night before, and the strange new feelings it had kindled in her. She couldn't remember ever wanting a kiss to begin again, not with any other man. But, of course, Gannon was an experienced man. She hugged her arms across her chest. She had to stop thinking about it nevertheless. She was his nurse, nothing more; she couldn't afford the luxury of getting emotionally involved with him. He was just passing time, but Dana was far too moral a woman to yield to temptation. Besides that, she didn't want him getting too close. It was a trap that would rob her of her peace of mind, that would make her vulnerable. She didn't trust emotions anymore. Especially she didn't trust her own. Her life, since her mother's death, had dissolved. She felt totally alone, and a part of her liked that aloneness. It would protect her from any more wounds; it would protect her from being hurt again.

"Dana! Wait up!"

She whirled, the wind catching her loosened hair, to find Dirk running along the beach toward her. He was wearing jeans and a knit shirt, and he was barefoot.

"You're fast, lady," he chuckled, sticking his hands in his pockets as he fell into step beside her. "What are you doing out here all alone?"

"Enjoying the view," she admitted. He was easy to talk to, and she smiled. "Isn't it just great? Sea breeze, all that ocean out there, and peace and quiet along with it. People tire me sometimes. I like solitude."

"Don't mind your own company?" he teased lightly. "You're a rarity. Most people can't stand to be alone."

"Your brother seems to like it well enough," she

mused, glancing up at him. "Is it only since the blindness?"

"Exactly. Oh, he's been a lone wolf most of his life in that he lives as he pleases." He frowned. "But he's never cared for solitude like this. There were always...friends with him," he added, and she wondered if he meant to say *women* instead of *friends*.

"We're all different," Dana sighed. "It's a good thing too. Imagine how dull it would be if we all thought alike?"

"There'd be fewer wars," he reminded her.

"Yes, but creativity would go down the drain."

"As you say." He pursed his lips and looked down at her. "Is he making much progress?" he asked.

She let her shoulders rise and fall. The comfortable jeans and sweat shirt she was wearing felt wonderful in the cool air. "I thought so until tonight. I really don't think it's a good idea that I go to Savannah with you—not if it's going to upset him like that. It's been a struggle just getting him out of the house."

He nodded. "I can imagine. But you mustn't let him make you into a puppet, Dana. He can do that, I've watched him."

"I won't. But he does pay my salary, and his track record with his nurses isn't super, I'm told." She lifted an eyebrow. "If he throws me out, who'll be brave enough to take my place?"

He winced. "What a horrible thought. Mother told me she begged your supervisor not to tell you everything about Gannon. She was afraid you wouldn't come."

Dana laughed. "I might not have. But once I got here, I wouldn't have left for the world. He challenged me, you see."

"If you want a real challenge," he said dryly, "you ought to wander into his study right now. I barely escaped with my skin intact."

"What did you do to irritate him?" she asked.

He chuckled, watching the ocean begin to darken as the sun set. "I breathed," he murmured. "He's thumping around the room, knocking over furniture and cursing everything from the color of the sky to the carpet that keeps tripping him up."

She drew in a slow breath. "Should I go in and see if I can calm him before your mother jumps off the balcony?"

"I see you've figured Lorraine out very well," he observed. "She's very nervous when he's in a temper—and he hasn't been any other way since the accident."

"At least you believe as the doctors and I do: that it's all a matter of making him realize he hasn't lost his sight permanently."

"Oh, I agree, all right. But Gannon's the one who has to be convinced. And, lady," he added with a grin, "that is going to be a full-time job, and not without hazards."

"I've already found that out," she said with a sigh.

"Won't you change our mind and come with me?"

She looked up at him thoughtfully. "If you'll take Mr. van der Vere along, too, I'll come."

He lifted his eyes helplessly to the sky. "What a horrible thought."

"Will you?"

He looked down, his head cocked, his eyes twinkling. "For you, lovely lady, anything."

"Not so lovely," she murmured, touching the scar.

"It hardly shows," he argued. "And it's healing.

You'll be left with hardly a memory of it in a few weeks."

"I suppose."

"Is that why you came here?" he asked quietly, stopping to watch her expression. "To hide your scars?"

She stared at the sand under her own bare feet. "I suppose I did, in a way. My mother died in an accident a few months ago, you see. She'd been drinking, and I let her drive...." Her shoulders lifted and fell. "I got a few scars and I had a concussion, but everyone seems to feel that I killed her."

"Do they?" he asked thoughtfully, "or is it guilt that's punishing you?"

Her eyes flashed. "Guilt?"

"Your eyes are tortured, Miss Steele," he said softly, studying them. "You're very young to try to live with that much guilt. I'm a fatalist myself. I believe that the hour of death is preordained."

She swallowed. "Is it?"

"Such things are best left to theologians and philosophers. But it seems to me a horrible waste to let guilt destroy your life along with your mother's. Was she a happy person?"

She shook her head. "My parents had divorced, my father had remarried and Mandy found it rough trying to live by herself." She stuck her hands in her pockets. "She couldn't cope. She wanted me to come back home, to take care of her." She laughed bitterly. "I couldn't even take care of myself...."

He caught her gently by the shoulders and turned her to face him. "Try living in the present. You can't change what was."

She felt her lower lip tremble. "The guilt is eating me alive."

"Then stop feeding it," he advised. "Stop hiding."

She searched his kind eyes. "Have you ever thought of becoming a psychiatrist?" she asked, forcing lightness into her tone.

One corner of his mouth curled up. "I studied psychology for three years before I decided I liked electronics better and transferred to a technical college," he confessed.

She burst out laughing. "I should have realized," she said. "You could probably do your brother more good than I have, you know."

"He won't listen to me or talk to me," he said, shaking his head. "But he'll listen to you."

"Only when I yell."

"It's a start. You really want to take him to Savannah? Okay. But you tell him. I'm not going back in there to save my life," he chuckled.

"I find that blatant cowardice," she murmured.

"No doubt. I call it self-preservation." He strode back down the beach beside her. "Have you told him—about the scars?"

"No," she said simply. She swallowed. "You... won't tell him?"

He glanced at her. "You're making too much of them, you know," he said softly. "You're a lovely woman. But if you don't want him to know..."

"It's not for any special reason," she said quickly. "It's just that, well, he doesn't need to know, does he?"

He turned away before she could see the tiny smile on his face. "No, of course he doesn't."

They walked quietly back to the house, and Dana gathered all her nerve before she knocked at the door of Gannon's study.

"Come in" was the harsh reply.

She opened the door, to find him sitting in his big armchair with tumbled furniture all around him, a black scowl on his face and a smoking cigarette in his hand.

"Who is it?" he asked shortly.

"It's me," Dana said.

The scowl blackened. "Back from your daily constitutional?" he asked sarcastically. "Did my brother go with you?"

"Yes, he did," she said coolly. "It was quite a nice change, to walk and talk without yelling."

He snorted, taking another draw from the cigarette. "Can you find me an ashtray?"

"Why?" she asked innocently, noting the pile of ashes beside the chair on the carpet. "Are you tired of dumping them on the floor already?"

"Don't get cute. Just find me an ashtray and bring it here."

She didn't like the silky note in his voice, but she got the ashtray and approached him warily.

"Where are you?" he asked, cocking his head and listening intently.

She set the ashtray softly on the arm of the chair and moved back. "Back here," she replied then. "Your ashtray is next to you."

He muttered something. "Afraid to come too close? Wise woman."

She shifted from one foot to the other. "It's my time off," she reminded him, "but I wanted to ask you something."

"I know it's your time off," he said curtly. "You remind me every day exactly how much you have and when you want it, so why the poor little slave girl act over the supper table? Playing on Dirk's sympathies? I might warn you that my brother is something of a play-boy: He likes skirts.''

"He's a nice, kind man, and you ought to be half as blessed with his good humor,'' she threw back.

"Shrew!'' he accused, sitting up straight. His face hardened; his eyes darkened. "If I could see you, you'd be in considerable trouble right now.''

"What would you do, take me over your knee?'' she asked.

His nostrils flared. "No, I wouldn't risk breaking my hand.''

"How discerning of you,'' she murmured.

His eyes searched in her direction, and something wicked flared in them. "I think I'd rather kiss you speechless than hit you.''

She couldn't help it. She flushed like a budding rose, gaping at him. Her knees felt strangely weak as the words brought back vivid memories.

"No comment?'' he murmured. "Have I shocked you? Or would you rather forget that last night in my arms you responded like a woman instead of a shrew?''

"I'm your nurse, Mr. van der Vere, not...!'' she began.

"You're a woman,'' he interrupted, "and somehow I think that fact has escaped you for a long time. You have the feel of fine porcelain, as if you've never been touched by human hands. Is it part of the shield you wear to keep the world at bay? Are you afraid of feeling too much?''

"I'm afraid of being accused of unethical conduct,'' she returned. "You aren't the first man who's made a pass at me, Mr. van der Vere, and, sadly, you probably won't be the last. Sick men do sometimes make a grab for their nurses if the nurses are young and not too unattractive.''

''The unattractive bit wouldn't matter to a blind man, would it?'' he asked shortly.

''The blindness is temporary,'' she said firmly. ''The doctors have told you that. Your sight will return; there's no tissue damage—''

He cursed roundly. ''There is!'' he shot back. He got to his feet and almost fell in his haste.

She rushed forward without thinking and helped him regain his balance, only to find herself trapped in his arms before she could move away.

''Mr. van der Vere,'' she said with controlled firmness, ''please let me go.''

But his fingers tightened, and a look of sudden pain washed over his features as her small hands pressed helplessly against his warm, broad chest. ''Dana, don't push me away,'' he said softly.

The quiet plea took the fight out of her. She stared up at him, hating what he made her feel, hating her own reaction to it. But how could she fight him like this?

His big hands ran up and down her arms. ''I wish I could see you,'' he said harshly.

''There's nothing uncommon about me. I'm just an ordinary woman,'' she said quietly. ''I'm not a beauty; I'm plain.''

''Let me find that out for myself,'' he said, letting his hands move to the sides of her face. ''Let me feel you.''

''No!'' She tried to move away, but his hands were too strong.

''What is there about my touch that frightens you?'' he asked harshly. ''I won't hurt you, I promise.''

''It isn't that...!''

"Then, what?" His face contorted. "For God's sake, am I such a leper? Does my blindness repel you...?"

Her eyes closed; her lower lip trembled. There was nothing for it now: She was going to have to tell him the truth or let him feel it, and she didn't think she could bear that. She didn't want him to know that she was disfigured.

"I'm...there's a scar," she whispered shakily, her eyes closed so that she missed the expression on his face. "Down my left cheek. A very long one."

His hands shifted, and he found the scar with its puckered surface and traced it from her temple down past her ear, traced it with fingers that suddenly trembled.

Her eyes closed even more tightly. "I didn't want you to know," she whispered.

"Dana." He searched her delicate features with warm, slow fingers, tracing her eyebrows, her eyes, her nose, her cheeks and, finally, her trembling mouth.

"It's like a bow, isn't it?" he whispered, drawing his forefinger over the line of her mouth. "Do you wear lipstick?"

"No," she admitted. "I...I don't like it."

"Firm little chin, high cheekbones, wide-spaced eyes...and a scar that I can barely feel, which must hardly show at all." He bent and brushed his mouth over the scar with such tenderness that her eyes clouded and tears escaped from them.

"Don't cry," he whispered.

She swallowed. "You make it seem so...so small a thing."

"It is. Beauty is more than skin deep—isn't that what they say? You have a lovely young soul...and a stubborn spirit that makes me gnash my teeth, even though

I respect it." He lifted his head. "Dana, I'd give a lot to taste your mouth again. But that wouldn't be ethical, I suppose, and we must above all be ethical."

She smiled at his cynicism. "Yes, me must," she murmured. She disentangled herself gently from his hands and he let her go with a sigh. "Now, about going to Savannah..."

His face darkened and he scowled. "I do not want you to go...."

"Oh, Dirk and I aren't going alone," she assured him. "We're taking you with us."

He blinked. "What?"

"We thought the ride would do you good," she murmured. "Help your disposition, as it were. Blow the cobwebs away."

He chuckled softly, then loudly, and she loved the masculine beauty of his face when it relaxed. "I can think of something that would do my disposition a lot more good than a drive," he murmured, tongue in cheek.

She cleared her throat and moved toward the door. "You just sit here and think about that. I'm going."

"Coward," he said silkily.

"Strategic retreat," she corrected. She paused at the doorway. "Thank you for what you said about the scar, Mr. van der Vere."

"My name is Gannon," he reminded her. "I'd...like to hear you say it."

"Gannon," she whispered, making a caress of it. She turned away from his set features. "Good night."

She barely heard his own "Good night" as the door closed behind her.

Chapter Six

Dana had never seen a city like Savannah, having spent most of her life around Ashton. She was overwhelmed by the history of the sprawling city, and when she and Dirk and Gannon had lunch at an eighteenth-century pirate inn, she almost swooned.

"Pirates really stopped here?" she asked in a whisper, staring around at the homey interior, which was crowded with lunch guests.

"According to legend, they did," Gannon murmured. "If I remember correctly, you can see the ocean from the window, can you not?"

She glanced out toward the horizon. "Oh, yes, you certainly can. What kinds of boats are those way out there?"

"Take your pick—shrimp boats, fishing boats, trawlers, tugboats.... It's a busy harbor," Dirk commented. "The seafood here is super."

"Something else we need to show her," Gannon said between sips of his hot, creamy coffee, "is one of the hidden gardens."

A flower-lover, her ears perked up. "Hidden gardens?"

"Little courtyards. Most of them are in private homes, but we have cousins here who love visitors. We'll drive by before we leave the city," Gannon told her. "I think you'll be impressed."

"I'm glad we didn't bring Lorraine." Dirk chuckled. "Every time she visits Maude and Katy, she wants to renovate the beach house."

"Maude and Katy are spinsters," Gannon continued. "Maude married, but her husband is dead, so she lives with Katy, who never married. They're sisters."

"You'll like the furniture especially, I think," Dirk added. "Most of it is mahogany. It came from the West Indies, where one of our ancestors made a fortune in shipping."

"Indeed he did," Gannon chuckled. "Raiding British ships. He was a pirate."

"Now I know why Gannon's so hard to get along with," Dana told Dirk with a wicked grin. "It's in his blood. I wonder how many people that pirate ancestor tossed overboard to feed hungry sharks?"

"Only one, as legends go," Gannon said, his eyes twinkling as they stared straight ahead. "His wife," he added on a low chuckle.

"Well, the old blackguard!" Dana exclaimed.

"He found her in his cabin with his first mate," he whispered, "and tied them together and pushed them from the starboard deck into the ocean."

She shivered. "What happened to him?"

"Nobody's sure," Gannon continued. "But at least one legend says that he went on to become a provincial governor in the West Indies."

"Injustice," Dana grumbled.

"That depends on your definition," Gannon reminded her. "Those were different times; there were different codes of honor. In those days it was suicide for a woman to be adulterous."

"And these days it's more the 'in' thing than not," Dirk nodded. "How times change."

"Not always for the better," Dana added. Her eyes widened as she saw the platters of seafood being brought by their waitress. "Food!" she exclaimed.

"I hope your appetite is up to it," Dirk teased.

"If it isn't, I'll go home with my pockets full," she returned, and was pleased to hear Gannon's laughter mingling with his brother's.

The happy mood lasted and seemed to increase when they reached the Victorian home of the sisters Van Bloom. Maude was tall and thin and Katy was short and dumpy, but they shared a love of people that went beyond their physical attributes.

Dana was amazed at the garden she saw when she walked through the black wrought-iron gate. The courtyard was floored with brick, and its size was about that of a medium-size living room. It was filled with flowers and potted shrubs and trees, and there was black wrought-iron furniture set near a small fountain positioned in front of a vine-covered wall. Dana could understand why Lorraine felt like redoing the beach house every time she came to the Van Blooms'. It made the most infrequent gardener's fingers itch to recreate it.

"Lovely, isn't it?" Gannon said from behind her. "I remember it very well."

"You may have appreciated it, my dear," Maude said shortly, "but that woman you brought with you last time most certainly did not. Did you hear her, muttering about putting in a bar and a hot tub...!"

Dana turned, frowning, and Gannon looked distinctly uncomfortable.

"Layn likes modern surroundings, Aunt," Gannon said curtly. "What kinds of flowers do you have in here?"

Maude hesitated before she let the subject of Gannon's former girlfriend drop. "Azaleas, my dear," she said. "Roses and sultanas and geraniums in shades of pink and red. I particularly like the red. How about you, Miss Steele?"

Dana sighed. "Oh, I just love them all," she said with quiet enthusiasm. "I don't think I've ever seen anything so lovely."

"You might try one of your own; it isn't so difficult," Maude encouraged.

"The nurse's home isn't the best place, I'm afraid," Dana said wryly.

"You're a nurse?" Maude burst out. "Why, so am I. I practiced as an R.N. for over fifteen years before I retired. Come, my dear, let's sit and discuss the changes over a pot of hot tea."

It was a long time before the two women finished, and then suddenly the others had joined them and it was time to leave. Dana climbed into the front seat with Dirk, while Gannon sat alone and quiet in the backseat and turned his head in the direction of the charming old home with a feeling of loss.

"Isn't it grand?" Dana sighed. "Are there many of those courtyards in Savannah?"

"More than you'd imagine," Dirk replied. "There's an active historical foundation here, with conscientious members who have a love of history and a sense of continuity. They've accomplished a lot, as you'll notice when we go through the downtown area. General Oglethorpe planned for gardens when he laid out the grid pattern of the first streets in the city, you see. He even established a sort of public nursery. Savannah is famous for its public squares as well.''

''It's a beautiful city. I wish we had more time to see it,'' Dana said.

''We'll come back again,'' Dirk promised with a grin. ''You're the kind of girl I like to take sightseeing, Dana: You have such a natural enthusiasm for new things.''

''I love beauty, that's all,'' she replied. ''Thank you for today, Dirk.''

''Today will be the first of many,'' the younger man promised. ''We'll do this again.''

In the backseat, Gannon's face grew darker and harder, and neither of the occupants of the front seat noticed that he wasn't taking part in the conversation. Dana was lost in the memory of what she'd seen, and Dirk was capitalizing on her interest to freeze his brother out of the running. He liked what he saw in this soft-voiced wildflower, and he wasn't planning to lose her to his freebooter of a brother. He was going to stake a claim while there was still time.

Dana, blissfully unaware of her companion's dark thoughts, was chattering away about the garden without a care in the world. The gaiety lasted until they were back at the beach house and inside, until Gannon called sharply for her to join him in the study. And when the door closed, the beauty of the day went into a total eclipse with his harsh outburst.

''Your job,'' he said without preamble, standing rigidly in the middle of the floor, ''is to look after me, not to flirt with my brother.''

She froze at the door, staggered by the attack. "I beg your pardon?"

"You heard me," he growled. "From now on there'll be no more of that. While you work for me, you do it exclusively. I will not have my routine interrupted by these charming little outings with Dirk."

"You came too," she burst out. "And I'll remind you that you only pay for my services, not my soul!"

"That," he said, "is debatable. Keep away from Dirk."

She drew herself up to her full height. "I will not," she said shortly. "As long as he's here I will show him the same politeness and courtesy that I show your mother. And if you don't like that, fire me."

"With pleasure. Pack your things and get out."

She hadn't been prepared for that. Wild thoughts whirled through her mind, the foremost among them being that she'd have to leave him, just when she was getting...used to him. But his face was as dark as thunder, and he had a look of a man who wouldn't back down half an inch to save his life.

"If that's what you want, Mr. van der Vere, I'll be pleased to leave you alone with your bad temper." She watched his rigid face twitch, as if her ready reply had come as a surprise. She could hardly resist a faint smile as she opened the door and went out. She'd had the last word, at least. But what would become of him now?

She started up the staircase when Lorraine appeared at the top of it.

"There you are," the older woman said with a smile. "What would you like for dinner? I've had the cook thaw some steaks—"

"I don't think I'll have time," Dana said quietly. "I'm going up to pack."

Lorraine paled. "But, my dear, you're doing so well with him. Won't you reconsider?"

"It's not me," Dana replied with a quiet smile. "I'd have stuck it out, but he just fired me."

The other woman blinked. "Fired you? Why?"

"I was flirting outrageously with his brother," was the amused reply. "Or so he said. I didn't know I had it in me."

Lorraine laughed softly. "Oh, my. It's not funny in the least, and I'm not laughing at you. But considering the length of time you've known my other stepson... Poor Gannon."

"Poor me," Dirk said from behind Dana. "I gather that something's afoot. Dana's been fired, and I'm the culprit?"

"I was flirting with you," Dana told him.

His eyebrows arched. "Were you? You might have told me about it; I didn't even notice."

"Dirk, do something," Lorraine pleaded. "Gannon simply can't fire Dana just when I've gotten used to her!"

"I'll see what I can do," Dirk sighed, giving the study door a long, hesitant glance. "But don't expect miracles."

"I, for one, will not. I'm packing." Dana started up the stairs. "Don't worry, Mrs. van der Vere, I'll find you someone tough to replace me—perhaps Mrs. Pibbs...?"

"I was thinking more along the lines of that big man on that adventure show I like on television"—Lorraine scowled—"The one who hires himself out as a bouncer in his spare time...."

Dana laughed softly. "Good luck." She went on up the stairs and into her room, closing the door gently behind her. It was just beginning to sink in that she didn't have a job or a place to go. Her job at the hospital had been filled out of necessity, and without it she couldn't move back in with her roommate. She'd just joined the unemployed of the world, and all because her employer had some strange idea that she'd been making a play for his brother.

The more she thought about it, the madder she got. How dare he accuse her of chasing Dirk? It was just as well that she was leaving. Let him sit here and stew all alone; it seemed to be all he wanted from life. Let him wallow in self-pity and convince himself that he was blind forever, and see if she cared.

The problem was that she did care—very much. The thought of the big man sitting alone in that room without trying to help himself made her want to cry. Nobody else would last with him. And most nurses would just throw up their hands and walk out: They wouldn't take the kind of abuse he handed out. She didn't like to think of strangers doing the things for him that she did; even handing him his medicine and leading him around obstacles had become a part of her life that she didn't want to surrender.

And she would keep remembering the way he'd kissed her.... It had been unethical, but so sweet. She'd felt necessary for the first time in her life—secure and protected and needed. All the color would go out of the world when she left this lonely house by the sea.

She started packing her few things with a heart that felt like lead. The sudden tap on her door interrupted her, and she went to answer it with a thudding pulse.

Dirk was standing just outside, his hands in his pockets and a disgusted look on his face.

"I'm afraid I made it worse," he said apologetically,

with a faint smile. "Not only wouldn't he relent, he went right through the ceiling and ordered me out of the house."

She sighed. She'd hoped…but what did it matter now? She returned the smile halfheartedly. "I'm sorry about that. He's in a nasty mood. I only wish I knew what was wrong with him."

"Are you quite sure you don't?" he asked with quiet suspicion. "He's very possessive about you. I haven't seen him this way since his early days with Layn, before he found out what a barracuda she really was."

Dana felt the blush work its way up into her hairline, and the fact that Dirk grinned wickedly didn't help it to fade.

"So it's like that," he murmured. "No wonder he was so angry when you decided to go to Savannah with me."

"It's not like that," she argued. "I'm his nurse. There is such a thing as ethics—"

"And such a thing as love," he interrupted. "What does ethics have to do with that? He cares for you— surely you've noticed it?"

Her eyes closed briefly. "I've notice that he's… attached to me," she corrected. "But you must remember that he's blind—temporarily or not. It makes him feel vulnerable, and he doesn't like it. What he thinks he feels for me may be nothing more than affection. I'm his anchor right now. If he regains his sight—and I'm convinced that he will—I will no more fit into his world than he will fit into mine."

"That might have been true once," Dirk agreed, "but he's changing."

That was true, he was, even if just faintly. But Dana was too wary to hope, and she said so.

"I still think that if you went downstairs and talked to him yourself, you might change his mind," he added.

She laughed softly. "I don't agree. And pride is my greatest fault; I'm not easily bent, you see." She shrugged her slender shoulders. "It's better this way. Mrs. van der Vere won't find it very difficult to replace me...."

"And you won't have risked an involvement, right?" he asked softly. "All right, it's your life. But I think you're making a big mistake."

"As you said," she reminded him quietly, "it is my life."

He nodded. "Well, take care of yourself. Although it's been brief, it's been nice knowing you. We may meet again someday."

She smiled. "It isn't likely. But thank you anyway. Good-bye."

"Good-bye."

She closed the door gently behind her and hated the quick tears that rushed into her eyes. She hadn't wanted to face what she was beginning to feel for Gannon van der Vere, but Dirk had forced her to. Yes, it was a good thing that it would end there. Because when Gannon did regain his sight, the last thing he'd want or need in his life would be a quiet, scared little nurse with inhibitions. And she was wise enough to realize it.

All the same, she paced the floor for what seemed like hours after she'd bathed and dressed for bed and finished gathering all her belongings into her suitcase. Her eyes felt bloodshot; her heart felt sore, as if wounded. She knew it was pointless to go to bed; she couldn't have slept.

The soft knock at the door seemed like a figment of her imagination, and she walked toward it like a daydreamer. Surely Dirk hadn't come back to say good-bye again?

She caught the doorknob, turned it and found a taciturn, weary-eyed Gannon standing quietly in the hall. He was wearing wine-colored pajamas with a long matching robe, and his blond hair was badly rumpled, as if he'd tried desperately to sleep and couldn't.

"Dana?" he asked softly.

Her heart jumped wildly at the sound of her name. "Yes?" she said in a taut tone.

He jammed his big hands into his pockets and leaned wearily against the wall, his eyes staring straight ahead. "Do you want to go?"

"Throwing the ball back into my court?" she mused. "Will it salve your pride if you can make me admit that I don't?"

He shook his head. "But it might make it easier for me to sleep. I...don't want to have to break in a new nurse now. I've gotten used to you. Warts and all," he added coolly.

It was insane, she told herself, to let herself be talked into staying. It would be better for both of them if she folded her tent and stole quietly away into his memory. But she looked at him and loved him; it was as simple as that. And the thought of leaving him became a nightmare.

"I'll only stay," she said firmly, "if you'll stop accusing me of things I haven't done with men I barely know."

His jaw tautened; his eyes flashed. But he sighed and nodded. "Very well. As long as you don't contemplate doing them," he agreed.

"If you could see me," she murmured, "just the

thought of my flirting with a man would amuse you. I'm not even pretty.''

"You have a lovely voice," he said, catching her by surprise. His fingers reached out and instinctively found her face, brushing lightly across her cheek and into her soft hair. His eyes closed in a scowl. "Don't go, Dana. You'd take the color with you."

"You'd very soon find someone to put it back," she told him, moving away from the disturbing feel of his fingers. "But if you like, I'll stay...a little longer."

He grinned then, and all the lines seemed to fall out of his hard face. "Until I fire you again?"

She smiled. "Until you fire me again."

"Get up early," he said, moving away from the wall. "I find myself looking forward to those walks along the beach with you."

"Yes...Gannon," she whispered, watching his face change, soften, mellow.

He nodded. "Yes. That's a start, at least. Good night, Dana."

"Good night."

He touched the wall until he reached his own room, and disappeared into the darkness. Dana stared after him quietly, surprised at the burst of joy she felt over what had happened. She didn't have to leave him. She stepped back into her own room with a silent prayer of thanks. At least she had his company for a little longer. She'd live on it all her life.

He was scowling when she appeared downstairs for breakfast the next morning, and Lorraine looked just as uncomfortable.

"Good morning, dear," she told Dana absently, chewing on her lower lip as she turned back to Gannon.

"Are they sure? They could be mistaken again, since…"

"He said they aren't," he growled. He muttered a rough word under his breath and gripped his cup tightly in both hands. "I told you," he said shortly. "I knew from the beginning that hysteria wouldn't cause so much pain. They'll find it now, too, since they've discovered what I knew all along."

"What is it?" Dana asked quickly, sensing disaster.

Lorraine sighed. "The X rays—there was a mixup: One of the new people at the hospital mistook Gannon's for another patient and mislabeled them. It wasn't really her fault; she was certain that someone else had made the mistake and was trying to correct it."

Dana felt her face whiten. Gannon was sitting very straight, quietly sipping his coffee.

"There was something on the X rays they'd wrongly linked to another patient," Lorraine finished wearily. "When they did a brain scan, it came back clear, so they repeated the X rays. That was when they discovered it. It's been weeks, you see, and they'd told the other patient that nothing could be done." She shrugged. "Oddly enough, his sight came back… It was only in one eye and was apparently truly hysterical in nature."

"Which mine isn't, apparently," Gannon growled. He set the coffee cup down so roughly that it sloshed everywhere, burning him.

Dana jumped up to dab at it and he pushed at her roughly.

She fell against the table with a gasp, and at the tiny sound he seemed to calm all at once.

"Dana?" He reached out. "Dana, did I hurt you? Dana!"

She rubbed her side. "I'm all right," she said quickly, shaking her head at Lorraine, who was rushing toward her. "I'm all right."

He moved closer, his whole look one of abject apology. "I'm sorry. I didn't mean to hurt you."

"You didn't. I collided with you, that's all." She let him find her hand and clasp it warmly. Surges of pure pleasure shot up her arm at his touch. "I'm really fine."

He drew in a steadying breath. "Come down to the hospital with us, will you?" he asked. "I need you."

No three words had ever sounded quite so sweet to her. "Of course I will," she said. "I'll be here as long as you need me."

Lorraine went to get her car keys, looking oddly relieved.

The next few hours seemed to drag on forever, and Dana felt cold fear eating away at her as Gannon went through test after test. Lorraine paced and muttered and looked increasingly more concerned.

Finally they were called into Dr. Shane's office, where the rotund little physician stated the evidence of the tests bluntly and without pulling his punches.

"It's shrapnel," he said quietly, watching Gannon start. "Apparently from the accident—a tiny sliver that lodged itself in the brain, affecting the optic nerve."

"Can you operate?" Gannon asked curtly.

"No."

Dana's eyes closed, hurting for him, because now it was permanent and now he knew it. She was already going over it in her mind before Dr. Shane continued, having seen that type of injury in war patients.

"The only chance you have to regain your sight," the doctor told Gannon, "is if the shrapnel should shift again. And it isn't completely impossible, you know. A sneeze is violent enough to dislodge it, although it isn't likely to. I'm afraid that's all the hope I can give you. If we were to try to operate, we could do irreparable damage to your brain. It's far too delicate and too great a risk. I'm very sorry about the mixup in the X rays, Gannon, but it would have made no difference if it hadn't happened. The condition is inoperable.''

Gannon stood up quietly and held out his hand, shaking the doctor's. ''Thank you for being honest with me. As you see,'' he added ironically, ''I was right all along.''

''Fortunately you have a nurse to help you cope,'' Dr. Shane reminded him, ''and a computer company to provide you with excellent assistance in those new techniques that help the blind communicate with the outside world. You'll do well.''

''Yes,'' Gannon said. ''I'll do well.''

He was putting on a great front. He looked like a man without a care in the world, but Dana didn't believe it, and neither did Lorraine.

''Stay with him,'' she pleaded, drawing Dana aside when they got back to the beach house. ''I'm afraid for him. He's taking it far too calmly to suit me, and you're the only person he's going to allow very close to him.''

''I'll take care of him,'' Dana promised. She touched Lorraine's arm. ''Please don't worry. I'll take care of him.''

''Yes, dear, I know you will.'' She smiled sadly. ''It's in your eyes whenever you look at him. But don't let him hurt you, Dana.''

''I haven't that choice anymore,'' she admitted softly, smiling before she turned and went into the study with him and closed the door.

''Would you like something to eat?'' she asked when

he stood out on the balcony, listening to the waves crash against the shore.

He shook his head. Behind him his hands were clasped so tightly that they looked white in spite of their tan.

"Can I do anything for you?" she persisted.

He drew in a deep, slow breath. "Yes. Come here and let me hold you."

Denying him was the last thought in her mind. She went to him as if she had no other function in life but to do and be anything he wanted of her.

He found her shoulders and pulled her close, wrapping her against his big, taut body. His body suddenly convulsed, and he buried his face in the long strands of loosened hair at her throat.

"Oh, God, I'm blind," he ground out harshly, and his body shuddered once heavily as the emotions poured out of him. "Blind! I knew it, I knew...Dana, what will I do? How will I live? I'd rather be dead...!"

"No!" She pressed closer, holding him, her hands soothing, her cheek nuzzling against him, her voice firm and quiet. "No, you mustn't talk that way. You learned to cope before; you can again. You can get used to it. I'll help you cope, I will. I'll never leave you, Gannon, never, never!" she whispered.

He rocked her against him, and she felt something suspiciously wet against her throat where his hot face was pressed. "Promise me," he ground out. "Swear to me that you won't leave me unless I send you away. Promise!"

It sounded very much like an ultimatum, and she was afraid of what he might do if she refused or argued with him. "Yes, I promise," she agreed softly. Her eyes closed and she savored the feel of him against her, the warmth of his body comforting, like the crush of his big arms. "I promise."

He seemed to slump in relief, and his fingers against her back soothed, idly caressing. "It was a blow," he confessed softly. "I had expected...I had expected them to find something operable, you see. I wanted a miracle."

"Miracles happen every day when people still believe in them," she reminded him. "You're still alive; isn't that a miracle in itself? You're big and healthy and you have everything in the world to live for."

"Everything except my sight," he said shortly.

"I'll remind you that there are many people in the world without sight who have accomplished quite a lot despite it," she said. "Singers, artists, musicians, scientists...nothing is a handicap unless you force it to be. You can accomplish anything you want to."

"Even marriage?" he scoffed, lifting his head. "A family?"

"That as well."

"And who would marry the blind man, Nurse? You?" he laughed, and his smile was cruel; his hands on her arms bit in painfully. "Would you marry a blind man?"

"Yes," she said with her whole heart, loving every line of his face, oblivious to what was happening, even to the words themselves as she drowned in the joy of being near him.

He blinked, and the hardness drained out of his face. "You would...marry me, Dana?" he whispered.

"Any woman..."

"You," he corrected curtly. He shook her gently. "Would you marry me, blind?"

"Gannon, if it's a rhetorical question…" she began unsteadily.

"Will you marry me, Dana?" he persisted, making each word clear and strong. His face hardened. "No more red herrings; just answer me, will you?"

"But do be sensible; we don't love each other," she pleaded.

"You love me," he corrected, smiling when she stiffened. "Oh, yes, it stands out a mile, even to an inexperienced man, and I'm not that. I know how you feel. You sound and smell and feel like a woman in love, and when I touch you this way, you melt against me. Professional compassion? No, Dana, it isn't that. Now is it?"

She swallowed, her lips parting. "It's…infatuation," she whispered. "You're so alien from any man I've ever known, and I know nothing of men. Is it surprising?"

He shook his head. "Not at all, but I'm going to take shameless advantage of it. Marry me, Dana. I can't promise you undying love, but I'll take care of you; I'll be good to you. And all you have to do in return is lead me around and keep me from blowing out my brains…."

"Stop it!" She pressed her hand frantically against his warm, hard lips and trembled when they pressed back into its palm.

"Would you care that much?" he laughed. "You don't even want my money, do you, little one? That in itself makes you an oddity in my world. Take a chance, Dana—say yes. I'll make it good for you, in every way there is."

She wanted to. She needed to. But it wasn't possible, and she knew that too.

"I can't," she whispered miserably.

He stiffened. "Why not?"

"Because there's every possibility that someday you'll regain your sight—the doctor told you as much—and what if you did and found yourself tied to someone like me?" she ground out. "You'd be ashamed—"

He stopped the tirade with his lips. She went taut under the hard, demanding pressure, feeling something unleashed in him that had been carefully controlled up until now. She pushed against his broad chest, but he wouldn't relent, not an inch.

"Ashamed of you?" he growled at her lips. "Never! Now, stop talking nonsense and kiss me back. We're going to be husband and wife, so you'd better learn to like this with me. We're going to do quite a lot of it through the years ahead. Come on, don't turn away. Kiss me."

"I won't marry you, I won't," she protested.

"Then we'll be engaged until I can make you change your mind," he murmured, brushing his lips maddeningly over hers, feeling the helpless trembling of her mouth at the newness of the caress. His hands dropped to her waist and brought her gently against him. "Just engaged," he whispered. "All right, butterfly? I won't even rush you to the altar. Just agree to that much and I'll stop talking about leaping onto the rocks...."

She shuddered at the thought of his body bruised and broken by those huge boulders. "Gannon..."

"Say yes," he whispered. His mouth bit at hers—warm, slow kisses that drugged her, that drained her of protest.

She reached up to hold his warm face between her hands, giving in to a pleasure she'd never known. "I shouldn't," she told him.

"But you're going to," he murmured, smiling. "Sweet little mouth, it tastes of honey, did you know? Now, stop talking and kiss me better. I've had a terrible morning. Make it better for me, can't you?"

She wanted to say no, she wanted to ignore the proposal, she wanted to run. But she heard her own breathless voice agreeing with him, felt her body lifting against the crush of his arms, felt herself go under in a maze of sweet magic as he kissed her long and tenderly. And then Lorraine was suddenly in the room, offering congratulations, and it was too late to protest, to take it back. Before she could open her mouth to deny it, she was drinking champagne as Gannon van der Vere's new fiancée.

Chapter Seven

Once Gannon decided to come out of his shell and cope with the reality of his blindness, he seemed to change overnight. He called in one of his computer experts and they locked themselves away in his study for the better part of a day. When the caller left, Gannon was grinning from ear to ear.

"I'd love to know what's going on," Dana ventured as she joined him, closing the door gently behind her.

"Progress," he said. He lifted his head. "Where are you? Come here."

She went to him as naturally as if she were walking into a room, feeling his big arm draw her close to his side with wonder.

"Did it happen?" he asked, his voice mirroring the same uncertainty she felt. "Did you really agree to marry me?"

She sighed and leaned her head against his shoulder. "I was out of my mind," she confessed. "I should have said no. You'll regret it...."

"Never!" He turned her into his arms and stood holding her tightly, his breath warm and soft at her ear.

"Never, not as long as I live. We'll have a good life together." He found her chin and lifted it. "Dana, you meant it? You do love me?"

She swallowed. Where was her pride, her caution? He'd as much as admitted that he didn't love her, that all he could offer her was companionship.

"Yes," she said anyway, studying the lines and angles of his face with soft, loving eyes. "Oh, yes, I meant it, Gannon."

His chiseled lips parted on a heavy breath and he seemed troubled. His hands moved up to her soft arms and stroked them idly. "I feel as if I'm cheating you," he confessed. "Perhaps...perhaps we should call it off—now, while there's still time."

She understood. He was telling her that he could never love her. But she was willing to settle for what he could give; even the crumbs of his affection would be more than she'd ever had in her young, lonely life.

"I'm willing to take the chance—if you are," she said after a minute, and the strangest expression crossed his hard features.

"I'll take care of you," he told her. "That may sound ridiculous, coming from a blind man. But if you trust me with your future, I'll do everything in my power to see that you don't regret it."

She smiled. Hesitantly, shyly, she reached up to touch his face, her fingers cool and trembling where they brushed against his cheek.

He flinched, and she started to tug her hand back, but he caught it and pressed it firmly against the warm, slightly abrasive flesh of his face.

"No, don't draw back, Dana," he said on a whisper. "You startled me, that's all. I like to be touched by you."

"Your face is rough," she murmured, studying it. "You have to shave twice a day, don't you?"

He nodded, smiling. "You'll discover after we're married that I feel like a bear early in the morning."

She blushed to the roots of her hair, and her breath caught. He heard it, laughing delightedly.

"Oh, bright spirit," he breathed. "What did I do in my life to deserve something as untouched and untarnished as you?"

She felt tears warm her eyes at the unexpected words. "I'm only a woman," she reminded him.

He shook his head, and his eyes sought the sound of her voice. They were dark with emotion, narrow, as if he'd have given anything at that moment to be able to see her.

"No, you're something completely out of my experience," he corrected. "The women in my life have been hard and jaded. I never realized that fact until we met. I think you've spoiled me, Dana. I didn't know there were people like you left in the world. God knows, my world wasn't peopled with them."

"Your world sounded very superficial to me," she said quietly. "As if people walked around without really feeling deeply, or thinking deeply, or participating in life."

"That was so." His hands moved up her arms to find her face and cup it. "I had nothing and never knew it. You make my darkness bearable, purposeful. I begin to understand what you said to me at the beginning about a life of service."

"You do?" she whispered.

"That man who just left? He was my computer expert. We are beginning research on a unit that will outperform our present equipment designed to assist the blind. It will be a unit that can convert the printed word into sound—that can read text to an unsighted person.'' He grinned delightedly. ''The first of many innovations, I expect. I think that I have never felt such pleasure as I feel at this moment, not only because such a device will assist me, but because it will assist so many others like me.''

She burst into tears. She couldn't help it. Such a statement, coming from the hard, cold man of her early days there, brought such joy that she couldn't contain it.

''Dana,'' he whispered, drawing her gently closer, rocking her. ''Doesn't it please you to have reformed me?''

She could hardly speak at all, she was so choked up. ''Oh, yes, it pleases me,'' she said fervently. ''Gannon, what a beautiful thing to do!''

''Contamination,'' he whispered wickedly. ''Being around you is making a civilized man of me. How do you like that?''

''I like it very much,'' she replied, pressing closer.

''So do I,'' he murmured. His hands smoothed down her tumbled hair. ''It is, at least, a beginning. For now, Pratt has left me a device that we marketed last year. Come, I'll show you how it works.''

She dabbed at her red eyes, following him to the desk, where a computer was sitting, along with a printer.

He sat down in front of the machine, booted up the system and fed a disk into it. Immediately, a mechanical voice began reading to him what was obviously a marketing report. He leaned back in his chair, grinning in her direction.

''What do you think?'' he asked, interrupting the program with a light touch on the keyboard. ''It gives me access to any company information I might need, at the touch of a finger. Even the disks have been coded with raised letters so that I can choose those I need. This terminal''—he tapped it—''is connected to the main computer at my office. With it I can access any information I need to send information back. Memos, letters and such. I can even contact other computers with the serial interface and a telephone modem.''

''Science fiction,'' she whispered, awed.

''The tip of the iceberg,'' he returned. ''The computer revolution has done more for the visually and audially impaired than anything else to date. And this is the bare beginning. Within ten years the entire industry as we know it will be so improved that this machine will seem obsolete.''

''But I thought your company specialized in electronic equipment?'' she murmured, standing close.

''It did. Now it's going to specialise in sensory aid devices for the blind and deaf,'' he said firmly. ''And the first order of business is going to be finding ways to cut costs and make that equipment easily affordable for the people who need it.''

''Oh, Gannon,'' she whispered, choking.

''Come here, waterspout,'' he chuckled softly, drawing her down into his strong arms. ''Don't cry all over me—you'll short-circuit my computer.''

''I'll try,'' she promised, cuddling close. ''Gannon, you're a nice man.''

''I suppose I can get used to being called that,'' he sighed. ''But bear with me, it's very new.''

''Yes,'' she agreed, laughing softly at the newness of being in his arms. ''It is.''

''How about getting me a cup of coffee while I go through this report?'' he asked. ''As much as I hate having you out of my arms for that long…''

''I'll be right back,'' she promised, getting to her feet. She left him with the computer and walked dreamily into the kitchen to get his coffee.

Apparently his good humor even extended to Dirk, because later that week he invited his brother down to help him work out some details on the new sensory equipment. Dana took the opportunity to go into town and shop, with Lorraine's guidance, for her wedding dress.

Dana's eye was caught by a striking brunette who was going through the boutique's collection of evening gowns, and she noticed Lorraine suddenly stiffening.

''Layn Dalmont!'' the older woman gasped.

As if the tiny sound caught her attention, the willowy brunette turned, her dark eyes flashing as they recognized Gannon's stepmother. She smiled, her attention shifting indifferently to Dana.

''Well, well, look who's here!'' Layn laughed, abandoning the dresses to float toward them, a vision in red chiffon.

''Hello, Layn,'' Lorraine said tautly.

''Hello, Lorraine. And who's this? The little fiancée I've heard about?'' she added, giving Dana an amused scrutiny. ''How fortunate for Gannon that he's blind, honey, or he wouldn't give you the time of day.''

It was what Dana knew already, but it stung to hear it put into words. She lifted her small face and smiled back. ''How nice to meet you, Layn,'' she said quietly. ''I've heard all about you.''

The other woman started, as if she hadn't expected such a polite reply, but she said nothing in return.

''How have you been, Layn?'' Lorraine asked, also politely.

''Bored, darling'' was the curt reply. ''Life without

Gannon is very dull. How is he, by the way? Still mourning me?''

"Hardly, when he's about to be married," the elderly woman said with sweet venom.

"On the rebound, no doubt," the willowy brunette said, with a cold smile at Dana.

"You're welcome to come to the ceremony," Dana invited, smiling back. "Any friend of Gannon's, as the saying goes..."

Layn cleared her throat. "I have other commitments. I'll be sure to send you a wedding present." Her cold eyes went to Dana's cheek. "Perhaps some veils...?" She turned and strode away, leaving Lorraine gasping.

"Oh, that woman!" Gannon's stepmother burst out. "How cruel!"

"How true," Dana corrected, unruffled. "Please, don't let it upset you. She may be troubled by her own conscience, and I can take care of myself, you know."

Lorraine visibly relaxed. "Yes, I've noticed that. Even Gannon doesn't get the best of you, my dear." She laughed. "It was delightful to see that Layn didn't either."

"I see what Dirk meant, though. She does remind me of a barracuda," she added unkindly, with a small laugh. "We'd better get home. I can shop for dresses another day, when the vibrations are a little less hostile. All right?"

"If you like, Dana. I'm sorry Layn spoiled this for you."

She shrugged. "I let her spoil it. Anyway, we haven't even set a date for the wedding yet, so it's no loss."

As they drove home, though, that realization began to bother her. Gannon hadn't liked to talk about actual dates, as if he were reluctant to set one. Perhaps he was no more sure of success than she was. Perhaps he really did miss Layn and regretted proposing to Dana. Layn was right about one thing: sighted, he'd never have preferred his plain little nurse to the other woman.

She steered away from the study when they got home and sought the solace of the beach instead. Her mind was troubled. Gannon had seemed to brood a great deal. Lately she hadn't been too concerned about that until that day—until she'd seen Layn. But what if he was regretting his hasty proposal? What if he'd only been searching for a way to keep Dana with him, and marriage was the only way he'd found?

He didn't act like a man in love; he'd admitted that he wasn't. He'd told her that he had nothing to offer except companionship, affection. Would that be enough to last them all their lives? What if he regained his sight? How would he react to being tied to a woman who paled when compared to his beautiful Layn?

She stood watching the waves crash onto the beach and she knew all at once that she couldn't go through with it. She couldn't marry him. But how was she going to go back into his study and tell him?

She'd have to leave. There was no choice about that. She'd have to go back to Ashton and find a job. She'd have to face her relatives....

Oddly enough, the grief over her mother's death was subsiding in the wake of her problems here with Gannon. She still felt an ache, a cold place deep inside that held loss and grief. But it was all beginning to fall into place. She was coming to grips with her own guilt, with the blame she'd transferred to her father, to the overreaction to her aunt's tactless remark. She seemed to have gone a little mad after the accident and was just now putting the pieces of her mind back together. Going home was no longer the terror it had been.

But still there was the problem of Gannon, the unwanted task ahead of explaining to him why she couldn't go through with the wedding. And along with it was the prospect of living her whole life without him. She closed her eyes, burning up with the love she felt for the big, bad-tempered man. She'd never felt so secure and safe in her life as she had with him, needing nothing more than his company, the pleasure of looking at him, holding his hand. Living without him was going to be almost as bad as losing her mother. How was she going to bear it? And most of all, how was she going to tell him?

She heard her name being bellowed from the steps that led to the beach from the house, and she smiled at the familiar voice that was audible above the crashing surf.

Barefoot, she joined him, her hair loose, and as she caught sight of his calm, relaxed face all her good intentions deserted her. *Let tomorrow take care of itself,* she decided. It would, and God would guide her steps. He always had, after all.

"Dana!"

"I'm here," she said, moving close. "I was just walking."

He smiled. "Walk with me, then. I've had all I can take of business for one day." He held out his hand, and she took it, feeling secure and warm all over at just his touch.

"I thought you were going to catch up on all the loose ends," she murmured.

He chuckled, a relaxed sound that pleased her ears. "I had good intentions. The drawback to the audio devices are that they wear you out. A sighted person can look back over a page of figures, but I had to do it by listening. It gets very repetitive.''

"The new devices are just the same, aren't they?" she asked.

"They are. It's one of the drawbacks. But it's the best thing we have, to date.''

"That new aid you mentioned, the one that reads printed material—was it your company that developed it?" she asked.

"We were one of several companies to hit upon the technology together, although we weren't the first to produce and market it," he told her. He grinned. "What is it they say, Dana, about great minds running in the same direction?"

She laughed with him, leaning companionably against his arm as they walked. He was so tremendous, so good to lean against, to depend on.

"Did you find your wedding gown?" he asked after a minute.

The question brought back unpleasant memories. "Not yet," she said quietly. "I'll go and look some more another day.''

He scowled in her direction. "What happened?" he asked curtly, immediately certain that something was wrong. "Come on, don't hedge. What happened?"

"We…we saw Layn Dalmont at the shop," she said after a minute.

He stiffened, as if he'd been slapped. "Did you?"

His own posture betrayed him, and she turned away to stick her hands in the pockets of her jeans while she watched the ocean. "She's very lovely," she said.

"Yes, she is." His head was cocked to one side, his

arms folded across his massive chest. "What did she say to you?"

"Very little," she replied honestly. "Mostly that she was bored to death without you."

He smiled faintly. "I'm not surprised. I spent a lot of money keeping her happy."

Her eyes closed, and she was glad that he couldn't see her face. "Lorraine told her that we were getting married."

That brought his head up attentively. "Did she? What did she say?"

Dana laughed. "She said she'd buy us a wedding present," she said, without mentioning the cruel way the other woman had put it.

"That doesn't sound like the Layn I know," he murmured. His eyes searched for her. "Where are you?"

"Here," she said, moving closer to him.

He caught her by the waist and drew her to him. "Did she bother you? I forget how unworldly you are. Layn can be dangerous."

"I can take care of myself," she reminded him. Her eyes studied his dark face. Was he regretting it all? Was he mourning for Layn?

"That's going to be my pleasure from now on." He suddenly lifted her clear off the ground so that her eyes were on a level with his sightless ones. "Kiss me, Dana."

Without thinking, she leaned forward and pressed her mouth very softly against his. He let her take the initiative, standing quietly while she savored the cool firmness of his lips against her own.

"You're very cool, darling," he whispered softly. "Mad at me?"

Her heart jumped at the endearment as well as the question. "No, of course not," she assured him.

"Then kiss me as if you mean it, Dana," he said, "not as if you're doing an unpleasant duty. Unless..." He frowned. "...unless it really is unpleasant?"

"Silly man," she whispered adoringly. She kissed him again, harder this time, lingering over his firm mouth until she felt the tension drain out of him, felt the warm response of his lips, the gentle hunger of his enclosing arms.

"Better?" she teased gently, clinging to him.

"Much better," he murmured, rubbing noses. "But that's enough of that," he added with a hard sigh, setting her firmly back on her feet. "I'm no saint."

She smiled. "You're doing very well for a man who isn't."

"Yes, aren't I?" he growled. He found her hand and held it warmly as they started walking again. "Dana, you do realize that things will be...different...when we're man and wife? I won't have a marriage of convenience at my age."

"I understand," she agreed. "I don't want an artificial marriage, either. I...I'd like to have children." Daydreams. Wonderful daydreams. She was refusing to face facts and she knew it, but wasn't she allowed to dream just a little?

His hand contracted painfully. "Children," he whispered. "I hadn't thought of that."

"Don't you want a son?" she teased. "I thought most men did."

"Of course I do," he growled, jerking her close to his side. "It's just that I hadn't expected...my wife didn't want them—did Lorraine tell you? She didn't want the inconvenience."

She smiled. "Perhaps if I were beautiful and gay and worldly...."

"No," he returned. "I think I know you quite well by now. No, it wouldn't matter. You'd have your own and a dozen orphans besides, wouldn't you, and never count the cost. You'd love the whole world if it would let you."

"You make me sound saintly, and I'm not," she countered. "I'm only—"

"—a woman," he finished for her. "Yes, I know. But what a woman!" he added, bending to brush his lips over her forehead. "No regrets? Will you be sorry that I can't see our children?"

Her heart stampeded at the sound of that. *Our children.* She smiled. "No," she whispered. "I'll describe them to you in minute detail. You won't miss a thing."

His jaw tautened. He stopped, dragging her into his arms, and kissed her suddenly, hungrily, shocking her into a wild response of her own.

He released her all at once and moved away. "I'm sorry," he said curtly. "It was thinking about children.... We'd better go back in. I feel odd."

"Are you all right?" she asked quickly, full of concern.

"Just my head. Dana, the headaches are so much worse lately," he said pensively as they turned back toward the house. "I'm taking more and more medication, hadn't you noticed?"

She had, but she was trying not to show too much concern. "We'd better call Dr. Shane, just to play it safe, don't you think?" she asked calmly. "It's probably just the hours you've been putting in lately. More stress. It's perfectly natural."

He seemed to calm at her own easy manner. "Yes, that's probably what it is."

"But we'll have him check you over. I'll call first thing in the morning."

He nodded. "Now, no more about doctors. Let's talk about houses. Where would you like to live?"

They spent the rest of the evening talking vaguely about houses and cities and holidays and schools for the children when they came along. But Dana didn't sleep well. The headaches weren't natural, and Gannon had to know it. They were playing a game, and she was afraid of the outcome.

The next morning she called Dr. Shane and described Gannon's symptoms. He asked her to bring in her fiancé that afternoon and let him run some more tests.

She drove him to the office and sat in the waiting room while the two of them talked. Gannon reappeared, taciturn and irritable, directing her to the hospital, where he was to be admitted overnight while Dr. Shane had the tests performed. Dana was concerned about that, and she had a suspicion that something was wrong. But Dr. Shane wouldn't talk to her, and neither would Gannon, since she was now in the position of a fiancée, not a nurse.

Lorraine paced with her, worried with her. But when the test results were in and Gannon was released from the hospital, he told no one what had been found. In desperation Dana called Dr. Shane, only to be told that what he'd found was privileged information, but that she needn't worry, he was certain everything would be fine.

She approached Gannon, but he wasn't talking. He only smiled and kissed her and told her that there was a chance, just a slight one, that his sight might come back. And then she knew what was wrong with him. He was going to see again—but he didn't want to be saddled with her when it happened. He wanted Layn, and now there was a chance he could get her back. But only if Dana was out of the way.

She imparted that information to Lorraine, who laughed at her.

"You're being ridiculous, dear," she chided. "He wouldn't want Layn now, not after the way she treated him. Don't be silly. He loves you!"

But he didn't. He'd already admitted it. And now Dana was worried, terribly worried. How was she going to survive if he sent her away? She loved him so much, how was she going to let go?

Chapter Eight

~~~

Dirk came down for the next weekend, and Gannon welcomed him with unusual fervor.

"I'm glad you came," he said, thumping his brother on the back. "You can keep Dana and Lorraine company while I work on the visual aid with Al Pratt. He should be here any minute."

"Shame on you," Dirk chided. "A newly engaged man..."

Gannon looked briefly uncomfortable, bearing out Dana's suspicions that he hated being engaged to her, newly or not. "I know, but time is money where this new device is concerned. We've got some innovative ideas we want to work up before somebody beats us to the punch. Oh, and I've invited a guest for Sunday dinner, Lorraine," he added.

"Anyone I know, dear?" Lorraine asked without looking up from her needlepoint.

"Yes. Layn."

There was a silence in the room so utterly sudden that the sound of the woman's name seemed to echo endlessly. Dana closed her eyes, feeling her heart shatter. It was true. Now she knew it was true.

"In that case," Dirk said quietly, "I think Dana and I will drive down to Savannah for the day on Sunday."

Gannon started to speak, stopped and smiled faintly. "Perhaps that would be just as well. You might take Lorraine with you. And you might stop sounding so suspicious while you're about it," he added, the Dutch accent emphasizing itself. "It's business. Layn and I have investments together in a shipping company. We're going to discuss stock and expansion. That's all. I haven't forgotten my own engagement."

"I'm so relieved to hear it," Dirk said curtly. "If it is an engagement."

Gannon blinked. "I beg your pardon?"

"Dana isn't wearing a ring," he observed, "and I haven't heard any mention of a wedding date."

Gannon coughed. "There hasn't been time. I've been busy."

"Sure," Dirk said shortly. He jammed his hands into his pockets. "Dana, care to go for a walk with me? Pratt's just driven up, and I know Gannon will have other things on his mind."

"Of course," she said in a ghostly tone. "Lorraine, would you like to come with us Sunday? Maybe we could go back to see Katy and Maude?"

"I'd like that," Lorraine said, struggling for composure.

While they discussed times and plans, Pratt came in to join Gannon, and the two of them vanished into the study behind the closed door.

Dirk was outspoken about the Sunday dinner and angrier than Dana had seen him since they became acquainted.

"Layn here," he growled. "And when he's engaged to you! He might consider your feelings. Lorraine told me what she said to you in town!"

"He doesn't know what she said," she told him quietly. "I didn't think it was necessary to tell him. I can handle Layn myself."

"So you think," he returned darkly. "She'd cut you into ribbons, and you know it. She's been after Gannon for a long time, despite the fact that she ran after the accident. I've always thought it was as much because she thought he'd blame her as because she didn't want to be around a blind man."

"Did he love her very much?" she asked.

"I don't know my brother that well. He's very good at disguising his feelings." He shrugged. "But they were together most of the time until he was blinded."

She felt sick all over. And now it was starting again: she was going to lose him. And there was nothing she could do. She didn't have the weapons to fight a woman like Layn.

"Maybe it really is business," she said softly.

"Maybe cows will run computers," he scoffed. "Don't kid yourself, honey; they don't need to meet here on a Sunday to do something they could manage over the phone."

Tears sprung to her eyes, but she blinked them away, too proud to let him see how hurt she was.

"I'm sorry," he said quietly. "I shouldn't have said that. It could be innocent...."

"You don't have to tell me something I already know," she said softly. "He doesn't love me; he said as much."

"But you love him very much."

She nodded. "Fortunes of war," she laughed bitterly.

"The first time in my life, and it had to be man like Gannon.... If only I were beautiful and worldly and sophisticated!"

"You wouldn't be the girl you are," he corrected. "I like you as you are. So does he."

"Like," she agreed. "Not love. And it wouldn't be enough, eventually. It's just as well. I'll be sad for a while, but I'll get over him."

"Will you really?" he asked, eyeing her.

She turned away. "Let's go look for sand crabs. They fascinate me, the way they dive into the sand to hide. Look, there's one...!"

He watched her with sad eyes, wishing there was something he could do to ease the pain she was trying to hide. But he was as helpless as she was.

Dana had been hoping that the other woman wouldn't show up until after she and Dirk and Lorraine had left the house on Sunday. But as luck would have it, Layn was on the doorstep before Lorraine had finished dressing.

"Well, hello, darling," she told Dirk as he answered the door. She was resplendent in a sea-blue dress with white accessories and a matching scarf tied over her hair, looking the fashion plate she was.

Layn's eyes darted past him to Dana, and she gave the other girl's simple white sun dress and sandals a distastefully quick appraisal.

"I'm not too early?" Layn murmured.

"Of course not, darling," Dirk replied with sweet sarcasm. "Gannon's waiting for you in his study. The rest of us are off to Savannah for the day."

Layn looked faintly shocked. "Leaving poor Gannon all alone with me?"

"We could load a gun for him before we leave," Dirk suggested.

Layn only laughed. "You might load one for me," she murmured, glancing at Dana. "Since he's been keeping company with the little saint, he may be desperate for some wicked company."

Dana's eyebrows lifted. "Think so? I'll have to remember to polish my halo more often."

Layn became angry when she couldn't get a rise out of Dana, then whirled on her heel and stalked off into the study.

Dirk was trying to smother his laughter and failing miserably. "You wicked lady!" he burst out.

Dana only shrugged. "Well, she asked for it. Shall we wait for Lorraine in the car?"

But just about that time Lorraine came quickly down the stairs to join them, and they left without even a good-bye to Gannon.

It was a long day. Dana, despite the fact that she enjoyed visiting Katy and Maude, spent most of the hours brooding on what was going on back at the house. Was Layn right? Would he be so desperate for a woman that he'd make a dead set at her? Was he tired of Dana's repressive ways? Was he trying to find a way out of the engagement? Why else would he have flaunted Layn in front of her?

They stopped at a restaurant for lunch, and while Lorraine was creating a salad at the salad bar, Dirk leaned forward earnestly.

"Worried?" he asked softly. "You've hardly smiled all day."

Dana smiled faintly. "Yes, I'm worried. How can I

compete with somebody who looks like Miss Dalmont?''

"Easily, since Gannon can't see her," he replied brutally.

"That's not what I meant. He's seen her; he's never seen me." She toyed with her napkin. "Besides that, he's not a saint. I must be a drag to him...."

"He adores you. It's even obvious to someone as thick-skinned as myself." He reached over and touched her hand. "Come on, spill it."

She lifted her shoulders. "I think he's trying to make me leave."

He frowned. "Why?"

"It's not something I can explain. But ever since he went back to the doctor, he's been distant with me. I can't get close to him." She looked up, worry shadowing her eyes. "They told him his sight was very likely to return—something about the shrapnel that they wouldn't tell me. What if he's beginning to see again?" she groaned. "Compared to Layn, I'm so ugly—and he loved her! Now she's back and he's asked her to dinner...."

He caught her hand in his and held it gently. "You're not ugly. You're a lovely woman, and any man would be proud to marry you. Even me, the confirmed bachelor, if I thought I had a chance."

She blinked, not believing him.

"Think I'm kidding?" he mused. "I'm not. There's a quality in you that I've never seen in another woman, and I like it very much. If Gannon didn't have a place in your heart, I'd give him a run for his money."

She blushed softly and lowered her eyes on a smile. "Thank you. You don't know what you've done for my crushed ego."

"I wasn't flattering you."

"Yes, I know." She lifted her eyes again. "He wants Layn, you know."

He sighed wearily. "Yes."

"I won't hold him to a promise he made in a moment of weakness. The minute his sight is restored, I'm going home to Ashton," she said firmly.

"You might consider fighting for him," he reminded her.

"With what?" She laughed. "I don't have potent weapons, and even if I did, I wouldn't use them. I'm not the type. No, he'd have to love me. And he's already admitted that he doesn't. It would be a very empty kind of relationship—don't you think?—if all the love was on one side."

He nodded solemnly. "I suppose so. Dana, if you do go home, I'd like to see you again."

She smiled. "I'd like that too."

He grinned. "Now we're getting somewhere. Tell me about your work."

They started discussing the advances in medicine when Lorraine joined them, and then the talk switched to flowers and gardens for the rest of the meal.

Gannon was alone when they returned to the house; he was preoccupied. He let Dana bring his meal and they sat in a cool silence for a long time while he finished it and asked her to pour him a second cup of coffee.

"Did you have a nice day?" he asked absently.

"Oh, it was lovely. Katy and Maude send their love."

He laughed bitterly. "Just what I need."

She paled, turning her attention to the coffee cup. "Did you get your business straightened out?"

He leaned back in the chair with the cup in his hands. "Yes. Layn's very lovely, isn't she?"

"Very," she agreed.

"Poised, sophisticated...with an excellent business head. The kind of wife a businessman could depend on to help him accomplish his goals," he added; his point seemed to have been made deliberately. He sipped his coffee. "What was she wearing?"

"Blue," she said, staring into her own cup. "Sea blue."

He chuckled. "One of her favorite colors. I remember a bathing suit she used to have, when I took her to Nassau...." His face clouded and he stopped abruptly, swinging forward in the chair. "Can you take dictation?" he asked suddenly. "I need to write some letters, and I'm not fast enough with the computer yet. Can you type?"

"Yes to both," she said agreeably. "I'll be glad to help you."

"Yes, I know," he said under his breath, and looked as if he were hurting inside. He leaned back wearily in his chair and closed his eyes. "It doesn't help the situation."

She moved closer to the desk, studying his lined face. "Gannon, is your sight returning?"

He made a curt movement, his sightless eyes opening on darkness. "What?"

"Are you beginning to see again?" she persisted. "I know something's happened—I can feel it. You're... you're very distant lately."

He laughed harshly. "Am I? And why do you suppose I am?"

She studied her feet. "Layn's very beautiful," she said quietly.

He sat breathing steadily, deliberately. "Yes."

"And you...you cared for her before you were blinded."

"That too." He cocked his head, listening. When she didn't say anything more, he seemed to slump. "She blamed herself, you know," he said finally. "She was driving the speedboat. It's taken her all this time to come to grips with it and realize that I didn't blame her."

Dana didn't believe that for a minute, but she kept quiet. More than likely, the knowledge that Gannon's sight was returning had a great deal to do with Layn's sudden interest in him.

"We're very different, aren't we?" she asked softly. "You and I, I mean. From different backgrounds, different worlds."

He was listening intently, his face shuttered. "Yes, we are," he said. "And I hate to say it, Dana, but when I...regain my sight, that difference is going to become even more apparent. I travel in circles you've never touched, full of wild living and unconventional people."

She watched him with a heart that felt near breaking. "And, too, there's Layn, isn't there?" she prodded. "Layn, who would fit very well—does fit very well—in that kind of world?"

His face tautened. "Yes."

She lifted her hands to her waist and clasped them there, very tightly. "Gannon, about the engagement..."

"Not today," he said curtly, as if the words were being dragged out of him, as if he hadn't meant to say them. "We'll discuss it some other time. Get that pad, please. Layn's driving me down to Savannah the day after tomorrow for a meeting about that expansion I mentioned at the shipyard. I'll be gone most of the day, and I need to have this correspondence out of the way before we get there.''

''Yes,'' she said quickly.

She turned and almost ran from the room, feeling as if something inside her had died. He wanted out. If she'd been blind herself, she'd have sensed it today, when he spoke so lovingly of Layn and seemed to hate the very thought of regaining his sight because he was tied to a woman he only needed because he was blind. And when he could see, he'd only want Layn....

By the morning Gannon was about to go off with Layn, Dana was more than ready to have the luxury of a day without his company. He was taciturn and curt and he began to pick at her as he had in the early days of their acquaintance. The engagement, while still apparently in force, was never referred to, and he treated her as his nurse, not his wife-to-be.

''I asked you to get Al Pratt on the phone half an hour ago,'' he snarled at her just before Layn arrived. ''Have you even tried?''

''Yes, I have,'' she said coldly. ''He wasn't in. I am not a miracle worker; I can't produce people at a second's notice.''

''You might be a little more diligent,'' he accused.

''I took my training in medicine, not business,'' she reminded him coldly.

''You have a sharp tongue,'' he growled.

''Yours is sharper, and you have no patience anymore,'' she shot back. She felt herself begin to slump. ''It's a good thing you're going out,'' she said wearily. ''Perhaps being with Miss Dalmont will improve your temper.''

His nostrils flared. "Perhaps it will. At least she tries to please me once in a while, miss."

So might I, if I knew what you wanted of me, she thought miserably. She moved away from him, her nurse's uniform making clean, crisp sounds in the silent room. She'd started wearing it again, because it made her feel more comfortable. He was treating her like his nurse, not his fiancée, after all, so what did it matter?

His head rose suddenly. "What's that noise?" he asked sharply.

"Sir?"

"That rustling sound...."

"My uniform," she said coldly.

He actually seemed to blanche. "I thought you were wearing street clothes now."

"I came here as, and still am, your nurse," she reminded him with dignity. "Is it surprising that I feel more secure dressed to fit the part?"

He stood quietly, breathing deliberately. "We're engaged," he said.

She laughed softly, bitterly. "No, sir," she told him. "That was a bit of fiction. An impulsive, quickly regretted and impossibly answered proposal that would be best forgotten by both of us."

"You don't want to marry me?" he asked, something odd in his tone.

"No, sir, I don't," she lied, her voice carrying a conviction that was not in her heart. "As we've already agreed, our worlds are too different ever to mix. And when you have your sight again, the last thing you'll want or need is a scarred, plain little..."

"Stop it!" he burst out, white in the face.

She caught her breath at the violence in the harsh words, at the expression in his blank eyes. But before she could say a word or question him, there was a loud knock at the door, and she went quietly to answer it.

Layn gave her a lazy, cool appraisal. "Back in chains, I see," she said pleasantly, chic in a white linen suit with a pale pink silk blouse. "Where's Gannon?"

"In his study, of course. He's expecting you," Dana said quietly.

"Do show me in," came the amused reply.

As if she needed showing. But Dana complied. There was no fight left in her.

"Miss Dalmont is here," Dana said to Gannon's rigid back.

He turned, staring toward the sound of her voice. "Layn?"

"Right here, darling," she cooed, going to him. She reached up and kissed him, and to Dana's amazement his arms went around her and he returned the kiss with a hungry fervor that was faintly embarrassing.

"What a nice greeting," Layn gasped when he let go. "Just like old times!"

"You smell delicious—just like old times," he murmured. "Ready to go?"

"Whenever you are."

Gannon took Layn's slender hand while Dana stood and watched them, hurting all the way to the heels of her comfortable shoes.

"You aren't taking your little nurse, I hope?" Layn asked.

Gannon flushed darkly and seemed about to say something, but stifled it. "No, Dana isn't coming with us," he said instead.

"Thank goodness," Layn murmured fervently. "Come, Gannon, the car's just outside. I hope we won't need an umbrella, because I didn't bring one. It's getting very dark and stormy-looking out.''

"Dana?" Gannon hesitated.

She swallowed, full of hurt pride and rejection. "Yes?"

He seemed to flinch. "Don't go out on the beach alone, will you? There are storm warnings out today."

"I won't," she promised quietly.

"I wish I could believe you," he said under his breath.

She didn't bother to reply, standing aside as he went out the door with Layn. Dana closed it behind them, just before she burst into tears.

"You're very quiet this afternoon," Lorraine remarked just before dinner that night as they sat together in the living room while thunder and lightning raged outside. "Does the storm bother you?"

Dana shook her head. "Not at all."

"Gannon's going out with Layn does, though, doesn't it?" the older woman probed gently. "Oh, Dana, if I only understood my stepson…"

"It's all very simple," Dana told her. She looked up with sad, quiet eyes. "He wants me to break off the engagement. He's done everything but toss me out the window to get his point across."

"But why?"

"His sight is coming back," she said, sure of it now. "He told me quite bluntly that I wouldn't fit into his world—the world he lives in when he has his sight. I could only belong in a world we made together, out of darkness. Layn is back and he wants her. And who could blame him?" she added bitterly. "She's perfect, so sophisticated and worldly…"

"So selfish and shallow," Lorraine countered angrily. "Your exact opposite in every way. It isn't like Gannon to succumb to that woman after the way she's treated him. He's much too proud. And he cares for you. It's in the way he speaks to you, the way he listens for your step and the way his face lights up when you walk into a room. No, there's something else, I'm sure of it."

But Dana wasn't convinced. Gannon's hunger for Layn had been all too obvious in the kiss she'd seen them share, and his manner with Dana had convinced her that all he wanted now was to be rid of her.

"When he comes back tonight," Dana said quietly, "I'm going to break off the engagement. It's what he wants, and now it's what I want too. If I'm right, he'll get back on his feet that much faster because he has Layn to look forward to."

"Dana, I wish you'd wait—just a little longer," Lorraine said softly.

"There's no point. If he felt as I did, it would be different. But I have no right to build my happiness on his sorrow. I won't."

"You must love him very much, my dear, to care so much about his happiness."

Dana's eyes clouded. "I'll never love anyone else. Not as long as I live. But I can't marry him, knowing how he really feels."

Lorraine looked as if she wanted badly to say something else, but she smiled sadly and went back to her needlepoint. There was no use.

Chapter Nine

It didn't help Dana's already damaged pride when Gannon called an hour later to tell Lorraine that he and Layn were going to spend the night in Savannah.

"He said Layn's afraid to drive back with the weather so bad," Lorraine related irritably. "If you want my opinion, she just wants Gannon all to herself."

"That's very likely," Dana said wearily. "Can you blame her?"

"For more than you know, I can blame her," the older woman said curtly. "Dirk's coming in the morning. Perhaps he can make some sense of all this. Heaven knows, I can't!"

But Dana could. Not that it eased the hurt. It made it worse.

The night was horrible. The thunder and lightning seemed to go on forever, and Dana couldn't sleep for its crash and roar. The ocean was boiling with the force of the storm, like the one raging inside Dana.

It seemed such a long time since she'd come there from Ashton, full of guilt and grief and despair. And while she was still aching from Gannon's rejection, she felt that she'd begun to cope very well with her personal problems. The sharp edge of grief was beginning to numb.

She went to stand at the window and watched the lightning flash down toward the water. Death was, after all, as natural as lightning, as the rain. It was the routine progression of things—birth, life, and death; a cycle that everything human had to follow. And somewhere in that natural progression was God's master plan. Even Mandy had had a part in that, and so did her death and the manner of it. It wasn't for Dana to question why. It was her part to do as God directed.

She wrapped her arms tightly around her thin night-gown with a ragged sigh. Perhaps her presence here had helped Gannon in some small way to rethink his own life. Even if she lost him forever, she felt that she'd helped him see a sense of purpose and meaning in his existence. And wasn't that worth a few tears? After all, love in its ideal form was an unselfish thing. If she loved him, she had to want what was best for him, didn't she?

A silent word to God, seeking His guidance, brought comfort. Resolutely she dried her eyes and went back to bed, and slept peacefully for the first time in days.

Dirk came in the door just as Lorraine and Dana were sitting down to breakfast, and slid into a chair between them to dig hungrily into bacon and eggs and home-made biscuits.

"I didn't realize how hungry I was," he chuckled, watching their amused glances. "Where's Gannon? Sleeping late?"

"He's in Savannah," Lorraine said tautly. "He and Layn didn't drive back last night. She said she was afraid of the weather."

"That's a laugh," Dirk scoffed. "Kidnapped him, did she?"

"Looks like it," the older woman replied. She glanced at Dana. "I don't know what's wrong with him lately; he acts so…strange."

Dana put down her napkin. "Excuse me," she said. "I'm through, and I do love to walk along the beach early in the morning. The rain's gone, and it's so lovely…" she realized that she was rambling, but she tacked on a quick smile and rushed out before anyone could stop her.

She'd only gotten halfway down to the pier before Dirk caught up with her.

"Hold up and I'll stroll along with you," he said. "How are things with you and Gannon?"

"Things aren't," she said shortly. "I broke the engagement."

"You what?"

"I had to," she burst out. "He was hating every second of it. Layn came, and the way he kissed her… Oh, Dirk, he loves her, don't you know?"

She burst into tears, and he drew her gently into his arms, holding her quietly while she got some of the hurt and pain out of her system.

"I'm sorry," she muttered. "I can't seem to stop crying lately."

"He really is blind if he can't feel how much you love him," he growled.

"He knows I love him. He can't help wanting Layn, can he?" she murmured quietly. She drew away and dabbed at her eyes. "I wish I could go home. Facing my kinfolk now isn't nearly as anguishing as having to live around Gannon day after day and knowing he wishes I were in some other country."

"Poor Dana," he said softly. "I wish there was something I could do to help."

She drew in a steadying breath. "But there isn't. I'll just have to wait it out. I can't leave him, not yet, not until he sends me away."

"As long as he needs you, is that how this goes?"

She nodded. "As long as he needs me." She smiled wanly. "I only hope it won't be much longer. I don't know if I can bear much more."

"That makes two of us," he muttered.

But she had her eyes on the horizon, and her mind was with Gannon. Where was he? Why didn't he come home?

The day passed slowly, and Dana's troubled eyes kept going to the driveway. But no car came. By the time the cook was putting supper on the table, Gannon still hadn't appeared.

When the phone rang, Dana rushed to answer it. Lorraine was still upstairs and Dirk had gone, and there was no one else around.

"Hello?" she said quickly.

"Dana?"

It was Gannon's deep voice, and her knees felt rubbery. She sat down in the chair beside the table. "Yes. Gannon, are you all right?"

There was a pregnant pause. "Yes," he said, his voice sounding strained and terse. "As a matter of fact, I have some rather exciting news, Dana. I've got my sight back."

"What!" she exclaimed, sitting up straight.

"We were rushing to get back to the hotel in the rain," he said quietly, "and I tripped and fell. The blow must have dislodged the shrapnel, because I can see."

Tears were rolling down her cheeks unashamedly. "Oh, Gannon, I'm so happy for you. So happy!"

There was another long pause, and a long, shuddering sigh. "Yes. Well, you do understand what that means?"

All the joy washed away in a torrent of cold understanding. Yes, she understood. She was out of a job. Sighted, he didn't need her anymore.

She swallowed down another burst of tears. "I understand," she said on a whisper. "You...you won't need a nurse now, will you?" she laughed.

"No," he said tersely. "Dana...about our engagement?"

"What engagement?" she asked bravely. "It's all right, you don't have to pull your punches. We agreed already that it was a mistake, that...that I wouldn't fit into your world, didn't we? Anyway, Dirk was here..."

His voice was colder than she'd ever heard it before. "Dirk? Well, well, how very convenient. Trying to get his bid in, is he?"

"That's unfair," she returned. "Especially when you as much as told me that you didn't want me anymore!"

There was a long, hot silence on the other end of the line. "Yes, I said that, didn't I?" he asked, his voice odd and deep.

"It's just as well. I...I miss my home," she said after a minute, her lower lip trembling. She controlled it with an effort. "It's time I went back, made my peace with my people."

"When did you plan to go?" he asked curtly.

She cleared her throat. "I...I thought...in the morning."

He sounded relieved. "That would be a good time. I...I plan to stay here with Layn for a few more days."

Her eyes closed on a pain so sweeping that she

thought she might fall to her knees. "Then it will work out…very well for you, won't it? She's so lovely."

There was a harsh, muffled sound. "It isn't because of the way you look!" he burst out. "Sweet heaven, Dana, I'd give anything to make you understand!"

"There's nothing to understand, and you don't owe me any explanations," she said quietly, gripping the phone like a lifeline. "I came here as your nurse. You were lonely and maybe a little afraid…. Didn't I tell you that most male patients make a grab for their nurses? I didn't take you seriously, of course."

They both knew it was a lie, but he was going along with the fiction to help save her pride. She hated knowing that.

"I'm glad of that," he said roughly. There was another pause. "If I can do anything for you, ever…"

"I can take care of myself," she told him proudly. "But thank you for offering. Shall I tell Lorraine and Dirk…?"

"No!" he said quickly. "No," he added in a more controlled tone. "I want to surprise them when I get back. Promise me you won't say a word."

"As you like," she agreed dully. "But why shall I say I'm going home?"

"Can't you invent an emergency?" he asked. "Or is telling a white lie too much for your snowy conscience?"

She swallowed down a hot retort. "I can manage that, I think."

"Good. Then do so. For all they have to know, this phone call could have been from your people. You don't have to say it was me, do you?"

"No," she agreed. "There's no one around right

now. I'll...I'll find an excuse to take the first bus out in the morning. Gannon...I'm very happy for you."

He didn't reply right away. "I hope things go well for you," he said finally, heavily. "Be happy, Dana. I'd give anything if..."

"If," she murmured. "What a sad word."

"Sadder than you know, little one," he whispered. "Good-bye, my...Dana."

"Good-bye, Gannon."

The line went dead. She put her head in her hands and cried until there were no tears left. It was over, all over. He didn't want her anymore, and he couldn't possibly have made it any plainer. He wanted Layn. Beautiful, poised Layn, who was sophisticated and physically perfect.

Dana heard Lorraine coming down the staircase minutes later, and was grateful that she'd had a little time to compose herself. She drew herself erect and tried to look calm.

"Did I hear the phone ring, dear?" Lorraine asked with a smile.

"Yes," Dana said, thinking fast. "It was my aunt. She's developed a serious medical problem, and there's no one but me to look after her. I don't know what to do..." She let her voice trail off and couldn't look at the older woman.

"Do? Why, you must go and see about her," Lorraine said quickly. "I can manage Gannon, with Dirk's help. We can do without you if we must," she added gently.

Dana felt dreadful. She'd hated telling the lie, but it was the only way she could think of to do as Gannon had asked. Besides, she thought miserably, when he came back home and Lorraine realized that he could see again, it would all come right anyway. And Aunt Helen did have a serious medical problem, after all—her sharp and unthinking tongue.

"I'd better pack, then. You'll…explain to Mr. van der Vere when he comes home?" she asked, pausing on the lowest step of the staircase.

"I can't tell you how sorry I am that things didn't work out for the two of you," came the soft reply. "Layn will never make him happy, Dana. She's too shallow to give anything of herself. But men are so strange, my dear."

Dana smiled wistfully. "I have to agree that they seem it sometimes. I hope you'll keep in touch with me; I'd like to know how Mr. van der Vere does."

Lorraine frowned slightly. "But surely you'll be coming back?"

Dana cleared her throat. "Oh, I'm planning to, of course," she lied calmly. "But one never knows how things will turn out. It could be days or even weeks before I can leave Aunt Helen. And she is my only remaining relative—except for my father."

"I've grown very fond of you, Dana." Lorraine hugged her gently and kissed her pale cheek. "Don't worry about Gannon, will you? I'll take care of him. And there's every chance that he'll see through Layn's wiles eventually. Isn't there a saying that all things come to he who waits?"

"If he who waits lives long enough, I suppose," Dana said with an attempt at humor. She drew away with a sigh. "Do let me hear how things go."

Lorraine nodded. "I certainly will. Give my love to Mrs. Pibbs, will you?"

Dana smiled, remembering her supervisor. With any luck at all, she just might be able to get another job at the hospital. Of course, she'd have to swear Mrs. Pibbs to secrecy, so that she wouldn't let anything slip about Aunt Helen being in the bloom of good health....

"I will. I suppose I'd better get packed. I'll want to catch the first bus out in the morning."

"Gannon may be home tonight," Lorraine mentioned.

Dana almost assured her that he wouldn't be, but she bit her tongue. "Yes, he may," she said instead, and managed a wan smile.

"Don't you want to eat first?" the older woman asked.

Dana hesitated. But her stomach did feel empty, and starving herself wasn't going to help the situation. "Yes, I think I will," she said. She followed Lorraine into the dining room. But she didn't taste anything she ate.

Chapter Ten

Ashton hadn't changed in the weeks Dana had been away: It was still slow-moving and provincial and charming. But she thought when she got to the bus depot that she was going to miss the sound of the ocean at night, miss the whitecaps on the beach. Most of all she was going to miss Gannon, and that was going to be the hardest adjustment to make.

She got off the bus, suitcase in hand, and called Jenny. Luckily she was at the apartment and not working.

"You're back!" her friend exclaimed. "Am I glad! My other roommate got sick of picking up after me and moved out, and I'm so lonely—and there's a job available if you hurry! Mrs. Pibbs would give it to you; I know she would!"

Dana smiled gaily. Every thing was working out fine; the path was being smoothed ahead of her. For the first time in two days she felt a ray of hope for her life.

Mrs. Pibbs was waiting for her in the spotless office, looking puzzled but pleased.

"All right, Nurse, let's start at the beginning, if you

please,'' she said curtly, leaning back in her chair to listen.

It was useless to put on a front with Mrs. Pibbs, who had a mind like a net. With a sigh Dana told her the whole wretched story, leaving out nothing.

''So I made up the fiction of Aunt Helen needing me and came home,'' she said quietly, avoiding the other woman's probing eyes.

''Are you certain that he was telling you the truth?'' the supervisor asked shrewdly.

''Why should he lie?'' Dana asked reasonably. ''At any rate he wanted to be rid of me and the fiction of our engagement, and now he is. And there's Miss Dalmont....''

Whatever Mrs. Pibbs was thinking, she obviously decided to keep to herself. She leaned forward. ''Very well, when I speak with Lorraine, I won't blow your cover. But in fact your Aunt Helen could use some support right now. She's grieving over what she said to you before you left Ashton. I think she'd be grateful for the opportunity to see you and apologize.''

Dana smiled. ''I'd like to see her, too. I've had a lot of time to think since I've been away. I think I've come to grips with it all now.''

Mrs. Pibbs lifted her eyebrows. ''God's will?''

The younger woman nodded. ''God's will. I won't question it anymore.''

''Just as well too. Now, here's the job that's open. It's only night supervisor on the east wing, but you'll make a go of it, I'm sure. You have only to readjust to the new schedule, or have you been keeping late nights anyway?''

''Mr. van der Vere liked to talk into the early hours,'' Dana confessed. ''I've been staying up relatively late, so it shouldn't be too difficult to get used to the eleven-to-seven shift again.''

"Good girl. And Jenny tells me she's without a roommate," she added, glancing at Dana's suitcase on the floor beside her chair.

"Yes, ma'am," Dana laughed. She got to her feet. "With your permission I'll dash over and stow my luggage. Do I start tonight?"

"With my blessing." Mrs. Pibbs actually smiled. "Welcome home, Dana."

"Thank you," she replied earnestly.

Dana unpacked, having barely enough time to say hello and good-bye to Jenny, who went on duty minutes later. Then, when she'd rested for a few minutes, she resolutely lifted the receiver of the phone and dialed Aunt Helen's number.

It rang five times before it was picked up, and Dana had almost given up when she heard her aunt's honeyed tones on the other end of the line.

"Aunt Helen?" she asked hesitantly.

"Dana! Dana, is it you? Oh, my dear, I've been sick to death about what I said to you.... Can you forgive me?"

"Of course I can, you were hurting just as much as I was," Dana said on a sigh. It was such a blessed relief to have things patched up again. "How are you?"

"Can you come over?" Aunt Helen asked, ignoring the question. "I'll make a pot of coffee and we'll talk, all right?"

"I'll be there in ten minutes," she replied.

It took fifteen, by the time she changed into jeans and a T-shirt, but her aunt lived only about two blocks from the apartment.

Helen's house was an old, rambling white frame Victorian, with a long front porch where white rocking chairs and an equally white porch swing invited visitors to sit among the potted flowers that lined the entire porch. Helen came rushing out, still wearing her apron, and grabbed Dana in a crushing embrace. She was crying, and Dana cried too.

Helen dabbed at her eyes through a smile and handed Dana a tissue.

"Silly women," she muttered. "Want to have our coffee out here?"

"I'd love it," Dana replied. "Can I help?"

"No, the tray's all fixed. My best silver, too, I want you to know."

"I'm honored!"

Helen disappeared into the house and returned with a huge silver tray laden with cake and cookies and coffee.

She put it on the white wrought-iron table by the rocking chairs and invited Dana to sit down. It was delightful on the porch, cool and quiet and homey. Dana could remember so many lazy summer days spent there while Mandy visited her only sister.

"How are you?" Helen asked while they sipped coffee and nibbled on homemade cookies.

"I'm better. Much better. And you?"

Helen shrugged. "Getting over it, I suppose. I still miss her, as I'm sure you do. But life goes on, doesn't it?"

Dana smiled wistfully. "Inevitably." She finished a cookie and took a sip of black coffee. "How's Dad?"

Helen gave her a sharp, probing look. "Hurting. He thinks you blame him for Mandy's death. He calls me once a week to see how you're doing."

That was painful. "It was hard," she said after a

minute, "getting used to being two families, when we'd been one most of my life. Always it was Mom and Dad. Now it's Dad and someone else, and no Mom." She sighed bitterly. "I honestly feel like an orphan."

"Dear, we've agreed that life goes on. Now answer me just one question honestly," Helen said, leaning forward intently. "Would you want your father to live all his life alone, with no one?"

Dana blinked. "Well, no, I don't suppose so."

"Would you want him to be a playboy and take out a different woman every night?"

"No!" Dana said, horrified.

"You've never even met Sharla formally," Dana was reminded. "She's a lovely woman, Dana. Very old-fashioned and sweet. She likes to cook and grow flowers and do needlepoint, and she loves the whole world. She's a...motherly woman. And she has no children of her own; she'd never been married before she met Jack."

That was interesting. Dana sat up straight, staring across at her aunt. "She hadn't?"

Helen smiled. "No, she hadn't. So, you see, marriage was a very special thing for her. She can't have children anymore, of course, and she was looking forward to having a grown daughter."

Tears stung Dana's eyes. She turned away. "That might be nice, to be wanted by someone," she whispered.

Helen frowned. "Whatever do you mean, darling?"

"Mother told me."

Helen blinked. "Told you what?"

"That because of me, Dad and Mom had to get married. That he never wanted me, that he blamed me for being the cause of a marriage they both hated,'' she said, letting the bitterness and hurt pour out.

Helen got up and drew the weeping girl into her arms. ''How could Mandy tell you such a thing?'' she ground out, rocking Dana slowly. ''It wasn't true! They'd been married over a year when you came along. And your father was the one who wanted you, my dear, as much as I hate to admit it. Mandy wasn't domestic, even in those early years. She hated the restriction of a child and refused to have another one. You spent so much of those early years with me, didn't you know?'' she added wistfully, tears welling in her eyes. ''Mandy would leave you with me while she partied. And since I had no children and no husband, you became the light of my life. You still are.''

Dana wept unashamedly. ''Why did she tell me that—why?''

''Because she'd grown bitter with advancing age, darling,'' Helen said soothingly. ''She was unhappy and afraid of being alone, and she wanted to make you hate Jack for her own misery. He did try, Dana, he did. But your mother was such an unhappy person. Eventually she turned to alcohol because she couldn't endure reality. Her whole life turned into a waking nightmare. She would have destroyed the entire family if she'd lived, and you know it. Don't you, Dana?''

Dana's lower lip trembled. ''Yes,'' she ground out. ''I knew it all along, but it hurt so much to admit it. And I felt guilty....''

''That was my fault. I always say the wrong thing, and I never blamed you; I was just hysterical.'' She drew back. ''Dana, it was God's will. He decides the hour of death, not you and I. And Mandy's so much happier now with Him, don't you imagine?''

Dana smiled wetly. "Yes, I imagine she is. I just miss her so!"

"I miss her too. But we want what's best for her, after all. And she's at peace."

Dana nodded, dabbing again at the tears. "How about some more coffee?" she asked.

"Suits me. Some more cookies too?"

"I'd like that." She sat back and accepted a second cup of steaming black coffee. "Aunt Helen, would you tell me some more about Sharla?" she asked after a minute.

Helen turned away to pour her own coffee, smiling secretly before she sat back and began to talk.

By the end of the second week Dana was back in the swing of things. The only hard moment had come when, catching a late-night newscast with Jenny, she'd seen Gannon van der Vere being interviewed by one of the anchormen.

"Say, isn't that the man you worked for? What a dish!" Jenny exclaimed, leaning forward to watch the screen intently.

Dana felt her face go white as she looked again into those deep-set eyes as Gannon's tanned face filled the screen. Her heart did a backflip just from her looking at him, looking into the eyes that could quite plainly see again.

"My own struggle with blindness," Gannon was saying, "taught me the value of proper tools to cope with it. This new device we're working on is a revolutionary concept. It will translate forms and shapes into a kind of braille that can be read by the holder's fingers, giving him the pattern of places and even people and traffic directly ahead of him. The impulses will be fed onto a screen in a piece of equipment about the size of a portable cassette player. In theory it's quite unique. We hope that theory will translate well into a useful product.''

"Amazing," the newsman murmured. "Mr. van der Vere, we've heard that your company may take a tremendous loss on this particular product to make it affordable to the general public.''

"That is so," Gannon replied quietly. "In order to be effective, it must be accessible to the people who need it. We're cutting corners to keep the cost of production down, and in cases of dire need we plan to have a loan program as well.''

"Would you term that good business?" the newsman asked dryly.

"A question of definitions," Gannon replied. "Our stockholders have no complaints about their profit, and one such sideline as this shouldn't have any disastrous effect on our finances. However, before I'll let the stockholders lose one penny, I'll pay for this new product out of my own pocket. I've been there, you see," he added softly. "I know what it is to be blind. I think those of us who are sighted and have access to the technology are morally obliged to help those less fortunate.''

"Philanthropy, Mr. van der Vere?''

He laughed softly. "God's business, sir," he replied with a grin.

The interviewer asked several more questions, but Dana didn't hear them. She was lost in the pleasure of what she'd already heard.

"Isn't he a dish?" Jenny said in awe when the interview was over and the screen was blank. "How in the world were you able to drag yourself away from him?''

"Oh, I managed," Dana hedged. She'd told Jenny nothing about what had really happened during her absence. And she wasn't going to. It was too painful to rehash.

Friday night came and she dressed very carefully for dinner with Aunt Helen. She chose an off-white shirtwaist dress with red accessories and a flashy red scarf, letting her long pale hair stay loose and free. She didn't know why her aunt had insisted on such formality, but then, Helen did occasionally get eccentric.

Of course, there was another possibility too—one Dana was afraid to ponder. She'd mentioned to Helen that she wanted very much to meet Sharla and make her peace with her father, but was too ashamed of her own behavior to approach him and risk another rejection. Helen had murmured something about things working out and had gone about her business. But this dinner sounded faintly suspicious.

Sure enough, when Dana got to Helen's house, there was a strange car parked in the driveway. She gripped her purse as if it threatened to escape, and forced herself to walk onto the porch and ring the doorbell.

Helen came rushing to answer it, her face flushed, her eyes apprehensive.

"There you are," she said, opening the door. "Come in, come in. Uh, I invited two more for supper…"

As Dana entered the living room, she came face-to-face with her father and Sharla, and she felt all the blood drain slowly out of her cheeks.

Chapter Eleven

❧

"Dana, I'd like you to meet Sharla," Helen said, faintly ruffled as she dragged Dana forward. "I think it's about time the two of you were formally introduced."

Sharla was tall and slender, with whitish-gold hair and pale blue eyes. She looked as nervous as Dana felt, but she looked delightful in a simple cotton shirtwaist that mirrored Dana's own unruffled style of dressing.

"Hello," Sharla said, extending a hand. She smiled hesitantly. "I…I wanted to meet you before, but…"

Dana nodded, taking the hand. It was warm and strong, and it was a hand that was no stranger to housework—a far cry from Mandy's delicate, well-manicured ones.

"How are you?" Jack Steele asked quietly, watching his daughter closely. "Helen said you'd completely recovered, and you…look well."

"I'm doing nicely, thanks," Dana replied. Her eyes scanned the familiar face, finding new lines and new gray hairs. He looked older, tired. But there was a light in his eyes when he glanced down at Sharla that she'd never seen before. The same light she knew was in her own when she'd looked at Gannon.

She glanced away, embarrassed.

"Sharla, why don't you help me with supper?" Helen said, with a meaningful glance toward father and daughter.

Sharla joined her quickly. "I'd love to."

When the other women were gone, Dana shifted from one foot to the other uncomfortably, searching for words.

"I've been worried," Jack Steele said finally, hesitantly. He shrugged. "I wanted to call you, but we've been so far apart for so long, and I knew I wasn't on your list of favorite people. I just let the time go by, I guess."

She nodded. She clasped her hands in front of her. "Yes, I know. That's how it was for me too."

"I didn't marry Mandy because I had to," he blurted out, avoiding her eyes. "I loved her. I really loved her, Dana. But when you came along, and she refused to settle down and take care of you—when she began enjoying parties and alcohol more than she enjoyed her marriage and her daughter—" He lifted his hands helplessly. "I don't even remember when it stopped being love. One day I woke up and realized that my life was too empty to bear. I thought if we divorced, perhaps she could find love again in someone or something. I didn't expect that she'd deteriorate so quickly. And by then there was Sharla...." His voice lowered with emotion. "Sharla. And I was in love, truly in love, for the first time in my life."

She studied his averted face and she understood. Because of Gannon she understood at last.

"It's a kind of madness, isn't it?" she asked wisely,

wryly. "It takes over your life and your mind, and you have no control whatsoever over what you do."

His eyes jerked up and he studied her for a long time. "You wouldn't have said that three months ago."

She shook her head. "I didn't know three months ago what it was to love. I was so superior to the rest of the world, you know."

He laughed softly. "Were you?"

"Smug and superior.... I could do without anyone. I'd lost Mandy, and the world along with her. I hated you." She searched his tired face. "Helen said that Sharla doesn't have any children of her own."

There was a tiny rustling movement from the doorway, and the older woman stopped just short of Dana.

"She does...now," Sharla said hesitantly, her hands lifting unsurely, her face quiet, hopeful.

With a tiny, aching cry, Dana ran into those thin arms and felt them enclose her, hold her, cradle her. And she cried until she thought her heart would break, because this woman was the mother she'd always wanted— needed. Without being disloyal to Mandy, whom she'd loved and whom she missed, Sharla was suddenly the rainbow after the storm.

Jack Steele cleared his throat, moving forward to separate the two women. "Let's eat something first," he murmured. "I can't cry on an empty stomach."

"Oh, Dad." Dana laughed through her tears and hugged him.

"Welcome home," he whispered huskily. "Welcome home, little girl."

It was the most wonderful night Dana could remember in years, sitting with her father and stepmother, learning about them, being with them. They were so good together, so secure in their love for each other.

Her opinion of marriage underwent a startling change just from watching them.

Jack didn't ask any pointed questions about the time Dana had been on the coast, but just before they left Helen's house, the two of them walked out ahead of the others and she felt him watching her.

"Helen said you were nursing a blind man," he said after a minute.

"Yes. Gannon van der Vere."

He whistled. "Quite a corporate giant, Mr. van der Vere. He's regained his sight, hasn't he? I saw him on the news the other night."

She nodded. "Yes, he's…he's back at work."

"And quite a changed man," he added dryly.

"Don't look at me—I was just his nurse."

"Really?" He turned, holding her gaze. "You love him, don't you?"

"Desperately," she admitted, feeling a surge of hunger so sweeping that it very nearly made her swoon.

"And how does he feel?"

She lifted her shoulders. "There's a woman…. They were very nearly engaged before his accident. Now they're back together again. He…he loves her, you see."

"I'm sorry," he told her. "Very sorry."

"Don't be. Loving him was an experience I'll never forget. It's enriched my life. In so many ways."

"Yes, I can see that," he replied surprisingly. "You're very different now, Dana. Another woman from the one who left Ashton those weeks ago."

She smiled. "A better one, I hope."

He grinned. "Why don't you go back down there and put a ring on his finger?"

She laughed. "Sounds simple, doesn't it? I'm afraid

he's not that kind of man. Our worlds are very different.''

"Worlds," he informed her, "can merge."

"Like yours and Sharla's?" she teased. Impulsively she hugged him. "I like my new stepmother."

"She likes you too. Let's not drift apart again," he added solemnly. "Let's be a family."

She nodded. "I'd like that very much."

"Dinner with us next Friday?" he asked.

She smiled. "Ask Sharla first."

"Sharla, can we have Dana to dinner next Friday?" he called.

"Don't be silly!" was the instant reply. "My daughter can come to dinner anytime she pleases without having to have invitations. Right, Dana?"

"Right…Mom," she replied softly.

Sharla smiled and turned quickly away, but not before Dana caught the gleam of tears in her eyes.

In the weeks that followed, Dana became a real part of the Steele family, and her life became bright and meaningful as she threw herself back into her work. But the longer she was away from Gannon, the worse the loneliness became.

When Lorraine called her unexpectedly one Wednesday evening, she felt shock wash over her. She'd only been thinking about Gannon and his stepmother a few minutes earlier.

"How are you, my dear?" Lorraine asked softly. "We haven't heard from you, and I just wanted to check and make sure you were all right. How is your aunt?"

Her aunt. The white lie. Dana swallowed. "Oh, Aunt Helen is much better," she said. "And I'm fine too. How about you?"

"I'm doing very well. You know that Gannon could see; you saw him on television? I meant to write you, but I was so excited, and then Dirk came back to help on the computer project.... The house has been overrun with technicians and scientists!"

"I heard about the new invention. I'm so pleased about what Gannon's done," she murmured.

"I'm shocked," Lorraine said flatly. "He's changed so. He's like another man, so caring and concerned. Except for missing you, of course."

"What?"

"Missing you."

"What about Layn?" Dana burst out.

"My dear, she brought him home from Savannah just after you left, and looked like a thundercloud. She took off in a blaze of glory and hasn't been seen since. Gannon hasn't even mentioned her."

"I don't understand," Dana said weakly. She sat down, her legs collapsing.

"Neither do I. And he wasn't staying with Layn in Savannah, by the way. Katy and Maude told on him. He was in the hospital."

"Hospital!"

"He fell, did you know?" Lorraine asked suspiciously.

"Yes," she admitted, feeling relief. "He asked me to leave and not say anything to you about his sight returning. It puzzled me at the time...."

"It's still puzzling me. I tried to pump his doctor, but I can't get anyone to tell me anything. Something's going on, Dana," she added quietly. "Something very strange. He doesn't look at women—not at all. And when he isn't working, he walks along the beach for hours at a time, looking so lonely that I ache for him."

"Maybe he misses Layn," Dana suggested.

"When he talks about no one except you?" Lorraine asked sadly. "My dear, he got his hands on a picture of you and he sits and stares at it like a starving man."

Her heart went wild. "A picture of me? Where?"

"He charmed Mrs. Pibbs out of it," Lorraine laughed. "I don't know where she found it."

Dana did. Mrs. Pibbs had asked for a photograph of her to add to some kind of brochure. Dana had thought it was an unusual request at the time, but she hadn't questioned it. And it had been for Gannon!

"Is he having any trouble at all with his eyes?" Dana asked quickly.

"No, that's the strange thing. No headaches, no blurring, no nothing. But he won't talk about that."

Dana sighed. "No, I don't suppose he likes remembering it."

"Why don't you come down for the weekend?" Lorraine asked.

Dana felt her pulse go sky high. "I don't think—"

"That's right, dear, don't think. Just come. You might consider going to see Dr. Shane while you're about it—and mention that you're going to be nursing Gannon and ask about procedure."

Dana gasped. "That would be highly unethical…" she began.

"Of course it would," Lorraine agreed. "But it would get the truth out of him. I'll take full responsibility. I've got to know, Dana, I've got to!"

She paused, hanging on to the receiver as if it were a lifejacket. "Well…" she began, her heart racing.

"Be daring," Lorraine taunted. "Don't you want to know what he's hiding? Dana, he loves you!"

Her eyes closed at the sound of those words. *He loves*

you. Heaven knew, she loved him—desperately! *God forgive me,* she murmured silently.

"I'll be there in the morning, after I get through at Dr. Shane's. Could you...sort of call him and pave the way?"

Lorraine laughed softly. "My dear, I'd be delighted. I won't tell Gannon, but I'll make sure he doesn't leave the house. Have a safe trip, darling."

"See you soon," she replied, and hung up. She was doing the right thing. But if Gannon was hiding something, she had to know what it was. She couldn't let him throw away their happiness without a sound reason. And nothing would be sound enough if it kept her from him—not now, when she knew how horrible life was going to be without him.

Chapter Twelve

Dana had anticipated some problems getting days off to go to the coast, but Mrs. Pibbs waved her off with a rare smile.

"The hospital will run as usual without you, Nurse," she said smoothly.

"How can I thank you…?" Dana began.

"Be happy," came the reply, sincerely. "Let me know how things work out."

Dana frowned slightly. "Have you been talking to Mrs. van der Vere by any chance?" she asked suspiciously.

"Now, why in the world should you think that?" Mrs. Pibbs asked tartly. "Run along and catch your bus, Dana, I'm a busy woman. Have a nice time."

"Thank you," Dana murmured, pausing at the door. "Are you sure…?"

"I'm sure. Good-bye, have a good trip."

She was suspicious about that pleasant grin, but she waved and closed the door behind her.

The hospital was crowded when she reached the

coast, and she had to wait an hour before she was allowed in to see Dr. Shane.

He looked harassed and not a little irritable, but he waved her into a chair and sat down heavily.

"Thank God," he muttered, "a chance to breathe. I understand from Lorraine that you're back to nurse Gannon? God knows why, nothing's going to change regardless of your nursing skill, but who am I to argue with him? I never get anywhere at all."

Dana almost grinned but caught herself in time. She folded her hands in the lap of her green shift with its pale green belt, feeling the nails bite into her palms.

"Exactly what is his situation, Dr. Shane?" she asked with forced calm.

He pursed his lips, studying her under a frown. "Lorraine assured me that you were here with Gannon's permission," he observed. "You do realize that if that weren't the case, I'd be breaching his confidence and my oath as well?"

She swallowed. "Yes, sir," she said. It was on the tip of her tongue to tell the truth, to be honest, but something kept her quiet and still.

He shrugged. "Very well, I'll have to take Lorraine's word for it. I wasn't even aware that he'd told her. But then, he's a strange man at times." He pulled a file toward him and opened it. "You know that the shrapnel is inoperable?"

"Yes, sir," she said, which was the truth. She sat stiffly, waiting.

"Well, nothing's changed there. The fall was a stroke of good luck, because it dislodged the shrapnel and relieved the pressure, returning his vision. However," he said, leaning back in the chair solemnly, to pin her with his eyes, "he has no guarantee that the same thing won't happen again and leave him blind."

Her heart stopped—stopped and then ran away. "He could become blind again?" she echoed numbly.

"Of course. There are new advances, you know. Every day we learn more and can do more. But for the present he has to go on living with that sword hanging over him."

"If the shrapnel shifts again," she said slowly, "it could do more than blind him, couldn't it?"

He lifted his hands. "As a nurse, you know as well as I do that anything lodged in the brain is a potential time bomb. But there's nothing medical science can do about it at the present time. I wish that weren't the case. But I'm afraid it is."

"And naturally," she continued, in what seemed a terribly slow voice, "he wouldn't want to ask anyone to share that risk with him."

"Marriage, you mean," he nodded. He sighed. "He said almost that same thing himself. I told him he was being absurd, but he wouldn't listen. Good heavens, Nurse, I could step off a curb and kill myself tomorrow, and there's nothing lodged in my brain!"

She managed a wan smile. "How very odd that he wanted to keep it to himself."

"Not odd at all. It's like him." He closed the file. "Well, that's all I can tell you, unless you want me to read you the medical terminology. He shouldn't participate in any daredevil antics, of course, and things like diving and violent sports are out. Otherwise he can lead a fairly normal life."

"A sneeze could dislodge it, couldn't it?" she asked quietly.

"Yes. Few people outside the medical profession realize how violent a sneeze is.'' He watched her pale face with interest. ''The best thing is not to dwell on it and not to let *him* dwell on it. There's a man in Vienna working on innovations in brain surgery right now; I expect a breakthrough any day. When it comes—and notice I said when, not if—I'll get in touch with Gannon.''

She smiled weakly. ''Thank you for telling me.''

''Does Gannon know you're here?'' he asked kindly.

''If I were here under false pretenses, would I answer that?'' she asked, standing.

''No. So I'd better not ask.'' He took her hand. ''Blast him out of his prison, girl. No man has the right to sacrifice himself on a gamble. That piece of shrapnel could stay where it is until he's a hundred and ten years old, for all you or I know.''

She nodded. ''Now all I have to do is convince him of that.'' Her eyes darkened. ''If I don't murder him first,'' she added coldly.

He chuckled softly. ''Let me know how things work out. I love happy endings.''

''His may not be so happy,'' she muttered, gathering speed as she walked out the door, thanking him again before she went stalking down the hall.

She took a cab to the beach house, fuming. He was going to spend the rest of his life living alone because of something that might happen. He was going to make her, and himself, miserable and shut her out of his life and deny her even the choice of staying or going. The more she thought about it, the madder she got. By the time she paid the cab and walked to the front door of the beach house, her face was hot with temper.

Lorraine answered it, and her thin face lit up. She grabbed Dana like a long-lost daughter. ''Oh, I was so afraid you'd change your mind, back out. I'm just be-side myself that you came anyway!''

"I'm glad too," she replied, hugging Lorraine back. "Dr. Shane told me everything. It's the shrapnel. He could become blind again."

The older woman closed her eyes with a sigh. "So that's it. It explains so much."

"Yes, it does. But it doesn't justify sending me away if he really does care," she added, frowning, because she wasn't sure that he did. She couldn't be.

"If you'll take an old woman's word," Lorraine said softly, "I think he does. Very much."

Dana sighed, afraid now, because the anger was wearing off and leaving desperation in its place. She could have misread the entire situation. It might be Layn he was sparing, not Dana.

"Why don't you walk down to the beach and find him?" Lorraine suggested, her eyes kind. "I think you'll be able to tell one way or another the minute he sees you. What he feels will be in his face, because he isn't expecting you and he won't be prepared."

Dana's heart leaped. "He's on the beach?"

Lorraine nodded. "About halfway down, sitting on a log, glowering at the ocean. Go on. Be daring. What have you got to lose?"

There was the question. She had nothing to lose, be-cause without Gannon there was nothing she minded losing. She pulled her shoulders back and laid her purse down on the hall table.

"Wish me luck, will you?" she asked the older woman. "I think I may need it."

"All the luck in the world, my dear." Lorraine gave her a push. "Go on. You'll never know until you face him."

"I may see you again very soon."

"If you don't, I won't wait lunch," came the dry reply.

Dana walked through the house and down the back steps with her heart hammering wildly at her throat. She paused at the top of the staircase that led down to the beach, and looked down until her eyes found Gannon.

His back was to her. He was wearing white slacks and a blue and white patterned tropical shirt, and his head was bowed in the sunlight. He looked so alone, so bitterly alone, that she felt like crying. That gave her the courage she needed to go down the steps and walk along the beach toward him. Her heart was hammering wildly at her throat like a trapped bird trying to be free, while the waves crashed onto the beach and the sun burned down on the white sand.

Dana's footsteps were muffled by the sound of the surf as she approached the big blond man sitting on the log. Her breath seemed to catch in her throat. Would he be glad to see her? Or would he just be shocked and annoyed?

She paused just behind him. Her hand lifted and then fell. "Gannon?" she called softly.

His head jerked up. When he saw her, he seemed to go rigid all over. His eyes took her in from head to toe and back again, noting the emerald-green dress, her face in its frame of pale, loosened hair, her wide, searching eyes.

"Dana?" he whispered, standing.

"Yes," she said simply. Her own eyes were busy reconciling the man she saw with her memory of him. He looked thinner somehow, worn, but the sight of him fed her poor, starved eyes.

"What are you doing here?" he asked.

"I, uh, I came to see Lorraine," she hedged, words failing her.

His chest rose and fell heavily. "Was that the only reason?"

Her lower lip trembled and she caught it between her teeth. "No," she replied with a shaky smile. "I...came to see you too."

"You look very thin," he said in a tight voice, studying her slenderness again. "Is that new?"

"The dress? No, it's an old one."

"The thinness, not the dress," he said harshly. "Why should I care about what you wear?"

"Why should you care about me, period?" she burst out, anger coming to her rescue. "Not a single phone call, not a card...I could have died and you wouldn't have known or cared!"

"That's a lie," he shot back, his face pale. "I kept up with you through Mrs. Pibbs. I knew how you were, at least. You couldn't even be bothered to write to Lorraine, could you?"

"Why should I, when you sent me away?" she tossed back, hurting all the way to her bones. "You sent me away!"

"I had to," he ground out, his face contorting as he saw the hurt on her eyes. "You don't understand."

"Yes, I do," she cried angrily. "You sent me away because of the shrapnel!"

He looked every year of his age. His powerful frame seemed to shudder. "Who told you?" he asked in a deadly quiet tone.

"I won't tell you," she returned. "But it's true, isn't it? You could go blind again."

His eyes closed on a weary sigh. "Yes," he said heavily. "I could go blind again."

She moved closer, looking up at him with soft, probing eyes. "I have to know," she said quietly. "I haven't much pride left—or much sense. I have to be told. Was it because of Layn that you wanted me to break the engagement, Gannon? Was it because of my scar...?"

He whispered something rough under his breath and his hands shot out. With an expression of pure anguish he dragged her against his big body and bent to her mouth.

"Don't talk," he said unsteadily, brushing his lips slowly, tremblingly, over hers. "Don't talk. Kiss me. Let me show you how it's been without you, Dana!"

She bent under the rough crush of his ardor, feeling the hurt and the heartache and the loneliness all wrapped up in his slow, fierce kisses. She clung to him with tears draining from her eyes, loving the touch of him, the feel and smell and taste of him, as the world seemed to turn to gold all around them, binding them together with skeins of pure love.

"I missed you," he whispered brokenly, wrapping her up in his big arms to rock her slowly against him. "I've been half a man since the day I sent you away. But I couldn't let you stay, knowing what I did. I only wanted what was best for you."

She hit his broad chest with a small, furious fist. "You stupid man," she whimpered, burying her face against him. "As if I cared about being protected. I'm a nurse, not an hysterical woman. And I love you quite desperately, in case you haven't noticed. You wouldn't even let me have a choice!"

"How could I, knowing what the choice would be?" he ground out, holding her even closer. "Dana, you're so young, with your whole life ahead of you."

"What kind of life am I expected to have, for

heaven's sake, without you?" she asked in anguish, lifting her red eyes to his. "Don't you even know that I only go through the motions of living without you? There'll never be anyone else, not as long as I live. So please tell me how to look forward to a lifetime of loneliness and grief—because I'll mourn you every day I live from now on!"

He tried to speak and made a helpless motion with his shoulders before he dragged her close again and bent his head over hers.

"I could die," he whispered.

"Yes," she managed on a sob. "So could I. A tree could fall on me while I was walking back to the house. Do you think life comes with a written guarantee?"

"I could be paralyzed."

"Then I'd sit with you," she whispered, lifting her head to study him with love pouring from her face. "I'd sit by your bedside and hold your hand and read to you. And I'd love you so much...."

The tears burst from his eyes and ran unashamedly down his cheeks as she spoke, and she reached up and tenderly touched each of them, brushing them back from his hard cheeks.

"I love you," she repeated softly, blinking away her own tears. "If we got married, I could give you children. And then, even if something dreadful did happen, we'd have all those happy years behind us; we'd have the comfort of our family around us. We'd have each other and the memory of loving."

He bent and kissed her eyes softly, slowly. "I love you," he whispered, shaken. "So much that I'd willingly give up my life for you. But what am I offering you except the possibility of a living nightmare?"

"If you won't marry me," she said after a minute,

"I'll live with you anyway. I'll move in and sleep in your arms and shame you for not making an honest woman of me." She drew back and looked up into his darkening eyes. "I'll follow you around like a puppy from now on, and you won't be able to look behind you without seeing me. I'll crawl on my knees if I have to, but I won't leave you now. Not until I die."

"Dana, for God's sake..."

"It *is* for God's sake," she whispered softly, smiling. "For God's sake and my own. Because all I know of love I learned from you."

His eyes closed. "Don't make it any harder for me," he pleaded.

"But I will," she replied, snuggling closer, feeling safe and secure for the first time in weeks. "You've given me back my family. Because I loved you, I was able to forgive them and love them again. I'm part of a family again, all because of you."

"I don't want you hurt," he whispered.

"Then don't send me away," she whispered back. She drew his face down to hers. "Because I'll never be hurt again if I can stay where you are."

"It's insane," he ground out against her warm, soft mouth.

She smiled. "Yes," she murmured. "Sweet insanity. Kiss me. Then I'll propose to you again and go and ask your mother for your hand in marriage...."

He burst out laughing in spite of himself. "Dana, you crazy woman...!"

"Be crazy with me," she tempted. She stood on tiptoe and kissed him again. And then she felt his arms contract, and he was kissing her. It was a long time before they could find words again.

"This isn't solving anything," he said finally, dragging himself away from her. "Here, sit down and let's try to talk reasonably."

She joined him on the log, sitting close, companionably, while he took a deep breath and sat, just looking at her.

"You look so different," he murmured.

"From my photograph, you mean?" she replied with an impish smile.

He shifted and looked uncomfortable for a minute. "Who told you? Lorraine?"

"Don't blame her," she pleaded. "I was clutching at straws. I thought you'd forgotten all about me."

He shook his head. "That was beyond me. I've sat here day after day, remembering the sound and smell of you." His eyes searched her quiet face and he smiled. "You're the most beautiful thing I've seen since I regained my sight."

She blushed and lowered her eyes. "I'm very glad you think so." She glanced up again, warily. "Gannon, the scar..."

He bent and brushed the soft hair away from her cheek and kissed the pale white line that ran alongside her ear. "We'll think of it as a beauty mark," he whispered. "We'll tell the children that you got it fighting tigers in Malaya, just to make it sound better."

Her eyes searched his. "You're going to let me stay?" she asked softly.

He touched her mouth with his fingers. "How can I let you go now?" he asked quietly. "But we may both live to regret it, Dana."

She shook her head. "Not ever."

She said it with such conviction that he averted his eyes on a heavy, ragged sigh. He caught her hand in his and held it tightly.

"I saw you on television," she mentioned, grinning. "You looked so handsome—my roommate said you were a dish."

He chuckled. "I didn't feel like a dish. I was missing you and hurting in ways I hadn't dreamed I could."

"Me and not Layn?"

He looked haunted for an instant, and the big hand holding hers contracted roughly. "I needed something to drive you away when Dr. Shane told me the truth. I couldn't bear the thought of subjecting you to what might happen." He shrugged. "It seemed the thing to do at the time. I knew you'd never go if you knew the truth." He glanced down at her. "You're far too caring a person to desert a sinking ship."

She nuzzled close to him, sighing. "You never really cared about her, then?"

"No. And she knew it—she knew exactly what I was doing. I'm still not sure why she went along with it, unless she thought she might have a chance with me again." He lifted his hand and let it fall. "She found out pretty quickly that she didn't. By that time I was so much in love with you that I couldn't see her for dust."

"There was something strange in your voice when you called me from Savannah," she confessed. "I couldn't help wondering at the time if you were really telling me the truth about being able to see again."

"Oh, I could see all right. And not just in any visual sense," he added on a hard sigh. "I could see you living with this time bomb in my head."

"We all carry time bombs around with us, Gannon," she said gently. "Of one kind or another. None of us knows the hour of our own death. It's just as well too: We'd never accomplish anything. You might survive me."

"Horrible thought," he said curtly. He looked down at her with all his heart in his eyes. "I wouldn't want to live without you."

"But you were going to condemn me to it, weren't you?" she accused. She reached up and touched his face as she'd longed to for so many empty weeks. "I want you to come home with me and meet my father and my stepmother and my aunt. I think—I hope—you'll like them."

"You've made your peace, I see," he observed.

She smiled. "I found that I quite like my stepmother. She's just what my father needed. I kind of like him too. We cleared up a lot of misunderstandings; we're closer now than ever before. And best of all, I've come to grips with my own guilt and my grief. I'll always miss my mother, but I realize now that she's better off."

"God does know best," he murmured, smiling at the look on her face. "Oh, yes, I've done my bit of changing. I've realized that there's much more to life than the making and spending of money."

She reached up and kissed him. "I've arrived at the same conclusion. When are you going to marry me?"

"You've only just proposed," he reminded her. "A man can't be rushed into these things, after all. I have to buy a suit and have my hair done...."

"Stop that," she muttered, hitting him lovingly.

"Well, if you don't mind an untidy bridegroom, I suppose we could get married Monday."

"That's only three days away!" she gasped.

He shrugged. "Well, we can do it sooner, I suppose; I just thought..."

"Monday is fine!" she said quickly, laughing. "Oh, Monday is just fine!"

"Then let's go and call my minster and see about

getting a license,'' he said. He stood up, drawing her with him. "Lovely, lovely woman. I'm the luckiest man alive."

"You're certainly the handsomest," she murmured. "What gorgeous sons we'll have!"

He chuckled, leading her down the beach. "Our daughters aren't going to be bad, either," he observed.

* * * * *

Dear Reader,

It is such a pleasure to see this book back in print again. *Blind Promises* is very special to me because I was going through some painful experiences in my own life when I wrote it, primarily the death of my mother. The book was a way for me to deal with her loss, and subsequent painful events in my life.

I know from my reader mail that many of you turn to fiction to escape painful realities, to find something to take you away from the pain, even for an hour or so. It may surprise you to learn that writers also escape into novels for the same reason. It is yet another bond between reader and writer, this need for a breathing space that makes us stronger and helps us to deal with the problems at hand.

One of the most comforting passages in the Bible is, to me, "…and this, too, shall pass away." Even the most painful things do, you know, and God is always there to catch us if we fall.

God bless all of you. Thank you for letting me share my own dreams with you.

Love,

Diana Palmer

LENORA WORTH

grew up in a small Georgia town and decided in the fourth grade that she wanted to be a writer. But first she married her high school sweetheart, then moved to Atlanta, Georgia. Taking care of their baby daughter at home while her husband worked at night, Lenora discovered the world of romance novels and knew that's what she wanted to write. And so she began.

A few years later, the family settled in Shreveport, Louisiana, where Lenora continued to write while working as a marketing assistant. After the birth of her second child, a boy, she decided to pursue her dream full-time. In 1993, Lenora's hard work and determination finally paid off with that first sale.

"I never gave up, and I believe my faith in God helped get me through the rough times when I doubted myself," Lenora says. "Each time I start a new book, I say a prayer, asking God to give me the strength and direction to put the words to paper. That's why I'm so thrilled to be a part of Steeple Hill, where I can combine my faith in God with my love of romance. It's the best combination."

LOGAN'S CHILD
Lenora Worth

To my best friend and neighbor,
Cindy Sledge, my own "Pig Pal."
And to all the mothers who love their children,
even when they can't be with them.
You are not forgotten.

Chapter One

A hot, humid September wind whipped across the flat countryside as mourners dressed in fashionable funeral black filed out of the small country church just outside Plano, Texas. Mingling together beside the expensive sports cars and chauffeur-driven limousines lining the graveled driveway, the elite crowd talked in hushed, respectful tones.

Tricia Maria Dunaway looked around at the cream of Dallas society, here to say their final farewells to her father, the famous bull rider, Brant Dunaway. Her mind was numb with grief and shock; her eyes hidden behind dark sunglasses that did little to relieve the harsh glare of the bright Texas sun. Beside her, her fiancé Radford Randolph III, looking as dapper as always in his dark navy summer suit, stood with one arm solicitously touching her elbow.

"C'mon, honey," her grandfather, Harlan Dunaway, said, his usually firm voice shaky. "We've got to get back to the Hideaway. People'll be coming around to pay their respects and it's up to us to be there to greet them."

Her mother, Pamela, pale and dark-haired, elegant and slender, in a black linen sheath and cultured pearls, nodded her agreement. "Granddaddy's right, Trixie. We wouldn't want to be rude to all these good people who came to your daddy's funeral."

Trixie looked straight ahead. "No, Mama, Dunaways can't ever be rude, can we? I mean, what would people think?"

Pamela's brown eyes held a glint as cold and hard-edged as the huge marquis diamond in her necklace. "I'm going to ignore that remark, Tricia Maria, only because I know losing your father has been a great strain on you."

With a halfhearted effort, Trixie reached up a black-gloved hand to touch her mother's still smooth cheek-bone. "I'm sorry, Mama. I know you gave up a trip to Palm Beach to make it to Daddy's funeral. I guess I shouldn't be mean to you."

"No, you shouldn't," Pamela retorted, her smile, ex-acted for the benefit of prying eyes, as intact as her unruffled classic bob. "Even though your father and I were divorced, I still had feelings for the man."

Trixie didn't respond. She'd heard it all too many times before. Too many times. Not even Rad's gentle endearments could bring her out of her deep grief.

She'd sat here in the church were she'd attended ser-vices all of her life and listened as Reverend Henry told them to rejoice in Brant's departure from this life.

"Be joyful," the good reverend told them. "'They that sow in tears shall reap in joy.'"

In spite of her faith, in spite of the strong Christian values she'd been taught, Trixie couldn't feel any joy today. After all those many years of riding bucking, angry bulls and fighting his way into and out of barroom brawls, Brant Dunaway had lost his life to the one thing even he couldn't fight off or sweet-talk his way out of— heart disease.

How could she find any joy in that cold, simple fact? How could she find any joy at all, when in her heart she kept thinking she should have stayed close to her father. She should have made him go to the doctor, take care of himself, live to be an old man. But…instead, she'd stayed away from the ranch in Arkansas where he'd spent his last years isolated and alone. Now she felt the remorse and regret that came with his death. So final, so harsh. So cold. Without even a goodbye between them.

And this was just the beginning. Tomorrow she had to take her father's body back to Arkansas, back to the ranch he'd loved more than he'd ever loved the fancy mansion near Plano that everyone called Dunaway's Hideaway. The mansion, Victorian in style and stark white and lacy in design, had been more like an over-decorated birthday cake to her father. His real hideaway had always been the crude, run-down ranch in Arkansas he'd inherited from his mother's side of the family.

The ranch where he'd requested to be buried.

The ranch Trixie had inherited from him.

The ranch where Logan Maxwell worked as foreman.

Logan. His name still brought little tremors of awakening shooting through Trixie's system. Would he be waiting there to greet her when she brought Brant home for the last time? Would he speak to her, acknowledge her, talk to her about the last eight years of his life?

Or…would Logan turn away from her in disgust, the way her father had turned away?

Harlan took her by the arm, gently urging her into

the waiting, black limousine. "Let's get going, Trixie. It's a long ride back to the house."

Trixie nodded absently, then allowed Rad to guide her into the roomy car, her thoughts on the man she'd have to face once again, come tomorrow. "Yes, Granddaddy, it is a long way back. A very long way." Then she closed her eyes and thought about Logan...and remembered.

"But where's Daddy?" Trixie had asked Pamela as they dressed for her coming-out ball that spring night so long ago. "He's supposed to be here with you, to present me."

"Brant won't be attending the ball, sugar," Pamela retorted, her chin lifting a notch, her eyes capturing Trixie's in the gilt mirror of the dresser where she sat. Trixie stood in the center of the elaborate bedroom her mother shared with her father, that is, when they weren't fighting. Pamela then turned away, patting her upswept curls, to stare down into the velvet-lined jewel case set out on the Louis XIV dresser.

Disappointed and steaming mad, Trixie stormed toward her mother, her white taffeta skirts swishing over the Aubusson carpet, her blond curls contrasting sharply with her mother's darker ones. "Daddy wouldn't do that to me! He promised he'd be here."

Pamela pursed her lips as she gazed into the jewel case. Making her selection, she lifted out a brilliant diamond necklace, then smiled over at Trixie. "Here, sweetie, wear this."

Trixie pushed the gaudy necklace away. "I'd prefer pearls, Mother, and I'd prefer you tell me what's going on here. Where's Daddy?"

Frustrated, Pamela snapped the jewel case shut.

"And I'd really prefer not to discuss your father. Especially not now, right before your coming-out ball." Spinning on the satin-covered vanity stool, she stared up at her daughter with beseeching eyes. "Oh, Trixie, we've waited for this night all of your life, darling. Tonight you'll become a part of the best of Dallas society. Let's not spoil things by talking about your missing father."

Trixie stood there, her gaze sharp on her beautiful, haughty mother. "You had another fight with him, didn't you?"

"I said I don't want to talk about Brant."

"That's it! You picked a fight with him so he wouldn't want to come to my cotillion. How could you do that, Mother?"

Pamela's expression quickly changed from sweet to steely. "It wasn't just me, young lady. You know how your father can be. And this time he pushed me too far." Waving a diamond-clad hand, she added, "If Brant isn't here tonight, it's his own fault. Your grandfather will present you. And that's all I have to say on the matter."

The matter turned out to be divorce. Of course, Pamela didn't reveal that to Trixie until after the season was over, until after she'd been to so many debutante parties, and danced with so many fumble-footed sons of oil tycoons and banking CEOs, that she thought she'd literally scream. No, Trixie found out the horrible, awful truth on the day of her graduation from high school, when Pamela lifted her wine glass in a toast at the formal dinner party she'd arranged for "just family," then presented Trixie with a trip to Europe as a graduation gift.

"We leave in a week, darling. Just you and me. I'll

show you all the best places, of course, and introduce you to my friends over there. We'll stay at a lovely chateau in France, and I've arranged for a private manor house in the English countryside. After we've done London, of course. You'll love Europe. I plan on introducing you to several very eligible bachelors."

Shocked, Trixie glanced around the long dining room of the Dunaway mansion, hoping to find some answers from either her beaming mother or her strangely quiet grandfather. "And what about Daddy?"

She didn't miss the meaningful gaze that moved between her mother and Harlan. In fact, she hadn't missed much over the past few weeks, in spite of being busy. Now she was sure something was going on. Brant hadn't even stayed for dinner. Her father, usually so carefree and talkative, usually so full of silly banter, seemed so distant, so quiet these days.

Earlier, he'd given her two beautiful graduation gifts, a golden heart necklace and one of his most prized possessions, his belt buckle from his last days as bull riding champ, and then he'd told her, "You know how much I love you, baby. But I've got to get on the road again. I just want you to know, Trixiebelle, how proud I am of you." She hadn't missed the catch in his voice or the sad look in his brilliant blue eyes.

Needing to know what was happening, and tired of being protected like a fragile child, she repeated her question. "I said, what about Daddy? I've hardly seen him in the past four months, and today he rushed in for my graduation, but couldn't even stay for dinner tonight. Why does he keep coming home, only to leave again on business? He hasn't traveled this much since his prime rodeo days. Will he at least join us in Europe, Mama?"

"Your father hates Europe," Pamela explained. "And besides, he wouldn't come if I begged him. In fact, now that you're through with graduation, you might as well know—your father has been spending a lot of his time up in Arkansas."

"Arkansas?" Trixie wasn't surprised to hear that, but she wondered what the big secret was. After all, Brant owned a huge chunk of land near Little Rock. "Is he finally fixing up the ranch? Is that it?"

Another stern glance from Harlan, but it didn't stop her mother. Pamela shrugged, then tightened her expression into a firm frown. "Well, he is wasting a fair amount of time and money on that broken-down hovel in the wilderness if that's what you mean. Trixie, your father has decided he wants to live up there permanently, and well…I can't agree to that. So I've put my foot down, and…we've decided it would be best if we go our separate ways and get a divorce—"

Trixie looked from her mother to Harlan. Her grandfather seemed to age right there in front of her. "I'm sorry, honey. I didn't want you to find out this way," he said, his eyes watering up, his accusing gaze shifting to Pamela.

Shrugging daintily, Pamela rushed on. "I've fought against it and tried to keep up appearances, of course, but this marriage can't be fixed. No amount of prayer or reasoning is going to change Brant Dunaway into a decent, reasonable human being. I've discussed this thoroughly with Harlan, and he's been very generous about letting me continue to live here, for your sake. I've had counseling with Reverend Henry, but it's just too late. Your father expected me to give up my life here, everything I've come to love, everything I've worked so hard to achieve for both you and for this family, to go up there and live in the boonies." She waved a hand. "I'm too old and too established here to start over."

"I can't believe this," Trixie said, turning to her grandfather for support. "Do you agree with her?"

Harlan cleared his throat and sat back heavily in his Queen Anne chair. "I'm trying to remain neutral. I know how much that land means to your pappy, so I can't keep him from doing something he's wanted for such a long time. Heck, he's got more money than he'll ever need, what with my holdings and his own money from endorsements, but he's determined to do this thing his own way. He's basically told me to stay out of it." He glanced down the table at Pamela again. "But he sure wanted your mama to come up there with him. Thought it might do them good to get away from everything…and start over."

Trixie stared at her mother's unyielding face. "Couldn't you just try it, for a little while, Mama? It sounds like Daddy really wants to make things up to you."

"Hah!" Pamela interjected, her brown eyes flashing fire. "He should have thought about that years ago when he left me for weeks at a time to travel the rodeo circuit. You're right, Harlan. He never needed the money. We could have had a good life together, if he'd only given it a chance."

"And what about you, Mother?" Trixie said in a low, trembling voice. "Did you ever give him a chance? You know how much he loved being a bull rider, yet you never once supported him or gave him any encouragement. Why did you marry my daddy, anyway?"

Pamela looked her daughter straight in the eye. "I've often asked myself that same question. But I can tell you this, young lady, because I'm a Christian, I tried to make this marriage work. I guess some prayers just can't be answered.''

Hurt and disgusted, Trixie turned back to Harlan. ''How can you sit there and let her talk about your only son that way?''

Harlan lifted up out of his chair. ''Your mother knows exactly how I feel about the subject of my son. I love Brant with all of my heart, and I'll continue to support his efforts up in Arkansas. But for your sake, and for the sake of this family, I can't very well put Pamela out on the street. We will continue to be discreet about this, and we will continue to act like Dunaways, regardless of any rift in this family.''

Trixie shot up out of her chair, rattling dishes and upsetting water glasses in a very unladylike fashion that made her oh-so-proper mother wince. ''I get it. Close ranks and put our best face forward, no matter how torn apart this family really is. Show the world the perfect life of the Dunaways, the family everyone in Dallas can model their own miserable lives after, right? Pretend we're good, upstanding Christians who attend church every Sunday and give a hefty tithe each and every month.''

''That's enough, Tricia,'' Pamela said. ''We are good people and we have nothing, nothing at all, to be ashamed of.''

''Except the truth,'' Trixie retorted. ''We're living a facade, a lie, Mother. And I for one, won't continue it.'' Slamming her linen dinner napkin down, she headed for the foyer, then turned to face her stunned mother and disapproving grandfather. ''And I won't be going to Europe with you. I'm going to Arkansas, to see my father, and I intend to stay there until this fall. But don't worry,

I'll be home in time for college. So you just keep on bragging to all of your friends. And while I'm gone, you can continue to keep up appearances to save face, Mother, since that seems to be so much more important to you than trying to save your marriage."

In the end, however, even Pamela's manipulations and sugar-coated half truths couldn't save face. When the Dallas press got wind of the impending divorce, things turned nasty, and Pamela turned vindictive. After demanding a multimillion-dollar settlement from Brant, Pamela went to Europe alone and made headlines by being seen with some very eligible men. Of course, Pamela managed to keep things highly proper and above reproach, stating that she loved her daughter and only wanted to protect Tricia Maria from all of this hurt and pain.

She never stopped to think how much she'd hurt both Trixie and her father. No, Pamela always managed to put a spin on the truth, to twist it to her advantage and to come out, as Harlan put it, "smelling like a rose."

So that summer Trixie went to Arkansas to find her own peace of mind, to regroup and reassess her life, to get back at her domineering, self-righteous mother, and to get reacquainted with the father she loved and adored.

And...wound up meeting a man who changed her life.

That summer Tricia Maria Dunaway fell in love with Logan Maxwell.

That fall Tricia Maria Dunaway did not enroll in college at Southern Methodist University, because she was expecting Logan Maxwell's child.

As the sleek limousine pulled into the long drive leading up to the mansion, Trixie glanced up to the sign over the white fretwork gate, proclaiming the surrounding thousand acres of prime Texas real estate to be Dunaway's Hideaway.

But Trixie knew in her heart, this was no hideaway. She knew she'd never be able to hide from the truth, no matter how secluded and protected her grandfather's estate might be, no matter how much power the Dunaway name carried in Texas, no matter how hard her mother had managed to put a pretty face on the worst of situations by guarding Trixie's great sin with all the alert attention and precise organization of a qualified damage control expert.

Even though no one, absolutely no one in Dallas, knew about the baby, especially not Rad's blue-blooded family, Trixie knew in her heart, knew in her soul, that somewhere out there she had a child. Once, she'd accused her mother of living a lie; now *she* had to live one each and every day of her life. Unlike Pamela and Harlan, and even her father, she couldn't forever stay in a state of determined denial. It was her great secret, her great burden to bear. She had yet to forgive herself for her one youthful indiscretion, or for allowing those around her to force her to let her child be sent away like a parcel of dirty laundry. Sometimes, she lay awake at night, asking God to show her the way, to give her comfort, to help her bear the sorrow of her secret. And she wondered, did God ever hear her pleas? Or like her misguided mother, was she praying for all the wrong things?

But tomorrow, tomorrow when she at last faced Logan again, as much as she now believed in the absolute truth, she hoped the truth wouldn't be plastered there on her own face. Because he could never know the truth.

Logan could never, ever know that she'd been forced to give his child up for adoption. Only she and her immediate family could ever know that great shame. Because of the Dunaway power, Logan hadn't had a say in the matter, at all. He had no idea that a baby had even been conceived.

Again, Reverend Henry's words came back to haunt her.

"They that sow in tears shall reap in joy."

Dear God, she silently prayed now, hidden behind her dark glasses, shielded by the touch of Rad's hand on her own, *Will I ever be forgiven? How can I face Logan, knowing what I did? How can I enter into marriage with Rad, with a such a devastating secret between us? How can I ever be whole again?*

Tomorrow she would take Brant Dunaway's remains back to the place he loved most. Tomorrow, she would come face-to-face with her past and the man she had once loved so fiercely.

As Rad helped Trixie out of the car, the unmerciful Texas wind whipped her hair and sang mournfully in her ear, holding her, pulling her close. But Trixie fought at the wind, her thoughts turning to the rolling green hills of Arkansas. And she desperately wished she could turn back time.

Chapter Two

Time might have changed Trixie, but time had not changed the ranch. The red-stained, open barn still stood at a slanted angle beside the dirt lane, looking as if the next strong wind might just knock it over. But Trixie knew this old barn had weathered everything, from gentle rains to fierce, whirling tornadoes. And yet it stood.

Off to the right were the big rectangular stables, their planked walls painted the same aged red shade as the barn. As the wind rushed through the long, cool stable corridors, the smell of fresh hay and pungent manure assaulted her senses and touched her with such a sensory remembrance, she had to close her eyes to keep the tears from falling. She could almost hear her father's deep-throated laughter floating along on that wind. She could see herself and Logan, young and carefree, walking the horses, cleaning the stalls, stealing a kiss in a dark, cool alcove.

Out beyond the barn and stables, out beyond the screened-in cookhouse and the narrow barracks that served as the bunkhouse, the pine-covered hills that formed the beginnings of the Ouachita Mountains lifted and flowed like a green velvet blanket tossed across a rumpled bed.

Everything about the place that Brant had simply called The Ranch, was rumpled and slightly off center. It was as run-down and down home as they came. Nothing fancy, no frills—just a good, solid working ranch that included cattle, sheep and pigs, along with corn, cotton, produce and hay. Certainly nothing to be ashamed of, but nothing to shout about, either, as her father used to say.

Pamela had always hated this place.

Trixie had always loved it.

And missed it.

Now she stepped out of the rental car she'd picked up at the Little Rock airport, to look toward the west where the small lodge stood on a pine-shaded hillside. Brant had built his modest house there, so he could wake up each morning with a perfect view of the surrounding peaks and valleys. Off in the distance the mountains presented a muted, watercolor vista of rock and trees. Brant had loved his view of this part of the Ozark Plateau. He had liked seeing his little domain as he stood on the wide, posted porch with his first cup of coffee.

Now, the A-frame, log-cabin-style house looked forlorn and lonesome, a bittersweet reminder to Trixie of all that she had lost. Her father had built the house as a retreat for Pamela, hoping to mend the great tear in their doomed marriage. But Pamela had shunned his gift and him. Trixie wondered if her mother felt any guilt or remorse over that now. She knew she certainly did.

In a few hours the meager staff would gather together not far from the brown-logged lodge, underneath a great live oak that stood alone like a sentinel on one of those rolling hills, to watch Branton Nelson Dunaway be put to rest in the earth he loved. Trixie had arrived early to make sure everything had been arranged. The funeral home in Little Rock would bring her father's remains in a few hours.

Right now she needed this time to readjust to being here, to steel herself against seeing Logan again. She just wanted to stand here in the sandy driveway and look out over what now belonged to her.

Rad wanted her to sell it, take the money and run.

"We won't have time to fool with some run-down ranch in Arkansas, darling. We'll be so busy with my law practice and your consulting work I don't see how you can be in two places at once."

"I won't have to be there, Rad. The Ranch has a very capable foreman."

"That Maxwell fellow? You don't even know him that well. For all we know he might decide to take you for a ride now that Brant's gone. From everything Harlan's told me, the place barely breaks even as it is. No, I think it'd be best to get rid of it. We'll invest the money. I'll call my broker first thing once you've taken care of the sale."

Trixie closed her eyes and leaned back against the rented Nissan, images of the past she'd tried to bury springing up like wildflowers in her mind. Was that why she'd considered selling the ranch—to get rid of any traces of her great shame? Now she had to wonder why she'd even agreed to sell it at all. How in the world could she tell Logan that she wanted to sell the land he loved so much, the only home he'd known since he was a teenager?

* * *

Logan Maxwell heard the slam of a car door on the other side of the barn. Dropping his paintbrush, he found a rag on a nearby shelf and tried unsuccessfully to clean the white paint off his hands. Then he headed toward the front of the building, his heart pumping, his nerve endings on full alert, his whole body coiled tightly against seeing the woman he knew would be waiting on the other side.

Trixie.

Then he saw her standing there with her eyes closed and her head thrown back as she invited the wind to kiss her face. She wore designer jeans and a pair of hand-tooled buttery tan boots—he would bet she'd had them specially made in Austin, and a bright pink-and-green-colored Western-style shirt—probably a Panhandle Slim—and she looked about as out of place as a Barbie doll at a G.I. Joe convention.

She also looked beautiful. Her hair was still that same honeyed hue of blond, although she'd cut it—no, she'd paid an overpriced hairdresser to cut it—to a becoming, layered bob that framed her face with sleek flips and soft swirls. Still tall and cool, still the darling of Dallas, still the belle of the ball. He couldn't see her eyes, but he knew the color was a deep, pure blue, same as the Arkansas sky over his head. He couldn't take his own eyes away from her, though, so he leaned there against the support of the rickety barn and allowed himself this one concession while he compared the real-life woman to the girl he'd watched walk away so long ago.

He'd had an image of this woman in his mind for the past eight years, an image that had warred within his subconscious, an image that at times had haunted him, at other times had comforted him. He'd tried so very hard to put Tricia Maria out of his mind. But she wouldn't disappear. It had taken her father's death to bring her back to him in the flesh.

Now he used bitterness as his only weapon against the surge of emotions threatening to erupt throughout his system.

He had so many questions; he needed so many answers.

So he remained silent and just stared at her.

Trixie opened her eyes, feeling the heat from the sun on her tear-streaked face at about the same time she felt someone watching her. It didn't take her long to figure out who that someone was.

Logan.

She stared across the expanse of the dirt driveway, to the spot where he leaned with his arms crossed over his chest, just inside the open barn doors. In her mind she held the memory of a young man in his early twenties, muscled and tanned, with thick wisps of brown hair falling across his impish, little-boy face. This Logan was the same as the one in her memories, yet different. He still wore his standard uniform of faded Levi's and chewed up Ropers she remembered in her dreams. A battered Stetson, once tan, now a mellow brown, sat on his head. The torn T-shirt, smeared with grease and dirt, told her he still worked as hard as anybody around there, and...he obviously still wore the attitude, the whole-world's-out-to-do-me-in attitude, that had attracted her to him in the first place.

Only now, a new layer had been added to his essence, along with the crow's feet and the glint in his brown-black eyes. He'd matured into a full-grown man, his muscles heavier, more controlled, broader, his expression hardened, more intense, deeper.

He looked bitter and angry and hurt.

He looked delicious and vulnerable and lost.

And he looked as if he'd rather be any place on earth except standing there with her.

"Hello, Logan," she said, her voice sounding lost and unsure to her own ears as it drifted up through the live oaks.

"Tricia Maria." He lifted away from the barn to stalk toward her, his eyes never leaving her face. When he'd gotten to within two feet of her, he stopped and hooked his thumbs in the stretched, frayed belt loops of his jeans. "Sorry about your daddy."

"Yeah, me, too." She looked away, out over the hills. "He wanted to be buried here, so..."

"So you had no choice but to come back."

"Yes, I had to—for him, for his sake."

Not for me. Not for my sake, Logan thought. Because she'd written him off a long time ago. And they both knew why. Yet he longed to ask her.

The questions buzzed around them like hungry bees. Logan wanted to lash out at her, to ask her why, why she'd left him so long ago. But he didn't. Because he knew the answer, knew probably even better than she did why she'd deserted him and left him, and lied to him. Instead he said, "C'mon. We'll get your stuff up to the lodge. When's this thing taking place?"

"Three o'clock," she said, understanding he meant the graveside service for her father. "Didn't anybody call you about it?"

He didn't look at her as he moved around her to get into the driver's side of the car. "Yeah, some fellow named Ralph, Raymond—"

"Rad. Radford Randolph. He's...we're engaged. I asked him to call ahead and let you know when we'd get here. Granddaddy's coming later."

Logan slid into the car, then patted the passenger's seat, his dark gaze on her face. "Get in. I'll drive you up to the lodge."

Trixie had no choice but to do as he asked. She remembered that about Logan. Quiet, alert, a man of few words. Dark and brooding. A rebel. A troublemaker who'd been turned over to her father for a job over ten years before by a judge who'd agreed with Brant, and Logan's mother, Gayle, not to send him to a juvenile home. He'd come to work off a truancy sentence, and he'd never left.

In spite of everything, Logan had not deserted her father the way she had, the way Pamela had. Somehow, that had comforted her and made her resent him at the same time. Logan had known Brant Dunaway better than Brant's own flesh and blood. She could tell he was taking this hard, too. Maybe that was why he had a scowl on his scarred, harsh face. Out of respect, Trixie didn't speak again. Besides, she didn't know what to say, how to comfort him. She'd prayed long and hard to find some sort of comfort for herself, but it hadn't come yet.

Logan pulled the car up to the long, square lodge that Brant had built with his own hands, then turned in the seat to stare over at Trixie. "Yeah, this Rad fellow was more than happy to talk with me a spell. Asked a lot of questions, too."

Frowning, Trixie said, "What kind of questions?"

Logan tipped his battered hat back on his head and wrapped one hair-dusted arm across the steering wheel, his eyes full of accusation. "Oh, about profit and loss, how much income we've been generating, how much I think the land is worth."

Trixie moaned and closed her eyes. How could Rad

be so presumptuous? This wasn't his land, after all. It was hers.

When she felt Logan's hand on her chin, she opened her eyes to find him close, too close. His touch, so long remembered, so long denied, brought a great tearing pain throughout her system. To protect her frayed nerve endings, and the small amount of pride she had left, she tried to pull away.

He forced her head around so she had to look at him. "You're gonna sell out, aren't you?"

She did manage to push his hand away then, but the current of awareness remained as an imprint on her skin. "I…I haven't decided."

Logan jerked open the door and hauled his big body out of the car, then turned to bend down and glare at her again. "I can't believe you'd even think of selling this place, but then again, maybe I should have seen it coming."

"What's that supposed to mean?" she asked, her hand flying to the door handle. When he didn't answer her, she rounded the car to meet him at the trunk. "Logan, explain that last remark, please."

Logan opened the trunk, then snorted at the many travel bags she'd brought along. "Still so cool, calm and collected, still the fashionable big-city girl, aren't you, Trixie?"

In defense of herself she said, "I wasn't sure how long I'd need to stay."

He lifted her suitcases out of the trunk, then slammed the lid shut. "Oh, I think I can clarify that for you, darlin'. Just long enough to shed yourself of this place, I imagine." When she looked away, he grabbed her arm to spin her around. "Am I right, Trixie? Is that it? Were you planning on pulling another vanishing act, like you did all those years ago?''

''No,'' she said, humiliation and rage causing her to grit her teeth. ''No.''

He pressed her close to the car's back. ''Yes. I say yes. As soon as you can sell this place to the highest bidder, you'll tuck tail and head back to Dallas.'' Hefting her suitcases up with a grunt, he added, ''After all, some things never change, do they, sweetheart?''

She was surprised to find that some changes had been made to the ranch, after all, such as the tiny white chapel Brant had built by the great oak where he wanted to be buried, and she was even more surprised by the large turnout for her father's graveside service. Trixie knew her father had a lot of friends back in Dallas, but here? She'd always imagined him alone and reclusive, once he'd lost touch with his family, but then again Brant Dunaway hadn't been the kind of man to be satisfied with his own company for too long. Brant had loved life; had loved moving and roaming and watching and experiencing. What was it Granddaddy used to say? He was a good ol' boy with a big ol' heart.

Only, Pamela had never seen that. She only saw what she termed Brant's weaknesses; his flaws and failings far outweighed his goodness in Pamela's eyes. Once the novelty of being married to the renegade rodeo hero son of an oil man had worn off, she'd judged him with a very harsh measure; he'd never stood a chance of living up to Pamela's standards.

Trixie had always been confused by her mother's double standards. Pamela professed to being a Christian, attended church each Sunday, did all the right things, yet she never seemed to possess the one basic trait that made anyone a true Christian. Pamela had never learned tolerance or acceptance. She'd tried to change Brant, and it had backfired on her. And she was now working hard on her daughter.

Right up till this morning, when, in a nervous tizzy she'd tried her level best to talk Trixie out of coming. "Trixie, I just don't think it's wise for you to go back to that place. Harlan can take care of the burial. Stay here with me, sugar, and help me plan your engagement party."

"I'm going, Mother, and that's final. I want to be there to see Daddy buried. And I have to decide about what to do."

"Get rid of that land as fast as you can. You and Rad don't need the bother, darling. You're going to be busy, too busy to have to deal with that old headache of a ranch."

Pamela would never come out and say it, but she didn't want her daughter anywhere near Logan Maxwell again. Pamela had erased the whole episode from her mind like a bad movie.

Now, as Trixie watched the long line of people marching across the hillside toward the spot where Brant would be buried, she was glad her mother would not be among the crowd. She needed this time alone with her father, one last time. Her granddaddy was here, though, right by her side as he'd always been, his old eyes watering up as he looked at the shiny new walnut-grained casket, encased with a set of brass bull horns, where his son now rested.

"Are you all right?" Trixie asked Harlan, worried about him. Her grandfather had started out as a wild-catter and had gone on to build an oil empire. He'd paid his dues; done his time. He was getting old. And his only son's death had aged him both physically and emotionally.

"I'm fine, honey. Just missing your father."

"Me, too." She looked down at the sunflower wreath lying across the closed casket. "I should have visited him more—stayed in touch. I should have let him know I cared."

"He knew you loved him."

"Did he? Did he really know that?" she asked.

"Yes, he surely did. I kept in touch with him, you know. After all, he was my son. And, thank the Lord, we made our peace with each other long before he died."

"Did…did he ever talk about me?"

Harlan lifted his gaze to her face, his blue eyes, so like his son's, full of love and compassion. "All the time, honey. All the time."

Trixie saw the hesitation in her grandfather's expression. He seemed to want to say more, but instead he just looked away, down at the ground. At least he'd told her that her father still thought about her and acknowledged her existence. Trixie found some comfort in that.

After she'd had the baby—they'd never allowed her to know whether it had been a boy or a girl—Brant had drifted further and further out of her life. Still numb, still grieving over the twist her life had taken, she went on to college, a year late. Determined to get her life back on track, she'd soon became immersed in her studies and her somewhat vague social life. She'd gone through all the motions—the sororities, the campus parties, the whirl of college life, but her heart, her center always came back here to her father…and to Logan. Ashamed, she'd felt as though neither wanted anything to do with her, so she hadn't made any effort to mend

the shattered relationships with the two men she loved
and respected most in all the world.

Logan stood now, apart from all the others, with a
group of about eight children of various ages. Watching
him, Trixie wondered again how this was affecting him.
Brant had been like a father to him. Logan's mother,
Gayle, had come to the ranch years ago, divorced and
struggling with a rebellious teenage son. Brant had
given her a job as cook and housekeeper, and promptly
had put her son to work on the ranch.

The arrangement had worked, since Brant hadn't
spent too much time at the ranch back then. He'd depended on Gayle and Logan to watch over things, along
with some locals he hired to tend the animals and crops.
By the time Trixie arrived that summer so long ago,
however, Brant was a permanent resident here, and he
and Logan had formed a grudging respect for each
other. That mutual respect had seen them through the
worst of times. The very worst of times.

Not wanting to delve too deeply into those particular
memories, Trixie turned her attention to the haphazard
group of children around Logan. "Granddaddy, who are
all those youngsters?"

Harlan cleared his throat and glanced in the direction
of the silent, solemn group. "They're living on the
ranch, Tricia Maria. They've been here for most of the
summer."

Shocked, Trixie stared hard at her grandfather.
"Why? I mean, are they helping out with the crops as
a project? Did Logan give them jobs?"

Harlan started to speak again when the preacher lifted
his hands to gather the group around Brant's casket.
Harlan leaned close and whispered, "I'll explain it all
later."

* * *

There was no easy explanation for death, especially when speaking to a child. Logan stood with the children he was in charge of and wondered again if he'd handled any of this in the right way. Granted, he'd had training in counseling youths from the minister who was about to conduct Brant's funeral service. But talking with children was never easy. Children demanded complete and total honesty, and sometimes adults, by trying to protect them, hedged and pawed around the truth. Logan certainly knew all about that.

Looking over at Trixie now, Logan felt a stab of guilt. He hadn't exactly been completely truthful with her, but then again, she had kept her distance, and her secret, from him all these years, too. As he watched her now, so cool and pulled together in her black linen pantsuit, he had to wonder what her intentions were. How could she come barreling in here again after all these years and rearrange his whole way of life?

Feeling a tug on the sleeve of his chambray shirt, Logan looked down to find ten-year-old Marco holding on to him.

"Hey, buddy," Logan said on a low whisper. "How ya doing?"

Marco, a beautiful Hispanic child whose mother had abandoned him when he was three, shook his shiny black-haired head and said, "Not too good, Mr. Logan." He put a hand to his heart. "It hurts here, inside. I miss Mr. Brant."

"Yeah, me, too, bud," Logan replied, his voice tight, his words clipped. "Tell you what, though. You just stand here by me and hold tight to my hand, okay? We'll get through this together. Then later I'll bring out Radar and let you exercise him around the paddock. Deal?"

Marco's sad expression changed into a grin. "I get to ride the pony?"

Logan gave the boy a conspiring wink. "You and you alone, partner."

Marco took his hand and held on. Soon, all of the children had shifted closer to Logan. Their warmth soothed the great hole in his soul and made him even more determined to hold on to what he'd helped Brant build here. Then he saw Caleb standing by Gayle. Motioning for the seven-year-old boy, Logan waited as the youngest of the group ran and sailed into his arms, then wrapped his arms around Logan's neck. Holding the boy close, Logan decided right then and there that he had to talk some sense into Tricia Maria Dunaway. He wouldn't stand by and let her sell this ranch. Not after everything that had passed between them. With that thought in mind, he glanced over at Trixie and held tight to the little brown-haired boy in his arms.

She chose that moment to look up, her eyes meeting his in a silent battle of longing and questions. Soon he'd have his answers, Logan decided. And maybe soon she'd have hers, too. Whether she liked it or not....

Then the minister preached to them about finding their answers through the word of God. "For the Lord is good, his mercy is everlasting, and his truth endureth to all generations."

The truth. Could it endure between Trixie and him? Was it time to find out? Logan stared across at the woman he'd tried so hard to forget and wondered if someone up there was trying to send him a personal message.

Much later, after all the mourners had paid their respects, after Harlan had headed back down the hill to the lodge to rest a spell, after the sun had dipped behind the distant live oaks and loblolly pines, Trixie stood alone beside her father's freshly dug grave and remembered all the good and wonderful things about Brant Dunaway.

And she cried. She'd never felt so lost and alone.

Until she felt a hand on her arm.

Turning, she saw Logan standing there, his eyes as dark and rich as the land beneath their feet, his expression a mixture of sympathy and bitterness. He didn't speak; didn't offer her any pretty platitudes or pat condolences. Instead, he simply stood there beside her and let her cry.

And finally, when she could stand it no longer, when he could hold back no longer, he took her in his arms and held her while the red-gold September sun slipped reluctantly behind the Arkansas hills.

Chapter Three

❧

"He used to bring me daisies on my birthday," Trixie said later as they sat on a nearby hillside.

The shadows of dusk stretched out before them, darkness playing against the last, shimmering rays of the sun. Off in the distance, a cow lowed softly, calling her calf home for supper. Trixie stared across the widening valley, her gaze taking in the panoramic view of the beautiful burgundy-and-white Brangus cattle strolling along, dipping their great heads to graze the grasslands.

"He always did like wildflowers," Logan answered. "Remind me to show you the field of sunflowers he planted just over the ridge. The wreath on his casket came from those."

Trixie glanced over at the man sitting beside her. Logan had brought her such a comfort, coming back up here to sit with her. "Thank you," she said at last.

"For what?"

"For not pushing me. For just being you."

He snorted, then threw down the blade of grass he'd been chewing on. Glancing toward her, he said, "I thought me just being me was the reason you never came back here.''

Not ready to discuss that particular issue, she ran a hand through her hair and leaned her chin down on her bent knees. ''I had a lot of reasons for not coming back here, Logan.''

He'd like to know each and every one of them. But he didn't press her. That wasn't his style. ''Yeah, well, we all have our reasons for doing the things we do, sugar.'' He looked away, out over the lush farmland. ''I take full responsibility for what happened back then, Trixie.''

Shocked, she glanced over at him. Did he know about the baby, after all? ''What do you mean?''

Logan looked back at her then, his dark eyes shining with regret and longing. ''Our one time together—I should have stopped before things got so out of control.''

''I played a part in that night, too, Logan.'' And paid dearly for it. She shrugged, hoping to push the hurtful memories away. ''Besides, it's over now.''

''Is it?''

She looked down at her clenched hands, not wanting him to see the doubt and fear in her eyes. ''It has to be. We were young and foolish back then and we made a mistake. We're adults now. We just have to accept the past and go on.''

He nodded, then lowered his head. ''Well, one thing is still clear—our lives are still very different. That much hasn't changed. Just like then. You were the boss's daughter, and I took advantage of that. I won't do it this time around.''

Ignoring his loud and clear message, she reminded him, ''No, you didn't do anything I didn't let you do.''

"Yeah, well, I could have been more careful." His voice grew deeper, the anger apparent in his next words. "Then you saved my hide by begging your father not to fire me. The rich girl helping the poor, unfortunate stable hand."

She realized where some of his bitterness was coming from. By asking Brant not to fire him after he'd caught them together, she'd only added insult to injury. "You needed your job. Your mother would have been heartbroken if Daddy had sent you away."

"So you went away instead." His eyes burned through her. "I've had to live with that all of these years. I've had to live with a lot of things."

Trixie reached out a hand to his arm, wanting to comfort him. What would he do, what would he think if he knew everything? "Logan, I'm sorry."

"Don't apologize! I'm the one who blew it!" Suddenly afraid of being this near to her, of being this intimate with her, he hopped up to brush the dirt off the back of his jeans. "C'mon. You must be hungry. Mama's probably got supper on the table by now."

Trixie took the hand he offered down to her, her eyes meeting his in the growing dusk. With a firm tug, he had her up and standing in front of him. Too close. Logan dropped her hand, then turned without a word to stomp away.

She followed, wondering if she'd ever be able to figure out Logan Maxwell. She'd seen him at the service this afternoon, watching her with that bitter expression on his face. And…she'd seen him with the children. He obviously cared about his little wards. Especially that little boy who'd clung to him the entire time. What a cutie. Trixie had only glanced at the child briefly and then he'd been lost in the crowd of people trailing by to pay their respects.

"Tell me about the children," she said now as she hurried to catch up with him. "Grandfather said he'd explain. But I want you to."

Logan stopped to whirl around and stare at her. "You mean, you don't know?"

"Know what?"

"That this ranch is now a part-time foster home for troubled kids?"

"What?" Shocked, she looked around as if searching for some sort of justification. "Well, no. No one bothered to tell me anything about that." Sighing, she added, "I'm so tired of everyone trying to protect me. Why don't *you* tell me all about it."

Logan kept walking, but slowed his pace to a comfortable gait. "Your father wanted the ranch to be a place where people could come and learn about nature and about life. Through a program with the local church, he set up a foundation called The Brant Dunaway International Farm. We grow food and livestock for underprivileged countries, and we train volunteers to go into the villages of these countries and teach the locals how to live off the land. Most of what we produce here is shipped out of the country to help these people."

Trixie had to let that soak in. Her father, the rowdy cowboy, doing missionary work for the church. "I don't believe it."

"I can't believe you weren't aware of it."

"The only thing I heard from the lawyers was that I had inherited this land. Everything else got lost in the fog shrouding my brain." Her head down, she added, "And well...I haven't exactly kept in touch over the years."

"Yeah, and who's fault is that?"

Frustrated and unable to tell him her reasons for staying away, she said, "Could we just get back to the children?"

He shot her a hard look. "Ah, the children. Does having them here bother you?"

She didn't miss the sarcasm in his question. "Well, no. I just want to know what's going on."

"These kids come to us through the church—from broken homes, from foster homes, from parents who've abandoned them, from law officers trying hard to save them. Most of them are juvenile offenders—petty stuff, like stealing from the local convenience store or vandalism. Small-time crimes that could lead to worse, if someone doesn't intervene. They've seen some ugly things out there beyond our front gates."

He stopped, taking a long breath. "We try to fix them—teach them pride and self-esteem, and how to be responsible and productive. We're like a summer camp, only," he glared over at her here, "only not for the rich and privileged few who can afford such luxuries. We cater to those who might never get a chance like this, and as corny as it might sound to someone like you, we try to teach them that there is some beauty and good in God's world."

"As hard as it might be for someone like you to believe," she said, her words tight and controlled, "I do have a social conscience, and I do care about the other human beings existing on this earth alongside me."

"Really?"

"Yes, really. I just had no idea my father had such...such lofty ambitions toward saving the world."

"He didn't try to save the world, Trixie. He just tried

to make a difference on his own little piece of earth. And he worked long and hard and gave a lot of his own money to accomplish his goals. Things here were just starting to turn around when he got sick.''

''He worked himself to death, didn't he?''

Logan heard the anguish in her question, but couldn't find any sympathy for her pain. It was too little, too late now. ''Yeah, Brant worked hard, as hard as anybody on this place. It was like…it was like he was trying to work off all his demons, you know.''

''I do know,'' she said, understanding more than ever what her father must have gone through. It didn't help to know some of his pain had come from her own foolish actions. ''I wish—''

''Too late for wishes, sweetheart,'' Logan said as they reached the house. Then he stopped just before the screened back door, and turned to face her. ''But…it's not too late for you to continue with your father's dream. That is, if you don't sell this place right out from under us.''

''I haven't made a firm decision yet,'' she said on a defensive note.

He smiled then, showing her the dimples she remembered so well. ''That's all I needed to hear,'' he said on a low whisper.

His whisper, so soft, so sure, and his nearness, so exciting, so frightening, told Trixie that she was in for a long, hard battle. And she wasn't sure if she had the strength to fight both Logan *and* her guilt.

She only hoped God would show her the right way to deal with this.

Gayle Maxwell was a petite, dark-headed woman who, because of the hard life she'd had, looked older than her fifty-one years. Trixie watched Logan's mother, physically feeling the woman's disapproval of her presence there. Gayle had not been pleased all those years ago when Trixie and Logan had formed an instant bond; she apparently wasn't pleased now to have Trixie back in their lives. And, Trixie had to remind herself, the woman was probably concerned that soon she might be displaced and unemployed. Well, Trixie was worried about that, too.

"Hello, Mrs. Maxwell," Trixie said as they entered the long, paneled kitchen of the lodge. "I'm sorry I didn't get a chance to speak with your earlier."

"Hello, Tricia," Gayle replied, her lips tight, her red-rimmed eyes looking everywhere but at Trixie. "Sorry about Brant. We'll all miss your daddy."

"Me, too."

Trixie knew Gayle had been avoiding her, but she wasn't prepared for the woman's evasiveness tonight. Gayle looked downright uncomfortable. Her movements were erratic and jittery. Her brown eyes darted here and there, as if she expected someone to burst into the room and interrupt their meal any minute. Maybe Gayle was still upset about Brant's death. They had always had a close relationship.

Wanting to soothe the older woman, Trixie asked, "Can I do anything to help with dinner?"

Gayle turned back to the stove. "No, everything's under control." Over her shoulder she said to Logan, "I've already fed all of the children. Samantha's with them down at the bunkhouse, helping them with their studies."

Trixie watched as Logan nodded, then told her that Samantha was a trained counselor who helped out during the summer. "She's also a qualified teacher. Some of the kids aren't ready to go back into the mainstream just yet, so we homeschool them.'' He glanced at her, then back to his mother. ''Where's…where's Caleb?''

Gayle dropped the spoon she'd been holding with a clatter. ''Down at the bunkhouse with the rest,'' she said, her gaze holding her son's.

Trixie didn't miss the look that passed between mother and son, nor did she understand what was going on. She was tired and still stunned by her father's death and having to be here again, but it was obvious that these two had mixed feelings about her visit to the ranch. Not wanting to ask too many questions too soon, she could only lift her brows in a questioning expression.

By way of an explanation, Logan turned to Trixie. ''Caleb's the youngest of the bunch, so he spends a lot of time up here with Mama.''

Trixie nodded. ''Oh, the little boy you were holding at the funeral.'' With a poor attempt at humor, she added, ''Goodness, he looks too adorable to be a juvenile offender. What's he in for?''

A dark look colored Logan's face. ''His mother abandoned him,'' he said in a low, tight voice.

Trixie fell down on a chair, all the energy she had left quickly pooling at her feet. Logan's words felt like a slap against her suddenly hot skin. Of course, he had no way of knowing how close to home his words had hit. ''How awful,'' she said, her words barely above a whisper. ''He's so young, so little.'' *So like the child I gave up.*

Gayle turned then to stare over at her, the look on the older woman's face full of fear mixed with contempt. ''Your Daddy told the boy he'd always have a home here. That is, unless you sell it out from under him.''

''Mama, hush,'' Logan said, shooting Gayle a warning glare.

Trixie stood up then, determined to be firm and fair in dealing with the Maxwells. ''I haven't made a decision regarding what to do about this place yet, Mrs. Maxwell. You see, I wasn't aware of the foundation my father had set up here.''

''You would have been, if you'd bothered keeping in touch,'' Gayle said over her shoulder. ''But I guess you had better things to do with your time.''

Trixie's gaze flew to Logan's face. He looked uncomfortable, but it was obvious from his cold, restrained look that he agreed with his mother.

''You're absolutely right,'' she said, her heart breaking all over again to think that Logan felt this way about her. ''I didn't stay close with my father, and I have only myself to blame for that, but now I'm trying to piece things together so I can make the right choice.''

Gayle whirled then, her eyes full of distrust. ''The right choice for all of us, or for yourself?'' Before Trixie could answer, the woman barreled ahead. ''I know all about your fancy degree, Ms. Dunaway. And I guess you're about as qualified and entitled as anybody to make changes at this place. Marketing consultant, is it? Fancy education, fancy title, fancy everything. But that don't make you smart. Not in my eyes, at least.''

Shaking her spoon at Trixie, she added, ''Your daddy used to say that it's better to be kind than wise and that true wisdom begins with kindness. Brant had both of those qualities down pat. Too bad his only daughter never learned them.''

Tears pricked at Trixie's eyes, but she refused to let

Gayle or Logan see her pain. After all, she couldn't just blurt out that she'd had a child out of wedlock with Logan and that her father had stopped talking to her afterward, and that was the reason she'd been forced to stay away from the ranch.

"Well, maybe I can learn all about kindness and wisdom while I'm here," she said in a quiet voice. "And I assure you, I won't make a hasty decision until I've weighed all of the facts."

Mustering what little dignity she had left, she carefully walked around the table, then edged her way to the open back door. "I'm not really very hungry, after all. If you'll both excuse me, I think I'd just like to go for a walk before I go to bed."

Then she was out the door, out in the night air. The wind hit her skin, cooling the heat that radiated from her face, soothing the humiliation that radiated from her soul. From inside, she could hear Logan arguing with his mother, bits of scattered words echoing out over the trees. Was he arguing in her defense, or was he simply warning Gayle to tread lightly while the wicked witch was on the premises?

Trixie didn't bother sticking around to find out which. Instead she headed down the sandy dirt lane to the stables, her feet taking her where her mind wanted to be. From the single security light shining out over the trees and shrubbery, she found her way to the looming structure to seek shelter from all of her problems, just as she'd done that summer so long ago.

As Trixie entered the corridor of the long building, a slender mare, a working quarter horse, greeted her with a soft whinny and a toss of her white mane.

Reaching out to rub the nose of the chestnut-colored

animal, Trixie cooed softly. "Hello, girl. How ya doing?"

The animal nudged her hand in response.

Looking around for a feed bag, Trixie said, "Let me see. I'll bet we can find you some sort of snack."

For the next few minutes Trixie stood letting the mare eat the mixture of oats, bran and hay she'd found nearby. As she watched the animal munch, she remembered other times she'd done this same thing, always with Logan by her side. He knew everything there was to know about horses, and he'd learned it all from her father. Again she felt that stab of jealousy and resentment whenever she thought about Brant and Logan, here together like a father and son.

"Maybe I should have been born a boy," she said to herself, knowing in her heart that Brant had loved her once just the way she was. No, she couldn't hold a grudge for something she had forced her father to do. She had asked Brant to allow Logan to stay on, had begged him not to fire Logan.

"It's all my fault, Daddy," she had said at the time. "I...I flirted with him. I wanted to be with him. If you send him away, Gayle will go with him. Then they won't have a place to live. Please, Daddy, don't do this. I'll go...I'll go back to Dallas, and I promise I won't have anything to do with Logan again."

She'd always believed she'd done Logan a favor. Now she had to wonder if instead she'd done him a great disservice by fighting his fight for him. But in the end it didn't really matter. She'd made the best decision, based on her love for Logan at the time.

Now she had the power to destroy everything that was left between them. She wanted to be rid of her past. That was why she'd been determined to sell this place.

And now she'd come face-to-face with that past again, but there was so much more to have to deal with, so much responsibility being thrown on her shoulders.

Her first instinct was to run as far away from this place as she could possibly get. If she got involved in Brant's dreams for this ranch, she'd be up to her eyeballs in something that might quite possibly become an overwhelming burden. Yet if she didn't at least think about keeping the ranch and continuing her father's work here, she'd never forgive herself.

Was she up to the task? Could she face down the secrets of her past with Logan, for the sake of her father's dream and for the sake of these children who'd been entrusted to his care?

Without warning, little Caleb's cherubic face came to mind. She couldn't get the picture of the little boy who'd been clinging to Logan out of her head. What would happen to Caleb if she sold the ranch?

How could she make such an important decision when she was so very tired and confused? The big mare snorted, her brown eyes giving away no secrets as she nuzzled Trixie's hand with her wet nose.

"Guess I need to pray hard," Trixie said to the animal. "That's what Granddaddy always tells me to do when I have a problem."

She let the mare finish the last of the mash, then dusted her wet hand against her pants before she walked on through the stables. When she came to the little tack room, Trixie stopped and closed her eyes against the intensity of her memories, the smell of saddle soap and horse sweat blending together in her mind. It was here in this very room, where Logan had first kissed her. She'd fallen in love that summer—her first love. But it wasn't meant to be. Now she had Rad and her life with him was all planned out. Everyone said they made a perfect couple.

Trixie closed her eyes. *Help me make the right decision, Lord.*

When she opened her eyes, Logan was standing in the doorway watching her, his own eyes devoid of any condemnation or judgment. For just a moment, it was as if time had stopped and they were back there, young and carefree and exploring the raging emotions coursing between them. But Trixie had to remind herself that that time was over.

Logan, however, had other considerations on his mind. He walked toward her with a purposeful look on his face, then took her into his arms without a word. Before Trixie could voice a protest, he kissed her, long and hard, stealing the breath right out of her body. Then he stood back and held his hands on her arms, his eyes bright with hope and longing.

"Stay awhile, Tricia Maria," he said, his breath ragged from the effect of the kiss. "Stay and see for yourself all of the good we're doing here. You owe me that much at least, before you decide what to do about this place."

"Is that why you kissed me?" she asked, her heart pumping, her voice raw with pain.

Logan's mouth came close to hers again. "No, I kissed you because I wanted to, because I couldn't stop myself. But I'm asking you to stay because I intend to fight you on this. I won't let you sell this place without at least putting up a good struggle. You said you'd consider everything and take in all the facts before you made a choice."

"I did say that," she admitted, thinking he was one

smooth operator. "And I can't make an informed decision without seeing how this place operates."

He leaned close again, his breath fanning her face. "Then you'll stay?"

She swallowed back the fear coursing through her system. Somehow she knew her answer would change both of their lives. "Yes, I'll stay," she said, her gaze holding his.

"Fair enough."

Logan let her go then, turning to get away from the overpowering urge to pull her back into his arms. He hoped he'd done the right thing by asking her to remain here for a while. He didn't really have any other choice. Somehow, he had to make Trixie see that this place could make a difference, not just in the lives of all of those children, but in her own life, also.

He would do that much at least for Brant's sake.

Even if it meant having to tell Trixie the truth at last.

Chapter Four

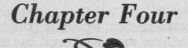

"**M**other, I've made my decision. I'm only going to
stay a few days, so don't worry." Trixie tried once
again to convince her mother that she wasn't being impulsive, then listened as Pamela's shrill words shot
through the phone line.

"Well, I am worried, young lady," Pamela said with
an impatient huff. "You have no business hanging
around with that…that field hand."

"Logan is the foreman of this ranch," Trixie reminded her mother, anger causing her to grind the
words out. "He's very capable of showing me what's
going on here."

"Oh, he's capable, all right. Apparently you've forgotten just exactly what that man is capable of doing."

Trixie closed her eyes, willing herself to stay calm.
They'd had this argument before. Pamela did not believe Logan Maxwell was good enough to even speak
to her daughter, therefore she couldn't dare acknowledge that he'd done much more, without laying the
blame at his feet completely.

"No, Mother, I haven't forgotten anything about Logan. But I'm asking you to trust me on this. I'm not here to stir up things with Logan again. I'm here to make a decision—an important decision—regarding what to do about this ranch.''

"Sell it!'' Pamela shouted. "It's that simple, Trixie. Harlan has left it up to you, and that's what needs to be done. No decision necessary.''

"I disagree, Mother,'' Trixie replied, her tone firm and controlled in spite of her trembling hand holding the phone. "Since neither the lawyers nor you told me the whole truth about this situation, I'm now forced to investigate things for myself. And that means I have to stay here longer than I'd planned.''

Trixie had already called her office and her assistant was prepared to cover matters there. She also had her client list with her, so she could handle any emergencies that came up, if necessary.

"Everything is under control,'' she told her mother.
Except my heart and your temper, Trixie thought.

"And what about your engagement party?''

"I'll be back in Dallas in plenty of time to tie up the loose ends for the party.''

"You have obligations, Trixie. It's expected—''

"I know, I know,'' Trixie interrupted. "People will talk and think the worst, and you might miss an opportunity to have your picture in the society pages.''

A long sigh. "Tricia Maria, that was low and uncalled for.''

"Mother, I'm sorry. Just let me do what has to be done and I'll be home at the end of the week.''

"I don't like this.''

"You'll get over it.''

"Well, I didn't get over it the first time.''

Trixie sat silent for a minute, counting to ten until

the sting of her mother's deliberate reminder had passed, then said, "No, Mother, neither of us did. And that's something you'll never let me forget, isn't it?"

Realizing she'd been cruel, Pamela tried to make amends. "Darling, I just want you to be happy. And Rad is such a wonderful man. I just want you home, to try on your gown for the party and to help me get all of this organized. You know I've reserved the entire country club, and of course I've invited so many people. Why, I've hired a firm just to address and mail out the invitations, and then I've got the caterers and the florists to deal with. I could really use your help, since this is all for you, anyway."

Automatically forgiving her mother's barbs and ignoring the excited pitch of Pamela's line of conversation, Trixie replied, "You'll do a great job on the party. You've always been one of the best hostesses in Dallas, whether it's for me or anyone else. And I promise I'll be there soon."

The compliment soothed Pamela's fragile ego enough that she gave in. "Oh, all right. Just shed yourself of that place, once and for all, so you can get on with your life."

Trixie hung up, wondering if Pamela had a clue as to what her daughter really wanted out of life. For years now, Trixie had let her mother steer the reins of her existence. And Pamela had taken full advantage of Trixie's disinterest, guiding her to what she believed to be all the right places and all the best people. Trixie had allowed it out of guilt, mostly, and because she herself didn't have the strength or the ambition to really care.

Now, however, Trixie felt the tides of her future changing. It had taken her father's death to cause her to see the light. She'd missed out on so much; she could have been here, by his side, helping him to realize his dream. It was such a big, lofty dream, yet with such a simple concept. He wanted to help others; he wanted to be fair and good and kind and nurturing. And Brant Dunaway had been all of those things. Too late, Trixie saw that now.

Now she was ready to take charge, to make her own decisions, to take a chance. She'd lived in fear over the past eight years, allowing her domineering mother to call the shots. Now, after discovering a whole new side to the father she'd lost touch with, she was willing to go on faith.

But what if she made another mistake?

A knock at her bedroom door brought her head up. Too late to worry about that now. She'd agreed to stay. She wouldn't go back on that promise, no matter how much her doubt nagged at her, right along with her mother, to go back home.

She opened the door to find Logan standing in the upstairs hallway, his hat in his hand, his feet braced apart as he stared down at her. Giving her a quick once-over, he said, "Didn't you bring any working outfits?"

Looking down at her short-sleeved, flower-embroidered blue cotton shirt and matching walking shorts, Trixie shrugged. "Sorry, I didn't bring the proper ranch hand attire. Any suggestions?"

Logan squinted, then made a face. "Well, it ain't what you're wearing, that's for sure."

Trixie frowned. What she was wearing consisted of the best in designer casual wear. "Should I change?"

He snorted, then dragged her out into the hallway with a hand encircling her wrist. "What, into something even more ridiculous than that? No, I kinda like it, even though it's way too fancy for slopping hogs.''

Trixie pulled back, her eyes going wide. "Slopping hogs? I'm here to *observe,* Logan. I don't plan on getting up close and personal with any farm animals."

He urged her on ahead of him, his cowboy boots clicking on the planked landing. "Oh, and how are you going to get a feel for this operation if you don't get some hands-on experience?"

Not liking the glee in his tone, Trixie cast a glance at him over her shoulder. If he thought she was going to do physical labor, he was in for a big surprise. "Can't I just watch and still get a feel?"

"Better to get down-and-dirty," he said, his grin telling her that he planned to make her time here a real learning experience.

"You're doing this on purpose," she chided as they marched down the open, planked stairway. "Is this your way of getting revenge on me?"

"Maybe," he readily admitted as they reached the long, spacious Western-style den. "Of course, if I wanted to really chap your hide, I could just kiss you again."

The minute he said it, the teasing light went out of his eyes to be replaced with something deeper and much more intimate. Maybe he was remembering that kiss they'd shared last night in the tack room. It had certainly caused her to remember other kisses and other such teasing conversations.

But since she'd just assured her mother that nothing was stirring between Logan and her, she felt obligated to fight him off. "I'll take the pigs," she retorted, half serious, half afraid he'd really kiss her again, just as punishment.

Logan shook his head, his dark eyes flashing. "Now, that sure makes me feel good about my kissing abilities." Then he turned completely serious again. "Maybe we should make a pact, though—to keep this strictly business."

Trixie saw the brief flash of need warming his dark eyes. Nodding her head, she said, "Good idea. Just show me the ranch, Logan, and I'll make a decision by the end of the week. Then I'll be out of your hair one way or another."

Wanting confirmation, he asked, "So does that mean if you decide to keep the place, you'll give me complete control on how to run it?"

"That depends," she replied. She hadn't thought that far ahead. If she kept the ranch, she'd have to put in an occasional appearance, to make sure the operation was run according to Brant's wishes. That could prove to be very awkward, especially if he tried to kiss her every time they were alone.

"On what?" Logan asked, his gaze direct and questioning.

Hoping to keep things light for now, she retorted, "On whether you make me slop pigs or not."

Logan managed a smile as he watched her move through the den to the kitchen. One week. One week of torment and torture, one week of having her near, and knowing she had to go back to her world and the man she'd pledged to marry. One week to convince her that she couldn't sell out her heritage. One week to show Tricia Maria Dunaway that she shouldn't sell out, or sell herself short, either. She could do this; she could gain a lot from this ranch. If she was willing to give a little.

And...he could do this. He could do what he had to do to keep this ranch, and his secrets, intact.

But as he watched her now, standing there in her expensive, baby blue ensemble, sipping coffee like a princess as she looked out over the blossoming dawn, Logan knew being with Trixie again would be one of the hardest things he'd ever had to suffer through.

Trixie looked at him then, her blue eyes a perfect match to her fashionable outfit, her cool attitude a perfect example of his notion of all she represented. He had no way of knowing she was a bundle of nerves and that sweat moistened the crisp cotton of her button-up blouse. He had no way of knowing that she was thinking this would be one of the hardest weeks of her life.

"Does Logan make you all work this hard every day?" Trixie asked Marco a couple of hours later.

They stood inside the hog pen, filling a trough with fresh water for the many sows and what looked like thousands of squealing, pink-nosed piglets. In spite of the chaos of animals and teenagers, the place was neat and tidy. The tightly wired fences stretched in symmetric order across the expanse of the paddock, and the animals looked healthy and well fed, their stalls full of fresh hay and clean, cool water.

Trixie only hoped she hadn't mixed up too many piglets when they'd moved the babies and cleaned the stalls earlier. How was she supposed to know which pig went with which sow, anyway? "That man put me in here on purpose. Well, we'll show him, huh, Marco?" That is, if she hadn't orphaned some poor piglet already.

Marco grinned, his black eyes squinting together as he stared up at his new blond-haired friend. "We call him the pigmeister," he said, his words meant for her ears only. "Mr. Logan wants us to learn responsibility," he added, his tone changing to somber as he reconsidered calling his boss/foster parent a derogatory name.

Trixie smiled down at the youngster. He was really sweet, if not somewhat street-wise. As were all of the half dozen children staying here. They ranged in age from sixteen to seven, from what she could tell. Kind of a patchwork family of personalities. And each one had a story to tell. Being a captive audience, she'd listened all morning, her heart opening with each child's tale.

Abusive parents or no parents at all, truancy charges, and some more severe charges, such as petty theft and robbery, colored each story and quickly, effectively turned her apathy into sympathy. These children needed some firm guidance in their young lives. She was proud of her father, and Logan, for providing it.

Now, she grinned back at Marco. "Mr. Logan seems like a tough taskmaster to me, but I guess it builds character, huh?"

"That's what he tells us when we whine," Marco said, giggling as several thirsty sows bumped each other to get to the fresh, cool water. "Only, Miss Trixie, we don't have to work all day long. As long as we do our assigned chores and attend the Bible study classes, we get free time each day."

"Great," Trixie replied, the sweat beading on her forehead making her wish she had some free time right about now. She was wilted and sweaty, not socialite material at all. "And what do you and your friends do for fun?"

"We head down to the swimming hole," Marco said

before running away to take care of more important pig business.

"That sounds like heaven," Trixie said to a pink-eyed sow who wanted first dibs on the water supply. Trixie obligingly moved out of the six-hundred pound animal's path, her eyes scanning the pen for Logan. He'd pushed her through the gates, told her to follow Marco's instructions, then had conveniently left.

As she stood there, wondering what the sharply dressed, sharp-minded women of the Metroplex Marketing Professionals would think of her now, she had to laugh. Right this very minute she didn't care what anyone thought. She was dirty and smelly and sweaty, and her white leather sandals would never be the same, but it felt kind of good to be back out in the thick of things—as long as she watched where she stepped.

Shaking her head, she grinned down at the thirsty sows. "Hold on, ladies, there's plenty of water for everyone."

"You're having way too much fun," Logan said from behind her, echoing her thoughts precisely.

Her grin turned into a grimace as the wind shifted. Giving him a level, daring look, she said, "Did you expect me to burst into tears and beg you to come in here and rescue me?"

"That would have been the highlight of my day," he said as he stepped through the gate and stalked toward her, a look of grudging admiration on his face. He should have known she'd rather die than give in to him. Trixie had always enjoyed a good challenge. Well, he wasn't quite finished with her just yet. "Looks like you've done a passable job here. Ready to move on to worming sheep?"

Trixie turned off the water hose, then stared across the trough at him. "You're kidding, right?"

"Nope. Has to be done, and as always, we could use an extra hand. You get your choice of which end you want to hold, though."

Her groan echoed out over the squeals and grunts of the hogs and pigs. "Logan, need I remind you that I'm still officially your boss? I think I'd just like a shower, then a tour of the ranch and a thorough report on the operation. And I think you've had enough fun at my expense for one day."

He watched her, his gaze rich with an unreadable emotion before he became glib again. "Testy, aren't you? What's the matter, Tricia Maria, break a nail or something?"

Swaying against the bumps of the sows, Trixie glared over at him. "Okay, I've had enough. I did what you asked—I hung out in the pig pen. And I don't mind lending a hand, but I won't stand around and take orders from you just so you can enjoy watching me make a fool of myself."

Logan quit smiling then, his expression hardening. "Why not? You certainly made me look like a fool all those years ago."

"Oh, is that what this is all about?" she asked, her hands on her hips as she leaned toward him. "You weren't the only one hurt by our brief encounter, Logan. I certainly paid a high price for my one indiscretion."

He inched closer, nudged by grunting snouts. "Oh, did you, now? Funny, I don't see it that way. You seemed to have bounced back pretty quickly, from what I've heard."

"And just what did you hear?" she asked, her breath stopping. Was he suspicious, or just being cruel?

"Your daddy kept tabs on you, Trixie. College, parties, the good life. You picked right up where you left off." He turned quiet, his eyes scanning her face. "I was just…a minor distraction while you slummed with the ranch hands."

His words hurt more than she'd allow him to see. Coming toward him, she tried to pass by, but his hand on her arm and the many grunting sows urging her forward only brought her straight into his arms. Trying to steady her, Logan held her with both hands now.

She looked up into a set of eyes as rich and deep and centered as the mountains behind them. "Is that really how you see me, Logan? As some socialite who used you, then dumped you?"

"Didn't you?"

Tears pricked at her eyes, but she refused to show him her pain. And she certainly couldn't tell him the truth. "How can you even think that? I didn't have any other choice. I had to go back to Dallas."

"Did you really? I think you had several choices, Trixie."

"What do you mean?" she asked, her voice a whisper on the wind, her whole body tense.

Logan stared down at her, his eyes softening only for a minute, his expression changing from harsh to forgiving as he lowered his hands to her back. She waited, knowing he wanted to say something, knowing he needed to tell her what was in his heart.

And then a big, greedy sow came barreling toward the fresh water, her pink eyes daring Trixie to stand in her way. Too late, Trixie and Logan heard the warning cries and high-pitched laughter coming from the young helpers.

"Look out, Miss Trixie," Marco called, clapping his hands together.

Trixie's gaze moved from Logan's face to the animal bearing down on her. Too late.

The sow charged into Trixie's legs like an angry steer plowing into a rodeo clown, taking Trixie completely by surprise. With a gasp of shock, Trixie lost her balance and since she was still holding onto Logan, pulled him right along with her as she stumbled back against the cold, sharp metal of the trough.

And toppled right back into the water.

Sows grunted and squealed, scattering in the mud as water splashed out over the trough's edge. Logan had no choice but to hold on and enjoy the fall, since Trixie's first reaction was to reach out for him in an effort to save herself.

He landed right smack beside her, laughing as she came up out of the water spitting and snarling.

"Oh, this is all your fault," she said, her face and hair wet and dripping. "Are you satisfied now, Logan Maxwell?"

Logan sat back in the cold water. Then reaching out to steady her, he hauled her close, his gaze sweeping her face. "No, not nearly enough," he admitted on a low growl.

Trixie saw the heat in his expression and felt that same heat pouring through her system. But she couldn't allow him to get too close, not when he obviously resented her so much. "Let me go, Logan," she pleaded, a catch in her voice.

That plea brought Logan quickly to his senses. He let go of her and stood up so fast he almost toppled over the side. Then he offered her a hand. "Sorry. For a minute there, I forgot that things have changed. It won't happen again.''

Trixie watched him while the children laughed and gathered around them, and she took all the chaos as an opportunity to regain her composure along with her balance. No matter how good she felt being in his arms, no matter how much she longed to kiss him again, she had to remember that things *had* changed for them. She was engaged to a wonderful, caring man, and Logan...well, Logan had his life here at the ranch. It wouldn't do for her to get caught up in some sentimental fantasy from the past.

After all, she had given up on Logan a long time ago. And with all the history between them, with her one big secret glaring her in the face each time she looked at Logan, things could only go from bad to worse. No, the best thing she could do was to make a decision about this ranch—soon—before she again did something she would regret.

His face blank, Logan helped her out of the trough, then said, ''I'll drive you back to the lodge. Get changed, and I'll give you a tour of the place, then we'll get serious about this.''

''Okay.'' She nodded, avoiding the look of regret she saw clearly on his face. Letting him guide her out of the maze of sows, piglets and young people, she looked straight ahead, ashamed and embarrassed and afraid of all the old emotions that had surfaced between them.

That's when she saw little Caleb running across the yard, his youthful face bright with animation, his deep blue eyes lighting up like the sky at dawn.

''Daddy, Daddy, I saw what happened. That was so funny! Was it cold? Did that big sow bite you?''

Logan's gaze shot over to Trixie, a look of guilt and

defiance coloring his expression. She stopped, her heart dropping to her feet right along with the water dripping off her body.

Daddy. Caleb had called Logan Daddy. Oh, Lord, was Logan married, then? Was that what he'd been trying to tell her? She couldn't speak. She could only stare over at him and wonder why with all this talk and action regarding kissing, he hadn't even bothered to tell her he had a wife and a son.

Then she remembered, Logan didn't owe her any explanations. Because she hadn't bothered to tell him that she'd borne his child so long ago.

Finding out that he had obviously gone on with his life so soon after only served as a brutal reminder—he could never know of her deceit. Her secret would have to remain intact, right along with any feelings she might still have for him. She'd have to, once again, bury her hopes. Because she belonged to another man now, and he belonged to another woman.

And a precious little boy.

Chapter Five

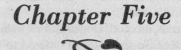

Trixie heard the pounding on her bedroom door the minute she stepped out of the shower. She knew it was Logan. She knew because she'd left the paddocks to run all the way to the lodge, then she'd stood in a hot shower, letting the water fall over her body, letting her tears fall at last, as she'd screamed a silent scream of longing and regret. The memory of Logan's kiss, of his arms holding her, was too much to bear now that she knew he had a family of his own. What kind of game was he playing with her, anyway? Was this his way of punishing her?

She didn't know why it hurt so much. After all, Logan deserved some happiness, and so did she. And the fact that they'd both found it with other people should make her feel better instead of worse. Maybe she was just jealous. Jealous because Logan had a child and she…she'd allowed their child to slip away.

She thought of little Caleb, and wondered how she'd missed it before. The same thick, wispy hair. The same facial features and body shape. Everything about the child looked like Logan, now that she put it together.

Except his eyes. Caleb had deep blue eyes, while Logan's were a beautiful chocolate brown. She supposed the blue came from the mother's side. And, where was that mother? What was going on?

She started crying all over again as she dressed hurriedly.

Trying to be rational, she reminded herself she'd just lost her father. No wonder this emptiness felt like a gaping hole that would never be filled again. She was still so grief-stricken, it was only natural to feel lonely and depressed and resentful. This would pass. Once she got back to Dallas, back to Rad and their plans together, this ache would surely go away.

The intense knocking at her door, however, didn't go away. "Trixie, let me in. We need to talk."

"Hold on," she managed to say, her voice raw, her words stiff and forced.

Grabbing a floral print sundress, she threw it over her underwear and slip, then ran a brush through her wet hair. Taking a minute, she willed herself to calm down, remembering all the etiquette coaching her Miss Manners mother had drilled into her over the years. Pamela had taught her to always remain a lady, even in the most critical times. For once she had to agree with her mother. She did not want Logan to see her like this. Her hands were still trembling, though, as she opened the door.

Logan filled the room with a caged presence, still in his own wet clothes, his expression guarded and worried. Bringing up a hand, then dropping it to his side, he said, "Ah, you've been crying. Trixie, I'm sorry. I didn't mean for you to find out this way—"

She halted him with a hand in the air. "It's all right. I'm glad for you, Logan. Really I am."

Surprised, he stopped his pacing. "What?"

She looked up at him, a fresh batch of tears welling in her red-rimmed eyes. "I don't know why you didn't trust me enough to tell me that you're married and have a child, but I understand how awkward this is for you."

Seeing the relief washing over his face, she stammered on, "And...I'd really like to meet your wife. Silly, why didn't you introduce us already? Caleb is such a beautiful little boy." Her voice broke in spite of the cheery smile she tossed out at him. "I'm sure his mother is just as beautiful."

Logan reached out a hand to wipe a single teardrop from her cheek. "She is," he said, his words hushed and choked. "But Trixie, there's something you need to know."

Trixie swallowed back another sob, the touch of his finger on her skin like a healing balm. Not wanting him to pity her, or be nice to her, she said, "What's that?"

Logan stood there, staring down at her, as if weighing just how much he should tell her. "I'm...I'm not married anymore."

She gazed up at him, her own relief so strong she almost fell into his arms. "You're not?"

Logan dropped his hand away from her face to stand back at a safe distance. "No. The marriage ended a long time ago. Actually, it ended before it really had a chance to begin."

Concern replaced the joy in her heart. But relief lightened her load considerably. "What happened? Did you make her slop pigs?"

The attempt at humor brought a wry smile to his face. "No, she liked living here. Ranch life agreed with her, but unfortunately, I didn't." He lowered his head, regret evident in his hushed words. "I...I married her straight into my first year of college…and I didn't really appreciate her or love her enough to make it stick.''

Trixie nodded her understanding. He'd obviously married someone else right after she'd left him. She could see the pain in his eyes. It mirrored the pain in her own heart. ''Where is she now?''

''Back in Little Rock, remarried and happy with a new baby, last I heard.''

She had to wonder, had to voice it. ''And…you got custody of Caleb?''

His head came up then. He hesitated, then slowly nodded. ''Yeah. This ranch is the only home he's ever known. He was real young when…when all of this happened. He doesn't know his mother at all.''

''You told me his mother abandoned him,'' she reminded him gently, her heart going out to both Logan and his son.

''She did,'' he said, a darkness moving across his expression. ''She left…not too long after he was born.''

Trixie closed her eyes, afraid he'd see the guilt of what she considered her own abandonment of their child written there. ''Does she ever see him now?''

He gave her a direct look. ''No.'' The harshness of the one word startled Trixie. But not as much as the simmering rage she saw in his eyes.

Sensing the evasiveness in his answer, she decided not to press him anymore about something so devastating. He was obviously still shaken, still angry, about the whole thing. This at least explained some of the bitterness she'd sensed in him.

The Logan she remembered rarely opened up; she should be glad she'd gotten this far with him. And to think, he'd managed to raise his child on his own, here on the ranch with his mother's help. Trixie's respect for him went up another notch. "Thank you for telling me the truth."

His head came up then, a look of disgust crossing his face. "The truth hurts, sweetheart. You should know that better than anybody."

Confused, she felt as if he could see straight into her heart. "I do, Logan. I do." Closing her eyes for a minute, she added, "But you're so lucky."

He grunted. "Oh, and how's that?"

Awe colored her words. "You have a beautiful child. You have a son. That's such a wonderful gift."

When she opened her eyes, the look he gave her made her take a step back. It was a mixture of pain and regret, and something else...anger. But instead of being directed toward his ex-wife, this anger centered on Trixie herself. She could feel it; could see it in his whole stance, in the way he curled his fists at his side.

"Logan?"

He backed out the door before she could recover, then pivoted in the hallway to give her a parting look. "Well, you'll be married soon yourself. Maybe you'll have a whole passle of kids."

"Rad wants to wait awhile," she blurted out, then instantly regretted it after Logan snorted and glared at her.

A smirk followed the snort. "Good idea. Keep it all neat and tidy. A workable plan where you can pencil them in when it's convenient."

"Logan, Rad isn't that way," she said, wanting to defend the man she'd promised to marry, even though Logan had summed him up pretty accurately. "He just knows what he wants out of life."

Logan stepped back into the room then, his eyes meeting hers, his words whispering across her skin.

"And do you? Do you know what you want out of life, Tricia Maria?"

Right now she wanted him to take her in his arms and hold her, but she knew that was wrong. And right now, with the mood he was in, she didn't think he'd be willing to let her cry on his shoulder.

"Yes, I do," she said, bobbing her head. "I just want to be happy."

He stood silent, weighing the anguish in her words, his anger and resentment misting around him like a heavy fog. "And this Rad…he's the man to make you happy?"

She didn't miss the hint of a dare in his question.

"I think so," she replied, her arms wrapped across her chest defensively.

At least, that's what everyone back home kept telling her, and that's what she kept telling herself. Thinking about it now, she felt a certain contentment, a certain comfort in knowing she had Rad to turn to. But she had to admit, her feelings for Rad were completely different from what she'd once felt for Logan.

But then, *that* had been so strong, so swift, so all consuming, she still held the scars from their brief encounter. Better to settle for contentment, rather than something so burning hot it felt like lightning shooting through her system. And scorched just as badly.

Logan picked up on her doubts like a wild mustang sniffing the wind.

He leaned close again, his dark eyes glowing with this new, intriguing knowledge. "Take it from someone who's been there, honey. You'd better be sure." With that, he turned, his boots clicking as he stalked out of the room. "I'm going to change, then I'll be downstairs waiting. Take your time."

Trixie had the distinct feeling he was referring to more than her getting dressed. Did Logan want her to take her time in making the right decision? Or did he just want more time before she pledged her heart to another man?

"'Reproach hath broken my heart, and I am full of heaviness, and I looked for some to take pity, but there was none, and for comforters, but I found none.'"

Logan finished reading the verse from Proverbs, then looked up at the faces of the teenagers and children listening to him. For a long while he simply sat there underneath the old oak tree where they held daily Bible discussions when the weather was nice, his thoughts automatically going out to Trixie.

He'd treated her badly since the little revelation in the pig paddock, dragging her around the ranch, his mood snarly and tight-lipped, his answers to her many questions clipped and precise. Sure, he'd seen the pain, the hurt in her blue eyes, but he didn't care. No, she'd caused him too much suffering for him to feel any compassion, any comfort, toward her.

But had he been wrong all this time?

Did she suffer from a broken heart, the same way he did? Up until now, he'd often wondered if she even had a heart. But something in the way she'd cried, something in the fresh-faced little girl he'd seen today, had brought a measure of compassion to his own hardened heart. Maybe he'd been unfair to her all of these years, blaming her for something she had no control over, blaming her for his own preconceived notions about the girl he'd known so briefly, yet so intimately. Brant had tried to tell him, had defended his daughter again and again, but Logan had never been listening, really.

Maybe because he wanted to think the worst of Trixie, maybe because it was just easier that way to accept that she would never be his.

He couldn't continue blaming Trixie, though, when he'd played such a big part in all of this himself. No, Trixie had had no other choice back then. Knowing her formidable mother from his many discussions of Pamela with Brant, Logan could understand the powerhouse of force Trixie had faced. No wonder she'd gone away and never tried to reach out to him again, in spite of their promises and pledges to each other in the heat of the moment.

Today, today, he'd seen that same Trixie who'd pledged her love to him, standing there in her sundress, her hair wet and smelling like summer rain, her eyes as blue as the September sky coloring the changing leaves. He'd seen the young girl, confused and afraid, reaching out to someone, something she could cling to and hold close for comfort. And he'd pushed her away, once again blaming her for things that had happened long ago when they were both young and impassioned. Why had he been so bitter all these years?

"Daddy, why do you look so sad?" Caleb asked from his perch on a gnarled oak root. "Finish talking, Daddy. It's 'bout time for supper."

"Sorry, pal," Logan said, regaining some of his composure as he stared down at his son. "Guess I got lost in thought there for a minute."

"I never been lost in thought," Caleb answered, his grin endearing. "Is it scary?"

Logan smiled, amazed at the simplicity children always brought to the complexities of life. "It sure can be, son," he said truthfully. "Sometimes, you know, we get so caught up in thinking about things, we stay all mad and pouting and we forget to take action to make things change.''

Samantha Webster, the youth counselor Brant had saved from the streets, nodded her head, her intricately braided hair shifting gracefully over her dark shoulders. ''Action speaks louder than words.''

''Right,'' Logan agreed, ''and I do believe that's what this particular passage of the Bible is saying.'' At the confused looks on the young faces before him, he added, ''Here is a person looking for someone to forgive him. He's sad, he's lonely, he's afraid, but no one wants to be bothered with his problems. So they turn away. How they act speaks louder than any words they might say.''

''They acted bad?'' Marco asked, his big eyes widening as he waited for an answer.

Logan nodded, thinking this lesson could sure apply to him. ''They didn't want to offer this person their help or their understanding.''

''That ain't nice,'' Caleb admonished, swiping his hand across his nose for emphasis.

''Sure isn't,'' Samantha readily agreed, her chocolate-colored eyes lighting up as she smiled down at Caleb. ''I've felt that way before myself, before Mr. Brant brought me here and taught me about loving other people. If he hadn't reached out to me and shown me some comfort, I wouldn't have changed my life. But I finished high school with honors and went on to college, thanks to him. If he hadn't taken action with me, I wouldn't be here today, that's for sure.''

''And you love us now, don't you?'' Caleb asked the young woman.

''I sure do.'' Just to prove her point, Samantha

grabbed the boy up and tickled him, causing him to squeal out in pleasure.

Logan watched, his own heart opening like a long-dormant flower. Caleb didn't care where Samantha had come from; he just knew she was his friend and teacher. His son was special that way. The little boy didn't have a mean bone in his body. His innocence always brought a sense of awe to Logan and a sense of fierce protection. Because he'd never known his own father, Logan had vowed Caleb would always be a part of his life, and he a part of his son's. He wasn't about to let anybody change that.

And that included Tricia Maria Dunaway. Okay, so maybe he'd been a little hard on her, but he still had a right to fight for this ranch and his son's future. And he'd do best to focus on his own obligations, rather than worrying about Trixie's welfare. She had old money and a new, powerful husband-to-be to take care of her. As he watched his son now, he knew he didn't have to be reminded of what was at stake here. Caleb would always be his first concern.

But as he ended the lesson, he prayed for compassion regarding Trixie. He would try really hard to give her the benefit of the doubt. Maybe she wasn't all bad; maybe she'd had her own reasons for leaving him behind so long ago. Being around her had certainly reminded him of the good in her, and today he'd seen that good in her tears and her open honesty.

But being around her had also reminded him of how much he'd once loved her. That love had turned out to be a huge mistake. Remembering that, he asked God for guidance. And he prayed that one day the truth would at last be told between Trixie and him. Maybe that would be the only way to find true compassion. Maybe that would be the only way to heal the burden of his own heavy heart.

From the kitchen window, Trixie watched as Logan finished the hour of Bible study. The gentle, patient man she saw out there now was a far cry from the rude, brusque man who'd reluctantly escorted her around the ranch for the past few hours. She'd realized over the course of the afternoon that Logan was mad at women in general, and especially her.

But how could he continue blaming her for what had happened, or what had not happened between them? True, she'd promised to spend eternity with him. She'd wanted nothing more than to stay here on the ranch and marry him. That had been their dream; their promise. But then, all of that changed when Brant found out just how far they'd taken things between them.

She'd been whisked away, and then she'd found out she was carrying his child. How many times had she thought about calling him, telling him the truth? How many times had she dreamed of them being together here with their child? But she couldn't tell Logan about any of her foolish dreams. And if anyone had a right to be bitter, it was Trixie.

He'd never even bothered coming after her. He'd just let her go, without a word between them. Well, she was here now. Maybe it was time for words, lots of words. Maybe if they could sit down and talk this through, they'd both find some sort of peace at last.

A rich golden dusk settled over the hills and valleys behind him, while he read and talked quietly to the children, his deep voice carrying out over the evening breeze. Again she was struck by his physical attractiveness. He looked right at home, sitting there on the ground in his Levi's and cotton shirt, fresh from an evening shower after a long day's work, his dark hair curling up in the wind, the laugh lines at his eyes crinkling whenever he stressed an important point, or cracked a joke.

It bothered her that she would even compare this man to Rad. But she couldn't help herself. Rad was clean-cut to a fault, always dressed in the finest and latest that money could buy, a picture-perfect version of the successful, up-and-coming associate of one of the oldest law firms in Dallas, a firm where his father just happened to be a senior partner.

"A perfect companion, a perfect gentleman," Pamela always told her friends. "Meant for my Trixie."

Funny, Trixie thought now. She'd once believed the man sitting out underneath that tree had been meant for her. Funny how her life had changed so much; how her attitude had changed so much. Watching Logan with his son only made her memories of their time together more poignant. Somewhere out there a child walked around with Logan's features and personality, mixed with her own.

Somewhere.

Maybe it was too late for them to find any peace, but it surely wasn't too late for her to continue her father's work here. Logan had at least opened up on that subject.

Brant had had big plans, but he'd died before he could finish them. He wanted to expand the ranch into a year-round school for underprivileged children, complete with certified teachers and the best in educational facilities. That would mean building a small school and more dorms; that would also mean more money needed and lots of hard work.

Could she do that? Trixie wondered now. Could she

commit herself to such a lofty task, all the while knowing she'd have to work closely with Logan?

"You can go out there and join them," Gayle said from her spot near the stove, her tone implying Trixie could use a good dose of gospel.

"No, I'll just stay in here with you, if you don't mind," Trixie replied, thinking she'd just have to weigh all of her options and make the right decision. Starting with winning over Logan's taciturn mother. "I wouldn't want to interrupt. Logan is so good with those kids."

Gayle kept stirring the pot of red beans and rice. "Logan is a good man."

"I know that," Trixie said, coming to stand by the older woman. "I've always known that, I think."

Gayle looked over at her, her hostile gaze sweeping over Trixie's face. "But not good enough for the likes of you, right?"

Startled by the woman's insistent hostility, Trixie asked, "What does that mean?"

Gayle shrugged, then checked the clock. "It means that you hurt my son a long time ago and that I'm worried you might do the same thing again."

Trixie waited a minute, forming her answer carefully. It wouldn't do for Gayle to become even more suspicious of her motives. "I never meant to hurt Logan. I cared about him, probably too much. And…we were very young."

"And foolish," Gayle admitted, her eyes softening a bit. "My son is as much to blame as you. I know that, and we've talked about his part in your little fling."

"It wasn't just a fling," Trixie said, wanting Gayle to understand that she had not taken her one night with Logan lightly. "I really cared about him, and I think he cared about me. But…we got carried away and then… circumstances pulled us apart.''

''Right.'' The coldness resurfaced in Gayle's eyes. ''Such as…you wanted a better life, with all the glamour and wealth your grandfather's oil money could provide. So you left in a great rush.''

Angry and tired, Trixie countered, ''Did you really expect my father to allow me any other choice?''

Gayle had the decency to look embarrassed. ''No, I know Brant was furious with both of you. I guess he did the only thing he could do. He sent you away. And of course, you did have your mother to deal with.''

Trixie nodded, the memories of her shame still like a sharp knife in her heart. ''I was so embarrassed and confused. My mother preached to me day and night about my sin, until she had me convinced of my unworthiness.'' She reached out a hand to touch Gayle's arm. ''But I did care about Logan.''

Gayle stared hard at her, her expression wavering only a fraction. ''Enough to beg your father to keep Logan on here.'' It was a flat statement, but a true one.

''Yes.'' Trixie lowered her head, wishing Brant were here himself so she could talk to him. ''I didn't want you or Logan to have to find work somewhere else.''

Gayle reached out a hand to pat Trixie's arm. ''I know how much you cared about my son, Tricia Maria. Logan cared about you, too. Why, you two were inseparable back then. Brant and I should have seen it coming, but, well…this place gets the best of you sometimes. But, I do appreciate your efforts toward calming your father down. Logan needed his job back then, just as he does now. I'm just worried…that's all. Seems like I've always got something to worry over.''

Trixie saw the concern in the dark shadows of fatigue

surrounding Gayle's eyes. "And now, it's about me selling?"

"That and—" Laughter from the yard brought Gayle's head up. "Oh, look at me, going on and on about things we can't neither one change. It's time for grub. Want to help me serve the kids out on those two picnic tables?"

"Sure." Glad that the woman was at least being somewhat civil to her, Trixie wondered what else Gayle Maxwell wanted to say to her. There was something going on here, some shared bond between mother and son, that Trixie was afraid she wouldn't be able to break.

What were they hiding?

Watching Gayle now, Trixie had a thought. Then, sure she'd hit upon part of the reason for Gayle's reserved attitude, she decided she'd have to ask some questions to find out if she had pinpointed some of the woman's real concerns. The answer was so simple, so obvious, Trixie wondered why she'd never seen it before.

Gayle Maxwell had been in love with her father.

And maybe that was why she'd been acting so strangely. She resented Trixie because now Trixie had the power to take away Gayle's only link with Brant Dunaway.

It was the only explanation.

And it was one more reason for Trixie to weigh the consequences of her actions very carefully. Saying a silent prayer, she asked God to help her. She had a feeling though, that no matter her decision, someone would wind up on the losing end.

It might be all of the children who needed this sanctuary. It might be Gayle and Logan and little Caleb.

Or it might turn out to be Trixie herself.

She'd lost once, based on other people's decisions. This time, though, the responsibility rested solely on her shoulders.

"I can't bear it alone, Lord," she whispered. "I'm asking for Your help."

For everyone's sake.

Chapter Six

"**G**randdaddy, what are you doing back here?" Trixie asked the next morning when she came downstairs to find Harlan sitting at the table, eating a hearty breakfast with Logan and Gayle.

He'd left right after the burial service, his old heart broken and heavy from the death of his only son. But Harlan Dunaway always bounced back, and he always looked on the bright side of things. Which is why his smiling face did a lot to boost Trixie's own sagging spirits. She could certainly use some reinforcements right about now.

Hugging him close, she thanked God for small favors. "I'm glad you're back, but why so soon?"

"Came to check up on you, girly," Harlan replied between bites of bacon tucked into a fluffy biscuit. "Your ma's fretting something awful over you being up here, while she's trying to get this engagement shindig organized."

"Good grief." Ignoring the way Logan's gaze heated her skin, Trixie headed straight for the coffeepot. She had not had a good night's sleep, and now this. Although she was thrilled to see her lovable grandfather, she didn't like hearing about Pamela's interference. ''Tell Mother to stop worrying about me. I'm a grown woman now.''

Harlan huffed a grunt at about the same time as Logan.

''Well, I'm glad you both agree on that,'' Trixie said, her eyes moving from her grandfather's amused face to Logan's stony expression.

''That's what's got her worrying,'' Harlan said, winking over at Logan.

Trixie saw the look that passed between the two men. Was Harlan warning Logan away from her in his own none-too-tactful way? Would her family ever let her make her own decisions?

Deciding to head him off at the pass, she said, ''You're sure in a good mood for a man bringing dire tidings of dread.'' Purposely turning away from Logan's frowning face, she sat down beside her grandfather and gave him a quick kiss. ''But I am glad for your company, and I could use your advice.''

Harlan just smiled and chewed. ''All I got is time, honey. I'll be happy to help in any way I can.''

''What'll you have?'' Gayle asked Trixie, her tone quiet and firm, her eyes wary and guarded.

''Just toast,'' Trixie replied, her gaze still on her grandfather.

Logan grunted again, louder this time, his scowling gaze slamming down on Trixie. ''Still eats like a bird.''

Harlan's chuckle jiggled his own ample belly. ''Habit, son. Always watching her weight, because of all those beauty pageants her Ma used to force her to enter—ruined her appetite for real food.''

Trixie turned up her nose, posing in true beauty

queen fashion. She'd hated being put on display back during her teenage years, and she and Pamela had had more than one royal battle when she'd announced to her frantic mother that she was retiring from the pageant circuit. "I won a few, but thankfully those days are over."

Logan's expression bordered on hostile while his searching gaze flickered over her face. "Well, then you don't have to starve yourself anymore to look good, Trixie. Eat something for goodness' sake."

Groaning, Trixie wished she'd stayed upstairs. She was in no mood to argue with the sanctimonious Logan Maxwell, or her playful grandfather. "If you two will quit fussing over me, I'll be perfectly fine. I'm not a big breakfast person."

Harlan shook his head, then chuckled again. "She always was grumpy in the morning."

"Rough night?" Logan asked, his eyes scanning her face. If misery loved company, he hoped she'd been as miserable as he'd been last night. He was beginning to wonder if asking her to stay had been the right idea after all.

Trixie hit him with a scathing glare, the blue in her eyes lighting like a flame's tip. "I've had better."

"None of us has been getting much sleep lately," Gayle said from her chair at the end of the plank table, her work-roughened fingers clutching a white coffee mug. She looked over at Trixie, her meaning evident. "Things are changing around here. First your father's sudden death, and now you…thinking about selling this place. It's all too much, I guess. That's why we're all so ornery."

Trixie wanted to scream, but Gayle had a point. To smooth things over, she said, "Yes, it's been hard on all of us. But I promised you both I won't make a hasty decision.'' Then she glanced at Harlan. ''Daddy sure had lots of plans for this place. Big plans. I realize there's a trust fund set up, and that regular donations come in, but I just don't know about the work involved. I could hire a consulting firm, or I could tackle it myself—that is if I decide to keep the ranch.''

Harlan nodded, then took a long swig of coffee. ''I trust you, darling. You'll do what's right.''

Gayle wasn't convinced. Slinging a dry dishrag over her shoulder, she shoved her chair back to go on about her daily business, her expression tight-lipped and unrelenting.

Trying to ignore Gayle's obvious disapproval and distrust, Trixie turned to her grandfather again. ''How long will you be here?''

''Long enough to bring back either you, or a convincing report, to your mother.''

Trixie would like nothing better than to go home, but she still had a lot to deal with and even more emotional trauma to work through. ''I'll be staying a few days longer,'' she said to Harlan.

Her grandfather's eagle eyes moved from her face to Logan's scowl. ''I see.''

Hoping to reassure him that everything was all right, Trixie said, ''Want to go for a ride with Logan and me? He promised we'd take a couple of the horses out, so I can see the rest of the place.''

And she really didn't want to be alone with Logan. Last night at supper he'd stared at her so long and hard, she'd felt a permanent imprint, like a brand, burning her skin.

She'd sat there, listening to the banter of the young people, listening to Caleb's infectious giggles, listening to the night sounds and the sounds of harmony and fellowship echoing throughout the cookhouse, only to have Logan remind her that she really didn't belong here in the first place.

And to make matters worse, he kept sending her mixed messages. One minute he was gazing at her like a man obsessed, and the next, well, if looks could kill....

"I'd enjoy that," Harlan agreed, rising up out of his chair, his knowing eyes moving between his granddaughter and Logan. "Provided, of course, Logan can find a mount with enough muscle to hold me."

Logan finally took his gaze away from Trixie long enough to form the makings of a grin. "I think I can manage that, sir."

"I'll be out in a minute," Trixie told the men. "I want to help Gayle with the dishes."

"No need," Gayle rushed to say. "Samantha will send one of the young people to help me after they've finished their meal out in the cookhouse."

"I don't mind," Trixie said, her tone firm, her eyes centered on the other woman. She might not get any answers from Logan, but she intended to corner his mother, at least.

Logan glanced over at his mother, concern apparent on his haggard features. "Is everything all right here?"

Gayle turned to give her son a reassuring look. "It's fine, son. Trixie and I are just getting reacquainted, is all."

Trixie noticed how reluctant he seemed to leave them alone, further confirmation that something wasn't quite right. But after giving her and Gayle a warning look, he left with Harlan, anyway.

Turning to face Gayle, she said, "Why do you hate me so much?"

"I don't," Gayle replied in her own direct way, busying herself with stacking their breakfast dishes in the sink. "I told you, I've got a lot on my mind."

"You miss my father, don't you?"

Gayle's expression softened at the mention of Brant. "Yes, I sure do. This place just ain't the same without him coming down those stairs, shouting for coffee and grits."

Bracing herself, Trixie lifted her head and asked, "Did you...love him?"

Gayle watched Trixie's face for censure, and seeing none, nodded. "Yes...I loved him so very much."

A sad sigh escaped through Trixie's parted lips. "I thought so. I could tell, by the way you say his name, by the way you smile when you're talking about him." Placing a hand on Gayle's arm, she asked, "Did he know how you felt?"

Gayle shook her head, her eyes watering up. "Brant only had eyes for your mother, Tricia Maria. I accepted that long ago, but I stayed here, watching out for him, taking care of him, because...I couldn't imagine doing anything else, going anyplace else."

Turning Gayle around with a hand on each of the other woman's sagging shoulders, Trixie said, "Why didn't you ever tell him?"

Gayle sniffed, then reached for a tissue from the box on the windowsill, that one action as telling as the sad frown on her face. "Oh, I tried, many times. But...so much had happened. He worried about you all the time, but he had to keep his distance. Your mother made it hard for him to hear any news of you. I'd watch him sometimes, late at night, standing out there underneath that great oak. He'd look off in the distance, his coffee cup in his hand. And I knew, I knew he was thinking of her. Always her.''

She gave Trixie a direct, daring look that reminded her of Logan. ''I lost one man to another woman, and I vowed I'd never be second best again. So, Brant and I stayed friends—close, compatible, comfortable. And every night I'd go into my room down here by the kitchen and he'd go up to that big bedroom he'd designed especially for her. I didn't have the guts to push myself on him, and I wouldn't dream of...of doing anything without the sanctity of marriage. It just wouldn't have been right.''

She stopped, seeing the dread and shame covering Trixie's face in a heated rush. ''I'm sorry.''

''It's okay,'' Trixie said, glad Gayle had told her about her special relationship with Brant. ''I agree with you completely.''

Gayle patted her on the hand, admiration showing in her eyes at last. ''It's hard, nowadays, living up to your convictions. There's a lot of temptation in this old world.''

Yes, Trixie thought. And her main one was out there saddling up a horse with her grandfather. Well, Gayle's honesty had opened her eyes to one thing at least. She wouldn't fall back into her old pattern with Logan. They had to behave like rational adults now, for the sake of this ranch and the example they had to uphold for the young people sent here for guidance. Just a hint of scandal could shut this place down, regardless of how she felt about keeping it open.

And, she reminded herself, she was promised to another. She wouldn't do anything to jeopardize her relationship with Rad. It was high time she practiced some of her convictions.

"My father was lucky to have your friendship, Gayle. And your love. Thank you for taking care of him."

"I did the best I could for him," Gayle replied.

"I'm glad we had this talk. It explains a lot to me about why you seemed so worried and resentful toward me. But I do want you to know, I'm also pleased that my father had you here. I'm sure it helped ease some of his loneliness."

Gayle didn't say anything. She only nodded and whirled to stare out the window. Then, her back still turned, she said, "Maybe, then, you can understand why I don't want Logan to spend the rest of his life pining away for you. Don't give him any false hope, Trixie. This time, I do believe it would destroy him for good."

Her heart pounding, Trixie knew what she had to do. Once again she would have to walk away in order to protect Logan and his mother...and what little dignity she had left herself. The decision was an easy one, based on lots of hard lessons.

"I'm not going to give him any false hope, Gayle," she said quietly. "But I am going to give him something else." When Gayle pivoted to her with questioning eyes, she held out a hand to the woman. "I'm going to give him total control over this ranch in my absence."

Gayle's hand flew to her throat. "You...you're not going to sell?"

"No," Trixie said, her smile bittersweet. "Once, long ago, I let go of something very precious, and I've regretted it ever since. I won't let it happen again. So, I'm going to keep the ranch and trust Logan to follow my father's stipulations regarding how things are handled. No, I'm not going to sell."

Tears of relief and joy fell down Gayle's face as she

took Trixie's hand in her own. "Oh, Logan will be so glad. You don't know how much this will mean to us."

Just then the screen door burst open and Caleb came running in, his cowboy hat tipped at a rakish angle, his deep blue eyes bright with the unexpected treasure he'd just discovered. "Nana, Nana, I found some baby kittens behind the barn. Wanna come see?"

"*I* sure do," Trixie said, wanting to cry herself for some strange reason.

Maybe because life on this ranch was so much more real, so much more poignant, than the life she'd always known, growing up in Dallas. She'd never been allowed to touch stray cats.

Except, she remembered now with brilliant clarity, once when she'd been around ten, and Brant had come sneaking into the kitchen, holding a finger to his lips and a tiny furry gray creature in his hand. "Look what I found out in the stables. Wanna hold the kitten, Trixiebelle?"

"Yes!" Trixie had leaped from her perch on a breakfast stool, dropping down to rub her hands over the soft, warm fur while her big father knelt and cooed to the frightened little animal. Of course, Pamela had come into the room, promptly breaking up the father-daughter conspiracy.

"Get that thing out of this kitchen, Brant Dunaway," her mother had insisted, a finger pointed to the back door. "You don't know where that cat's been. It's filthy and germy, and I won't have my daughter exposed to it."

And sadly, Trixie thought now, that had set the tone for most of her life.

"Well, come on," Caleb said, bringing her out of the bittersweet flashback. "I know right where they're hidin', but you have to be careful. They scratch.'' Proudly he held out a hand to show her a spot where he'd been clawed.

"Wait just a minute.'' Gayle's brief joyous attitude changed immediately back into one of wariness and distrust. "You better get on out there for your morning ride,'' she reminded Trixie, her arms going around her grandson in a protective, loving gesture.

"I will, after Caleb shows me the kittens,'' Trixie said, bending down to smile at the little boy. He looked so much like Logan it took her breath away and brought another rush of great pain to her heart.

"I don't think that's a good idea,'' Gayle insisted as she shoved the boy behind her skirts, her stance guarded and defiant.

Surprised, Trixie stood up to stare over at her. "And why not?''

Gayle sniffed back the last of her happy tears and said, "Because, quite frankly, I don't think Logan wants you around his boy.''

Stunned and hurt, Trixie could only stare over at the woman. When Caleb's big curious eyes shifted from his grandmother to Trixie, she backed down. It wouldn't do to upset the little boy by provoking an argument with his stubborn grandmother.

Bending down again, she said in a controlled voice, "Tell you what, Caleb. Since your Daddy is waiting on me, why don't you get that scratch cleaned up and then take Grandmama to see the kittens, and when I get back from my ride I'll peek in on them, okay?''

Caleb let out an exaggerated sigh, then plopped his rickety hat down on the table. "Oh, okay. Know what, Miss Trixie?''

"What, sweetie?''

"If one of 'em's a girl kitten, I'm gonna name her Trixie, after you."

The tears did come then, unbidden and uncensored, but Trixie swallowed them back. Reaching out a hand to touch Caleb's thick tousle of hair, she managed to say, "Thank you. That's very sweet." Then she stood and rushed out the door, gently closing the screen between them.

"What's the matter with Miss Trixie, Nana?" she heard Caleb say.

"Nothing for you to worry about," Gayle replied softly.

When Trixie turned to look back inside, Gayle was hugging her grandson close. Over the child's head, her eyes met Trixie's. And that's when Trixie saw something else there in the other woman's gaze.

Fear.

Because both Trixie and Logan were in rather dark moods, it was left to Harlan to do the talking as the trio walked their horses down the fenced dirt lane that cut through the pastures and hills of the ranch.

Everywhere around them the trees and grasses were slowly changing from green to brown. Soon the surrounding hills and mountains would be radiant with the colors of fall.

To Harlan's way of thinking, however, there was already a chill in the air between these two. They'd just finished surveying most of the acreage, and as the sun climbed to lofty heights, so did his granddaughter's haughty attitude toward the brooding, tight-lipped foreman.

"Fine morning, ain't it?" Harlan said to the wind, since neither of the two young people on either side of him had seemed to notice the golden haze of late September settling over the earth. "Indian summer's here. Then those crisp, cool days of autumn. God's handiwork, children—it always amazes me."

"Right," Logan grunted, his hat slung low over his brow, his back straight in the saddle.

"Beautiful," Trixie replied, her gaze focused on the distant mountains, her mind focused on Gayle's strange behavior back in the kitchen.

"Gonna get hot before the day's out, though," Harlan continued, referring to much more than the weather. Glancing over at Trixie, he said, "And might I add, you look like sunshine yourself in that yellow outfit, Trixiebelle."

"Why, thank you." His compliment brought a measure of triumph to Trixie's hurting heart. In pure defiance of Logan's "work clothes" rule, she'd worn a button-up yellow cotton shirt that had embroidered sunflowers plastered across the bodice, and the matching knee-length shorts with sunflowers rimming the full legs. Let him make fun of that!

He did. "Yeah, she looks like a regular walking garden. Guess we ought to take her over to Brant's sunflower patch and throw her right smack dab in the middle."

"Good idea," Harlan agreed, his chuckle laced with a tad too much cheer. Deciding to change the subject to business only, he said, "Let's see—we've seen the sheep, the cows and pigs, the farm equipment—all of that seems in working order. We've talked about the harvest—corn's just about ready to be pulled, fall produce looks excellent. And the counselors you're hired are doing a great job with the young 'uns. Looks like you've got everything under control, Logan."

"Except who's gonna wind up being my boss," Logan said in a huffy breath, cutting his gaze to Trixie.

Trixie hadn't told him her decision yet. Her mind was in such turmoil she couldn't think straight. And especially with him riding that horse like a born cowboy, making her heart turn all mushy and her breath stop in her throat. Memories of another time, and this same man, only added to her misery.

She remembered the first time she'd seen Logan. She was standing in the stables, fresh off the plane from Little Rock, petting a mare and her new foal while she waited for her father to come in from the pastures. The late-afternoon sun cast a burnished sheen through the arched gateway, framing the humid air in a glistening stillness. She looked up to see a darkened shadow of a man approaching, but the man certainly wasn't her father. He looked mysterious and dangerous, his hat slung low over his brow, his jeans dirty and snug, his eyes… his eyes burning with a knowing, cynical fire.

A cowboy, home from mending fences, his attitude as intact and intense as the barbed wire surrounding the far pastures.

A young socialite, innocent and searching, searching for something, someone, her whole world shattered by her parents' divorce.

Oh, Logan, she thought now, afraid to look at him, *we were so young, so afraid, so anxious to find some sense of comfort and peace. We had no way of knowing our whole lives would change that autumn.*

Reminding herself that she'd decided to live by her convictions, she stopped her horse and called out to the two men riding up ahead of her. "Granddaddy, I need to talk to Logan. Do you mind?"

Harlan whirled his sturdy mount around with expert

agility. "Heck, no, honey. Don't mind at all. 'Bout time for my lunch and my nap, anyway. I'll just go visit your pa's grave for a spell, then head back to the house." Then he brought his horse close to her own. "Like I said at breakfast, I'm trusting you to make the right decision. And I know you will."

Trixie smiled up at him, loving him so fiercely she wanted to hug him close. "I'm glad somebody trusts my judgment."

"Oh, I do." Harlan eyed Logan as the younger man trotted his horse a few yards ahead of them, then slid to the ground to check a rickety fence post. "And…I also trust you to marry the right man."

Surprised, Trixie saw the expression of hope in Harlan's eyes. "You don't have to worry about Rad and me, Granddaddy. Please, don't let Mama get you all in a dither about this."

Harlan grinned. "I can handle your mother, Tricia Maria. You just take care of the rest." With that he nudged his mount into a brisk trot, throwing up his hat in a final farewell as he hurried back up the lane toward the chapel and Brant's grave.

Deciding everyone around here was acting as if they'd all taken a bad case of sun poisoning, Trixie urged her mare up to the fence where Logan struggled with the weak post. He looked so right standing there, his hat covering his curling hair, his jeans snug fitting and faded, his boots dusty and mud caked. He *was* a born cowboy, just as Brant had been. Logan belonged to this land, needed this land, to keep him strong, to keep him centered. She understood that about him, in a way Pamela had never understood about Brant.

As she watched Logan now, she knew she'd made the right decision. Pamela would be beside herself, of course. And Rad...well, she'd deal with Rad when she got back to Dallas. Right now, even though her heart was breaking, even though she knew she'd always love Logan in that special way that only first love could be cherished, she knew what she had to do. She would give him the land he held so dear, and then she'd leave him again.

When Logan looked up at last, he saw the love reflected there in her eyes, saw the struggle she'd been fighting since she'd set foot back on this place. And he decided right then and there, that no matter what she planned on doing, he had to at least offer her some comfort. He owed her that much, for Brant's memory, if nothing else.

"So you wanna talk, huh?" he said, his tone soft and yielding as he squinted up at her.

Trixie swallowed hard, gathering her strength. "Yes. I've seen enough of this place. It's time to settle things."

He walked up to her, holding her mount steady as his gaze held hers. He'd just have to go on faith, hoping that she'd made the right choice regarding her father's legacy and land. And the rest...well, he'd have to settle for what the Lord handed out. "How about I show you your daddy's sunflower patch?"

The sweetness of his suggestion washed over her with all the warmth of the morning sun, making her forget her anger and her convictions. Right now, she only wanted a truce between them, however brief.

"I'd like that," she said. Then she laughed. "Promise you won't throw me in the middle and leave me, though?"

Slinging a long, blue-jeaned leg over his saddle, he

grinned then. "Oh, I might throw you down in the flower patch, but I'd never leave you."

Trixie knew he meant it. He'd always been right here, waiting maybe, through all the years and all the doubt and pain, through his own bitterness and anger. And now she would be the one doing the leaving.

Again.

She would leave Logan to his work and his life with his son.

She would leave her heart here, too. In this land, in his hands. Always.

Chapter Seven

The legendary sunflower patch was out past one of the far ridges, away from the hustle and bustle of the main ranch. Logan rode the spotted pinto named Rocky ahead of Trixie, guiding the way up to a jutting dirt-and-rock formation. "Here we are," he said, turning in the saddle to wait for her.

Trixie stopped her mount at the edge, then looked out over the field of bright yellow and green giant flowers spread out like a floral quilt below, a small gasp of pleasure leaving her body. "Logan, it's...it's so pretty."

Acres and acres of big, fat sunflowers lifted their heads to follow the sun, dancing and swaying in the warm wind. She'd never seen anything like it. And to think, her rough-and-ready father had planted them there. It made him all the more special in her eyes, and filled her heart with regret.

"People come from miles around to see them," Logan said, pride evident in his words. "We always have an open house during peak blooming season. For a donation, they can come and take all the pictures they want, and stay awhile to enjoy the view. People have picnics, brides have their pictures taken. Word's spread and now it's becoming a tradition.''

"What a great idea.'' She smiled over at him, thinking he had some marketing talent himself. "I couldn't have planned a better public relations coup myself.''

He lowered his head, the hardness leaving his face as he gazed down on the flowing, rippling field. "We just used the only draw we've got—the land. And the community is glad to give, to help the children and our mission cause.''

"And you're doing a good job. The financial reports seem in order and the records are meticulous.'' She'd looked them over last night, when she couldn't sleep. "Of course, I did spot some places where we can improve things.''

She didn't miss the glance he shot her way. "Nothing wrong with our record keeping, Tricia Maria.''

Giving him a level look, Trixie retorted, "I didn't say that, Logan. I just said—oh, never mind.''

Relaxing a bit, Logan told her, "Well, maybe we could be more efficient, but we've come a long way. Mama single-handedly learned how to run the new computer Brant had installed a few months ago. She took to the new system, after telling Brant and me she'd never get near the thing.'' He had to laugh. "Now, she's a net surfer. Thinks we need to build our own Web site.''

Trixie laughed then, the idea of Logan's quiet, reserved mother playing around in chat rooms too paradoxical to resist. "Modern technology is frightening, but necessary. And she's right—you do need your own Web page. Especially here, where you need to be connected to some of the most remote places in the world, since you're shipping livestock and goods internationally.''

He looked at her from underneath the shade of his tattered old hat, wondering if she would want to overhaul everything about the ranch—that is, if she kept the place. "Yep."

Trixie watched him, saw the doubt in his expression. "I guess you probably aren't looking forward to having me as a boss, huh?"

Logan tipped his hat back. "You know, I haven't really thought about that." Giving her a look full of promise, he added, "I can see both advantages and disadvantages in the situation. But I'd rather deal with you than some stranger who might run us all off."

And, Logan told himself, he'd just have to deal with his worries and concerns one at a time.

As the casual conversation died down, the tension mounted. Even the horses could sense it as they pranced impatiently and snorted into the humid wind.

"It's getting hot out here. Want to go down and get a closer look at the field before that sun climbs any higher?" Logan asked at last.

"Sure."

When he came around to help her down, Trixie's heart puttered and moaned, not so sure. Why did she always feel so safe, yet so scattered, in Logan's arms? Sending him a shaky smile after he set her down, she allowed him to hold her hand. "Thank you."

"Careful," he said over his shoulder. "This ridge is slippery even on a dry day."

Trixie held on, taking her time as they followed the path that led down to the open field beyond. "How do you handle all the tourists?" she asked breathlessly.

"They come in through the back way—a dirt lane

that leads to the field. We just held open house a few weeks ago when the flowers were at their peak. Then Brant got sick and...we decided to cancel the second weekend.''

Trixie didn't say anything. Thoughts of her father brought a great, ripping pain to her chest. She could just see him, standing here in his jeans and his cowboy hat, watching as people poured in to see the sunflowers. Such a simple thing—planting a field of flowers. Yet he'd touched so many lives by doing it. He'd brought a small measure of beauty and tranquillity to those who came here to view his creation.

She regretted that she hadn't been a part of all this, and she was once again reminded of the preacher's words about those who sow in sorrow. Had her father done that, hoping to find his joy in these beautiful, serene flowers?

By this time they'd reached the bottom of the ridge. Trixie let go of Logan's hand to rush forward and touch a flower. ''They're so tall,'' she said as she tilted her head to view one of the massive six-foot-high blooms.

''Watch for bees,'' Logan warned, enjoying the way she blended in with the flowers in her yellow outfit. He didn't follow her, but chose instead to stand back and enjoy just seeing her in this field. He'd certainly pictured it enough in his mind. ''He knew you loved sunflowers,'' he called out to her.

Trixie turned then, her eyes locking with his, her heart hammering a beat as erratic as the buzzing bees lost in the midst of the hundreds of golden petals. ''He planted this for...for me?''

Logan stepped closer then, his expression full of sadness and regret. ''It was his way of remembering, I guess.''

She let out a long sigh. "And I always thought he'd forgotten." She couldn't bring herself to tell Logan that she'd forgotten, too. She'd forgotten that little girl who used to run wild and free amidst the bluebonnets, with her handsome father chasing her. Now she had to wonder what had happened to that child?

Logan saw the pain in her eyes and the wistful expression crossing her face. Not stopping to think, he strode toward her, then pulled her into his arms, his expression fierce with a love he'd long denied. "How could anyone forget you, Tricia Maria?"

Before she could respond, he yanked his hat off and kissed her, the heat of his mouth rivaling the heat of late September. Trixie fell into the embrace, her whole system going haywire as she allowed herself to be drawn into a wonderful dream. Too soon, however, reality pierced its way back into her consciousness, bringing with it her great shame and regret.

Pulling away, she said, "Logan, we can't do this."

His breath ragged, Logan held her with a hand on each arm, his gaze searching her face. "No, we can't, can we, because of the past, because of Rad, because I'm not good enough for you."

Seeing the hurt and anger in his eyes, she shook her head. "Is that what you think? Is that why I never heard from you again—you think you're not good enough for me?"

He gently eased her away. "Well, I know I'm not good enough for you, and…your parents sure thought that. Your mother made that quite clear from the beginning. And yes, that was one of the reasons I never tried to find you again."

"*I* never thought that. I certainly never thought about you in that way," she admitted, tired of the lies and the

deceit and all of the wasted time. "I...I loved you, Logan."

He stood there, his heart bursting with pain and love,
his whole world tilting and unbalanced. Telling himself
he was stepping into trouble, reminding himself he
needed to be as far away from her as possible, Logan
couldn't stop the need to hold her again. Just once
again.

So he did, hauling her close so he could see the blue
of the sky reflected in her eyes. "And I *still* love you,
Tricia Maria. I will always love you."

Stunned, Trixie clung to him, her eyes going wide,
her heart breaking into a million pieces. "Why didn't
you come for me?" she asked, tears softening her
words. "I used to lie awake at night, hoping, praying,
that you'd just come to Dallas and get me and bring me
back here."

"And we'd be married," he finished, a hand coming
up to touch her face. "I had that same dream. I dreamed
of you standing right here. I dreamed of us building a
house right over there." He motioned his head, his eyes
as moist as hers, then spun her around, his hands encircling her waist as he pulled her body back against
his. "Your daddy gave me this ten acres, free and clear,
to build a house on. But I...I never could bring myself
to build anything there. I didn't have you, so what was
the point?"

Trixie looked out over the valley, thinking she'd
never seen a more beautiful spot. She could envision it
all, her hopes, her dreams, a house with a yardful of
wildflowers and sunflowers, the mountains off in the
distance, cows lowing, bees humming. And...a child
running to meet his father.

Her heart broke in two, because she'd given up all

of her dreams the night she allowed them to take her baby away.

"Oh, Logan," she said, "we lost so much, so much."

"I know, sugar," he said, his words gentle on the back of her neck. "And...we can't get it back. It's too late now. You...you don't belong with me. You have your life mapped out, and I keep telling myself it can be a good life. I keep telling myself I can't stand in your way. I don't have the right—"

She turned then, falling back into his arms, her words ragged and torn. "No, *I* don't have the right, Logan. I don't have the right to make you miserable again. And I promised your mother—"

Logan lifted her chin, his eyes filling with alarm. "What? What did my mother tell you?"

Seeing the genuine fear and dread in his eyes, she could only shake her head. "Nothing, except she doesn't want you wasting your time on me." Then, because she was hurting so much, because she needed to know, she added, "And she told me...she told me you don't want me around your son."

He pulled her head down, his hands moving over her shoulders, then her hair. "That's not true. It's just—" He hesitated, struggled, fought against himself. "Caleb gets attached to people very easily. Sometimes he has a hard time with all the comings and goings here on the ranch, the other children passing through for a few weeks at a time. I'd hate for him to get attached to you, and then—"

Trixie finished his sentence. "And then I'll be gone out of his life for good, just like his mother."

Logan nodded, the lump in his throat almost suffocating him. "You will go, won't you? You can't bear to be here, where you committed your greatest sin with me. I remind you of your shame each time I hold you and kiss you, don't I?'' The torment in his eyes increased with each question. ''You're going to sell this place and never look back, right?''

She didn't have the answers to all of his questions. So she told him what was in her heart, because she couldn't tell him her real reasons for walking away. Stepping back, she lifted her gaze and stared up at him. ''I'm not going to sell the ranch, Logan. In fact, I'm going to do just the opposite.''

At the look of hope on his face, she held up a hand. ''I want to put you in charge completely. I'll trust you to do all the things my father set out to do, but—''

''But you don't want to be involved.'' This time he finished her statement, his expression torn between relief and regret.

''I can't be involved,'' she stressed, her hand on his arm. ''There's just too many memories, Logan. Too much water under the bridge for us—and too much temptation between us right now. I'd only be in the way here, and I don't want you to wind up resenting me.''

''So I'm still not good enough for you.''

Wrapping her arms around her waist, she shook her head again. She wanted to tell him that she wasn't good enough for him, after the horrible thing she'd done. ''I didn't say that. I told you, I've never felt that way.''

''But you never bothered to come back to me. And now, you're planning on leaving me again. Does it matter that I still love you?''

She heard the doubt in his voice, saw the hard edges of his bitter smile. ''More than you'll ever know,'' she said as she started back up the ridge, afraid she'd crumble and confess if she didn't get a grip on herself.

He caught up with her, urging her around with a firm tug. "Then stay. Stay here with me, Trixie."

In that one moment Trixie saw everything with a brilliant clarity. She did belong here, and she did love Logan. She'd never stopped loving him. But he could never know that. Because if he knew what she'd done, he'd never forgive her. Her secret, her choice, would destroy him.

And so she didn't tell him what was really in her heart.

When she didn't respond, Logan let her go, dropping his hands to his side in defeat. Then he looked off into the distance, to the empty patch of land her father had deeded to him. "Guess I'll never get that house built. I don't want to live in it alone."

When he pushed past her, she tried to stop him. Maybe she should just go ahead and tell him the truth. It would certainly change his opinion of her and stop him from pining away, as Gayle had feared. "Logan?"

But Logan was beyond listening now. She'd made her choice, and once again he wasn't included in her plans. Really, he should be glad, relieved, that she wouldn't be hovering around here. He didn't need her here, and he sure didn't want her here. He only wanted to protect his son. "I'm grateful that you aren't selling, Trixie," he said from his perch on the rocks. "And I won't let you down. I'll take care of things here. I'm not going anywhere."

"Thank you," she said, the coward in her relieved that she hadn't had to open up and reveal her great secret to him. "I appreciate that."

He reached out a hand to help her climb back up to the horses. When they reached the top, Trixie looked back out over the field of sunflowers and wished she didn't have to go back to Dallas. But what choice did she have? She still loved Rad, but she would *always* love Logan. This situation really wasn't fair to either of them.

Logan waited as she mounted her horse, then he turned to her, his gaze focused and blank. "This is for the best. Like I said, you don't belong here."

With that he trotted the pinto ahead of her, leaving her alone on the ridge while a great, sighing wind rushed through the yellow field of flowers down below. Trixie listened to that hot, moaning wind, then sent up a prayer for help. Had she made the right choice?

"You're wrong, Logan," she whispered. "I do belong here, but I can't stay. I can't."

Unless she told everyone the truth at last, including Rad. What if she simply confessed her great sin to everyone and let God handle the rest? It would be risky; she could wind up losing both Rad and Logan. But at least she'd be free, free and clear, to have a future with hope, a future with no shame and no secrets. And maybe a little forgiveness.

She turned her prancing horse and stared out over the elegant sunflowers, her mind at peace for the first time since her father's death. "Thanks, Daddy," she said.

She knew what she had to do now.

"What should we do?" Samantha asked Logan later that afternoon as they tried to round up a flock of about fifty sheep that had burst through the weak place in the fence Logan had spotted earlier that morning.

"I'll saddle a horse," Logan said, watching as the timid sheep spilled out into the lane and headed for the back forty. "You and one of the older kids can take the four-wheeler."

"Can I ride the four-wheeler, Daddy?" Caleb asked, always his father's shadow when Logan was anywhere near the main house.

Logan bent to scoop his son up in his arms. "Nope, you know the rules. You aren't old enough yet to ride the four-wheeler with anyone but me, son." Seeing the disappoint in his son's eyes, he added, "How 'bout you ride shotgun with me on Rocky?"

Caleb's eyes lit up. "Let me get my hat."

In spite of sheep milling around where they weren't supposed to be, Logan grinned. Caleb was a little cowboy himself, following a long tradition. And chomping at the bit to follow the bigger kids around the ranch on their various chores. Gayle had to watch the kid every minute, or he'd try to sneak by her and go off to the far reaches of the ranch. Since his grandmother was overprotective by nature, Caleb rarely got a chance to get into any heavy mischief. But when he did, it made up for the rest.

"How'd this happen, anyway?" Logan asked Samantha, speaking of mischief. He had a sneaking feeling one of his young charges probably provoked the sheep to stampede.

Samantha threw her long cornrows off her shoulder and gave him a beseeching look. "Promise you won't scream?"

"Just tell me the truth," Logan said, holding on to the last shreds of his patience. If he hadn't been so distracted with Trixie, so busy confessing his undying love to her, he would have fixed this when he'd first spotted it. Glad this had happened in spite of the mess, he reckoned he'd needed a wake-up call. This ranch was his first priority. He'd better remember that.

"It was during the worming," Samantha began. "We

had four adult volunteers helping, including Mr. Harlan, but you know how that goes. Mr. Harlan knew what to do, but the rest—''

''Yeah.'' Logan nodded. Volunteers were sometimes more of a pain than a help. ''Somebody get skittish or something?''

''One of the ladies saw a big spider out behind the worming station,'' Samantha tried to explain.

''And she screamed bloody murder?''

''No, actually, she was pretty calm. Her husband did all the hopping up and down and screaming. Just enough to cause the sheep to get jittery and run for the nearest fence.''

Logan sighed as he headed to the stables in a backward trot. ''I get the picture. Hurry, now, and bring the four-wheeler. And keep those volunteers away from the herd.''

''Right.'' Samantha turned to head to the open garage behind the barn, afraid to tell Logan that Mr. Harlan had already taken the volunteers down the lane on foot to waylay the anxious sheep. Spotting Trixie coming toward her, she waved. ''Gotta go, Miss Trixie. Sheep on the loose.''

''I wondered what all the fuss was about,'' Trixie said, her gaze on the renegade animals heading gleefully to freedom. All afternoon she'd been cloistered in the tiny office in one corner of the lodge, going over the computer printouts and farm reports with Harlan, in order to keep her mind off Logan. After giving her his blessings and telling her he was fully behind her decision to keep the ranch, Harlan, always the rancher himself, had come out earlier to help with the chores.

Now, Trixie had stepped out for some fresh air and exercise only to find chaos. ''Want some help?''

Samantha looked skeptical. Since Logan seemed to tense up every time Blondie was around, she wasn't too sure about accepting Trixie's well-intended services. "Logan told me to keep all the amateurs away."

"I've been on cattle drives," Trixie replied, affronted. "I think I can manage a few sheep."

"Well, come on, then. I gotta hurry."

Trixie followed her to the shed to get the four-wheeler, thinking sheep herding was a little different from cattle herding. Her Daddy had always relied on a horse. Spying Logan and Caleb already following the sheep astride Rocky, she smiled in spite of her earlier morose mood. Caleb was enjoying being with his daddy up on the spotted beauty. And his hat was about as ratty and stained as Logan's. The two looked so beautiful, so perfect riding atop the great horse, that her heart again felt heavy with regret. That little boy needed a mother.

And she…she suddenly realized she needed a child.

Maybe she could convince Rad to reconsider his stance on waiting, so they could have children soon. Maybe that would replace this great emptiness in her heart.

"Hang on," Samantha warned as they headed after the sheep, the four-wheeler whirling and circling back to change the flock's erratic course.

Snapping to attention, Trixie did as she was told, since her body bounced and hopped with the terrain. Soon, however, Samantha and Logan and the few other daring souls under Harlan's experienced hand, had the reluctant runaways corralled back in the broken paddock.

Caleb stood proudly with his daddy, holding the fence together with the help of some of the other workers, while Logan temporarily patched the damaged spot back together.

Watching them, Trixie remembered Logan's earlier words, wishing it were as easy to fix broken relationships. "I still love you." She'd tried so hard to block those words out of her system this afternoon, through tedious reports, through phone calls back to her own office, through thoughts of her upcoming wedding. But Logan's words and his kisses haunted her and held her. Even Harlan had wondered if something else was bothering her. Her grandfather was shrewd; he would figure things out soon enough if she wasn't careful.

She needed to go home. After all, there was really nothing holding her here now that she'd made her decision. Except the memory of Logan's kiss and the fact that he still loved her. How long would that love last, though, if he knew the truth?

As the dust settled, Trixie came off the four-wheeler with a wave, unsure about Logan's reaction to her help since they'd parted on such uncertain ground this morning.

But instead of frowning at her, he started laughing. "You look like you've been rode hard and put up wet," he chided as he reached out to wipe a smudge of dirt off her face.

Realizing she was covered in dust and grit and that her hair had been completely rearranged from the wind and humidity, Trixie had to smile. "Guess I look pretty stupid, all decked out in sunflowers and covered with mud. Kind of wilted and dusty, huh?"

Logan's eyes burned softly, while his tone became intimate. "You look all right to me, but the dust…well, that's another thing all together. I think you better let Mama wash that outfit for you."

Seeing the mud spots and various other stains splattered across her intricately woven sunflowers, Trixie shook her head and wrinkled her nose. "It has to be hand washed. I'll do it myself."

Caleb tugged on her grimy shorts. "Miss Trixie, wanna see those kittens now?"

Trixie looked over to Logan for approval. When she saw the grudging admiration in his eyes, along with some other unreadable emotion, she hesitated. "I don't think—"

"It's all right," Logan said, dusting off his forever dusty hat before he plopped it back on his dark curls. "In fact, I'd like to see those kittens myself. Mind if I tag along?"

Caleb reached out a hand to both his father and his new friend, tugging the two of them along as he walked between. "We don't mind, do we, Miss Trixie?"

Trixie's gaze met Logan's over the boy's head. "Not at all."

In spite of the brittle smile on his face, she once again sensed a hesitancy in Logan. Was he coming with them to make sure she didn't do or say anything to upset his son? Or was he worried about something else entirely?

Trixie didn't have time to ponder that puzzle. From up the lane toward the lodge, someone called her name.

"Tricia?"

Her heart did a quick jolt. Only one person ever called her by her first name, without the Maria. Still holding Caleb's hand, she turned to find Radford Randolph heading toward her, his silk suit coat tucked over one arm, his face covered with sweat and irritation.

"Rad?" She whispered the name, a panic setting in to make her blood run faster and her heart pump harder. Her gaze flew to Logan's. She didn't miss the condemnation in his eyes as he lifted one brow in a daring question.

"Who's that dude?" Caleb asked with the innocence of a seven-year-old.

"That *dude* is no one for us to worry about," Logan said, tight-lipped. "Show me those kittens, son."

Caleb held back, his big eyes lifting to his father. "But what about Miss Trixie?"

Logan shot her another scathing look. "Miss Trixie has unexpected company. Let's leave her alone so she can have some privacy with her intended."

Torn, Trixie felt Caleb's little hand slip away from her own. She stood frozen in place, her eyes on Rad, her heart heavy with guilt as Logan's words replayed over and over in her mind. "I still love you."

But she'd promised her love to Rad. And now he was here. Watching helplessly as Caleb and Logan headed toward the stables without her, Trixie decided she'd had enough of the deceit. After all, she couldn't possibly expect to start a new life with Rad without telling him the truth.

It was only fair. And he loved her. He'd forgive her. He had to.

Because she couldn't stay here.

As Logan had pointed out so bitterly, she didn't belong here. She belonged with Rad. She'd just have to take her chances and hope she was doing the right thing for both of the men she loved.

Or, she told herself with a wry smile, maybe she was doing this because she was afraid of happiness.

She certainly didn't believe she deserved any.

Chapter Eight

❧

"Hello, darling," Rad said, reaching out to give Trixie a hug. The look of her ruined outfit stopped him, though. Instead, he leaned toward her in an awkward position, staring at her as if he'd never seen her before. "Good grief, what happened to you?"

"Sheep stampede," she said, still in shock and wishing she could just drop through the earth. "It's a long story."

Rad nodded, then shot her an unsure smile. "Well, you'll be fine once you get cleaned up. Right?"

Annoyed that he didn't even want to kiss her hello, Trixie started walking toward the lodge. Rad was a germ freak, afraid to leave his apartment at the slightest hint of anything odd in the Metroplex air. "Don't worry, Rad, it's not contagious."

He hurried after her, his chuckle as brittle as his thick, sandy blond hair. "Of course it isn't. And I'm sorry if I seem a little…surprised. It's just that I've never seen you this way."

Trixie turned to face him, glad to see him in spite of her ill temper. She couldn't blame him; she'd never allowed him to see her at anything but her best. Another of Pamela's rules—never leave home without your makeup or your hair perfectly in place. "It's all right. I guess I do look like a fright. What on earth are you doing here, anyway?"

He shifted his feet, stepping gingerly so his Italian loafers didn't sink into anything mushy or smelly. "I was worried about you. You've been here a few days now, and you haven't returned any of my calls. "Pamela—"

Trixie groaned, so frustrated with her mother's misguided interference, she didn't bother telling him she'd tried to return his calls but kept missing him. "Don't tell me she sent you to check up on me, too. Granddaddy's already here."

"Harlan's here?"

Hearing the worry in his question, Trixie had to smile. Rad had always been intimidated by her grandfather. And she knew Harlan reveled in that intimidation, just to keep her fiancé on his toes. Funny, Logan seemed to get along quite nicely with Harlan. But then, very little intimidated Logan.

Mentally shaking away the comparison, Trixie continued. "Yes, he's here. He's in the paddock, trying to worm sheep."

A look of distaste twisted Rad's handsome, clean-cut face. Carefully touching a hand to her arm, he said, "Why are you doing this, Tricia?"

"Doing what?"

"Hanging around this rundown old ranch. I thought we agreed to sell it right away."

Tired, dirty, smelly and completely out of whack, Trixie glared up at him. "*We* didn't agree to anything,

Radford. You wanted me to sell, but I told you I wanted
to think about it. And...I have.''

He smiled, then, oblivious to her frustrations. "Good.
Then my timing is perfect. We can fly home together.''

Not in a mood to be manipulated, Trixie dug her
heels in. "I'm not ready to go home.''

"And why not? If you've arranged for a buyer—''

Bracing herself for what was about to come, she said,
"I'm not selling.''

Rad's face went from pasty to pink. "What did you
say?''

"I said, I'm not selling this ranch. I've done enough
research to get a handle on things around here, and I
like what I see. My father was providing a much-needed
service to a lot of less fortunate people, and I intend to
see that his work here continues.''

Swatting a fly away impatiently, Rad placed a hand
on his hip. "You can't be serious? You know you don't
have time for all this do-gooder stuff. What about your
position back in Dallas? You worked very hard to become head of marketing, and well, something like this
could ruin all of that.''

Anger coloring her words, she asked, "Are you referring to my position as a marketing consultant, or my
position in polite society?''

"Well, both. I mean, think of all the time you'll be
forced to invest in this—this money pit. If you want to
donate to your father's favorite charity, sell this place
and set up a trust or something, so we can write it off.''

Leave it to Rad to find some way to justify being
generous! "I don't want to do that,'' she said, her tone
firm. "I've made my decision, and I've put Logan in
charge. My father's mission work will go on as planned,
and I intend to be involved in it as much as possible.''

Rad looked at her as if she had the plague. "When did you get so high-and-mighty?" he asked with a snort.

Keeping her hurt feelings to herself, Trixie said, "When I realized that my father was a better Christian than I'll ever be."

Lifting a finger to point in her face, Rad gave her a look of indignation. "You could have at least discussed this with me, Tricia. You know how I feel about being saddled with this place."

"It's my place, Rad," she reminded him kindly, though she felt anything but, "and it was my decision." Giving him a disappointed look, she added, "And I knew you'd try to talk me out of it. But it's final. I'm going to tie up a few loose ends, consult with the local lawyers Daddy hired, then I'll be home by the end of the week."

He stepped closer, his nose turning up at the smell of animal all around them. "Does this have something to do with that Logan fellow?"

Shocked, Trixie immediately became wary. "What makes you think that?"

Rad studied her face, his own expression disapproving. "Pamela told me you once had a crush on him. Of course, she said she nipped it in the bud right away."

Furious at her mother's deliberate betrayal, Trixie wanted to tell him the truth right then and there. But when she spotted Logan and Caleb walking toward them from the stables, she held herself in check, knowing that would be a fatal mistake.

Instead, she simply said, "My mother would say anything to discredit Logan. She's never liked the ranch or any of the people who work here. But then she's never bothered to come up here and see exactly what I've seen."

Rad rolled his eyes heavenward. "Well, I'm here and I'm not overly impressed. And I'd really like to know what's going on. Just what have you seen, Tricia?"

Trixie stepped closer then, hoping to keep her words low pitched, so Logan wouldn't hear her. "I don't like the implication of your question, Rad."

"Why? Do you have something to hide?"

What would he do when she told him the truth? Right this minute she didn't care. He was being so callous, so condemning, she didn't like him at all. And he had once again sided with her mother. That hurt the worst.

Before she could respond, Rad pushed her away. "That smell is going to cause me to start sneezing. Please, go and change, so we can talk like two sensible adults."

That's when Logan stalked across the yard, his eyes blazing fire, his temper boiling. "Hey, Ralph, the lady's had a hard day. Cut her some slack."

Rad glared over at Logan with complete disgust. "The name's Radford. Radford Randolph. And who are you?"

Logan's tone was mocking. "Logan. Logan Maxwell—the one she *used* to have the crush on."

Trixie realized their voices had carried out over the trees and that Logan had heard enough to get him riled. Afraid he'd say more than she wanted him to say, she placed a hand on his chest. "I can handle this, Logan. Thank you."

"Can you?" he asked, the accusation in his question only rubbing her already-raw pride.

"Yes, I can," she said between a clenched jaw. She was getting a splitting headache, and she needed a long, hot shower. "Rad's right. I need to clean up. He can cool his engines in the cookhouse while I change."

Looking over at Rad, she suggested on a more level tone, "Why don't you spend the night, and in the morning I'll show you around." Maybe if she showed him the work being done here, she could make him see why she wanted to keep this place.

Logan interjected, "You're welcome to bunk in the camp house. It's not too crowded right now. Only 'bout a half a dozen teenagers."

Rad lifted a hand in dismissal, his gold Rolex glinting in the waning late afternoon sun. "Forget that. I doubt either Trixie or I will be staying past supper."

Trixie whirled to face him, her voice impatient. "I told you, I'm not ready to come home yet."

Rad looked from her to Logan. "And whose idea was that?"

Logan held out his hands, palms up. "Hey, fellow, Trixie makes her own decisions. Or hadn't you even noticed?"

"Stop it," Trixie said, stepping between them as they both pawed the ground like two raging bulls about to butt heads. "Logan, your son is watching from the porch."

That got Logan's attention, forcing him to shut down his overactive temper. "Yeah, thanks for reminding me."

Trixie sensed a hidden meaning in his words, but she let it go. With Rad here, she had more than enough to worry about. And it would get much worse once she told him everything.

"It wasn't right of your ma to send him up here," Harlan said later as he huddled close to his granddaugh-

ter in the cookhouse. All around them, teenagers sat
laughing and talking to the few remaining volunteers,
their mouths full of Gayle's famous spaghetti and garlic
bread, their eyes full of hope and contentment. This was
the Wednesday-night ranch supper, a celebration for
both the students and the volunteers who'd helped that
day, so everyone was included, and expected, to be
here.

Trixie had readily agreed to help out, and she'd actually looked forward to her meal with the youth and
the volunteers, that is, until Rad had shown up. Now
she was torn between giving her attention to the camp
kids and her cranky fiancé.

Watching him now, she whispered to Harlan, "I'd
better get back to him. He's waiting on his glass of iced
tea."

"He can get his own drink," Harlan replied, frowning.

Trixie ignored him and went to sit back down beside
Rad. "Did you enjoy the spaghetti?"

Rad pushed the remains of his meal away. "The
sauce is a little too sweet for my taste."

Wanting to make amends, Trixie said, "How about
dessert? Gayle makes wonderful chocolate chip cookies."

Giving her a look of disdain, Rad retorted, "I don't
want a cookie. I'm not some waif off the street, you
know. I just want you to come back to Dallas with me."

Needing some answers, Trixie asked, "Did you come
up here because you missed me, or because my mother
talked you into coming?"

He glanced down at his plate. "Well, I do have a
pretty heavy caseload. That's why I have to get back,
tonight if possible."

"You didn't answer my question."

He took her hand then. "You should already know the answer. Yes, I missed you, but Pamela did suggest—"

Trixie pulled her hand away. "Just as I thought."

Offended, Rad said, "Hey, don't get mad at your mother. She's worried sick about you, and after seeing the looks of some of these delinquents, I can understand why."

"They are not delinquents," Trixie said, keeping her voice low. "These are children, Rad. Children who needed some guidance and some love to set them on the right path. They're not bad kids—they've just had some bad breaks."

"If you say so."

Getting up, she gave him a sad smile. "I know so. The people who work here have done wonders with the children who pass through this ranch. That's one of the reasons I don't want to change anything."

"You've obviously been impulsive," Rad told her. "You've let some sort of sentimentality cloud your better judgment."

Hurt and aggravated by his attitude, Trixie said, "Yes, I guess I have. But I'm not going to sell this ranch. And that's final."

Her heart swelled with pride, knowing that her father had saved so many young people from a life of crime and abandonment. She'd seen the pictures of past Camp Dunaway participants, and she'd read the letters students had sent to her father, thanking him for taking the time to help them out. Somehow she knew in her heart God was giving her an opportunity to make a difference, and to find the right priorities in her own life. She couldn't just walk away from a challenge and responsibility of that magnitude. She'd just have to make Rad see things her way.

"Can't you understand how important this is?" she asked him.

"No," he said, a pout distorting his face.

Losing her patience, Trixie said, "I'm going to talk to Granddaddy."

"What about us? What about leaving?"

"I'm not leaving tonight, Rad," she repeated, gritting her teeth with each word.

Coming back to Harlan, who'd witnessed the whole exchange with an eagle eye, she said, "I can't really blame Rad. He's just concerned about me. And you know how mother is. When she wants things to go her way, she pulls out the stops. Especially when it comes to interfering in my life. So I'm not surprised she talked him into coming up here. I am surprised, though, that she didn't book you two on a flight together, or better yet, fuel up the company jet."

Harlan snorted, then lowered his head, looking guilty. "Well, actually, she had planned it that way. Only I jumped the gun and took off without him. I didn't think he'd have the gumption to come on his own, though."

Amazed at her grandfather's devious ways, Trixie could only stare at him, thinking perhaps Brant had inherited his good-ol'-boy charm naturally. "Thanks for trying, Granddaddy," she said. "You'll be in trouble when you get back home. We both will."

"We'll cross that bridge when we come to it," Harlan replied sagely. "*Are* you going back with him?" he asked, his voice low and gruff as he eyed Rad, who sat sulking in a corner.

Rad had not been happy when Trixie informed him they had to share dinner with the entire group. He'd wanted a more intimate meal. And to top things off, Logan was conspicuously absent, which meant he was probably off somewhere stewing.

Her headache pounded against her temple with each pulse beat. "No, I'm not," she replied to Harlan's question. "That's why he's over there pouting. I plainly told him I can't leave until the end of the week—probably Sunday."

Harlan winked over at her. "A lot can happen before Sunday, sweetheart."

"A lot has happened already," she admitted, knowing she could trust her grandfather. "I've discovered so much about my father, and myself for that matter, that I didn't know. And I'm so proud of him. I want to do the right thing. And I believe keeping the ranch is right. It's what he would have wanted me to do. But it will be a tremendous responsibility. I...I just need to sort through it all, I guess."

Harlan nodded. "This place has a way of doing that to a person. Really makes you think about what matters most in this old life." He patted her arm affectionately. "And I, young lady, am very proud of you. Always have been. If you're worried about the burden of running this place, you know you can count on me. I only wish your father had turned to me more."

"Me, too," she said, her thoughts misting over with regret. "He did all of this on his own, maybe because he was so hurt by Mother's rejection, maybe because he needed to carve out his own special niche in the world. He was a good man—I know that. I think I always knew it. But I sure wish he'd...he'd stayed closer to all of us."

"Too late for worrying about that," Harlan replied, his words gruff with emotion. "My son was full of conflict and contradictions—a cowboy who had a hard time with rules and regulations, which is why your mama could never tame him.''

Without thinking, Trixie said, "Logan's a lot like that.''

Harlan gave her a scrutinizing look, then nodded. "Yep. A good man, proud and stubborn, and willing to work hard to keep this place intact. You're smart to put him in charge of things. He won't let you down.''

Surprised by her grandfather's impassioned praise, Trixie glanced toward him. "Why, Granddaddy, I had no idea you admired Logan Maxwell so much.''

Harlan's aged eyes grew intense with meaning. "Like I told you, I want you to marry the right man.''

Confused, Trixie shot him a questioning look. "If I didn't know better, I'd think you're suggesting I marry Logan instead of Rad.''

He shrugged. "I didn't say that.''

"Uh-huh. And what you don't say always tells me more than what you do say.'' Pausing, she glanced around, then whispered, "How do you really feel… about Logan?''

Harlan chuckled low. "I've got a better question. How do *you* feel about Logan?''

"Granddaddy, you sly old thing,'' she admonished, glad that he'd always been honest with her, even if he could read her like a book. Then, turning serious, she said, "I still care about him. I guess I always will. But we both agree that it's for the best if we just go our separate ways.''

"You sure about that?''

Watching Rad, she had to wonder. "Right now, I'm not sure about anything.''

"Better be sure before you make a mistake you can't

fix,'' Harlan warned her. ''Constant prayer and careful consideration, that's my advice. Now, I'm going back for seconds on that spaghetti.''

Trixie sat still, thinking her grandfather's words echoed the same warning Logan had given her. If she were honest with herself, she'd admit she wanted to tell Rad the truth to test him, to see if he would stand by her. She had the sinking feeling he wouldn't. It made her realize that all the money and position in the world couldn't bring her what she really wanted.

She wanted someone to care enough about her to fight for her, really fight for her, in spite of her shortcomings. She'd always tried to be the perfect daughter, putting on a proper face for society, putting up with her mother's requests and reprimands, yet always believing she was loved and cherished. But when she'd failed, when she'd digressed, Pamela had hidden her away in shame…too afraid of a scandal to stand by her daughter or show any compassion for Trixie's feelings. And even her father and Harlan had gone along with it, to keep things quiet, to protect the Dunaway name. Would Rad stand by her because he truly loved her? Or would he too turn away in shame and disgust?

Wanting to rekindle the good she'd seen in him when Pamela had first introduced them all those months ago, she got up to go sit by him again. ''I'm sorry,'' she said in an attempt to console him. ''I know all of this had been hard on you, and I really want to make you understand why I'm doing this. Do you want to go for a walk and talk?''

Rad pushed his fork through his half-eaten spaghetti. ''Is there anyplace around here that doesn't smell like a cow pasture?''

''Not really,'' she said, laughing. ''We could go back

to the lodge and sit on the screened porch. It's down-wind from the paddocks, and the flies can't get to us there.''

"Okay." His eyes still on her, he rose from his seat, then turned to grab his coat. His hand moved over the silk, then stopped. "Trixie, my watch is gone."

Alarmed, she looked around. "What? Are you sure?"

"Yes, I'm sure," he said impatiently. "I took it off when we all had to freshen up camp style earlier. I put it in my coat pocket."

"Maybe it fell out of your coat."

Rad immediately panicked. "No, I'm telling you it's gone." He glared at the suddenly quiet teenagers who'd been watching him shyly all evening. "Who took my watch?"

Hearing him, Gayle walked around from the kitchen area, her expression full of contempt. "What's the problem?"

Rad shouted at her. "I'll tell you the problem. Somebody took my watch from the pocket of my coat." His gaze accused each and everyone of them.

Trixie hissed at him. "Rad, don't be silly. Let's look for it."

"I don't need to look," he said, anger blotching his face. "Somebody had better start talking, or I'm calling the sheriff. That was a very expensive watch."

Wondering where Logan was, Trixie tried to hush Rad again. "Please, don't jump to conclusions. Where did you last have the watch?"

"Near that big basin outside where everybody washed their hands," he replied hotly. "If I'd been allowed to go to the lodge, this wouldn't have happened. I took it off because I didn't want it to accidentally go down that big, dirty drain."

Thinking the watch was waterproof and built to stay put, Trixie remembered Logan had deliberately insisted Rad stand in the wash line to the outdoor sink so all the adults could set an example to the young people—no one got special privileges here. His way of getting the upper hand, she supposed. And just to show him what an inconvenience it had been, Rad had purposely taken his watch off and rolled up the sleeves of his white shirt. But surely none of the children had stolen Rad's precious piece of jewelry.

"Then let's look outside by the washing basin," she suggested, her tone soothing and sure.

Rad stomped away while Trixie explained to the puzzled teenagers what had happened. Samantha started an immediate search, a worried expression on her face. Harlan, skeptical and keen eyed, joined in with the rest of the volunteers. Gayle huffed, then went back into the kitchen to clean up.

But where was Logan?

Racing around the cookhouse, Trixie searched the grounds for him. It wasn't like him to be late for supper with the kids, especially a celebration supper where he expected everyone to be on equal footing and their best behavior.

Then she saw him there in the red rays of the sunset, and her heart stopped. He'd had a shower and now wore a clean set of faded jeans and a fresh T-shirt, his hair still wet with dark, damp curls springing up around his temples. He stood oblivious to the commotion off in the distance, because he was intensely busy with his own secretive work. He was hanging her sunflower shorts out on the clothesline behind the lodge.

The outfit was obviously damp and…completely

clean. Not a bit of mud remained on the bright garments. They looked brand-new.

"Logan?" she called as she hurried toward him. "What on earth—"

He turned then, guilty and sheepish, his eyes rich with a sweetness that took her breath away. "You said hand wash."

Trixie stopped, her gaze moving over his face. "You washed my outfit?"

He didn't answer. Instead he gave her an indifferent shrug, then turned around to finish pinning the clothes to the line.

"That's the sweetest thing anyone's ever done for me," she said, her heart opening like a flower bud finding the sun.

"Don't go around talking about it," he replied drily. "I've got a reputation to maintain."

She smiled as he turned to face her. "I won't tell."

For a long time they just stood there, looking at each other, the brilliant rays of the evening sun falling all around them in golden shards, neither one of them able to say what was really on their minds.

And there in that knowing light Trixie discovered what her soul had been shouting at her from the first time she'd seen him again—she loved him with all her heart. And she wanted to tell him. Not only that, but she wanted, needed, to tell him the whole truth, and hope, pray, for his forgiveness. Her grandfather had said Logan wouldn't let her down. She'd find out, one way or another.

"Logan—"

"Why, you little punk!"

Rad's angry shout brought her head around, forcing her to forget about telling Logan anything for now.

"What's going on?" Logan asked, pushing past her to head to the cookhouse where Rad stood with a cluster of teenagers. Soon Harlan and Gayle and the others had joined them.

Trixie followed Logan, meaning to stop him from provoking another fight with Rad, or worse. She hoped Rad hadn't been right. She didn't believe anyone had taken his watch, but it might have proved too tempting for someone who'd never seen such an exquisite piece of jewelry before.

She prayed none of the children had given in to that temptation. And she prayed neither Logan or Rad would do anything foolish or rash if they had.

Chapter Nine

$\sim$

Horrified, Trixie watched as Rad yanked little Caleb by the arm, his face distorted with anger, his whole body rigid with accusation.

"You took my watch, didn't you?"

Before Rad could question the boy further, Logan pushed between them, the force of his hand on Rad's arm causing Rad to glance up.

"Let him go. Now," Logan said on a steely calm breath.

Rad pushed Logan's arm away in irritation, but realizing everybody was watching him manhandle a child, he reluctantly let Caleb go. The frightened child burst into tears, then ran to his grandmother's arms.

Logan glared at Rad, then turned to the little boy. "Caleb, did you take Mr. Randolph's watch?"

Caleb gulped back a sob, then stared wide-eyed up at his father before handing the missing watch over to Logan. Trixie could see the fear in the boy's eyes. Even if Caleb had stolen the watch, Rad had no right to be so cruel to a child....

Logan squatted down in front of his son, then touched

a gentle arm to Caleb's shoulder. "Just tell the truth, son. I promise you aren't in trouble unless you did something wrong."

A look of trust slowly emerged through the tears Caleb couldn't hide. "I...I found it, Daddy," he said, his words filled with a plea. He pointed to the wall of the cookhouse. "Over there by the flower bed."

Logan looked around the group, his voice calm in spite of his racing heart. "Did anybody else see anything?"

Marco stepped forward, shifting his weight from foot to foot. "He's telling the truth, Mr. Logan. When Mr. Randolph told us his watch was missing, we all came out to look...and Caleb found it over in those yellow mums by the washbasin."

Rad hissed, then placed both hands on his hips. "You don't actually believe that, do you?" Pointing an accusing finger at the two young boys, he said, "I saw those two huddled together, snickering. I'm telling you—they took it."

Marco shook his head. "No, sir, we were happy because we were so glad we'd found it. Caleb couldn't wait to show it to you."

Caleb, embarrassed now, hid his head against his grandmother's apron.

Trixie's heart went out to him. She knew from being around him, and hearing his grandmother talk, that Caleb was inclined to be impish at times, but she didn't think he had deliberately taken Rad's watch.

Rad still looked skeptical though. "I'm sorry, I just don't believe that. You both looked guilty when I caught you with it."

"That's because you seemed so mad when you

shouted at us," Marco said, his voice low and shaky. "You scared us."

Logan stood up, his nose inches from Rad's, his level tone belying the heated look in his eyes. "If they say they didn't do it, then I believe them." Touching Caleb on the shoulder, he added, "My son's been taught to tell the truth, and Marco knows the rules regarding other people's property."

Rad looked surprised to learn the little boy was Logan's son, but the knowledge didn't stop his ranting; it only added fuel to his self-righteous fire. "Well, you know how kids can be, especially if they're allowed to run around *unsupervised*." His condescending tone and the way his eyes glinted when they centered on Logan indicated that he didn't think highly of Logan's parenting skills, or this whole setup. "We all know why most of these children wound up here, anyway. Maybe your son's learned a thing or two from some of them. I think he's just afraid to admit he took it."

Shocked and embarrassed, Trixie stepped forward to touch his arm. "Rad, Caleb wouldn't do such a thing. Besides, he was being supervised, as are *all* of the children entrusted here. Caleb was in the cookhouse kitchen with Gayle most of the evening, so he never had an opportunity to go through your pockets."

"I was sitting right by the kitchen door," Rad shot back, his tone defensive. "It would have been easy for him to sneak around and take it." Scowling at her, he added, "Why are you defending these people, anyway?"

Trixie looked from the man she had pledged to marry, down to the confused little boy in baggy denim shorts and a baseball shirt, still clinging to his grandmother's skirts. Her eyes soft and gentle on Caleb, she said, "Because I believe Caleb when he says he found the watch. Everyone saw you take it off right in that very spot, Rad. Be reasonable. The watch slipped out of your coat pocket, and I for one, think you owe Caleb and Marco an apology."

Rad snorted, then threw his hands up in the air. "Fine, fine, have it your way." Leaning forward, he said in an exaggerated voice, "I'm so sorry. Now, could I just have my watch back."

Logan shoved the glinting gold at him, a look of contempt etching his face. "The excitement's over, folks," he said to the awkward, embarrassed crowd. Giving Rad a meaningful look, he added, "Let's all be more careful with our valuables from now on."

Rad started to retort, but at the warning look from Harlan, decided better of it.

As the crowd dispersed, Trixie headed over to Caleb. "Are you okay, sweetie?"

Gayle, for once, didn't pull the child away. Instead she nudged Caleb forward. "Tell Miss Trixie thanks for sticking by you, Caleb."

"Thank you," the little boy said, his eyes still bright with tears. "I did find it over there, Miss Trixie. My Daddy taught me not to steal, and besides I got a Cal Ripken, Jr., watch for my birthday, anyway. Mr. Brant gave it to me. I don't need another one."

Placing both hands on the boy's shoulders, Trixie smiled. "Cal Ripken, huh? Well, he's a baseball legend. You're right. Your watch is much more valuable than that plain old gold one."

Distracted from his woes, Caleb perked up considerably. "You like baseball?"

"Astros and Rangers," she answered, glad she'd taken his mind off this humiliating situation. "Jeff Bagwell is my favorite Astros player. Maybe they'll make it to the play-offs, huh?''

"Sure hope so. My friend Matt, he loves Jeff Bagwell. He's got all of his cards." With that, the little boy ran off into the sunset, his tears forgotten.

But his father hadn't forgotten. Logan watched as the last of the young people and volunteers sauntered off to the bunkhouse to watch a video, then turned back to Rad.

Getting in the man's face so Rad could see the mad in his eyeballs, Logan said, "If you ever lay a hand on my son again, I'll personally see to it that you lose more than your Rolex."

Rad looked unsure, then scoffed, quickly recovering. "You're in no position to be ordering me around, Maxwell. Pretty soon, I'll be co-owner of this ranch. I suggest you keep that in mind before you make any idle threats."

Gritting his teeth to keep from belting the man, Logan used every bit of confrontational counseling he'd been taught over the years, as well as a deep reserve of inner strength. While it galled him to let this idiot get away with a slur like that, he knew he had to maintain his cool for his son's sake and for the benefit of the other kids here.

His eyes on Trixie, he said, "Don't remind me." Then he turned back to Rad, his stance unyielding. "You might eventually own this ranch through marriage to Trixie, but neither one of you will ever own me. Just stay away from my son."

But Rad didn't know when to quit. "Hey, Maxwell, I've got a better idea. Why don't you and your brat pack up and get off this property! Sure would save all of us the trouble later."

Logan's hand on Rad's throat was a blur of motion. Trixie watched as he shoved Rad up against the wall of the cookhouse, rattling the screen door in the process.

Gayle's shocked gasp echoed out over the night, causing Trixie to bolt into action.

Rushing forward, with Harlan on the other side, she managed to pull Logan off Rad. "Stop it! Stop this. What kind of example are you both setting?"

That calmed Logan enough that he backed away, clearly disgusted with himself for letting this self-absorbed snob get to him. Then he turned to her, his eyes blazing. "Do *you* want me and Caleb to go?"

She shook her head. "No. Of course not." Reaching a hand out to touch his arm, she said, "Logan, you haven't done anything wrong."

Rad took her defense of Logan as a personal affront. Groaning loudly, he said, "Surely you aren't going to let him stay on? The man attacked me, Tricia!"

Trixie whirled on him. "Yes, after you attacked his son." Her tone firm, her eyes bright, she said, "Get this through your head, Radford. I'm not going to sell this ranch, and I'm not going to fire Logan."

Clearly frustrated, Rad threw up his hands. "I just don't get it. Ever since your father left you this stinking place, you've turned into Lady Bountiful. Are you so sure it's the land you want to hang on to, or do you still have a thing for him?"

He pointed to Logan, causing Logan to snarl and move toward Rad.

Before Logan could get very far, Harlan stepped forward, his bulky frame becoming an effective barrier between the two men. "I've had just about enough of this bickering between you two."

While the two men stared hotly at each other, Harlan

said in a calm, authoritative tone, "Now, boys, this is
the way it's gonna be. Tricia Maria is the sole owner
of Brant Dunaway Farms International." Giving Rad a
scathing glare, he continued, "She's made a firm decision to keep the ranch, and she's put Logan in charge
of things in her absence. That's good enough for her ol'
grandpa, so I say it's a done deal."

Turning to Logan, he said, "You, get a grip on that
attitude. We're on your side, son." Then he frowned at
Radford. "And you, get your tail back to Dallas and
mind your own business. Trixie knows what she's doing."

His anger refueled, Rad glared hotly at Trixie. "Do
you?"

"Yes, for the first time in a long time, I do," she
replied quietly, her gaze shifting toward Logan.

An angry flush rose on Rad's face. "Well, we'll just
see about that. I have some very influential friends, you
know. I wonder how Social Services would react if I
put the word out that your so-called foreman has a very
dangerous temper?"

Dazed, Trixie could only stare at him in shock. "Rad,
you can't be serious. You provoked him, and besides,
we have witnesses to the whole thing. Stop spouting
idle threats."

"Oh, it's no threat," Rad said, his expression smug.
"And I'm telling you, Tricia, if he doesn't watch it, I'll
call in all my markers."

Trixie put her hands on her hips, then turned to Logan. "I won't let that happen. Logan, you have my
word on that."

Logan gave her a hostile look, then ran a hand
through his tousled curls. "Sorry, but I can't go on your
word right now, Trixie." His eyes shooting fire, his ex-

pression daring, he glared at Rad. "Do what you gotta do, but you stay away from my son. I've got things to take care of. See y'all in the morning."

Harlan watched him stalk away, then cleared his throat, his eyes on Rad. "I need a big glass of sweet tea to get this bitter taste out of my mouth. I'm going in the cookhouse to help Gayle tidy up."

That left Trixie and Rad in an uncomfortable silence.

Finally she looked over at him, her tone quiet, firm, and determined. "We need to talk."

He smirked. "I'll say. *You* need to come home with me right away. Do you realize you're acting so irresponsibly that you're seriously jeopardizing our whole relationship?"

She laughed bitterly at his twisted logic. Why had she never seen this shallowness in him before? Maybe because she hadn't wanted to see it? Maybe because it reflected a side of herself she didn't want to acknowledge?

"Oh, yes," she answered, "I realize a lot of things." Taking him by the hand, she led him toward the luxury rental car he'd parked out away from the main house. "I realize you have a nasty side that I don't like. I realize that you won't ever let me run this ranch the way I think it should be run. And I realize that, thanks to my mother's biased opinions, you hate Logan."

They made it to the car, and now Rad swung around to lean on the shiny gray metal, crossing his arms over his chest as he scowled at her. Ignoring her first two accusations, he went right to the heart of the matter. "Well, sure. You're engaged to me, yet you defended that…that hillbilly."

"He is not a hillbilly," she said, shaking her head. "Logan graduated from the University of Arkansas with a business degree and a minor in agriculture, and he's had training in youth counseling. He knows his stuff, but he does have a temper. You're lucky he didn't whip your pants off back there.''

''All the more reason to press charges,'' he countered. ''That man needs to be held accountable for his actions.''

Frustrated, Trixie groaned, then threw her hands in the air. ''Please, Rad, don't threaten Logan, or me, for that matter. If you did something irrational like that, you could very well close down this whole operation. And I won't let that happen. My father and Logan have worked too hard on this.''

Rad stared down at her as if he were seeing her for the first time. Then, realization dawning in his self-involved system, he said, ''You still care about him, don't you?''

Too tired to hide it any longer, she said, ''Yes, Rad. Yes, I do. And that's one of the things I need to talk to you about.''

Shaking his head, he gave her a patronizing chuckle. ''No, no. You just need to come home. You can't think straight in this place.'' Pleading with her, he said, ''We're engaged, remember? You're wearing my ring. I love you.''

Trixie looked down at the perfect solitaire nestled on her finger, then lifted her gaze back to him. ''No, Rad, you love the idea of being with me. You love us as the fashionable up-and-coming power couple around Dallas. You love our image, what we represent, and I have to admit, I once enjoyed all of that, too. But…now I understand things about myself…things I've tried to deny for so long. And you're right. I have changed since my father's death.''

She hesitated, then took a deep breath. "You see, I've stepped out of my self-centered shell and I've taken a good hard look at my life. Seeing this ranch, knowing what my father tried to do here, has made me aware of the outside world, the world my mother has tried so hard to shield me from. But now that I've seen the work being done here, I think I want to be a part of all this." She lifted a hand to include the ranch. "I might be making a mistake, but I need to stay here awhile. I need to find some sort of peace."

"You're not making any sense," he said, impatient with all this soul searching.

Trixie gazed up at him, wishing, wishing they'd shared more intimate talks, wishing they'd shared a closer spirituality with each other. But now that she thought about it, she and Rad had never really had any heavy, meaningful conversations. No, they'd always been too busy seeing and being seen. Their whole relationship had been built on a carefully cultivated facade, orchestrated by Pamela to always put them in the best light.

Now Trixie wanted that facade to end. "Yes, Rad, I am making sense. Finally I'm taking charge of my own life." Touching a hand to his arm, she added, "And unfortunately, that means I can't marry you. It wouldn't be right now, because I don't love you anymore, not in the way I should."

He grew quiet then, his hand clinging tentatively to hers. "Because of him?"

"Yes, partly." She took another long, calming breath, then lifted up a prayer for strength. "But partly because something happened to me a few years ago, something that I've kept a secret from the world. And because of that, I can't love anyone completely. That's why I want you to know the truth.'''

He attempted a grin. "What'd you do, avoid paying your taxes or something?"

He would figure money into it. Rad just didn't have a clue as to any type of emotional depth. Which would make it even harder for him to understand what she was about to tell him.

"It has nothing to do with taxes," she began. "But, I did pay a high price for something. I…I used bad judgment, I suppose. I lost control and wasn't thinking straight, and…I paid dearly for it."

In an effort to soothe her, he placed a hand on each of her shoulders, his gaze full of affection and concern. "Tell me, honey. We'll work through it together, then things can go back to normal. I love you, Tricia. We can handle all of this if you'll just come home with me."

Wishing it were that simple, she touched a hand to his cheek. "Rad, listen to me and try to understand what I'm saying. Eight years ago, I spent the night with a man and…and I got pregnant."

Rad's breath hissed right out of his body. Slowly, as if he'd touched something filthy and distasteful, he dropped his hands away from her shoulders. "What did you say?"

"I…was with a man once, and I got pregnant," she said again, her head down. Then lifting her gaze to his, she said, "And I was forced to give the baby up for adoption. My mother and Brant and Harlan are the only ones who know. They made me agree to the adoption, and…I think we've all been in denial since."

Rad stood silent, then. Trixie watched his face, saw the disgust and disapproval coloring his expression, much in the same way they'd colored her mother's face when she'd been forced to tell Pamela the truth years ago.

Oh, how it hurt to have to relive this all over again, especially with Rad. Yet, even through her hurt and humiliation, she felt an inner peace emerging to give her the strength to face him without shame. So she waited, hoping he'd show some compassion and at least try to understand.

Rad might not be good at intimacy or compassion, but he was good at numbers. It didn't take him long to put two and two together. "It…it was him, right? You…you and Logan Maxwell?"

She flinched away from the look of utter revulsion in his eyes. "Yes," she said, swallowing back the pain, the humiliation she'd worn for so long. She refused to be ashamed any longer, and she certainly wasn't ashamed of Logan. "He doesn't know about the baby, though. But I intend to tell him." *That* would be the hardest test.

Rushing on, she added, "We were only together that one time, then my parents made sure it would never happen again. Logan went on to college and, well, he was married briefly. They got divorced and now he has custody of their son, Caleb.

"That's why I can't sell the ranch. I won't displace that little boy, and I won't shut down a place where troubled teenagers can come and find hope. I've already lost one child because of everyone telling me I had no other choice. I won't do that to Logan and his child, or any other children who might need a temporary shelter here."

To her amazement, instead of condemning her, Rad laughed in relief. "Is that what this is all about? You think you owe Logan Maxwell something simply because you gave his bastard up for adoption! You're worse off than I thought!"

The slap sounded out over the hot, still dusk like a shutter flapping in a harsh whip of wind. Appalled at both Rad and herself, Trixie backed away, her stinging palm covering her mouth. The imprint of her hand spread like a bright red stain across Rad's stony face.

"I'm sorry," she said, shaken and heartbroken, all her hope for the last shreds of their shallow relationship dying with the final rays of the sun. Handing him the one-carat diamond ring he'd given her just months before, she said, "I think you'd better leave."

"Good idea," he retorted as he yanked open the car door. "I'll be glad to tell your mother the engagement is off." Before she could respond to that dig, he added, "Oh, and don't worry. Your tawdry little secret is safe with me. After all, I do have some dignity left, and I certainly don't want people to find out you dumped me for some low-life field hand who didn't even have the decency to acknowledge his indiscretion."

Fighting back tears, she repeated, "He never knew, Rad. But I'm going to tell him the truth before I leave here."

A triumphant smile crested on Rad's red streaked face. "Yeah, and then we'll see who's the better man. We'll see if Logan Maxwell will be so willing to work for you once he finds out you used your money and power to get rid of his baby. You're making a big mistake, but then, like Harlan so clearly pointed out— you're calling all the shots. I wish you lots of luck. You're going to need it."

"And lots of prayers, too," she whispered as she watched him pull away, the cruelty of his taunts tearing at her heart while she stood there in the dusty lane, her arms wrapped across her chest, her head bent.

In spite of Rad's callous observations, she managed to pull herself together. Lifting her head toward the afterglow of the setting sun, she sent up another prayer. And she decided she'd never be ashamed again.

Yes, she'd made a mistake, but now she was going to get past that by dedicating her life to her father's work. Tonight she'd done something she should have done a long time ago. She'd told the truth. That gave her a very liberating feeling, as if a tremendous burden had been lifted from her shoulders.

As she strolled out toward the stables, she found a new sense of purpose. This was a turning point in her life, but this was only the beginning. Now she had to tell Logan the same thing she'd just told Rad. It was the only way to start fresh and find that second chance she needed so desperately. It was the only way to salvage the love she and Logan still had for each other.

She had set things in motion, and now she was willing to turn the rest over to God.

Hours later Logan watched and listened from his perch on the porch, worry creasing his brow as he waited for Trixie to come back. It was well past dark, and still no sign of her.

Would she come back? Or had dear, wonderful Radford, with all his charm and cunning, conned her into leaving with him?

And why, Logan wondered, did he care?

Because he loved her. In spite of everything, he still loved her. But would that be enough? Would his love carry them through when things got even tougher between them? Would he have the strength to lay it all on the line, to take a chance with her again? Or would he let his pride stand in the way once more?

The Bible said to trust in the Lord. He'd just had an evening devotional with the youth, his son at his side. Because of what had happened earlier, they'd talked about accusation and anger, and how to control the two.

"For his anger endureth but a moment; in his favour is life: weeping may endure for a night, but joy cometh in the morning."

The verse from Psalms had hit the nail right on the head, as Harlan had so tactfully pointed out before he'd gone off to bed. Logan got the impression Harlan, and maybe the Lord, too, were both trying to hit him on the head with something.

Was he too stubborn, too bitter, to get it?

He sat there in the rocking chair, listening to the night sounds, trying so very hard to hear the echo of his own wounded heart. He heard the moaning of the humid wind as it merged with the gentle lowing of a cow. A set of pewter wind chimes hanging from a nearby rafter played a pretty, tinkling tune, its melody telling him to forgive, forgive, live, live. The rich smell of the earth mixed with the scent of fresh-baked bread and the night dew. And off in the distance a streak of lightning highlighted the starless sky. A storm was coming across the Arkansas countryside.

Where was Trixie?

Torn between duty and need, Logan knew he wouldn't have the strength to hold out much longer. He wanted to tell her everything at last. He wanted the answers to the questions that had haunted him for eight long years. He wanted to put an end to the bitterness and the accusations, and the pain.

He wanted. He wanted to find joy in the morning.

His eyes misty with stubborn tears, he whispered to the night. "There's so much, Lord. So much I need to tell her...so much I need to ask her. She has her secrets, and I have mine. I don't want any more secrets between us. I only ask for a second chance." His voice, his prayer trailed off into a humble plea. "I only want redemption."

The wind picked up. The chimes danced and jingled. The thunder grew closer.

And then the screen door squeaked open and Trixie stood there in her floral dress, her blond hair windswept and moon kissed, her eyes glistening like beckoning stars in the gray-black darkness.

"Logan?"

Logan hastily wiped his eyes, and without a word came up out of the creaking rocking chair to take her into his arms. Silently, softly, slowly, he pulled her to him. If he spoke now, he'd blurt everything out. And he needed time, time to collect himself, time to brace himself for what was to come.

Because when he told her the truth, he could very well lose her forever.

But not tonight. Not now. Tonight he only wanted to cherish the sweet victory of having her here still. Tonight he wanted to close the door on his conflicted soul and find that little bit of joy he felt each time she was in his arms. Tomorrow would be soon enough for the truth.

As a soft rain began to fall all around them, he held her close and waited and hoped and prayed.

And remembered.

"Weeping may endure for a night, but joy cometh in the morning."

Yes, in the morning he'd tell her everything.

And then he'd leave the rest up to God.

Chapter Ten

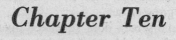

The storm worsened during the night, so the morning brought a whole new set of problems. While tornado watches prevailed across the state, heavy rains poured over the land, making the paddocks and pastures a muddy river of dirt and water. The animals huddled together, trying to find comfort and warmth in each other, while the humans went about their work in yellow rain slickers and heavy rubber boots. All across the ranch, pine limbs and oak branches lay broken and tangled, snapped from tall trees by the force of the winds.

Trixie took up residence in the office just off the den, where she called in to her own Dallas office to see if anything major had happened in the few days she'd been away on bereavement leave. Luckily her assistant and secretary were so efficient and organized that everything back in Dallas was well under control. Just a few questions to answer and some quick calls to clients, then Trixie was left to sit and watch the rain falling in spattering rivulets off the eaves of the wraparound porch.

Sipping another cup of strong coffee, she once again

thought about everything that had happened to change her life over the past few days. She'd lost her father, inherited a ranch and found a part of herself that had been missing for a long time now. She was no longer engaged to Radford Randolph and—she was still in love with Logan Maxwell.

While those revelations summed things up in a nutshell, the complications of each resounded in her head like the rain hitting the shingles out on the slanted roof.

How would she ever find the courage to tell Logan the truth? And especially after last night, when he'd held her in his arms as if he never wanted to let her go. Finding him there on the porch, waiting for her to come home, had been just the balm her wounded soul had needed. He'd hugged her close, rocking his body against hers, soothing her with softly whispered endearments, then he'd turned and gone inside without another word between them.

Now, she couldn't help but remember Rad's condemning words. Would Logan be so forgiving, so willing to continue working here, once he found out the truth?

Sitting here now, in the worn leather chair where her father must have spent hours, she glanced around, savoring the spirit her father had left everywhere in the paneled, cluttered room, hoping to find the courage to face Logan again. Hoping he would be able to forgive her at last.

Honors and awards, plaques and belt buckles, were displayed here and there, on every available surface. Professional Bull Riders Champion, 1977 and 1978. Rodeo Hall of Fame, 1994. PBR Ring of Honor—a circle of diamonds and gold, locked safely behind a glass case. National Finals Rodeo Champion, 1981. PRCA 1984

World Bull Riding Champion. The room was a testimony to Brant's love for the rodeo life, and his talent for riding the bulls.

Trixie sat back, closing her eyes as warm memories flooded through her mind. Her father had always been a cowboy. He'd never been interested in going into town with Harlan to learn the oil business. No, sir. No skyscrapers and silk suits for Brant Dunaway. Her father preferred mountains and mesquite trees to mergers and million-dollar deals. Brant could always be found out in the corrals and stables at Dunaway's Hideaway, riding, roping and hoping.

"From the time he was five years old..." Harlan said from the doorway now, as if reading his granddaughter's thoughts. "Your daddy sure loved riding those bulls and broncs."

Trixie opened her eyes, then sat up straight. "And mother hated it? Why?"

Harlan lowered his girth down onto a plaid wing chair nestled by a broad window. "Think about it, sugar. Bull riding is a very dangerous sport. Oh, she went to watch in the early days, when he was just setting out at every rinky-dink rodeo between Dallas and Oklahoma City. Pamela loved the romance, the glory, associated with being married to a handsome bull rider. But...one time, when you were about three years old and safe at home with your grandmama, God rest her soul, your ma watched your Daddy take a gore from a crazy-mad bull. Sliced through his gut and...well, he almost bled to death before they got him to the hospital. Had to remove his spleen."

Trixie looked around the room at the many pictures of her father during his heyday. "I never knew."

"She didn't want you to know. And she spent the

rest of their marriage trying to forget. That's why she hated what he did. Pamela was so afraid he'd get killed.''

Marveling at all the undercurrents she'd never been aware of in her parent's relationship, Trixie said, "So she did love him."

"Still loves him."

"But why did she drive him away?"

Harlan shook his head. "She nagged him away. Brant was a proud man. He wasn't about to let a goring stop him from becoming the best he could be. And he surely wasn't going to let a worrisome wife turn him into a coward."

Trixie scowled at that. "Men and their pride."

Harlan countered, "Women and their demands."

"Expectations," she corrected. "We have high expectations, and sometimes—"

"Sometimes a man can't live up to that kind of pressure," her grandfather finished for her. Changing the subject with a briskness that equaled the wind outside, he asked, "Did Rad live up to your expectations?"

"No," she said, lowering her head to stare at a photograph of her father with little Caleb on his knee. A shard of pain and longing hit her as she gazed at the framed picture. Brant had lost his own family; he'd turned to Logan's son for comfort, she supposed. And somewhere out there...

She refused to think about the child she would never know. Instead, she looked up at her grandfather. "Rad and I broke up last night."

Harlan nodded, then said, "Well, now you can 'dance with the one who brung you.'"

"And what's that supposed to mean?"

"You and Logan," he said, rising up with a huffing

breath. "You two have some unsettled business between you, I believe. And I say, now's the time to settle
it."

"What if it's too late?" she asked, the hope in her
voice edged with fear.

"It's never too late, if you tell the truth and trust in
the Lord."

"I'm trying, Granddaddy. I'm trying."

Harlan leaned his meaty hands against the burgundy
leather desk pad. "Tricia Maria, I know we don't speak
about what happened much—heck, we never talk about
it. But I want you to know that…that I'm sorry I didn't
fight harder for you back then."

Trixie stood up to come around the desk. Hugging
her grandfather close, she said, "I certainly don't blame
you. You were up against both Mother and Daddy, same
as me. I just wish—"

"Me, too," he said, his eyes misty and full of regret.
"I wish a whole lot of things. Maybe that's why I'm
so determined to see that you and Logan at least try to
get things straight between the two of you."

Patting him on the back, she said, "I plan on telling
him…everything, as soon as I can work up my nerve.
Where is he this morning, anyway?"

"Out rounding up stock and cleaning up debris, I
imagine," Harlan said. "That weather turned nasty during the night. Fences down, trees blown over. Frightened animals to tend. The rancher's life is a tough one,
even on good days, but Logan will get things under
control."

"He's a lot like Daddy, isn't he?"

"Yep. He's stubborn and prideful, but determined to
do his best."

She stared at the rain for a minute, then said, "Rad

isn't like that. He only does what he has to do to make the best possible impression. It was never real between us. It was all carefully calculated, all part of the overall plan. Even his feelings for me were superficial and based on what he could gain from being with me. And I'm ashamed to admit it, but I felt the same way toward him. He was the perfect choice, so I went along with it." Shrugging, she added, "I almost made another mistake, didn't I?"

"You stopped it in time," Harlan replied, then winked. "'Course, your ma will be fit to be tied."

"I'll deal with her," Trixie assured him. "I do believe it's high time I stood up to her."

"That's the spirit. You've got a lot of your ol' daddy in you, Trixiebelle."

"Thanks, Granddaddy," she said as she waved him out of the office. Somehow, in spite of the dreary day, in spite of her breakup with Rad, she did feel stronger.

Maybe being here, amidst her father's things, helped. Maybe knowing Logan still loved her helped. But would he still love her when she told him everything?

Just then the door creaked open and Trixie found herself staring at a pint-sized set of six-guns. Playing along, she raised her hands. "Oh, my. Am I being held up by a bandit?"

Caleb sauntered into the room, dressed in brown imitation chaps and his ever-present cowboy hat. "Yes, ma'am," he said in his best cowboy drawl. "I come to take all your valuables."

Pretending to be frightened, Trixie waved a hand. "Please, take whatever you'd like, sir. I don't want to get shot down in my mangy tracks."

Caleb giggled, then put his dangerous looking fake weapons on the desk. "I ain't gonna shoot you, Miss

Trixie. Mr. Brant taught me guns are for hunting, not killing people.''

"He told you that, did he?" she asked as she scooped the little boy up on her lap. He smelled of life, all warm and sweaty, with just a trace of sugar cookie lingering around him like a halo. "Mr. Brant was a very wise man."

"Yeah, and he was smart, too," Caleb replied with big-eyed innocence. "He taught me how to ride, you know?"

"Did he now?" Trixie's heart went all soft and mushy at the thought of her father patiently teaching little Caleb all about the rodeo. "But not those nasty old bulls, I hope?"

"Sure I want to ride bulls, just like him," Caleb answered, looking at her as if she'd just fallen off the turnip truck. "But I like the broncs, too."

"Even worse," she said, her hand touching tentatively on his back. "A very dangerous sport."

He shrugged. "Girls always say that. Nana thinks the same way."

"Nana's about as smart as Mr. Brant," Trixie replied, afraid to move, afraid he'd run off into his fantasy land again and leave her here to deal with reality. It just felt so nice, so special, to be holding a child in her lap.

Caleb sighed long and hard, then dropped his shoulders. "He was your Daddy, huh?"

She smiled at the boy's sweet innocence. "Yes, he was. I didn't get to see him very much, since I lived so far away. But he was still my Daddy."

Caleb grew quiet then. When he looked up at her, his eyes were wide and completely honest. "I miss him."

"Me, too," Trixie said, her voice barely above a whisper. "He was a special man."

Caleb lifted a finger to point to the ring nestled in a velvet box behind the glass case. "Know what? He told me he'd give me that ring one day. Told me I ought to have it."

Surprised that Brant would be willing to part with such a prestigious and valuable award, she looked down at the little boy. "Are you sure it was that particular ring?"

Caleb bobbed his head, causing his hat to tip back. "Oh, yeah. His Ring of Honor. He told me only real all-around rodeo cowboys could wear that ring."

She smiled down at him, thinking she'd never seen a cuter cowboy in her life. And she'd seen a few in her time. "Well, you certainly are a real all-around cowboy, aren't you?"

His nod was swift and confident. "Yep. I'm gonna be the best. I'm gonna be just like Mr. Brant."

Realizing her father and this precious little boy must have had a special relationship, Trixie once more pushed back the hurt of never knowing her own child. Brant should have been able to share things with his own grandchild, but none of them had taken the time to think about that back when they were so concerned about the Dunaway name and position. Instead they'd hurriedly sent her child away, in the name of maintaining the family status and dignity. Lord, would she never be able to forgive herself?

Staring down at Caleb now, she said, "I promise you—one day you will have that ring."

"Okay," he said as he shoved off her lap, his trust in her as complete as the few minutes of quiet he'd spent here in this room. "Mr. Brant said when I grow up and prove myself, then I can have it." He twisted his face in a confused grimace. "What do you have to do to prove yourself, anyway?"

Trixie shifted in the chair, feeling empty now. "Well," she said, her eyes focused on the little boy waiting for an answer, "you have to be honest and hard-working, and you have to care about other people and...you have to always respect others as well as yourself." Sighing, she added, "Sometimes, proving yourself is a tough job."

He grinned then. "I can do all of that. My daddy's proved himself a whole bunch, 'cause he does all of that stuff."

Trixie's smile was bittersweet. Maybe it was time she proved herself, too. It would be worth it, just to win Caleb's praise. And Logan's. "Your daddy is a special man."

"Just like Mr. Brant was," Caleb reminded her. Then, in typical cowboy fashion, he tugged his battered hat low over his brow and gave her a determined look. "I want that ring. I'm gonna work hard, I promise."

It was a long time before Trixie could reply. "Then it's a deal."

"What's a deal?" Logan said from the door.

Trixie looked up to find his dark eyes centered on her, that worried look she'd come to recognize and dread moving like a thunderstorm across his damp, mud-smudged face. He looked so powerful, so all male, standing there in his heavy twill rain duster, with his hat dripping water, that she had to agree with little Caleb. Logan had more than proven himself. He'd saved this ranch. And maybe her, too.

"It's a secret," Caleb said, turning to Trixie for support in this new game.

"Yes, a special secret," Trixie replied, amused by

the wary look in Logan's eyes. "Don't worry, we're not planning anything illegal or illicit."

"What's ill—illis—it?" Caleb asked.

Trixie laughed then. "It means something underhanded and shifty. But not you—you're not in trouble."

"Not yet, anyway," Logan said, relaxing a little bit. "Scoot off to the kitchen and get you some beef stew, sport."

Caleb picked up his guns and rushed past his father, but not before Logan grabbed his hat and tousled his hair a little bit.

"He's so cute, Logan," she said, nervous now that she was alone with him again. "And smart as a whip."

He watched her for a minute, the hesitant expression on his face telling her more than words ever could. Trixie waited, half expecting him to say something, to tell her what was on his mind. But the blankness returned, curtaining his feelings like the gray clouds outside, hovering, moving, misting over whatever he'd been about to say.

"That's my boy," he replied finally, lifting a shoulder off the doorjamb. "Hope he wasn't filling your head with tall tales."

"No, just telling me he wants to be a bull rider."

Logan's grin was weak with worry. "Yeah, we're still negotiating that matter." He took off his slicker, then sat down. In a quiet voice he said, "Your father was his hero."

"So I gathered."

They sat for a minute, staring, very much aware of each other, the rain, falling more gently now, the only sound between them.

Finally Logan said, "Hey, I was wondering…I mean, when this bad weather is over and…I've got some free time…I was wondering if we could get together and maybe get away from here for a couple of hours.''

Touched by his invitation and his nervousness, Trixie lifted her brow and said, ''Are you asking me out on a date, Logan?''

He tugged his hat off, ran a hand through his damp curls, then sighed long and hard, the glint in his dark eyes taking her breath away. ''Yep. I guess you could call it that.''

She ruffled some papers on the desk to hide her own jitters. Getting away from the ranch for a quiet talk would be better for her, too. She could tell him what she needed to say without any interruptions. ''That would be…nice.''

He pulled himself out of the chair then, his hat in his hands, his gaze on hers. ''It's just…we need to talk, about the ranch, about us, about everything.''

Trixie stood, too, mostly to keep busy, her hands in her shorts pockets. ''I agree. I guess you figured out I broke up with Rad last night.''

She saw the relief in his eyes. But she also saw something else—that same wariness she'd witnessed so many times, over the past few days. Well, it was only natural for him to be on guard around her. They had a highly intimate history. She was still treading lightly around him herself.

''I can't say I'm sorry,'' he admitted, tipping his head to one side as he gazed over at her. ''He was a first-class—''

''Careful,'' she warned, her smile a little sad, a little happy. ''Remember, you have to set a good, upstanding example for the young people.''

''Yeah, right.'' He nodded, then turned to leave, his

long slicker hooked with a thumb over his shoulder and floating out behind him. "See you at lunch."

"I'll be there." Then, "Logan, do you need any help?" She motioned toward the window. "It's so bad out there—I could ride fences or check on those adorable piglets."

He grinned, then shook his head. "Nope. You just stay here and keep Mama company...until I get back. She could use a hand with Caleb. He gets kinda restless when he can't play outside."

"All right."

"All right. See you later."

Trixie waited until he'd stomped down the hall before hugging her arms to her chest, thankful that Logan didn't seem to mind her being around Caleb so much anymore.

Then a terrible thought occurred to her. Would he want her around his son once she told him the truth?

Would he ever want her again, once he found out she'd given up his child without even telling him?

By the end of the day Trixie did get to go out and help with the cleanup work. In fact, every available hand was needed in order to corral skittish animals and secure broken fences. The electricity had gone out during the afternoon, so she couldn't get much work done in the office, anyway. She'd spent most of her time trying to entertain Caleb while his grandmother had gone about her regular daily chores. The little boy had stolen her heart, much in the same way his father had when she'd first met him.

Then, leaving Gayle to man the cellular phones and feed the workers cold sandwiches, she headed out with Logan and Caleb in the misting rain.

Cloaked in a bright yellow slicker and a rain hat, she rode a docile mare around the perimeter of the corrals, checking one last time for strays or places in the fence they might have missed earlier. Off in the distance, she could hear the four-wheeler revving up. Samantha would take the lane and check the far pastures before dark set in.

Up ahead, riding with his father on Rocky, Caleb shouted to Samantha as she whizzed by. "Can I come?"

Samantha slowed the four-wheeler down, then lifted a questioning hand to Logan. "I don't mind, if you don't."

Logan stared down at his son, then seeing the hopeful expression on Caleb's face, nodded. "Go ahead. I'm too tired to argue with you." As Caleb scrambled down to race to the off-road vehicle, Logan called, "And put on that helmet stashed under the seat!"

Samantha saw to it that the boy followed his father's instructions, then with Caleb sitting firmly on the wide seat with her, headed slowly off down the lane.

"He loves to ride that thing," Logan replied as Trixie coaxed her horse up beside his. "He's been begging me to let him drive it, but I haven't had time to teach him."

"He's certainly all boy," Trixie replied, as glad to be out of the house as Caleb, even if it was still a nasty day. "You've done a good job with him, Logan."

He glanced over at her, his eyes lifting underneath the brim of his hat. "Mama's helped out there a lot."

Noticing that cautious, guarded look in his eyes again, Trixie said, "It must have been hard on you—after your wife left, I mean."

Logan looked straight ahead, his face as blank and stony as the weathered posts of the wire fence stretching out beside them. "It was. Donna and I met in our first year of college...right after—"

"Right after you and I," she finished, understanding dawning in her eyes, regret pooling in her heart. "You must have really fallen for her."

He grunted. "I didn't fall at all. I didn't really love her the way I should have. Oh, I thought I loved her. I wanted to love her. But—" He stopped, looked off into the distance, his eyes swirling with the same dark intensity as the clouds curling and churning over the horizon. Then with a hard, cold look that left her breathless and afraid, he pinned Trixie. "I was still so in love with you, I couldn't think straight. So I used her to ease the pain. I cared about her, and I needed her. But, she knew. She always knew. So she left me."

And her child. Shocked, Trixie stared over at him. If this were some sort of declaration, it didn't make her feel any better, knowing she'd caused so much heartache. The condemning look in his eyes contrasted sharply with the gentleness she'd seen in him last night, only adding to her confusion and her fears.

"You still resent me, don't you?" she said, hurt in spite of her understanding. She didn't dare chastise his ex-wife for leaving Caleb. She'd done no better herself, after all. "Why, Logan?"

He couldn't tell her exactly why he resented her even while he loved her, so he only nodded and said, "I resent a lot of things. I resent your money and your mother. I resent your indifference to your father. But mostly, Tricia Maria, I just regret...so much."

They'd reached a small copse of trees at the corner of one of the pastures. Having seen no fences that needed his immediate attention, Logan slipped off his horse then turned to Trixie.

Before he could touch her, though, she dropped down and tied the mare's reins to a low branch, more intent on getting some much-needed answers than making sure her animal was secure.

Her eyes blazing blue fire, she said, "Logan, you're a constant contradiction. One minute you tell me you still love me, then the next you seem so distant, so bitter I can't reach you at all. What's going on?"

Tired, frustrated, yearning, Logan pulled her into his arms, his hands knocking her hat off so he could pull her head up. "You," he said, the one word half endearing, half hateful. "You—coming back here to stake a claim on everything from my heart to the ground I'm standing on. I've fought against you for so long, Trixie. I've blocked you out of my mind all these years, for reasons I can't even begin to explain now, and yet, here you stand. Here you are, in my arms, where I've always dreamed you should be. And I want you…I've prayed for you to be mine, but—"

"But?" She saw the torment in his eyes, saw the disgust on his face. He was fighting a battle, against her, against himself. "What is it? What did I do that was so terrible?"

He looked away, his grip on her still firm and sure, even if the doubt in his eyes told her he wasn't so sure. "You gave up," he said simply.

Wanting him to understand, she placed her hands on his face, the roughness of his five-o'clock shadow grating the nerve endings on her fingers. "Logan, I wanted to stay here with you. I wanted…"

She couldn't tell him she'd wanted nothing more than to come to him and tell him she was having his child. She'd wanted nothing more than to marry him and raise that child here on this ranch with him. But, ashamed, confused, humiliated—and taunted by her mother's hateful, insinuating words—she *had* given in and given up. Too soon. Too late.

And how, dear God, was she supposed to tell him the truth now, when he still seemed so torn whenever he looked at her or touched her? The truth would turn him away forever, no matter how much he loved her.

"Do you love me now, Logan?" she asked, her hands on his face urging him to look at her. "Do you love me right this minute?" She had to know, had to take what little she could find. "Look at me and tell me the truth."

He did, his eyes locking with hers, his heart breaking with loyalty and honor, and his love for her. "Yes," he said. "I love you."

She was crying now. She had to tell him. She had to let go of all of the pain and the heartache, and she would make him understand somehow. But first...

"I love you," she said, her hands stroking the hard lines of his jaw. "I never stopped loving you, and...in my own way, I was using Rad just like you said you used Donna. We've both been playing these games, the games other people expect us to play. I left you because I had no choice, no choice. My mother made me feel dirty, sinful, full of contempt for myself. And since then I've prayed to God to forgive me, to forgive me for everything." She stopped, her breath hitching between sobs. "I did more than leave the man I loved. I gave up everything, Logan. Everything."

He waited, holding his breath, his eyes never leaving hers, the expectation, the anticipation on his face making him look harsh and hopeful all at the same time. "Tell me about it, Trixie. I really want to understand."

Oh, how she wanted to do that very thing. How she

wanted to unburden herself to him, to tell him the horrible, honest truth at last. Would she find her redemption then, she asked the heavens. Or would she just be alone all over again, without any forgiveness or compassion?

Something in his eyes told her to trust him, to trust herself, to trust God. It was almost as if Logan knew all of her secrets and yet wanted to hear them from her lips just to confirm the strength of their love.

Impossible. He didn't know. He couldn't know. He just thought she'd dumped him because she was shallow and afraid. And maybe that had been true once, but not now. Not anymore.

Because she loved him so much, because she knew she might not ever get another chance, she pulled his head down and kissed him with a tender urgency, needing to feel his lips on hers just once more, needing to know that he loved her for this moment, in this place, standing here on this land. Just once more.

"I love you, Logan," she said after lifting her mouth from his. "Please remember that. I love you." Then she stepped back, distancing herself from him, from the pain. "And because I do love you, I want you to know the truth."

Logan let out a deep, shuddering sigh, then dropped his hand away from her hair. "I have some things to tell you, too." His eyes went soft again, then he trailed a finger down her cheek. "But you first."

Trixie hitched another breath. "We were supposed to do this over a candlelight dinner."

"We've got the rain and the wind," he said. "And the darkness."

She shook her head. "I've been in the dark too long now. It's time to come out into the light."

"Then come on," he said. "I'll find some candles and a dry spot."

She took his hand, ready to face the sure knowledge that he would soon hate her all over again. Ready to test her faith and their love for each other.

That's when they both heard the roar of an engine off in the distance, followed by a crash.

And after that, all they could hear was a long, keening scream.

Chapter Eleven

❧

Everything after that became a nightmarish haze to Trixie, a shock-filled, dreamlike groping to see clearly, and to remember. She remembered running, running to her horse, with Logan close on her heels. She remembered galloping down the lane, toward the place from where the sounds, the horrible, telling sounds, had come.

And then, hours later, as she sat in the cold, sterile hospital waiting room, she had to put her hands to her face to block out the sight of little Caleb lying so still, so silent, in the mud of a shallow rocky ravine, with blood, so much blood, coming from the split on the side of his skull while the overturned four-wheeler's tires moved, spinning, spinning to nowhere.

She closed her eyes, trying to stop the inevitable tears, trying to block the memory of the stark terror on Logan's face as he scrambled down the slope to reach his son. How could she ever forget the way he'd bent over his child, unable to take Caleb in his arms for fear of hurting him worse, one hand tentatively touching the deep cut on Caleb's head as Logan told him over and over, "It'll be all right. It'll be all right. Daddy's here."

And Daddy had done all the right things, in spite of his own shock. Logan had administered CPR like a pro; he'd been trained for just such an accident. Once he was sure Caleb wasn't hurt anywhere else and that no apparent bone fractures existed, he'd carefully checked the head wound, cautious not to make it bleed even more. But because Caleb was unconscious, they all knew the seriousness of the situation. Still, somehow, Logan had remembered what to do.

So much to remember, so much had changed in one split second of tragedy.

Samantha had come running, tears falling down her face, mud streaking her clothes. "He...I got off to check on a lamb. We saw it down in the ravine...we heard it crying. I thought it might be hurt. He...Caleb stayed on the vehicle. He'd taken his helmet off to...to scratch his head. His head was itching."

Trixie had held the girl, trying to calm her, trying to put the image of that sweet, still little body out of her mind. "What happened, Samantha?"

"I...I think he tried to drive the four-wheeler. I heard the engine. I turned around and..." The girl held a fist to her trembling lips. "It just took off, shot off right into the ditch. Caleb flew through the air and...he hit his head on those rocks." Falling against Trixie, she said, "Oh, Miss Trixie, I'm so sorry. What have I done?"

"Shhh," Trixie had said, soothing, touching, her gestures nervous and erratic as she'd watched Logan moving like a zombie up the shallow, muddy incline. "It's not even that deep here. How could...?"

She'd let go of Samantha to walk slowly toward Logan, her eyes searching his face, her heart dropping with the weight of fear and dread. How could she ever forget the look on his face, so cold, so stony, so…accusing. "Logan?"

He didn't answer her. He just keep walking, faster now, never stopping until he'd reached his horse. With a walkie-talkie he pulled from his saddle bag, he radioed Harlan back at the house and told him in a clipped, calm voice to call 911. Then he slid back down into the ditch, doing what he could for his son.

Horrified, Trixie stared down at the scene, her arms hugging her chest as she watched Logan carefully cushion his son's neck with a rolled-up saddle blanket for support. Then he covered Caleb with his heavy twill duster.

The tiny hand Logan touched with his bigger hand drooped like a broken feather. In spite of Logan's calm, reassuring words, Caleb's eyes remained closed. His face, so pale and serene, looked, other than the bright red spot of blood congealing at the base of his skull, like that of a sleeping angel.

"Logan?" She realized she sounded panicky and frantic, but she rushed down to him, oblivious to the mud and slippery rocks, pulling Samantha along with her. "Logan, please, tell me—is he still—"

"He's alive," Logan growled, his words low and full of a misery she would never, ever be able to forget. "We…*I* have to get him to the hospital." With that, he turned away, giving all of his attention back to his son.

"I'm coming with you," she said as she fell down beside him, her eyes on the little boy lying between them.

Logan didn't look at her or answer her. He just sat

there holding on to his son, willing the little boy to hang on, his whispered encouragements becoming more and more urgent with each moment.

Trixie thought she would go insane with the waiting. Time seemed to stop. It seemed as if the whole ranch stilled, waiting, hoping. The rain slowed to a fine, silent mist. The air was still as the minutes slid slowly by. The only sound was that of water dripping off the yellow-green leaves of nearby trees.

"Where are they?" Logan finally asked, the impatience in his voice tempered with a hint of fear as he checked Caleb's pulse yet again.

Finally, off in the distance, they heard the screaming sirens crashing through the still silence, the urgency of their whine only mirroring the urgent scream inside Trixie's pounding head.

"I'm coming with you," she repeated, her eyes searching Logan's face.

He whirled, the look he shot her full of venom and anger. "No."

"Logan?" Her whole body trembled with fear, with a tragic sickening. "Logan, I want to help you."

He didn't answer her. Instead, Logan hopped up, motioning with waving arms to the approaching ambulance. Then he rushed toward the paramedics, explaining what had happened, the urgency of the situation his only focus now. He ignored Gayle's frantic calls as she jumped out of the ambulance cab and ran toward them; he ignored everything and everyone except his son. He waited, letting the experts do their stuff, then he followed them as they hurriedly lifted the stretcher into the ambulance, then he hopped in after them without a word to anyone.

Trixie watched, her heart shattering, when Logan

once again took his son's hand and began crooning softly to him. With a look of hope and a gentle touch to his son's forehead, he wrapped the fresh blanket the emergency crew had provided over Caleb's body.

Gayle climbed into the ambulance with Logan before Trixie could. When she would have protested, both Gayle and Logan glared at her with such a harsh, pronouncing statement, she backed away, her hands to her mouth, her eyes filling with tears.

They were both obviously too distraught for her to argue with them right now. Besides, Caleb belonged to them; they had every right to be there with him. While she, she was an outsider who had no right, no reason to ride in that ambulance. Except that she cared.

"We'll take your car," Samantha said, seeing the worry on Trixie's face. The youth counselor became the calm one now, the one who knew what had to be done. "C'mon, Miss Trixie. Just let me leave someone in charge of the other kids. I'll get one of the adult volunteers."

She rushed off, her braids flowing out behind her.

Then Harlan pulled up, jumped out of his car and came trudging up the lane, surprise and concern etching his wrinkled face. "What in the world? Logan didn't give me all the details, and I'm too old to make this long walk in a hurry."

He took one look at Trixie's face and placed both arms on hers to steady her. "What's happened, girl?"

Trixie swallowed, shuddered, fell into his open embrace. "Caleb—he had an accident on the four-wheeler. He...he won't wake up. Granddaddy, he won't wake up."

"Let's go," Harlan said, not even stopping to get his Stetson. After convincing Samantha to stay on the ranch with the other frightened children, he insisted on driving, since Trixie was too shaken to maneuver the slippery highways.

So now here she sat, in a corner, in the cold, condemning lights of a sharp-angled, steel-encased waiting room. Waiting. Waiting.

It seemed she'd been waiting for something, someone, since the day she'd left another hospital's maternity ward so long ago. Now she only wanted Caleb to wake up and tell her that he was the best all-around cowboy in the world. *Just that one thing, Lord,* she prayed over and over again. *Just let him be all right.*

It didn't matter right now that Logan was as distant and cold as he'd been the day she'd returned to the ranch. It didn't matter that Gayle sat dry-eyed and silent, her eyes staring straight ahead, her expression grim. It didn't matter that she couldn't break through their pain, their hostility, except to know that they were hurting, afraid, dreading what the doctor might tell them any minute.

Trixie wanted to offer comfort; indeed, she'd tried. But Logan had only pushed her away. She had the sinking feeling that he blamed her, because he'd been with her at the time of the accident. But right now she didn't care about that. Right now she only wanted Caleb to be all right.

She got up to try again. Logan stood looking out a huge window at the end of the hall, his hands braced so tightly against the window frame, she could see the white of his hair-dusted knuckles underneath his permanent tan.

"Logan?"

"Not now," he snarled without even turning to see her.

She wanted to touch him, wanted to hold him close and promise him that Caleb would pull through, but his rejection pressed at her and tore through her, making her see that in spite of how much he claimed to love her, he was still holding back from her. He couldn't share this with her, because he still wasn't ready to let her be a part of his life.

Telling herself that now wasn't the time to wallow in self-pity, she sat back down. Now...now she had to concentrate on praying for Caleb. Now she had to be strong and quiet, for Logan's sake. Soon, Caleb would be just fine, and she and Logan could have that long talk they'd wanted to have. They could whisper by candlelight and make plans for the ranch and for...

For what? she had to ask herself, the glaring reality of her secret sin shouting down the efficient hallway at her. Did she really believe she could have a future with Logan? They'd never really gone beyond admitting their love for each other. And today, just when they were making progress, this terrible tragedy had happened to remind them that they'd always been dangerous for each other. What now? What next?

What if Caleb didn't make it?

She heard the doors from the examining room open. Dr. James Arnold, the neurologist assigned to Caleb's case, came marching out of the set of double doors leading from the operating room down the hallway, his face stern, his eyes guarded and dark with knowledge and secrets.

Logan turned, his gaze sweeping over the doctor, his hand reaching out. "Tell me," he said, his voice raw, his words a rasp.

Dr. Arnold, tall, with a thick head of wispy brown hair, stood with his hands behind his sterile hospital scrubs. "I'm not going to beat around the bush with you, Mr. Maxwell. Your son suffered a traumatic head wound, but the good news is—the brain wasn't affected as badly as we first thought. His wounds were serious, though—there was some swelling in the brain. We found a small blood clot, so we had to fix that to relieve the pressure."

"Surgery?" Gayle said, her hand going to her heart. Because her son couldn't bring himself to ask it, she did. "Will…will there be any…brain damage?"

Trixie closed her eyes, willing, praying, telling herself that couldn't happen. That just could not happen.

The doctor's features softened, but the look in his eyes was honest. "It's too soon to tell. In a perfect world, the swelling will go down and the brain will mend on its own. And little Caleb will wake up and be fine."

Logan turned with a grunt and hit the edge of his fist against the side of a soft-drink machine, the echo of his frustration and helpless rage resounding down the hallway.

Rubbing his throbbing hand, he said, "But this isn't a perfect world, is it, Doc? And you can't tell me that my little boy is going to be the same when he wakes up. You can't even tell me if he's going to live or die."

Dr. Arnold didn't reprimand Logan, but he didn't back down, either. "Hope springs eternal, Mr. Maxwell."

Logan's laugh was bitter and hard edged. "Yeah, right. Hope. There's always hope, isn't there?" He looked around then, at his mother, at Trixie, at Harlan. "I've been clinging to hope for so long…I'm tired, you know? Just plain tired.'' Then, he stepped close, his face inches from the doctor's, his eyes bright with tears he refused to allow or acknowledge. ''But, I'll tell you this. I won't give up on that little boy in there.'' He pointed down the hall, toward the ominous looking double doors, toward the room where his child lay. ''I won't give up on him. You see, he's the only thing I've got left.''

The doctor took Logan's impassioned declaration in stride. He'd seen it before so many times. ''The power of hope,'' he said, his voice low and filled with compassion, ''the power of prayer, Mr. Maxwell, can sometimes move mountains that mere doctors have to walk away from. I could use your help with that.'' He looked around the small group. ''All of you.''

Trixie never thought she could hurt any worse. She'd thought giving her own child away had been the worst pain imaginable, but she'd been wrong, so wrong. Watching Logan now, seeing him go through this terrible grief, this waiting, this not knowing, was killing her slowly and softly. Well, she wasn't going to let it happen.

Without a word she stalked down the hall, intent on finding the hospital chapel.

Harlan rushed after her, his old eyes haggard with worry. ''Where you going, child?''

''To pray,'' she said simply.

Her grandfather nodded, then turned back to comfort Gayle.

When Trixie turned at the elevator, she saw Logan staring at her, his expression harsh and hard, unyielding. Whatever resentment and bitterness he felt toward her, whatever silent, secret pain he now suffered, she understood. And for once in her life, for once, somehow, she intended to make things right.

She'd pray Caleb well.

And then she'd get as far away from Logan as possible.

Because she could never, ever put him through this kind of hurt again.

Which meant she couldn't possibly tell him the truth.

Logan stood by his son's bed, holding one tiny hand in his bigger one, hoping that little bit of contact would bring Caleb out of his unconscious state. He couldn't help but relive the nightmare of the past few hours, couldn't help but take on the guilt of not being there when his son had needed him the most.

No, instead, he'd been kissing Tricia Maria Dunaway, and pledging his undying love to her yet again. And again that love had cost him.

His son was in a coma.

Maybe it was time he just told her the truth.

He wanted to blame someone; might as well be Trixie. After all, he'd certainly blamed her all of these years, and he was sure blaming her right this minute. Why not just go ahead and get it all out of his system?

Would that save his son?

Would that save his soul?

Holding Caleb's hand tightly in his, he talked in a low, shaky voice. "There's so much, son," he began, wishing, hoping he could find the courage to see this through. "There's so much I need to tell you. Do you know how much your Daddy loves you? Do you?"

The little body didn't move a muscle. The eyes remained closed behind the lush brown lashes. Caleb's face looked so peaceful, so calm, while his father's

whole body screamed with a silent, taut tension that
begged to be released.

"C'mon, Caleb," he tried again, determination willing the hitch in his voice to go away. "Wake up, cowboy. Gotta get back up on that horse. Isn't that what
your...isn't that what Brant used to tell you when you
fell down and skinned your knee?"

Logan stopped, waiting, watching, his eyes misting
over in spite of his resolve not to cry. With a stubborn
swipe of the back of his hand across his face, he dashed
the tears away. "Courage, son. Courage. And I don't
mean the kind where you act the fool. I mean real courage. You don't have to be a bull rider, son. Not for
me." Gripping Caleb's hand, rubbing his son's arm
with his other hand, he added, "All you have to do is
find the courage to wake up. Just wake up, Caleb."

Courage. The one word resounded like an echo
through Logan's frazzled brain. Here he stood, demanding, begging, his son to wake up, when he himself
had been asleep for so long. Did he have the right to
teach Caleb about courage, when he'd never known the
meaning of the word himself?

Gayle came into the room then, her eyes red rimmed,
her expression wilted and tired. "Let me sit with him
a spell," she said, dismissing her son with a pat on the
arm. "I'll call you right away if he wakes up, I promise."

Logan nodded, then turned to face his mother. "I do
need to take care of something."

"Logan?" she asked, her eyes lifting to her son's,
frightened and filled with worry.

"I have to do it, Mama," he replied, knowing her
question before she even asked it. "It's high time I own
up to my responsibilities."

Gayle didn't try to stop him. Instead, she touched a hand to his hair, lifting the wispy strains away from his forehead much in the same way she'd done when he was young. "I think you're right. Maybe it is time to let go of all the lies and the heartache."

Lies and heartache. Trixie sat in the quiet hospital chapel, a small, square room with a white altar, mauve silk flowers and soft lightning. A room full of peace and calm, a beacon for all the confused souls that came screaming and shouting to God in their time of need.

Did God listen to someone like her? she had to wonder. Did He answer the prayers of the unworthy, of those who'd only brought lies and heartache with them to his altar?

"I'm asking You now, God," she said, her head lifting to the stained-glass window rising over the altar. "I'm not asking for myself, but for Caleb. I'm asking You to make him better, to help him to wake up."

She sat silent for a minute, groping for an answer. "This child...this child means so much to his father, to his grandmother, to me. Please, Lord, let him be okay. Just let him be all right."

From the back of the room, Trixie heard a noise. Twisting in her spot on one of the smooth wooden pews, she turned to see Logan standing there, the double doors swinging behind him. The look on his face, that look of torment and dread she'd seen so many times these past few days, was evident as he stalked toward her.

"Where were you?" he asked, anger pulsating through every vein of his body. "Where were you, Tricia Maria, when Caleb needed you the most?"

Thinking he was angry with her because he'd been

with her when Caleb got hurt, she lifted her gaze to him. "I'm sorry, Logan. I know you feel guilty for not being there when...when Caleb took off in the four-wheeler—"

"Yeah, I feel guilty. You're right about that. I shouldn't have turned my back, but I did. For you. Always for you. But I'm not talking about what happened today, Trixie."

Trying to find some measure of calm amidst her confusion, she asked, "Then what are you talking about?"

Logan pushed his way to her to stand over her, then he pointed an accusing finger in her face. "I'm talking about what happened between us eight years ago. I mean, where were you when he was a baby? Where were you when he had to be fed in the middle of the night? When he cut his first tooth? When he learned to walk?"

A stunning, sickening realization poured through Trixie's entire system. Even as the magnitude of Logan's condemning questions swept through her, she brought her hands up to her mouth, then shook her head in denial. "I don't know what you mean."

He yanked her up then, his face inches from her own, his eyes condemning and full of judgment. "Yes, you do. You know exactly what I mean. You see, I know all about it, Trixie. I know you gave our son away right after he was born."

If Logan hadn't been holding her, she would have fallen to the floor and fainted. She felt the blood rushing away from her head, felt her pulse increasing to a dangerously high level, felt the imprint of his hands on her arms, steadying her, holding her up even as he held her body away.

"You know?" she managed to ask, stunned that he'd

kept it a secret all of this time. Stunned with understanding. This, this was why he'd resented her so much! He'd known, dear God, he'd known from the very beginning. And if what he was telling her now was the truth—

"Oh, yeah, I know," Logan said, the confession pouring through him like a rushing river tearing through a dam. "I've known since the day your father brought Caleb to the ranch when he was only a few days old—to his home, to me." Holding her close, his hands gripping her arms, his eyes boring into her, he said, "I know, because, you see, I'm his father. But you already know that, of course. At least that much isn't a lie."

He let her go then, stepping back to run his hands through his hair, his anger at both himself and her boiling down to a slow simmer. Then he looked her in the eyes and told her in a voice quiet with honesty, "But what you didn't know, what I didn't tell you is—you're his mother."

His mother! Images, blurred and hazy, rushed through Trixie's numb mind. This couldn't be true. This had to be some sort of cruel joke.

"No!"

At her gasp of shock, Logan nodded, watching as she gripped the back of the nearest pew for support. "That's right. That's the truth, at last. The little boy lying in that hospital bed is the child you gave up, Trixie. Caleb is your son."

Chapter Twelve

The cruelty of his words struck her with the force of a cold, hard slap.

And then the reality of what he'd just told her set in, causing her whole world to shift off its carefully built foundation.

In that instant all the time she'd spent with Caleb came rushing back, poignant and sweet, flashing through her consciousness like the pages of a photo album. And so did the evasiveness she'd seen in both Logan and Gayle, the distrust she'd sensed from both of them. That image tainted her world, her whole outlook, while it explained so much.

So much. So much time wasted, so many lies told.

Backing away, she shook her head again, her hands covering her mouth. "No, you're lying. That can't be possible. That can't be true."

Logan belatedly realized what he'd just done. He'd let his own rage and guilt color his judgment. Now, seeing the tortured look on her beautiful face, he instantly regretted his actions. He'd never meant to be so blunt, so insensitive.

Reaching for her, he said, "I'm sorry, Trixie. I didn't want to tell you like this, but...well, with everything that's happened..." Groping for the right words now, he finished with a defeated sigh. "I'm so worried, I wasn't thinking straight."

Trixie pushed at him, instinctively trying to get away, then, as the full impact of his words hit her, she came at him with both fists, beating her hands against his chest with all her might. "How could you do this? How could anyone be so cruel, so callous? How? Why?"

Logan stood stoic and still, letting her beat out all of her frustrations and helpless anger on him. He certainly deserved it. And the physical blows didn't hurt half as much as the dejection and hurt in her blue eyes. That was the part he couldn't take.

Funny, he'd always envisioned this very moment, when he would tell her the truth about Caleb. He'd always dreamed of it, thinking he'd feel some small measure of vengeance and triumph. Now, he only felt empty and lost, bitter with himself, guilty for all he'd been a part of, for how he'd made her suffer. And until this very moment, he'd never fully realized just how much she must have suffered. But her misery, her anguish, was there on her face, bruising her, changing her, making her look so vulnerable and afraid. And destroyed.

Now he had to wonder why he'd ever agreed to any of this. Too late. Way too late to start wondering now.

Up until now, he'd laid all the blame at her feet because he'd believed she didn't care enough to fight for their child, for their love. Well, he'd played a big part in this deliberate charade, and because of that he'd probably lost her forever. Because of that his son might not ever know his real mother.

Logan stood there, seeing Trixie in a new light, seeing the girl who'd become the woman, seeing the innocence of ignorance, blissful ignorance, stripped from her face, along with what little pride she had left.

He wouldn't make her suffer anymore. It was time he told her everything. High time he learned to trust in God and his own faith. He could only hope he hadn't learned too late.

So he stood, holding her while she fought against him, holding her while she cried and sobbed and finally, went completely limp in his arms. Then he pulled her close and hugged her, trying to give comfort where none could be found, trying to find comfort in the arms of the woman he loved.

Finally he lifted her chin with a thumb, and looked into her eyes, for the first time with complete, absolute honesty. "I've wanted to tell you for so long."

Trixie still shook from the shock of it. But through the shock, through the numbing realization, came a little bit of sheer joy. "Caleb is my son," she said on a whispery, breathless voice. "Caleb is my son."

Logan guided her back to one of the pews, then sat down beside her, his arm still around her shoulders. "Yes, he certainly is."

He'd seen that little bit of her in Caleb each and every day of the boy's life. In the blue of his big eyes, in the impish way he tried to get the best of both his father and his grandmother. In the way he'd doted on Brant Dunaway. She was there, had always been there in Caleb's very essence. Each time his son laughed or cried, Logan was reminded of the woman who'd given birth to him, the woman who'd been forced to give him up.

Logan understood that now. Just like him, Trixie had

been forced to choose. And it felt good to be able to share this with her at last. At long last.

She got up. "I have to go see him."

"I want you to see him," he said, pushing her back down. "But first, I want you to know everything."

"Why?" she said, her eyes lifting to his. "Why didn't anyone tell me?"

Logan knew the truth was far from being told. There was still more hurt to wade through.

"Well," he began, ripping a hand through his hair, trying to tell her straight, "after you and I...after Brant caught us together, well, you remember how you pleaded with him not to fire me?"

She nodded. She remembered every impassioned word. "I told him I'd never see you again, if he'd just let you keep your job."

"And he did. He never could resist anything you asked of him, and he was a very forgiving person. So it only stands to reason that when you asked him to help you save your baby—"

Trixie hitched another sob. "He did," she said, love for her father pouring through her battered system. "He...he saved my son." Her eyes widened, filled with tears again. "I begged him to. But...he never told me what he did. He never told me."

Logan nodded, then ran a hand over the beard stubble on his face, feeling so drained, so very tired. "But it cost him, Trixie. It cost all of us."

She gripped his arm, a steely determination keeping the anger at bay, keeping the impact of this latest revelation at a distance, until she knew the whole story. "Tell me, Logan. I want to hear all of it."

Logan leaned back against the support of the pew, weary to the bone, his voice raw and raspy. "Pamela called him and told him you were pregnant. She blamed him, of course, for letting you run loose on the ranch, for not watching you, for not watching me. Of course, he didn't tell me any of this until later.''

''So you didn't know about the baby right away?''

''No. All I knew was that I loved you and that your father hadn't shot me on sight.''

She almost smiled. ''He was pretty mad at both of us.''

''Yeah, but your mother was even madder, especially at Brant. She made him feel so guilty, especially when she found out he hadn't fired me. She claimed he was putting my welfare above yours.'' He paused, weighed his next words. ''She also accused him of doing it to protect my mother. Or as she termed it, his mistress.''

Trixie gasped, stunned. ''But that's not true. Your mother told me how things stood between her and my father.''

''Yes, but Pamela wanted to think the worst.''

Trixie closed her eyes, a terrible scene playing in her mind. How Logan must have hated her when he found out the truth. And Gayle. No wonder the woman had been so hostile toward her. Lowering her head, she said, ''I can't believe this.''

Logan's next words were rough with emotion. ''Brant took her badgering pretty calmly, but when Pamela insisted that you had to give the baby up, he fought for you. He told me all of this later, after…after he'd forgiven both of us, after he'd seen his new grandson. He fought for you, Trixie.''

Trixie gazed over at him, wishing she had known, wishing she had had even a glimpse of her baby. Bitterness choked her words. ''But mother won, as usual.''

''Yeah, I think he had a hard time turning her down,

too. He was rough and tough, but he had the softest heart. He went off into the mountains and he didn't come home until he thought it all through. He wanted to do what was right and fair. And, he wanted to protect his daughter.''

Logan's words, spoken in such a loving reverence, only added to Trixie's own anguish. She sat silent, remembering bits and pieces of things she'd long ago buried. ''So when I called him, begging him to help me, he came, and he had both my mother and me to contend with.''

Logan nodded, calmer now, determined to tell her everything. ''He was torn. Pamela wanted to hide you away and then get rid of the baby as quickly and quietly as possible.''

That hurt. That hurt so very much. But Trixie was used to her mother's misguided shame. It had been her own for so long now. ''They never once allowed me to call you or see you, Logan, or to even give you a say in the matter. She told me she'd make it hard for you and your mother. And she would have.''

He nodded again, then frowned. ''You don't have to remind me of Pamela's power. She wielded it over Brant and over your grandfather.''

Shocked, Trixie stared at him. ''Granddaddy knows?''

''Everybody knows but you,'' he admitted. When she would have said more, he held up a hand. ''Just let me finish. I need to get this all out of my system.''

She sat back, silent and brooding. All this time she'd felt so guilty, so worthless for her deceit. And all this time, she'd been deceived by the people she'd trusted the most. ''Go on,'' she said in a small voice.

''They argued, a lot. Harlan and Brant wanted to raise

the child as a Dunaway. Pamela refused. She threatened, she manipulated, she promised to make life unbearable for everyone involved. Finally Brant told her that he would raise the child here in Arkansas, on the ranch. Once he made up his mind, he was pretty determined, from what he told me later. Pamela knew when to call it quits, but she also saw this as a prime opportunity to get her way."

Shuddering, Trixie doubled over, the pain of her feelings so physical, it racked her stomach. "He did it to help me. He wanted to help me."

"Yes, but Pamela made sure he paid a price for his request. You see, she was concerned about me. She hated me."

Trixie nodded her understanding. "No, she wouldn't want you involved, even if she didn't care enough about the baby to raise it herself."

She refused to think about all of that now. Right now, she only wanted the complete truth, no matter how painful.

And the pain got much, much worse.

Reaching out to take her hand, Logan continued, his words deadly calm, too calm. "They struck up a deal. You would give birth to the baby, then they would take it away. To protect you, they wouldn't allow you to see it or even know if it was a boy or a girl."

The tears flowed down Trixie's face, silent and purging, while she listened and thought about Caleb's beautiful little face and the big blue eyes that looked exactly like Brant Dunaway's. If she hadn't been so preoccupied with the ranch and Logan, she might have seen it earlier. The truth she'd wanted, needed, so badly, had been staring her in the face all along.

Logan's grip on her hand tightened. "Brant agreed

to take the child and bring it to the ranch. He would tell me the truth and allow me to be with my child.''

Trixie heard the raw pain in his voice, felt the tension in his hand on hers. ''And?''

''And in return for that favor, for that privilege, neither Brant nor I could ever have any contact with you again. Even if you tried to see either of us or visit the ranch, we had to turn you away. Oh, and I could never tell you the truth. Never. That was the only way I would be allowed to raise my own child. If I hadn't been so angry and hurt, I would have fought them all, but all I could think about was that you didn't want our baby.''

Trixie turned to face him, the blur of tears that clouded her eyes matching the misty regret she saw in Logan's gaze.

''I'm sorry,'' he said, tears flowing down his face now. ''So very sorry.'' Wanting, needing her to understand, he said, ''Do you know how hard that was—to have to make that choice? But…I never knew my father. All I knew was that he had abandoned me, left my mother and me. Trixie, I just couldn't do that to my son. I couldn't. So, I chose him over you. You weren't the only one who gave everything up. I had to give you up, so I could have my son with me.''

''Oh, Logan.'' She pulled him to her, holding him, rocking him in her arms. ''What other choice did you have? I know all about the power and persuasion of the Dunaway dollars. I know you would have done anything, anything to protect Caleb.''

''Except tell his mother,'' he said, the weight of his guilt suffocating him. He raised his head, then brought his hands up to her face. ''Do you know how much I loved you? You can't know how many times I thought about taking Caleb and running away, to find you. I wanted to, so bad. Then I remembered that I was just a field hand and you—you had this wonderful, bright future that didn't include a bum and a baby. So I went off to college at Brant's insistence, and I left my baby with him and my mother—I only saw Caleb on weekdays and holidays. Then I married Donna, just to ease the pain, just to have someone, anyone to share my beautiful boy with. And the whole time I thought about you, and how you'd just given him up without a fight.''

Trixie smoothed his hair off his hot brow. ''And I bet my mother made sure you heard all about me, or at least her version of my life.''

''She kept Brant posted, and because I was so bitter, I assumed you just didn't care, that you had put all of this behind you, that you never really wanted the baby. So I let my anger be my shield, and I took it out on Donna. I hated you, so I made her life miserable.''

''So she left you, too. And that's why she doesn't have anything to do with Caleb.''

''Yeah. Donna loved the baby, but she couldn't stick around to be a mother to him. We both—Caleb and me—we were a constant reminder of you.'' He lowered his head, then glanced over at her. ''And the whole time, the whole time, I thought you didn't care. Brant tried to tell me, but I wouldn't listen. All of these years, I thought you didn't love our child or me.''

''No,'' Trixie said in defense of herself. ''I always wanted our child. Always. All those years ago, I dreamed about being with you and our baby. Then, as time passed, I had to give up on that dream. I thought it could never be possible after what I'd done, and so I let my mother rule my life, because I just didn't care anymore.'' Her voice barely above a whisper, she added, "And she knew. All of this time, my mother knew."

Logan couldn't bring himself to voice how he felt about Pamela Dunaway. Instead he said, "She'd send money, but she never even asked about Caleb. Not once. I think she considered that her way of paying me off, for my silence. But I never wanted her money. Brant put it in a trust fund for Caleb, though. He said that it was Dunaway money, and it belonged to his grandson."

Trixie closed her eyes, willing the anger and pain to stay away just a little longer. "All of this time, I thought my daddy didn't love me anymore. I thought he was ashamed of me, the same way my mother was ashamed. But he did love me. He loved me enough to make sure my child, his grandchild had a safe, loving home. He gave me up so he could protect our baby. He kept his promise."

Reaching her hands up to cover Logan's, she gulped back another sob. "Oh, Logan. Logan, help me, help me. I don't think—"

"I'm here," he said, pulling her into his arms again. "I'm here now, Trixie, and I promise I won't desert you or hide away anymore, like the coward I've been. Caleb is our son, together. No more secrets or lies. And no more placing blame."

She held tightly to him, his strength, his courage making her feel so much better. Then she lifted her head, "But he's so sick. Logan, he has to pull through."

Logan stared up at the altar, his expression grim. "I wonder…is God punishing us for all this? Is this His way of showing us we can't play with people's lives?"

She rubbed her hand over his, horrified that he could even think such a thing. "No, no. God wouldn't do that, not to Caleb, anyway. He's so innocent in all of this. We have to believe that, Logan. God wouldn't let him die, not now, not when I've finally found him again.''

Without another word between them, they held hands and turned toward the stained-glass window shining down on them. And together they prayed for their son's life.

"One more chance, Lord," Logan said. "That's all we ask of you. One more chance to make things right with our son."

A gentle silence flowed around them, offering comfort, offering honesty, offering hope.

Offering redemption, at last.

The silence didn't last long, however. Pamela showed up bright and early the next morning, decked in jewels and jealousy, determined to get her daughter out of the clutches of what she termed "these Arkansas heathens."

Spotting Trixie and Logan as they came out of pediatric intensive care, she swept across the hospital corridor in crisp blue linen, her eyes flashing fire at Logan before she turned a pouting face toward her daughter. "I've come to take you home."

Trixie didn't know whether to scream or cry. She'd just spent the past few minutes with her son, watching him, touching him, crooning to him, hoping against hope to make him hear her, see her, know her. That had been her ritual all during the night, standing by her son's bed, along with his father, in the few precious minutes when they were allowed in to see him.

Her son.

Even now, hours after Logan had told her that remarkable truth, after she'd walked into Caleb's room with that new, bursting knowledge and touched a tentative hand to his, she still felt a surge of joy rushing through her system each time she said the words in her head.

Her son.

Her son, who now lay in there, so alone, so deep in a dream world, so at peace even when those around him seemed to be falling completely apart, even when his world was changing with each passing minute. Her son, whom her mother had kept away from her all of these years, a little boy who'd been bartered and used, to gain what Pamela believed to be the best for her daughter.

And now, Pamela was here, without a thought for him, demanding that she come home? Suddenly she knew where her home was, and that she would never leave it, or Caleb, again.

"What kind of mother are you?" Trixie said to Pamela in a deadly level tone, her eyes centered on her mother's shocked face. Logan's hand on her arm steadied her enough to keep her from lashing out even more.

"The kind who cares about her daughter's reputation," Pamela replied evenly as she raked her gaze over Logan with unabashed disdain. "Rad is inconsolable, of course, and everyone is talking. This behavior is scandalous, Tricia Maria, and I won't stand for it any longer."

"Tough, because I'm not going anywhere with *you*," Trixie replied, letting go of Logan to push past Pamela before she did something that would really give people cause to talk.

"Tricia Maria, don't do this!"

She could hear her mother's high heels clicking on the hospital tiles, right behind her. It seemed as if that sound had followed her all of her life, taunting her with guilt and blame, haunting her with regret and reprimand.

Waiting until they were out of earshot of the others, Trixie turned to face Pamela, the look on her face causing her mother to step back. "Mother, I don't think I can discuss any of this with you right now. In fact, I want you to leave."

Her mother took one look at her face and suddenly realized the cause of Trixie's unbridled hostility.

"Oh, oh, you know, don't you?" Pamela said on a small gasp of breath. Lifting her chin, she glared down the corridor at Logan. "Of course, *he* couldn't wait to tell you."

Shaking her head, Trixie said, "He waited over seven years, Mother. He waited from the day Caleb was born until now, when he's lying in there near death. Isn't that enough punishment, even for you?"

Pamela lifted her head, surprise temporarily replacing snobbery. "What do you mean, near death? No one would tell me anything when I arrived at the ranch. They just said the boy had had an accident and you were here."

Amazed at her mother's self-involved existence, she said, "Yes, I'm here. Finally. But I should have been here long ago. I'm here, but now it might be too late. The boy, Caleb—his name is Caleb—hit his head after he crashed a four-wheeler, Mother. The boy, who happens to be your grandson by the way, might die."

The impact of that statement stopped Pamela in her kid leather handmade pumps. "Oh, my. Oh, my," she said as she sank down in the nearest chair. "How awful."

Trixie stared down at her, her tone harsh. "Yes, how awful. Another messy tidbit for you to try and clean up and hide under your self-righteous carpet. Hurry, Mother, run fast so you won't be caught associating with this group of sinners and losers.''

Appalled, Pamela said, ''Now, there's really no need to be so vulgar, Tricia.''

''Vulgar?'' Trixie hissed the word at her mother. ''Vulgar? I'll tell you what's vulgar! Vulgar is the way you manipulated my father and Logan into doing this. Vulgar is the way you cajoled my grandfather into going along with this scheme of yours. Vulgar is the way you used a child, *my* child, Mother, to get your own way. When are you going to stop playing with people's lives? When?''

Pamela didn't speak. Instead, she just sat looking up at her daughter. Finally, with a long-suffering sigh, she said, ''I only did what I thought was best. And I'm truly sorry that the child is hurt. But, think, Tricia, think. You can't possibly tell that boy who you really are. Not now.'' Her shrug was as indifferent as it was elegant. ''Why, it's way too late now. You would only make things worse for him, and for yourself, too, of course.''

Without taking a breath, without stopping to see the pain her words were inflicting on her daughter, Pamela rushed on, ''No, let's just leave things the way they are. I'll take care of all his hospital expenses, of course. He'll have the best of care. But you, you need to come on back home to Dallas, darling, and patch things up with Rad—I've already smoothed the way there for you. He loves you, so he's willing to forgive and forget. Then you can put all of this behind you for good. It's really for the best.''

Trixie gasped in horror as she realized that once again, her mother was trying to manipulate her life. Once again, Pamela was willing to pay any price to keep all of this a secret. And she was also willing to pull out all the stops to keep her daughter away from Logan and the baby Trixie had given up so long ago. Oh, she knew exactly which buttons to push. Only this time she'd pushed too far.

But she was right. How could Trixie just march into Caleb's room and announce, ''Oh, glad you're all right and by the way, I'm your mother.''

The brief period of joy Trixie had felt at finding out the truth was gone now, replaced by the cold, ugly glare of her mother's spiteful, pointed observations. How would she ever be able to face her son? How could a mother tell a child that she'd let him go and now she was back to make up for all the lost time, all the lost dreams?

The anger, the shock, the delayed reaction to everything that had happened in the past few days and hours, hit Trixie squarely in the face as she stood there looking down at her mother's beautiful, deceitful, hypocritical face, every nerve in her body going into overload.

''Was it best,'' she began, spitting the words at Pamela, her hands shaking, her mind raging, ''to take a child from its mother? Was it best to make Logan and my own father choose between that child and me? Was it best to have everyone involved in the situation lie, including me? How can you actually sit there and say that to me with a straight face, Mother? How can you spout out platitudes about Christian values, when you've never applied those values to your own life? How?''

Pamela stopped pretending then. Frightened, she stood to try and touch her daughter, to offer comfort. But Trixie was beyond comfort. With a growl she shook

Pamela's hand away. "If Caleb dies, I will never forgive you."

With that she headed out the door, out of the hospital, away from the pain and the agony of all that she had lost, of all the minutes and hours of tiny pleasures she'd been denied with her son. She longed to go to him, to shake him awake, to make him see that she loved him so very dearly. But in her heart she felt she didn't deserve to be here. She didn't deserve his love, and she certainly didn't deserve Logan's love. No wonder he'd hated her all of these years. It was no more than she hated herself right now.

And, for his sake, for her son's sake, she would probably never be able to tell Caleb that she was his mother. If he even lived to see her face again.

She headed out the lobby, mindless of Logan calling to her.

"Trixie, wait. Wait, please. Trixie, come back. Caleb needs you. I need you."

Meeting Harlan on the steps, she said, "Give me the car keys."

Her grandfather looked her over and shook his head. "No. You're in no condition to drive."

Angry at him too, she retorted, "And you're in no position to stop me."

Hurt, Harlan reluctantly handed her the keys. "I'm sorry, child," he said as he watched her hurry away.

Trixie turned back, respect for her grandfather overriding her own frustration. Running back to grab him by the arm, she said, "I don't blame you. I blame myself. I should have fought harder. I should have come back here to Logan."

"I know that now," Harlan said, his eyes watering up. "I wasn't thinking straight back then. I was only worried about the Dunaway name. I forgot to worry about the Dunaway family. I should have stood by you.''

"I understand," Trixie said. "And...I just want to go to my father's grave, just for a little while. I have some...some things to say to him."

Harlan let her go then, with a loving pat on the arm. "Okay, but be careful. And, Trixie, remember that he loved you above all else."

"I know that now," she replied as she walked away. "Granddaddy," she said over her shoulder, her voice hitching, "stay with him, please. Stay with Caleb until I can...until I can face him again."

"I will," Harlan replied. "But...you come on back when you're feeling better about things, okay?"

Trixie didn't answer him. She wasn't sure if she'd ever feel better about things.

Logan, however, wasn't going to let her get away so easily this time. "Trixie, wait," he said as he headed her off at Harlan's car. "Don't leave."

She lifted her gaze to his, saw the pain of her soul mirrored in his troubled eyes. "I have to...I have to think about all of this. I...I don't think I should be here when he wakes up. I don't want to confuse him."

Logan touched a hand to her face. "You won't. He needs you. You're his mother. Right now that's all that matters. We'll work out the details later."

She looked down at the door handle. "But he doesn't know that—he doesn't know me. How can we ever tell him that?"

"We'll work it out somehow," Logan said, his rough hand soft on her skin. "Will you come back inside?"

She shook her head, then looked down. "I can't. I'm so ashamed."

Pulling her close, Logan said, "We all played a part in this, honey. And I won't let you go off alone in this shape." Anger coloring his next statement, he added, "And I won't let your mother do this to you, to us, again. Don't listen to her, Trixie."

Running a hand through her hair, Trixie whispered, "I just need some time alone. I can't be in the same room with my mother right now." Then, "Logan, I want to go see my father. I need to talk to him, I need to be near him right now."

Understanding dawning in his eyes, Logan nodded, then backed away. "Okay. Fine. You need to be near Brant? Then come on back and stay by your son's side. That's where a part of your father will always be. I mean it, Trixie. I won't let you go this time."

She had to know. "Even if Caleb dies?"

Logan's face turned ashen. "He won't. Remember, God didn't bring us this far without a reason. I'm counting on that to save my son's life. And I'm counting on you, to stay here this time. Don't run away again."

Trixie watched as he reached out a hand to her.

She didn't want to leave Caleb. But after the sickening conversation with her mother, she felt dirty and disillusioned. Caleb had Logan to watch over him. He'd always had his father. Always. And thankfully he'd had his grandfather for a few years at least.

But he might not ever have his mother. And the fact that he might not even have her in the last hours of his young life only added to her agony. He might die, never knowing, never seeing, how much she loved him.

Unless she was there by his side, regardless of the outcome. Gulping back fresh tears, she took Logan's hand. She couldn't leave Caleb. Even with her mother's cruel words ringing inside her head, she still couldn't leave her little boy.

Logan let out a relieved breath, then guided her across the parking lot. Without a word, they went back inside the hospital to stand by their son's bed.

"Mommy's sorry, baby," Trixie said, tears flowing down her face as she rubbed his little arm. "Mommy's so sorry. But I promise, I'm going to be right here with you from now on."

This time she would follow her heart.

Chapter Thirteen

Logan watched Trixie as she sat by Caleb's side, memories of all that happened to them racing through his weary mind. Things might have turned out so differently back then, if he'd known she was carrying his child. For one thing, he would never have let her get away. But they had both been too young and afraid to take matters into their own hands.

This time, he promised himself, *this time I won't let her go.* This time it would be different.

But before that could happen, Caleb had to get well.

Feeling completely helpless, Logan walked out into the quiet hospital corridor. He might not be able to hold on to Trixie just yet, and he alone certainly didn't have the power to bring his child back, but there was one thing he could do right now that would make him feel a whole lot better. Logan needed to have a long-overdue talk with Mrs. Pamela Dunaway.

He found Pamela sitting in the same spot where Trixie had left her, mainly because Harlan had ordered her to stay there. Logan came into the waiting area near pediatrics to find Harlan standing over a pouting Pamela like a raging bull about to charge.

"You aren't going to bully her—not this time," Harlan said. "You've badgered that child all of her life, trying to turn her into a replica of yourself. And I've stood by and watched you, only because I thought you had her best interest at heart." He paused, swallowed. "But the things Gayle told me you said to Trixie here today, the way you made her ashamed to face her own child—that was just downright underhanded, Pamela. I can see now what I should have seen long ago. You don't care about your daughter's happiness. Your only interest is in protecting yourself. Apparently you only care about something when you can gain from it."

Pointing his forefinger at his daughter-in-law, he told her, "All of these years I allowed you to stay a part of this family, because I believe in family and because I thought it was in Trixie's best interest to have her mother around. But not anymore. Not anymore.

"She's a grown woman now, and she has a good head on her shoulders, and a fine, big old heart just like her daddy's. I won't let you ruin her chance to find some peace and happiness with her son and Logan, the way you ruined your own chance with Brant. Do I make myself clear?"

Pamela's round eyes widened in utter surprise. "Perfectly," she said, her legs crossed primly, one foot swinging in an angry arc of anxiety. Harlan might be an old softy, but he still wielded the power that paid her bills. She knew when to tread softly with him. Beseeching him now, she said, "So, what am I supposed to do? Just sit here and watch her throw her life away?"

Logan had had enough at this point. Stalking toward Pamela, he said, "What makes you so all-knowing?

What makes you the one who gets to call the shots in Trixie's life?''

Giving him a look of total disdain, Pamela continued to swing her foot. ''I'm her mother. Isn't that reason enough to stop her from making a tragic mistake?''

Logan scoffed, then stared down at her. ''No, being her mother doesn't give you the right to control her life, even if you believe she may be heading down the wrong road. But that's what you've done ever since you lost Brant. You used your daughter to punish him, and then you used your own flesh and blood—your own grandson, to control all of us.''

Mad now, Pamela rose off her chair with all the grace of a queen, then waved a hand in dismissal. ''Somebody had to be rational. Brant always was too sentimental and emotional. I had to be the calm one. I had to be the one who always played the heavy. I'm sorry if that offends you, Mr. Maxwell.''

Logan stepped closer, his eyes flashing darkly. ''What offends me, Mrs. Dunaway, is the fact that you think you're above reproach, that you think you're such a perfect Christian that none of the rest of us can possibly keep up with you or even aspire to ask your forgiveness.''

Pamela hissed, ''What you did to my daughter was unforgivable.''

''I agree,'' he said, nodding, ''but if you had been willing, Trixie and I could have made a decision to do right by our child. Sure, we got carried away, we made a mistake in judgment, but we were both willing to own up to that mistake. Only, you refused to let that happen. You didn't even let us decide what to do about our own child.''

She glared at him, disgust evident in her words. ''No,

because I always expected my daughter to do better than the likes of you. I couldn't allow her to marry so young and to a man she barely knew.''

Logan threw his hands up, then dropped them at his side. ''I was good enough for Brant. I was good enough to raise my son. And I'm good enough for Trixie. You see, she loves me. So, frankly, your opinion of me means very little to me at this point. But for Trixie's sake, I do wish you'd try to step out of that narrow-minded notion of yours.''

Pamela lifted her shoulders, then turned away. ''My notions are based on my values and my beliefs.''

Pulling her back around, Logan replied, ''Then, lady, you have a really skewed idea of what the word of Jesus Christ is all about. You just don't get it, do you?''

Lifting her chin to a haughty level, she said, ''No, Mr. Maxwell, I guess I don't. Why don't you set me straight on something I've been taught all my life, since you seem to know so much more about my own religion than I possibly could.''

Thoroughly fed up, Logan took her by the arm. Lifting her up off the chair she'd been perched on, he practically dragged her down the hospital hallway. ''All right, you want to know what I'm trying to tell you? Then, follow me. I'll show you the real meaning of the love of Jesus Christ.''

Harlan let them pass, his eyes full of admiration and apprehension for Logan. Let the boy have his turn. He'd certainly waited long enough, and now his son was near death. It was high time they all accepted their fate and learned to love again. He just prayed it wasn't too late.

Gayle, too, just sat there, watching, wondering, hoping that maybe Logan could talk some sense into that high-handed, overblown socialite. Then she prayed for both of them.

But most of all she prayed for her grandson.

"Let go of me!" Pamela demanded, furious at being manhandled by this field hand in a public place. Glancing around to make sure none of the busy nurses had seen anything, she hissed, "Where are you taking me?"

Logan stared straight ahead, his hand on her arm light but firm. "To see your grandson—and your daughter," he replied over his shoulder, the dare in his voice too real to miss.

"No." Pamela tried to pull back at the doors of the pediatric intensive care unit, a horrified look marring her wrinkle-free face. "I...I don't think this is wise."

Logan whirled to give her a harsh stare. "Why? Because 'out of sight, out of mind' is the way you want to keep him? Or maybe because he'll remind you of Brant too much, and that might actually make you feel just a pinch of guilt?" Tugging her through the doors, he dared any of the nurses to try and stop him. In a low whisper, he continued, "Or maybe, just maybe, you'll recognize Trixie in that little boy in there, and that might be too much for even your hardened soul to bear."

Trying to pull back, Pamela said, "Don't make me do this. I won't go in there."

Logan refused to let her go. But...there was real fear in her eyes. That surprised him; he'd always pictured Trixie's mama as such a formidable, fearless person. Perhaps there was a soft spot somewhere behind that haughty demeanor, after all.

More gently he said, "You need to see your grandson. He might not make it, unless we all pull together and show him we love him.'' Leaning close, he added, ''And please, think about Trixie for once. She just found out she's his mother. She needs your support right now, not your criticism.''

Pamela's alabaster skin turned even more pale as she stood there, frozen. Finally she looked up and glanced around, her eyes full of sincere appeal. ''You don't understand. I...I can't tolerate hospitals. Ever since Brant—''

Logan saw it all so clearly now. ''Ever since Brant got hurt in the rodeo?''

She nodded, a brisk bobbing of her head, then closed her eyes tightly shut. ''All the blood, all the stitches. I thought...I thought he was going to die. I begged him to give it up, but he loved the rodeo more than he loved me.''

Feeling a strong sympathy for her in spite of all she'd done, Logan said, ''You're wrong there. He loved you more than anything. He loved you till the day he died.''

''How do you know that?'' she asked, her eyes bright with stubborn tears as she looked directly at him for the first time.

''He told me,'' Logan said, his voice calm and sure. ''He told me to tell Trixie he loved her, then he told me to take good care of his grandson.'' His hand tender on her arm now, he added, ''And the last thing he said was, 'And Pammy. You know, son, I sure do love my Pammy. Wish I could see her pretty face one more time.' And then, he died.''

The tears came then, falling down her face in soft rivulets. And with the tears, her heart opened just a little, like a shy flower. ''But...he left me. I gave him an ultimatum and he...he chose the ranch and the rodeo over me.''

"No," Logan said in a whisper, "you drove him away by demanding perfection, by trying to make him into something he could never be. You see, Brant loved you just the way you were, flaws and all. But you refused to meet him halfway. So the rodeo and his ranch were the only things he had left, except Trixie. And then, you even managed to take her away from him."

Logan's voice, usually so deep and firm, cracked with the weight of a broken heart. Pointing to the room where Caleb lay a few feet away, he said, "That little boy in there was Brant's only consolation. And Brant loved him—he gave all the love he still had for you and Trixie to his grandson. And now, all I'm asking of you, all I want from you, is a little consideration for that love. Let go of the grudge, let go and let God take over. Open your heart, Mrs. Dunaway, and help me to save my son—your grandson." Giving her a gentle nudge, he added, "Or do you want to risk losing Trixie, too?"

Pamela actually looked humble, and more than a little ashamed. She stood there, so silent, so unmoving, her expression changing from stubborn and resentful to understanding and hopeful. Glancing up at Logan, she said, "But...he's so tiny, so young. And he doesn't even know me."

Logan heard the hidden message in her plea. She didn't want to get too attached to someone she might lose. He could sure understand that feeling. He'd protected Caleb all this time for that very reason. He'd worried about losing his son to Trixie, to her way of life. Selfishly, he'd been glad that Caleb didn't know his mother. And now he realized, too late, none of that was important.

Brant had died without being able to tell Caleb that he was his own flesh and blood. Now Caleb might die, never knowing how very much he was loved, never knowing he had a mother who'd sacrificed so much because she loved him.

He turned back to Pamela now, hoping to make her see what he'd been too blind to see. "It doesn't matter. He'll know you're there. A few precious moments of happiness are a lot more important than holding a grudge and blaming everyone for one mistake. My son was not a mistake. He was a beautiful gift, and I'm just thankful that God saw fit for me to be a part of his life. And if he makes it, he can get to know you, and you and Trixie can finally be in his life, too."

Pamela still looked skeptical and confused. "Won't that only make things worse?"

Hearing the catch of doubt in her question, Logan pushed on. "How can loving a child make that child's life worse? Love heals all wounds, Mrs. Dunaway. Love brings joy and pleasure and hope. Haven't we all paid the price of sin and sorrow? Isn't it time…isn't it time to put all of that behind us and do what's right for Caleb?"

She looked up at him then, her eyes devoid of any hostility. "And Trixie," she said, her tone gentle and meek, awe filled. "I need to do right by my daughter, don't I?"

"That's the idea," Logan said, relief washing over him. He knew in his heart that Trixie wouldn't be able to love her own child until she felt worthy in her mother's eyes. Oh, she loved Caleb. That came without saying. But she didn't think she deserved to be near him.

But Caleb deserved all of the love this family could offer him.

Starting now.

"Come on," he said. "Just hold his hand. Help Trixie and me to bring him back."

Pamela stepped forward, then dried her eyes, a new look of determination dawning across her face. "All right. I'll try."

Logan guided her into the room, his gaze falling across his son's face before sweeping over all the tubes and machines that were keeping Caleb alive. His eyes meeting Trixie's, he whispered, "I brought someone with me."

Trixie looked up, her red-rimmed eyes going wide at the sight of her mother standing there. Her first instinct was to tell Pamela to get out, but something in the gentle, confused expression of her mother's face stopped her.

"Oh," Pamela said, her hand flying to her mouth as she gazed down on Caleb's peaceful face. "Oh, the poor baby."

Logan took one of Caleb's little hands, rubbing it tenderly, a smile holding his own tears at bay. "Hey, sport, you've got a special visitor. This is—" He looked over at Pamela for support.

Taking Caleb's other hand, she tentatively stepped closer to the bed, her gaze touching on Trixie's face before she looked down at Caleb. "Hello," she said, her voice hitching. "I'm…I'm your…I'm your other grandmother. And I sure hope you wake up so we can get acquainted." She was silent for a minute, then with a bright smile, she said, "You know, I would just love to spoil you rotten. Why, I'll take you to Disney World and the giant water park all the kids love so much." She dashed the tears off her face with one bejeweled hand. "I'll buy you the moon, if you'll only wake up."

Logan didn't say anything. He couldn't speak. He

looked over at Trixie's amazed expression, his gaze reassuring. He'd worry about Pamela Dunaway spoiling his son later. Right now, he had to agree with her. Right now, the lump in his throat was about to burst wide open. One prayer answered, he thought as he watched Pamela's expression change from tentative and unsure to determined and uncondemning.

Logan felt as if he and Trixie had just witnessed a miracle. As she held her grandson's hand for the first time, Pamela's expression changed from harsh and unyielding to soft and maternal, all in the space of a few precious minutes. She was a beautiful woman, always had been. But what he saw there in her eyes now was an inner beauty that came from a certain peace, and a certain acceptance. Pamela Dunaway still had the fight left in her, only now she would fight for Caleb and for Trixie.

"He looks so much like Brant," she said, a gasp of awe sighing through her words. Then looking over at her daughter, she added, "And you, darling. He looks a lot like you. He's a beautiful little boy."

Trixie couldn't speak. Instead, she reached across the bed to take her mother's outstretched hand.

"Yes, he is," Logan agreed. "And he needs his mother."

Pamela looked over at Logan then. "Do you love my daughter, Mr. Maxwell?"

Logan returned her intense stare. "Always have."

"Does she love you?"

"I believe so."

Trixie spoke then, her words husky and thick. "Yes, I do love him, Mother. And, I love my son, too."

Pamela stood silent for a while, her fingers tracing a line over Caleb's limp wrist, her beautiful ageless face changing, shifting with each warring thought. Finally, she said, "Then I think you'd better grab hold of that love, while you still have a chance."

Coming around the bed to hug Trixie close, she started to cry. "I'm so sorry, honey. I was wrong. You should be with your child...and with the man you love."

"Do you mean that?" Trixie asked. "Will you stop interfering and let us just be happy together?"

"I'll do my best," Pamela said honestly. "It won't be easy. I'm very set in my ways, and I'm very used to getting my way."

Logan shot Trixie a reluctant grin. At least she was being straight with them. "We'll help you," he said, his eyes touching on hers with a new respect.

"All right then," Pamela replied, her old spunk returning. "That's settled. You two need to find a quiet corner and talk—get something to eat."

Trixie shook her head. "But—"

"No buts. I'll stay here with...with Caleb. And your mother and Harlan are still here. We'll watch over him."

"No fighting?" Logan asked, already reaching for Trixie.

Pamela scoffed. "Mr. Maxwell, I don't cause scenes in public." Then she smiled wryly. "No more fighting. I promise." She looked up at him, her gaze completely serious. "We'll be much too busy praying."

Logan nodded, then taking a shocked Trixie by the hand, tiptoed toward the door.

"Oh, and one other thing," Pamela called in a hushed voice. She gave Trixie a meaningful look. "After you've rested a bit, I'd like to talk to you."

"All right, Mother," Trixie said, still awestruck by her mother's amazing attitude change. "I'll be here."

"So will I, darling. So will I."

Trixie stood on a small open terrace overlooking the busy hospital parking lot below, watching as the evening sun shifted lazily behind the mountain range to the west. The distant vista was colored in muted hues of gold, green and red, glistening and glinting with a warm autumn fire that took her breath away.

In that brilliant autumn beauty, she found some of her strength again. *Please, God, take care of my son. Let him find the sun again. Let him live.*

She'd cried. Oh, how she'd cried. Sitting by her son's bed, she had, as Logan had suggested, found a part of her father. So she'd poured out her heart to him at last.

"I love you, Daddy. And I want to thank you for taking such good care of my son. He's so like you— it's only right that you turned out to be the one to help raise him."

Maybe God had formed a plan for all of them, she thought now as she listened to the bees humming around the carefully-tended hospital flower beds and heard squirrels frolicking in a nearby oak. Off in the distance, the loblolly pines swayed in the crisp fall breeze, soothing her soul with a lullaby sent straight from the heavens.

Maybe God had known that Caleb would grow and thrive right here where he'd been conceived. Maybe Logan had been the right one to raise their child. Caleb had been safe here in Arkansas's gentle hills, nurtured, loved, protected much in the same way as Brant's beloved sunflowers. Knowing that he had been in a safe and loving environment gave her some comfort. Yet she'd missed out on so much of his life. So much.

She looked past the clutter of buildings, to the valley leading out to the hills, watching as a few early golden and orange-colored oak leaves let go and fell gracefully to the earth, and she dreamed a beautiful dream.

In her mind, there stood the house Logan had described to her, all whitewashed and country fresh, with geraniums growing in large pots by the open front door. And in the yard Caleb rode a spirited pony while Logan instructed and encouraged and taught his son the cowboy way. She stood on the porch watching and laughing; loving the two most important men in her life.

And off in the distance, high on a mountain that reached almost to the clouds, she could imagine her father sitting astride a big roan, his hat dipped low over his brow, his laughing blue eyes bright and clear as he called out to his grandson. "Go, little cowboy. Ride that horse. Get back up now. Gotta try again, son. We're all rooting for you, Caleb."

The tears came again. Blinking, she wondered if she'd imagined the scene; it seemed so very real. But the valley was far away in the distance, and the only sounds she heard were those of the traffic, followed by the rustle of falling leaves blowing across the asphalt parking lot below. The sky was rich with the promise of another brilliant sunset.

Would she ever stop crying?

Earlier, she'd gone to the little hospital chapel again and prayed there amid the pine benches and paneled walls, there in the cool darkness of a peaceful, quiet sanctuary. At last, a sanctuary.

Please, Lord, forgive me for what I did. Forgive me

for giving my child away, for letting them take my child from me. Did I have a choice? I didn't think so.

But now she did have a choice. Now she'd been given this wonderful, miraculous second chance.

And she was scared to death.

What if Caleb died?

What if he lived, yet didn't want anything to do with her?

What if she could never, ever tell him the truth?

There were other problems to consider, too. Would Logan be willing to share their son with her? He'd had Caleb to himself for so long. Would he be willing to let her take over some of the responsibility?

None of that mattered now, she told herself as she sat there on the terrace, waiting for Logan to bring their dinner.

Just let him live.

That's all she asked now. She'd figure out the rest as it came along. And with God's help, she'd find a way.

Just let him live, Lord.

Did the angels hear her?

She looked up then at the sound of boots clicking on the stone walkway. Looked up and saw Logan coming toward her, his dark eyes rich with unspoken promises, his expression as sure and grounded as the mountains, his hat shading his face so she couldn't really tell what he was thinking.

Trixie got up, her heart pumped with a mixture of pride and longing. She couldn't bear it if—

"Logan?" She rushed to meet him, reaching out a hand to touch his arm. "Logan?"

Logan dropped the sandwiches he'd picked up in the hospital cafeteria, then held her tight against him.

"Don't look so worried, baby. Your mama knows where we are. If anything happens, she'll send word."

Trixie fell against him, savoring the warmth, the strength he offered, a great relief washing through her. "I still can't believe my mother's actually—"

Logan lifted her away, then cupped her face with his hands. "Listen to me, Tricia Maria. This is real. Your mother saw the love in that room—that's what changed her."

"That has to be it," Trixie agreed. "It's like a miracle. She changed, right there before my eyes. She took one look at our child and…her heart opened."

"Love does that," Logan said, his own eyes watering up in spite of his best efforts to hold back. "I always wanted your family to…to just accept me. And now, because of Caleb, your mother's done just that."

Trixie saw the pride in his eyes, but she also saw the pain he'd suffered for so long. Softly, gently, with all the love in her heart, she pulled his head down on her shoulder, cradling him as he cried. How long had he held these tears? How long had he played the part of the tough cowboy, always out mending fences when he'd desperately needed someone to help him mend his own broken heart?

Determined now, Trixie held him close. "Logan, I love you. I love you so much."

He could only nod, but she knew he loved her, too. He'd loved her enough to raise their son; he'd loved her enough to confront her mother. He'd loved her enough to wait for her all these years.

She tugged his head up, then wiped his tears away with her fingers. "And I tell you this, I refuse to let our son die. You're right. This isn't about me or how sorrowful I feel. I don't have time to feel sorry for myself.

And it isn't about whether Caleb will accept me or not. Right now I just want to be with my son, even if…even if it's only for a little while." She smiled through her tears. "It's all so simple, really. I've been searching for answers, when the answer is right here, in my heart. I've been handed a second chance, with you and Caleb."

Logan touched a hand to her face. "I love you."

He kissed her then, his touch as soft as the sun's glow to the west, as full of warmth and promise as the rich mountains off in the distance.

With that kiss, with his firm declaration, Trixie found the strength she needed to face her son. "I love you, and…I will make Caleb see that I love him, too. Somehow."

Logan flapped his hat against his jeans, then wiped a determined hand across his wet face. Giving her another quick kiss for luck, he said, "Well, let's hurry up and eat, so we can go back and tell him."

For the first time since she'd learned that Caleb was her son, Trixie felt a certain peace. They'd get through this, with a little help from above. Hopeful, she looked off toward the west, envisioning the spot of earth where her father lay buried. Envisioning the sunflowers.

Chapter Fourteen

Trixie walked back into the hospital, a new determination coursing through her blood. She would not leave her son again. Ever.

Pamela was there, watching over Caleb, quiet and serene, the same determination her daughter possessed pushing her beyond herself as she harassed the doctors and made sure the nurses weren't neglecting her grandson. She took turns with Gayle and Harlan, each of them cooing to Caleb, talking to him, singing sweet songs to him, telling him to come back, to wake up and make mischief. Each of them telling him to live, that he was loved. Each of them praying, hoping, that he'd wake up.

Trixie stood now, tired, but unyielding, unwilling to surrender the son she'd just discovered to death.

"You are so precious," she whispered as she stroked Caleb's head just underneath the bandage protecting his wounds. "And I called Samantha and had her bring you something. I know you think you have to earn this, but I've decided to go ahead and give it to you."

She placed the small open box on the bed by Caleb's

still little hand. "It's the Ring of Honor that your...that Brant promised you. You are a true all-around cowboy, and you deserve this."

She looked down at the glittering ring, wishing with all of her heart that it would provide the healing power needed to wake her son up. The big ring sparkled and winked, its diamonds like beacons as she lifted it high to show Caleb this coveted treasure. "It's yours, all yours."

Her son remained asleep.

Trixie tried again. "Look, I brought your cowboy hat, too. You can wear it again, once that sore spot on your head gets better. Caleb, can you hear me? You need to wake up and put this hat on."

He looked so peaceful, so perfect. Where was he in his dreamland? Was he out riding the range with Brant, roping stray steers? Was he sitting at the Astrodome, watching his favorite baseball player hit a home run? Was he down at the pond reeling in a big, fat bass, or high up in the mountains watching her from above? Could he hear her voice, see the love she wanted him to find?

"Caleb," she said, her hands touching here and there on his still body. "Caleb. Mommy loves you so much. I know I let you go, so long ago. I didn't want to. I wanted to keep you near. I wanted to hold you and rock you and smell your sweet baby smell while I kissed the top of your head. I missed out on all of that, but I'm here now. And I won't leave you again. Can you hear me, Caleb? Do you know how much I love you and your daddy? Please, baby, please let me have a second chance."

Logan stood at the door, his own heart shattering in two as he watched Trixie trying desperately to bring their son back to them. If he'd had any doubts about her, or his love for her, those doubts were now gone.

He loved her. Completely. Unconditionally.

And he wondered why he'd blamed her for so long. Why had he let his pride hold him back, hold his son back, from her? Brant had tried to tell him, but he hadn't been willing to listen. He wanted to believe the worst about Trixie.

So much wasted time, so much bitterness. Now none of it seemed so important. Now he only wanted her and their son to be with him.

Stepping into the room, he touched Trixie on the arm. She looked tired and forlorn, worn. Her hair hung limply around her face and dark circles marred her usually bright blue eyes. "Come on," he said. "You need a break."

She held tight to Caleb's hand. "I don't want to leave him."

"Your mother will take over. Just for a few minutes. I have something I want to give you."

Her eyes widening, she looked up at him. "Sounds intriguing, but I'm not interested. Especially if it's another cup of hospital coffee."

"I think you'll appreciate it," he said, the warmth of his words assuring her that this surprise would be a good one. "We'll be just outside, I promise."

Pamela came in then, looking about as frazzled as Trixie had ever seen her. She'd pulled her sleek hair back in a prim ponytail at the nape of her neck, and in spite of being wrinkled, her clothes still hung in graceful lines around her slender body. Her face was haggard, most of the carefully applied makeup now faded and streaked.

Trixie never remembered her mother looking more beautiful.

"Go with Logan, dear," Pamela said, her smile gentle. "I'll stay with him for a while."

"Okay." Still amazed at her mother's change of heart, Trixie squeezed Pamela's hand, then turned and gave her son a kiss. "I'll be right outside and I'll be back soon, sport."

She watched as Pamela picked up Brant's ring box. "I remember this."

"He promised it to Caleb," Trixie explained, hoping Pamela wouldn't argue about it.

Pamela laughed, then looked down at Caleb. "He'll have to do some growing to fit it on his finger."

She glanced back up at her daughter then. Their eyes met in a silent promise and a guaranteed truce. Mother and daughter, fighting on the same side, instead of against each other, at last.

"Go on, honey," Pamela said. "When you get back, we'll…we'll have a nice talk."

Trixie nodded. "Thank you, Mother."

Pamela shot her a surprised smile. It had been a long time since she'd heard those words from her daughter's lips.

Once they were outside the pediatric ICU, Logan took Trixie to a quiet corner of the deserted waiting area. It was near midnight and most visitors had gone home long before.

"Mama and Harlan went down to the cafeteria for a few minutes," he explained.

Wary, Trixie gave him a worried look. "Why all the mystery? Is there something the doctors haven't told me?"

"No, no," Logan said, reassuring her with a quick hug. "I just wanted to show you this...and I thought you might like some privacy while you look it over."

He handed her a large album. "It's Caleb's baby book, complete with pictures from the day he was brought home till now. You missed out on all of that, but Brant...well, he was a stickler for keeping scrapbooks."

Trixie bobbed her head, her heart racing. "Daddy had tons of scrapbooks—all his awards, from 4-H and Cub Scouts, to the rodeo. He and mother made me keep one, too."

"Well, he did the same thing for his grandson," Logan said, his voice hushed. "And I want you to have this."

Touched beyond words, Trixie took the thick, leather-covered book in her arms, hugging it close to try and absorb the essence of her son. "Thank you, Logan," she said, her voice hitching. "I thought I'd cried all my tears, but this—"

She couldn't finish. Logan hugged her again, then whispered, "Take your time. You look it over, then if you have any questions, I'll be glad to tell you all the stories about your son. I won't leave anything out."

Trixie took the book in her lap. For a few minutes she just sat there, running her hands over the smooth burgundy leather. Caleb's initials were etched in its center, in gold. C. L. M.

Caleb Logan Maxwell.

Her child.

Carefully she opened the book, restraining herself from tearing through the many pages. She was so hungry for a glance into her son's life, but she also wanted to savor each and every minute of this precious gift.

And she did. Time seemed to flow into one smooth, complete line as Trixie stared down at the beautiful baby in the pictures before her. Caleb, sleeping in baby blue, in a small crib. Caleb, smiling at the camera, sitting up, his first tooth front and center. Caleb, crawling across the kitchen floor, his chubby little knees smudged with dust and dirt.

Her son. Taking his first steps, with Logan grinning in the background.

Her father, holding Caleb on his knee, Brant's leg bouncing as Caleb rode the imaginary pony and laughed. Brant and Caleb, both in cowboy hats, at Christmas, opening presents underneath a majestic, brightly decorated cedar tree.

Logan with Caleb, up on Rocky, looking like partners in crime. Only, she knew these two were the good guys. Grinning. Playing. Loving.

So many pictures. So many moments snapped and held, cherished. Fishing trips. Campouts. Cub Scouts. Football. Baseball. Bike riding. Horse riding. Swimming in the pond. Worms. Crickets. Frogs. Bugs. Muddy tennis shoes, dirty cowboy boots. Dirt-streaked faces. Grins and smiles. Laughter. Tears.

And finally, Caleb standing in the sunflower patch, holding on to a fat, yellow blossom that stood as tall as him. A little boy doing all the things little boys did.

Her child. Her little boy.

The same little boy who now lay so still, so quiet in a hospital room, with tubes and machines keeping him alive.

She reached the end of the book, and flipped it over, only to start all over again, memorizing each moment, imagining in her mind what it would have been like to be there with him. She read and reread the pictures, adding her own version of each scene, playing out Caleb's young life over and over in her mind, until she knew in her heart that she would never be able to get enough of this, of him.

"He can't die," she said to the empty hallway. Night wore on, dawn was coming. Trixie waited for the sunrise, and the hope of a new day. "He can't die."

Pamela came out to sit by her, silently taking her hand, holding Trixie's fingers interlaced through her own.

"We won't let him die," she told her daughter.

For a minute Trixie believed her. After all, Pamela Dunaway always got her way. For a moment Trixie wanted to hate her mother all over again, but the fight was gone now. The only fight she had left was for Caleb.

"Why, mother?" she asked, her voice raw and raspy. "Why did we send him away?"

Pamela clasped her daughter's hand tightly in her own. "I've asked myself that question a lot over the last few hours. And believe it or not, I've often wondered that very same thing over the years since…since all of this happened. I can only tell you that I was afraid."

Trixie understood that emotion, but she needed more. "Afraid of what?"

Pamela looked at her daughter, then reached up a hand to stroke Trixie's hair away from her temple. "Afraid that my friends would talk, afraid I'd lose my standing within the community, afraid of things that seem so silly, so trivial now. But mostly, I think, I was afraid of losing you to your father. You see, I would have been left with nothing then."

Trixie saw the desolation in her mother's beautiful eyes. "I'd never desert you, Mother."

Pamela lifted her shoulders in an elegant shrug. "Your father did, or so I thought. I was bitter and lonely, and I wasn't so sure about your loyalty, so I fought for you the only way I knew how. I wasn't sure about anything, except my need to protect you and myself."

"We were selfish," Trixie said. "I was afraid, too. I was afraid to fight for my own child."

Pamela's arm tightened around her shoulder. "No, you were young, darling. And confused. We did what we thought was right."

Trixie stared over at her, desperation apparent in her words. "We could have loved him, Mother. We could have provided him with everything. No one would have questioned that."

"Maybe," Pamela agreed, "but...I would have resented him. I would have punished you and him. I did punish you, darling, and I'm so very sorry."

Trixie couldn't answer that. She'd longed to hear those very words from her mother for so long, yet the wounds were still too fresh, too raw, for her to accept them now. They'd all punished each other enough with this horrible deception, though.

"Too little, too late," Pamela said for her. "I know that now. I lost your father, and I had too much pride to come up to the ranch to try and win him back. So I became vindictive and bitter. And I used that bitterness against him when you got pregnant. I had the perfect weapon, the perfect opportunity to make him see that I'd been right all along."

Trixie held the album tight, then closed her weary eyes. "It's not all your fault. I was indiscreet and I was too ashamed, too confused, to own up to that indiscretion. But I should have fought harder to keep my child. I should have run away, back to Logan.''

"We can go over and over this," Pamela said, her pragmatic side still burning strongly, "but facts are facts. We did what we had to do, to protect you and our name and our family. Maybe that seems shallow and self-serving now, but back then I suppose those were two of my main attributes.''

Surprised, Trixie glanced up. "And now?''

"And now, I've had a lot of time to think about this. All it took was one look at that little boy's face." Pamela shifted, crossing her long legs and straightening her skirt, a daring look crossing her face. "And now, my darling, I am not ashamed anymore.

"So what if I have a grandson pop up out of the blue? Miriam Grisham has a daughter who's an alcoholic. She's having to raise her two teenaged granddaughters all by herself while their poor mother tries yet another rehab clinic. And I hear they're a real handful. I didn't turn away from Miriam at the country club, even though she tried to keep it hush-hush.

"And Reba Gallaway has a son who had to go to jail for shoplifting. She asked all of us to pray for him at church not two weeks ago. All of my friends have their own problems, in spite of their money and their big fancy houses. And I still consider them my friends—I worry about them, I feel for them and I do pray for them. I think I've just been praying in all the wrong ways, asking for the wrong things.''

In spite of everything, Trixie couldn't help but laugh at her mother's misplaced logic. Comparing family crises at the country club! Now, there was a new one! Well, at least now Pamela was willing to admit there was a crisis in the Dunaway clan. And she was willing to do something about it. That willingness to let go of some of her iron-clad control and cold, firm denial endeared Pamela to Trixie in a way nothing else ever could.

"Oh, Mother, you are priceless," Trixie said now, some of the sadness leaving her for a brief moment.

Pamela held her head high, like a queen on a throne. "I have nothing to be ashamed of. I refuse to be ashamed of that beautiful child lying in that hospital bed. Besides, I'm getting too old and too impatient for all this pettiness. If my so-called friends can't support me in this, then pooh on them."

"Mother?"

Seeing the genuine surprise and shock on her daughter's face, Pamela shrugged, then turned serious. "It was like...like a light coming on. Seeing that little boy, realizing he was my own flesh and blood. I was ashamed, all right. But not ashamed about what my friends might think. I became quite ashamed of myself. I tried to deny one of my own." Sitting up to pat her hair, she added, "Dunaways do not turn family away. We stick together. And it's high time I remember that."

Trixie handed the album to her mother. "I wish Daddy could hear you saying that. He'd be so proud."

"Me, too," Pamela admitted. "You know, I miss your father so much. We could have grown old together, only I was too full of pride to forgive him, or to ask him to forgive me."

"I think he knows," Trixie said. "I think he always knew that you loved him in your heart."

"I hope so," Pamela replied. Her eyes settling on her daughter's, she added, "Do you know, Logan told me that Brant talked about me the day he died?"

Amazed that Logan and her mother had even had a civil conversation, Trixie said, "Really?"

"Really. He said Brant told him that he missed his Pammy. And that he loved me."

"That's so sweet, Mother. You have to remember that."

"I will, always." Looking down at the scrapbook, she said, "Now, what's this?"

"Pictures of your grandson," Trixie told her. "And, there's some of Daddy, too."

"Oh," Pamela said, her eyes widening, tears springing up in their depths. "Oh, that Brant. He always was a big ham."

"Our big lovable ham," Trixie replied. "Look at the pictures, Mother. And while you're looking, try to forgive yourself."

Pamela nodded. "I will if you will."

Trixie stood up, the little bit of laughter her talk with her mother had inadvertently provided gone now as the solemn weight of her son's accident hit her squarely on the shoulders. She turned to give her mother a parting glance. "I'll forgive myself when my son is safe and well."

Worried, Pamela stood up to follow her. "Trixie, don't blame yourself for this, sugar. It was an accident."

"Was it, Mother? I wonder. Was it an accident, or was it meant to happen exactly this way?"

Appalled, Pamela hurried after her daughter. "No, darling. You can't think like that. We have to keep the faith and hold fast."

Trixie bobbed her head then. "I'll hold fast—to my son. And this time, I won't let him go."

* * *

"She blames herself," Harlan told Logan the next afternoon as they sat in the waiting room.

The doctor had given Trixie, Logan and Harlan a full report, and Trixie had rushed back into Caleb's room, visibly upset.

"Five days in a coma, and no response. That is cause for concern, but we're still optimistic," Dr. Arnold had said to them in his monotone way a few minutes earlier.

"Doctors," Logan said, worry causing him to lash out at the very ones who'd helped keep his son alive. "They talk in such riddles."

"They're doing everything they can, son," Harlan assured him. "But I still say we can move him to Houston. I'll round up a passle of the best specialists money can buy."

Logan appreciated Harlan's offer, but resented the power of his money. "You've already brought in a specialist from Little Rock," he reminded Harlan. "And he told us the same thing as Dr. Arnold. They've done everything they can. Now we just have to wait and hope."

"And pray," Harlan reminded him. "Some things even my money can't buy."

Logan wondered if he'd been asking God for the wrong things himself. He only wanted God to save his son, but maybe it was time to accept that he had no control over that. Maybe it was time to just turn it all over to the Lord and accept whatever happened. That wouldn't be easy, but he was running out of options.

"I'm going in to see him," he told Harlan as he pushed up off one of the many comfortable chairs provided in the waiting area.

He found Trixie in her familiar spot, sitting by her son's bed, her hand intertwined with Caleb's, her face drawn and desperate, her voice pleading and firm at the same time.

"Get well, honey. We all miss you so much. Please, Caleb, open your eyes and talk to me."

Logan came to stand by her side. He was worried about her; she hadn't left the hospital in over twenty-four hours. First her father's death and now this. No one could stand up to that much stress for very long.

"Tricia Maria," he said, his voice low and coaxing, "why don't we go back out to the ranch for a while. You can get some sleep, and I'll make you some of my famous chili."

"No." She didn't look at him. Her eyes remained on her child. "I'm not tired."

Logan knew what she was trying to do. She was pouring seven years of lost time into what might be her last hours with her son. "Trixie, honey, you're making yourself sick. You can't keep up this pace."

Turning to him at last, Trixie stared hard into his eyes, tiredness making her edgy with resentment. "I refuse to leave him," she said, a frown marring her face. "I left him once. I promised him I won't do it again."

She was stubborn, that was for sure. And still angry.

"He knows you love him, Trixie. He has to know that."

"Does he? How can he, Logan, when he never even knew I existed?"

He didn't miss the accusation in her words. They'd all reached the end of their ropes and tension was bound to make them say things they'd regret later. Taking a minute to calm himself, he tried to reason with her again. "Listen, honey, it was wrong of me not to tell you about him, but we've been through all of that."

Hating herself for her harsh words, Trixie looked

back down at her son, wishing with all of her heart she could just let go and turn things over to God. But she still had too much fight left in her. She wasn't quite ready to relinquish control.

Her voice soft now, she said, "When were you planning on telling me about him, Logan? If my father hadn't died, would I have ever known about my son?"

A valid question. A hard question to answer. But she needed answers, and she'd hit on one of the things that had been eating at him the most.

"I honestly don't know," he admitted as he came to stand by her. "When you came back to the ranch, I was so afraid you'd find out. So we tried to protect him from you."

She gave him a quick glance, then returned her concentration to Caleb, her eyes darting here and there over her son's face. "That much I've figured out. You must have really wrestled with that one. If I sold the ranch, you could possibly be booted off the place, but if I kept the ranch, you risked my finding out the truth."

"Yes, and I'm not proud of it...or the way I treated you."

She lifted her eyes to his, slamming him with a look of anguish and hurt. "How long would this have gone on?"

Logan lowered his head, the guilt of his deception coloring his face. "I don't know. But I do know that one thought has been uppermost in my mind since the accident."

Trixie heard the regret in his voice. Immediately she felt remorse for her angry, accusing words. "Oh, Logan. I'm sorry. You're right, I am so very tired. And trying to lay blame won't help Caleb now."

Logan knelt, them placed his hand on top of hers over

Caleb's. "If it's any consolation, I had planned on telling you everything that night at dinner, the night of the storm."

"The night of Caleb's accident," she said, awe filling her words. "Isn't life ironic? I was going to tell you that night that I'd given your child up. I figured we could never be happy together with such a horrible secret between us."

"I felt the same way," he said, his eyes holding hers. "I only knew we had to forgive, before we could ever forget and move on with things. Do you think we can ever get over this, Trixie?"

She looked down at their hands. Logan's big hand covered hers, while her fingers held on to Caleb's smaller hand. It seemed so bittersweet that they were together now. But they were, and that gave her a small measure of hope.

She watched Logan, hoping he'd see the love in her heart. "Think about it. We were willing to risk losing each other again, by telling the truth at last. That has to count for something."

Logan grinned then, relief washing over him. "You're so smart."

"Not smart," she said. "Just tired of fighting against my heart." She pressed her lips to his jawline, then sat back. "I do love you, Logan. That is the real truth. And I know we've got a lot to work through. If…if Caleb doesn't make it, I don't know if we can, either."

Logan understood what she was saying. The pain would be too great, the loss too overwhelming, for them to ever find happiness together again. Suddenly he knew what they had to do.

"Trixie, listen to me," he said, his voice low and full of pain. "We've been praying for the wrong things.

We've asked God to spare our child, but it's not up to us to ask that.''

Shocked, she raised her eyebrows. "Well, I intend to keep on asking, whether it's my place or not."

"Hear me out," he said, his hand on hers tightening. "Maybe we should just turn it all over to God. Maybe instead of blaming each other, and rehashing all the old hurts, we should just let go and give this burden to the Lord."

"Just give up?"

"No, honey. We won't be giving up. We'll be letting go—of all the pain, all the sins and the lies, all the bitterness. Maybe that's the only real way we can help our son."

Tears pricked her eyes. "Now look who's so smart."

Logan shook his head. "No, actually I've been a fool. We know we love each other, but we forgot one important element of love."

"What's that?"

"Trust," he replied, his gaze slipping from her to his son. "We forgot to put our trust in each other, and in the Lord."

He was right. All of these many years, she'd believed she was in total control, while all along she'd let others control her life. Pamela. Harlan. Radford. Never once had she turned things over to God, not in the real sense of the word. And she'd never really trusted anyone, because all of those around her had let her down so many times.

Except God.

Somehow He'd brought her back here to be with her son. Somehow, through all of the pain, He'd shown her the truth.

"Okay," she said, "I'm willing, Lord. I'm turning

this burden over to You. I leave my son in Your hands. And whether he lives or dies, I trust You to protect him and watch over him.''

''Me, too, Lord,'' Logan echoed.

They both let go of Caleb's hand, then turned to each other, a new hope, a new peace apparent in their expressions as they held each other close.

''I love you,'' Logan said.

''I love you, too.'' Trixie held tight to that, even as she gave up control. Then she whispered, ''And I trust you—completely.''

''Enough to eat my chili?'' he asked, his eyes bright with tears and laughter.

''Yes,'' she answered, laughing. ''Even that much. But another time. I'm not leaving the hospital.''

''Still stubborn,'' Logan whispered. But he took her hand, and together they sat, watching over their son.

Much later, Gayle came back in, ready to take over the constant vigil.

''Your mother and I had a long talk,'' she informed Trixie, her tone as firm and unyielding as ever. ''I think we've reached an understanding.''

''I'm glad, I think,'' Trixie said, wondering just what kind of understanding these two very different women had reached.

Trying to reassure her, Gayle smiled. ''Your mother is a very strong woman. I admire that much about her. I think I can tolerate her, after all.''

''Another miracle,'' Logan whispered.

Chapter Fifteen

Gayle sat huddled near her grandson's bed, her hand in his. Logan stood in the corner, his eyes never leaving his son's face. Trixie watched from outside, through the glass window to her son's room. She'd sent Pamela back to the ranch earlier to get her a suitcase of fresh clothes. They were all afraid to leave the hospital now.

Caleb wasn't responding to any of the treatment the medical staff had tried. As the minutes turned into hours, Trixie's heart began to sink once again. She had to accept that Caleb might not ever wake up.

And still she prayed. Still she held out hope as she gazed at her child. So small. So very innocent.

How should she ask God for help?

Should she promise to walk away, if only He'd spare her child? Should she beg, plead, bargain, barter, threaten, or should she simply get down on her knees and hand it all over to Him?

"I'm so tired, Lord," she said, her eyes on Logan. "So tired. I can't bear this alone. I've fought against this for so long, holding my sin in my heart. And now, the truth has come out. Don't make my son suffer anymore. That's all I ask. And please, help me to forgive and to understand why they kept my child from me. And help Logan to heal, too. Help me, help us, Lord.''

She turned away from the window, unable to watch Logan's tortured face any longer. Harlan was there, with outstretched arms. Trixie willingly ran to him, letting him tug her close in the comfort and security of his arms. "Granddaddy, I don't think I'll make it if he dies.''

"Hang in there, honey," Harlan said, his tone sweet and encouraging. "It ain't over till it's over. As long as there's breath in him, there's still hope.''

"But will it ever really be over?" she asked as he guided her to a chair. "I mean, if Caleb does make it, we still have so many problems to deal with. Logan and I held our secrets so well—how can we learn to really trust each other again?''

"Love," her grandfather replied simply. "Love, darling. That's the miracle.''

"I don't think there are any miracles left," she said, laying her head on his shoulder.

"You rest, then," he replied, his big hand patting her arm. "And leave the miracles up to the man in charge.''

Logan came out into the hallway, his gaze scanning the area until his eyes settled on Trixie. "Can we talk?''

Harlan rose out of his seat, then glanced down at his granddaughter. "Do you want me to stay?''

"No. I'll be okay.''

"Then, I'll go in and see my great-grandson," he said as he shot Logan a worried glance.

Somewhere across the way, a television set blared the evening news. A car commercial came on, the pitch man spouting out the deal of a lifetime. Logan glared at the television as if it were the cause of all of his problems.

"What is it?" Trixie asked, bracing herself for the worst.

He took her hand, his eyes gentle. "I just wanted—"

But Trixie's gaze was fixed on the television now. "Logan, look. It's my mother."

Pamela stood on the back porch of the ranch house, her tasteful jewelry glittering in the late afternoon sun. "And I'd just like to clarify the entire situation. I repeat, Mr. Logan Maxwell, foreman of Brant Dunaway Farms International, has in no way jeopardized or neglected any of the children in his care. In fact, a social worker just finished investigating these unjustified allegations and I believe her report will indicate that the rumors regarding this ranch are unfounded and clearly false."

"What?" Logan glared at the television, in shock. "What is she talking about?"

Trixie could only shake her head. "I have no idea."

The camera moved to another woman standing with Pamela.

Logan groaned. "That's Mrs. Wilder, the social worker for the ranch. She comes by periodically to check on things and make sure the children are okay. But what's she doing with your mother?"

"Mrs. Dunaway is correct on all counts," the young woman said, her stance confident. "I've interviewed all of the children here, as well as the counselors and volunteers, and I feel confident that these allegations are totally false. Mr. Maxwell hasn't been neglecting his duties here. He's been at the county hospital with his son. The boy was involved in a four-wheeler accident."

Trixie looked over at Logan, her mouth open in amazement. "Rad," she said, realization sweeping through her. "He threatened to make trouble, and apparently he did just that."

Logan shook his head. "I'd better head out there to see what this is all about."

"Wait," Trixie said. "Knowing my mother, that might not be necessary."

When the camera panned back to her mother, Pamela beamed. "Of course, Ms. Wilder is just doing her job based on the unsubstantiated rumors she's heard, but I can assure the good citizens of Arkansas that the Brant Dunaway Ranch is a strong, viable refuge for troubled teens and other children with special needs. My family has contributed largely to this project, and we have always been completely satisfied and pleased with the work here. Logan Maxwell is a good man, and a hardworking, highly trained individual. And I, along with several of the best attorneys in the state, dare anyone to prove otherwise."

"She's obviously delusional," Logan said, the black humor breaking some of the tension he'd felt all morning. "I mean, since when does your mother go around defending me?"

Trixie looked into his eyes. "I'm sure we'll hear all the details later. But I believe my mother just stood up for you because she realized that you are a good and decent man, and that I love you."

"How?" he asked, the awe in the one word causing him to hang his head.

"How what?" Trixie lifted his chin with a finger. "How can she defend you? How can I love you?"

"That about sums it up," he said, his hands settling on her shoulders. "I've been such a—"

"You've been worried about your son and the ranch," she interjected. "And I've been holding back."

"Another secret?" he asked, forgetting the drama unfolding on the evening news.

Trixie took his hand. "Not really a secret. Just a little bit of resentment. I resented you for keeping Caleb away from me. But I know in my heart, I wouldn't have wanted him to be raised by anyone else. You are his father, after all."

He looked away, down at the floor. "But it was cruel to keep him from you. You have to know how I feel."

"I do," she said, her hand moving over his face. "I know that we love each other, and Granddaddy says that's all we need. But, Logan, we have a lot to work through. I don't even know if I'll ever be able to tell Caleb the truth."

"Your granddaddy's right," Logan replied, his own hands coming up to touch her face. "Our love has to be strong, Trixie. We'll do it right this time—we'll get married. We'll take it a step at a time. And the first step is to hold tight to each other, while we pray for our son. Nothing else matters right now—not even the ranch."

She nodded her agreement. "With my mother in charge, I can assure you the ranch is in good hands, no matter what Rad or anyone else tries to pull."

Logan managed a weak grin. "There's a scary thought."

"Trust me," Trixie reminded him. "If Rad did try to stir up trouble, my mother would set him straight good and proper."

Logan tugged her into his arms, then closing his eyes in a silent, gentle prayer, all of the anger leaving him as he leaned on the strength of her love.

Trixie held to him, letting him anchor her there, letting him tell her with his touch and his kiss that he would always forgive her, no matter what.

They would fight, together, for the ranch, for their child, for their love. And with God's help, they'd survive.

A commotion all around them brought them out of their embrace.

"The doctors," Logan managed to shout, his face going pale. "They're headed into Caleb's room."

"I called them," Gayle replied from behind them. "Oh, Logan, he's awake. Caleb's awake."

Tears of gratitude and joy fell down Trixie's face as she followed Logan into the room, their hands held tightly together while several doctors hurried to examine their son.

"Daddy?" Caleb called, his voice weak, his eyes widening at the sight of his father.

"I'm here, pal," Logan said, moving to the bed as doctors rushed past him to check all of Caleb's vital signs. "How ya doing?"

"Okay, I guess. Where's my hat?"

Trixie stood there with Logan, laughing and crying at the same time. "It's right here," she managed to say as she held up the battered cowboy hat.

"What happened?" Caleb asked, his little boy eyes bright with a million questions.

Logan looked from his son to Trixie, heaving a sigh of relief. "That, son, is a long story."

"Okay," Caleb said, drowsy again. "Hey, Miss Trixie, when we get home, will you finally, finally come and see my kittens?"

Trixie leaned close to place a kiss on her son's forehead as she reaped the joy of a new beginning. "I sure will. I love stray kittens."

Epilogue

One year later

"Come on, sport," Logan called to his son. "We got a new crop of volunteers to break in."

Trixie and Caleb both came down the porch steps, laughing and giggling as the morning sun lifted its shy head over the eastern horizon. Samantha followed close behind, her grin as wide as the sun.

"You two behave now," Logan warned his wife and son. "Don't want to scare them off before they even get to enjoy pig duty."

Caleb stepped up by his father, taking Logan's hand in his own. Then he turned to Trixie, reaching out a hand to her as several people piled out of trucks and cars, eager to spend a few days helping on the ranch.

"Hey, folks," he said before Logan could utter a word. Pulling Trixie and Logan forward, the little boy grinned. "This is my daddy, Logan." Then he looked up at Trixie, his eyes as vivid and blue as the autumn sky. "And this is my mama, Tricia Maria. You can call her Trixie."

Everyone laughed as Trixie bent down to hug her son close. "And you, silly boy, can go in and finish your breakfast."

Caleb giggled and ran toward the house where Gayle waved, then Samantha took charge with the new volunteers, leaving the little boy's parents to gaze into each other's eyes. It had been a tough year, full of struggles and changes, but they had made it through.

Pamela had headed Rad's accusations off at the pass that day on the steps of the ranch house. She and the formidable Mrs. Wilder were now the best of friends. And Pamela was one of the most visible patrons of The Brant Dunaway International Farms. Her work here had brought Trixie's mother a certain amount of fame in both Texas and Arkansas. Pamela, in true socialite fashion, was having the time of her life. And so was her daughter.

Trixie smiled over at her husband, then patted the baby just beginning to grow inside her stomach. Soon they'd be in their new home, near the sunflowers, near the mountains.

"It's going to be a wonderful harvest, Mr. Maxwell," she said, all the love in her heart shining in her eyes.

Logan touched a hand to her stomach. "Every day's wonderful with you and Caleb here," he said. "And our little Harlan Branton Maxwell in there."

"What if it's a Pamela Gayle Maxwell instead?"

Logan rolled his eyes skyward. "Perish the thought."

Trixie snuggled close, kissing his jaw. "You know you love both of them."

"I know I love you," he replied. Then he kissed her. "Now, let's get to work."

"I'm ready," Trixie replied, her eyes scanning the distant mountains as she thanked God for blessing her with this second chance. Then she remembered one other very important person who would always hold a special place in her heart. "Thanks, Daddy."

The warm September wind lifted her hair away from her face, and one perfect golden leaf glided down from the great oak standing in the yard. Trixie caught it, smiled, then let it go, her heart filled with love.

And at long last, joy.

* * * * *

Dear Reader,

This book is all about second chances. Sometimes we make decisions that will ultimately change our lives forever. And sometimes we regret the choices we are forced to make. There are people out there who suffer each and every day for choices they made long ago. But I believe hope springs eternal. We might not be able to go back and change the past, but with God's help, we can move forward to the future. We have to look for the joy, and when we do get an opportunity to make things right, we have to take it and know that God is watching over us always.

This book was a joy to write because I've actually been on a ranch similar to the one in this book. That's where I got to know Cindy, who has turned out to be one of my closest and dearest friends. We had pig duty and yes, we did meet "The Pigmeister" himself, a handsome, intense young man who was determined to show the volunteers from the big city what ranch life was all about. After a massive attack of allergies, we survived and still laugh about our adventures today.

We found the joy of friendship.

Hope you find yours, too.

Until next time, may the angels watch over you while you sleep.

Lenora Worth

LOREE LOUGH

A full-time writer for many years, Loree Lough has produced more than 2,000 articles, dozens of short stories and novels for the young (and young at heart), and all have been published here and abroad. An award-winning author of more than thirty-seven romances, Loree also writes as Cara McCormack and Aleesha Carter.

A comedic teacher and conference speaker, Loree loves sharing in classrooms what she's learned the hard way. A mother of two grown daughters, she lives in Maryland with her husband and an old-as-dirt cat named Mouser (who, until this year—when she caught and killed her first mouse—had no idea what a rodent was).

SUDDENLY DADDY

Loree Lough

To Carolyn Greene, Cindy Whitesel,
Robin Morris, Mike Sackett and Carla Butler,
for their faith in the story, and to Anne Canadeo,
whose faith in my "talents" made this *book* possible.

Chapter One

Like gunfighters of the Old West, they faced each other in the middle of their living room, intent, it seemed, on making their first fight a humdinger.

"Don't be so naive," Mitch shouted. "Things like this don't happen every day. Besides," he added, jabbing a forefinger into the air, "you *knew* what I did for a living when we met."

Ciara matched his ire, decibel for decibel. "Isn't *this* a fine way to celebrate our one-month anniversary… hollering and yelling and—"

"Well, pardon me all the way to town and back," he retorted sarcastically, "but nobody ever told me I was an idiot for becoming an FBI agent before." He threw his hands into the air. "I sure didn't expect to hear nonsense like that *from my wife!*"

"I never said you were an idiot. I said if anything like what happened to Abe ever happened to you…"

He crossed both arms over his chest. She'd never seen him this way before, so it surprised her that her soft-spoken young husband's eyes darkened when he was angry.

Ciara held her ground. Narrowing her eyes, she said, "Abe died in the line of duty, and you have a bullet wound in your left side…pretty good evidence, wouldn't you say, that *you* could…"

He sighed heavily. "I've told you and told you—I was in the wrong place at the wrong time. It was a flesh wound. And it happened years ago, when I was a dumb kid, straight out of Quantico."

Her eyes widened. "Is that supposed to *comfort* me?"

Shaking his head, Mitch's shoulders slumped. "I don't know Ciara. I honestly don't know."

"It's just that I thought…I hoped once we were married, you wouldn't want to take risks like that anymore."

He plowed his fingers through his hair. "Oh for the luvva Pete. Now you're being downright silly. I don't *want* to take risks, but…"

The tears of frustration and fear she'd been fighting since their argument began, now threatened to fill her eyes. Life had taught her that crying accomplished little more than to make her nose stuffy. If she won this debate, it would be because she had *right* on her side, not because Mitch couldn't stand to see a woman cry. She covered her face with both hands and prayed for control of her emotions.

Mitch's hard stare immediately softened, and he crossed the room in three long strides. "Ciara, sweetie," he said, his voice thick and sweet as syrup, "don't look at me that way." He bracketed her face with both hands. "Aw, honey, I don't want to fight with you."

She looked deep into his brown eyes. *This* was the man she'd fallen in love with…warm, caring, understanding. Ciara was about to tell him she didn't want to fight, either, when he said, "Except for that little mishap, I was always careful—" he wiggled his brows suggestively "—even before I had a beautiful wife waiting for me at home."

He stood a head taller than she, outweighed her by seventy pounds, yet she'd bowled him over with one misplaced pout. *Lord, we both know he's nothing but a big softie. Please don't ever let me take advantage of that.*

She laid her hands atop his. "I *love* you, but I don't know if I can…" Her hands slid to his shoulders, and she shrugged, a helpless little gesture. "I'm not like your mother or your grandmother or your brothers' wives." Unable to meet his penetrating gaze, she glanced at the packing boxes still stacked all around the room. "We haven't even finished unpacking yet, and already we're making plans to attend an FBI funeral."

"I know it's hard, sweetie, but—"

Ciara wagged a finger under his nose. "Don't you *dare* tell me that his wife knew what she was getting into."

He grabbed her finger, kissed it. "Ciara…"

Her voice grew raspy, and she bit her lower lip in an attempt to stanch a sob. "I don't know what I'd do in her place. If anything ever happened to you…"

He held her tighter. "I love you, too. And nothing is going to happen to me, I promise. In a year or two, you'll be so bored with my nine-to-five routine, you'll wonder what all this fuss and bother was about." He kissed the tip of her nose. "In the meantime, you've got to remember that I know how to take care of myself. I don't take unnecessary chances."

She looked directly into his thick-lashed eyes. "I'm asking you not to take *any* chances."

The brown of his eyes went black again as he deciphered her meaning. "You're a cop's daughter, Ciara. You of all people should understand. It isn't just a job—being a special agent is my life."

She jerked free of his embrace. "According to the vows you took four weeks ago, *I'm* supposed to be your life!" Lifting her chin, Ciara added, "You're the center of mine...."

Mitch knuckled his eyes. "Look," he groaned, arms extended beseechingly, "can't we discuss this like grown-ups? Why does it have to be 'either/or'?"

"It doesn't get any more 'grown-up' than this, Mitch. If you keep doing what you're doing, it's just a matter of time until—"

Ciara perched on the arm of the sofa. "If only you could find a safer line of work..."

"Like *what?*"

She ignored his sullen pout. "I don't know. But there must be something...something that doesn't put you in the line of fire quite so often."

His frown intensified. "Well, I could always be a receptionist. Or a secretary, even!"

She ignored his scorn. "Save the sarcasm, Mitch. That's not what I meant and you know it. But at least you're on the right track." Ciara tapped a fingertip against her chin. "My dad left the department," she said thoughtfully, more to herself than to Mitch, "started teaching Law Enforcement at the University of Maryland when—"

"I'd go nuts," he blurted out, "staring at the same four walls all day, every day."

Was he being deliberately mule-headed? Or had this

been part of his character all along? Ciara completed her sentence through clenched teeth. "When he realized his job was worrying my mother to death. Dad left the department...because *he cared* about her."

The frown became a scowl. "I care plenty. Why else would I be standing here, trying to justify why I need to bring home a paycheck to support my family!" He paused, looked at her long and hard. "Go ahead, flash those big blue eyes all you want. Getting mad at me doesn't change the facts—your dad quit...because your mom henpecked him into it."

Ciara gasped. "My father is *not* henpecked. And he isn't a quitter, either!"

Mitch clapped his palm over his eyes. "I'm sorry. I shouldn't have said that. But cut me a little slack, will you? I'm still trying to figure out what pushes your buttons."

She had to admit, they *had* gone through the normal courtship process faster than most folks. A *lot* faster. Ciara wondered how many other couples found themselves at the altar three months after their first meeting.

Gently, Mitch gripped her upper arms, gave her a little shake. "I don't know what to say, Ciara, except I love you."

"And I love you. But I want to grow old with you. How can I do that if you end up like Abe?"

He stomped over to the window, leaned both palms on its sill. "You might be just a little slip of a thing, but you've got a stubborn streak wide enough for an NFL linebacker." He faced her, tucked in one corner of his mouth. "I'd never ask you to give up *your* job."

Ciara harrumphed. "I'm not in any danger from my fourth-graders."

He poked his chin out in stubborn defiance. "Give me a break. Those kids are crawling with germs."

She couldn't suppress a giggle. "Nothing that would kill me—" her smile faded "—and make a widower of you."

He pocketed his hands, stared at the toes of his shoes. "Frankly," Mitch said softly, "I'm disappointed. I expected better from you. You seemed so different from other women I'd known. That's why I fell forehead over feet in love. You were more than the most beautiful thing I'd ever laid eyes on, you had a heart as big as your head, and—" Mitch shook his head "—I never expected you to make me choose between the two most important things in my life."

He was a gun-toting, badge-carrying FBI agent, for goodness' sake; couldn't he see the evidence that was right under his nose! *I'm so afraid, Mitch,* Ciara wanted to shout, *I'm terrified of losing you!*

Exasperated, she rolled her eyes. "And here's a 'button' you can avoid in the future, Mahoney—I wouldn't have married a man who could be henpecked. I am not 'making' you do anything."

"Listen, Ciara," he said, massaging his temples, "I can't talk about this right now. I need to find a neutral corner, where I can think, and—"

"Fine," she said, heading for the stairs.

"'Fine' yourself!" he countered at twice the volume. "I'm going to the office for a couple of hours."

Simultaneously the bedroom door and the front door slammed.

It would be the last sound either of them would hear from the other for a very long time.

Ciara ran back down the stairs. He'd locked the bolt from outside, and her hands were shaking so hard it took three tries to get the door opened. "Mitch! Wait!"

But he hadn't heard her, for he was already backing down the drive. He must have been furious, she admitted, to make it that far in so little time. Standing in the open doorway, shivering in the wintry wind, she prayed he would look up and see her there on the porch, pull back into the drive....

Her pleas did not reach God's ear. If they had, the shiny red convertible wouldn't have peeled away from the curb like a speedster in the Indy 500. Probably, when she retrieved the morning edition of the *Baltimore Sun,* she would likely find skid marks from his '66 Mustang stuck to the asphalt, pointing like an accusing finger in the direction he'd gone.

Ciara retreated into the house they'd owned for one whole week and locked the door behind her. Her heart tightened as the bolt slid into position with a metallic *thunk;* it seemed such an ominous, final gesture.

She passed the first half hour pacing back and forth in front of the picture window, elbows cupped in her palms, heart lurching every time a pair of headlights rounded the corner, heart aching when they didn't aim up the drive.

There in the corner, amid to-be-hung pictures and stacks of books, stood their foot-high Christmas tree. Since they hadn't unpacked the ornaments yet, Ciara and Mitch had made do with several pairs of her earrings, a couple of his cuff links, curly ribbon, and a big red bow on top. It had looked adorable when they'd finished it last week—Christmas Eve. It just looked sad now, and Ciara resisted the urge to cry. She should be dry-eyed when he came back, not teary and sniffling, like a spoiled little girl....

It wasn't until she'd chewed a cuticle and drawn blood that Ciara decided to do some more unpacking. The activity, she hoped, would keep her from doing further damage to her fingernails. More important, it would draw her focus from the ever-ticking clock.

She arranged the good dishes and silverware in the glass-doored china closet, stood brass candlesticks on the mahogany sideboard, put a centerpiece of burgundy silk peonies on the table. Ciara had promised that on Sunday she would serve Mitch his favorite meal at this table—lasagna and Caesar salad. Surely things between them would be right by then.

Ciara tossed the empty boxes marked "dining room" into the attached garage, then got started on the family room. On either side of the flagstone fireplace she hung the carved wooden plaques and framed parchment awards he'd earned during his years at the Bureau, stood his guitar and banjo on one side of the hearth, his collection of walking sticks on the other. She filled the bookshelves with hard-bound adventure stories by his favorite authors, Dean Koontz and Jack London, and arranged his assortment of ceramic wolves.

Taking a break, she dropped into his brown leather recliner, which sat in its special place, facing the TV. It was an ancient, cavernous thing that had seen better days, but Mitch loved it, and the deep impressions, permanently hollowed into its cushions, were proof of that. Though it didn't match anything in the room—not the pale oak tables or linen-shaded lamps, not the blue-checked sofa or the white tab-topped draperies—the ugly old chair *belonged.*

She pictured him in it, size eleven feet on the footrest, one hand behind his dark-haired head, the other aiming the remote as channels flicked by at breakneck speed.

How many times had she looked at him in this chair, and felt her heart throb with love, her mind reel with amazement that an exciting, adventuresome man like Mitch Mahoney had actually chosen her as his own?

Could she make a man like that happy…for the rest of his life?

Not if tonight was any indicator.

Why did you ask him to choose between you and the agency? she asked herself. Didn't you learn anything from Mom and Dad's mistakes?

They'd been three days into the two-week church-sponsored cruise when her mother found out how much time Ciara had been spending with Mitch. "He's a cop," her mother had said. "You want to live the way I have for thirty years? You want to be miserable all the time, worrying every minute that—"

"He's FBI, Mom," Ciara had gently corrected. "And besides, we're just *seeing* one another. It doesn't mean we're going to get mar—"

"He's a flatfoot, just like your father. You want to know how he got that name? By stepping all over *me*, that's how!"

Eyes narrowed by fury, her mother had concluded the tirade through clenched teeth. "Why waste your time, *seeing* him at all…unless you're hoping to end up at the altar?"

Ciara glanced at his big, empty chair. He should be sitting there now, she told herself, rather than in some stuffy office…alone and angry and—

She could only hope that when he came home they could resolve the problem, ensure nothing like it ever happened again. Otherwise, scenes like that would become a habit, as it had with her mom and dad.

She remembered her college roommate, whose parents seemed more in love after twenty-five years of marriage than Ciara's parents had likely ever been. Surely Kelly's mom and dad weren't lovey-dovey *all* the time; in quiet private moments, their *real* feelings for each other surfaced. "They fell head-over-heels in love," Kelly had said dreamily, "just like in the movies." Love at first sight? Ciara had thought. *No way!*

And she'd kept right on thinking that way, until she first caught sight of Mitchell Riley Mahoney....

He'd been in the pool with a half dozen rambunctious youngsters. Judging by his height, his broad shoulders, his muscular arms and legs, she'd decided he must be a professional football player. And when he'd answered "Polo!" to a little boy's "Marco!" Ciara felt certain he was probably a loud, clumsy fellow. "Hey," she'd heard him shout, "play fair. It isn't your turn...it's *mine!*" *Self-centered*, she'd added to her list, and maybe even a bit of a bully.

No one was more surprised than Ciara, when Pastor Boone introduced them at dinner that night. His soft-spokenness, his sense of humor, his intelligence, surprised her as much as the polished manners and thoughtfulness that had him pulling out chairs, opening doors and fetching a refill of punch before she'd emptied her cup.

Like Cinderella, she'd fallen in love before the clock struck twelve.

Smiling, she snuggled deep into his recliner and inhaled its faint leathery scent. Running her fingers over well-worn arms, she closed her eyes and remembered the little boy who'd clung to the pool's ladder that first day. She'd thought it unfair at the time, a bit mean, even, the way he'd ignored the child. But when the game ended and the older kids headed off to catch a movie in the theater, she understood *why* he hadn't interfered...the child was terrified of the water.

Somehow, Mitch convinced him to let go of the ladder. Holding the boy close, he'd walked back and forth in the pool's shallow end, letting the youngster's toes drag the water's surface. The kid hadn't seem to notice, as he giggled in response to whatever Mitch was whispering into his ears, that he was being taken deeper, deeper...

Two hours later the kid was doing an awkward breast stroke...on his own.

Mitch had taught her about lovemaking in that same gentle, patient way. The size of a man, she learned that day, was not a barometer of his capacity for tenderness. Even now she only needed to remember their wedding night, when she had trembled, like a child afraid of the water, for proof.

Ciara had always taken pride in her strength, physical and emotional. What she lacked in height and weight, she believed, she more than made up for with something her grandpa had called *gumption*. But surrounded by Mitch's muscular arms, she had felt precious, treasured, like a piece of priceless porcelain.

Inwardly she gave a halfhearted smile. It's your own fault, Mitch Mahoney, that I've become the kind of woman I've always despised...weak, whining, clingy....

Sighing deeply, she rehashed their argument. If I had it to do over, she thought, I would never have brought up the subject of his job.

Mitch had always been forthright about everything, especially his work. He'd told her how long and hard he'd worked to earn his current status within the Bureau. And she had thought she was being honest with him. "I'm a cop's daughter," she'd told him when he'd pointed out that being married to an FBI guy wouldn't be easy. "If *I* don't know what to expect from marriage to an officer of the law, who does?" She'd gone into the relationship with her eyes wide open, thinking her strength—her gumption—would see her through those trying, worrisome times when he was late and didn't call. She would not whimper and nag, not even in the name of love, as her mother had done....

The trouble was Ciara had not counted on loving him *this* much. Everything changed when she realized that without him life would be empty, meaningless, terrifying. It would be easier now for her to be more understanding of her Mom, she knew.

So what had she done, the very first time she was put to the test? She'd acted like a spoiled brat, that's what. Ashamed—and a little embarrassed—Ciara hid behind her hands. You asked him to give it all up, because—

Because she'd turned on the tiny TV in the kitchen, hoping to catch the evening news as she'd loaded supper dishes into the dishwasher. It hadn't mattered that she'd never heard of Special Agent Abe Carlson before. The story affected her as much as it would have if the stranger had been Mitch's best man, or if he'd lived next door. The live footage of him, young and handsome...and dying in the arms of a fellow agent...had sent a tremor through her that had made her drop the saucepan she'd been holding. "What are those reporters thinking?" she'd asked Mitch. "What if his wife sees this film clip? Or one of his kids? They'd have that picture in their memories, forever...."

Mitch's gaze had been glued to the screen, too, and she'd watched his expression of horror turn to grief as he put his plate in the sink and silently left the room. She hadn't asked if he'd ever met Abe. Instead, she'd followed him into the living room, and like a pampered little girl, told him to give it all up, just like that.

"You knew what I did for a living when we met," he'd said. And he'd been right. As a good Christian wife, didn't she owe it to him to at least try to be supportive and understanding?

The question gave her new resolve. When he returned—soon she hoped, peeking at the clock—Ciara would show him that she'd married him for better or for worse. You never complained about the "better"— the thoughtful little things he did, the constant praise, the sweet lovemaking—so stop whining about the "worse."

"I've always been careful," he'd told her, "even before I had a beautiful wife to come home to." Being loving and understanding, even when it was tough, couldn't help but improve his chances out there in the mean streets. She would give her handsome young husband plenty of reasons to survive the day-to-day dangers that were a routine part of his job, because underneath it all—beneath the fear that he'd be hurt—or worse—*she loved him.*

Lord, she prayed, *please give me the strength to prove it—help me become the wife he deserves.*

Lieutenant Chet Bradley knew better than to question the Colombian. He'd ordered men killed for slamming doors, for interrupting telephone conversations, for talking out of turn. No one dared cross him; to complain was tantamount to suicide.

He'd been paid well for doctoring files and losing the evidence that would have sent the gangster back to his homeland, not in cash, but in pure, uncut cocaine, whenever and in any amount he requested, no questions asked.

Since the recent deaths of several mules, the Colombian and the U.S. governments had increased the pressure on transport of the white gold. "It's no longer worth the risk," Pericolo explained, ushering Bradley to the door. "Don't be a glutton," he added, handing the agent a small pouch, "for you'll get no more from me."

He'd had to be careful to keep his "fast lane" life in the shadows, so his top-of-the-line stereo equipment, designer clothes, and upscale vacations were things he'd had to hide from fellow agents. If he allowed even one of them to see the way he lived, they'd know in a minute he was on the take, because his life-style was impossible on an agent's salary alone.

No one knew that better than Bradley.

He supposed he could get used to living within his means again, as he had when he'd joined the agency. But he didn't *want* to.

And now, his money supply was dead.

"You look like you just lost your best friend," said Pericolo's next-in-command.

"Not yet," Bradley said, "but it could be terminal...."

"Naw," Chambro said, dropping an arm around Bradley's shoulders. "There are things we can do to, shall we say, save you."

Hope gleamed in Bradley's green eyes. "Yeah? What?"

"Let me walk with you to your automobile, Mr. Agent," the younger Colombian said, "let us talk."

In a hushed voice, Chambro spelled it out: He wanted control of the Pericolo empire, and he could get it...if he got rid of the boss. A few "favors" for Chambro—information leaked, files misplaced, evidence that would get Pericolo out of Chambro's way permanently—and Bradley would be guaranteed a continued supply of ready, untraceable cash. The would-be ruler leaned on Bradley's car door. "I'll leave the details to you, Mr. Agent. I am sure you can come up with a way we can—how do you Americans put it?—kill two birds with one stone." He gave Bradley a jaunty salute, and left him to consider his options.

Three days, Bradley said to himself. You've got three days to figure out how to get rid of Pericolo....

And then he knew.

Something Chambro had said reverberated in his head: "Two birds with one stone," he said, grinning. "Two birds with one stone...."

Mitch never left his office desk lamp on, so the dim light glowing from his cubicle puzzled him.

Lieutenant Chet Bradley hunched over Mitch's desk, riffling through his Rolodex. "Hey," Bradley said, holding up a card that read "Mahoney, Mitch." "I was just about to call you."

Mitch slid his briefcase onto the desktop, glanced at his wristwatch. "Good thing I'm here, then, 'cause it's nearly ten. Kinda late to be calling me at home, isn't it?" he asked, relieving Bradley of the card and returning it to the Rolodex.

He didn't know why, but being around this guy always gave Mitch an uneasy feeling. Maybe it's that weird grin, he told himself; shows every tooth in his head, but it never quite reaches his eyes....

But his mistrust of Bradley went deeper than any grin and farther back than he cared to remember. He'd hoped that once Bradley assumed his role as boss, the resentment would fade.

It had not.

The proof? He'd gone a long way in his years with the Bureau, but since being assigned to Bradley, Mitch had been given only the dullest, most routine cases, instead of the "newsmakers" he'd grown accustomed to working on. It seemed Bradley was trying to bore him to death…or kill his career.

Bradley made himself comfortable in Mitch's chair and pointed to a thick manila file folder. "Have a seat, Mahoney."

Mitch sat in the chair across from his own desk.

"It's like this," Bradley began, thumb and forefinger an inch apart, "we're this close to nabbing Giovanni Pericolo."

Mitch knew that for years the agency had been trying to put the Colombian away—or, at the very least, have him kicked back to his homeland at the end of a steel-toed boot—but like a greased pig, Pericolo had always managed to slide through the system before they could even issue a warrant that would stick. "What's the charge this time?"

Bradley adjusted the knot of his navy tie. "Tax evasion."

"Like Capone?" Mitch chuckled quietly, despite the fact that his head still ached from having argued with Ciara. "You've gotta be kidding."

"It'll stick, provided we can get copies of certain, ah, financial documents."

Understanding dawned on Mitch. "Ahhh, so that's why you're here. You want me 'inside.'"

Like a rear-window doggy, Bradley nodded. "Philadelphia, to be specific."

If this don't beat all, Mitch grumbled to himself. I'm lookin' down the barrel of the best case he ever offered me, but— But how could he accept it, after what had just happened at home? Ciara had been harping on the dangers of his job ever since their wedding night, when she'd noticed his bullet wound. Maybe if this case wasn't going to be dangerous...

Mitch scrubbed a weary hand over his face. It had all happened so fast. How would he explain to his boss that during his two-week vacation to the islands, he'd seen Ciara onboard ship and gone completely nuts. Except for the hours between midnight and 6:00 a.m., they'd spent every minute of the cruise together, and it had been pretty much the same story once they'd gone home. Two months to the day after he'd met her, he'd put a ring on her finger. One month later they'd been married, quietly, because that's the way they'd wanted it. And what with shopping for a house and packing and moving, he hadn't been able to find the time to tell his boss about it.

"I don't know if you heard, but I just got married...."

He couldn't tell if Bradley was very surprised or very angry. Mitch sensed an imaginary noose hovering over his head.

"I've been meaning to tell you," he added, "but—"

"Is this the little woman?" Bradley asked, picking up the photograph on Mitch's desk.

He nodded, and the loop dropped onto his shoulders.

The lieutenant's wolf whistle pierced the silence. "How'd you get a beauty like that?" he asked, putting the photo back.

Mitch's heart lurched as he glanced at her sweet, smiling face framed in silver. She was everything he'd ever wanted in a woman and more. I wonder how *she'd* answer that question, if it was put to her right now? he asked himself. "Just lucky, I guess," he said, and meant it.

"I guess you know this puts us in a bind, Mahoney. We don't like sending married men under...not for stuff like this."

He swallowed as the rope tightened.

"But you're the best man on my team."

Mitch shot the lieutenant a look that said "What?"

"You were handpicked for this one, Mahoney." He tapped his forefingers together.

Mitch sat up straighter. "To be frank..."

"But I have to warn you, this won't be an easy one."

He'd been around long enough to know what *that* meant; it was FBI code for "high risk." Which was exactly what had bothered Ciara about his job. And, too, he couldn't get Bradley's threat, made years ago on the obstacle course at Quantico, out of his mind: "One of these days, *I'll* have the upper hand, and *you'll* know how it feels to be bested." Mitch had "bested" other guys on the gun range, in footraces, on exams, and *they* hadn't taken it personally....

Now I'm supposed to believe he thinks I'm the "best man" to haul in a guy at the top of the FBI's Most Wanted list? Maybe he isn't trying to kill my *career*, maybe he wants to kill *me*....

Mitch ran a finger around the inside of his collar. "How long would I be, ah, in Philadelphia?"

"You know that's impossible to predict. But if I had to guess, I'd say a week, maybe two."

He couldn't leave Ciara that long. Not after what had just happened between them. Besides, he'd told her he would be back in a couple of hours. "Sorry, boss. No can do," he said emphatically. "Get yourself another man, because—"

"Let me make something perfectly clear, Mahoney— we don't have time to get another man. You're goin' in, and I'm gonna be your point man or else. Get the point?"

Mitch bristled. He wouldn't have trusted Bradley to get a black-coffee order straight, let alone act as his only means of communication with his wife and the people who could pull him out if things got rough. He nodded at the file folder. "How much time will I have to prepare if—"

The lieutenant pulled back the cuff of his left shirtsleeve and glanced at his watch. "Not *if...when.* And you're already a day late and a dollar short," he growled.

Instinct—and intense curiosity—compelled him to pick up the folder. Paging through its contents, Mitch found himself biting back the urge to wretch. He'd seen plenty of ugly sights in his years with the agency, but *this...*

He scanned the black-and-white pictures, hand-penned notes, fading faxes and speckled photocopies that depicted Giovanni Pericolo's life of crime. He would have a hard time forgetting any of it, particularly the photo he held. Pretty, petite, blond, the young girl reminded him of Ciara.

Mitch's eyes glazed as he stared at the file, unconsciously clicking his thumbnail against his top teeth. The file was full of reasons to put this guy away, but the government didn't have a shred of evidence to connect Pericolo with these heinous crimes. Like a giant squid, the Colombian's tentacles had reached across oceans, sucking the life from thousands of innocents.

He seemed to have no particular method by which he chose his victims. Did he throw darts? Toss a coin? The girl who looked like Ciara...what if Pericolo's random selection pattern had zeroed in on *her* instead?

This was no ordinary thug. Pericolo was bad to the bone. If Mitch *did* manage to get in close, he'd have to keep his back to the wall at all times, because Pericolo wouldn't hesitate for a heartbeat when deciding whether or not to kill him. The material in the file was proof of that.

For the second time in as many minutes, he realized he'd named Ciara's greatest fears.

Mitch knew this case was a career maker. Truth was, if he'd been offered this carrot six months earlier, he'd have snapped it up so fast there'd have been an orange streak down the boss's palm.

But a lot could happen in six months. Heck, a lot could happen in half that time—he'd met, fallen in love with and married Ciara in three. Before that he'd been responsible for himself and no one else. Now he had a wife who depended on him, and soon, he hoped, they'd have a family. What better inspiration did an officer of the law need for putting guys like Pericolo away for good?

Mitch turned the question over in his mind. Was protecting his family the reason he wanted this assignment, or merely an excuse to do what he would have done in an instant...if he hadn't let himself be swept off his feet by love for a five-foot, two-inch spitfire?

He wanted to do the right thing, for the Bureau, for Ciara, for himself. But what was the right thing? Mitch drove a hand through his hair. *Lord God in heaven, show me the way....*

"Maybe you could give me a little advice, here. See, my wife—"

"Don't look to me for marital advice," Bradley interrupted, hands up in mock surrender. "My old lady took off for parts unknown years ago."

"Ciara saw the Abe Carlson thing on the evening news."

Bradley snorted his commiseration. "Leave it to the media to make a bad situation worse."

"And she knows I got myself winged back in '90." He shrugged. "She put two and two together, and—"

"—came up with one dead hubby." Bradley shook his head. "It's tough, finding a woman who understands. When my wife left, she said right out that she didn't have the backbone for the undercover stuff."

"Well, let's face it. Hazardous duty isn't an easy thing for a wife to live with."

"Don't get me wrong, Mahoney, I'm really enjoying our little heart-to-heart, but we've got a narrow window of opportunity, here, and we need you in Philly, like, *yesterday.*" Grinning crookedly, he tried to lighten the mood by adding, "You're a CPA, with an impeccable record, and you speak fluent Spanish. You're perfect for the job."

Mitch forced a thin smile. *"Gracias, ser muy mandamas,"* he said guardedly.

"I can't *force* you to take the case, but look at it this way—we both know there's no love lost between us. Go to Philly and consider the hatchet buried."

Mitch shifted uneasily in the chair. He'd faced leather-jacketed thugs in dark alleys. He'd been shot, beaten, kidnapped...had looked Death straight in the eye more times than he cared to remember. But none of it had stressed him as much as the pressure being put to bear on him now.

"You bring Pericolo in, and you're sure to get another medal." Smirking, he added, "And I'll get a feather in *my* cap, too, for being the guy who hand-picked you."

He gave his words a moment to sink in. Mitch's mouth had gone dry, and he licked his lips. A big mistake, as it turned out, because the lieutenant read it as hunger to go under.

"First order of business…get rid of those sideburns. No more collarless shirts, no pleated trousers. Wingtips, not Italian loafers. You've got to look the part of a pencil-necked geek." He hesitated. "Let's face it, you're the Clark Kent of accountants. Just do the best you can, stay away from kryptonite, will ya?"

Mitch did not join in Bradley's merry laughter. "The wife and I, we ah, left things in a bit of a muddle tonight. I only came down here to clear my head."

"You had a fight?" Bradley asked. "After just three weeks of marriage?"

"Four," Mitch corrected.

The lieutenant shook his head. "Tough break, pal. You'll be lucky if you even *have* a wife if you get back from this one."

Mitch stared hard at him. *If?* Thanks for the vote of confidence, pal.

Standing, the boss handed Mitch a five-by-seven manila envelope. "Your new identity," he said, then pointed at Pericolo's file. "You know what to do with that."

It was a copy, of course, and once he'd memorized pertinent information, Mitch would burn it.

Bradley's matter-of-factness did little to blot Ciara's

image from Mitch's mind. Every time he blinked, it seemed, he saw the way she'd looked just before she'd rushed up the stairs. He remembered thinking about that as he'd headed for headquarters. Just last week he'd been forced to cock back his arm and punch a thug to get him under control. In those first, tense seconds after fist connected with cheek, the perp's eyes had widened with shock and pain. Ciara had worn the same expression....

He didn't want to leave her, not for a moment, especially not this way. He knew he could get out of going "in." But Bradley had said this case would put a feather in his own cap. He ain't gonna be tickled if you take that feather away, Mitch thought. He'll bump your rank back so far, you'll *never* catch up.

But what if Bradley was right? What if Ciara *wasn't* waiting for him when this was over? What difference did it make if he reached the top if she wasn't there to share it with him?

He needed to be part of this mission, but he needed to know she'd be there, waiting for him, loving him still, when it was all over...because he couldn't afford to be distracted, not this time. And what could be more distracting than wondering whether or not the job might cost him Ciara?

He posed the question lightly, as if it were a mere afterthought. "I won't breach security, of course, but if I could give my wife a quick call, feed her some innocuous details, so she won't worry...."

Laying a hand on Mitch's shoulder, the boss shook his head. "Sorry, Mahoney," he said, almost gently. "You know the rules—the less she knows, the safer you'll both be in the event that..." His mouth and brows formed a "you know what" expression.

Mitch fingered through the contents of the envelope. Passport, driver's license, credit cards, a library card. "It's just...we didn't part on a very pleasant note," he said without looking up.

He gave Mitch's back a brotherly thump. "Now, don't you worry, 'cause ole Uncle Chet is gonna take good care of your little lady."

The thought of it wrapped around him like a cold, wet blanket. Mitch shook off the feeling. He had to keep a clear head.

Every man in his family was or had been a cop. Ciara's father, too. They'd understand. They'd explain it to her, they'd be there for her. She'd be fine....

Still, it was a strange, foreign thing, this feeling of resentment bubbling in the pit of his stomach. He'd never before felt torn between duty and—

"There's a blue Ford Taurus downstairs," he said, grabbing Mitch's wrist, plunking a set of keys into his palm, "and a reservation at the D.C. Sheraton in your, ah, new name." Almost as an afterthought, he asked, "Did you go to church today?"

He nodded.

"Good."

Mitch heard the implication loud and clear. *You'll need all the Divine intervention you can get.*

"Now head on over to your hotel and get a good night's sleep. First thing in the morning get yourself to the nearest mall."

Mitch nodded again. Outfitting himself for undercover assignments had filled his closet to overflowing. Too bad his aliases never had his taste in clothes.

"Pericolo's expecting you, one o'clock sharp," Bradley added, "so when you get your new laptop, have the sales clerk load it up with all the latest accounting software...general ledger, spreadsheet, the works.''

"I'm a CPA," Mitch snarled, "I think I know what I need."

"We're gonna get him this time, Mahoney," he continued, ignoring Mitch's pique. He aimed both thumbs at the ceiling. "I can *feel* it!"

Mitch shuffled woodenly back to his desk, plopped the file and envelope near the phone, picked up the receiver. If Bradley hadn't been standing there, watching and waiting, he might have called Ciara, to explain...or try to, anyway. He took a deep breath, shook his head. It's better this way, he reminded himself. She's safer, and so are you....

He dialed nine for an outside line, then banged the receiver into its cradle. "What am I thinking? I can't call a florist—it's nearly eleven, and they'll all be closed."

"So? Write her a note instead."

Mitch met the man's steely gaze, and despite himself, decided there was truth in his words; a note would be better than a handful of cut flowers and a terse message penned by some unknown saleswoman.

He pulled a yellow legal pad and black felt-tip from his desk. "Dearest Ciara," he wrote, "I'm sorry for upsetting you tonight. First chance I get, I'll explain *everything,* I promise." He underlined *everything* three times, hoping she'd read the message between the lines. "Trust me, sweetie—I need that now. Don't ever forget that I love you more than life itself, and I always will." He signed it "Your grateful husband."

He folded the letter, sealed it in a plain white envelope and wrote her name across its front. With a deep sigh, he handed it to the lieutenant.

A chill coiled around Mitch's spine as Bradley tucked it into the breast pocket of his suit coat. It was like watching it go down a rat hole. He shook off the disheartening thought as Bradley said, "You're my responsibility, and I take that very seriously. I won't let you down. You have my word."

He wanted to spell out exactly what he thought Bradley's "word" was worth, but thought better of it. *He's not much, but he's all you've got. You can't afford to rile him now....*

He grabbed the file and the envelope containing his new "self", and they rode the elevator down to the lobby. The silence between them continued as they stood on the sidewalk outside headquarters.

Mitch turned up his collar to fend off the wintry December wind. For a moment he stood on the corner of Ninth and Pennsylvania, oblivious to the screaming sirens and honking horns around him. Far in the distance, pinpricks of light winked from the windows of houses in the D.C. suburbs, reminding him that forty-some miles away, a light glowed in a window in Ellicott City, too. And if he knew Ciara, she was standing in that window right now, watching for him....

Mitch straightened his back. Cleared his throat. Bradley had said two weeks. *Two weeks,* he reminded himself. *Maybe less. Not so long, really....* "Well, I'd better get a move on," he said, and headed for the car.

"Two for the price of one...I'm here for ya, pal," Bradley called after him.

Without turning around, he threw a hand into the air, as if to say, "Thanks." But the thought in his head was, *Uh-huh, and the last horse to win the Derby was a mule.*

Mitch believed he understood what Chicken Little must have felt like, and gave a cursory glance toward the sky...just to make sure it wasn't falling....

Chapter Two

A shaft of sunlight, slicing through the bay window, slanted across her face. Ciara came to gradually, and slowly acknowledged every kink and cramp in her joints. She'd fallen asleep in Mitch's chair, cuddling the fluffy pillow he liked to tuck behind his lower back.

She headed for the front door. "Please, God," she prayed as she went, "let his car be out there, where it belongs."

Her sporty white Miata looked smaller and sad, parked alone at the top of the drive, as if it missed the companionship of the little red Mustang.

Ciara didn't know whether to be angry or hurt or terrified. She half ran to the kitchen, grabbed the telephone and dialed his direct line. She didn't know what to say when he answered, but she knew this: it would be a relief to hear his voice. Angry or pouting or tired from spending the night at his desk, at least she'd know he was all right.

She counted ten rings before a man said, "Hullo..."

Once before, another agent had picked up Mitch's

phone. But that had been a weekday afternoon, not six o'clock in the morning. "Is Mitch Mahoney there?"

"Hold on, I'll check," said the gruff, unrecognizable voice. And a moment later he said, "I don't see him. Want I should take a message?"

Ciara sighed. "No, thanks. I'll try back later."

"Okey-dokey," he chimed merrily, and hung up.

She showered and dressed and called again. And again an hour after that. "Parker, here," said the agent who answered this time.

Briefly Ciara introduced herself. She didn't want the guys at the office knowing their private business, and so she said, "He left a folder on the table. I just wanted to let him know it's here."

"If I see him," Parker said, "I'll tell him."

"Is there any way I could find out where he is?" Ciara tried not to sound anxious. "I really need to speak with him."

"You could ask his lieutenant. Lemme see if he's in his office."

She put on a pot of coffee while she waited on Hold, made it extrastrong, the way Mitch liked it, in case he came in before she got answers to her questions.

"Lieutenant Bradley doesn't usually get in till nine. I left a message on his desk to call you, Mrs. Mahoney."

A minute later she found herself standing with receiver in hand, staring into space. Ciara hung up, hoping she'd had the presence of mind to thank the man for all his trouble.

"Where could he be?" she whispered.

Chester, who'd been staring out the low-slung bow window in the breakfast nook, trotted over to his mistress. She'd more or less been aware that, as she paced back and forth with the phone pressed to her ear, the dog had been pacing, too…from window to window. He sat back on his haunches and whimpered for some attention.

Distractedly she patted his honey-colored head, then opened the back door. "No digging under the fence, now," she warned, wagging a finger. Chester sat in the open doorway, cinnamon brows twitching, caramel brown eyes pleading for a moment of affection.

On her knees, Ciara wrapped her arms around his fuzzy neck. "You're worried about him, too, aren't you?" she asked, smoothing back his shaggy ears. He'd taken an immediate liking to Mitch—something not one of her former boyfriends could claim—so much so that she'd felt a pang or two of jealousy as the dog followed him from room to room. "Don't you worry. I'm sure he's fine."

Chester responded with a breathy bark, then bounded out the door.

Ciara stood on the small porch and watched him, scampering after a squirrel. "If only I could stop worrying that quickly," she said to herself.

Something told her it wasn't just the late-December weather that sent a shiver up her back.

"Come in, Mr. Lewis, please, come in." The swarthy man grabbed Mitch's hand, shook it heartily. "My friend and your cousin, Buddy Kovatch, recommends you highly."

Your friend, Mitch thought grimly, is a stooge. But at least he's earning the big bucks the government pays him to be a stooge. Buddy Kovatch had been a trusted Pericolo employee for nearly two decades. His last bust would have sent him up to Jessup for ten-to-fifteen if he hadn't agreed to help put his boss away for good. The government buried the charges against Buddy, and in exchange, he put in a good word for the agency's "plant." And now Mitch, posing as Buddy's cousin Sam, would "keep" Pericolo's books until he gathered enough evidence to arrest him for tax evasion.

Smiling, Mitch bobbed his head good-naturedly. "Please. Call me Sam."

Though he wore a wide, friendly smile, Giovanni Pericolo's dark eyes glinted with icy warning. "Very well, then, Sam it is." He gave Mitch's hand a tight squeeze and added, "I hope for your sake, Sam, that you can live up to your stellar reputation...."

He took a new deck of cards from his jacket's inside pocket, unwrapped it, and handed the cellophane to a white-gloved manservant. "Pick a card, any card," Pericolo said. Except for a hint of a South American accent, he reminded Mitch of every sleight-of-hand expert he'd seen on "The Ed Sullivan Show." Without looking at the card he'd chosen, he handed it back to Pericolo. The Colombian gave it a cursory glance, replaced it in the deck and, silent smile still frozen on his face, led Mitch into the dining room, repocketing the deck as they walked.

"Darling," he crooned, "I'd like you to meet Sam Lewis, our new accountant. He'll be spending a lot of time around here from now on." He pulled her to him in a sideways hug. "Sam, this is Anna, my lovely wife."

The shapely blonde patted her husband's ample belly, her wide smile barely disturbing her overly made up face. "It's a pleasure to meet you," she said. "Won't you have a seat? Dinner will be served momentarily."

Pericolo's chest puffed out like a proud peacock's as

he moved to stand behind a teenaged boy. "My son, David," he said, gently squeezing his look-alike's shoulders. "He's a big boy for fourteen, don't you think? David, say hello to Mr. Lewis."

"Hello, Mr. Lewis."

The boy would not meet his eyes, a fact that made Mitch tense. "Good to meet you, David. You on the football team at school?"

David shook his head.

"Basketball?"

He glared openly at Mitch. "Don't like team sports," he snapped.

"Don't have the grades to make the team, you mean," said his sister.

David cut her a murderous stare that not only immediately silenced her…it chilled Mitch's blood as well.

"And this," Pericolo interrupted, concluding the introductions, "is my beautiful daughter, Dena."

Mitch guessed her to be sixteen, if that. Her bright red fingernails exactly matched her highly glossed lips, her hair dyed two shades lighter than her mother's. The minidress and mascara-thick lashes told Mitch she had not been taught to dress for dinner by a church-going mother.

She tilted her head flirtatiously to say, "Good evening, Mr. Lewis. It's a pleasure to meet you."

"Same here," he said carefully.

Mitch followed Pericolo's move and took a seat, resisting the urge to excuse himself, find a powder room and wash his hands. Pericolo looked like he'd just stepped out of the shower, so why had the brief handshake made Mitch's palm itch, as if he'd smashed a spider bare-handed? He reminded himself that Pericolo had a reputation, too. Not just *any* spider, Mitch told himself, wiping his palm on his pants leg, a Black Widower.

Bradley and the director had spelled it all out during the meeting last evening. Tax evasion would be the *charge* they'd hang Pericolo with, but it wasn't the reason he'd made the FBI's Most Wanted list. Mitch didn't know of an instance when anyone ·had violated the law…man's or God's…the way Pericolo had.

His crimes were far more sinister, more evil than any Mitch had seen to date. And he'd seen some grisly things in his years with the Bureau—drug kingpins, hit men, bank robbers, kidnappers, hijackers—tame as pussycats, in Mitch's opinion, compared to Pericolo. Once he'd heard the details of the Colombian's ghastly crimes, how could he turn his back on the assignment?

Like many young men who dedicate their lives to fighting crime, Mitch, too, had started out with typically high-and-mighty ideals. Maturity, and the things he'd witnessed firsthand, had made him leave most of those lofty sentiments by the wayside. But so far, thankfully, he had managed to hold on to one objective: to do his small part in creating a safer, healthier life for kids. Those he and Ciara would have one day, even Pericolo's kids, deserved that kind of protection.

Rumor had it that Pericolo had no shame about what he did for a living, seeing himself as an "entrepreneur" who provided a certain group of "consumers" with a much desired product. Never mind that Pericolo had become one of the wealthiest men in the world by exploiting the weakest, most pitiful side of human nature.

Mitch had to take this assignment. If he didn't, he wouldn't have been able to live with himself if someday, one of Pericolo's "hollow bodies" turned out to be that of a friend, the child of a friend, one of his own loved ones....

"A toast," Pericolo was saying, "to the newest addition to my business family." Shimmering light, raining down from the Tiffany chandelier like thousands of miniature stars, glinted from the facets of his Waterford goblet and the bold gold-and-diamond rings on his long, thick fingers.

Mitch lifted his glass, glanced at Mrs. Pericolo. Was it a carefully disguised warning...or smug satisfaction...that chilled her smile? How much did she know about Pericolo Enterprises? Did she understand *how* her husband acquired the wealth that put her in this thirty-six-room mansion? He'd seen two Rolls Royces when he parked the rented Ford in the circular drive...was Anna's the silver or the gold one? Surely she suspected *something,* and if so, how had she taught herself to look the other way?

Mitch measured the atmosphere, chatting amiably when he thought it appropriate, nodding somberly when he felt he should. At the conclusion of the long, leisurely dinner in the elegant dining room, Pericolo's wife and children excused themselves, and Giovanni invited Mitch to join him for coffee in his study.

"Please, make yourself comfortable," he said, gesturing expansively toward twin bloodred leather chairs that flanked the massive mahogany desk.

Mitch chose the chair on the right, where he could keep an eye on the door...and keep his back to the wall. Pericolo lifted the lid of a teak humidor. "Cubans," he whispered harshly, tilting the box so Mitch could peek inside.

"Never touch the stuff," Mitch said, holding up a hand, "but thanks."

As Pericolo removed a long, fat cigar, Mitch said, "Mind if I ask you a question?"

Pericolo sat beside him, gold lighter in one hand, hundred-dollar cigar in the other. "You can ask," he said smoothly, his accent a bit thicker now that he'd downed a bottle and a half of Chateau Mouton-Rothschild. Swirling the cigar's mouthpiece between his lips, he ignited the lighter. "But I cannot promise to answer."

Mitch nodded and sipped his coffee. "What was the card game all about, Mr. Pericolo?"

"We needn't stand on ceremony, Sam," he mumbled around a mouthful of cigar. "Starting tomorrow, you will have your nose in the pages of my most personal, ah, shall we say 'affairs'? Please, call me Giovanni." His lips popped as he drew air through the cigar's tip. "Now, back to your question. You were referring to the card I asked you to pick, no?"

Another nod.

He lounged in the chair, broad shoulders nearly touching each curving wingback, shining black hair matting against the buttery leather. "Ah, yes," came his satisfied sigh. "You're sure you wouldn't like to light one up?"

Smiling thinly, Mitch shook his head.

Pericolo blew a perfect smoke ring, poked the cigar's glowing tip into its floating center. "I have asked many men to choose. Not one has asked me why." His dark gaze bored into Mitch's eyes. And then he laughed, a short staccato burst of snorts and grating snickers. "Perhaps that's because so few *could*."

Crossing his knees, he took another thoughtful drag from the cigar. "You drew a red card. Queen of Hearts, to be exact." Through cold-as-death, narrowed eyes, he studied Mitch's face for a moment. Grinning, he slurred, "You are not satisfied with this answer?"

Mitch shifted carefully in the chair, so as not to spill his coffee. "Ever since I was a boy, I've had this incurable need to know why."

"I understand completely. I have the same...shall we say...affliction." He shrugged. "I have accepted it as a trait of intelligent, ambitious men." He raised one eyebrow as his upper lip curled in a menacing snarl. "Still...it's sometimes smarter...and safer...not to know the answer." The well-practiced smile was gone, and his voice, which had been smoothly polite until now, dropped an octave, growled out as if his throat had been roughened by coarse sandpaper.

To this point Pericolo had been the perfect host, generous, humorous, magnanimous. But this, Mitch knew, was the *real* Giovanni. He felt a bit like he'd walked unarmed into a lion's cage, and found himself face-to-face with a recently captured, seasoned killer that the zookeeper hadn't bothered to feed in a week. To meet the old beast's golden irises meant certain death, for it could read fear in a man's eyes just as certainly as it could smell it emanating from his body. The difference? The lion killed to satisfy his hunger; Pericolo killed *because he enjoyed it*. The similarity? Once their bellies were full, neither gave another thought to their prey.

Mitch pretended to study the delicate rose pattern decorating his Wedgwood teacup. "Perhaps it's because I'm an accountant," Mitch continued, trying to appear nonplussed by Pericolo's not-so-veiled threat, "that I've always believed the devil's in the details. I like to dot all the *i*s and cross all the *t*s." He drained the coffee. "So if you'll indulge me...why ask me to pick a card?

And what's the significance of the red queen?'' Only then did he meet the beast's eyes.

Pericolo sniffed, gave a nonchalant wave with his cigar hand. ''No significance of any importance, really. A man in my position must be careful...I'm sure you understand....''

''I'm afraid I don't.''

Another chuckle. ''Well,'' he said, reclaiming his former suave, distinguished persona, ''then allow me to explain. One inaccurate assessment of a man could mean—'' He drew a finger across his throat. ''It has been my experience that people seldom are what they appear to be.''

Pericolo, he knew, had taken this roundabout tack to make him nervous. This wasn't the first time he'd been eye to eye with a cold-blooded killer, but it was the first time he believed he might be killed just for sport. Mitch took a slow, quiet breath to ease his fast-beating heart.

''I do as much checking of the backgrounds as I can when bringing a new man aboard,'' Pericolo continued, shrugging one shoulder. ''At best, it's a fifty-fifty proposition. Some will be who they say they are, and others...'' He shook his head, hands extended in a pleading gesture. ''Despite my Oxford education—or perhaps because of it,'' he said, laughing softly, ''I'm a very superstitious man. The cards, if you'll pardon the pun, are my ace in the hole.''

''I'm a thick-headed Irishman, Giovanni,'' Mitch said, feigning a jolly laugh at his own expense. ''I'm afraid I don't have a clue what you're talking about.''

Straight-faced, Pericolo reached out slowly, deposited the smoking Cuban into the foot-square ivory ashtray on the corner of his desk. Mitch found it interesting that, despite what this man did for a living, the hand did not tremble, not in the least.

"Allow me to clarify it for you, then," he began. Settling against the chair's tufted backrest, he calmly folded his hands in his lap.

"If you had picked a black card, you would be dead right now."

Pericolo spoke so matter-of-factly, he may as well have been reading yesterday's baseball scores, or repeating the weatherman's prediction. Mitch leaned forward to put his cup and saucer on the desk, more to have a moment to compose himself than because he'd finished the coffee. He had never been fooled—not about men like this. Every last one of them were capable of look-you-in-the-eye, drop-you-where-you-stand murder, but...

"You are a lucky man, Sam."

His best bet, he decided, was to go for broke. "You would have killed me...for picking the wrong color?"

Pericolo's feral stare was all the answer Mitch needed. Yet the man felt inclined to add, "I have nothing more to say, Sam, except that life is fleeting."

Sitting back, Mitch leaned both palms on the chair, careful not to squeeze the armrests too tight, lest this proficient beast of prey sense his fear. "I've never been much of a card player," Mitch said, grinning sardonically, "but I've suddenly developed a strange fondness for them. Red queens, in particular."

The sound of Pericolo's boisterous laughter echoed in his ears long after Mitch went to bed.

It was 9:05 when Bradley read the pink "While You Were Out" message on his desk. "Call Mitch's wife," Parker had scribbled. Frowning, Bradley wadded the slip of paper into a tight ball, tossed it neatly into the metal wastebasket beside his desk. He'd done the very same thing last night with the letter Mahoney had written to his wife.

If Mahoney hadn't put in for the same promotion, none of this would be necessary. As it was, he'd made himself the unwilling pawn in Bradley's dangerous game against Giovanni Pericolo.

Two for the price of one, he thought, slouching in his chair.

Except for Buddy Kovatch, no one but Bradley knew where Special Agent Mitch Mahoney was right now. And Kovatch wouldn't be doing any talking. Not if he wanted to stay out of prison. He clasped his hands behind his head and smiled. "Sure is nice, bein' boss," he said to himself.

He didn't like admitting that if his uncle hadn't risen through the ranks to a position where he could pull strings, down in personnel, he wouldn't *be* boss.

His uncle's hands had been tied by that very same string—too many promotions would alert the rest of the brass to what was going on downstairs. Mahoney was Bradley's only competition for the upcoming administrative job slot, and there wasn't much doubt in Bradley's mind who'd get the job. Especially if the big dumb guy pulls off this case the way he's pulled off others in the past....

Well, Lady Luck had kissed Mitch Mahoney for the last time, Bradley thought, sneering. And if the fickle gal felt inclined to pucker up for him again, Bradley would be there to see that her lips never made contact.

Bradley had gone undercover once himself, and knew from personal experience that an agent had better not let anything distract him from the task at hand. And nothing, he'd discovered, was more distracting than a rift with a spouse.

His grin grew. Two for the price of one....

He had no intention of being Mahoney's message boy. Or his wife's delivery man, for that matter. He wants to make fast tracks to the top, let him do it without my help!

Mahoney would nab Pericolo, all right. Bradley would be surprised if he lasted three days after bringing in the evidence the U.S. Attorney needed to convict the Colombian. If Pericolo didn't give the order—from his prison cell—to make a door knocker out of Mahoney's head, Bradley had plans of his own for the Irishman....

Two for the price of one....

He snapped the mini-blinds shut, effectively closing himself into his ten-by-ten office. He propped the heels of his wingtips on his desktop and leaned back in his highback chair.

His thin lips curled into a malicious grin.

Two for the price of one....

Chapter Three

❧

When he got the call and heard the agent say he was on his way home, Bradley knew he'd better act fast. As he made the forty-minute drive from D.C. to Ellicott City, he slammed a fist into the steering wheel. You should have done this weeks ago, he reprimanded himself. It isn't like you didn't have plenty of opportunity....

Grinning crookedly, he recalled the many times he'd visited pretty little Mrs. Mahoney. That first time in particular stood out in his mind. It had been a week to the day after Mahoney went undercover. She'd looked like a high school kid in her faded jeans and oversize Baltimore Orioles T-shirt, long blond hair tied in a ponytail on top of her head. The whites of her big blue eyes were pink from crying, and there had been a box of tissues tucked under her arm when she opened the door. When he flashed his badge, she would have slumped to the floor for sure...if he hadn't reached out to steady her.

"I thought...I thought you were here to tell me he'd

been…killed,'' she'd stammered once she'd regained her balance.

He'd given her a moment to calm down before explaining how things worked. ''Mitch has left town, on…well, let's just say…company business.''

''Left town? But…but we were just married.'' Several silent seconds passed before she said, ''I suppose you sent Mitch because you had to. I mean, there wasn't anyone else avail—''

''Actually, Mitch volunteered. Seemed quite eager to go, in fact.'' Shaking his head, he'd added, ''I think he's out of his ever-lovin' mind, 'cause *nothing* could have made *me* leave a pretty little thing like you at home.''

She had paid absolutely no attention to his blatant flirtation. Ciara's bright eyes had brimmed with tears as she stood wringing her hands, trying hard not to cry.

''Now, just to make sure everybody stays safe,'' he'd continued, ''there can be no direct communication between you two.'' He had to sound convincing, because one thing Bradley didn't need was a hysterical wife phoning the director, asking when her husband would be home.

She could write letters to her husband, he instructed, as many and as often as she wanted, and Mahoney could answer, when and if his situation permitted. In any case, all messages would be written in Bradley's presence…and immediately destroyed by him once they'd been read.

Her eyes filled with tears again, and she'd looked so much in need of a comforting hug that Bradley gave her one. ''I have a feeling you have what it takes to be patient,'' he'd added, stroking her back.

Even now, seven months later, he remembered how

she felt in his arms. She'd trembled, like a baby bird that had fallen from its nest, felt so small, so delicate, that he had to force himself to hold her gently, taking care not to press her too close. Too bad she has to be part of the plan, he'd thought. But the reality of it was that without her, he couldn't pull it off. It was as though she'd read his mind, because no more than a second, perhaps two, ticked by before she'd stiffened, wriggled free of his embrace. The look on her face reminded him of the time when, at sixteen, he'd been caught, red mouthed, kissing Mr. Cunningham's daughter. Hands pressed to her tear-streaked cheeks, Ciara had seemed ashamed to have allowed another man to touch her, even in a gesture of comfort.

Now, as he peered at his reflection in the window beside her front door, Bradley admitted that he'd told one truth that day. "If I had a woman like her waiting for me at home…" The memory of her pretty, sad-smiling face flashed in his mind. If she was *your* wife, he told himself, a lot of things would be different today….

The hostility he'd harbored toward Mahoney intensified as he acknowledged that, yet again, he'd been bested. The grudge went way back, to the days when Mahoney outshot, outran, outscored him at Quantico. These months of watching his wife's devout fidelity only served to sharpen his prickly envy. Would a woman ever love *him* that much? Bradley wondered. Never a woman like Ciara…beautiful, warm, intelligent, endlessly devoted to her man.

He blinked, shook his head. You can't afford to feel anything for her, he admonished. Not admiration, not respect, certainly not concern! It would mean letting down his guard, and to do that around a guy like Pericolo…well, he may as well put a gun to his own head.

Two for the price of one, he reminded himself. Two for the price of one.

Bradley straightened his tie, ran a hand through his reddish blond curls, nervously tugged the cuffs of his sports coat and rang her doorbell. As he waited for Ciara to answer, he rehearsed the plan…one more time.

"Lieutenant Bradley," Ciara said, smiling when she opened the door. "Please, come in." Once he was inside, she asked softly, expectantly, "Is there a letter this time?"

He could have said no and let it go at that. Could have shaken his head sadly, feigning commiseration. "I told you, this is just the way Mitch *is* when he's on assignment." Winking, Bradley lowered his voice. "He says if his babes worry enough, he's guaranteed a memory-making homecoming!"

Sometimes he got the impression that once he'd told her there was no word from Mahoney, she simply tuned out everything else he said. This time, Ciara's silence—and the heat emanating from her blue eyes—told him she'd heard every word.

"I'm sorry. Guess I shouldn't have said that."

As always she shrugged it off. "Then…if there's no news…"

If there's no news, why am I here? he finished, gritting his teeth. I was wondering how long it would take you to get around to saying it this time.

The third or fourth time he'd visited her, Bradley had brought a bouquet of flowers. It had surprised him more than a little to discover that neither his corrupt behavior nor the people he'd been hanging around with lately had snuffed out his conscience. If she hadn't been so doggoned *sweet,* maybe he wouldn't have felt so bad about using her. Guilt had nagged him into popping for two dozen long-stemmed white roses. She'd thanked him. Said he shouldn't have. And stuck the box on the foyer table. May as well have tossed that hundred bucks in the trash, he reprimanded himself, because he had a feeling the prickly green stems would never see water. Not because she was an ungrateful sort. Quite the opposite, in fact. Ciara Mahoney would consider it improper to display flowers given by a man who was not her husband...particularly when that husband had vanished from her life like chimney smoke.

A couple of months back, he'd brought donuts and coffee, hoping this less extravagant, more friendly gift would help her warm to him, even slightly. Ciara had arranged the treats on a blue-flowered plate, poured his coffee from the paper cup into a matching mug and placed a white cloth napkin beside it. Two bites of a cruller and a sip of coffee later, he realized she had no intention of joining him. She sat stiffly across from him, smiling politely, her gaze darting to the kitchen clock every few seconds, as if counting the minutes until he'd leave. She was too polite, too kindhearted to say it straight out, but Ciara Mahoney wanted no part of Chet Bradley.

"Just stopped by to see how you were doing," he said, forcing the bitter memories from his mind. He sighed resignedly as if his message wouldn't be an easy one to deliver. "And to tell you that I saw Mitch again yesterday."

Well, you don't have to look so all-fired pleased about it, he thought when her eyes lit up. You haven't heard a word from that bum in seven months, but *I've* been here every week, like clockwork!

"He looked great," Bradley continued, "happy, healthy, well rested. Seems our boy is having a grand old time on this assignment, so don't you worry your pretty little head about him, you hear?"

He watched a myriad of emotions play across her delicate features before worry lines creased her smooth brow. "When will this nightmare ever end?" she whispered, and he suspected she hadn't intended to ask the question aloud. Her shoulders rose on a deep breath. "Can I get you something? Coffee? Lemonade?"

He plastered a practiced look of concern on his face. "Can't stay. I only came by to make sure you were okay. Is there anything I can do? Something I can get you?"

"No, but thank you, Lieutenant."

Grinning, he took her hand, gave it an affectionate pat. "'Lieutenant?' Ciara, you're breakin' my heart!" He chose his words carefully. "I've spent more time with you than your husband has these past seven long months. It wouldn't be improper for you to call me Chet, would it?"

She gave it a moment's thought. "You're right, of course...Chet."

He placed a mental check mark beside Part One of his plan. And now for Part Two:

"Did you hear something?"

His tense, slightly crouched posture had the desired effect. Ciara hovered near the wall, cringing, hands clasped under her chin, eyes wide with fright. "No, I—"

A forefinger over his lips, he warned her to be quiet. "Now, don't you worry," he whispered. "Chances are practically nil that Mitch has tipped his hand...and that's the *only* way those goons would know how to find you.''

Assuming the 'ready, fire' position, he unholstered his weapon, and as though he really believed a gun-toting bad guy had invaded the second floor, Bradley slowly made his way upstairs, darting into doorways, aiming the Glock at imaginary felons skulking along the hall, as if he truly expected an assassin to pop out and draw a bead on him.

The moment he ducked into Ciara's room, he straightened, calmly reholstered his service revolver. Smirking, he reached into his pocket and withdrew a small vial of Homme Jusqu'au Dernier. ''Now for Part Three,'' he said, his voice echoing quietly in the white-tiled master bathroom. '''Man to the Last,''' he translated the cologne's gold foil label. Opening the medicine cabinet, he placed the decanter on a glass shelf and gently closed the door.

Swaggering toward the hall, he pocketed both hands. It was all he could do to keep from whistling a happy tune. Pericolo was safe behind bars. ''One down, one to go,'' he singsonged.

First chance he got, Bradley would pay the newlyweds a little visit. If he knew Mahoney, he wouldn't be in the house five minutes before the subject of the cologne came up. They'd have words over whose fingerprints were all over pretty Mrs. Mahoney.

It wouldn't take much to convince Internal Affairs that the man of the hour had snapped after all those months in Pericolo's headquarters. Bradley's story that he'd killed the enraged husband in self-defense would go uncontested.

''One down, one to go,'' he repeated, grinning. ''One down, one to go....''

* * *

Mitch spent the first day and a half of his freedom down at headquarters, typing up the detailed report that outlined the case. He'd turned down the chance to be there when they picked Pericolo up; he'd seen enough of the Colombian to last several lifetimes. He glanced at the clock. They'd have him in custody by now.

He's probably already complaining about the way his orange jumpsuit clashes with his complexion. His Italian mother had been a fashion designer in Milan; maybe that explained why Pericolo was so focused on outward appearances. Ill-fitting prison garb was Giovanni's problem, and Giovanni was the U.S. Attorney's problem from here on out.

Mitch had troubles of his own, starting with the fact that he'd been away from home a long, long time. He'd known from the start that Bradley had underestimated the amount of time he'd be gone. *But seven months?*

The lieutenant had not been in touch once, a fact that had deeply concerned Mitch at first. But he'd been in situations like that before, and knew how to handle himself. It turned out to be a blessing, really, that he hadn't been able to make a single contact with the outside world once arriving in Philly; he may well have picked a red card from the Pericolo's slick deck, but the Queen of Hearts hadn't squelched the man's suspicions....

The phone in Mitch's room had been bugged, and he couldn't drive to McDonald's for a burger and fries without spotting a "tail." Whether brushing his teeth or watching TV or adding up columns in Pericolo's ledger books, he got the sneaking suspicion that he was being watched. Two-way mirrors...or paranoia?

Mitch discounted anxiety when, on a warmer-than-usual January day—the kind that gets folks hoping for an earlier-than-usual spring—he made it to a secure phone. He'd dialed FBI Headquarters in Washington, D.C., but Bradley hadn't been in, so he'd talked to Parker instead. "What's the weather like down there?"

"Same as there, I reckon…ice, snow, freezing…."

Mitch hadn't wanted to break the connection. He'd been in Philly for over a month by then, and the stress of being on Pericolo's payroll was beginning to take its toll. He hadn't been sleeping. Had lost ten pounds. And Ciara was never far from his mind….

He was about to leave a message for Bradley, when he spotted a black Cadillac rounding the corner. He'd seen that car in the rearview mirror nearly every time he'd climbed behind the wheel of his Ford. Mitch banged the phone into its cradle and quickly blended in with the crowd of people milling around the hot dog vender's cart. It had been a close call. Too close. And Giovanni must have agreed, because his men pressed in closer still after that.

Like a babe in the woods, Mitch had no protection in Philadelphia. He had no way to ask for help if he needed it. Didn't even have a weapon. He couldn't risk another phone call…until last week, when he finally got hold of Bradley to say he was in the Philadelphia Metro station. "Had to leave the car, the clothes, the laptop behind," he'd explained, "but I've got photocopies like you wouldn't believe. There's enough in my wallet to get me back to D.C. on the Amtrak. I'll call you when I get in."

Prayer had helped get him that far. Mitch hoped it would be enough to get him through this phone call.

"Hello?"

It felt so good to hear her voice that Mitch found himself swallowing a sob. "Hi, Ciara."

He heard her gasp. "Mitch? Is that…is it really you?"

Thank you, God, he thought, because she sounded genuinely pleased to hear his voice. He hadn't expected that. Not after the way they'd parted. Not after seven whole months apart. You don't deserve a woman this understanding, he admitted.

"I—I thought," she stammered, "it's been…you were…I just—" After a slight pause, her voice tightened. "Where have you been?"

He said it softly, gently, because that's exactly how he felt. "Sweetie, I wrote you…." At least he'd managed to get that one message through before Philadelphia had swallowed him up. Mitch thanked God again.

"Give me credit for having *some* intelligence, Mitch. I admit my behavior that last night was a little out of line, but to punish me this long…"

"Punish you?" He sat forward in his chair. What on earth is she talking about? He took a calming breath. "I know the letter was vague, but I couldn't give you any details. It would have been too dan—"

"What letter, Mitch? I never saw any letter. The only explanation I got about your disappearance was from your father and your brothers. 'All in the line of duty,'" she singsonged, the quote thick with sarcasm.

"But…" Now he understood why that sense of dread had loomed over him when he'd handed the envelope to Bradley.

"But *nothing.* All I can say is, thank God for Lieutenant Bradley. He stopped by every week to see if I needed anything…and tell me you'd missed another rendezvous. Which told me one of two things—either you were in too much danger to keep the appointments, or you didn't *want* to keep them." There was a long pause before she added, "He never said it outright, but I got the impression he believed it was the latter."

"Bradley's a bald-faced liar," he blurted out. "I can't believe he never gave you that letter!"

Until the pencil he was holding snapped, Mitch hadn't realized how tense he'd grown. He dropped the pencil halves and ran his hand through his hair. Bradley had put him out there alone, and he'd left Ciara the same way. Burning anger roiled in his gut. He didn't know what Bradley had to gain by his blatant lies—and he'd obviously told Ciara a pack of them—but he knew this much, he thought, balling up a fist, he had better not run into him, because what he would do to him would cost him his badge.

Mitch gulped down a mouthful of cold black coffee. He would deal with Bradley later. "I can be home by noon."

Home. The word reverberated in his mind like gentle rain, defusing his fury.

"Don't hurry on my account," she snapped. "You've been away from *home*," she said, putting an entirely different emphasis on the word, "for seven long months. What's another couple of hours?"

He stared at the buzzing receiver for a moment before hanging up. She had a perfect right to be upset. He only hoped when the time was ripe, God would feed him the words that would make things right.

He never would have agreed to take the case if he'd known he would be gone so long, but once he'd gone in, one week became two, and before he knew it, months had passed. There had been no turning back then. Not if he'd wanted to survive.

An icy sense of dread inched up his spine as he recalled the last thing Pericolo had said to him. "I'm fairly certain that the last words of men who dared to betray me were 'I'm sorry.'" His near black eyes had glittered when he made his hateful promise. "I have a long memory, Mr. Sam Lewis, and an even longer reach. Don't *you* become one of the 'sorry' ones."

Did the Colombian pack enough power to extend that "reach" beyond the walls of his prison cell? The U.S. Attorney didn't think so. "He's a has-been," the man assured Mitch. "Eduardo Chambro has been chomping at the bit to get control. Kovatch told me he said he owes you a debt of gratitude for getting Pericolo out of his way."

Mitch could only hope the lawyer had been right…and pray that all of Pericolo's soldiers were now loyal Chambro followers.

A moment ago he'd wanted nothing more than to get his hands on Chet Bradley. Now he only wanted to cuddle up with Ciara, close his eyes and let her kiss his worries and fears away, as she'd done on their wedding night, when the horrible dream woke him. Tiny as she was, she'd wrapped him in her arms and made him feel safe and secure and *loved*.

He refused to focus on her angry words, chose instead to remember the relief he'd heard when she'd said, "Mitch? Is that you?" The melody of her voice had been enough to raise goose bumps on his flesh. If it had been that good to *hear* her, Mitch could only imagine how much better would it be to *see* her. And once they were face-to-face, the misunderstanding would fade away.

After rushing through the final paragraphs of his report, he filed it, then drove like a madman around the D.C. beltway toward their home in the Baltimore suburbs. He'd spent a total of four nights in their new Cape

Cod-style home on Sweet Hours Way before their argument…before going undercover. It would be good, so *good*, to sleep beside her tonight in their low-ceilinged room at the top of the stairs.

It wasn't quite 10:00 a.m. when he pulled into the drive. She wasn't expecting him till noon. Mitch glanced at the window on the second floor. Their bedroom. Was she up there, getting ready for him, applying mascara, spritzing herself with perfume, brushing her long, lush hair?

He ached to see her, hold her, kiss her sweet lips.

Mitch slid the wallet from his back pocket and withdrew the photograph he'd been carrying for nearly a year now, the one his brother Ian had taken during the church-sponsored cruise. Mitch's big fingertips gently caressed her glossy image—as they'd done thousands of times since he'd left her that cold, bleak night—and smiled tenderly.

There had been other pictures he might have chosen to carry with him—Ciara, looking like a fairy princess in her wedding gown; Ciara in the pink suit she'd worn after the reception; Ciara in sweats and a baseball cap on the day they'd moved into this house. But this, by far, was his favorite.

Weeks after his family and hers had walked away from the cruise ship, long after the film was developed, Ian would look at this picture and remark, ''Y'know, you two look good together. You're a perfect fit.''

Mitch couldn't deny it then. He couldn't deny it now.

Everything about them was different—size and weight and coloring, and the contrasts were good. She was femininity personified, he, man to the bone, and the balance was right.

He recalled the events leading up to the taking of this

picture. They'd been too busy swimming, sight-seeing, playing shuffleboard, to watch the sun set. Once, she'd been sitting in a deck chair, so caught up in her book that she didn't hear the gaggle of kids headed her way. If he hadn't scooped her up, they'd have run right into her. "My hero," she'd said, grinning and fluttering those long, dark lashes of hers.

That night they scheduled a time to watch the sun set. Arm in arm, they'd positioned themselves at the boat's bow, waiting to see the blazing fireball slip behind the horizon and disappear. When it finally disappeared, like a coin in slow motion, sliding into a slot, she'd faced him, and in a womanly, wifely way, tucked his windblown necktie back into his jacket. She hadn't removed her hands once she'd finished. Instead, Ciara had looked up at him and smiled. From the dreamy, wide-eyed expression on her face, he had expected her to say, "It's such a lovely evening," or "Isn't the view spectacular?" Instead she'd grinned mischievously. "My stomach's growling like an angry bear. What say we hunt ourselves up a snack?"

"You're a little nut," he'd said, gently chucking her chin.

She'd bobbed her head and launched into her own musical rendition of the once-popular candy bar commercial: "Sometimes I feel like a nut—" her silliness slipped away, like the sun's fading light "—sometimes I don't...."

That quickly the mood shifted, from lighthearted merriment to something he hadn't been able to identify. He only knew that his heart was thumping and his pulse was pounding as she looked into his eyes.

They skipped dinner that night, preferring instead to stand at the prow until the earth darkened and the black sky above the cruise ship was haloed by the glow of the midnight moon. The boat rocked gently as it slogged through the inky island waves. She'd pointed toward the horizon. "The water is so bright, so clear blue during the day. Amazing, isn't it, that now it looks like black velvet."

He'd grasped her shoulders, turned her to face him. It was as he gazed into her eyes...eyes as bright and clear blue as the daytime Caribbean, that he knew how to define that look—love. And he'd kissed her, long and hard, as if to seal it between them for all eternity.

He'd walked her to her cabin, kissed her again in the narrow hall outside the door. "Let's do this again tomorrow," he'd whispered.

"Which," she'd asked, wiggling her brows suggestively, "the walk around the deck or the kiss?"

"Both."

And so they had. The very next evening, Mitch missed the sunset altogether, because he hadn't been able to make himself focus on anything but Ciara. After an hour or so of gazing into her eyes, listening as she talked about the kids in her fourth-grade class at Centennial Elementary, as she told him about her golden retriever, Chester, he wrapped her in his arms, pulled her close.

"Oh, my," she'd gasped, fanning her face with a delicate hand when the kiss ended. "You're getting pretty good at that."

Grinning like a love-sick schoolboy, he'd placed a hand upon her cheek, and she'd copied his movement.

That's when Ian snapped the picture.

Looking at this photo of them, outlined by the amber-orange sky, had brought him countless hours of comfort, had given him immeasurable peace in Philly, as he crossed the days, the weeks, the months off the calendar pages.

She was a vision, brighter and more beautiful than any sunset ever photographed. Her hair riffled by the breeze, billowing out behind her like a sunny sail as sun-sparkled waves danced in the background. It was a profile shot, a silhouette almost, with the fire yellow light of evening shimmering around her head like a golden halo.

He'd worn an ordinary summer suit. Nothing ordinary about Ciara's outfit! Even if he didn't have the picture to remind him of it, Mitch knew he'd never forget that dress. It was pale blue, and made of a flimsy material that floated around her shapely calves on salty air currents. She'd wrapped a matching gauzy shawl around her narrow shoulders, and with every slight draft, it fluttered behind her like angels' wings.

He hadn't seen his bride in seven long months. Their last evening together had been little more than an accumulation of angry words and misunderstanding, and they hadn't communicated, in any way since that night...thanks to Chet Bradley. He wanted their reunion to be so much more...the fulfillment of seven months of yearning and loneliness and dreams.

Would she be his angel still?

Would he be her hero?

When he walked into headquarters, that's exactly what Parker had called him. And so had the TV reporter who'd wanted to interview the man who'd snagged Giovanni Pericolo. Admittedly the case had ended well, with everything falling neatly into place. But Mitch knew he couldn't have done it without Pericolo's help.

Smart as he was, Giovanni had made a stupid mistake: because he'd outwitted the Feds so often, he'd begun to believe himself invincible. Feeling cocky and full of himself, he'd boldly marched down to the Immigration office and applied for U.S. citizenship. And because he'd never been formally charged with any crime, he had as much right to pledge allegiance to the flag as any other immigrant. He greased a few palms, cutting through the usual red tape, and two weeks before Mitch uncovered the final piece of evidence to convict him, Giovanni Pericolo stood among several hundred soon-to-be Americans, raised his right hand and swore to honor his new nation.

The U.S. Attorney's office would have had a long, expensive fight on its hands, had Pericolo still been a full-fledged Colombian when the charges hit the fan. But Giovanni's dream of becoming a U.S. citizen became his nightmare; he would never enjoy the perks of being a free American from his four-by-eight-foot prison cell.

The praise of Mitch's comrades and a few extra dollars on his paycheck were worthless if he couldn't have Ciara. He needed her steady, sure love now more than ever, to help blot the grotesque images of this case from his mind. He remembered how she'd reacted to the scar on his rib cage, to the news of Abe Carlson's death. It wasn't likely he'd ever tell her any of the details of the Pericolo case. If it messed up a hard-nosed Fed like you this much, he told himself, think what it'll do to a sweet little thing like Ciara.

Mitch tucked the photo back into his wallet and checked the time. Ten-thirty. Too early to knock?

He glanced at the front door. It had been painted black when he'd left home. Ciara had given it a coat of rust-red, and it reminded him of the bright, welcoming doors of Ireland's thatched cottages.

A lot had changed around here in the months he'd been gone, Mitch noticed. Spindly tree branches that had been brown and bare on the cold December night when he'd left now combed the clouds with leaves of every verdant hue. And in flower beds that once sat barren and bleak beneath the many-paned windows, white daisies and pink zinnias bobbed their brightly blossomed heads. She'd planted clumps of hosta along the shaded, curving walkway, yellow tea roses beside the privet hedge.

All by herself she'd transformed what had been an ordinary yard into a warm and welcoming retreat. He could only imagine what magic she'd performed inside, what more she might have been able to accomplish…if he'd been here, at her side.

Mitch got out of the car and slammed the door, wondering what to say when they were face-to-face for the first time in so many months. *How are you? You're looking well. Don't shoot…I'm unarmed,* he added with a wry grin.

Hands in his pockets, he debated whether to ring the bell or use his key. She had no doubt grown accustomed to her solitary status; he might frighten her if he barged in as he would have done before their fight.

He shook his head, hoping the hundreds of prayers he'd said while undercover had inspired the Lord to soften Ciara's heart. Taking a deep breath, he straightened to his full height and rang the bell.

Ten seconds, twenty ticked by before impatience made him ring it again.

"Don't get your socks in knots," came her voice from the other side of the door, "I'm movin' fast as I can.…"

Mitch grinned. At least that hasn't changed, he thought. She's still the same little spitfire.

The light coming through the peephole darkened. His heart hammered with anticipation; maybe she would decide not to open the door when she saw who was standing on her porch.

But the door did open, slowly, and she peeked out from behind it. "Mitch," she whispered, blue eyes wide, "you're early."

He wanted to take her in his arms and hold her close, inhale the fresh clean scent of her soap and shampoo, kiss her as she hadn't been kissed…in seven months. "Didn't take as long as I thought to finish up the report."

Ciara stepped back, smiling a bit as she opened the door wider. "Well, come on in. The electric company already gets enough of my hard-earned money without air-conditioning the front yard, too."

Mitch glanced around the sunny foyer. Last time he'd been in this part of the house, the floor had been piled high with as-yet-unpacked boxes. Now he could almost see his reflection in the highly polished hardwood. "Smells like pine," he remarked, shoving his hands back into his pockets. "Nice…reminds me of my grandma's house."

The way she stood, half hidden by the door, Mitch had barely seen her. He yearned for an eyeful, and faced her now, fully prepared to apologize, eat crow or humble pie, or whatever else it took to get back into her good graces. He wanted to tell her how awful these months without her had been, how sorry he was for having left the way he had, how many thousands of times he'd thought of her. His gaze started at her tiny, white-sneakered feet, climbed to the shapely legs inside the black stretch pants—

And froze on her protruding abdomen.

"What's the matter, haven't you ever seen a pregnant woman before?"

He forced himself to look away from her well-rounded belly. Her eyes seemed bigger, bluer, longer-lashed than he remembered, but there were dark circles beneath them now. And despite her swollen stomach, Ciara appeared to have lost weight. "Well, sure I have. It's just, well…"

"I'm eight months along," she said, answering his unasked question. "You were gone a month when I knew for sure."

He did the math in his head. "So…so you were—"

Ciara nodded. "We didn't know it then, but we were 'in a family way' on the night you left."

To learn that he was going to be a daddy, in this sudden, unexpected way, was by far the biggest shock Mitch had ever experienced. A myriad of emotions flicked through his head. One moment he was overjoyed at the prospect of fatherhood, the next, terror thundered in his heart, because, what did *he* know about being a dad? On the one hand it thrilled him to know that the girl of his dreams was carrying his child, on the other, his stomach churned as it dawned on him that she couldn't have informed him.

She had gone through all this alone.

Mitch didn't know whether to throw his arms around her or get on his knees and beg her forgiveness or continue standing there, gaping with awe at the sight of her.

Ciara headed for the kitchen. "I'm going to have some lemonade. Can I pour you a glass?"

Mitch stood alone in the foyer a moment, staring after her, then followed her down the hall. "Are you all right? Is everything okay? With you and the baby, I mean?" he began, falling into step beside her. "Gee, Ciara, I wish I had known...."

She opened the refrigerator door, wincing as though the slight effort caused her discomfort. "I *tried* to tell you," she said again. Ciara inclined her head and placed a fingertip beside her chin. "Goodness. It seems our devious Lieutenant Bradley has been scheming on *both* sides of the street!"

The sarcasm rang loud, and Mitch knew it was proof she didn't believe he'd written any letter. Mitch clenched his jaw, fully prepared to tell her what he thought of Lieutenant Bradley. But when he noticed her, struggling to lift the half-full pitcher from the fridge, his ire died.

This isn't like her, he told himself. She was always such a sturdy little thing. Instinctively, he relieved her of it. "Sit down, will you, before you fall down," he scolded. Frowning, he added, "You look..."

"Terrible?"

"Yeah." His cheeks reddened as he realized he'd unintentionally insulted her. "No, of course not. Well, gee whiz, Ciara," he fumbled, "haven't you been taking care of yourself at all?"

"Well, golly gee, Mitch," she mocked, hefting her bulk onto a long-legged stool at the snack bar, "you sure are great for a girl's ego."

He grimaced. "I didn't mean to— It's just that you look like you haven't slept in—"

"I *haven't* slept in days."

"In your condition," he continued, "shouldn't you

be paying more attention to your health? You know, eating smart, taking vitamins, getting plenty of rest...."

"*You* try sleeping with a watermelon superglued to your body, Mahoney, see how well you rest!"

Ciara pointed to the cabinet above the dishwasher. "Since you're so determined to '*do*' for me," she said, "the glasses are in there. And while you're pouring, give this some thought, Secret Agent Man—you can't just waltz in here after all this time and start bossing me around." She aimed a forefinger at him. "And stop pretending you're so concerned about my well-being. I might have appreciated it...*seven months ago!*"

Anger had put some color back into her pale cheeks, and the flash had returned to her blue eyes. If she didn't look so all-fired beautiful, he might have shouted his response. As it was, Mitch's defense was barely audible. "I'm not pretending anything. I wrote you, the night I left, and I tried—"

She tucked in one corner of her mouth and raised a brow. "Maybe it would have been a good idea to attend a couple of those meetings Chet scheduled, so he could have delivered your concerns." Ciara tucked a wayward lock of hair into her ponytail. "He warned me you'd have a list of lame excuses for not having been in touch."

He'd known the guy more than a decade, and even *he* didn't call him Chet. Mitch rummaged in the freezer for a handful of ice cubes, dropped them noisily into the tumblers. "*Chet?*"

"He asked me to call him by his first name," Ciara explained, "and I agreed because—" she frowned, crossed both arms over her chest "—because at least *he* was here for me, every week of the seven months you were gone."

"Here for you?" he thundered. "If he didn't deliver my letter to you, and he didn't give you any news at all, exactly what was he here *for,* Ciara?" He glared at her for a moment, then poured the lemonade and shoved a glass toward Ciara. He sat the pitcher down with a thud, splattering the countertop with drops.

"So you're saying you wrote a letter," she said, grabbing a napkin to blot up the mess, "personally handed it to Lieutenant Bradley, and he didn't bother to deliver it."

"That's what I'm saying."

"And you expect me to believe that?"

"Yes, I do."

His words hung in the air like a spiderweb, intricately taut, yet fragile enough to disintegrate with the slightest disturbance. The last time he'd spoken the words, he'd stood in front of the altar at the Church of the Resurrection. "Do you, Mitchell Riley Mahoney, take this woman to be your lawfully wedded wife?" Pastor Rafferty had asked. Heart pounding with anticipation, and love, and joy, Mitch had gazed deep into Ciara's eyes, taken her small hand in his and breathed, "Yes, I do."

Her voice brought him back to the present. "I'm surprised you're having so much trouble with the numbers...considering you have an accounting degree and all. When you left me seven months ago, you said you'd be back in a few hours." She wasn't smiling when she tacked on, "Were you lying to me then, or are you lying to me now?"

"I've never told you a lie, Ciara. And I don't see how you can say I—"

"There's a lot you don't see, Mahoney, because you've got your blinders on again, just like...just like the lieutenant said."

Mitch snorted, knowing she'd hesitated because she'd wanted to say "Chet" instead of "lieutenant." "Your buddy *Chet* doesn't know diddly about me, Ciara, but it's beginning to look like even *he* knows me better than you do."

She shrugged. "Can't get to know a man who isn't around."

He planted both palms flat on the counter, leaned forward until they were nearly nose to nose. "Listen, I don't know what he told you—or why—but I know this—I had a tail on me every minute. If I had tried getting in touch with you, we'd both be—"

He clamped his jaws together, knowing he'd just put himself between the proverbial rock and the hard place. By admitting he couldn't contact her, he was supporting her claim that his job was too dangerous.

Just tell her you love her, Mahoney. That's what she needs to hear right now; you can work out the rest of this mess later. He opened his mouth to do just that when the tight, skeptical look on her face stopped him cold. His lips formed a thin straight line. "Seven months ago you asked me to choose. Sounds to me like *you've* chosen to believe that slimeball Bradley over me." He ground his molars together. "Believe whatever you want," he snarled. "Everything I've said is true."

Her eyes misted, and she swallowed. "While you were gone, I saw a movie about an agent who went undercover. *He* managed to call his wife. Even managed to sneak off and *visit* a few times!"

"This isn't Hollywood, Ciara. In the real world we do things by the book...or *die.*"

"It was based on fact."

"Did your buddy *Chet* tell you that story, too?"

Ciara only stared at him, eyes blazing and lips trembling. "You know what, Mitch?" she said after a moment. "I was an independent woman before we met, and believe it or not, I managed quite well after you left...once I got used to the idea. I'll admit, those first couple of weeks were pretty rough, but look around you," she added, upturned palms drawing his attention to their surroundings, "I got a lot accomplished, *all by myself.* This house is a home now, thanks to the endless hours I've spent working on it...*alone.*"

Suddenly she was on her feet, pacing back and forth across the black-and-white linoleum tiles, arms swinging, eyes flashing. "What was I to think, when you vanished like something from a magic show...and never came back?" she demanded, coming to a halt in front of him.

"I've given it a lot of thought and prayer since you stormed out of here that night." Hands on her hips, she raised her chin slightly. "I think it would be best if you just packed your things and moved out."

In response to his grim expression, she tossed in, "I can afford the mortgage on this place, thanks to my teacher's salary, so don't you worry about how I'll manage. In fact, every time one of your checks arrived from the Bureau, I put it into *my* bureau, uncashed. I didn't need your help turning the house into a home, and I don't need your money to stay in it. And I *am* staying, because it's a nice, safe neighborhood, with plenty of children, and good schools, and..."

She has every right to be angry, he told himself. She's been alone for a long time, not in the best of health, listening to Bradley's lies. Maybe if he sat quietly and let her vent, the anger and resentment would fade, and she'd look at him the way she had on the cruise ship, as she had at the altar, on their wedding night....

The cruise ship, the marriage, the separation, the pregnancy. All these things had happened in less than a year, yet it seemed like an eternity to him now.

Mitch leaned against his stool's backrest, wondering what she'd do if he just gathered her up in his arms and silenced her with a big kiss. But before he had a chance to put his plan into action, she plunged on, fingers drawing quotation marks in the air, reminding him of something he'd said the night he left:

"So don't feel 'duty-bound' to take care of me. I know your old-fashioned need to meet your responsibilities is supposedly the reason you work as hard...and as *long* as you do, but..."

Was it his imagination, or had her face paled even more in the last few minutes? All this ranting and raving couldn't be good for her *or* the baby. Suddenly it didn't matter who was right and who was wrong. Calming her down, that was all that mattered.

"Ciara, I know I said those things," he began, his voice softly apologetic, "but I never meant it to sound as though taking care of you is a burden. Bottom line— I love you. Have since the day we met, will for the rest of my life. Providing for you will always be an honor, a privilege." He grinned slightly. "Believe me, I've had plenty of time to think about that while..."

Oh, how she *wanted* to believe him! But Ciara had convinced herself that she must focus on the pain his absence had caused in those early days, when she'd been forced to admit the ugly truth: the oath he'd taken for the Bureau meant more to him than the vows he'd made to her. She loved him with everything in her, but if she was going to survive, if her heart was ever to heal, she must stand firm on this issue. She could *not* give in simply because he was standing there, looking at her with those sad brown eyes of his, imploring her to be something she believed she could not be.

She forced a cold, careless tone into her voice that she did not feel. "I'm sure you *did* have lots of time to think while you were away. Well, guess what, James Bond? While you were off living your life of adventure, I had a little time to think, too, and…"

He held up a hand to silence her. "I want to show you something," he said quietly, pulling out his wallet. Slapping her photograph on the counter, he said, "You see that? *That's* what kept me going for seven months. *That's* what gave me the incentive to think smart, to do whatever it took to drag my sorry self home.

"I won't deny that before I met you, I liked the danger and excitement of undercover work, but back then, getting the job done was the only focus." Mitch shrugged, then emphasized his point. "That's why I took unnecessary chances. That's how I accomplished in nine years what it takes most agents twenty. Because who was I, that my passing would make such a difference?"

She picked up the photograph. He must have held it in his big, strong hands hundreds of times, and the proof was that the paper it had been printed on now felt soft and supple as cotton. Her aching heart pounded. All right, so maybe he loves you a little bit after all, she thought.

But wait…something he'd said pinged in her memory. He couldn't possibly believe his life had no value, that his existence wasn't important to anyone. He mattered plenty—to his parents, his siblings and their children—to *her*.

Ciara handed back the photograph, tensing when their fingers touched, for she yearned to hold him, to be held by him. "Everyone would miss you if you were—" Ciara hesitated, unable to make herself say "killed in the line of duty." She began again. "A lot of people would be very upset if anything happened to you."

He dismissed her comment with a flick of his fingers.

Ciara straightened her back, reminded herself that she'd decided she couldn't, *wouldn't* go through that agony again. Even if she had the strength to survive the next case—and the next, and the one after that—their children deserved a full-time dad.

"I saved some of the boxes from our move," she began, looking anywhere but into his haunted eyes. "They're in the garage. If you like, I could pack for you. I wouldn't mind...." She was rambling and she knew it, but seemed powerless to stanch the flow of words. "Your brother, Ian, has an extra room, now that Patrick is off at college. Did you know he was accepted at Stanford? Of course you didn't.... Well, I'm sure Ian wouldn't mind if you stayed there until you found a place to—"

"Shut up, Ciara. Just *shut up*."

He'd never spoken to her in such a vulgar, vicious way before, and she felt a sharp pain, deep in the pit of her stomach.

"I realize I've messed things up pretty well," he said, "but I think we can work this out." He took her hand in his. "Give me a chance to make all this up to you." Mitch stroked her fingertips. "Please?"

Hang tough! she reminded herself. Be strong, or these seven months that are behind you now will be a road map of the rest of your life. "Maybe you'd rather do the packing yourself," she continued, as if he hadn't spoken at all. "Or, we could do it together, to make the job go easier and faster."

"I don't believe this!" he bellowed, dropping her hand. "I know we didn't have much time together before—" He stopped. Took a deep breath. And, hands on her shoulders, he started again. "We had something special once. At least, I thought we did. I think it's worth fighting for. Let me prove that to you."

Ciara couldn't believe how much intense physical pain a moment like this could cause. Though she'd rehearsed it and rehearsed it, she'd never imagined it would ache this much.

In response to her strained silence, he walked away from her, stood his empty glass in the sink. "All right. I'll leave, if it's what you want. But…"

She doubled over and gripped her stomach with both hands. "Mitch," she groaned, slumping to the floor, "it hurts. Hurts bad."

Ciara had always been the type who poked fun at people who whined and complained about everyday aches and pains. He knew she must be in considerable agony to have admitted it straight-out like that. Kneeling, he wrapped his arms around her. "It's way too early for the baby, isn't it?"

She nodded. "Call 911."

"No time for that—could take the ambulance an hour to get here." He spoke in a calm, reassuring voice that belied the terror he felt…raw, surging fear like he'd never experienced on the job.

Mitch grabbed the telephone, seeing that she'd jotted her obstetrician's number on the tablet beside it. He dialed, explained that they were on their way to the hospital and hung up. "The nurse says Dr. Peterson will meet us there," he said, gently helping her to her feet.

And as if she weighed no more than a baby herself, lifted her in his powerful arms and carried her to the front door.

She melted against him like butter on a hot biscuit. Unconsciously he pressed a kiss to her temple. "Have you been taking childbirth classes?" he asked, kicking the door shut behind them. He wanted to kick *himself*, because he should have been beside her at those classes.

She burrowed her face into the crook of his neck. "Yes," came her hoarse reply.

"Who's your coach?"

"Mom."

"What would she be doing," he asked opening the car door, "if she were here right now?"

Ciara began to sob uncontrollably. "I don't want to lose the baby, Mitch. I love it so," she said, one arm hugging her tummy. "I don't think I've ever been more afraid...."

He'd never seen her cry before. He wanted to hold her this way forever. Comfort her. Tell her whatever she needed to hear. But there wasn't time for that now. Gently he put her into the car. "You're not going to lose the baby, sweetie." He ran a hand through her hair. "The best thing you can do is stay calm. Right?"

Nodding, she wiped her eyes as he pulled the seat belt around her. Ciara grabbed his hand as he clicked the buckle into place. "I don't know how well I'd be handling this if I were alone."

Without even thinking, he placed a quick kiss on her cheek. "You're never gonna be alone again, sweetie, not if I have anything to say about it."

As he ran around to his side of the car, she couldn't help but admit how much she wanted to believe him.

Oh, Mitch, please don't give me false hope, especially not now....

It was as he shifted into Reverse that Ciara noticed her blood on his hands. He followed the direction of her gaze and gasped involuntarily.

"'It's nothing,'" she rasped, quoting word for word what he'd said when she'd first noticed his bullet wound, "'a flesh wound. No big deal.'"

Mitch turned on the flashers and the headlights, and prayed for all he was worth: *No traffic, no potholes, no red lights,* he begged God as he pealed away from the curb. He glanced over at her, held his breath when he saw how much blood had already soaked the seat. *Get us to the hospital, Lord, and us get there fast!*

Chapter Four

"**W**hat do you mean, I can't go with her?" Mitch demanded.

The nurse was nearly his height and likely outweighed him by fifty pounds. She tilted back her red-haired head and held up one hand like a traffic cop. "You'll only be in the way. Now have a seat," she ordered, pointing to the chairs against the wall.

Mitch didn't want a confrontation with this woman. He just wanted to be with his wife. He'd promised never to leave her alone again. He couldn't let her down. Not now.

Ciara had looked so frail and fragile when the orderlies put her on the gurney, so pale and drawn it was hard to tell where she ended and the starched white sheets began. She'd reached out her hand as they wheeled her past, but in the flurry of activity, he couldn't get close enough to take hold of it. The last thing he saw were her teary eyes, wide with fear and pain.

"Listen, lady," he ground out, "that's my *wife* in

there, and she needs me. No amount of your self-important hoo-ha can stop me from going in there.''

He took a step, and she blocked it. Crossing both arms over her ample chest and tapping a white-shoed foot on the shining linoleum, her eyes narrowed. ''I'm calling Security,'' she snapped.

''You do what you have to do,'' he shot back, shrugging, ''and I'll do what I have to do.'' With that he barged into the emergency room. Almost immediately he felt guilty for having behaved like a caveman, but he'd have done whatever it took to be near Ciara.

''Did you see where they took my wife?'' he asked the first nurse he saw.

''Little blonde, pregnant out to here?'' she asked, making a big circle of her arms.

He nodded.

''Second bed on the right. Now, stop lookin' so worried, hon. Women have babies every day…I've had seven, myself. Trust me,'' she said with a wave of her hand. ''It's a cakewalk.''

He didn't bother to point out how elaborate and difficult cakewalks had been for the slaves who'd competed for slices of dessert…. ''Thanks,'' he said, and headed for his wife's cubicle.

''Mitch,'' she sighed when she saw him. ''I heard all the ruckus. I didn't think you'd ever get past her….''

He kissed her cheek, then flexed his bicep to lighten the tense atmosphere. ''Hey, it's gonna take more than one coldhearted nurse to keep me away from you, especially now.''

She smiled feebly, gave his hand a grateful little squeeze.

''So how're you feelin', sweetie?'' he asked, pulling a chair closer to the bed.

"I'm okay," she whispered.

But she wasn't, and he knew it. Smoothing wispy blond bangs from her forehead, he looked into her blue eyes. It was hard to tell the agony from the fear. He felt incredibly powerless, because she was bleeding and in pain, and there wasn't a thing he could to help her. Where were the doctors? And the nurses? Did they intend to let her lie here and bleed to death? Did they...

Well, there was *something* he could do!

Mitch leaped up and stomped toward the pastel-striped curtains. "Hey," he hollered, half of him in the cubicle, the other half leaning into the hall, "can we get some help in here? My wife is—"

A blue-smocked man blew past Mitch. "Mrs. Mahoney?"

Ciara nodded weakly.

"It's about time you got here," Mitch snarled, letting the curtain fall back into place.

Ignoring the husband's grumbling, the doctor stepped up beside Ciara. "First baby?" he asked, a knowing smile on his face.

Another nod, and a small smile, too.

"Well, don't you worry, little lady. We're gonna take real good care of you, I promise." He pulled the blood pressure cuff from a hard plastic pocket on the headboard. "You see, there was a six-car pileup on Route 95 about a half hour ago," he explained, his voice calm and reassuring as he fit it to her upper arm. "The paramedics brought in the last of the injured just minutes before you arrived." A half shrug. "Contusions and abrasions for the most part, but the nurses are hotfooting it, just the same."

He stood silent for a moment, reading the gauge, then put everything back where he'd found it. "You don't mind a lowly resident working on you, do you?" he asked, scribbling a note on the file attached to the clip-board he held.

"It takes a lot of hard work to become a resident," Ciara said, smiling. "There's nothing 'lowly' about your position."

She's lying there getting weaker by the minute, Mitch thought, and he's making small-talk! Frustration got the better of him. "It's been my experience," Mitch inter-rupted, "that chitchat can't stop hemorrhaging...."

"Mitch," Ciara protested, a restraining hand on his forearm, "it's all right, I'm—"

"First of all, Mr. Mahoney," the young doctor said, writing another note in Ciara's file, "your wife is losing some blood, but she's not in immediate danger. Sec-ondly, I have a wife, and a kid, myself. If either of them were here now, I'd be breathing fire, just like you are." He clicked off his ballpoint and slid it into his shirt pocket. "Trust me," he said, meeting Mitch's eyes squarely. "We're going to do everything in our power for your wife and baby."

He didn't wait for Mitch's agreement or approval. Instead, he plowed through the curtains and began bark-ing orders, commanding attention, demanding assis-tance. When he returned a moment later, shoving a tool-laden cart, he looked at Mitch. "How well do you handle the sight of blood?"

"He's an FBI agent," Ciara answered on his behalf. She sent Mitch a crooked little smile. "My husband has seen more than his share of blood."

The doctor snapped a pair of surgical gloves over his hands. One corner of his mouth lifted in a grin. "Stand over there, then, near the wall. If you don't get in the way, maybe I'll let you stay."

Mitch crossed both arms over his chest, fully prepared to follow the doctor's orders to the letter. He'd been away from her long enough. No way he would leave her now, especially not now. He pressed a knuckle against his lower lip, and watched.

He'd been on the scene when emergency medical technicians tended the victims of shootings, stabbings, near drownings. Once, he'd been the only one available to help a woman give birth to twins. Always before though, as his adrenaline had pumped and his heart raced, he'd managed to keep a professional distance from the lifesaving—or life-giving—experiences. Keeping an emotional arm's length from them had been easy, because the people involved had all been strangers.

Admittedly, he hadn't known the beautiful young woman on the gurney very long, but she was his wife, and the great bulge beneath the sheet that covered her was his unborn child. Unconsciously he began to gnaw his thumbnail.

As a small kid his mom was forever admonishing him to keep his fingers out of his mouth. By the age of seven, he'd left the habit behind, along with his night-light and Peppy, the stuffed bear. And no matter how stress- or pressure-filled the situation, he hadn't chewed his fingernails since, not when he took his SATs, not when he sat for the CPA exam, not before the final test at Quantico.

A tiny stab of pain told him he was back at it again. Mitch searched for a napkin, a paper towel…anything that would blot the bloodstain from his thumb. He spotted some tissues on the small counter against the wall and plucked one from the box. Wrapping it around his thumb, he squeezed.

He tried to see Ciara. She was all but hidden from

his sight as doctors, nurses, interns and residents gathered round. He felt like that seven-year-old nail-biter again. He'd been through terrifying situations. He'd faced death at point-blank range. Through it all, he hadn't shed a tear for himself, or anyone else involved. So why was he on the verge of tears now?

Because you could *lose* her, he admitted.

For the first time, Mitch understood how the bad guys must feel once they'd been snagged, frisked and cuffed, because *he* felt caught—smack between his career-focused, solitary life-style and the reality that without Ciara life would be meaningless.

Snap out of it, Mahoney! he berated himself, gritting his teeth. Pull yourself together, for Ciara's sake.

Mitch chanced a glance over his shoulder, caught a glimpse of her between the broad shoulders of the young resident and the shower-capped head of a nurse. He'd seen blood—his own, fellow agents', criminals'— hundreds of times. So why did the sight of Ciara's make him feel as if a tight band had been wrapped round his chest?

Mitch swiped at the sweat that had popped out on his forehead, discovered that his palms were damp, too. His ears started to ring, the room started to spin, and he realized if he didn't get out of there fast, he'd keel over.

He took another look at her: eyes closed, jaw clenched, fists bunched at her sides. She hadn't uttered a word of complaint since he'd cradled her, there on their kitchen floor, when she'd admitted how badly it hurt. You weak-kneed wimp, he chided himself. She's the one going through this, so why are you swooning like an old woman?

Mitch closed his eyes again, took a deep breath and prayed the extra oxygen would clear his head.

It didn't.

Pressing his forehead to the wall, he prayed the dizziness would pass, at least long enough for him to make it into the hall. He turned and headed for the curtain.

"Mitch," came her exhausted voice, "you're pale as a ghost. What's wrong?"

Humiliation washed over him like a tidal wave. Even in her weakened condition, and surrounded by half a dozen medical professionals, her thoughts were of him, not herself. He didn't know what minor miracle had prompted her to say yes when he'd asked her to marry him, but he knew he'd never done a thing in his life to deserve a woman like Ciara.

Too ashamed to meet her eyes, Mitch looked at the young doctor instead. "I, ah, I..."

"Get out of here, Mr. Mahoney," he said, frowning over his round-lensed glasses. "The room's too crowded as it is. I'll come for you when we're finished here, bring you up to speed."

With a nod of gratitude, and another of relief, Mitch hurried out of the cubicle. He slumped into the first chair he came to, a ghastly orange thing of molded plastic, being held up by four aluminum legs. What in God's name is the matter with you? he demanded of himself, an elbow resting on each knee. Mitch hung his head, stuck his face in his hands and prayed for all he was worth.

"Let her be all right," he whispered into the warm dark space between his face and his palms. "Give me a chance to show her how much she means to me...."

"You're doing fine," Dr. Peterson said, patting her hand.

"I'm so glad the hospital was able to get hold of you," she admitted.

"Relax, now. Everything's under control."

But was it?

The baby hadn't moved, not once, since—since right after Mitch had come home. She remembered the exact moment because, when she'd felt the baby stir, she had wanted to interrupt him, in the middle of explaining that he *had* written, to say, "Mitch...our baby is moving...give me your hand...."

Instead she'd stared into the handsome face of the man in her kitchen...her husband, yet a virtual stranger. Had she refrained from sharing that warm "baby" moment with him because he'd left her alone for seven long, lonely months? Or had she kept it to herself...to *punish* him for those months?

A little of both, she admitted, a twinge of guilt knotting in her heart.

"You doin' all right?" Peterson asked.

Ciara nodded.

"Then why the big sigh?"

"Oh, just talking to myself. I do it all the time."

He grinned. "Well, keep it down, will ya? We're tryin' to concentrate here."

His teammates snickered. "Yeah. You're noisier than a gaggle of geese," a nurse said.

"What's the matter," said another, "aren't you gettin' enough attention?"

Ciara smiled weakly. She knew the purpose of their lighthearted banter was to keep her calm, and while she appreciated their attempts to reassure her, she could have saved them the bother. Nothing could calm her as long as she was worried....

She was terrified, right down to the marrow of her bones, that the baby had stopped moving because something terrible had happened.

And what if Mitch didn't want the baby?

Possible, she thought, but not likely. He'd been so sweet and understanding during the drive from the house to the hospital, saying all the right things, patting her hand lovingly, concern flashing in his big brown eyes. But had it all been a joke, like those the doctors and nurses had been telling, to keep her quiet and still? If not, why had he dashed out of the room just now, looking like a deer with a hunter hot on its trail? And why had his usually ruddy complexion gone ashen? Perhaps because the sudden news had overwhelmed him....

She'd known from the moment he'd seen her belly that he would need time to come to grips with the fact that he'd be a father soon. She'd had *months* to get used to the idea—he'd had half an hour before the bleeding started.

Since they'd arrived at the hospital, she'd been lying there telling herself that, in time, Mitch would be as overjoyed and exuberant about the prospect of parenthood as she was.

But what if he wasn't?

Ciara's lower lip began to quiver, and she bit down to still it. Her eyes welled with tears, and she squeezed them to keep new ones from forming. Stay calm, she scolded herself, for the baby's sake.... But the lip continued to tremble, and the tears fell steadily.

"We're almost finished here, Ciara," Dr. Peterson said.

Sniffling, she summoned enough to control to say, "Um...the baby...hasn't moved, not once in all this time...."

"Perfectly normal under the circumstances. You've gotta give the little tyke credit...he's already smart enough to know when to lay low."

He?

Ciara's heart lurched as she pictured a miniature Mitch, running around the house on chubby bare feet. "So…the baby's all right?"

"We've had him monitored the whole time. If there was a problem, I'd have brought in a neo-natal specialist, stat. Trust me."

His words calmed her, soothed her. She thanked God and all the saints and angels. Thanked God again.

So why on earth are you making a spectacle of yourself, she thought, embarrassed by the tears, the hiccuping sobs. Ciara crooked an arm over her eyes, like the child who thinks because he can't see his mama, mama can't see him, either.

"Get her husband back in here," the resident said to the nurse beside him. "He was lookin' a little green around the gills when I kicked him out. You'll probably find him in the men's room.…"

"You know," the nurse said, cocking an eyebrow, "you're gonna be a fine surgeon someday."

He gave her a grateful grin. "You think so?"

"Uh-huh." Smiling, she shoved through the curtain. "You're a natural…already a master at barking out orders and making nurses feel like peons."

He met Peterson's eyes, then Ciara's. "Nurses," he huffed good-naturedly, "can't live with 'em, can't live without 'em."

Ciara giggled nervously, and she didn't stop until Mitch wrapped his big warm hand around her small, cold one.

Once things were under control, Mitch stayed with Ciara while she slept, and Peterson left to make a few phone calls. When he returned, seeing that Ciara had fallen asleep, Dr. Peterson said, "I have a few questions, but I don't want to wake her." He stood at the foot of her bed, reading her chart. "Tell me, Mr. Mahoney, has she been staying off her feet, like I told her to?" he asked without looking up.

Mitch's heart pounded. She'd been told to stay off her feet? How long ago? And why? If she'd been told to rest, how did he explain the flower gardens, the spotless house, the—

Peterson was looking at him now, a puzzled frown furrowing his brow. Mitch knew it was a simple enough question. Knew, too, that the doctor was probably wondering why Ciara's husband didn't have a ready answer for it.

"It's my understanding that you've been out of town," the doctor said, peering over his half glasses at Mitch. "Maybe she hadn't had a chance to tell you everything…yet."

Mitch swallowed. *The man thinks you're a no-good husband…because that's what you are.*

"We've been carefully monitoring the baby for several weeks now, ever since Ciara started spotting." Narrowing his eyes, he said, "She didn't tell you *any* of this?"

He hung his head. "I'm afraid not." She hadn't told him anything about the pregnancy, because he hadn't been around. The thought of her going through this alone caused a nagging ache inside him.

"Well, she does tend to be a secretive little thing, doesn't she?"

It was Mitch's turn to frown. "How do you mean?"

"Most young mothers—particularly first-time mothers—love to talk about their plans. You know," he said, shrugging, "the nursery, baby names, whether or not to breast feed...." He looked at Ciara. "Not your wife." After a long pause, Peterson met Mitch's eyes. The doctor cleared his throat. "What happened today is proof she hasn't been taking proper care of herself."

"What *did* happen, exactly?"

"Placenta previa. The baby gets its nourishment and eliminates its waste by way of the placenta, you see," he explained. "In Ciara's case, the placenta began separating a bit. That's what caused the bleeding."

His gaze fused to Mitch's. "She'll have to stay off her feet for the duration of the pregnancy. That means she'll need someone with her at all times." He glanced at his patient again. "From here on out, she cannot be left alone. Not even for short periods of time."

"That's impossible," Ciara said, her voice thick with drowsiness. "My parents are touring Europe. I couldn't get in touch with them, even if I wanted to."

Why can't *you* take care of her, Mr. Mahoney? was the question written on the doctor's face. He turned to Ciara. "Do you have a sister? An aunt? A grandma, maybe?" he asked instead.

"I'm the only child of only children," she stated, "and my only living grandmother is in a nursing home."

"Hmm. Well, that pretty well covers it, doesn't it." He thought for a moment, then said to Mitch, "You could hire a live-in nurse."

Ciara sighed. "They're bound to cost a small fortune." Passing a trembling hand over her worried brow, she added, "I know my teachers' insurance won't cover that. I doubt the agency's will, either."

Mitch was still bristling over the fact that the resident

had also zeroed in on what he construed to be a problem between man and wife. Who does that little twerp think he is, sticking his nose in where it doesn't belong? "Doesn't matter if the insurance covers it or not," Mitch all but snarled. "We won't need any live-in nurse. I'm perfectly capable of taking care of my wife."

The doctor removed his glasses and gave Mitch a hard, appraising stare. "Day in, day out...."

What does he expect from me? Mitch asked himself. I come back from seven months undercover—life on the line every day of it—see my wife for the first time, and she's eight months pregnant! And during our first hour together, she collapses. "I have some R and R coming. I'll be there round the clock."

"I'll be back after I finish my rounds," he said, and headed for the door. He left nothing behind but the memory of his smug, know-it-all smirk. Harrumphing under his breath, Mitch remembered his dad's quote: "Give authority to a fool, and create a monster."

But in all fairness, the entire medical team had done a fine job. Mitch couldn't hold any of them accountable for the guilt roiling in his own gut...or for the shame boiling in his head.

You're the fool, he told himself. And if anybody's a monster, it's you. Because, hard as it was to admit, if he hadn't left Ciara alone all those months, she wouldn't have felt obliged to turn their house into a home all by herself. All that work, no doubt, put a terrible strain on her, mentally, physically....

He leaned his forearms over the bed's side rail, clasped his hands together and watched her sleep. He'd watched her sleep on their wedding night, too. Then, as now, she'd breathed so lightly, he'd had to strain to hear her inhale and exhale, the whisper softness of her sighs, he imagined, were what angels' wings might sound like. What had he ever done in his life to deserve an angel for a wife?

Just before she'd collapsed, Ciara had asked him to pack his things and leave. He hadn't wanted to do anything of the kind at the time, and he certainly had no intention of doing that now.

Well, they'd be spending a lot of time alone together in the few weeks to come. With God's help, Mitch hoped, he could earn Ciara's forgiveness, could make up for the many months he'd left her alone. He would take better care of her than her mother would. Mitch fancied himself a fair-to-middlin' cook, and his stint in the navy had taught him a thing or two about keeping his quarters shipshape.

He tucked the covers under her chin, smoothed the bangs from her forehead. Lord, but she's lovely, he thought. Her gracefully arched brows set off the long, lush lashes that dusted her lightly freckled cheeks, and her perfectly shaped full lips drew back in the barest hint of a smile.

What are you smiling about, pretty lady? he wondered, tucking a tendril of honey-blond hair behind her ear. *You married the village idiot, and now you're stuck with him...at least till our baby is born.*

Our baby....

Gently, so as not to wake her, he laid a hand on her stomach. "Hey, little fella," he whispered. "How's it goin' in there? You don't know me yet, but I'm your—"

The baby kicked, and Mitch's heartbeat doubled. He'd never experienced anything quite like it in his life...the sudden, insistent motion of his child, squirming beneath his palm. Ducking his head, Mitch leaned in closer and lifted his hand, like a boy who'd captured a butterfly might steal a peek at his prize.

The breath caught in his throat when he saw something—a tiny knee? a little heel?—shift beneath Ciara's pebbly white blanket. The egg-sized lump reminded him of the way Scooter the hamster looked, scurrying beneath Mitch's little-boy bedcovers. Grinning like the Cheshire Cat, his hand covered the mound yet again, following its passage, until the baby finally settled down.

If he knew he had an audience, would he continue to smile? Would he keep his hand pressed to his wife's stomach? Would his gaze remain glued to the stirring of the child—*his* child—alive inside her?

Ciara didn't think so. And so she continued to watch him through the narrow opening between her eyelids. *Thank you, Lord,* she prayed, *for showing me that Mitch* does *want this baby as much as I do.*

They were going to be spending a lot of time together in the next few weeks. Perhaps in that time, with the Lord's guidance, they could find a way to repair the damage they'd done to their marriage. A girl can hope and pray, she told herself.

Chapter Five

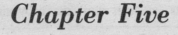

Peterson insisted that Ciara spend the night in the hospital, where she and the baby could be constantly monitored. At midnight, as the floor nurse was busy taking Ciara's vital signs, the doctor ushered Mitch into the hall.

"If you're smart," he said under his breath, "you'll go home, right now, and get a good night's sleep, because starting tomorrow, she's going to need you for everything." There in the dim hallway light, he'd lowered his voice to a near whisper. "I don't want her on her feet *at all*."

Mitch nodded.

"I know it's none of my business, Mr. Mahoney," the doctor added, "but it's obvious that *something* isn't right between you two." His voice took on a tone that reminded Mitch of his dad, scolding the four Mahoney boys when they allowed anything to interfere with school. The doctor continued, "Whatever your problems are, set them aside. Doesn't matter who's at fault or what it's all about. The only important thing right now is that we keep Ciara healthy so we can to take that baby to term.''

Mitch remembered the thirty-six-week explanation: it's the critical time, the doctor had said, after which the baby's vital organs are mature enough for survival outside the womb without requiring mechanical assistance.

Peterson's voice had come to him as from a long, hollow tube. He shook his head to clear the cobwebs and focused on the man's words. ''You realize she's lost a lot of blood....''

Another nod.

''And she may lose more....''

He met Peterson's eyes. Suddenly Mitch understood why, despite the belly, it seemed she'd lost weight. ''I thought the bleeding had stopped.''

''It has, for now. But placenta previa is a progressive condition,'' he said matter-of-factly. ''She'll have good days and bad days.''

''Until the baby's born?''

The doctor nodded somberly. ''I'm afraid so.''

''Not as much as today....'' Four more weeks of that, and she would waste away to nothing....

''I want you to understand the gravity of Ciara's condition, Mr. Mahoney.''

As he waited for the doctor to explain it Mitch's stomach twisted into a tight knot. He gritted his teeth so hard, his jaws ached. And deep in his pockets, his nails were digging gouges in his palms.

''If the placenta should tear, even slightly more, Ciara could hemorrhage.'' He paused, giving Mitch time to wrap his mind around the seriousness of his words. ''If it should separate completely, it will mean instant death for your child.''

Mitch's head began to pound. "Wouldn't…wouldn't she be better off here, in the hospital, where you guys could keep an eye on her? I mean, if something like that happened at home…" He ran a hand through his hair, scrubbed it over his face. "At least here, she'd have everything she'd need—"

Shaking his head, Peterson said, "I disagree. Placenta previa is a very stressful disorder. The mother is constantly aware that one wrong move could be fatal, for the baby, and possibly for her as well. It's been my experience that mothers-to-be rest and relax far better in their own homes, surrounded by the things—and the people—they love."

Despite the air-conditioning, Mitch began to perspire. He couldn't get his mind off the possibility that, if he hadn't left her alone, none of this would be happening. "What causes plug…ah—"

"Placenta previa," Peterson said, helping him along. Shrugging, the doctor shook his head. "There's no cause or reason for it that we can determine. We only know that it's there, to one degree or another, from the beginning of the pregnancy."

"Should we…should we take precautions so she won't have this problem in the future?"

"Are you asking whether or not the condition will repeat itself in future pregnancies?"

Mitch nodded.

"Despite the way things look now, Ciara is a healthy young woman. There's no reason to believe her next pregnancy will be anything but perfectly normal, with absolutely no complications."

Mitch breathed a sigh of relief. *So if you can pull her through this one, Mahoney…* "I don't mind tellin' you, doc, I'm scared to death. What if I mess up? I mean, there are two lives on the line, here…my wife's and my child's. I can't afford to make a mistake. Not even a small one." He met Peterson's eyes. "You're sure she's better off at home? Because I want to do whatever is best for Ciara."

Peterson smiled for the first time since he'd met the man. "What you said just now is all the assurance I need that she'll be in the best of hands at home."

"But…but what if something goes wrong? What if the spotting turns into something more? What if—"

"I'm going to put in a call right now, so the equipment will be ready for delivery when you get home tomorrow."

"Equipment? What equipment?"

"The home monitor. Hooks up to the telephone and the TV, so we can get a look at what's going on without Ciara having to endure the trauma of driving back and forth for tests. Plus, every other day or so, a visiting nurse will stop by to see how things look, do a blood count. It's costly, but…"

"I don't give a whit about that. I only want what's best for Ciara and the baby." He hesitated. "How reliable is this equipment?"

Peterson's smile widened. "It'll do its job. You do yours, and everything will turn out just fine."

Mitch had undergone years of extensive training to become an FBI agent. Had never felt anything but capable and competent, even in the most dangerous of situations.

So why did he feel totally inept and inadequate now?

For the first half hour, Mitch walked through the house, turning on lights and investigating the contents of every room. Even his staff sergeant would have been hard-pressed to find a speck of dust anywhere. Everything gleamed, from the old-fashioned brass light fixtures hanging in the center of every ceiling to the hardwood and linoleum floors beneath his loafered feet.

He flopped, exhausted, into his recliner—a treat he hadn't enjoyed in seven long months—and put up his feet. From where he sat, he could see every award and citation he'd ever earned, hanging on the flagstone wall surrounding the fireplace. His guitar and banjo stood to one side of the woodstove insert, his collection of canes and walking sticks on the other. The ceramic wolves he'd acquired from yard sales and flea markets held up his hard-cover volumes of Koontz, King, Clancy and London.

The knowledge that, despite the way they'd parted, despite their many months apart, she'd turned this into "his" room swelled his heart with love for her...love and gratitude that she hadn't given up hope...no thanks to Bradley.

He grabbed the chair arms so tightly his fingertips turned white at the thought of his lieutenant's part in their separation. But one glance at their wedding portrait, framed in crystal beside the photo of Mitch taken as he trained at Quantico, cooled his ire. You can deal with Bradley later, he thought, grinding his molars together. Right now, you have to concentrate on Ciara.

Mitch closed his eyes and pictured her as he'd seen her last.

After thanking Peterson, he'd headed back to her hospital room, to tell her good-night and let her know he was heading home. Her eyes were closed, and thinking she was asleep, he'd started for the door.

"I'm glad to see you have *some* sense in your head,"

she'd said, her voice whisper-soft and drowsy. "It's about time you went home and got some rest."

He'd pulled the chair beside her bed closer, balanced on the edge of its seat. "How're you doin'? Feeling any better?"

"A little tired, but otherwise I'm fine." With a wave of her hand she had tried to shoo him away. "Go on, now. Get some sleep."

"I will," he'd said, taking her hand, "in a minute." He held her gaze for a long, silent moment. "You had me pretty scared there for a while." He kissed her knuckles. "It's good to see a little color back in your cheeks."

She'd smiled, sighed. "I'm sorry to be such a bother."

He kissed her knuckles again. "You must be delirious, because you're not making a bit of sense."

"I'm just trying to see things from your point of view. You come home from seven months of terrifying, dangerous, undercover work, and what do you find? Your wife, eight months pregnant and grouchy as a grizzly bear. And then—''

Gently, he'd pressed a finger over her lips. "Shhhh. You should be sleeping."

"True. At home. In my own bed. I know it's irrational, but I've always hated hospitals!"

"Dr. Peterson says you can come home tomorrow."

"But I feel fine. Why can't I—"

She'd looked so small, so vulnerable, lying there in that tilted-up hospital bed, that he couldn't help himself. Mitch leaned forward and silenced her with a tender kiss. A quiet little murmur had escaped her lips as she pressed a palm against his cheek. "You could use a shave, mister," she'd said, grinning mischievously as she rubbed his sandpapery whiskers, "unless you're go-ing for that Don-Johnson-Miami-Vice look."

He'd assured her he wasn't, and promised to be clean shaven when he came to pick her up, first thing in the morning. Smiling now, Mitch opened his eyes and glanced at the carriage clock on the mantel. Two-thirty-five. And he still hadn't done anything to prepare for her homecoming....

Mitch dropped the recliner's footrest and got to his feet. Was the linen closet in the upstairs hall? Or was it the extra door in the main bathroom? He didn't have a clue, because they'd spent the first two weeks of their marriage traipsing back and forth between his condo in the city and her apartment in the suburbs as they'd waited for the former owners of the house to move out. And even after settlement, they'd spent alternate nights in his place or hers, too exhausted after putting in a full day at work, then packing all evening, to make the trip to their new home in Ellicott City.

They'd only been in the house, full-time, a few days when Mitch had left on assignment. And what with pic-tures leaning against every wall waiting to be hung, and stacks of books cluttering the floors, he'd spent most of that time picking his way through the mess.

Taking the stairs two at a time, he went in search of linens for Ciara's daytime bed.

The extra door in the bathroom, as it turned out, was where Ciara stored bathroom linens. Beneath neatly folded towels and washcloths, the shelves had been lined with muted green and blue plaid paper that matched the shower curtain. There had been a hideous black and silver wallpaper in here when they'd bought the place, and a putrid gray rug on the floor. Now, the walls were seafoam green, the door and window frames dusty blue. Like the family room, she'd chosen patterns and colors that were neither overly feminine nor masculine. "A man's home is his castle," she'd said when they'd discussed the changes they would make in the house. "When he comes home from a hard day's work, a man shouldn't be made to feel like he's about to be smothered by ruffles and chintz."

Mitch grinned and headed for the hall. He was beginning to understand why she'd been able to sweep him off his feet.... The things she'd said during their three-month courtship had dazzled him. No woman he'd known had ever talked of being there for him, of doing for him, of taking care of him. As he looked around at square-edged shams that topped off tailored comforters, at fabrics and carpeting and bold-framed prints—each that had been carefully selected and positioned—he realized Ciara had meant every word.

A pang of regret clutched his heart. You could have been enjoying this all these months. And where were you instead? Playing cops and robbers.

He opened the linen closet door, where sheets and pillowcases, blankets and comforters had been tidily folded and stacked. He'd seen department store displays that didn't look half as orderly. On a high shelf he saw that she'd stowed away a delicate-looking pink-and-lavender-flowered sheet set. Beside it, a set with a bright blue background and big bold sunflowers. She'd put a lot of thought into making this house a home he'd be comfortable in. The least he could do was give equal care to which sheets he'd put on the bed where she'd be spending endless hours. The soft-toned floral pattern reminded him of Ciara...feminine, dainty, utterly womanly. But the sunflowers were like her, too, in that they were spritely, happy, youthful.

You could play it safe…put plain white sheets on the bed…. He bounced the idea around in his mind for a moment. In college, he'd learned a thing or two about the psychology of color. White symbolized purity, cleanliness, and often served as a pallet, an enhancer for other colors. It enlivened, energized, expanded spaces. Shades of purple offered comfort and assurance, while yellow created an atmosphere of energy and cheerfulness….

He grabbed the sunflowers and headed downstairs.

During his three-year stint in the navy, he'd learned a thing or two about making up a bed. Those lessons were for naught, since the sofa bed's mattress was too thin to turn sharp hospital corners, or tuck the ends under, ensuring a snug, smooth fit. But it would do for resting during the day.

During the drive home, he'd worked it all out in his head: at bedtime, he'd carry her upstairs and tuck her into bed, and in the morning, he'd carry her back down to the sofa bed. Because if he'd been the one who'd been confined to quarters for an entire month, he would go stir-crazy, alone in an upstairs room. Besides, she'd spent enough time all by herself already, thanks to him.

Mitch turned back the bedcovers in a triangle, as the maids on the cruise ship had done, smoothed them flat, then stood back to admire his handiwork. Nodding with approval, he headed for the kitchen. As he filled a tumbler with the lemonade she'd made that morning, Mitch noticed a red circle around today's date. It's three-fifteen in the morning; yesterday's date, he corrected, yawning, that's *yesterday's* date…. He squinted, read the reminder she'd printed in the date box. "Pick up Chester at Dr. Kingsley's."

He hadn't given a thought to the dog, and wondered

what malady had put the retriever into the vet's office. Fleas? Ingrown toenails? Mange? He'd never been overly fond of canines, and Chester could be a miserable pest, sitting beside the bed at five in the morning, whining until Mitch or Ciara got up to let him out. Just one more of the compromises he'd made in order to get Ciara to agree to marry him.

She hated big-city life, so he'd sold his condo in the singles building near Baltimore's Inner Harbor and agreed to live in the suburbs. He didn't want a dog, but she'd had Chester for five years and couldn't part with him. He'd wanted to honeymoon in a johnboat on the Patapsco River, where he could spend a lazy week casting for trout; she'd wanted to luxuriate in the islands, where they'd met. And so they'd gone to Martha's Vineyard, spent two days fishing and two days walking on the windy beaches. Mitch had a feeling that in the weeks to come, he would experience *compromise* on an entirely new level.

He swallowed the last of his lemonade and headed upstairs, set the alarm for seven. Four hours' sleep would do; he'd gotten by, plenty of times, on less. After a quick shower and shave, he would look up Kingsley's address in Ciara's personal phone book. Wouldn't she be surprised when she got into the car, to find her shaggy pup hanging over the front seat to greet her!

Mitch stepped into the closet with the intention of grabbing the jeans and a short-sleeved pullover to wear the next day. But when he flipped on the light, he could only stare in wonderment at Ciara's handiwork. She'd given him the entire left side of the walk-in, and had hung his suits and sports coats on the rack above his shirts and jeans. Casual and dress shirts had been grouped by color and sleeve length. His neatly folded jeans had been stacked on an eye-level shelf, sweaters on the next, shoes in a precise row on the bottom. Ties and belts had been given their own sliding racks, to make one-at-a-time choosing easier.

How long ago had she organized this? he wondered, moving to the dresser in search of socks and briefs. There, too, her homemaking skills were evidenced by the systematic placement of tennis shorts, T-shirts and pajamas. She couldn't have been serious when she'd said he should pack up and leave. If she *had* been, would she have aligned his possessions in such a creative way?

Mitch didn't think so. She loves you—whether you deserve it or not—and the proof is all over this house! Sighing, he dropped the clothes he'd been wearing into the clothes hamper, pulled back the dark green quilt and maroon blanket and climbed between crisp white sheets. The minute his head hit the pillow, the scent of her— baby-powder light, yet utterly womanly—wafted into his nostrils. He fell asleep, a half grin slanting his mouth, hugging that pillow tight.

"Me and you, and you and me, no matter how they tossed the dice, it had to be," the Turtles crooned, "happy together, so happy together...." Mitch slapped the alarm's Off button and, rolling onto his back, yawned heartily. After a moment of noisy stretching, he climbed out of bed and padded into the bathroom to adjust the spray for his morning shower, humming the melody of the oldies but goodies song that had awakened him. "...and you're the only one for me," he sang off-key. If you've got to have a song stuck in your head, at least this one is appropriate, he told himself, belting it out, then grinning as the sound of his own voice echoed in the master bathroom's tiled stall.

Here, too, Ciara had seen to it there would never be a doubt whose house this was. The walls were white and the trim the same dusty blue she'd used in the hall bath. Like a professional interior designer, she'd carried the color scheme throughout the house, creating a feeling of organized unity that was both warm and welcoming. How'd you get a woman like that? he wondered as he toweled off.

Bradley had paid him a similar compliment that night in his office when Mitch had been given the undercover assignment. The lieutenant had taken one look at the picture of Ciara on his desk and said, "How'd you get a beauty like that?"

Mitch felt his blood boil just thinking about Bradley.

One thing was certain, Mitch knew, as he swiped steam from the mirror, not even nepotism was going to net Bradley the job they'd both been drooling over for over a year. The lieutenant's uncle may have wielded enough power to garner him a grade hike in the past, may have packed enough punch, even, to get him the job that put him in charge of a dozen field agents, but—

"Enjoy it while it lasts, *Chet,*" Mitch said, smiling to himself, "''cause when the director hears what you did to me, you'll be history."

It had been Bradley's job...no...his *duty* to act as the go-between for husbands under his command and the wives they'd left behind. He had lied, repeatedly and deliberately, about the letters that should have gone from Mitch to Ciara and back again, and he'd done it to set Mitch up.

At first Mitch blamed the chill snaking up his back

on cold air from the floor vent. But he knew better. The creepy ''somebody's watching'' feeling had nothing to do with air-conditioning. Bradley hated him...enough to see him dead. That's what caused the sensation.

He was hoping that not hearing from Ciara would screw up my head, distract me, make me mess up. Didn't much matter whether those mistakes would cost the government its case...or Mitch his life. Either way, Bradley's competition for that job...and any other down the road...would be forever eliminated.

If he could do it to Mitch, Bradley was just as capable of putting other agents in harm's way...if he saw them as a threat of any kind. Mitch owed it to the agency to see to it Bradley never got the chance to repeat his crime. He was aching to get the old ball rolling...right over Bradley, if possible. But filing reports, verbalizing complaints, setting things in motion would take countless hours down at headquarters. And his place was beside Ciara now, not avenging a wrong.

There'll be plenty of time to see that Bradley pays, Mitch thought, opening the medicine cabinet. ''Good gravy,'' he said aloud, ''she's alphabetized this, too.'' Grinning, he recalled the pantry, where canned goods and cracker boxes had been lined up in *A, B, C* order. Same for the spices. ''So my Escada would be...'' His forefinger drew a spiral in the air as he tried to guess which of the bottles held his favorite aftershave.

The first, Armando, then Comandante, and beside it, a travel-size flask of Homme Jusqu'au Dernier. ''What's this?'' he asked aloud. ''Hamma Jooo Aw...?'' But try as he might, Mitch could not pronounce the fancy French name. ''So, Mrs. Mahoney,'' he said, rearranging the bottles, ''you're not perfect after all...*E* comes before *H*....''

Curiosity compelled him to unscrew the foreign bottle's cap and take a whiff of the cologne she'd added to his regular stock. "Bleh-yuck," he complained, coughing as he peered into the tiny opening.

Half-empty? That's odd....

Even if Ciara had bought it the day after he left, it wouldn't have evaporated this much in seven months. Eyes and lips narrowing, he asked himself why the aroma seemed so familiar. The rage began slowly, then escalated, like an introductory drumroll: It was that no-good Bradley's brand. What's *his* aftershave doing in my—

With trembling hands, Mitch recapped the container and pitched it into the wicker wastebasket beside the vanity. Heart pounding and pulse racing, his mouth went dry, and despite many gulps of water, it stayed that way. He had a hard time swallowing, because his throat and tongue seemed to have swelled to three times their normal size. A vein began throbbing in his temple, and his ears were ringing. His hands became suddenly clumsy, knocking over the toothbrush holder and the soap dish as he attempted to hold a paper cup under running water.

Unable to stand still, he began pacing in the small space, his big feet tangling in the scatter rug on the floor. Mitch steadied himself, one hand on the counter, the other pressed tight to the wall. "What's Bradley's aftershave doing in my medicine cabinet?" he demanded, his hoarse whisper bouncing off all four walls.

Ciara's face came to mind, all sweet and smiling and big-eyed innocence. She'd been a devout Christian girl when he'd left her. Had loneliness and despair driven her into another man's arms? Had she turned to Bradley for comfort, and—

''No!'' he bellowed, bringing his fist down hard on the sink. ''That's *my* kid she's carrying, *not* Bradley's!'' The mere thought of her in another man's arms started his stomach turning. Because she'd asked him to pack his things and leave, even after he explained everything....

But it had been *his* hand she'd reached for in the emergency room, and *his* gaze she'd locked on to for encouragement and support. He thought of their goodbye kiss in her hospital room the night before and the way she'd so tenderly touched his cheek, looking into his eyes as if she believed he'd hung the moon.

She *had* believed that once, before he'd gone to Philadelphia. Did she believe it still? Or had her love for him been strangled by the choking loneliness of endless days and nights without a word from him?

No...she'd genuinely seemed to need him, there at the hospital. But then, she'd been scared to death, for herself *and* the baby. If Bradley had been there instead, would she have clung to *his* hand? Would she have looking lovingly into *his* eyes?

Everything around him, every towel and curtain, every knickknack and picture, every stick of furniture, screamed out that she loved him. What more proof did he need than the way she'd turned this place into a haven for him in his absence?

He ran both hands through his damp hair, held them there. A strange grating sound caught his attention, and he attuned his ears, trying to identify it. He exhaled a great huff of air when he determined that what he'd heard had been the rasps of his own ragged breathing.

He remembered that moment in the foyer, when she'd announced in her calm, matter-of-fact way that she'd been carrying his baby on the night he left. His baby.

Of *course* it was his baby! She'd been so proud to be his wife that in those first weeks of their marriage he'd found things all over the house—envelopes, lunch bags, the TV listings—covered with her fanciful script: "Mrs. Mitchell Riley Mahoney. Ciara Neila Mahoney. Ciara Mahoney. Mrs. Ciara Mahoney."

And what about the way she'd trembled virginally in his arms on their wedding night, when he'd made her his wife in every sense of the word? It had taken time, but his soft-spoken words and gentle touches and tender kisses soothed her fears. "I'll never hurt you," he'd vowed. "Trust me, sweetie...."

Their eyes had met—hers glistening with unshed tears of hope and joy and anticipation, his blazing with intensity—and she'd sent him a trembly little smile.

He'd absorbed the tremors of fear that had pulsed from her, returned them to her as soothing waves of love and comfort. "It's all right, sweetie," he'd crooned, stroking her back. "We'll take our time...."

He'd kissed her eyelids, her cheeks, her throat, his fingers combing through her lovely silken hair. "I love you, Mitch," she'd breathed. "I love you so much!"

And then her touches, her kisses, her words of love rained upon him, as if she sought a way to show him that she'd meant it when she'd said that she trusted him, that she loved him with all her heart.

And for the first time in his life, Mitch understood why God had decreed that marriage was a sacred and blessed thing. The Lord intended this kind of loving warmth as a gift...a physical illustration of His own intense love for His children.

In the morning, he had awakened first, rolled onto his side to watch his sleeping bride. Her cheeks were still rosy from the night's ardor, and he'd reached out to draw a finger lightly down the bridge of her lightly-freckled nose. Her long-lashed eyes had fluttered, opened. "I love you, Mitchell Riley Mahoney," she'd whispered. Then she'd snuggled close.

Later, as she lay cuddled against him, Ciara had said, "Remember what you said last night...?"

He'd met her eyes. "You mean that verse from Ecclesiastes, 'Enjoy life with the wife whom you love.'"

"Yes," she'd whispered. "Marriage to you is going to be very romantic, I think...."

Now, in the distance Mitch heard the dim notes of the carriage clock on the family-room mantel and counted eight chimes. He couldn't have stood there, lost in memories, for nearly an hour! But he hadn't dawdled when the alarm sounded at seven; he'd leaped out of bed and stepped straight into the shower.

Taking a deep breath, he faced the sink. "She loves you. Of *course* she loves you," he told the wild-eyed man in the mirror. Either that, or she's the best actress ever born.

One bottle of aftershave was no proof of any wrongdoing. It might not even be Bradley's...perhaps her father had spent a night or two in the house, to help out, keep an eye on his daughter's failing health. Maybe—

Lord Jesus, he prayed, *I don't* want *to believe the worst, but—* "You're a special agent with the Federal Bureau of Investigation," he said to himself, squirting an egg-sized dollop of shaving cream into the palm of his left hand. With the right, he painted it over the lower half of his face. "If you can't get to the bottom of this," he added, touching the razor to his cheek, "you don't deserve to carry the badge."

One bright splotch of red bled through the white

foam, then another, as his quaking hand dragged the blade over his skin. Mitch barely noticed. The stinging, biting sensation of the tiny razor cuts was nothing compared to the ache in his heart.

Chapter Six

The golden-haired retriever scooted back and forth across the linoleum like a pendulum counting the happy seconds until Mitch managed to attach the leash to the dog's collar. "C'mon, fella," he said, ruffling Chester's thick coat, "let's go get Mom."

Chester whimpered.

"I know, I know," Mitch said, unlocking the car door, "I miss her, too."

And he did. He'd decided on the way to the veterinary clinic that it must have been a horrible coincidence that Chet Bradley's brand of aftershave had ended up in his medicine cabinet. Maybe Ciara got a free sample in the mail, he thought. Wrinkling his nose, he thought of its odor, which reminded him of rearview-mirror air freshener and horseradish. He could only hope if the freebie had come with a coupon for a bigger bottle, Ciara hadn't saved it.

By the time he had parked in the hospital parking lot and passed through the main entrance, Mitch believed his head was in the right place. At least he hoped it was. It had better be, he warned himself, or this next month is going to be miserable, for both of you.

As he strolled down the hall toward her room, he heard the melodic notes of Ciara's girlish laughter. The lilting sound of it thrilled him…until the grating tones of a man's chortle joined it, sending waves of heated jealousy coursing through him. "If your husband ever gets bored with you," the young man was saying when Mitch entered the room, "give me a call, 'cause women like you don't grow on trees." He spotted Mitch, leaning on the door frame, one foot crossed over the other, hands in his pockets. "You Mr. Mahoney?"

A tight-lipped grin on his face, Mitch nodded.

The blood technician scribbled Ciara's name on two white labels. "Lucky man," he said. "Where's a woman like this when *I'm* in the market for a relationship?" He stuck the labels to the vials containing her blood samples, lifted his case and walked toward the door. "The lady I'm dating now thinks *man* and *diamonds* are synonymous," he said from the hallway. And with a quick glance back at Ciara, he repeated, "Lucky man," and headed for his next patient.

Not once in the months he'd been gone had Mitch considered the possibility that she'd violate their marriage vows. *One lousy bottle of stinking cologne,* he told himself, *is no cause for mistrust now.* He had no reason to be jealous of Ciara, because she'd given him no reason to be.

The image of that cologne, standing on the glass shelf in the medicine cabinet as if it belonged, flashed in his mind. And right on its heels, the blatantly flirtatious comments of the good-looking young man who'd just left her room. So he told himself: you'd better get used to guys flirting with your wife; it's what you did, first time you saw her. Besides, what did you expect when you married a knockout? Mitch grinned despite himself, and looked at his wife. Yeah, she sure was a knockout.

Despite a night's sleep, Ciara still looked pale and drawn, but she was smiling and seemed happy to see him. "Good morning," she said brightly, her eyes still puffy, her voice early-morning raspy. "Did you sleep well?"

"Like a baby," he answered, the memory of her scent, clinging to the pillowcase, hovering in his mind.

Ciara raised a brow. "Are you aware that babies wake up every two hours?"

Mitch chuckled. "You trying to scare me? 'Cause if you are, you'll have to try harder."

She sent him a knowing grin that was both motherly and wifely. "I'm glad you slept well." The grin became a soft, sweet smile as she leaned back against her pillows. "I remember the way you always prepared for bed. I used to think if it wouldn't mar the woodwork, you'd have cross-barred every opening with two-by-fours and ten-penny nails. It's a wonder you get any sleep at all, worrying the way you do."

Some might call his before-bed ritual eccentric to the point of psychotic. Not Ciara. Even the first time she'd witnessed it, she had treated his fussiness matter-of-factly, as if all the men in America bolted every door, locked each window, pulled the blinds...and checked twice to make sure he hadn't overlooked anything. He'd never explained it, and Ciara had never asked him to. But Mitch had been out there, had seen the vile and vicious things human beings could do to one another. He wasn't about to take any chances. Not with his wife's safety.

She'd viewed it as routine, like showering and shaving. Which amazed him, considering his recurrent nightmare.

It had disturbed his sleep almost hourly those first months after he'd been kidnapped. Gradually it plagued him less often. By the time he met Ciara, the horrid images only came to him when he'd skipped a night's sleep or went to bed more tired than usual.

They'd been married exactly two days, and he'd gone to bed that second night of their honeymoon. The excitement of the wedding, all that dancing at the reception, the long drive to Martha's Vineyard…Mitch should have expected it, should have warned her. But he'd been so happy, so content with his new life that he hadn't even thought to bring it up.

When she'd roused him, he'd almost slugged her, because in that instant between sleeping and waking, he'd mistaken her for the unseen enemy of his nightmare.

He'd felt a deep, burning shame when she'd seen him that way, trembling, breathing like he'd just run a mile, on the verge of tears like a small helpless boy. The man of the family was supposed to protect his wife, he'd chided himself as the tremors racked his perspiration-slicked limbs; the husband was supposed to comfort and reassure the wife after a nightmare, not the other way around.

But her strong yet delicate hand, gently shaking his shoulder, had brought him to, and her soft, sweet voice, had pulled him from the nightmarish haze. Ciara had snuggled close, her cool fingertips smoothing the sweat-dampened hair back from his forehead. "You were having a bad dream," she'd whispered, "but it's all right now. Everything is all right."

Amazingly, it had been. Relieved to be in her arms, he clutched her to him and moaned into the crook of her neck. "Thank God," he'd rasped. "Praise Almighty God."

And she'd rocked him, kissing his tightly-shut eyes. "Shhh. It's all right," she'd crooned. "It's all right."

He remembered thinking at the time that she'd be a terrific mother someday, because she was certainly good at this comforting stuff.

Until she'd begun kissing away his tears, he hadn't been aware he'd started to sob. Her soft touches, her tender kisses, her soothing words of love rained upon him and slowly washed the agony away. The festering sore of his fear healed that night; he hadn't had the dream since. *God in Heaven,* he prayed, *I love her...love her like crazy.*

It had been on the morning after she'd witnessed the aftereffects of his nightmare, as she drew lazy circles in his chest hair, that Ciara had discovered the gunshot wound on his rib cage and he'd told her the story of how it had happened. She'd been shocked, horrified. "It's such a *dangerous* job, Mitch," she'd said, on the verge of tears. Between that and what had happened to Abe Carlson, the idea of his leaving the Bureau was never far from her mind after that.

The sound of her voice reached his ears, bringing him back to the present, and Mitch wondered how long she'd been happily chattering there in the hospital bed, while his mind had been wandering.

"And I don't suppose you got one decent night's sleep the whole time you were gone," she was saying in that affectionate, scolding way that made him feel loved and protected and wanted, all rolled into one. She shrugged, then aimed the finger at him again. "How could you, when the job required that you sleep with one ear perked and one eye open the whole time?"

Mitch chuckled. "You make it sound like I was fighting a war."

She wasn't smiling when she said, "You *were*."

This was the Ciara he had thought about day and night, the Ciara he'd dreamed of while he'd been away. *This* was the Ciara he'd fallen in love with…caring about his every need, even in her very delicate condition. How could you have even suspected her of being unfaithful? he asked himself.

She's as innocent as that baby she's carrying; either that or she missed her calling as an actress.

The dark thought hovered there in his mind for a moment, blotting out the joy the bright one had given him. Her innocence, her sweetness…could it be nothing but an act?

"I've taken care of the paperwork," he heard her say, "so you wouldn't have to bother when you got here." Ciara sighed, and smiling, a hand on her big tummy.

"Thanks," he said, forcing a grin. "You're too good to me."

"I hate to admit it," she said, her eyes alight with mischief, "but I didn't do it for you." She patted her tummy. "I just can't *wait* to get us home!"

"I have a surprise for you…in the car," Mitch said, and pictured Chester, who was no doubt slathering the rear windows of the Mustang with what Ciara lovingly referred to as "joy juice."

"I don't know if I can handle any more surprises," she said, a half smile on her face.

He sat beside her on the edge of the bed, a hand atop her stomach. "I did this while you were sleeping last night," he said, "and this kid of ours did quite a dance for me. Any chance I'll get a repeat performance?"

She patted his hand. "The little imp wakes me up

every morning between five and six. Sorry, but you missed the first show.''

Unable to hide his disappointment, Mitch screwed up one corner of his mouth.

''Don't pout, Mahoney. There's usually a matinee right around lunchtime.'' She tilted her head, studied his face for a quiet moment. ''Free admission for dads only,'' she added, winking.

''I'll be there, front row center,'' he said, looking into her beautiful, exhausted face. ''Now what say we get you dressed and go home?''

Ciara nodded and threw back the covers.

''You were dressed under there?''

''I've been ready since dawn.'' Then, sending a glance toward the door, she whispered, ''They must set the thermostat at ten above freezing. I was shivering in that flimsy T-shirt and stretch pants!''

He tucked a tendril of hair behind her ear. ''Then you'll be happy to know it's still a pleasant seventy-five degrees at home,'' he said. ''Now you sit tight, while I scrounge up a wheelchair.''

Ciara rolled her eyes and harrumphed. ''Wheelchair? I'm going to hate this.''

He held up a silencing hand. ''I know that lying around for a whole month is going to be tough on a go-get-'em gal like you, but you'll do it...for the baby's sake.'' He drew her to him in a sideways hug. ''Why not look at these 'lady of leisure' weeks as a gift from heaven?''

Ciara leaned her head on his shoulder and nodded. ''I suppose you're right. I'll be getting all kinds of exercise once the baby is born, won't I?''

Suddenly she bracketed his face with both hands. ''No matter what I say, you stick to your guns, you hear? Keep a tight rein on me, even if I give you a hard time…and I think we both know that's possible.''

"Possible!" he said, laughing softly, then kissing her temple. "You may as well say 'It's possible the sun will rise in the east. It's possible spring will follow winter, it's possible—'"

"I'll try to be a good patient, Mitch."

He rested his chin on top of her head. "'Course you will. And I'll be the best doctor stand-in you ever saw." He wagged a finger under her nose. "But I feel it's only fair to warn you…I'm going to be a tough taskmaster where your health is concerned."

She nodded. Sighed. "So go get the wheelchair, Doctor Killjoy," she said, grinning. "I want to go *home*."

Mitch carried her into the family room and gently deposited her on the sofa bed, got onto his knees and began untying her white sneakers. Their trip home had been swift and Ciara's reunion with Chester had been well worth the trouble of bringing the big guy along.

She grabbed his wrists. "Mitch, you don't have to—"

He sent her a silent warning that silenced her.

Ciara rolled her eyes. "I never thought I'd see the day when I'd be so helpless I couldn't even take off my own shoes," she complained.

"Look at it this way—once they're off, you won't be putting them on again, so you were only 'this helpless' once."

She grinned. "When did you start seeing the silver lining? I thought you were the type who just saw dark clouds?"

Mitch shrugged. "Things aren't always what they seem. You know what happens when you judge a book by its cover?'' he smirked good-naturedly. ''You bite the hand that feeds you, that's what.''

''Please—'' she laughed, hands up in surrender ''—one more bad cliché, and I'm liable to explode.''

He patted her tummy and twisted his face into a pleading frown. ''Please, don't. At least not till the equipment arrives.''

''Equipment? What equipment?''

''Didn't Peterson tell you? He put in an order for a home monitor. You're gonna be on TV, pretty lady!''

Ciara frowned. ''What in the world are you talking about? Dr. Peterson didn't say anything to me about—''

''The machinery will be delivered today. Way I understand it, we're to plug you in to the monitor, then plug the monitor into the phone and the TV, so Peterson can read the printout that'll come out at his office.''

''A fetal heart monitor?''

He shrugged. ''Guess so. I never thought to ask what kind.'' He plunged on. ''Plus a nurse will be stopping by every other day to do a blood count—'' he winked ''—make sure you're not melting or anything. You'll get used to it. Maybe you'll even grow to like it.''

She'd harrumphed. '' 'Fetal' attraction, huh?''

''There's more than one way to kill a rabbit.'' He held up a hand to forestall another cliché warning. ''Sorry,'' he said. ''But technically, that was a pun, not a cliché.''

Ciara rolled her eyes. ''It's going to be a long, long month....''

''No way, honey. Time always flies when you're having fun. And I'm going to see to it you have plenty of fun. Now sit still so I can get your shoes off. You're supposed to keep your feet elevated as much as possible.'' He tugged at the snow-white shoelace. ''First chance I get, I'm gonna write a letter and complain about the condition of the roads in this county. There are more potholes between here and the hospital than a zebra has stripes. That trip home is likely to have—''

She laid a hand alongside his cheek. ''No need to waste a stamp on my account. I'm fine. Tired, but fine.''

She must have read his mind again, and knowing he was about to say she didn't *look* fine, Ciara glanced around her.

''When did you find time to do all this?'' she asked. ''You must have been up all night. The bed's made up all nice as you please, and you've moved the end table forward so I can reach it, even while I'm lying flat on my back,'' she said. ''You've thought of everything…tissues, books, magazines, the remote.''

She met his eyes, her own wide with surprise. ''Wait just a minute, here…you're giving *me* control of the clicker?'' Ciara tilted her head and propped a fist on a hip. ''Why, Mitchell Riley Mahoney, are you flirting with me?''

The way you flirted with Bradley while I was away?

Mitch shook his head, cleared his throat. Where did *that* come from? he wondered, surprised by the sudden intrusion of the suspicious thought. He forced a smile. ''I was hoping you'd be sleeping a lot, and I could slip it out from under your hand now and then.''

He pointed at the summer-weight gown and matching robe he'd laid out for her. ''Let's get you into your pajamas, and once you're all tucked in, I'll see what I can rustle us up for lunch.''

When Ciara glanced at the nightclothes, Mitch noticed the slight flush that pinked her cheeks. They hadn't had much time together as man and wife, but he'd seen her in a nightie before. Surely she wasn't still feeling timid and shy, as she had on their wedding night. I'll bet you weren't this modest with— He stopped himself, wondering where on earth those thoughts were coming from.

"How 'bout I start lunch, let you slip into these…by yourself."

She bit her lower lip. Rolled her eyes. "You must think I'm the silliest thing on two feet." Hiding behind her hands, she mumbled, "It's just— I'm…I'm so *huge,* Mitch. Last time you saw me, I had an hourglass figure, and now I look like a—"

"You've never been more beautiful. Don't you say one negative word about my gorgeous, very pregnant wife," he scolded, "or I'll have to arrest you."

They hadn't been together long, but had managed to develop a private joke or two. Ciara had always known that despite outward appearances—tough-cop sternness, badge and gun, the sometimes violent things he'd been forced to do in the line of duty—Mitch was nothing but a big softie.

Ciara leaned her cheek against his upheld palm, nuzzled against it, like a house cat in search of a good ear scratching. He'd been sitting on his heels and rose to his knees now. "If you don't stop looking at me with those big, blue eyes…" Those big blue *loving* eyes.…

"Can't help myself," she sighed. "I'm just so glad to be home." Ciara hesitated, then added, "I'm glad you're back, Mitch."

His arms went around her, as naturally as if he'd been doing it dozens of times daily for the past seven months, and hers slipped around him just as easily. Their lips met, softly at first, and what began as a gentle kiss intensified.

Oh, but it felt good to be with her this way, as man

and wife again. He'd missed her while he'd been away, but until this moment—now that her condition had stabilized and she was out of danger—he hadn't realized exactly how much.

She pulled away, inhaled a great draft of air.

Like a man too long in the desert yearns for water, his lips sought hers again.

"Do you still love me?" she murmured against his open mouth.

A palm on each of her cheeks, he sat back to study her face. Surely she wasn't serious.

The raised brows and pouting lower lip told him she was. Did she really think it was possible for him to *stop?* "Ciara, sweetie, I've always loved you. From the minute I first saw you, looking out to sea at the rail of that beat-up old cruise ship, I loved you...."

"Beat-up? I'll have you know that was once *The Love Boat.*"

"Yeah. Right. Like they had such things a century ago. But you can't distract me that easily," he said, an eyebrow cocked. "Every minute that passes, I love you more. I've never stopped. Not for a heartbeat. Couldn't if I tried." Not even if I find out that you and Bradley— Mitch swallowed. His ping-ponging emotions were sure to make him crazy...if they didn't give him a heart attack first.

"Thank you," she said, her voice thick and sweet as syrup.

"Thank you?" he echoed, a wry grin tilting his mouth. "You've been to the movies. You know how it's supposed to be done." He held a finger aloft and began the lesson. "I say 'I love you,' and you say 'I love you, too.' Not 'thank you' but 'I love you.'" Mitch chuckled, tenderly grasped her lips with the fingertips of both hands, and gently manipulated her mouth. "'I love you,'" he said, as if he were the ventriloquist and she his dummy. "Go on, now you try it, all by yourself."

She kissed his playful fingers. "I *am* grateful, Mitch. What's wrong with admitting it?"

She branded him with an alluring, hypnotic gaze. His heart ached and his stomach flipped. There's nothing wrong with admitting that, he wanted to tell her, but it isn't what I need to hear right now.

After a seemingly endless moment, Ciara closed her eyes. "I love you more today than yesterday," she whispered, reciting the old promise with heartfelt feeling, "but not as much as tomorrow."

He held her, and she melted in his arms, her rounded little body feeling warm and reassuring as it pressed tightly against him. "It's good to be home," he admitted, putting aside his worries that she might be carrying another man's child. "I'm sorry I was gone so lo—"

She silenced him with a kiss.

The memory lapse was short-lived.

Did she kiss Bradley? The ugly thought took his breath away, and he ended the intimate moment. Mitch sat on the edge of the sofa bed with his back to her and ran both hands through his hair. What's wrong with you, Mahoney? One minute you're sure as shootin' she couldn't have cheated on you, the next you're just as sure she did. What's it gonna take to make up your mind!

He could ask her, straight-out, for starters. If she was innocent, she'd be shocked, hurt, furious, that he hadn't trusted her. But if she was guilty, didn't he have a right to know?

Mitch shook his head. Asking her was out of the

question. At least for now. If you haven't figured it out by the time the baby's born... He gulped down the last of the coffee he'd brought her. Until then, she's to rest and stay calm.

If the child was his, he wanted to ensure a healthy birth. Even if it wasn't, well, the baby hadn't played a part in the duplicity that led to its conception. It deserved nothing but good things, no matter who its father was.

"Fine waiter you are," she teased, "bringing me fresh-brewed coffee, then drinking it yourself."

He looked over his shoulder at her sweet, smiling face. "I'll get you a refill."

Let it be my kid, he prayed as he headed for the kitchen. *Please let it be my kid....*

Ciara listened to Mitch in the kitchen, clattering pots and pans and utensils, and remembered that kiss. Guilt hammered in her heart. She would never have deliberately hurt him, but she had, and the proof had been the abrupt way he'd ended their brief intimacy.

She'd said a lot to hurt him yesterday. Maybe after lunch they could discuss it a little more quietly than they had the night he'd left, or yesterday morning when he'd phoned from headquarters, or later, before she'd collapsed.

That old spark is still there, strong and bright as ever. Ciara touched her fingertips to her lips, remembering how wonderful it felt to be in his arms again, to be kissing him again. She hadn't realized how much she'd missed him, until the old familiar stirrings of passion erupted within her.

But I need time, she thought, time to forget all those months alone, time to be sure he won't do it again.

Every wifely instinct in her had made Ciara want to reach out and comfort him when he'd ended the kiss, turned away from her and held his head in his hands. But what would she have said? What might she have done? Since nothing had come to mind, she'd chosen instead to make light of it, to behave as if she hadn't noticed at all. "Fine waiter you are," she'd teased when he drained her cup in one gulp.

You're not in this alone, you know, she reminded herself. It's hard for Mitch, too. She sipped the refill of decaf he'd brought her and sighed. Their love had been as deep and wide as the Montana sky, bright with joy, deep with companionship, hot with passion. Will we ever get back to that? Ciara slumped against the cool, pillowy backrest of the sofa bed and closed her eyes. *Please God, help us find our way back.*

Right from the start, she and Mitch, like the boy and girl next door who'd known each other a lifetime, had felt relaxed and at ease in each other's presence. It had been that factor more than any other that told her it would be safe to fall in love so soon after the pastor's cordial introduction.

Ciara missed that serenity, the satisfaction born of the comfort they shared. Not take-you-for-granted comfort, but the old-shoe-dependable kind that she sensed would wrap around them—warming, soothing, nourishing their love—for a lifetime. She'd heard all about the fireworks-and-sparks kind of love, and had never wanted any part of it. I'll take charcoal over flash paper any day, she'd thought, because paper burned hot and quick...and died the same way. Coal might not heat up as fast, but it stayed warm a whole lot longer. She likened Mitch to charcoal—steady, sure, lasting. No one had been more surprised than Ciara to discover that her calm, dependable guy turned out to be a hot-blooded, passionate man.

You can't judge a book by its cover, he'd said earlier that day. But Ciara had said it first…on their wedding night.

Once they'd passed that initial test, she and Mitch had not needed the traditional "getting to know you" time her married friends had warned her about. It was a miracle, Ciara believed, that they'd *started out* feeling like lifemates. Their time apart had all but destroyed that comfortable, companionable feeling. But the passion was still there; that kiss proved it. Perhaps that was God's way of telling them the rest could be salvaged, if they were willing to work at it.

Ciara prayed for all she was worth. "Lord," she whispered, "I love him, Lord. Help us." She shook her head. "Help us repair the damage, so that our child will never know the loneliness that comes from living with parents who aren't in love."

Her mom and dad had always claimed to love each other deeply, and from time to time, they'd actually put on a pretty good show of it. She suspected things weren't quite right before she was seven. By the time she turned ten, Ciara had seen through their ruse. She didn't want her child wondering the things that she'd wondered as a girl: had their love for *her* been an act, as well?

"I hope you're cooking up an appetite," Mitch called from the kitchen, breaking into her thoughts, "because I'm cooking up one special lunch out here…."

He'd fixed her a meal once, days before he left. Breakfast, as she recalled, chuckling to herself. She'd been in the front hall, trying to decide whether to store their winter hats and gloves on the shelf in the closet or in the sideboard near the front door. "Sweetie," he'd called from the kitchen, "I hate to bother you, but—"

She'd had to jam a knuckle between her teeth and bite down hard to keep from laughing when she walked into the room. Covered by a red-and-white gingham apron, his jeans-covered legs had poked out from the bottom, and the bulky sleeves of his University of Maryland sweatshirt stuck out from its ruffly shoulders. He held a pancake turner in one hand, hot dog tongs in the other. If he'd worn the outfit to a Halloween party, he'd have won the Silliest Costume Prize, hands-down.

"What?" he'd asked, mischievous dark eyes narrowing in response to her appraisal.

"I just missed you," she'd replied, "because you're the most handsome husband a girl ever had."

He'd grinned. "You think?"

"I do." She wiggled her eyebrows flirtatiously, wrapped her arms around his aproned waist. "In fact," she'd said, winking, "I'm giving a lot of thought to kissing you, right here, right now."

The turner and the tongs had clattered to the floor as he pressed her closer. "And they say aggressive women are no fun...."

After their warm embrace, Mitch started digging in a box marked "Kitchen." "Can't make my home fries till we find the big black skillet."

She'd glanced at the counter, where he'd piled enough peeled-and-sliced potatoes and onions to feed the Third Regiment. Ciara opened one box as Mitch popped the lid of another. "I've already looked in that one," he said, poking around inside another. "If you find the vegetable oil, salt and pepper, and Old Bay seasoning, let me know."

"Old Bay?" she'd asked, incredulous. "That's for

steamed crabs and shrimp, not potatoes and—'' At the startled, almost wounded expression on his face, she'd quickly added, ''Isn't it?''

''Just wait till you taste 'em, sweetie,'' he'd said, licking his lips and scrubbing his hands together. ''They're gonna spoil you for anybody else's potatoes. From now on, you won't be able to settle for anything but Mitch Mahoney's breakfast spuds.''

He'd given her dozens of memories like that one…before that awful night. Memories that had lulled her back to sleep when a bad dream awakened her, memories that gave her the energy to unpack every box in their new house within the first week, so he'd have a proper homecoming…*when* he came home.

Night after night as she'd headed for bed, Ciara had stood at the foot of the stairs, one hand on the mahogany rail, the other over her heart, listening for the sound of his key in the lock. Day after day she woke hoping that when she walked into the kitchen, he'd be sitting at the table, reading the morning edition of the *Baltimore Sun,* lips white from his powdered sugar donut as he grumbled about the one-sidedness of the newspaper's politics.

When the nights and the days turned into weeks, it got harder and harder to find a reason to hope he might be there waiting when she got home from teaching, a big smile on his handsome face. ''Where have you been!'' she imagined he'd ask. ''I've been dying to see you!''

Every time Lieutenant Bradley's car pulled into the drive, her heartbeat doubled…maybe this time he'd have a letter for her. Ciara played her tough-girl routine to the hilt. She would show the seasoned agent that she knew a thing or two about bravery. She'd prove she knew how to handle being married to the Bureau. Because when Mitch *did* come home, she wanted him to be proud of the way she'd conducted herself.

In truth, her bravado had been almost as much for Bradley as for herself. "I'm so sorry, Ciara," he would say every time, taking her hand, "but Mitch missed another meeting." And every time, she'd pull free of his pressing fingers and focus on the look on his face. It could mean one of two things: Bradley was truly distressed to have delivered unpleasant news...again, or his wingtips were two sizes too small.

She'd never given a thought to the possibility that he'd deliberately kept her and Mitch apart. Why had it been so easy to believe him, instead of her husband? Oh, he was a smooth one, all right, starting out in complete defense of his comrade, slipping in a little doubt here, casting a bit of suspicion there, until he had her thoroughly convinced that the only possible reason Mitch hadn't written was because he hadn't wanted to. But she'd *let* him put those mistrustful thoughts in her head.

Those first unhappy weeks, she'd spent so much time on her knees, hands folded, it was a minor miracle she hadn't developed inch-thick calluses. She had gone over it in her mind a hundred times: from those first, thrilling stirrings of love, she had beseeched the Almighty to show her a sign; if Mitch wasn't the man He intended her to spend the rest of her life with, she would take her mother's advice and stop wasting her time.

And then Mitch had taken her in his arms and kissed her, and it had felt so good so right. How else was she to have interpreted the emotions, except as God's answer to her heartfelt prayer!

She'd waited a long time to meet the right man. Had

she jumped into the relationship because she'd been lonely? Had she misread God's response? Maybe it had been nothing but hormones, she'd fretted, dictating her interpretation of the Lord's intent.

The pastor had said, more than once, that prayer alone is not enough to prevent doubt. It takes faith and lots of it, he'd insisted, to forestall suspicion, to keep uncertainty at bay. It was a lesson, Ciara realized, that she'd have to learn the hard way, through time and trial; for try as she might to look for reasons to believe Mitch would contact her—or come home to her—hope faded with each lonely, passing day.

And just about the time she was about ready to give up altogether, Dr. Peterson confirmed what she had suspected for weeks: Ciara was going to have a baby. *Mitch's* baby! The news changed everything. Surely when he heard their baby would be born the following summer, Mitch would do everything in his power to come back. She wrote a long, loving letter, outlining her hopes and dreams for this child growing inside her. When she handed it over to the lieutenant, Ciara had wanted to believe that Mitch would find a way to be with her, to share the joyous news, face-to-face.

But Lieutenant Bradley returned the very next week, wearing that same hang-dog expression she'd come to expect of him, and she set all hope aside. Her mother had been right: he was a cop, first and foremost, and would always put his job ahead of everything—every-*one* else—including their unborn baby.

"Mitch missed another meeting," he'd said, hands outstretched, as if imploring her to forgive *him* for her husband's transgressions.

One of the teachers at Ciara's school was married to a divorce attorney, and on the day Dr. Peterson let her hear the baby's heartbeat, she made an appointment to see the lawyer. For the child's sake if not her own, she had to make plans. If Mitch never came back, she had to ensure a stable, secure future for her child. If he did return, it wasn't likely he'd be a dedicated father, and she must protect the baby from such callousness.

She had no one to talk to about the situation. Who would understand such a thing! Certainly not her mother, because from day one, the woman's bitterness against Ciara's father spilled onto Mitch as well.

"He'll never love you as much as he loves his job," she'd said when Ciara showed her the sparkling diamond engagement ring. "The only enjoyment he'll get from life will be related to his work."

Judging by the furrows that lined her father's handsome brow and the way his mouth turned down at the corners when working a case, Ciara found it hard to believe her dad loved his job at all. She'd put the question to him on the night Mitch asked her to marry him.

Her father had answered in his typically soft-spoken way. "All I ever wanted was to see right win out over wrong."

"That doesn't happen very often," she'd countered. "It's in the news all the time…the way criminals get away with murder."

He'd nodded his agreement. "That's true far too often, I'm afraid. But it's so satisfying when the system works as our forefathers intended it to," he'd said, dark-lashed blue eyes gleaming as he plucked an imaginary prize from the air and secured it in a tight fist. "And you forget when the D.A. botched up, or the lab lost evidence, or the arresting officer forgot to read the suspect his rights. You forget that a lot of the time, everything goes wrong, because you're able to focus on what went right.''

Her father didn't love his *job,* Ciara understood when the conversation ended, he loved *justice.*

During her first weekend home after finishing up her freshman year in college, Ciara and her mother had been alone in the kitchen, chatting quietly as they'd washed the supper dishes. The contrast had reminded her of the weekend she'd gone home with her roommate, Kelly, to a cozily cluttered house that throbbed with the cheerful sounds of a big family. It hadn't been the first time Ciara had compared other households to her own—somber as a funeral parlor, quiet as a hospital. If her parents were that unhappy, why not get a divorce? she'd often wondered. She hoped they hadn't spent nineteen miserable years together for her sake, because if *she* was the reason they'd endured all that misery...

Perhaps they'd stuck it out because of the ''for better or for worse'' line in the marriage vows. But was that what God intended? That two individuals—who made a promise while they were too young and too foolish to understand the gravity or longevity of it—spend the rest of their lives locked in an unhappy union?

Ciara had always seen marriage as a loving gift, hand delivered by the Father. Her parents' marriage had been more a jail sentence than a gift of any kind. When *she* married, Ciara had decided, it wouldn't just be for love. No, she'd consider the future, as her parents obviously had not, because she would not, could not inflict a bitter loveless marriage on any children she might have. Ciara knew only too well what that could be like. If only she had siblings, maybe things wouldn't have seemed so bleak....

She dried the plate her mother had just washed. "Mom, why don't I have any brothers or sisters?"

The answer had come so quickly, Ciara figured out much later, because it was something that was often on her mother's mind. "I didn't think it would be fair to bring more children into this world, children who'd feel neglected and slighted by their own father."

"I've never felt anything but loved by Daddy," Ciara had admitted.

It had been the wrong thing to say to her mother.

Following a disgusted snort, she'd said, "Kids are adaptable. Besides, how would *you* know a good father from a bad one? You have nothing to compare him to."

"My friends' fathers spent as much time at work as Daddy did when he was a cop," she'd said, more than a little riled that her own mother had put her in the position of defending her father, "and they weren't policemen."

"Kids are adaptable," she'd repeated, "and they're good at justifying what's wrong in their lives, too. Well, I'm *not* so good at those things." She'd jammed a handful of silverware into the cup in the corner of the dish drainer. "Now you know why you're an only child."

"Why are you so *angry* with Dad?"

Her mother had stared out the window above the sink for a long moment, as if the answer to Ciara's question hung on a shrub or a tree limb. "I'm angry because I asked him to give it up, to do something safer—for my sake—and he refused."

"But he *did* give it up."

"I asked him to quit long before he was shot, Ciara. You weren't even born yet when I told him how hard it was for me, worrying every minute he was on the job, scared out of my mind if he was five minutes late, imagining all the terrible things that might have happened to keep him from coming home on time." She hesitated. "I found a solution to my worrying."

"What?"

"I taught myself not to care."

Now it all made sense. She'd been eleven when her father had been wounded in the line of duty. The injury to his hip would heal, the doctors had said, but he'd walk with a permanent limp...and because that would put him in harm's way on the job, he was forced to retire.

Strange, Ciara had often thought, that though he worked fewer hours at a far less stressful job, teaching at the university seemed to tire him like police work never had. Stranger still, before the second anniversary of his retirement, his dark hair had gone completely gray and his clear blue eyes had lost their youthful spark. And in addition to the gunshot-induced limp, he began to walk slightly bent at the waist, as though the burden of being unable to make his wife happy was a weight too crushing to bear, even for one with shoulders as broad as his.

One line from a poem she'd read in her English Literature class popped into her mind, "Joy is the ingredient that puts life into a man's soul, just as sadness causes its death." Her father, though the doctors claimed his vital organs were strong and healthy, was dying of unhappiness.

In the kitchen making her lunch, Mitch finished singing one Beatles tune and immediately launched into another, his voice echoing in the cavernous room. From her place on the sofa bed, Ciara smiled. He sounded happy, despite their predicament, and she wanted him to stay happy. The only way she knew to accomplish that goal was to set her own needs aside and let him continue the dangerous undercover work he seemed to love so much.

Could she do that? Should she, now that there was a baby to consider?

"I hope you're hungry," he called to her, "'cause I've made enough food for two Boy Scout troops and their leaders."

She closed her eyes. Oh, how I love him! she admitted silently.

But she couldn't allow love to blind her, not when the baby's future, as well as her own, was at stake. She wouldn't spend decades chained to a loveless marriage, as her mother had done. Had her parents stayed together, simply because of the vows they'd exchanged? Ciara and Mitch had spoken those same words. "What God has joined together, let no man put asunder," the preacher had said.

Ciara closed her eyes. "Lord Jesus," she whispered, "I want to do Your Will, but You'll have to show me the way."

"Ciara, sweetie," Mitch said, poking his head into the family room, "you can finish your nap later." He popped back into the kitchen. "Make a space on your lap for the breakfast tray." His face reappeared in the doorway, a confused frown furrowing his brow. "Ah, do we *have* a breakfast tray?"

"Yes," she answered, giggling softly. "It was a wedding gift from your Aunt Leila, remember?"

"Oh, yeah. Right," he said, nodding before he disappeared for the second time. In seconds he was back again. "Um...where do we keep the breakfast tray?"

She was reminded of an episode of "I Love Lucy," when Ricky insisted on making breakfast so his pregnant wife could sleep in…but continued to call Lucy into the kitchen to find this and that. Grinning, Ciara mimicked Lucille Ball. ''Oh, Ricky, it's in the cabinet under the wall oven, standing with the cookie sheets and pizza pans.''

''What?''

And after a terrible clatter, she heard him say, ''Bingo!''

Yes, Mitch seemed happy. But was she wife enough to keep him that way? Was her faith strong enough to stick with it and to find out?

Chapter Seven

❧

He hadn't been deliberately eavesdropping later that day, but the kitchen and the family room shared a common wall with an open vent. He made a little more noise with the ice cubes and lemonade, hoping to drown out Ciara's mother's nagging voice:

"I just don't understand why you couldn't have married someone like that nice Chet Bradley. He's always so—"

"Mom, please," came Ciara's harsh whisper. "Mitch is right in the next room. You want to hurt his feelings?"

Kathryn laughed. "Feelings? Please. He's a cop, and as we both know, cops don't *have* any feelings."

A moment of silence, then, "He left you alone for seven months, Ciara. Alone and carrying your first child. And a difficult pregnancy to boot!"

"It wasn't his fault," countered his wife. "He was just following orders."

"That's not what Chet said...."

He heard the rustle of sheets. "What are you talking about, Mom?"

"Did you know that Chet is single?"

Ciara had told Mitch that her mother was English, through and through. There must be a wee bit o' the Irish in 'er, he thought, 'cause she's answerin' a question with a question....

"Not single, divorced," her daughter corrected. "There's a difference...not that it matters. I'm a married woman, and pretty soon now, I'll be a mommy, too."

His mother-in-law's bitter sigh floated to him. "Don't remind me." She clucked her tongue. "I just hope you're happy, young lady, because now you're stuck in the same leaky boat I was in for two solid decades."

Kathryn had never made a secret of her feelings for Mitch, insulting him at every turn, trying to make him feel small and insignificant every chance she got. Obviously, he thought, my little "vacation" hasn't improved her opinion of me.

"If you had listened to me and married a man like Chet, you wouldn't be in this predicament now. At least he has some breeding, unlike certain Gaelic immigrants." She snorted disdainfully. "Chet wouldn't have left you high and dry. He—"

"He's a cop, too, don't forget."

"True. But his job doesn't put him on the front lines. His ego isn't all wrapped up in how much attention the 'big cases' give him."

"Lieutenant Bradley is Mitch's superior officer. He's the guy who made Mitch go away."

"That's not the way he tells it."

"You skirted this question earlier, and if you don't mind, I'd like a straight answer to it now. What do you mean, 'That's not the way he tells it'?"

If he stood just to the right of the stove and crouched

slightly, Mitch could see their reflections in the oven window. He saw Kathryn narrow her eyes and incline her head. "Where *was* Mitch all those months, anyway? I distinctly got the impression from Chet that—"

"That doesn't answer my question. And besides, when have you had an opportunity to discuss Mitch with him?" Ciara asked, sitting up straighter.

Kathryn waved a hand in front of her face, as though Ciara's question were a housefly or a pesky mosquito. "Last time I stopped by, he was here when I arrived, remember?" She tucked a flyaway strand of dark blond hair behind one ear, inspected her manicured fingernails. "That was the time he brought you roses, to cheer you up." She smiled brightly. "Such a caring, thoughtful, young man!" She straightened the hem of her skirt and added, "We were in the kitchen, fixing coffee, remember? I didn't see any harm in asking him a few questions. You're my daughter, after all. If I don't have a right to know the details about something that affects you so directly, who does?"

Roses? He brought *roses*…to cheer Ciara up? Mitch ground his molars together. It was understandable that his wife would be down in the dumps, considering the way they'd parted and all, but… How often had good old Chet been in his house, anyway? Often enough to feel comfortable upstairs…in the master bathroom?

Ciara's voice interrupted his self-interrogation. "What did he tell you?"

He knew Ciara well enough to recognize annoyance in her voice when he heard it. She was annoyed now.

Kathryn huffed. "All right, Ciara. I guess a child is never too old to be reminded to mind their manners. I'll thank you to keep a civil tongue in your head when you're talking to me, young lady. You may be a married woman now, but I'm still your mother!''

"I'm sorry if I sounded disrespectful, Mom. Blame it on cabin fever.''

She has been in the house an awful lot these past months, Mitch thought. And she always loved to take long walks...must be hard, being cooped up this way....

"You should try your hand at writing mysteries,'' Ciara added, giggling, "because you're a master at dropping hints and clues. I admit it, you've hooked me. Now *please* tell me what Chet said about Mitch!''

Kathryn joined in on what she believed to be her daughter's merriment. Mitch knew better. Shouldn't a mother be able to recognize when her daughter is getting angry? He'd only known her a few months before leaving for Philly, and even he recognized that Ciara's laughter was rooted in frustration.

"Well,'' Kathryn said, a hand on Ciara's knee, "it was like this.... It seems Mitch came to Chet late one night with this ego-maniacal idea for capturing a man on the FBI's Most Wanted list. Notorious criminal, Chet said. Mitch had it all worked out, right down to the kind of clothes he would wear. He'd pretend to be a CPA to trick the man.

"Chet didn't want to let him go, once he found out that you two had just been married, but Mitch insisted.'' Kathryn sighed. "Chet tried and tried to talk him out of it, but in the end, he had no choice but to admit that Mitch *had* come up with a good plan....''

"Interesting,'' Ciara said.

And Mitch could tell by the way her fingers were steadily tapping against her tummy that she was chomping at the bit to hear the rest of the story. Frankly, I'd like to hear it, too, he admitted.

"Chet didn't hear from Mitch the whole time he was undercover. Did you know that? It's his duty to report to his commanding officer, and he didn't phone in once! If he's that irresponsible about his job, think what a wonderful father he'll be."

Her voice dripped with sarcasm and bitterness. *I love you, too, Kathryn,* was his snide thought.

"I've told you and told you," Ciara said, "Mitch *couldn't* call. They were watching him night and day. One false move, and he might have been—"

Kathryn patted her daughter's hand, turned to face the kitchen. "Mitch! What's keeping you?" she called. She leaned forward and lowered her voice. "Send him to the kitchen for lemonade, and he's gone a half hour. Send him on a week-long assignment, and he's gone seven months."

That low-down lout, Mitch thought. *What was he doing telling her the details of a case that hadn't even gone to court yet?*

Kathryn snickered behind her hand. "Being elusive must be part of his nature. Now, if you had married a man like Chet..."

He'd heard about all of that he could handle. Straightening from his position in front of the oven window, Mitch left the glasses of lemonade on the kitchen counter and barged into the family room. "I don't mean to be rude, Kathryn, but Ciara looks awfully tired."

Ciara shot him a grateful look.

"I promised her doctor that at the first signs of fatigue, I'd make her take a nap." Gently he grabbed Kathryn's elbow and helped her up. "Why don't you come back in a day or so and bring Joe next time. I haven't seen him in—"

"In over *seven months!*" his mother-in-law finished, jerking free of his grasp.

Mitch handed her her purse and walked toward the front door. One hand on the knob, he smiled politely. "Why don't we make it Sunday afternoon. I'll fix a nice dinner. I'm sure Ciara will be rested up by then. Won't you, sweetie?"

Her blue eyes were twinkling when their eyes met, but when her mother faced her, she slumped weakly against her pillow. "I don't know...maybe you'd better call first, Mom, just to make sure I'm up to having company...."

Kathryn laid a hand on her chest, eyes wide and mouth agape. "Company! Your father and I aren't 'company,' we're *family!*"

"Thanks for stopping by," Mitch said, opening the door. "As always, it's been...an experience."

"'Here's your hat, what's your hurry?'" Kathryn quoted, snatching her purse from his hands. "You'd better not let anything happen to my daughter," she snapped, shaking a finger under his nose. "I intend to hold you personally responsible for—"

"Kathryn," he said, calmly, quietly, "you have my word that I won't let anything happen to your daughter. She happens to be the most important person in my life."

She huffed her disapproval. "You sure have a funny way of showing how you feel."

Smiling thinly, Mitch said, "You know, you're right about that." He opened the door and with a great sweep of his arm, invited her to step through it. "See you Sunday?" he asked once she was on the porch. "How does two o'clock sound?"

"I'll..."

"Drive safely now," he added as the door swung shut, "and be sure to give Joe my best."

Whatever Kathryn said in response was muffled by the closed door.

"Is she gone?" Ciara whispered when he came back into the family room.

Nodding, he sat on the edge of the sofa bed.

"Thank goodness. I love her, but she doesn't make it easy sometimes."

Mitch flexed a thick-muscled biceps. "You want her to stay out, it'll be my pleasure. *Trust me.*"

Ciara giggled. "I couldn't keep her away. She means well, it's just that she has—"

"The personality of vinegar?"

She pursed her lips. "Well, lemons, maybe...."

He stood, picked up the empty cookie plate he'd brought out when her mother had arrived. "I'm going to throw a load of sheets into the washer," he said, bending down to kiss her forehead. "How 'bout catching a catnap while I'm gone. You look like you could use it."

Yawning and stretching, she smiled. "I might just do that."

He started to walk away.

"Mitch?"

He stopped.

"What are we going to do? After the baby is born, I mean?"

Mitch held his breath. His heartbeat doubled, and his pulse pounded in his ears. She'd turned onto her side, making it impossible for him to read her expression. Was the question a throwback to her suggestion that he pack up and leave?

"You're taking such good care of me...of everything...that I'm going to be spoiled rotten by the time this baby gets here.''

Relieved, he exhaled. ''You've done more than your share, turning this house into a home all by yourself. You deserve to be spoiled rotten.''

She lifted her head and grinned.

''At least until the baby is born,'' he finished, winking.

She snuggled into her pillow and in moments was fast asleep.

I didn't tell you the whole truth, he admitted to his peacefully sleeping wife. *I have no intention of spoiling you rotten just till the baby comes. I'm going to treat you like a queen for the rest of your life.*

The next few days passed quietly and without incident. The lines of communication between them were beginning to open, as he took her temperature, brought her her vitamins, saw to it she drank plenty of water....

Ciara admired him, for although he had a different way of doing things, he accomplished every task with productive efficiency.

He had a plan for everything—usually written out on a five-by-seven tablet—and made so many checklists, Ciara believed all the ballpoint pens in the house would run out of ink before he had accomplished every task.

Mitch had written up his first list the night before he brought her home from the hospital. Once he helped her get settled the next morning, he whipped out a little notebook and sat on the edge of the sofa bed. ''Breakfast at nine, lunch at one, supper at seven, a light snack at ten, lights out by eleven. You can read or watch TV in between, but I want all the power off a couple of hours in the morning, again in the afternoon, so you can catch some shut-eye. What do you think?''

The dog sidled up to him and nudged Mitch's hand with his nose, as if to say Where do I fit into the plan?

"Don't worry, boy, I won't neglect you." Mitch flipped to the second page in his tablet. "See," he said, as if Chester could read what he'd printed in bold black letters, "you'll get yard time while your mommy, here, takes her naps." Patting the top of the dog's head, he'd added, "I'm afraid long walks around the block are going to have to wait till she's up and at 'em, 'cause we can't leave her alone."

Chester's silent bark seemed all the approval Mitch needed. "It's settled, then." To Ciara he added, "I've already put clean sheets on our bed, so…"

"I don't really have to go to bed at eleven," she said, hoping he'd agree because she'd said it so matter-of-factly.

His stern expression told her that she did have to retire at eleven.

"But…but I like to watch the eleven o'clock report on Channel Two before I turn in," she protested. "Besides, it isn't like I'll be doing anything to wear me out. Staying up late won't hurt me."

Unconsciously he ruffled Chester's thick coat, frowning as he turned her words over in his mind. "I hate TV news—nothing but a serving of pap for the feel-good generation, if you ask me. So…"

"I didn't ask you," she interrupted, grinning.

He held up a hand, and she'd giggled.

"How 'bout we make it an every-other-night thing," he had continued. "Tonight, the news. Tomorrow, bed at eleven."

She hadn't heard anything but *bed*. The word echoed

in her mind. She hadn't shared anything with him—not conversation or a meal, their home, *certainly* not a bed—in seven long months. Did he really expect her to pick right up where they'd left off, as if he'd been away on some fun-filled, weekend fishing trip with the guys? Didn't he understand that during nearly every moment of their separation, she had reviewed thousands of scenarios that would explain his lengthy absence—shootings, stabbings, beatings, kidnappings—horrible, torturous images.

She blinked those images away. "There's no reason for you to cart me upstairs every night, then back down in the morning." Consciously, deliberately, she phrased it as a statement of fact.

"You can't get a decent night's sleep with a metal bar diggin' into the small of your back," Mitch pointed out. "You'll sleep upstairs on a real mattress or—"

"I'll be fine, right here on the couch."

He crossed his arms over his chest, lifted his chin a notch. Mitch was not smiling when he said, "We can compromise on TV or not TV, but this subject isn't open for negotiation." He paused thoughtfully. "Well, I suppose I ought to give you *some* say in the matter...."

She should have waited a tick in time to display her victorious smile.

"You have two choices—sleep upstairs or stay upstairs. It's entirely up to you."

His stern expression, his cross-armed stance, his no-nonsense voice made it clear she would not win this battle, and yet Ciara couldn't help thinking what a wonderful father he'd be if he disciplined their children with the same gentle-yet-firm attitude. She got so wrapped up in the concept that she didn't give a thought to the fact that if she gave in on this point, they'd be sleeping together every night, like any other married couple.

And they were nothing like other married couples....

Chester looked back and forth between them and whimpered, reminding her of how helpless and afraid she'd felt when her parents argued.

"You'd really leave me up there," she asked breathily, "all alone, all day?"

"I'd much rather have you down here, where you can keep me company, but we'll do it that way if we have to."

And so the deal was struck.

Ciara snuggled beneath the crisp top sheet, remembering the way he'd carried her up the stairs that first night. Her heart had drummed and her stomach had clenched. After all those nights alone, clutching her pillow...and pretending it was him...what would it be like, she'd wondered, lying beside the real thing?

Chester, who had become Mitch's four-legged, shaggy shadow, had tagged along and flopped in a graceless heap on Ciara's side of the bed. Almost immediately he'd rested his chin on his paws and fell asleep.

If only *I* could get comfortable that easily! she'd thought as Mitch tucked her in and turned out the light. It had been a dark night, without so much as a moon sliver to brighten the room, and for those first few seconds, Ciara blinked into the blackness, listening....

Silence.

Had he decided to sleep downstairs? Had he made up the guest bedroom for himself?

By then her eyes had adjusted to the darkness, and she'd seen his shadow pass in front of the window. Almost immediately, he'd been swallowed up by the blackness, and she'd strained her ears. First, the sound of heavy footfalls, padding across the carpeted floor, then a muffled *clunk* as his belted trousers had landed on the upholstered bedside chair. The mattress dipped under his weight, the sheet billowed upward, like a plaid parachute and settled slowly over them.

Then he'd rolled onto his side and slid his arms around her. "G'night," Mitch had whispered, kissing her temple. "Sweet dreams." He'd tucked a hand under his cheek, rested the other on her tummy. "G'night, li'l sweetie," he'd added.

More silence.

Then the unmistakable, comforting sound of his soft snores.

Ciara didn't know how long she'd lain there, snuggled against him, but listening to his steady, deep breaths had relaxed her, lulled her. Before she'd known it, the bright light of morning had beckoned her.

The morning after his return, Ciara had at first thought she'd been dreaming again, that he wouldn't be there when she opened her eyes, and then she'd seen him there, flat on his back, gentle breaths counting the seconds. One hand had rested on his slowly heaving chest, big fingers splayed like a pianist's. The other, he'd tucked under his neck. A lock of dark hair had fallen across his forehead, and the shadow of a night's growth of whiskers dusted his cheeks and chin. She had needed to use the bathroom, but he'd looked so peaceful—like an innocent boy, without a care in the world—that she hadn't wanted to wake him.

Instead, she'd tucked the misplaced curl into place. His thick black lashes had fluttered in response to her touch. He'd focused on the ceiling and frowned, as though trying to remember where he was. A tiny smile lifted the corners of his mouth, and he'd slowly turned to face her.

"G'mornin'," he'd said, the bass of his sleepy voice guttural and growly. He'd worked his arms around her. "Sleep well?"

Ciara had tucked her face into the crook of his neck. "Like a log," she'd answered. "And you?"

"Terrific." And as if to prove it, Mitch had yawned deeply. He climbed out of bed and thumped groggily around to her side, and carried her into the bathroom. "I'm going to go down and start the coffee," he'd explained. "I'll only be a minute, so don't you move from there, you hear?"

"I hear," she'd agreed as he closed the door.

Almost immediately, she'd noticed the milky white bottle in the wicker waste basket. "Homme Jusqu'au Dernier," she said, reading the label aloud. Mitch had never worn that brand before he'd left.... Ciara couldn't reach it without getting up, so she didn't know if she liked his new cologne. She would ask him about it when he came back for her.

The clatter of cabinet doors and canister lids, and the sound of running water had blotted the question from her mind. And true to his word, he was in their room in minutes, opening and closing drawers and doors, his big bare feet thudding as he crossed from closet to dresser and back again.

One sleeve of his white T-shirt had rolled up, and the legs of his boxers had wrinkled during the night; his dark waves were tousled, his cheeks sheet wrinkled when he burst into the bathroom. "Finished?"

The little-boy, rumpled look had been so appealing

that Ciara had been forced to look away to diminish the passion stirring deep inside her. She mumbled a polite "Yes, thanks," and just like that, he'd lifted her into his arms and sat her on the edge of the bed.

On his knees, he'd gently gripped her wrists, held them above her head and slid her nightgown off. The nothing-but-business expression warmed as he focused on her naked stomach. Lifting his gaze to hers, he'd smiled tenderly, blinking and shaking his head slightly. He'd broken the intense eye contact, looked at her broadened waistline again and stroked its roundness.

The heat of his hands, pressing against her taut skin, sent eddies of desire coursing through her. "You're beautiful," he'd rasped, kissing every inch of her stomach, "so very beautiful."

And then his eyes—dusky chocolaty eyes that blazed with need and yearning—had met hers. It seemed to Ciara that he hadn't wanted her to read his mind and discover the longing there; why else would he have slowly, slowly dropped the densely lashed lids?

No, she'd thought, almost sadly, don't shut me out. She'd placed a palm on each whiskered cheek, thumbs massaging the tight muscles of his jaw. She'd been stunned when he opened his eyes again, to see the thin sheen of tears glistening there. "I'm so sorry, Ciara," he'd husked. "I should have been here, right from the beginning."

His arms had slid around her, his ear cleaving to her midsection. "Can you ever forgive me?"

There had been moments, while he'd been gone, when Ciara had said she despised him. It would have been easier, accepting his absence, if only she could hate him. But try as she might, the words had never rung true. On the day they'd met, she'd fallen in love with his silly jokes and his opinionated politics and his bighearted nature. Standing at the altar of God, she'd vowed to love him for better or for worse, and no matter how many miles and months separated them, her last words on this earth would likely be "Oh, how I loved him!"

She had felt the dampness between his skin and hers that morning, as Mitch had nestled his face against their unborn child. Any anger she had felt for him was swallowed up by his heartfelt tears. Every maternal instinct inside her had risen up, and she'd held him near, fingers gently raking through his plush chestnut curls.

One day soon, she would ask him about the assignment that had put time and space between them. But for those few moments, it hadn't mattered where he'd gone, or why. He had come home, had come back to her.

He had sniffed, and shaken his head, then sat back on his heels to gather up the clothes he'd set out for her. He'd given the big white T-shirt—one of his own—two hearty flaps, and slipped it carefully over her head. She picked up the brush that had been hidden under the shirt. Mitch had held out his hand, and she'd handed it to him and, standing, he'd run the boar bristles through her hair, one hundred strokes; she'd counted them. "Shines like the sun," he'd said, then he'd lifted her in his arms and carried her downstairs.

Though he'd daubed a light kiss upon her cheek each time he brought a cup of coffee, a plate of cookies, Mitch had not repeated any part of that lovely scene since…despite the countless hours she'd spent wishing and hoping that he would. Was it something hormonal, induced by her condition, she'd wondered, that made her ache for the intimacy of his touch? And why had he stoically withheld it?

They'd been back together for four days now, and Ciara decided the best way to divert her attention was to focus on the burning questions—where he'd been, what he'd been doing—that had plagued her while he'd been gone. When the time was right—and she'd have to trust God to tell her when that moment arrived—she would ask Mitch about the assignment. Had he wanted to take it, or had it been foisted upon him? The answer would make all the difference in the world....

Now as Ciara watched him folding towels as he sat on the foot of the sofa bed, grinning as Chester wrestled with a Lambchops doll, she said, "Mitch, let me help. Folding clothes is hardly strenuous activity, and I feel so useless."

He looked at her and said, "Since I'm the one sitting here doing it, I know for a fact that the job requires the use of stomach muscles. You're not doing anything that puts any strain on that baby." Smoothing the washcloth he'd just doubled, he added it to the neat, colorful stack. "Got it?"

She flopped back against the pillows he'd stuffed behind her. "Got it," she droned.

He reached for the laundry basket. "When I'm finished putting this stuff away, I'll—"

Changing positions, Ciara winced slightly.

"What...?" He leaped up so fast, he nearly toppled his tower of towels. "What's wrong?" His big hands gripped her upper arms. "Are you in pain?"

"Goodness gracious sakes alive, Mitch," she said, frowning slightly, "my back is a little stiff from all this inactivity. It was a muscle cramp, that's all." Shaking her head, Ciara rolled her eyes and punched the mattress. "I *hate* being completely helpless. It makes me feel so…so."

He stood for a moment, pinching the bridge of his nose between thumb and forefinger, then heaved a deep sigh. "You scared me half to death." He stuffed the linens into a wicker laundry basket and grinned. "Mrs. Mahoney," Mitch said, rubbing his palms together, "get ready for the best back rub of your life."

She grinned. "I've never had a back rub, 'best' or otherwise."

Mitch's brows rose. "Never?"

Ciara shook her head. "Never."

"Never say never. Now, roll over, Beethoven."

She wouldn't have admitted it—not until she knew he loved her as much as she loved him—but having him near was like a dream come true. Ciara did as she was told. Hiding her face in the pillow, she closed her eyes and bit her bottom lip to gird herself. Those moments in their room, when he'd so lovingly held their unborn child, haunted her. He hadn't left her side, had taken such good care of her, all without a word of complaint. She had worried in the hospital that he might not want this child; what had motivated his loving ministrations…love for the baby, love for her, or both? Until she knew, Ciara could not admit how much his physical presence meant to her.

He lay down behind her, hiked up the oversize T-shirt and ran his palms over her skin, paying particular attention to the small of her back. His fingers slid up, kneaded her neck and shoulders, then moved down to rub her biceps.

Ciara relaxed her grip on the pillow, as unconscious sighs slipped from her lips. Her mind was wandering in a half awake, half asleep state, floating, soaring, surrounded by yards of satin under a sky full of puffy clouds when Mitch leaned forward and brushed her ear with his lips. "I love you," he whispered. And lowering his dark head to hers, he kissed her cheek, softly, then more urgently as moved down the side of her neck.

He pressed so close, that not even the barest wisp of a breeze could have passed between their bodies. She was his, and he was hers, and at the moment nothing mattered except her fierce love for him. She trembled as his fingers played in her hair, shivered as his palms skimmed the bared flesh of her back, tingled as his lips nibbled at her earlobe.

He climbed over her then, putting them face-to-face, and placed his palms upon her cheeks. Raw need glittered in his eyes as he held her gaze, analyzing her expression, studying her reaction. She blinked, feeling light-headed, and hoped he wouldn't read the passion smoldering inside her.

"I love you," he said again, a tinge of wonder in his voice.

She looked away, shifted restlessly, but the look of helpless uncertainty on his face wasn't that easily forgotten. He loved her. He loved *her!* Ciara ignored the voice inside her that warned her to be still, to be silent. It was surprisingly easy to admit the truth, once the words started tumbling out: "Oh, Mitch, I've missed you so." She wrapped her arms around his neck, drove her fingers through his thick curls. She kissed his cheeks, his chin, his eyelids, punctuated each with a heartfelt "I love you."

He cupped her chin in his large palm, his eyes scanning her face, as if to read her thoughts. "Do you?" he asked. "Do you really?"

She didn't understand the pensive darkness in his

eyes. Ciara held his face in her hands. "You know I do."

"Just me? *Only* me?" he asked through clenched teeth.

He'd been so confident in her love before he'd gone away. What had he seen or heard or experienced to shake his trust in that love? Till now, she'd been struggling with her own emotions, trying to hold on to some semblance of pride. None of that mattered now. Ciara wanted nothing but to comfort and assure him, to restore his faith in her. She put everything she had into it, every happy memory, every heartache, every nightmare, every dream she'd had while he was gone. Would she have gone through all that if she *hadn't* loved him? "I love *you*, Mitch Mahoney. Only you, and no one *but* you."

He closed his eyes and heaved a great sigh. She hadn't thought it possible for him to gather her closer, but he did. The rhythmic thumping of his heart lulled her, soothed her and quieted the child within her.

He was smiling slightly when she tilted her face up to his. His dark eyes burned fervently into hers for a silent moment. His kiss caused a small gasp of pleasure to escape her lips. Her blood surged, her pulse pounded. "Mitch," she rasped. "Oh, Mitch…" She loved him hopelessly, helplessly, blindly; the most powerful emotion she'd ever experienced. Heart and mind and soul throbbed with devotion as she pressed her pregnant body against his. He belonged to her and she to him, and this baby was theirs. "Mitch," she sighed, "I wish…"

"Shhh," he said, a fabric softener-scented finger over her lips. His fingers combed the hair back from her face, and he looked deeply into her eyes. What *was* that expression on his beautiful face? Fear? Regret?

And then she knew: Guilt.

Mitch felt guilty for having left her alone. No doubt he blamed himself for the complications of her pregnancy, as well. Hadn't Dr. Peterson explained it to him? Hadn't he told Mitch that her condition had been there, right from the moment of conception?

Something told her this was a situation she must handle carefully, delicately, or his ego could be forever damaged. Ciara would not do to Mitch what her mother had done to her father. She would not subject him to a lifetime of misery for not having done everything her way. Somehow she had to find a way to let him know there were no hard feelings, nothing to forgive, everything to forget.

Ciara snuggled close, closer, until his lightly whiskered cheek bristled against her throat. They lay that way for a long time, Mitch stroking her back, Ciara running her fingers through his dark waves as his warm breaths fanned her. Finally she felt him relax. There's no time like the present to tell him he has nothing to feel guilty about, not now, not ever again. Ciara wriggled slightly, shifting her position so that she could meet his eyes.

She had to hold her breath in order to stifle the giggle…because she didn't want to wake him.

It wasn't until something cold and wet pressed against her cheek that she realized she'd fallen asleep, too…had been out quite a while, from the looks of things.

Chester's fur was still damp. "So you've had yourself a bath, have you?" she asked, rumpling his shining coat. I must have done something mighty good in my childhood, she thought, to have earned a husband like this.

Mitch bent over to pick a speck of lint from the carpet, noticed her staring. "What...? Do I have spinach on my teeth or something?"

"No. I'm just trying to decide if you're real, or a very pleasant mirage."

Grinning, he walked over to her, leaned down and kissed the tip of her nose. Her cheeks. Her lips. The kiss lasted a long, delirious moment. "Could a mirage do that?"

Sinking back into the pillows, she sighed, a dreamy smile playing on her freshly kissed mouth. "If it can, I don't know why folks are so all-fired disappointed when they discover they've seen one."

"I'm making your favorite for supper," he said, changing the subject.

Unconsciously she licked her lips. "Gnocchi?"

Mitch frowned slightly. "I thought breaded cubed steaks were your favorite."

"They're great," she replied with a wide smile. Maybe too wide, she quickly realized. *You are an insensitive boob, Ciara Mahoney. Now you've gone and hurt his feelings.* "Oh, *that* favorite," she quickly added.

"I don't even know what a naw...a no...what is it, anyway?"

"Nyaw-kee," she pronounced the Italian pasta. "And it's plural, because just one wouldn't be the least bit satisfying. They're fluffy little potato dumplings that melt in your mouth. They sell them, frozen, at the grocery store. They're not nearly as tasty as the ones they make at Chiaparelli's, down in Little Italy, but they'll do when a craving strikes."

He jammed the handle of his feather duster into a back pocket, leaned over to clean up her snack plates. "So, you're having cravings, are you?"

She shrugged, thinking of their massage session. "Maybe one or two...." Then, giggling, she added, "You look like a rooster, with that thing sticking out of your pocket."

He shook his bottom and cock-a-doodle-doo'd for all he was worth, sending Chester into a feather-chasing frenzy. Mitch and the dog rolled on the floor for a moment, playfully wrestling over the cleaning tool. "You two are going to make a terrible mess," she warned, laughing. "You'll be cleaning up feathers for a week."

"But," Mitch groaned, chuckling as he tugged on the plastic handle, "he won't let go."

"Chester," Ciara ordered, "sit."

Immediately the dog obeyed.

"And only one feather out of place," she boasted, buffing her nails against her chest.

He plucked the peacock blue feather from the carpet, tucked it behind her ear. "Did I ever tell you how beautiful you are while you're sleeping?"

"You're pretty cute with your eyes closed, yourself," she said.

Mitch smiled. "I've got to get back in there before the meat burns. Can I get you anything? Your wish is my command."

She couldn't think when he looked at her with that dark, smoldering gaze. "I can have any wish I want?"

"Any wish you want."

I wish we could make love, she thought, remembering their recent intimacies, *the way we did before you left me.* "Is it too late to whip up some of those fantastic home fries of yours to go with the steaks?" she asked instead.

Chapter Eight

"Don't pull the plug till I get back, 'cause we don't want you going down the drain...."

Ciara grinned with disbelief. "Six months ago, maybe, but now? Down the drain? I can barely fit in the tub, so you've got to be kidding." She adjusted her headset and snapped an Amy Grant tape into place, then waved him away. "Go on, read your morning paper and leave me to my bubbles."

"Back in ten," he said, smiling as he pulled the door shut behind him.

From the semicircular window in the landing, he could see all the way to the end of their driveway, where the mailbox stood. Earlier, Ciara had sent him outside to put a card in the box and flip the flag up. "Can't forget Ian's birthday," she'd said, grinning, "not this year. It's the big four-oh, y'know."

Mitch craned his neck; if the flag was down, it would mean the....

Instead of the red flag, Mitch spotted a sleek black Ferrari, parked behind Ciara's Miata. One of Pericolo's goons drove a car like that.... Every muscle in him tensed as he took off down the stairs. In the foyer he breathed a sigh of relief. All's secure here, he thought, jiggling the bolted knob. Now for the back door…. He headed for the kitchen by way of the family room and stopped dead in his tracks.

The man in Mitch's recliner wore a black suit, maroon tie, and peered over the pages of the newspaper he held in one hand. "Well, now," he said, assessing Mitch's summery attire, "aren't you the picture of suburban life…deck shoes, Bermuda shorts, madras shirt." With a jerk of his head, he indicated the side yard. "Don't tell me…there's a cabin cruiser out there with 'Mahoney's Bah-lo-nee' painted across its back end, right?"

Mitch's fingers balled into fists. "What're you doin' here?" he demanded, planting himself in front of the chair.

"Just paying my weekly visit to the little woman." He shrugged. "You don't expect us to go cold turkey, just 'cause you're home, do you?"

Mitch leaned both palms on the arms of the recliner. "I don't know what you're up to, Bradley, but it ain't gonna work. Now beat it." He straightened. "Way I'm feeling 'bout you, this is a dangerous place for you to be…."

Bradley shifted uneasily in the chair. "Hey," he said, grinning nervously, "is that any way to talk to your boss?"

"*Ex*-boss. I made a couple of phone calls, and—"

The grin became a scowl. "You tryin' to scare me, Mahoney? 'Cause if you are…"

Mitch's upper lip curled in contempt, his arm shot out as if it were spring loaded, and he grabbed a handful of Bradley's collar. "*If* I was tryin' to scare you," he snarled, twisting the shirt tight against Bradley's throat, "I wouldn't need a telephone."

Bradley shrank deeper into the chair cushions, eyes wide with fright as frothy spittle formed in the corners of his mouth. The hand that had been holding the newspaper went limp, and the sports section of the *Baltimore Sun* fluttered to the floor like a wounded gull.

Through the thin material of his T-shirt, Mitch felt something cold and hard pressing against his ribs. Looking down, he saw that Bradley's other hand, sheathed in a surgeon's glove, held a chrome-plated, pearl-handled .35 mm handgun.

The face-off lasted a terrifying moment, Mitch increasing the tension on Bradley's collar, Bradley stepping up the pressure of the gun. "Like I said," Bradley husked, his face reddening further from lack of oxygen, "just stopped by to see how the missus was doing."

In response to the unmistakable *tick-tick-tick* of the hammer being pulled back, Mitch unhanded Bradley's shirt and slowly straightened, held his hands in the air. The man had a loaded weapon trained on him, and he could see by the wild glint in his eyes that he was fully prepared to use it. "Nice piece," he spat. "New?"

"Yes and no." He smirked. "It shoulda been tagged as evidence, when our boys busted Pericolo last week." Shrugging, he added, "It got kind of, ah, misplaced."

Mitch's brow furrowed. "You stole it from the evidence room?"

"You're not as smart as everybody thinks, are ya, Mahoney? It never—"

"Never made it to the evidence room?"

Using the gun as a pointer, he answered, "Have a seat, Mr. High and Mighty, and keep your hands where I can see 'em."

Ciara was upstairs in the tub, alone, naked, vulnerable. Stress was as potentially deadly for her and the baby as that gun in Bradley's hand. *You've got to get that weapon,* Mitch commanded himself. *Somehow you've got to disarm this son of a—*

Still standing, he said, "They're on to you down at headquarters. Anything happens to me, or to Ciara, they'll know exactly who to—"

"A bluff like that might be useful in poker..." A sinister smile cracked his face. "Speakin' of cards..." He slid a pack of Bicycles from his jacket pocket, slammed it onto the coffee table. "Pick a card, any card."

Mitch's lips formed a thin, stubborn line.

"Do it," Bradley demanded, leaning forward in the chair, tapping the deck with the .35 mm.

He wouldn't know about Pericolo's trick unless—

Stay calm, he warned himself. You lose your cool and you're a dead man. And Ciara... Mitch didn't want to think what Bradley might do to her in his present state of mind. He took a breath to steady his nerves, reached out and grabbed a card.

The ace of spades.

"You know what old Giovanni says about black cards...."

Mitch knew, only too well. He'd passed the sociopath's test that first night, but during his months in Philly, he'd seen two men fail it. Something told him he'd hear their screams of anguish and terror till he drew his last breath.

Bradley reached out, flipped the deck over. Skimming a hand over them, he spread the cards in a neat arc, displaying the ace of spades...times fifty-two.

Then he laughed, a sound that chilled Mitch's blood.

"So where's your pretty little bride?" Bradley asked, interrupting Mitch's worrisome thoughts.

He stood taller, squared his shoulders, pretended not to have heard the question. He'd do whatever it took to keep Bradley's focus off Ciara, even if it meant stepping in front of a—

"Don't look so worried, Mahoney. I'd never do anything to hurt her." He snorted. "Won't have to. Once you're out of the way, she'll come with me willingly…she and that…baby she's carrying." He smirked. "Who do you think the little guy'll look like?"

His blood turned to ice, freezing in his veins. It isn't true, *can't* be true, Mitch told himself. Because if it was, everything he believed, everything he held dear about their relationship had been a lie.

And there sat the one man in the world who knew the ugliest fact about him. Mitch was filled with such fury that he wanted to teach him a lesson he wouldn't ever forget.

But Mitch had no proof of her sin. None…except the word of this…to call him a cur or a swine would be to insult all pigs and dogs! Mitch thought. He wanted to punish the smooth-talking, low-life predator. But having no weapon at the ready, he settled for a mild insult. "Come with *you?* Have you taken a good look at yourself lately? You're nothin' but a good-for-nothing hunk of garbage."

"Shut up," Bradley snarled.

"So when did you turn, Bradley? Or have you always been like this, even as a rookie?"

"Careful what you say," Bradley interrupted, waving the gun in the air, "or I'll…"

He was beyond reason now. Nothing scared him as

much as the thought of this animal touching his wife. "Or you'll *what?* Take me out? How're you gonna explain *that?*"

Bradley licked his. lips, wiped perspiration from his forehead with the back of his gun hand.

Mitch's fingers splayed, and he tensed, ready to grab it.

"I wouldn't if I were you," came Bradley's gravelly warning. His green eyes glittered, like a panther ready to pounce. Then he rested an ankle on a knee, balanced the gun there.

"I could always say I stopped over to see how you were doin'," he said, answering Mitch's question. He laughed softly. "Does this have post-traumatic shock written all over it, or what? I mean, think about it from the point of view of those knuckleheads down in Internal Affairs...guy like you, undercover all those months with a maniac like Pericolo...." He shrugged nonchalantly. Chuckling, he added, "Here's the cherry on the sundae—I could plug you, call it self-defense, and you'd still get a hero's burial. Wouldn't be *your* fault you went nuts."

The way Bradley was quivering, Mitch believed he could wrest the gun from his hand, if he could just get in closer....

"Naw, that's way too complicated. There'd be a hearing, I'd be on administrative leave while IA investigated. Truth is, you ain't worth all that bother."

He tilted the weapon left and right. "For your information, this little number here has Pericolo's prints all over it." He grinned proudly. "I've got this one all tied up with a pretty red bow, eh, Mahoney?" He stared hard, as if debating whether to answer his own question or pull the trigger.

"The weapon may have Pericolo's prints on it, but the guards on his cell block will give him an airtight alibi—or did you forget that small detail, Bradley?"

Bradley got to his feet. "Enough conversation, wise guy. Turn around."

Mitch lifted his chin defiantly and, crossing both arms over his chest, planted his feet shoulder width apart.

"You never did like taking the easy way, did you, Mahoney?" Bradley took a step closer, prepared to forcibly turn Mitch around.

It's now or never.... He grabbed the deck of cards. "Mind if I shuffle and draw again? Might improve my odds."

Bradley chortled. "What's the point? You know they're all—"

Mitch flicked the deck in Bradley's face, and as his hands instinctively went up to protect his eyes, Mitch's left hand shot out, grabbed the gun barrel and pointed it at the ceiling. In a heartbeat, he elbowed Bradley in the Adam's apple, socked him in the stomach, stomped on his instep, rammed a hard shoulder into his nose.

Bradley doubled over, wheezing and moaning. Mitch had the gun now, and he knew it. Holding up the gloved hand, he choked out, "Don't...don't shoot...."

Mitch snorted with disgust. "You're not worth the mess," he ground out. "Now assume the position, while I—"

He heard a thump overhead, and Ciara's muffled voice: "Mitch...what's going on down there?" Mitch cut a quick glance toward the ceiling, and Bradley used that tick in time. Hot on his heels, Mitch ran for the back door and saw the lieutenant leap the fence and duck into the yard next door, where the neighbor's toddlers were splashing contentedly in their blue plastic wading pool.

Mitch drew a bead on Bradley's left shoulder, squeezed back on the trigger, slowly, slowly...

Just then, one of the twins jumped up, putting herself directly in the line of fire. "Mine!" she squealed, grabbing an inflatable horse from her towheaded brother.

Mitch eased up on the trigger as the little boy pulled her back into the water. "No," he insisted, "mine!"

Squinting one eye, he zeroed in on Bradley's shoulder once more, every muscle tense and taut as he held his breath. And then the kids were up again, right in his sights, hollering for their mommy.

From the other side of the forsythia hedge, Bradley saluted and disappeared.

The car...he's gonna circle 'round to get the Ferrari.

Slamming the back door, then bolting it, he blasted through the house. Cursing the knob lock and the dead bolt, he struggled to yank open the front door.

Somebody was out there, all right, standing behind the Ferrari's back bumper. "Good morning, Mitch," said Mrs. Thompson. "How's Ciara this morning?"

Heart hammering, Mitch ran a hand through his hair, jammed the gun into the belt at the small of his back. "Fine...you?"

"Oh, my arthritis is acting up, but in this humidity, what can a seventy-two-year-old expect?" She nodded at the Ferrari. "Fancy car...."

"Belongs to a—" He couldn't make himself say *friend.* "One of my co-workers left it here." The .35 mm wasn't Bradley's, and neither was the car. The lieutenant couldn't afford to come back for either. Mitch knew that now, like he knew his own name. "I think I hear my wife calling," he said, closing the door. "You have a nice day."

Mrs. Thompson smiled, waved. "Tell Ciara I said hi."

Mitch's shoulders slumped and he walked back to the kitchen. He hid the gun in the cookie jar on top of the fridge and grabbed the phone, dialed Parker's extension down at Headquarters. The guy didn't seem the least bit surprised when Mitch filled him in on what had just happened.

"He's never been wrapped too tight," Parker admitted, "but lately..." He whistled the "Twilight Zone" theme.

"You've gotta find him," Mitch interrupted. "My wife's—"

"I know, I know...Bradley told us all about her condition."

"Listen, Parker, he's still out there. I've got his weapon, but he won't have any trouble getting another."

"Okay, okay, Mahoney. Settle down."

"Don't tell me to settle down! If my guess is right, now that I know he's been on the 'take,' and his reputation is ruined, he's got nothin' to lose. I don't have time for your patronizing—"

"Sorry, Mitch. I didn't mean to." He paused. "Look, I know it won't be easy, but you have to settle down, for your wife's sake."

Mitch took a deep breath. "When you call in the APB, get a tow truck out here to pick up this Ferrari in my—"

"Ferrari?" Parker snickered lightly. "Did you get a raise for this last caper, buddy?"

"It's Bradley's...or else it belongs to whoever he's

workin' for. You've got to get it out of here. If Ciara sees it, how am I gonna explain…?''

"I'm on it, Buddy."

"Keep me posted, will ya?"

"You bet."

"And send somebody to—"

"I'll get a surveillance guy out there, pronto."

"'A guy'? I put my neck on the chopping block to nab Pericolo. You'll send more than 'a guy'! Who knows what kind of backup Bradley's got…or where he got it. I'm a sittin' duck out here, and—"

"Sit tight, Mitch. I'll see what I can do."

He exhaled loudly, ran a trembling hand through his hair. "Keep me posted, will ya?"

"You bet," Parker said, and hung up.

Mitch glanced at the wall clock. When he came downstairs earlier, he had promised to get Ciara out of the tub in ten minutes. Amazingly, he had three whole minutes to spare. Three minutes to calm down and get up there and pretend everything was hunky-dory.

"Sweet Jesus," he prayed aloud, "give me strength."

Chet Bradley was a bald-faced liar. A turncoat, possibly a burglar—since he'd picked the back lock to get into the house—and a killer. The pampered little rich boy had never wanted for anything in his life—the fact that he was Mitch's boss without having had to pass the customary tests, was proof of that—so, was it any surprise that faced with temptation, he'd shown no self-control, snatching up bribe money with both hands? His whole life was a story of instant gratification…why should that change now?

In Mitch's mind, men like Bradley were worse than

the Pericolos of the world; at least folks knew where they stood with a guy like Giovanni. Bradley was repugnant, foul, lower than a gutter rat. He'd come to the house for the express purpose of murdering Mitch, to keep him from testifying against him at an interdepartmental hearing…or in a courtroom. If he'd had to take Ciara down first to get to Mitch, he'd have done it in a whipstitch.

He raised the book he'd been pretending to read, glanced over its pages at Ciara, who absentmindedly twirled a length of flaxen hair around her forefinger as, word by word, she filled in the blocks of her crossword. Suddenly she exhaled a sigh of vexation, pencil eraser bouncing on the puzzle. The feminine arch of her left brow increased, the gentle bow of her lips smoothed, dark lashes dusted her lightly freckled cheeks as she slid a dainty fingertip down a column of definitions in the dictionary.

She was, in his opinion, the loveliest woman on two feet. Pregnancy had only enhanced her beauty, filling out the sharp angles and planes of her girlish face in a womanly, sensual way.

Sensual enough to reach out to Bradley for physical comfort in her husband's absence?

He remembered the things her mother had said, things that made it clear Bradley had spent countless hours in this house, alone with his wife. Mitch felt the heat of jealous fury rise in his cheeks, took a sip from the glass of the ice water, standing on a soapstone coaster beside him, hoping to cool his temper.

Is she the innocent young thing you married, or a passionate woman? She's both, he admitted, the edge of his uncertainty sharpening.

Mitch now pressed a thumb to one temple, his fingertips to the other, effectively blocking her from view, and remembered their wedding night, how she'd stared up at him, willing him to hold her close with nothing more than the silent draw of her long-lashed crystalline eyes.

The moment he'd slipped his arms around her, he knew…knew he'd be with her till the end of his life. Mitch knew it now, too, even if he discovered that every one of his ugly suspicions were true.

He'd lived a rough, rugged life, and his women had been a reflection of that, because he'd had neither the time nor the inclination for love. Life was mean, and so he lived it that way. Tenderness? Compassion? A lot of romantic nonsense, in his opinion. Besides, what did a man like him, who had committed himself to spending his days dogging bad guys and dodging bullets, need with love? He couldn't afford to fritter away even one precious moment, seeking something he believed he should not have.

And so he'd guarded his heart with extreme caution. Built a sturdy wall to protect himself. If he couldn't accept love, why bother to give it? But Ciara had burrowed under that wall. Yes, life was mean…past tense. She had changed all that. He'd built a wall around his heart, all right, but he hadn't built it nearly tall enough or strong enough, because he hadn't counted on meeting a woman like Ciara.…

When she laughed, her whole body got involved. And if something saddened those close to her, it was apparent to anyone with eyes that she felt the pain, too, all the way down to her size-five feet.

That night on the cruise ship, when she'd looked into his eyes, he realized that she saw him as the man he'd always wanted to be. No need for a fancy suit or a

Boston education. No need for pretense or pretty words, not with Ciara!

She could read his moods by something as insignificant as a quirk of an eyebrow or the slant of his smile. Mitch strongly suspected she could read his mind, too, for on more than one occasion she'd spoken aloud the thoughts pinging around in his head.

She seemed to sense how alone he felt, despite the fact that he had three burly brothers and two sisters, parents, grandparents, aunts and uncles and cousins. She had taken one look at his college graduation picture, crinkled her face with compassion and said, "Oh, Mitch, why do you look so *sad?*"

When his mother had seen the photo, she'd said, "Such a handsome boy, that youngest son of mine!" And his dad had agreed. "He's got the Mahoney jaw, all right." Why hadn't the people he'd known all his life been able to see the quiet fear, the desperation burning in his eyes, yet Ciara, who'd known him mere weeks the first time she'd viewed the portrait, had spotted it right off?

Mitch had marveled at that, because until she'd pointed it out and followed it up by dispensing her unique brand of all-out love like warm soothing salve, *he* hadn't admitted it!

Starting on their wedding night, without regard for her own needs and desires and fears, she gave what *he* needed. And in her tender, feminine embrace, he felt at once sheltered and exposed, strong and weak, manly and boylike.

And more alive than he'd ever felt in his life.

Doggone if she isn't some kind of woman! he thought. Li'l thing whose head barely reaches your shoulders, becoming the biggest thing in your life....

Mitch had never felt any regret about leaving places or people when his cases ended, and it was time to move on. But Mitch knew if he ever had to leave Ciara, he'd miss her more than he would miss water.

The breath caught in his throat as he recalled the sensation of her slender fingers, weaving through his hair on the night the preacher made them man and wife. Her whisper-soft sighs had floated into his ears as she responded to his touch, and her heart—the same heart that had beat hard and angry when faced with life's injustices—thumped wildly against his chest as he held her close.

The first time he'd said those three words on the cruise ship deck, he'd asked himself, Are you crazy? Shut up, man! Say whatever she wants to hear, but don't say that! And he'd shrugged, thinking that when a man thought a thing a thousand times or more, wasn't it just natural to say it out loud? He'd spent his whole adult life avoiding that phrase, words that, until Ciara, had been fearsome. Yet they'd linked together and rolled off his tongue so easily and naturally, all he could do was hope they'd spilled out quietly enough that she hadn't heard them.

"What did you say?" she'd asked, her voice husky.

He couldn't very well repeat it, now could he? It wouldn't have been fair to either of them, since he knew full well he wouldn't be seeing her once the trip ended, no matter how much he'd meant what he said.

Oh, how she'd *moved* him! She'd reached places in his heart and soul and mind that he would have bet his last dollar were impossible to reach...if they existed at all.

"What did you say?" was her quiet, honest question. Mitch wouldn't have hurt her for all the world. He'd rather die than cause her a moment's pain. So he'd stood there, trying to conjure up a similar-sounding phrase that would answer her...painlessly. No matter what he said, *he'd* be hurt....

If she hadn't branded him with that loving, longing look as she traced his lips with her fingertips right then, Mitch might have summoned the strength to pull it off. But that intimate, yet innocent, gesture was the final hammer stroke to the already crumbling wall he'd built around his heart.

He'd watched her with his nieces and nephews, doling out instructions and admonitions and compliments with equal care. He'd seen her minister to her elderly aunt, and to her parents, with a compassion he'd once believed reserved only for God's angels.

He had never let anyone see him cry. Not even the threat of dying in the trunk of a car had pushed him that far. But gazing into her eyes, seeing the purity of her love looking back at him, woke emotions long asleep. And once awakened, those feelings bubbled up and boiled over like a too-hot stew pot. He'd never wanted anything in his life more than he wanted her and her pure, unconditional love.

So he'd gathered her close, closer, whether to hide his tears from her or hide her from his tears, Mitch didn't know, and rested his chin amid her mass of soft, pale curls. "I'd better get to my cabin," he'd said, his voice gruff and hard from biting back a sob. And he'd walked away, just like that, without a backward glance or a by-your-leave.

And the night stretched on endlessly.

He'd exposed his most vulnerable self to her. How could he face her again, knowing she'd seen his weakness? Mitch fretted about it all through the night. Yearning, he understood, was an emotion born of experiencing perfection, and he wished he'd never begun this dangerous game of flirtation-turned-fondness-turned-love. Because he didn't believe he deserved the devotion of one so fine, so pure, so innocent. Didn't believe he'd earned the loyalty of a woman that fine.

He'd been like an animal these past years, like a mole, always seeking shadows as he moved from place to place in search of safety, in search of peace. Survival of the fittest, he'd heard, was the law of the land. Well, he'd survived top-secret cases, but to what end? To find safety and peace in Ciara's arms, only to discover he didn't deserve it? Far better never to have tasted fine wine at all than to have it snatched away, forcing him to live forevermore without even the smallest sip.

He had learned to accept the fact that, because of his career choice, he'd never have a family. A home. The love of a good woman. But could he learn to live without Ciara's love, now that he'd tasted the sweetness of it?

A sob ached in his throat, and Mitch buried his face in the pages of his book. If she shared herself with *him*, he thought, gritting his teeth, even if it *was* because she was lonesome, and scared, I'll—

"Mitch? What's wrong?"

Like the angel she was, Ciara had read his heart. "Nothing," he said, holding the book high, to hide his teary eyes.

"I'm cold," she said, patting the mattress. "Would you hold me…get me warm?"

He put down his book, crossed the room in two strides and settled beside her. He buried his face in her neck and wrapped both arms around her, holding this fragile flower who had planted the seed of her love deep in his heart, as the wild rose vine plants its seed even in the craggiest outcropping of a snow-covered mountaintop. He would hold tight to perfection for as long as he could, so at least he'd have these moments to remember, in case she'd meant it when she told him to pack up and leave.

Placing a tiny hand on either side of his face, she brought him out of hiding. Tears shimmered in her eyes and glistened on her long, lush lashes when she said, "I love you, Mitch." She pressed her lips to his, softly at first as she combed delicate fingers through his hair, more urgently then, as those dainty fingers clutched at his shoulders, his back, his neck, with a strength that belied her size and condition.

Oh, how he wanted her! Wanted her with every echo of his soul, with every beat of his heart. But he dared not want....

He'd seen film footage of the floods in the midwest the summer before, when the rivers rose and threatened to devour every building and barn, every mortal man or mammal for miles. The surging water's awesome power humbled him as he watched it sluice through the streets, hissing like a giant turbid snake.

What emanated from Ciara, who felt so small and helpless in his arms, was far more powerful than the river's rage. And though she didn't know it—and certainly wouldn't have intended it—she stirred more fear and apprehension in him than the roiling waterway.

Mitch had survived numerous near fatal experiences, but with nothing to live for or look forward to, death had no authority over him. Even Bradley, brandishing his loaded gun, hadn't terrified him as much as this tiny woman in his arms. She loved him. He could see it in her eyes, in her smile. Could feel it in her touch, taste it in her kiss. And he loved her more than life itself. If she *had* succumbed to temptation, it had only been because he'd left her alone for so long....

He looked inside himself for the strength to turn away from the love so evident on her face, and rested his hands on her thickened waist.

They were strong hands. Hands that had not wavered, no matter how strenuous the task. And yet, when he put those work-hardened hands on this woman, they trembled, the way a crisp autumn leaf shivers at winter's first icy blast.

He looked into her eyes, read the love there. Hesitantly he ran a hand down her back, and when he did, a rough callus caught on the finely woven fabric of her nightgown. He stopped, pulling abruptly away, embarrassed that his big clumsy hand had damaged the pretty gown.

Yet again she read his heart. "It's all right," she whispered.

But it wasn't all right. Nothing would ever be all right, until he knew for certain whether she had betrayed her vows. Because he loved her like he'd never loved anyone, like he'd never known it was *possible* to love, and the moment he admitted it, Mitch was doomed.

She pressed his "offending" hand to her chest. "See? I'm nervous, too...."

He felt the wild thrumming of her heart, felt it vibrate through his palm, past his wrist and elbow, straight to the core of him. They were connected, for the moment, by hard-beating hearts, by desire that coursed from her into him.

In a move that stunned and surprised him, she boldly reached out and grabbed his shirt collar, drawing him near, her soft yet insistent kisses imprinting on his heart as surely as a cowboy's branding iron sears the rancher's brand to his cattle.

His mind whirled as a sweet, soft moan sang from deep within her, its music moving over him like wind ripples on a still pond, and he returned her kiss with equal ardor.

"Easy," she sighed. "Easy...."

Misunderstanding her intent, Mitch immediately withdrew. Ciara read the hurt and humiliation burning in his eyes. "I said *easy*," she smiled mischievously, "not *stop*."

His left brow quirked and his lips slanted in a grin. "You weren't really cold, were you?"

Ciara shrugged. "Would I have said I was if I wasn't?"

He nodded. "I think you would."

Her fingertip traced his eyebrows, his cheekbones, his jaw. "Are you saying you think I'm dishonest?"

"Never intentionally," he said.

Frowning, she gave him a crooked grin. "What does *that* mean?"

You're a passionate woman, he told her mentally. You're not the kind who can be left alone, to wilt and die without—

"Mitch," she said, interrupting his reverie, "what's going on in that head of yours? You've been acting strange all day. Is there something you're not telling me?"

I could ask you the same question, he thought. And then Bradley, the gun, the knowledge that the fool was out there somewhere, carrying a heated vengeance around in that sick, twisted mind of his, blotted out Mitch's response.

She backed away to arm's length, gave him a stern

look. "I'm not a child, Mitch. If there's something I should know…"

Mitch wasn't about to upset the apple cart. Her blood count, the readouts Peterson had been getting by way of the monitor, everything had been going fine, up till now, and he intended to keep it that way. "I'm just worried about you," he said truthfully, pulling her closer, resting his chin atop her head.

Worried that this baby is going to die, or kill you, and wouldn't that be ironic if it isn't even mine….

"Mitch?"

"Hmm?"

"I love you…."

He closed his eyes tight. *Dear God in Heaven, give me strength….* "I love you, too, sweetie. I love you, too."

Chapter Nine

*T*he bright blue sky warmed the mourners who stood in a tight semicircle, heads bowed and hands folded, as sunlight glinted off the polished brass handles, pointing toward heaven like luminescent arrows. And Ciara, dry-eyed and tight-lipped, stared at the white enamel casket, trying to focus on the preacher's powerful voice.

"And our time comes to an end like a sigh...." He closed his eyes, smiled serenely and began reciting from the Book of Job: "'Thine hands have made me and fashioned me together roundabout; yet thou dost destroy me. Remember, I beseech thee, that thou hast made me as the clay; wilt thou bring me into dust again?'" Closing the Holy Book, he bent down, scooped up a handful of freshly-dug dirt and sprinkled it into the hole. "'You shall return to the ground,'" he quoted Genesis, "'for out of it you were taken; you are dust, and to dust you shall return.'"

Ciara wanted to shake a fist at the sky. Why, God? she wanted to shout. Don't You have enough cherubim and seraphim? Did You have to take *my* baby boy...?

She had not cried over the death of her child, had

not shed a single tear. Would tears bring him back to life? Would sobs revive him? Would the ache in her heart matter at all to the One Who had taken him?

Absentmindedly she kneaded her stomach, where so recently the infant had nestled in her nurturing womb, taking quiet comfort from her steadfast love. He had moved inside her, each strong jab and kick proof of his vitality and vigor.

In a flash, the bright blue sky turned blinding white, and Ciara was in the delivery room, perspiring and panting as the contractions contorted her face.

It's all right, *she told herself.* The pain is only temporary. When this is over, you'll have a beautiful baby boy....

She didn't know how she knew it was a boy, but she knew.

She knew....

Soon, the doctor would lay him on her chest, kicking, crying, arms akimbo. She'd smooth back his wet hair, count teensy fingers and toes, inspect every tiny joint, every minuscule crevice, each contour and curve and line of his warm little body. She'd soothe and comfort him, and his small, hungry lips would seek nourishment from her milk-laden breast.

"Just a few more minutes," the doctor said. "Just a few more minutes."

Pride and joy and thankfulness filled her eyes with tears, put a sob in her throat. Just a few more minutes, *she repeated, smiling.* In a few minutes, I'll be a mommy.

She made herself focus on the bustle of activity in the blindingly bright delivery room—shuffle of paper-shoed feet, the rustle of surgical gowns, banter of the staff, clank of tools against stainless steel trays—instead of the pain, the gripping, never-ending, powerful pain....

Then, for a half second, maybe less, silence—deep and still and falsely calm. No one moved or spoke or breathed, as if the world had stopped spinning and everything, everyone in it had ceased to exist.

In the next eyeblink, life!

Ciara knew—though she didn't understand how she knew—that during the instant of deadly quiet, her baby boy had died. She knew because the pain of childbirth had ceased, and in its place, heartache like none she'd experienced.

The doctor gave her knee an obligatory pat, pat, pat. "I'm so sorry, Mrs. Mahoney, but..."

Her heartbeat doubled, tripled.

"We did everything we could, but," he said softly, so very softly that Ciara thought perhaps she'd imagined it; perhaps it had been part of a pain-induced hallucination. "There's no easy way to say this, I'm afraid... but your baby is dead."

With every beat of her heart, every pound of her pulse, the word echoed in her head. Dead. Your baby is dead...dead...dead.

The eye-blinding white light warmed to a golden glow, and she found herself in the cemetery again, eyes locked on an ivory coffin hardly bigger than a breadbox. Any minute now it would be lowered into the rectangular hole carved into the earth by shovel and pickax. The hole was hardly bigger than the casket, yet it seemed to gape and yawn like a ravenous, savage beast, hungering to swallow up her newborn son, forever.

Ciara forced her gaze away from her boy's eternal bed, focused on the faces of the people who had gathered around: her mother, daubing her face with a lace-trimmed hanky; her father, staring stoically straight ahead; sniffling in-laws; sad-eyed neighbors and co-workers; a few of her students, looking bewildered by this thing called Death; and their parents, whose expressions said, I'm sorry, but better you than me.... Everyone had shed at least one tear for the infant whose birth caused his death.

So why not Ciara? People will think you didn't love him; people will think you don't care. And that was a lie, the biggest lie ever told.

Ciara had never held him to her breast. Had never looked into the miracle that was his face. Had never inhaled the sweet scent of his satiny skin. Would not hear his soft coos or his demanding cries. Could never feel the miraculous strength of his tiny fingers, wrapping around her own. But she loved him, and oh, how she missed him!

It began as nothing more than a solitary thought in her head:

No....

And became a soft whisper that no one, not even those right beside her could hear: "No...."

Then heads turned, and the monotonous din of voices, joined in prayer, quieted when she said more loudly, more firmly, "No."

"No!" she screamed, falling across the coffin. "No, no, no, no, no...."

A man's voice, deep, powerful—her father's?—floated into her ears. "Ciara, sweetie, don't—"

Don't what? Don't grieve for my baby? Don't make a scene? Don't make the rest of you uncomfortable?

She gripped the little casket tighter. "You can't have

him, Lord!'' she yelled. "You can't take him, because he's mine!''

Then, utter silence.

Ciara looked around her, surprised that the other mourners were gone, all of them.

Car doors slammed.

Engines revved.

The grounds crew stepped forward. Where had they *come from? And a beer-bellied man in a grimy baseball cap stuck out one gloved finger, pressed the red button and started up the machine that would carry the casket down, down into the dark, damp dirt.*

Rage roiled inside her. Don't! *she ordered.* Stop that, right now! *But the motor continued grinding.*

Ciara wanted to grab his fat wrist, crush every bone in the hand responsible for beginning her son's slow, steady descent into the cold, unwelcoming earth.

The mournful moan started softly at first, then escalated in pitch and volume, like the first piercing strains of a fire engine's wail. She couldn't pinpoint the source of the grief-stricken groan, and, frightened by it, Ciara clapped her hands over her ears. The keening call echoed all around her, bounced from marble headstones, granite angels, trellised tombstones and returned, like a self-willed boomerang to its genesis.

"No-o-o-o-o-o-o-o…''

Then, big hands, strong, sure hands gripped her shoulders.

"Ciara? Ciara…''

"Where's Mitch?'' she sobbed. "Where is my husband? Why isn't he here? Why!''

"I'm here, Ciara, I'm here, right here, right—''

"That was some dream," Mitch said when her eyes fluttered open. He slipped an arm under her neck, pulled her near. "Aw, sweetie," he sighed, kissing her temple, "you're trembling." He tugged the sheet over her shoulder, tucked it under her chin. "How 'bout a cup of warm milk?" he asked, holding her closer. "Maybe that'll relax you, help you get back to sleep..."

"I hate milk," she mumbled, her voice sleep drowsy.

Something you should know after eight months of marriage, he scolded himself. Holding her at arm's length, Mitch cupped her chin in a palm. "You want to talk about it?"

Ciara shook her head, then buried her face in his shoulder. "You weren't there," she whispered brokenly. "You...weren't...*there.*"

She sounded so forlorn, so frightened, like a child lost in the woods. His heart ached, because once again, he felt powerless to comfort her. "I wasn't *where,* sweetie?" he asked, brushing the bangs from her forehead.

Ciara shook her head. "Nothing...just, just a dream..."

Nearly every inch of her was pressed against him, yet Mitch felt as though someone had built a brick wall between them. Her taut muscles, her refusal to tell him about the nightmare, the way her voice trembled when she'd said, "You weren't there..."

He held her a long while, not talking, not asking her to. A shaft of moonlight had slipped under the window shade, cutting an inch-wide slice of light through the blackness. It lit the room just enough for him to see her sad, still-sleepy eyes.

"I know I wasn't here," he said at last, a tremor in his own voice. "I can't tell you anything that'll undo what's already done, but I can tell you this—I'll be here for you from now on. I promise."

He waited for a reaction of some kind: a nod, a sigh, *something*.

Either she's asleep, he told himself, or she doesn't believe you.

Tears stung his eyes, and he held his breath to keep them at bay. He had done this to her—he, and the Bureau—and if she *had* strayed during his absence...

He held her a little tighter, kissed the top of her head.

"What're we going to do, once this baby is born?" she'd asked earlier, worried he might spoil her, waiting on her constantly.

The question became a chant in his wide-awake mind: What're we going to do? What're we going to do?

Her health was precarious, at best.

The baby, if it survived, might not even be his.

And Bradley was out there somewhere, fully convinced that the only way to stay out of prison was to silence Mitch...permanently.

Mitch shivered involuntarily. He certainly didn't want to die, especially now that he and Ciara were so close to getting back what they'd once had. If something happened to him now, who would look after her?

Lord Jesus, he prayed, *what am I going to do?*

She couldn't get that dream out of her mind until the baby moved inside her. Even then, the eerie aftereffects flashed in her mind.

Ciara put her full attention on the cross-stitch she'd been working on. Better that than try and make small talk with Mitch, she thought. "I'm just tired, that's all," she'd fibbed, when he'd asked if she was feeling okay. "It's nothing," she'd answered, when he'd wanted to know if something was wrong. "Thanks, but I'm fine," she'd said, when he'd offered to bring her a snack. What else *could* she do...admit she was furious at him for something he'd done or hadn't done...in a *dream?*

Mitch made a few calls on the kitchen phone, pacing as far as the twelve-foot cord would allow, talking in low, steady tones, rousing her curiosity and more than just a little of her suspicion. Who was he talking to, and what topic demanded such privacy?

Had he met a woman while he'd been undercover? Someone who had made his lonely days more bearable; someone who hadn't been so easy to say goodbye to?

Or were there loose ends, still unraveled, ends that could choke him if he didn't tie them up?

This job of his is going to be the death of me, she fumed.

The thought distracted her from the needlework, and she pricked her finger. "Ouch!" she said, popping it into her mouth.

Holding the phone against his chest, Mitch stuck his head into the doorway. "You okay in there?"

She held her finger up, as if testing the direction of the wind. "Stuck myself," she said, rolling her eyes. "No big deal."

Nodding, he smiled. "Whistle if you need me," he said, and popped out of sight again.

She could have picked up the portable, pretended she'd forgotten he was using the extension. Perhaps a snippet of conversation would answer her questions. Maybe a word, a phrase, overheard before he realized she'd joined him on the line, would ease her fears.

Or you could act like a grown-up, and ask him straight-out, she told herself. No...just because he's your husband doesn't mean you have a right to know *every* intimate detail of his life.

Intimate?

Could a man like that have sought comfort in the arms of another woman? Ciara shuddered, shook her head. Not Mitch. Anyone but Mitch. She had never met a more fiercely loyal man. He was devoted to his family. Dedicated to his job. Unwavering in his reasons for choosing a career in law enforcement.

"What are you making, there?" Mitch asked.

Gasping, Ciara lurched with fright.

He was beside her on the sofa bed in an instant. "Are you all right? Geez, I'm sorry, sweetie. I didn't mean to scare you."

"It's okay," she said, patting her chest, as if the action could slow the rapid beating of her heart. "It wasn't your fault." She had always liked working in complete silence, without radio or stereo or TV to interfere with her private thoughts. And at the moment when his voice had cracked the stillness of the afternoon, her thoughts had been very private, indeed.

He turned his head slightly, regarding her from the corner of his eyes. "You sure you're okay?"

She nodded.

"And you don't want anything? More tea? A cookie? Some—"

"I'm fine, honest," she interrupted.

Mitch continued to study her face for a moment more. "All right, if you say so."

The glint in his dark eyes told her he didn't believe a word of it. "You want the truth? Really?"

His brows rose in response to her terse tone. Blinking innocently he said, "Well, I asked, didn't I?"

Ciara narrowed her eyes, set her needlepoint aside, crossed both arms over her chest. "You asked for it...."

He lay on his side facing her, drove his elbow into

the extra pillow, and propped his head on a palm. "Go on. Start talkin'. I'm all ears."

You weren't there for me in the dream, and you weren't there for me in real life, she thought, the stirrings of anger niggling at her. Ciara remembered the day she discovered she was going to have a baby. The first person she had wanted to tell, naturally, had been Mitch. And where were you? she demanded mentally. You were off somewhere making like James Bond.

And when the doctor had diagnosed her condition, warned her to stay off her feet. Where were you then? Where *were* you!

He had been so gentle and affectionate, so tender and loving when the nightmare had awakened her. He had been that way, practically from the moment they'd met, and those very qualities had made being without him all those months so much harder to bear. Ciara seemed to remember muttering and mumbling noncommittal responses to his quiet questions. But what would he have done if you'd told him the truth? she wondered. How affectionate would he have been then?

"What are you trying to do," he asked, grinning, "win the Alfred Hitchcock 'Keep 'Em in Suspense' award?"

Their gazes fused on an invisible thread of tension...his the result of confusion, hers caused by steadily mounting anger.

Mitch reached out slowly, gently laying a palm against her cheek. "You look so tired, sweetie," he said. "Let me hold you so you can take a little nap, right here on my shoulder."

She planted both palms on his chest, locked her elbows and managed to keep him at arm's length. "Do I smell beer on your breath?'' she asked, narrowing one eye suspiciously.

He held up two fingers. "I had two. That's all. While I was cleaning up your lunch dishes." He snickered. "Just two…on an empty stomach."

Ciara looked into his eyes. He was right…he hadn't had a bite to eat all day. He looked so cute, so helpless; how could she lambaste him in this condition!

"So, what do you say? You want to take a little nap?"

"I'm not sleepy, Mitch. I'm…I'm bored, and I'm tired, and I'm achy from lying around like a hundred-year-old house cat all day. I'm sick of looking at these four walls, and I'm—"

"Tomorrow is the Fourth of July, you know."

She gave her head a little shake, drew her brows together in a frown. "What?"

"Oh, sweetie, I've got it all worked out! First, we'll have a big country breakfast…pancakes, home fries, eggs over easy. After your bath, we'll get you into some real clothes for a change, watch the parade on TV. This evening we'll have a cookout—steaks, potato salad, baked beans—the works! And after that, we'll lounge around in the deck chairs, watching the sky get dark.…" Mitch wiggled his eyebrows. "Did you know that we can see the fireworks from the mall in Columbia from our backyard?"

Smiling, Ciara shook her head, so caught up in his excited recitation that she almost forgot why she'd been mad in the first place. "You're a grown man, Mitch Mahoney. How can you get so caught up in a light show?" she asked affectionately. "Besides, how do you know that?"

"I don't see anything wrong with looking forward to

some stars and spangles,'' he said defensively. And just as quickly he added, "Old Mrs. Thompson told me the other morning. She's comin' over for the barbecue and bringing her grandson. He's four.'' Squinting one eye, he looked toward the ceiling. "His name is Nicky or Ricky or something like that. Your folks are coming, too, and so is the entire Mahoney clan.''

Ciara's eyes lit up. "You're kidding. When did you plan—''

"This morning. I made about a dozen phone calls while you were working on...'' He leaned forward. "What *is* that thing, anyway?''

She clutched the fabric to her chest. "I don't like people looking at my needlework until it's finished.''

He went back to resting on his palm. "You've been working on it for days,'' he grumbled good-naturedly. "When is it going to be finished, anyway?''

He looked like a little boy, Ciara thought, when he pouted that way. Grinning maternally, she answered him as if he were one of her fourth-graders. "It'll be finished when it's finished, young man.''

Mitch grabbed the finger she was shaking under his nose. "Didn't your mother teach you it isn't polite to point?'' he asked, kissing it.

"She did. But I wasn't pointing. I was scolding. There's a difference.''

"Not when you're on the receiving end, there isn't.'' He kissed her palm. "Besides, 'When you point a finger at me, you're pointing three more right back at you.''' Pressing his lips to her wrist, he added, "I learned that in the second grade, when I accused Carrie Butler of putting a valentine card in my tote tray.''

"Carrie Butler, eh?'' Ciara asked, one brow up in mock jealousy. "You sure pulled that name out of the air pretty quick, considering how long ago you were in second grade.''

"Hey," he mumbled into the crook of her elbow, "watch it. It wasn't *that* long ago."

"I'd say a quarter of a century ago is a long time." She giggled. "Mitch. Stop that. It tickles."

"What...this?" he teased, kissing the spot again.

"Yes, that. Now cut it out," she insisted, laughing harder. "I mean it now...."

"Okay. Sorry. I was just trying to distract you, is all."

She looked into his handsome face. "Distract me? Distract me from what?"

"From asking any more questions about Carrie." He winked, then sent her a mischievous smirk. "I asked her to marry me, you know."

Grinning now, Ciara gasped, pressed a palm to her chest. "But...but you said *I* was the first woman you proposed to...."

"You were the first *woman.* Carrie was the first *girl.*" He rolled onto his back, tucked both hands under his neck and exhaled a dreamy sigh. "I met her in kindergarten, in the sand pit. She beaned me with a red plastic shovel. It was love at first strike."

Another gasp. "You said she was the *first* girl...there were others?"

He shrugged. "Oh," he said lightly, inspecting his fingernails, "one or two."

She grabbed a handful of his shirt. "How many others? I want names and addresses, mister, 'cause I aim to hunt them down, every last one of them, and—"

"Whoa," he interrupted, hands up in mock surrender. "I've never seen this side of you before."

"What side?"

"The jealous, vindictive side."

She blew a puff of air through her lips. "Jealous? I'm not jealous. I'll have you know I don't have a jealous bone in my body."

He looked almost wounded. "You don't?"

Shaking her head, she announced emphatically, "Not a one."

"So it doesn't bother you that Carrie was my first?"

She giggled. "Not in the least!" After a moment she added, "Your first what?"

"My first love, of course."

Grinning, Ciara rolled her eyes. "You weren't in love. You were *seven*."

"I wasn't seven."

"Everybody is seven in the second grade. Didn't you just say you asked her to marry you in the second...."

"Yes, but I asked her again when we were in high school."

This wasn't funny anymore. He'd known this Carrie person since kindergarten, had asked her to marry him in high school. "So what did she say?"

Mitch blinked. "What did who say?"

Ciara gave his shoulder a playful slap. "Carrie, silly. When you asked her to marry you...the second time...what did she say?"

"She told me to take a flying leap." He did a perfect Stan Laurel nod of his head.

"But...but you must have been sweet and handsome even then. *Why* did she say no?"

"Did I say she said no?"

"You said she told you to—"

"Take a flying leap. That's right."

Ciara exhaled a frustrated sigh. "If that isn't a rejection, I don't know what is."

"We were both on the gymnastics team. I was on the parallel bars. She kept pesterin' me to get off, give her a turn. And I said, 'Gosh, Carrie, you sound just like a wife. Maybe we should get married.' And she said, 'Mitch Mahoney, why don't you—'"

"'Take a flying leap?'" they finished together, laughing.

They lay there cuddling in silence for a moment before Ciara said, "What did this Carrie girl look like?"

"Mmmm," he growled, "she was hot stuff. Blonde, blue-eyed, with the cutest nose I ever—"

"Sounds like you're describing me!"

"Hmmm." He rubbed his chin thoughtfully. "I hadn't noticed...."

She quirked a brow. "Did you ever ask her to marry you again? After the uneven bars incident, I mean?"

"As a matter of fact, I didn't."

"Why not?"

"Hey, I wasn't the brightest bulb on the tree, but nobody coulda called me dim-watted, either."

"Dim-witted," she corrected with a twinkle in her eye.

Mitch sighed. Clapped a hand over his forehead. "*Carrie* always got my puns." He peeked between two fingers. "She thought they were funny, too."

Ciara sniffed indignantly. "Well, she must have had a very strange sense of what's funny." She paused. "Did you *want* her to say yes?"

"Maybe, but only a little."

She clucked her tongue, then said, "Say, our names are awfully similar...Carrie, Ciara...why you can barely tell them apart!"

"Hmmm." He went back to massaging his chin. "What do you suppose it means?"

"That you were searching for a Carrie replacement…for *years*…and you found it in *me!*"

He wrinkled his brow. "You think so?" He gave it a moment of consideration. "Naw. I don't think so."

"I wonder what Sigmund Freud would say about it?"

"He'd say, 'Mitch, if you have a lick of sense, you'll get your high school yearbook and show your pretty little wife what Carrie *really* looked like, before she boxes your ears.'"

"What are you talking about?" she asked, when he climbed off the sofa bed.

Mitch rummaged on the bookshelf, slid the black volume from between three other yearbooks. He flipped to the back, skimmed the glossary, chanting, "Butler, Butler, Butler…ah, there she is. Page two-sixteen."

He opened the book to the right page, handed it to Ciara.

She slid a finger over the glossy paper, stopping beside the postage-stamp-size black-and-white photo of Carrie Butler. The girl had short dark hair, a monobrow, and a slightly hairy upper lip. "'French Club president, Math Club, Chess Club,'" Ciara read. She eyed him warily. "You really asked her to marry you?"

"What can I say? The guys were always pickin' on her."

Her heart thumped with love for him. "You mean, you risked being teased by the other kids, because you felt sorry for her?"

He shook his head. "Shoulda let you go on thinking Carrie was your twin, 'cause this is embarrassing."

His reddened cheeks told her he hadn't been kidding. "Mitch, I don't think I ever loved you more than I do at this minute."

He tucked in his chin. "Why?"

"Because," she said softly, "you have a heart as big as your head, that's why."

And a man with a heart like that, she told herself, smiling happily, couldn't cheat on his wife.

Chapter Ten

Ciara looked around her at friends and family who had gathered in response to Mitch's invitation. On blankets spread on the lawn, in deck chairs, at the umbrella-shaded patio table, they sat, sipping iced tea and munching hot dogs.

"How's my girl?" Joe Dorsey asked.

She held out her hand to the tall, gray-haired man who sat in the chaise lounge beside her. "Better than I've been in a long time, Dad."

He squeezed, then patted her hand affectionately, his blue eyes glittering. "I have to admit, you look good. You look happy."

"I am happy." Ciara turned slightly in the chair to face him more directly. "Am I crazy, Dad? Am I out of my ever-lovin' mind to feel this way?"

He frowned slightly. "Of course not. You're young and beautiful and a wonderful human being. You have every right to be happy."

Sighing, she glanced across the yard, where Mitch stood, tossing a softball back and forth with his nephew. The gentle July breeze riffled his dark curls, giving a boyish quality to the masculine angles and planes of his handsome face. Sunlight, dappling through the leafy trees overhead, sparkled in his dark eyes. His smile reminded her of the way she felt whenever, after days and days of gray skies and rain, the clouds lifted and the sun would come out. *Lord, how I love him,* she prayed silently.

But he'd left her, with no word or warning. Had put himself in harm's way to apprehend an unknown criminal who'd committed some heinous crime.... Would he ever tell her where he'd been? What he'd been doing? Why he'd left the way he had?

Ciara sighed. "I love him," she said softly, squeezing her father's hand. "Maybe I *am* crazy, because I don't know if I have what it takes—"

"To love him? Of course you have what it takes. Look at you," he said with a nod of his chin, "sitting there. You've been sitting around, doing nothing, for two solid weeks now." One graying brow rose as he added, "I know that must be tough, real tough, for a bundle of energy like you. But you're doing it, because..." He waved a hand, inviting her to complete his sentence.

Smiling, she said, "Because I love this baby, that's why."

"And no sacrifice is too great for one you truly love."

She gazed into his blue eyes. When she was a girl, they'd often played the "whose eyes are bluest" game. "Your eyes are so blue, the cornflowers will be jealous," she'd say. "And yours are so blue, the sky wants to duel at dawn." Shaking her head fiercely, Ciara would respond, "Mother robins could mistake your eyes for baby eggs." "And the miners in the sapphire mines come home depressed," he'd counter, "because they can't find any stones as blue as your eyes."

"Was it hard, Dad? Leaving the department, I mean."

He nodded so slowly it was scarcely noticeable. "I've done easier things, I suppose."

Ciara watched him glance around, saw that when he focused on his wife, his jaw automatically tensed and his lips tightened.

"She was miserable," he said in a barely audible voice. "You were too small to remember, I suppose, but there were times when I thought she might have a nervous breakdown." He met Ciara's eyes. "I couldn't let it go on. I had hurt her for so long already. I had to do something to stop her pain."

"You loved her a lot, didn't you?"

His eyes crinkled a bit when he smiled. "You say it in the past tense. What makes you think I don't love her still?"

"Oh," Ciara sighed, "I'm sure you love her...the way Mitch loves Ian, the way I love you." Slowly she shook her head. "But you don't love her in a romantic way."

For a moment—such a fleeting tick in time that Ciara would have missed it had she blinked—she read the gut-wrenching pain he'd buried in his heart for so many years. Her father tore his gaze from hers, stared at the dark green clover leaves between his sneakered feet. She had done more than strike a nerve with her observation. For the first time in her twenty-eight years, Ciara saw him not merely as her father, but as a flesh-and-bone man, with needs and dreams and yearnings like any other man had.

"You never did love her that way, did you, Dad?"

The corners of his mouth twitched as he struggled to retain his composure and control. "Ciara," came his raspy whisper, "she's your mother. You haven't the right to say things like that."

"I'm sorry, Dad. I just want to hear the truth…from you."

"Well, *I'm* sorry, because I will never say anything disrespectful about her. She did a spectacular job raising you, and—"

"And you're grateful for that. You even *love* her for that." Ciara paused. "It's all right, Dad. I'm not a little girl anymore. Lately," she said, looking over at Mitch again, "it's hard to believe I ever *was* a little girl."

She sighed, returned her attention to her father. "I saw more than you realized. I know you both tried to hide it from me, but I knew, I always knew, that whatever you had wasn't what some other kids' parents had."

He faced her, his eyes boring deep into hers. "What are you saying, Ciara?"

"That I love you both for what you did. You mentioned sacrifice a little bit ago. 'No sacrifice is too great for one you truly love.' You didn't leave the department because you were worried about Mom. You left because you loved *me,* and since Mom was mostly in charge of me…"

His broad shoulders slumped, and Ciara wanted to climb into his lap as she had when she was tiny, snuggle into the crook of his neck and hug him tight until everything was all right again. But she couldn't do that now, because she'd grown up and married, and soon she'd be a parent herself. If you didn't learn anything else in these seven months alone, she thought, eyes on

Mitch again, it's that it takes a lot more than a hug to make everything all right again.

"If I'm even *half* the parent you've been," she said, patting her tummy, "this little tyke will be the luckiest baby ever born."

He swallowed. Blinked. Took a deep breath. "We were so young when we met, Ciara." Shrugging, he said, "I had no idea what love was at sixteen. Never had another girlfriend. Never had a chance to..." He cleared his throat. "And I was too stupid to get down on my knees, ask the Good Lord if she was the woman He intended for me." He shook his head again. "I don't mind telling you, I did a lot of praying since you met Mitch."

"Praying? Whatever for?"

A mist of tears shimmered in his eyes when he looked at her. "I prayed that you weren't making the same mistake...handing your entire future over to someone who might have ulterior motives, to someone who saw what they could get and—"

He was angry now. Very angry. Ciara knew, because it was the only time he made that tiny pucker with his lips. Almost immediately he reined in his emotions. Taking a deep, cleansing breath, he cleared his throat.

"Ulterior motives? What ulterior motives would Mitch have had?"

"By taking all you had to give and giving nothing in return," her father continued. "By choosing their needs over yours, without another thought—" He clamped his jaws together suddenly. "I've said enough." He held one hand up as if to silence himself. "Said too much." He sandwiched her hands between his own. "I'm sorry, sweetie. I shouldn't have burdened you with—"

"You haven't told me anything I didn't already know."

His brows rose at that. "But how could— I worked so hard to hide it from you. And to give her her due, I think your mother did, too."

Ciara shook her head. "Don't get me wrong, because I love Mom, but contrary to the old cliché, love isn't blind."

The furrow between his brows deepened.

"I know what she is. I know what she's done. I know, because she told me, Dad. A long, long time ago."

"What are you saying, Ciara?"

He already looked so miserable, how could she tell him that she knew *why* he had so quickly agreed to leave the department. He'd been wounded in the line of duty, and the injury would have prevented him from front-line work, but it wouldn't have forced him into early retirement. He'd given it up because her mother had found out about his one marital misstep....

Ciara, still in elementary school at the time, had come home to find her mother crying at the kitchen table. Kathryn had wrapped her arms around her little girl and the words tumbled out in a puzzling, dizzying swirl. Words like *betrayal* and *affair,* and phrases like *stabbed in the back* and *best years of my life.* She'd been too young to understand fully...and just old enough to be afraid, more afraid than she'd been to date.

That night, through the wall that separated her room from her parents', she heard their muffled voices in heated debate. And heard more confusing, scary words, like *ultimatum* and *divorce,* and one phrase that would echo in Ciara's mind for a lifetime: "We'll disappear, and you'll *never* see her again."

A week later her father had handed in his badge and gun.

A week after that, he'd begun teaching at the university.

She remembered those months just prior to the confrontation. It was the only period in her memory when her father had seemed truly happy. Had the "other woman" put that joy into his eyes? Had she opened up the part of him that had been sealed off by loyalty and vows spoken, and shown him what a good and lovable man he was? Ciara knew she should hate this woman who had come between her mother and her father. But how could she hate the one person who had made him realize his self-worth, who had made him smile...*with his eyes?*

She had overheard him once, sitting at that same kitchen table with his brother. They'd tipped a few bottles of beer, loosening their lips, and her father had poured out his soul.

It didn't matter that Kathryn belittled and criticized him at every opportunity. Or that in place of the big family she'd promised, Kathryn coldly announced she would never have children. Years later, seeing the 'I'm leaving' handwriting on the wall, she appeased him by consenting to give him one child.

And it didn't matter that she'd always put her own needs ahead of his, spending money faster than he could earn it, stuffing their house full of ancient, ugly things despite the fact that he'd made it clear he preferred a simpler, sparser life.

What did any of it matter, her father had asked his brother. *Kathryn* had committed no "sin," and there was no getting around the fact that *he* had committed one of life's most grievous transgressions. Little-girl

Ciara, still hiding behind the pantry door, had whispered to herself. But being mean is a sin, and pretending is the same as lying, and lying is a sin....

She had replayed that conversation in her mind, many times, and in Ciara's opinion, her mother's icy anger was also a sin, a sin all its own. For decades, Kathryn's acrimonious, acerbic feelings for her husband throbbed and seethed just beneath the surface, visible to friends, relatives, neighbors. Hadn't Kathryn gotten the meaning of Matthew, Chapter Seven, Verse One: "Judge not, that you not be judged"? Didn't she believe, as Ciara did, that God was all merciful, all-loving...no matter how great a man's sin? If a small child could understand this, and the Almighty could extend the hand of forgiveness, *why couldn't Kathryn?* Her father had admitted his sin, had atoned for it tenfold. The moment he acknowledged his wrongdoing, God had cleansed him of it, freeing him from further punishment. How long did his wife intend to penalize him!

"What are you saying?" her father repeated.

Ciara would not add to the burden that had bent him over, a little more each year, by telling him she knew what he had done as a younger man.

Ian stepped up just then. "You two must be discussing the stock market," he said. "I don't know any other subject that would put scowls on such handsome faces."

Admittedly, the conversation had forced Ciara to take stock....

"Are you staying to watch the fireworks with us?" she asked her brother-in-law.

"Wish we could, but I promised the kids we'd go down to the Inner Harbor this year." He rolled his eyes. "If it were up to me, we'd watch the fireworks in air-conditioned comfort on TV, but they've got their hearts set on it, and—''

"And as I've been telling him for years," his wife interrupted, wrapping her arms around him from behind, "our kids are nearly grown. This could be the last time we see the fireworks with them.''

They're so much in love, she told herself, after all these years together, they're still crazy about each other, and it shows. Mitch had told her that Ian, the oldest of the Mahoney boys, had married at twenty; Gina had just turned nineteen. Theirs, too, had been a whirlwind courtship, speeding from a chance meeting to a date at the altar in less than a year. Isn't it ironic, Ciara thought, that Mom and Dad went steady for three years, were engaged for two more before they said I do. If anyone should have been sure of themselves, it should have been the two of them....

She remembered something her father had said earlier: he'd been too young to know, too foolish to ask for God's guidance. All the time in the world, she acknowledged, can't give us the peace and assurance that comes from a moment of heartfelt prayer.

Gina directed her attention to Ciara's father. "You're looking good, Joe. What have you been doing...taking vitamins or something?''

He shook his head. "I guess the prospect of becoming a grandpa agrees with me. You know, seeing a part of me living on in a new generation.''

"Well," Gina huffed, "you don't look old enough to be a grandpa, if you ask me." Playfully she elbowed Ian. "I say that because Patrick has a steady girl now, and things seem to be heating up. *We* could be in your shoes in a year.''

Ian chuckled. "Who, me? A grandpa?'' Smiling serenely, he added, "Maybe I'd better reread *Grimm's Fairy Tales*. It's been a while since I told a good story."

"Oh, give me a break," Gina teased. "You tell a story every morning of your life, when you say I'm the loveliest thing you've ever seen."

Opening his eyes wide, he tucked a finger under her chin. "Sweetheart," he said, doing his best Jack Nicholson impression, "you can't handle the truth." He punctuated his comment with a kiss to the tip of her nose.

"Ian, really," Gina scolded, smiling and blushing like a young girl, "you know how I feel about—"

"'Public displays of affection.' Yes, I do. And you know I don't give a whit who sees how I feel about you." As proof, he kissed her again, on the lips this time.

Giggling, she shoved him away. "So tell me, Ciara," she said breathily, "how're you feeling?"

Ciara grinned. Like I'm watching an X-rated movie, she thought. "Well, let me put it this way," she said instead. "If this baby doesn't get here soon, Mitch is going to have to hog-tie me, 'cause all this lying around is driving me nuts!"

"Hey," Gina advised, "enjoy it while it lasts." She winked at Ian. "Trust me, when that baby has you up every couple of hours, you'll be asking yourself why you were complaining!"

"Complaining?" Mitch knelt beside Ciara's chair and slipped an arm around her shoulders. "I'll have you know this girl hasn't uttered a word of complaint, not once in the two weeks I've been home." He kissed her cheek. "She's a real trouper," he boasted.

"Well, all I can say is you're lucky you didn't marry *me*," Gina admitted. "I'd be whimpering and whining every five minutes if I had to stay off my feet for four solid weeks." She wriggled into her husband's arms. "Isn't that right, honey?"

"Oh, I don't know. Hard as it is to get you out of bed on a Sunday morning..."

"Much as I hate to admit it," Gina said, bobbing her head, "he's right."

"Say, Joe," she put in, "tell your motorcycle story. I tried to tell it the other day, but I couldn't remember the punchline...."

Ciara's father rubbed his palms together and grinned, blue eyes twinkling merrily. "Okay, you asked for it..." Standing, Joe held a finger aloft, and began:

"There were two Irishmen," he said with an exaggerated brogue, "travelin' the A-1 on a motorbike. 'Tis mighty cold, McAfferty,' said the one on the back. 'Well, no wonder, Casey, ye've got yer coat on backward.' McAfferty parked, turned Casey's jacket 'round, and zipped it up the back. 'There, now,' he said, tucking the fur collar under Casey's chin, 'that'll keep ye warm.' They took off again, and after a bit, McAfferty noticed Casey wasn't there, and headed back the way they'd come. He spied a couple of farmers, starin' at somethin' in the middle of the road. 'Why, it's me friend, Casey,' McAfferty said. 'Is he all right?' 'He were fine when we got here,' one farmer said, 'but since we turned his head 'round the right way,' said the other, 'he ain't said a word....'"

Their laughter acted like a magnet, attracting Kathryn. "There you are, Joseph, I've been looking everywhere for you." The words, if printed on a page, might have convinced bystanders his wife felt something akin to affection for her husband. But Ciara had heard that "why do you torture me so?" tone in her mother's voice before, too many times to count. Had seen that look, too, hundreds of times…one brow up, lips pursed, shoulders slumped in long-suffering exhaustion. "Has he been telling that awful motorcycle story *again?*" she asked. Rolling her eyes, she sighed heavily. "Thank goodness I walked up when I did! If you only knew how many times I've heard that stale old story."

Gina, Ian and Mitch smiled stiffly in response to her obvious insult. Ciara had seen *those* looks before, too…looks that blended pity for Joe with disapproval for Kathryn. How long will she make him pay for his mistake? Ciara wondered.

She couldn't have known that her mother's contemptuous treatment of her father had started long before she'd learned of his affair, but evidence to support that fact was there, etched in the tired lines and weary smile on his sad-eyed face.

I won't live that way, she told herself. Better to let Mitch go…better to *send* him away than to condemn him to a life of arm's-length neglect and open disdain.

Mitch was looking at her when she tore her gaze from her mother's hostile expression, from her father's lethargic acceptance of it. He shook his head, a small smile lifting one corner of his mouth as he winked. "Don't worry," was the message emanating from his brown eyes, "we won't let that happen to us."

Her heart fluttered in answer to his promise. Ciara wanted to believe him, wanted to grasp it as truth.

Still…

So far, they had all but walked in her parents' marital footsteps. Dread and fear hammered in her heart. Is there any way to avoid other stumbling blocks along the way?

She loved him with every cell in her body, with every

pulse of her heart. But like her father, she had not been wise enough to seek Divine Guidance in choosing a mate. What price would she pay for that foolishness? Was it too late to right that wrong, or could their marriage yet become what it might have been...if she'd had the foresight and the insight to ask the Lord what *He* intended for her future?

She looked at her parents, read the indifferent compliance that yoked them to each other, then looked at her in-laws, and saw the esteem, the friendship, the respect and admiration they felt for one another. *That* is what she wanted to see in Mitch's eyes, twenty, thirty, *fifty* years from now.

"What God has joined together, let no man put asunder," the preacher had said, sealing the vow that made Ciara and Mitch husband and wife. Surely, now that they were married in the eyes of God and man, He would show them how to make theirs a strong union, rooted in faith, nourished by steadfast devotion. If they could accomplish that, how could their love do anything but grow, like Ian and Gina's, as the years went by?

The words of a hymn hummed in her head: "Let there be peace on earth, and let it begin with me."

Mitch grasped her hand, gave it a hearty squeeze as Ian said, "Well, thanks for the eats, but we've got to make tracks."

"We ought to hit the road, too," her father said. "I have lesson plans to write."

She watched the two couples leave, walking side by side through the gate and out of the yard. How similar, yet how different, Ciara thought, biting her lower lip. Unconsciously, she gave Mitch's hand a little tweak. She thought she knew the secret that had given Ian and

Gina years of happiness…and her parents decades of misery.

Teach us to love selflessly, Lord, she repeated, echoing the words of the song, *and let it begin with me….*

"What time is it?" she asked, her voice whisper soft.

"Don't know," Mitch answered. "Can't read my watch."

"Shouldn't the fireworks have started by now? It's been dark for an hour."

"You're a grown woman, Ciara Mahoney," he teased, quoting what she'd said the day before. "'How can you get so caught up in a light show'?"

There was just enough moonlight to allow him to see her playful sneer. He rolled onto his side, propped his head on a palm. "Yeeesh," he said, grimacing, "if looks could kill, I'd be worm food."

Ciara rolled over, as well. "Don't say things like that, not even as a joke," she scolded.

He drew her to him. "I'm sorry, sweetie. I keep forgetting…"

She laid a finger over his lips to silence him. "Shhh." She raised the same finger into the air. "Listen…I thought I heard one."

"Heard one what?"

"A firework, silly."

"'Firework?'" he quoted. "*Now* who sounds silly?"

"Well, if all of them are fireworks," she said, accenting the *s,* "doesn't it make sense that one is a—"

Chuckling, he nodded. "Okay. All right. 'Firework.' You're the teacher, after all."

"And don't you forget it," she said, smiling as her

forefinger drew lazy circles in the chest hair poking from the vee of his shirt.

They lay on a makeshift bed he'd created from two thick quilts, a crisp bedsheet and three overstuffed pillows for each of their heads. Beside her, a foot-high table was laden with decaffeinated sodas, a bowl of strawberries, a plate of cheese and crackers. Beside him, nothing but a fly swatter. All the stars in the universe winked at them from the inky sky above. And all around them, crickets and tree frogs chirped.

"This is nice," Ciara told him. "I'm glad you thought of it."

He pulled her closer. "Me, too."

"I thought Mrs. Thompson was going to watch the show with us and bring Nicky."

Mitch shrugged. "Guess she changed her mind...or Nicky changed it for her."

"She's something, isn't she? Seventy-two and doesn't look a day over fifty. I hope I age that gracefully."

"Are you kiddin'? You'll be the envy of every old woman in the retirement home."

"Only because every old woman will be wishing they had *you*."

He grinned. "You think?"

She nodded. *"I know."* Ciara yawned, stretched. "If the fireworks don't start soon," she said, "I'm liable to sleep right through them."

"If you doze off, I'll set off a firecracker near your ear."

"You just try it, Mister Big Shot, and I'll...I'll...I'll fire *your* cracker!"

"What in the world does that mean?"

"I have no idea...."

Their laughter blended in sweet harmony, as Ciara snuggled closer, closed her eyes. "This is nice," she said again.

And he nodded. "Yep, nice." Two minutes, perhaps three, passed before her breathing slowed and shallowed, telling him she'd fallen asleep. He leaned back a bit, so he could see her face. The soft breeze combed through her hair, fluttered the ruffle at the collar of her blouse. Long lashes curved up from her pale cheeks, and soft breaths passed her slightly parted lips. He knew it might wake her, if he touched her, but Mitch couldn't help himself. Gently he pressed a palm to her cheek and marveled at the miracle in his arms.

Miracle, because she was lovely and sweet, and good to the marrow of her bones. The baby kicked, and he felt the powerful little jab against his own stomach...a subtle reminder that soon, he might be forced to call another man's child "son."

Mitch held his breath, ground his molars together. Why, he asked himself, when you've been praying like crazy for weeks, can't you get that thought out of your head?

Because of what Bradley had said, that's why: "She'll go with me willingly." And "Who do you think the baby will look like?"

Headlights panned the yard, distracting him, and Mitch squinted into the brightness. They'd considered themselves fortunate to have found a corner lot...the appearance of twice the land, with only one neighbor to contend with, but it had its negative aspects, as evidenced by the beams of every passing car.

Hey...that's the same car that went by not ten minutes ago, he told himself, staring harder at the four-doored black sedan. It's just someone looking for an address, he told himself, someone lost in the maze of streets that comprised the neighborhood.

Ciara sighed quietly as the car slipped out of sight. He rested his chin upon her head and relaxed a bit—but only a bit. A quiet *pop*, followed by several more, told him the fireworks had begun. "Sweetie," he whispered, kissing her cheek, "they're starting...."

Wriggling, she blinked. "Hmmm?"

"The fireworks," he repeated, gently shaking her shoulder, "hear 'em?"

She rolled onto her back, smiling as the sky brightened with starbursts of red and blue and white. "It's beautiful," she said. "Isn't it just beautiful?"

He hadn't noticed. He was too busy watching her face, painted in shades of pink and gold and green by the reflected light. "It's beautiful, all right," he agreed. "Most beautiful thing I've ever seen."

If not for the darkness, he'd have seen a blush, Mitch knew, for her big eyes fluttered in response to his scrutiny. "Pay attention," she scolded sweetly, "you're missing all the good stuff."

"That's a matter of opin—" The black car crept by, choking off the rest of his words.

"What's wrong?" she asked, eyes on the sky.

"Nothing," he lied, levering himself up on one elbow as the car inched past. "I'm having the time of my life. How 'bout you?" He could almost feel the intense gaze of a back-seat passenger boring into him through the blackened windows. Had Bradley rounded up the troops? What better night to pull a stunt than the Fourth of July, when explosions in the sky competed with Roman Candles and other assorted firecrackers on the ground? Who'd notice a gunshot amid all the rest of the noise?

"This is the most fun I've had in—" She gasped. "Mitch, what is it?"

He was torn between keeping his eyes on that car and looking into Ciara's face to reassure her. The hammering of her heart against his rib cage decided it. "Just a little headache," he fibbed, wanting to calm her, soothe her, because a rise in blood pressure could be deadly.

"Are you sure? Because you look like you've just seen a ghost."

He kissed her cheek, gently turned her face toward the sky show. "It's no big deal. I'll get an aspirin when the fireworks are over."

He felt her relax in his arms. "Well, if you're sure...."

"I'm sure." And with the tip of his forefinger, he gently pushed her chin, until she was looking up into the sky again. "Wow," he said, "I felt that one all the way to my toes!"

Ciara giggled. "The rib-rackers are my favorites. Those, and the ones with the squeaky little squiggles...."

The night had swallowed up the car again; either its driver had found the address he'd been looking for...or had found a place to park, where he could watch the Mahoney house, undetected.

Except for the half-dozen or so strange phone calls he'd intercepted, Mitch had no reason to believe he was in any danger. The U.S. Attorney had pretty much assured him Pericolo's men, relieved to have gotten rid of the boss with the hair-trigger temper, had lined up behind Chambro. And it wouldn't be very smart for Bradley to show his hand, not with everybody from the dog catcher to the CIA looking for him.

Mitch remembered that old saying: "Just because

you're paranoid, doesn't mean they're not out to get you.''

But who was *they,* and what would they get him *for?*

Ciara had been right; his job was dangerous. In the past he'd been the only one in harm's way. Now, simply because she'd chosen to stand beside him through life, she stood in the line of fire with him.

If anything happens to her because of my job…

Mitch clutched her a little tighter to him, pressed a kiss to her temple as she oooh'd and ahhh'd at the skylights. *Lord Jesus,* Mitch prayed, *thanks for protecting her from reading my fears. I'm counting on you to keep her safe and sound.*

Clenching and unclenching his fists, David Pericolo sat in the blackness, counting to ten, taking deep breaths. It was natural to be a little nervous, even though he'd taken every precaution. He recalled his last visit with his father at the penitentiary, how his father had laughed at his plan. Well, he'd prove himself worthy of respect yet. He'd make his father proud. For weeks, he'd been watching Mahoney from his hiding place across the street.

It was time to make his move. And this time, there would be no slip-ups, as there had been a week ago…

You got too sure of yourself, and it made you lazy, he told himself. You overlooked something, all wrapped up in memories the way you were….

He'd been thinking of his grandfather, who'd been a demolitions expert during World War II. If the old man could see you now, he'd thought.

What was the expression his grandfather had used? ''A rude awakening,'' that's it! He'd lifted the black lid of the boot box on the dresser, wiggled a red wire, jiggled a black one. Agent Mitch Mahoney, he thought, smirking, is in for a rude awakening.

He had waited until the letter carrier filled Mahoney's box with a handful of mail, slipped the bomb inside, carefully attaching the wires to the hinged door. Then he'd climbed back into the car, wondering as he waited if, like himself, Mahoney had ever wanted to be an astronaut. The minute you open that door, kaboom! you're gonna experience space flight, first hand.

Then some kid in baggy jeans shorts and a backward baseball cap had sauntered up, and slipping the top flyer off the pile of bright blue papers tucked under his arm, and opened the Mahoney mailbox. It had taken every bit of control he could muster to keep from hollering ''Get away from there, you little jerk!'' He rolled the window down an inch, intending to distract the boy, offer him a couple bucks for his bundle, and send him safely on his way.

But he hadn't been quick enough. ''Cool,'' he'd heard the boy say, grabbing the bomb. ''Hey, Gordie,'' he called to his buddy, who was delivering flyers on the other side of the street, ''check this out.'' The boys stood, cap brim to cap brim, muttering under their breaths for a minute before the taller one said, ''It ain't nothin' but a hunk of junk.'' The first kid shrugged, then tossed the bomb into a nearby trash can.

Junk!

He had rolled the car window back up. *It took me three hours to build that ''hunk of junk''!*

Now, in the steamy darkness of this July night, he stared at the Mahoney house and grinned. *This bomb was no hunk of junk.*

He had never missed the fireworks before...but then,

if everything worked as he expected it would, he wouldn't miss them this year, either.

Any day now, Mahoney would open his front door, reach for his morning paper, and get the worst news of his life.

Chapter Eleven

Ciara looked up from her needlework when the doorbell rang. "Who could that be? It's nearly supper time."

Mitch shrugged. "I didn't feel much like cooking tonight, so I ordered us a little something special."

"Pizza?" she asked expectantly. "I haven't had pizza in weeks. I hope you got two large ones, with the works, 'cause I'm famished."

Grinning, he fished his wallet out of his pocket and headed for the door. After a moment of front-porch small-talk, she heard the door close, bolts click into place, Mitch's bare feet padding up the hall and into the kitchen. The clatter of dishes and the clank of silverware inspired her to call out, "No need to get fancy, Mitch. Paper plates will be—"

He was back before she could complete the suggestion, positioning a tray table over her lap, putting a neatly folded napkin on the left side of her plate, arranging a knife and fork on the right. "I made lemonade and decaffeinated iced tea. Which would you prefer?" he asked, bowing low at the waist.

"Lemonade, with—"

"Lots of ice," he finished. "I know."

When he returned this time, he balanced a crockery bowl and a basket of bread on the tray carrying the drinks. "This," he said, removing the towel that hid the bowl's contents, "is to calm a craving."

Her eyes widened with surprise and delight. "Mitch! Where did you—"

And then she read the label on the napkin that lined the bread basket. "Chiaparelli's? You ordered gnocchi from Chiaparelli's?"

"None other," he said, spooning a huge portion onto her plate.

She waved a hand over the steaming dumplings to coax the tempting aroma into her nostrils. Closing her eyes, she sighed. "How did you know?" she asked, looking at him. "Surely not from that little slip of the tongue the other day...."

"That," he admitted, "plus you talk in your sleep."

"I do not." She speared a gnocchi.

Nodding, Mitch sat in his recliner and balanced his plate on his knees. "Oh, yes you do. It's just a good thing we have air-conditioning, because I don't know what Mrs. Thompson would think if she heard you moaning through the open windows, 'gnocchi, gnocchi, *gnocchi!*'" he said, pronouncing each louder than the first.

"She'd think you have a very strange appetite," Ciara explained, wiggling her brows suggestively. Then she popped a pasta into her mouth, and uttered a satisfied "Mmmmmm."

"Is it good?" he asked, taking a stab at one.

"Better than good," she breathed. The fingers of her left hand formed a small tulip. *"Delicioso!"*

He bit into one, chewed for a moment, nodded thoughtfully. "Not bad," he affirmed, eating the other half. "Not bad at all."

She gobbled up a dozen more dumplings before saying, "I have a feeling when Donna comes to weigh me tomorrow, I'm going to tip the scales!"

"Gimme a break. If you come in at a hundred and twenty, even in your condition, I'll be surprised."

"I was a hundred and thirty-five day before yesterday, I'll have you know."

"A hundred and thirty-five? You don't say!" He chuckled. "There's probably not a woman within a one-hundred-mile radius of this house who'd say a thing like that with such pride in her voice." He smirked, patted her tummy. "Come to think of it, *you're* almost a hundred-mile radius...."

"Stop it," she said, giggling, "and let me enjoy this. It's the most I've weighed, ever."

"Well, since you seem to like it so well," he said, pinching her big toe, "maybe I oughta just keep you barefoot and pregnant *all* the time."

Her smile waned, her eyes filled with tears, and she hid behind her hands.

He leaped out of the chair, nearly overturning his plate when he deposited it on the cushion. "Sweetie, what's wrong? Did I say something? I'm sorry if..."

"Stop it," she sniffled. "It isn't your fault my hormones are raging out of control."

"But you were fine till I..."

She blotted her eyes with a corner of the napkin. "You didn't do anything wrong, I'm telling you! It's me. All me." Ciara thumped a fist onto the mattress. "It's because I've been cooped up inside so long, getting no exercise. I'm trying to stay current...reading the paper, watching the news…but my mind is turning to mush. I'm becoming the kind of woman I've always despised, Mitch, weak and wimpy and whiny and—''

"Aw, sweetie," he said, taking her in his arms. "You're the strongest woman I know, and the proof is the way you're handling this situation. You're a hundred months pregnant, for goodness sake. Cut yourself a little slack, why don't you?''

She mulled that over for a moment, then started to giggle. "A hundred months?" she repeated, her voice muffled by his shirt. "Even elephants have babies in less time than that." She shook her head. "Sometimes I think I'm doomed to stay this way for the rest of my life.''

Ciara leaned back slightly to meet his eyes. "Oh, Mitch," she whimpered, "do you think your baby will *ever* be born?''

His eyes widened slightly. *My baby?* Would she have said it that way if she suspected Bradley might be the father? Mitch didn't think so. She'd blurted it out without even thinking, so it must be true. *My baby,* he repeated, kissing her tears away, struggling to hold back tears of his own. *My baby!*

"Shhh," he soothed. "Your gnocchi is getting cold.''

"Do you really want to have more children with me?" she asked, her voice small and timid, like a child's. "What if I'm like this every time I get—''

"Ciara, listen to me now," he said, tapping a finger against her nose. "I mean, think about it…a lifetime with whoever that is in there," he added, patting her tummy, "for a few weeks of inconvenience.''

"Easy for you to say," she teased, "I have to lie here like a lump while you get to empty the trash and do the dishes and—''

"I'll be more than happy to turn all the fun stuff over to you after the blessed event," he said, laughing. "Promise."

"So you really wouldn't mind going through this all over again?"

"Peterson assured me the chances of this happening a second time are practically nil, but no, even if the whole thing repeated itself exactly, I wouldn't mind. Not a bit." He pushed a pink satin nightgown strap aside to kiss her shoulder. "Look at it from my point of view—how many other husbands get to see their wives in gorgeous lingerie all day, every day, for weeks on end?"

Another soft giggle, then, "How many times?"

"How many times would I do this?"

She nodded.

He kissed her shoulder again. "Until my lips wear out."

"No, silly, I mean…"

"Six," he said without hesitation, "just like we discussed before we got married."

"Half a dozen," she sighed. "We'll have to add a whole wing onto the house."

"Or buy a bigger one."

"In the country, maybe," she said dreamily, "where we can have cats and dogs and—" Ciara looked around. "Speaking of dogs, I haven't seen Chester all afternoon. Is he out back?"

Mitch nodded. "He treed a cat out there, and I couldn't get him to come in, not even for a rawhide bone."

Ciara frowned a bit. "I wonder what he'll think of the baby."

Snickering, he said, "Are you kiddin' me? He's

gonna make that big-hearted old nanny mutt in Peter Pan look like Cujo. Now eat your gnocchi, before I do.''

Ciara stuck her fork into a dumpling. ''I don't suppose there's dessert....''

''As a matter of fact,'' he said, picking up his plate, ''there is.''

''Cheesecake?''

He sat in the recliner. ''With cherries on top.''

''How big a piece?''

''I went for broke. We've got a whole cake to ourselves.''

She licked her lips. ''If I break the visiting nurse's scale,'' she asked, grinning mischievously, ''will our insurance pay for a new one?''

''Blood presh-ah and pulse rate are fine,'' Donna said, her Boston accent making the details of the routine exam sound far more interesting than it was. ''Your blood count is a little low, but nothin' to worry about.'' She strapped the monitor into place. ''Now, let's see how the little one is doing....''

The machine clicked and beeped quietly for a few minutes as the nurse squinted at the screen. A thin green line of phosphorescent light blipped, counting the baby's heartbeats. ''Lookin' good. Lookin' real good....'' The diminutive woman had small, deceptively powerful hands. With firm gentleness, she palpated Ciara's stomach. ''Hmmm. He's dropped some since I was here day before yesta-day. If I had to guess, I'd say you have a week till you join the ranks of mothahood. Maybe less.'' Propping a fist on a hip, she narrowed one blue eye. ''You experiencin' any cramping?''

Rolling her eyes, Ciara shook her head. ''Not unless

you count the ones in my rear end, from sitting on it hour after endless hour.''

"Well, don't you fret. It won't be much longah now."

"You're not sugarcoating things to keep me calm, are you?"

"Oh, right…I've stayed in this line of work all these years 'cause I enjoy fibbin' to my patients." Then she got serious. "Stretchin' the truth makes everything seem scarier, no mattah how good or bad the situation really is." The perky blonde winked at Mitch. "I'll leave the shugahcoatin' to your hubby, here. He looks like a man who knows how to lay it on thick.…"

"Now, wait just a minute here," he said, grinning in mock self-defense. "I believe in telling it like it is." Then, in a more serious tone, "You'd tell us if something wasn't quite right…even slightly?"

"I would indeed. You two have got to stop all this fussin', now, 'cause everything is fine. And do you know why?"

Like obedient students, husband and wife shook their heads simultaneously.

"Because *you*, Mistah Mahoney, have been doin' a bang-up job takin' care of the missus. There oughta be a medal for husbands like you. I've seen plenty of men go through this, but not one of 'em handled things like you have." She gave an approving nod. "No mattah what time of day I drop by, this house is squeaky clean from top to bottom, Ciara's sheets are always fresh and crisp, and by the looks of those roses in her cheeks, you must be a dandy cook, too."

"It'll probably take me two years to get my girlish figure back!" Ciara agreed.

"Well, don't let this one out of your sight, missy,"

was Donna's advice. "He's a prize, and I know a dozen gals who'd snap him up in a heartbeat!"

"They might *think* they want to snap me up," he said, slipping an arm around his wife, "but none of 'em would have the *stomach* for me." He patted her tummy. "Would they, sweetie?"

"Yeah, well, if they try, they'll have to go through me first!"

"Might be a bit difficult, in your condition," Donna pointed out. "Aren't you glad he's the trustworthy sort?"

She nodded, met his eyes. "Yes. I'm glad," she said in all seriousness. "And thankful, too. He hasn't left my side for a minute, not once in sixteen days."

"Cut it out, you two," Mitch said, smiling sheepishly, "or I'm going to have to make all the doorways keyhole shaped, so I can fit my swelled head through 'em."

"Joke if you want to," Donna said matter-of-factly, "but men like you are one in a million. I've seen my share...personally and professionally...I know what I'm talkin' about." Hefting her nurse's bag, she headed for the door, waving to Ciara. "See you day after tomorrow." As she passed him, she whispered to Mitch from the corner of her mouth, "Stick close by from here on out. She could blow any day now!"

Blinking, he stood gap-jawed in her wake. Any day now? he repeated. Yup, any day now, you'll know for sure who that baby's daddy is....

He had tossed and turned so much through the night that Ciara didn't think either of them could have slept more than two hours. What had he been dreaming about as he'd writhed so fitfully, moaning and groaning under his breath? Was he reenacting scenes from his under-cover days? Reliving the day he brought the bad guy in? Experiencing a near-death experience, like the time he'd been locked in the trunk of a car?

Today is the day, she decided, that you'll ask him to tell you about the case. Good or bad, his answers would be a blessed relief, because anything was better than not knowing at all!

Mitch was sleeping peacefully now, and she turned on her side to get a better look at him. Once, before he'd left her, she told him he had the most amazing profile she'd ever seen. Totally masculine, it was Michaelangelo's *David* and Rodin's *The Thinker* all rolled into one. She had traced it with a fingertip, saying, "I wish I were an artist, so I could sculpt it from clay, or carve it from wood. That way, I'd have it to look at, even when you were at work...."

She looked at his profile now, the strong forehead, the patrician nose, the powerful jaw that was boldly, wholly *man*. Long, thick lashes fringed his eyes, giving him a boyish quality that softened the look, kept him from appearing too severe, too stern. And his lips, those full, well-rounded lips, only added to his very male appeal. Lightly, lovingly, she skimmed the backs of her fingers over his whiskered cheek. "I hope our baby looks exactly like you," she said in a voice so soft, even she barely heard it.

Ciara rested her hand on his chest and, assured by the steady *thump, thump, thump* of his heart, drifted into peaceful slumber and dreamed of a chubby-cheeked infant with dark curly hair and enormous brown eyes, and a smile that could charm the birds from the trees....

He'd been dreaming he was walking through their house, pointing out things of interest to the baby boy in his arms. "Now son, this is your mom's favorite afghan," he said. "Her grandma brought it over from Italy, so whatever you do, don't spit up on it. And this," he added, plucking the strings of his guitar, "is your dad's git-fiddle. Maybe when you're older, I'll teach you to play...."

He hadn't known know what woke him...Ciara's feathery touch, tickling over his stubbled cheek or her rustling sigh: "I hope our baby looks exactly like you." All he knew was that her touch, her words washed over him like warm Caribbean waves.

I love her, and I love that kid because it's part of her. If she'd transgressed—and it was beginning to look less and less like she had—it had only been for want of him; could he begrudge her a stolen moment of comfort? Would it have mattered, really, whether he or Bradley had fathered her child? In truth, it would have mattered a great deal. But he thought he knew the truth now. "And the truth shall set you free."

Smiling, he pressed a palm to her roundness, hoping to feel forceful little feet or the powerful punch of a tiny elbow. After a moment of absolute stillness, Mitch admitted, regretfully, that the child, like its mother, was at complete rest.

When he was a little boy, his mother would listen to his prayers, tuck the covers under his chin and sing a verse from a song she'd learned as a child: "May the Good Lord grant you beautiful dreams and send a legion of angels to watch over you," she'd croon, brushing back his wild, wayward curls. He sent the same prayer heavenward on Ciara's behalf, then succumbed to drowsiness himself.

But not before this soughed from his lips:

"I love you, Ciara Mahoney, and I always will."

* * *

They woke slowly, gently, to the distant trilling of the phone. "Who can be calling at this hour?" he grumbled, reaching for it.

"Mitch, it's after ten o'clock! How could we have slept so late?"

Stretching, he said around a yawn, "Must have needed it, that's all I can say." And then, into the telephone's mouthpiece, he muttered a groggy "Hullo?"

Silence.

He cleared his voice and said more firmly, "Hello." Nothing.

"Who is it?" Ciara asked.

He banged the receiver into the cradle. "Wrong number, I guess."

But he knew better. This hadn't been the first such call they'd received; it was the eleventh or twelfth, by his count. At first, he'd dismissed it. Could be some kind of computer error down at the phone company, he'd told himself, or maybe one of Ciara's students has a crush on his pretty teacher and he's calling just to hear the sound of her voice.

He had learned to trust his gut instinct, and his gut was telling him not to blame coincidence or accident or happenstance.

But who had been calling…and why?

Could be Bradley.

One of Pericolo's men.

Some other felon he'd arrested….

Truth was, he could think of a hundred possible explanations for the silence on the other end of the phone; *trouble* was, the more explanations he came up with, the more nervous Mitch became.

A week or so ago, while Ciara was napping, he'd tiptoed upstairs, taken his trusty Rossi completely apart and thoroughly oiled every piece. After he'd reassembled it and loaded six rounds into it, he'd listened to the reassuring *whirr-tick-tick* of the spinning chamber, then snapped it shut with a flick of his wrist. Paranoid? he'd asked, sliding the revolver onto a high shelf. Probably, he'd answered, but better safe than sorry....

Hopefully, he'd never have to use it. But just in case, every now and then he rehearsed his trip upstairs to fetch it. He was in the kitchen now, fixing breakfast, when he went over it again. If he took the stairs two at a time, he believed he could get into the closet and back downstairs again in thirty seconds flat. If he could figure out a way to explain it to Ciara, he'd practice physically as well as mentally.

She had asked for a bowl of corn flakes this morning, and he topped them off with a sliced banana and cold milk. He'd put strawberry slices in her orange juice, to surprise her when she finished it off. He'd plucked a rose from the shrub beside the back fence, too, broke off the thorns and tucked its stem into her napkin.

"When I'm on my feet again," she said when she saw the tray, "I'm going to spoil you so rotten, you're going to stink!"

"My mom used to call me a little stinker. Maybe she's clairvoyant?"

"She's a mother, and mothers know things."

"Is that right?" He settled in his recliner and waited for Ciara to tell him what she knew about their baby. *Their* baby. *His* baby. She'd said so in the middle of the night, when she thought he was asleep.

"I know, for instance, that this baby is going to be brilliant and musically gifted and kind and..."

"How do you know all that?" he asked, chuckling good-naturedly. "Did the Baby Fairy tell you?"

"Make light of it if you must," she sniffed, "but it's all very scientific, actually."

"Scientific?"

Ciara began counting on her fingers. "You're very intelligent, and I'm not exactly a dull bulb, so the baby *has* to be smart." She held up a second digit. "I play a pretty mean piano, and you play just about every other instrument God ever created." The ring finger popped up. "And the way you've been taking care of me, well, if I didn't already know you were a kind, big-hearted man before I was quarantined, I know it now. Isn't it natural to assume our baby will have a blend of our finer qualities?"

He merely sat there a moment, nodding as he assessed what she'd said. Ciara hadn't mentioned one trait that even closely resembled Chet Bradley. And why would she? It's your kid....

"You know, when you put it that way, why wouldn't our kid be terrific?" He smiled. "But I hope he looks like you."

"And I hope he'll have your *character.*"

Chuckling, he nodded at the plaques and awards hanging on the fireplace wall. "Don't you mean my reputation? I've won—"

"'Reputation is what men think you are,'" she quoted. "'Character is what God and the angels know about you.'"

She had fixed him with that no-nonsense, all-loving stare of hers, so he couldn't very well argue with her, now could he? And so he said, "Well, this *character* is gonna go down to the end of the driveway and see which shrub our paperboy has hidden the newspaper under this morning. And then he's gonna refill his coffee cup, and put up his feet, and make like a man of leisure till he's read every last page."

Ciara patted the mattress. "I'd like to ask you a question first...."

She'd been behaving strangely all morning. Till now, he'd chalked it up to her condition, to cabin fever, to being forced to stay off her feet. Mitch perched on the edge of the sofa bed. "Ask away, li'l lady," he drawled.

"When are you going to tell me where you were, when we're both old and gray?"

He frowned. "Where I was?"

"You know perfectly well what I'm talking about."

She wasn't teasing. He could tell by the lift of her left brow, by the slight narrowing of her wide eyes. Their hands, flat on the sunflowery sheets, were nearly touching. He inchworm-walked his forward until his forefinger rested atop hers. "The case, you mean...."

"Where were you? Why didn't you write, or call?"

"I tried, remember?"

She rolled her eyes. "So you've said. Didn't you wonder why, if you wrote so many letters, I never answered them? Didn't you think it was strange, that after one little fight, I'd completely write you off?"

"Didn't seem so little to me."

Ciara sighed. "It was the first time we'd ever disagreed about anything." She crooked her finger around his. "You didn't expect us to spend our whole marriage in a state of harmony, did you?"

Mitch shrugged. "My folks never fought."

"Maybe you never heard them fight, but they disagreed, I'm sure. Every married couple does. It's normal. It's natural. It's...unavoidable."

He met her eyes. "I guess…I guess I just hadn't gotten used to the idea."

"We did sort of rush things, didn't we?"

Their eyes locked on a thread of understanding. "Do you still think it was a mistake?"

The pain in her voice was matched only by the agony shining in her eyes. Mitch pulled her to him. "Sweetie, I've *never* thought it was a mistake. From the moment I first saw you, I knew…."

She pressed a palm to each of his cheeks, her eyes searching his with fierce intensity. "Then why did you let them send you away? Why would you go undercover, and leave me here to wonder where you were… how you were?"

"Because I'm a proud, thick-headed, know-it-all."

Her brow crinkled with confusion. "A know-it-all?"

"I'd been hearing about Pericolo for ages. I knew it was going to take some fancy footwork to get him. The agency wasn't about to send some rookie in there to nab a guy like that. I guess I felt sort of proud they'd picked me."

"I see," she said softly, nodding.

"Well," he shrugged, "that, and Bradley made it pretty clear that if I didn't go *in*, I was on my way *out* at the Bureau."

"You could have found another job…what made you so sure I'd still be here when you came home…*if* you came home?"

"I wasn't." He exhaled a heavy breath. "Till recently, that is."

She leaned against the pillows and hid behind her hands. "I must need a nap already, because I'm not following you."

"I thought…." Mitch licked his lips. He wished she

hadn't pulled away, because nothing felt so reassuring, so comforting as having her in his arms. He looked at his empty hands, filled them with hers. "I thought maybe you found a way to replace me."

A tiny, nervous giggle popped from between the tightly-clenched fingers that hid her face. A second passed in utter silence. She folded her hands in her lap. "Replace you? How?"

"Bradley." The word ground out of him like a monosyllabic growl.

"Bradley?"

And then the light of understanding gleamed in her eyes. Ciara gasped, touched her fingertips to her lips, shook her head. "Mitch...you don't mean...." Her brows lifted and her eyes filled with tears. "You thought...." She bit her lower lip. "You thought I had...."

"Just look at you, trembling and tense. Forget I ever said anything. I'm a total idiot." He tried to gather her in his arms.

"Stop it," she said, one hand up like a traffic cop. "Just give me a minute to wrap my mind around this thing." Ciara took a deep breath. After a moment, she rested crossed arms on her ample belly. "What had I ever done to make you think such a thing?"

"Nothing. And I didn't think it. Not once in the whole time I was gone." He held up both hands in a gesture of defensiveness. "I knew I'd have a price to pay for leaving the way I did, for staying gone so long, but I figured we could work it out. I figured eventually, we'd...."

She lifted her chin. "What changed your mind?"

He took a deep breath. "Aftershave."

Ciara rubbed her eyes. "You're not making any sense...."

"Bradley's brand. In the medicine cabinet in the master bathroom.

She inclined her head. "Bradley's brand," she repeated, more to herself than to Mitch. And then she began nodding, tapping a finger against her chin. "So *that's* why he insisted on going upstairs that day....'

Mitch rested a hand on her thigh, and listened.

"He came over one day to see if I needed anything...and to tell me you hadn't been in touch, as usual...and acted as if he'd heard a noise upstairs. Drew his weapon and everything!" Lips narrowing with suspicion, she added, "Now I understand why he spent more time in our room than...."

"When?" Mitch demanded. "How long ago?"

"Right before you came home." A note of alarm sounded in her voice, and panic brightened her eyes. "Why?"

"Because it had been part of his plan all along. We were both pawns in his little game of 'kill two birds with one stone.'"

"What?"

"He used me to get rid of Pericolo, so Chambro could take over and Bradley's pay-offs would continue. He never figured I'd survive being underground with a maniac like that, and when I did...." He emitted a low groan of frustration. "And he used you to drive me over the edge."

"By planting the aftershave."

Mitch nodded.

"What I don't understand is why you believed I could have done such a thing."

He met her eyes, still damp from her bout with tears.

"You're a beautiful woman, Ciara. Beautiful and warm and loving...." He shrugged helplessly. "You saw my mom's prized roses. She spent hours tending them every week."

"They're spectacular, but what do they have to do with...."

"She says the lovelier a creature of nature, the more time and attention it needs."

"I don't know whether to be flattered at being compared to a rose, or insulted that you think I'm so high maintenance."

"Not high maintenance, Sweetie, just deserving of some tender loving care."

"I suppose I can't fault you for doing the very same thing I did, can I?"

"Me? When would I...."

"I didn't know where you were, what you were doing. For all I knew, you'd been sent undercover to guard a beautiful singer, like in the movie that came out a couple years ago, where the bodyguard fell in love with his charge...."

"I never so much as looked at another woman," he said, hand forming the Boy Scout salute. "I swear."

"And I never looked at another man," she responded, mimicking the gesture. "So tell me, what changed your mind?"

"How do I know that baby's mine, you mean?"

She gasped again, and hugged her tummy. "You thought our baby...? You thought...*Bradley?*" Ciara shuddered. "Now I *am* insulted. How could you think so little of me, Mitch? Was it because I fell for you so quickly? Was it because I let you talk me into getting married after only a three-month courtship? Was it because...?"

"I already told you why," he said, grasping her hands. "I'm an idiot."

When she blinked, a silvery tear broke free of her long lashes, landed on the back of her hand. Mitch kissed it away. Kissed away the tears remaining on her cheeks, in her eyes. "I'm sorry, Ciara. About everything. If I could go back in time and do it all over, I'd...."

"Would you still take the assignment?"

"Not if I knew then what I know now."

"What do you know now?"

He cupped her cheeks in his palms. "That—cliché as it sounds—I love you more than life itself, and nothing, no one, is more important than you." He wrapped her in his arms. "I can't live without you, Ciara. I'm so sorry for everything I put you through. It's all my fault you're in the shape you're in."

"Is that what you think?" she asked, pulling away.

"How else do you explain it?"

"Didn't Dr. Peterson tell you there's no known cause for this condition?"

"Well, yeah, but...."

"And didn't he tell you there's no predicting who it'll affect and who it won't?"

"Yes, but..."

"But nothing. It just happened, and you know what?"

"What?"

"I think it was a blessing."

"A blessing! To be practically flat on your back for over a month, worrying every minute whether...."

"It brought you closer to me than anything could have. And Mitch," she said, voice softened and warmed by tears, "it taught me so much about you."

"About *me?*"

"That's right, Daddy." She smiled. "It taught me that, despite the fact that you wear a big gun to work, and despite the fact that you talk tough, you're as gentle as Mary's little lamb. I couldn't have chosen a better husband and father if I'd ordered him from a catalog. I love you, you big idiot!" she teased, and kissed him soundly.

"I love you, Ciara."

"Now why don't you get the morning paper, and I'll 'scissors-paper-rock' you for the sports section."

Grinning, he headed for the door. He was on the porch when he said, "Do we have a new paper boy?"

"Not that I know of. Why?"

"Because the regular kid likes to chuck it into a shrub or halfway up the crabapple tree, and today it's lying smack in the middle of the driveway."

"Stop complaining," Ciara called from the living room, "get that newspaper so we can see how the Orioles did in last night's game...."

"Good morning, Mitch," sang Mrs. Thompson. "And how are you on this beautiful morning?"

"Couldn't be better," he said, stooping to pet her toy poodle. "How're ya doin', fella?" Mitch ruffled the dog's curly ears. "Tell me, how is it that you're always so cheerful?"

The old woman smiled brightly. "I'm seventy-two years old, lived through five wars, the birth of three kids, eight grandchildren and two great-grandchildren. I buried two husbands and a business enterprise or two. After surviving all that, the world seems like a happy, peaceful place. Why wouldn't I be cheerful?"

"I like your outlook," Mitch admitted. "And I like

your pup, here, too." Standing, he added, "I'll bet he could last a year on one bag of Chester's dog food."

"You'd be surprised how many Kibbles my little Bruno packs away." She clapped her hands, and the poodle leaped into her arms. "Isn't that right, sweet-ums? You eat Mummy right out of house and home, don't you?" Mrs. Thompson unclipped Bruno's rhine-stone leash and draped it around her neck, then put the dog back onto the ground. "He hates to be tethered," she explained, heading for the porch. "How's that pretty little wife of yours today?" she asked, one foot on the bottom step. "I must say, she looked lovely yes-terday. And you take such good care of her!" She pat-ted her stomach. "By the way, the cookout was splen-did. That potato salad of yours was scrumptious. Maybe you'll share your recipe...."

"There's a huge bowl of the stuff in the fridge. You'd be doing me a favor if you took some of it off my hands."

She grinned. "Oh, that would be lovely!"

He started for the house. "I have a memory like a colander. If I don't do it now—"

"Bruno, you leave Mr. Mahoney's paper alone now, you hear, before I—"

Mitch had no time to react. He looked back in time to see bits of smoking, flaming debris raining down from the sky.

In a heartbeat, he was beside the old woman. "Mrs. Thompson, are you all right?"

"I'm fine," she said, as he helped her sit on the top step of her porch, "but where's Bruno?"

He'd been on his way back inside when the explosion had cracked the peaceful July morning—hadn't seen what happened. But the last thing he'd heard was Mrs. Thompson, scolding the dog. If that was the case—

Act fast, he told himself. Ciara is inside alone....

"You sure you're okay?" he said.

Nodding, Mrs. Thompson clung to the wrought iron railing.

Mitch breathed a sigh of relief as he spied the dog, shivering under an azalea bush. "Found him," he called, pointing.

"Bruno," Mrs. Thompson cried, clapping her hands. "Bruno, you come here this instant!"

The dog was on her heels in an instant.

The old woman gripped the wrought-iron rail so tightly that her knuckles turned white. Mitch helped her to her feet and guided her through her front door.

"Just sit tight, Mrs. Thompson," he said. "As soon as I check on Ciara, I'll come back to see how you're doing."

"Yes, that would be best. You must go to Ciara. I'm perfectly fine," she said.

"Now then," she said, as he dashed out the door. "Lighten up! You don't want to frighten Ciara with that sour expression, do you?"

Frightening Ciara was the least of his worries right now. *Saving her*—from whomever was trying to even a score—*that's* what he was worried about....

Chapter Twelve

No one had made an outgoing call since the telephone woke them earlier that morning. Mitch dialed "star sixty-nine" and waited for the operator to identify the caller. "The last number to call your line was 410, 555-1272," said the smoothed-voiced recording. He scribbled the digits on a sheet of scrap paper and handed it to Bob Knight, the lead investigator from the Howard County Police Department.

Knight was tall and wiry, with coal black eyes and a shock of thick, nappy hair. "Maybe you oughta tell me about this case you were workin' on, Agent Mahoney."

Mitch snuck a peek at Ciara, who had been listening intently. "I'm cool as a cucumber," she said, crossing both arms over her chest. "And I agree with Officer Knight. It's high time we heard about this case you were working on...."

Mitch studied her calm face, her relaxed demeanor. He had to give it to her; she'd kept a tight rein on her emotions after the blast, and he knew that couldn't have been easy. Not for a woman whose feet left the floor if someone walked into a room and surprised her....

Ah, what a mother won't do to protect her young, he thought wryly.

"Really, Mitch," she added, trying to sound more convincing, "I'm fine. In fact, I think it'll be good for me to hear it...finally."

"The night I left here," he began, sitting beside her on the sofa bed, "I went straight to headquarters."

Knight made himself comfortable in Mitch's chair. "Go on...."

"Bradley was at my desk when I got there. He had Giovanni Pericolo's file and my undercover identity with him." Shrugging, he cut to the chase. "He told me the Bureau locked Pericolo up, but they couldn't stop Pericolo from doing business."

"It's sad but true," the cop agreed. "Guys run drug rings from prison every day."

Ciara sighed heavily. "And this is the man you were 'up close and personal' with for seven months."

Mitch nodded. "I posed as an accountant. Kept his books."

"How'd you get inside?" Knight wanted to know. He'd stopped taking notes. His interest was personal now.

"We busted one of Pericolo's right-hand men for trafficking, cut a deal with him. He'd get me into Pericolo's organization, we'd let him stay outside the federal pen."

"It's a miracle you're still with us," Ciara said, her voice trembling slightly. "You see why I was so afraid? Do you understand what—"

He squeezed her hand. "Yes. I admit it. I'm in a dangerous business."

"That's putting it mildly," Knight said. "You've got your neck in a noose every time you go under. Why don't you come to work for us? I happen to know we need a few educated, well-trained guys, right here in Howard County.''

"Do you send men undercover?" Ciara asked.

"Uh-huh, but it's rare, and even then, only the narcs and homicide guys do stuff like that. What your husband, here, would be doin' would be relatively safe, all things considered.''

"'Relatively safe'?" Ciara's brow furrowed with confusion. "'All things considered'?"

"Nothing comes with a guarantee these days, little lady, least of all a cop's safety. Every time you pull a guy over for speeding, you wonder if—"

Mitch saw her frown with resignation and roll her eyes, as if to say Where have I heard that before? and decided it was time to change the subject. "So what's your take on this, Knight? Based on what you've already got, that is.''

"Well, whoever set the bomb wasn't an expert, that's for sure.''

"How can you tell?"

"For one thing, amateurs always want to use too much explosive. It's like they think if a gram will go "Pow," then an ounce is sure to go 'Boom!' But they don't take that into consideration when they're putting the rest of the thing together. It was sheer luck it went off at all.''

Knight took a deep breath and got to his feet. "Well, I've done all I can do here for the time being." He handed Mitch a business card. "Give me a call if you can add anything that'll help. And give some thought to ditchin' the agency and comin' to work for us.''

Mitch tucked the card into his shirt pocket, shook the officer's hand. "I'll do that. Thanks, Knight."

"I'm putting round-the-clock protection on you guys." He chuckled. "Till the Feds bully their way in and take over, anyway. I hear they like to take care of their own."

"You hear right."

"Yeah, well, that ain't nothin' to be proud of, way I see it. Doesn't make much difference what the emblem on your badge says, we all took the same oath."

He looked at Ciara. "So when's that baby of yours due?"

"A week, maybe two...*never,*" she said, rolling her eyes.

"I have three young'uns myself, five, six and seven. My wife just takes it in stride. Except for the big tummy, you'd hardly know she was havin' a baby at all!"

"I hope next time I'll be that way, too."

Mitch walked Knight to the door. "Can she hear us from here?" the cop mouthed when they reached the foyer.

Mitch nodded.

He grabbed Mitch's forearm and leaned in close. "Stay away from the windows," he growled softly, "you hear?"

"No way. When did they find the body?"

At the mention of the word *body,* he saw Ciara's needle hover over the cream-colored linen square she held.

"I'm not surprised," Mitch said, "considering. Still, it seems a shame. He was a good agent...once."

He watched as she tried to pretend she wasn't listening. What was it his Italian grandma used to say when he pouted? "You face, she gonna freeze-a that way!"

The old wives' tale seemed to fit Ciara's present condition....

"He did what?" he asked Parker. "You've gotta be kidding." Shaking his head, he said, "Ironic, isn't it?" Then, "Yeah, I'll kick in ten bucks, but who's gonna see it? Yeah. Okay. Thanks for calling."

"Who was *that?*" she asked the moment he hung up.

He slumped onto the edge of the sofa bed, flopped back on the pillow beside hers and linked his fingers behind his neck. "Parker. Down at headquarters. They found Chet Bradley...."

"Found him? I didn't even know he was missing. Did the Bureau send him undercover, too?"

"Hardly," Mitch groused. "He's been workin' both sides of the street for years now. That's why I got sent to Philadelphia."

She put her needlework aside, snuggled against him. "I don't get it."

He'd never told her about his set-to with Bradley, right there in their living room. If she had known the guy had broken into their house, planning to murder him... Mitch didn't want to think about what might have happened.

"He worked a case, couple years back," he explained, "busted Pericolo for possession of cocaine, distribution, the whole nine yards. But the slimeball got off, thanks to our sophisticated immigration system. Anyway, it seems Bradley decided he could make a few quick bucks if he didn't turn in all the evidence. If he sold what he held aside on the street." Mitch took a deep breath. "The fool taste tested his own merchandise, got himself hooked but good and ended up having to make a deal with Pericolo."

"Chet Bradley?" She seemed surprised, then shook her head. "Well, he's a liar, why not a coke-head, too?"

Mitch turned slightly to read her face. If the news had secretly upset her, she was doing one fine job of masking it. He stared at the ceiling again. "He started doing odd jobs for Pericolo—muffing up investigations, losing evidence, running errands...."

"And Pericolo provided him with the cocaine."

"Uh-huh. Had himself a four-hundred-dollar-a-day habit at the end. You know how many favors a guy has to do to satisfy an addiction like that?"

"But why did he send you to Philadelphia? Were you involved in that drug bust all those years ago? Did you know something that would—"

He shook his head. "He had a falling out with Pericolo, and the boss man cut him off, cold turkey. Bradley was desperate to ensure his supply, so he cut a new deal...with Eduardo Chambro, Pericolo's next in command."

"How do you know all this?"

"Seems his upbringing got the better of him, and he made what you might call a deathbed confession." Mitch shook his head. "Nobody thought much of Pericolo, it seems. Chambro would have taken over years ago if he hadn't been scared witless of the guy."

"But...if Chambro was on Pericolo's side, what did he have to fear from him?"

"Plenty, believe me. I saw Pericolo waste a guy for interrupting a phone call. Heard that he'd done the same thing to men who dared to question his judgment or entered his office without knocking. The man had no heart, no soul, I tell you. Life meant nothing to him...except his own."

"So the lieutenant made a deal with Chambro," she

said, bringing him back to the point. "How did you fit in?"

"He called me the best man on his team. Said I was perfect for the job. Not to sound arrogant, but he was right, and he knew it. The deal he cut with Chambro was to get me inside so I could take Pericolo out of the picture. And when Chambro took over..."

"He'd continue to supply Bradley with bribes," she said, thinking out loud. "A lot of things make sense suddenly."

He rolled onto his side. "Things like what?"

She met his eyes. "I had no reason to believe his lies. I'm ashamed to say I wanted to. It was easier to hate you that way, for leaving me here alone, for not getting in touch, for not being with me when—"

He pulled her to him. "Sweetie, I'm sorry you had to go through all that alone. Hindsight is twenty-twenty—I guess it got to be a cliché for good reason...every word of it is true—but if I had known then what I know now—"

"You would have come home that night? You wouldn't have accepted the assignment?"

"Exactly," he said firmly and without hesitation. "How could I have left my beautiful wife, pregnant or not? No amount of glory is worth a sacrifice like that."

"My dad said something like that the other day," she told him. "He said no sacrifice is too great when it's made for love."

"Smart guy, your dad." He kissed her cheek.

"Were you ever in any danger in Philadelphia? From Pericolo, I mean?"

He thought of that first night, when Giovanni had asked him to choose a card. "If you had picked a black card, you'd be a dead man now."

"Not really," he fibbed. "I was acting as a numbers man. A pencil pusher. A four-eyed geek. I suppose I didn't look like much of a threat, so—"

"Didn't look like a threat!" she stopped him. "As big and muscular as you are? As handsome and intelligent and—"

"I'd better get to work on those door frames," he said, laughing. "Any more of this flattery and my ego won't fit through the door."

"Mitch…"

"Hmm?"

"That explosion was intended for you, wasn't it?"

Every muscle in him tensed. Tell her the truth, and risk sending her blood pressure sky high. Tell her a lie and risk the trust she's beginning to put in you again. "It's possible," he said carefully.

"Who do you think was responsible…if you were the intended victim, I mean?"

"Truthfully?"

Ciara nodded.

"I have no idea.

"I suppose Pericolo might have had *one* loyal follower, but I don't think so. And it can't be Bradley, unless he's operating from the grave." Eyes and lips narrowed, she exhaled a sigh of frustration. "It could be anyone you ever arrested, or a family member of someone you locked up, or…"

"Sweetie, it's not good for you to get worked up over this. We're safe."

"For now. How long can that last? The cops won't hang around here forever. Whoever planted that bomb will wait until they leave, come back and finish what he started."

She voiced the fears that had been on his mind every moment since the explosion.

"Ciara, let's not talk about this now. It's not good for you to get upset, honey."

"You can't sweep it under the rug, Mitch. It's bigger than both of us. You can't deny it anymore. Like it or not, you have responsibilities now, to me, to this baby of ours. You can't just keep running off, playing cops and robbers. Not when it can backfire, blow up your family!"

He sat up. "Ciara," he said, his voice stern and scolding, "this isn't doing you any good. Let's—"

"Hiding from it isn't doing me any good, either," she said, sitting beside him. "Have you given any thought to what Officer Knight said?"

"Quitting the Bureau, you mean, to become a Howard County cop?"

She nodded, the barest hint of a hopeful smile playing at the corners of her mouth.

"Yeah. I've thought about it," he said dully. "I've thought about how I'd like to stop arresting nationally renowned criminals and start writin' speeding tickets. I've thought how nice it would be to give up apprehending drug lords and murderers, and spend my time shooing teenagers off the street corners after 11:00 p.m. instead." On his feet now, he added, "I'd be about as happy as your dad has been all these years, pretending that what I'm doing is what I *want* to be doing."

"But, Mitch," she said, her eyes welling with tears, "what about the baby and me? What will we do, if something happens to you?"

The smiling, the laughing, the playfulness…it had all been an act, and he'd known it all along. Worse, he'd *let* her put on the act, because it had made it easier for him to deal with his own guilt.

She was a tough little thing, and he knew if it weren't for everything that had happened—this illness, being confined to bed, the explosion—she wouldn't be crying right now. And he felt like a heel for being the one to put tears in her beautiful blue eyes. But she had asked him a straight question, and after all those months of silence, deserved to hear a straight answer. But did you have to make it *that* honest? he asked himself. He could blame the very same occurrences for his thoughtlessness, but the truth was he had no excuse for behaving like a self-centered lout.

And she deserved better than that.

He climbed back onto the sofa bed, took her in his arms. "Aw, sweetie. Seems all I ever do is apologize for hurting you. Sometimes I wonder why you married me. I'm sure as heck not very good for you." And the awful thing was, he believed it was true.

Ciara gripped his forearms, gave him a little shake. "You *are* good for me!" she insisted, her eyes blazing with unbridled affection. "You're the best thing in my life, if you want to know the truth. *That's* why I married you. That and the fact that I love you like crazy."

She felt so good, so right in his arms. She was the most beautiful woman he'd ever seen, the most affectionate and loving. Why wasn't it enough? Why did he feel he must have her *and* the Bureau to be happy?

"I did some thinking last night," she said softly, "about something Dad said at the cookout yesterday."

"You're all flushed, sweetie," he said, all but ignoring her. "Lie down, will you, before something—"

She did as she was told, but continued talking. "I know how unhappy he's been all these years, sacrificing the job he loved for his family. But he seemed to have derived some sort of satisfaction for having done the right thing. That's why he said no sacrifice is too great, if—''

"If your love is strong enough?"

Ciara nodded. Then she grabbed his wrists, forced him to place his hands on her stomach. "*This* is what's important, Mitch. *This* is your future. I know you're a good agent, one of the best. Of course the Bureau recognizes that and appreciates who you are and what you do...."

She placed a hand alongside his cheek. "But, Mitch, the FBI doesn't *love* you! If you die, they'll add your name to the already-too-long list of agents killed in the line of duty. They'll give me some sort of medal to lay on your grave, another plaque to hang on the wall. And by week's end, another agent will take your place." Her voice trembled, and fresh tears filled her eyes when she said, "*I* won't be able to replace you, Mitch, not if I live to be a hundred."

What *was* so all-fired important about his precious agency? he asked himself. *Why* couldn't he just give it up, walk away from it, without looking back?

She was right about one thing—he had a lot of thinking to do.

His big hands bracketed her face, his thumbs wiping the tears from her cheeks. "I don't deserve you," he said after a while.

"You deserve the best that life has to offer, which is why I intend to try and be the best wife who ever lived." She managed a tremulous smile, her voice whispery. "I love you, you big lug! Can't you get that through your thick, Irish skull? I love you, and I don't want to live a day of my life without you."

"I'm half Italian, don't forget," he said in a feeble attempt to lighten the mood, change the subject....

"And so am I."

He was aware of her scrutiny, aware that she wanted—no, needed—to hear him say he'd leave the agency. In truth, Mitch wished he *could* say it, because he wanted and needed to comfort and reassure her. Guilt ached in his chest like a huge painful knot. He looked away, feeling restless and uncomfortable with the fact that he couldn't tell her what she wanted to hear.

Ciara's small hand cupped his chin, turned his face and forced him to meet her eyes. Her tears were gone now, and she spoke slowly, with careful dignity. "You don't have to make up your mind right now. You have two weeks of R and R left. Please say you'll use that time to think about it, at least."

Mitch set his jaw. He could give her that much, couldn't he?

It was quietly disturbing to even consider leaving the Bureau, and his stomach knotted with tension. His voice began as a hushed whisper, then he spoke in neutral tones. "I'll give it some thought," he promised, his mouth tight and grim.

"And some prayer?"

"And some prayer."

"Thank you," she said, gently, serenely. "Thank you."

When she snuggled close, he felt the rhythmic pounding of her heart against his chest, and the strong, sharp kicks of the baby against his stomach. "*This* is what's important," she had said.

And it was.

For the first time in days Ciara put aside her secret needlework project and spent every moment, it seemed, making lists.

She had spent hours fixing up every room of the house, and it showed. But for a reason she couldn't— or wouldn't—explain, she hadn't done a single thing in the nursery. And now, it seemed, she was in a frenzy to get it all done before the baby came.

She insisted that Mitch sit beside her and help her pick out the furniture for the baby's room. Everything had to be neutral, yet stimulating, a concept which thoroughly confused him. "Nothing frilly or girlie, but nothing too strong or masculine, either," Ciara explained. "Colors capture babies' attention and help them learn faster."

They decided on a pale oak crib and ordered a dresser, changing table and toy box to match. He suggested the teddy bear wallpaper border. "Lots of color, without being masculine or feminine." Rather than repeating the print in the baby's bedding, Ciara ordered bright red sheets, a deep blue quilt, fluorescent yellow curtains and an emerald green bumper pad.

Portable phone in one hand, department store catalog in the other and list in her lap, she placed the order. "For an extra twenty-five dollars," she told him, "they'll deliver it tomorrow. Should I tell them to go ahead?"

It was by far the happiest he'd seen her since returning from Philly—small price to pay, in his opinion, for her pink-cheeked complexion and wide smile.

The next day when everything arrived, Mitch had the deliverymen put the boxes into the white-walled room across from the one he shared with Ciara. When they were gone, he took one of the chaise longues from the deck and dragged it upstairs, outfitting it with a downy quilt and pillow. And once he had her settled comfortably in it, he hung the wallpaper border and continued to focus on it as he hung brackets and rammed rods through the pockets of a pair of tailored curtains.

Then it was on to a more interesting—and difficult—project: assembling the crib.

"This manufacturer must be from Timbuktu or something!" Mitch growled. "I can't make heads or tails of these instructions. And what're all these nuts and bolts for? There aren't half as many holes to stick 'em into!"

"Sweetie," she said, repeating what he'd told her a day earlier, "it isn't good for you to get so worked up."

He shot her a narrow-eyed smirk. "Careful, lady," came his mock threat, "'cause I'm the guy in control of the cheesecake...."

Amazingly, she seemed to know what fit where without ever having so much as glanced at the directions. And once he got over the humiliation of being bested in a construction project...by a woman...the crib went together in no time flat.

She had him rolling the thing to every conceivable spot in the ten-by-twelve-foot space, and finally settled for putting the crib against the only blank wall in the room. The changing table, she decided, looked best under the window, and the dresser simply *had* to stand on the short wall, just inside the door, with the toy box right beside it.

Ciara clasped her hands under her chin when it was finished. "We'll have to get another catalog," she gushed, "and fill that toy box to the brim!"

"That's what Christmas and birthdays are for," he muttered, hanging the last picture on the wall.

"Oh, don't be such a Grinch," she scolded playfully. "Besides, his *birth* day isn't very far off, you know...."

Mitch tried to read her face, but couldn't tell if the silly expression was part of her excitement at having completed the nursery, or some strange way of masking pain. "Are you okay?" he asked, kneeling beside her chair.

"This has been driving me crazy for weeks. Now that it's done, I feel so much better!"

The doorbell rang, and Mitch grinned. He couldn't have timed it better if he'd tried.

"You didn't order in from Chiaparelli's, did you?" Ciara asked, narrowing one eye.

"Nope. Now you stay put, while I see who it is."

How the women for the baby shower had all managed to arrive at the same time boggled his mind. Leave it to Gina to get a bunch of women organized, he thought, grinning.

Gina had her back to him when he opened the door, and Mitch would have bet his last nickel that folks clear on the other side of the street had heard her severe "Shh-hhh-hhh-hhh!"

Silently he waved the ladies inside, nodding and smiling as they passed, each carrying a brightly wrapped package. "Get back upstairs," Gina whispered, "and turn on a radio or something so she won't hear us putting up the decorations."

"How will I know when to bring her down?"

"I'll send Chester up to fetch you," she whispered, smacking his bottom. "Now git! Before I take a broom to the seat of your pants!"

He ducked into their bedroom and turned the clock radio on full blast before returning to the nursery. "Who was it?"

"Wrong house number," he fibbed.

"Wrong—"

"Somebody looking for the Smiths. I think they were on the wrong street. I hope I didn't get them lost...." And without another word he scooped her up and carried her into their room.

"Goodness, Mitch," she said, hands over her ears, "aren't you a little young to be experiencing your second childhood? What's with the loud—"

"Didn't you ever get an itch to dance?" he asked, spinning in a dizzying circle, still carrying her. "Listen to that," he added, swaying to and fro in time to the music. "Ain't it a shame? They just don't write 'em like that anymore."

"I think you must have clunked your head on something while you were putting the furniture together," she observed, giggling. "You're acting very—"

She cocked an ear toward the doorway. "What was that? Did I hear voices downstairs?"

"Maybe...I left the TV on in the family room." He danced her farther from the door, danced her back again and kicked it shut.

"Put me down, you big nut," she scolded, "you're starting to perspire. I'm not exactly a featherweight these days. All we need is for you to develop a hernia right—"

"I'm fine," he interrupted. "Now stop being a spoilsport. Who knows when we'll get another opportunity to go dancing?"

"What's that noise?" she asked, a finger aloft.

Mitch plunked her gently on the bed and turned off the radio. "Scratching?" He opened the door. "Hey, Chester. What're you doin' up here, old boy?" He ruffled the dog's thick coat, then hoisted Ciara in his arms once more and hurried down the stairs.

"Mitch, I wish I knew why you're acting so—"

Her eyes widened as both hands flew to her mouth. "Balloons, streamers, cake," she said, taking it all in, then seeing the women. "When did all of you— How did—"

Giggling, she buried her face in the crook of his neck and whispered, "How's my hair?"

"Can you believe all these wonderful presents?" she asked, holding up a tiny terry cloth jumpsuit. "We'll have enough diapers to last for months, and all these T-shirts and booties and…"

He'd been stuffing wrapping paper and bows into a gigantic lawn and leaf bag when he noticed she'd stopped talking. Mitch peered over his shoulder, surprised to find her crying. Dropping the trash, he wrapped his arms around her.

"I'm so lucky," she sobbed into his shoulder. "I have such good friends and so many wonderful relatives, and you…you're the best husband any woman could ever hope for!"

"But those are good things, sweetie. Why are you crying?"

She settled down a bit to say, "Because… because…because I'm so happy, that's why."

"I sure will be glad when this baby gets here," he teased, handing her a tissue, "'cause you're costing me a small fortune in blotting materials!"

Giggling, she blew her nose. "You could always buy stock in the company.…"

He popped a kiss onto her forehead. "That's what I like, a woman with business sense who isn't afraid to cry."

"I hate crying," she admitted, sniffling. Then, eyes wide with panic, Ciara added, "What if I never go back to the woman I was before I got pregnant? What if I've turned into a big fat crybaby forever? What if—''

''What if I start hauling some of this loot up to the baby's room while you take a nap. You're looking a mite pooped, if you don't mind my saying so.''

''You know, I think I'll take you up on your offer,'' she said, snuggling under the covers. ''Two parties and a bomb blast in three days can be exhausting!''

He plucked a trash bag from the box and chucked a load of stuffed animals into it, filled another with miniature shorts and hats and shoes, and dragged both up the stairs behind him. It isn't like her to give in so easily to a suggestion to take a nap, he told himself. And she did look paler than usual....

Should he call Donna? Peterson? His mother? What could they do that you're not already doing? And the answer was, Nothing.

He continued making trips upstairs until every gift had a new place to call its own. She'll be happy to know the baby's toy box is filled to the brim, he thought, smiling as he left the last of it. Mitch stood in the doorway, arms crossed over his chest, and looked at the nursery. Soon, a baby boy or girl would call it home. Soon tiny cries would wake them from a sound sleep, demanding food or a fresh diaper or a dose of affection.

The telephone interrupted his reverie, and he crossed the hall to answer it in the master bedroom.

''Hey, Parker,'' he said, ''what's up?''

''Well, I have the answer to your question, for starters.''

''Yeah?''

''Bradley's blood type is AB Negative.''

The news made him weak in the knees, and he sat on the edge of the bed. The card in his wallet said he was O Positive. And according to Donna's chart, Ciara was O Positive, too. Peterson had "typed" the baby weeks earlier, so they'd have a plentiful supply on hand in case of an emergency...and the baby's blood matched his mommy's and his daddy's.

His mommy's...and his daddy's!

How could he have ever doubted her? He felt terrible about it now.

The heat in his cheeks and the buzzing in his ears had usually accompanied bad news. Not this time. *Thank you, Lord,* he prayed. *Thank you!*

"What did you need that information for?" Parker wanted to know.

"Uh—confidential at this point," Mitch replied curtly. He wasn't lying. He'd no interest in sharing his suspicions about Ciara with anyone.

"Gotcha," Parker said.

"You said the info was 'for starters'?"

"Well, it'd be nice if you'd fill us in once in a while, Mahoney. How's that gorgeous wife of yours?"

"Tired, but holding her own. I think it's going to be soon. Very soon."

"Want some friendly advice?"

"Sure..."

"Get all the shut-eye you can, while you can, 'cause once that little one gets here, you're gonna need a dictionary to remember what *sleep* means."

Sleep? Mitch thought. I don't know what that is *now,* what with all that's been going on around here. Chuckling, Mitch thanked him and hung up. Then he headed down the stairs to climb into bed beside his sleepy wife and try to take Parker's advice.

* * *

"Mitch," Ciara whispered, shaking his shoulder. "Mitch!"

He draped an arm over her middle. "Mmmm?"

"I think I heard something...."

"Where's Chester?"

"Right here at the foot of the bed. There it is again...in the kitchen...."

"Can't be," he muttered, opening one eye, "there are half a dozen cops outside. Houdini couldn't get past 'em undetected." He yawned. "But I gotta admit," he said, wiggling his hips against hers, "I like the benefits of comforting a frightened—"

"Did you hear that?"

He laid a finger over her lips and nodded, then held the finger in the air, as if commanding her to listen.

"What do you—"

One sharp look from his worried eyes silenced her. "Don't say another word," he instructed, his whisper hoarse and stern. Mitch handed her the phone, where he'd taped Bob Knight's cell phone number. "You hear anything funny in there, call him. Okay?"

Wide-eyed, Ciara nodded. She grabbed his hand. "Please," she said, a hitch in her voice, "be careful...."

Trying to appear cavalier, he sent her a wink.

"Mitch," she added as he got to his feet. "I love you."

"Love you, too," he whispered, and headed for the stairs.

He took them two at a time, as he'd planned, then ducked into the closet and grabbed the Rossi. *Lord,* he prayed, switching off the safety, *I think we both know I'll use it if I have to. Don't let me have to....*

Mitch crept back down the stairs and peered around

the double-wide doorway leading from the foyer to the family room. Hiding the gun behind his back, he caught Ciara's eye. "He still in there?" he mouthed.

Ciara nodded.

Thumb to his chin and forefinger to his ear, he pantomimed, "Did you call Knight?"

Another nod.

He blew her a kiss and headed up the hall. It seemed to take hours, rather than seconds, to reach the kitchen. Since he could see the reflection of a dark-haired man in the black glass oven door, the man could see him, too. Mitch flattened himself against the wall, heart hammering as he tried to plan his course of action.

Where are those confounded County boys? he wondered. They must have been asleep on the job. How else had this guy penetrated their line of defense? It happened so quickly, he never saw it coming...the karate chop that sent his service revolver clattering to the hardwood floor. He gave it a solid kick, sent it careering to the end of the hall. If I can't reach it, neither can—

A fist crashed into his jaw, killing the thought.

In the next seconds, amid the flurry of fists and arms, Mitch managed to grab hold of the man's T-shirt.

Pericolo's men never went out in public without a shirt and tie. But who was he to complain; the soft, cottony fabric of the T-shirt was a whole lot easier to grasp than a starched white collar. In a heartbeat, Mitch wrestled the intruder to the floor, straddled him and attempted to disable him with a wrestler's hold.

The high-pitched whimper made him stop just long enough to look at the face he'd been beating.

A boy's face.

David Pericolo's face.

Mitch pinned the kids' wrists to the floor. "What are you doin' here?" he demanded.

"You put my father in jail," he said haltingly, his lips swollen and bloodied. "'Eye for an eye,'" the boy added. "'Eye for an eye.'"

Bob Knight burst through the back door just then, and three uniformed officers came in on his heels. "Cuff him," Knight ordered, "wrists *and* ankles."

Shaking, Mitch got to his feet and leaned both palms on the kitchen table to steady himself. "Meet David Pericolo," he said to Knight.

"You'll pay," David whimpered, as Knight's fellow policemen secured the handcuffs.

"Get him out of here and keep him quiet," Knight barked, shaking a big fist in the air.

Once they'd dragged David off, kicking and screaming, Knight closed the kitchen door. "You okay, buddy?" he asked, patting Mitch's back.

"I'm fine." His gaze shot daggers into the cop. "How'd he get in here, anyway? Your boys oughta be ashamed of themselves."

Knight shook his head. "That number you gave me…the one you star sixty-nined?"

Mitch nodded.

"Pericolo's…car phone."

"I see."

"Heads are gonna roll for this one," Knight said, "trust me."

"You're just lucky nothing happened to my wife."

At the mere thought of her, Mitch tensed. "Ciara—" He ran into the family room and gathered her in his arms. *Thank God she's all right.* "You okay, sweetie? How are you feelin'?"

"Not so hot," she said in a small, shaky voice. "I've

already called the hospital. They're expecting us.'' She buried her face in his shoulder. "Oh, Mitch, I was so scared. I thought...I thought...."

"Shhh," he soothed, stroking her back. "Nothing happened, and—"

"*This* time." She sat back, eyes bright with tears, and faced him down. "You're not a cat, Mitch. You don't have nine lives." Her lower lip quivered when she added, "If you were, I imagine you'd have used up at least six of them by now. How much longer do you expect your luck to hold out? How much—"

Gripping her stomach, she winced with pain.

"Ciara, sweetie, what is it?"

She met his eyes. "It's time, that's what it is...."

She was right. It was *time*. Time to stand up and act like a man. Not a gung-ho, macho, hot-doggin' FBI agent, but a man, who took his responsibilities seriously. He only hoped it wasn't too late....

Ciara took a deep breath and said on the exhale, "Could we...could we continue this later, do you think?" she said, smiling past clenched teeth. "Because if it's all the same to you, I think I'd rather have a baby right now."

Epilogue

Ciara snuggled deep into the pillows on her hospital bed, smiled contentedly into her newborn's face. "Your daddy went to get me a cup of soda," she cooed, kissing the tiny fingers that had wrapped around her thumb. "He'll be back any minute now."

And when he comes back, she thought, I'm going to tell him that it doesn't matter to me *what* he does for a living or where he does it; all I care about is that he's happy, and healthy, until the Lord calls him home.

She closed her eyes, hoping to blink away the horrible scene that had taken place hours ago. Until the sounds of the life-and-death struggle penetrated her brain—when she knew and understood that she could lose him, right there in her very own kitchen—Ciara had not realized just how much she loved having him in her life. *Whether you have a week or a year or a lifetime more with him,* she told herself, *you'll enjoy every moment, and thank God for it!*

How could she say that she loved him, really loved him, and demand that he give up the Bureau? He had worked too long, too hard, to leave it all behind now.

No doubt she would keep a careful eye on the clock until he arrived home from work safe and sound, but she would lose no sleep over his absences, because faith would see her through. "When I'm afraid, I will look to the Lord," she paraphrased Micah, Chapter Seven, Verse Eight. "I will wait for the God of my salvation, and He will hear me."

The coins dropped into the machine with a metallic *chink-chink-chink*, and Mitch pressed the button that said All Natural Orange Juice. That oughta hold her over till they bring her supper, he thought, nodding when the can hit the tray with a hollow *thud*.

Those hours in the delivery room, when it was touch and go for a while, he knew what he had to do. You could have lost her, he reminded himself, but you didn't, and you'd better thank God for that!

Ciara had asked him to think about changing jobs. He could tell by the way she'd phrased the question that she fully intended to stand by him, regardless of his answer. He also knew that, even if he decided to stay with the Bureau, she would never do to him what her mother had done to her father. And you haven't earned devotion like that…yet….

While the nurses were getting Ciara and the baby cleaned up, he pretended to need a breath of fresh air. Instead, he placed a phone call, straight to the director's office. The director took the call, not so surprisingly, considering what Mitch had just accomplished on behalf of the agency. He would put in his resignation, here and now.

"What can I do for you, Mitch?"

"Well, I have a big favor to ask, sir."

"If it's within my power, it's yours. We owe you that much, son...."

Wait till Ciara hears the news, Mitch thought later, grinning. Merely imagining her reaction caused him to quicken his pace down the corridor. That and the fact that he couldn't wait to hold his firstborn in his arms....

"I'm so proud of you. You're the bravest woman I've ever known."

Ciara giggled. "You act like I'm the first woman on earth to have given birth."

"You're the first woman to give birth to *my* child." How good it felt to say that, and know for certain that it was true. Mitch knew that he would spend the rest of his life making it up to her for so much as *thinking* that she could have betrayed him.

"She's so beautiful," Ciara sighed. "Just look at her, Mitch."

"She's beautiful 'cause she takes after her mommy."

She met his eyes. "What are we going to call her? I didn't think up many 'girl' names—everybody kept saying 'he' and 'him' and 'his,' and I guess I got caught up in it myself."

"How 'bout Carrie, for old-time's sake?"

She branded him with a playfully hot glare. "You think I want a reminder, right under your nose, of your first love? No way, José."

He kissed the baby's round little head. "She smells so sweet. We could name her after a flower...Rose or Tulip or Daisy...."

"I'm glad you're having fun with this. At least *one* of us should be, I suppose."

"I want her to have a strong name. Something memorable. Like Hannah or Eden or Shana."

Ciara nodded. "Now that's more like it. Let's look them up in my baby book...."

Mitch dug around in her overnight bag. "It opened to the *M*s," he said, narrowing one eye suspiciously, "all by itself."

"Well, I have a confession to make," she said, flushing. "I *did* sneak a peek at a *few* girls' names...just in case...."

"Is that so?" He placed the book on the edge of the bed. "Let's see if I can figure out which name you chose." His thick finger ran down the pulpy paper page. "'Mildred' means 'gentle strength,' but I don't think so. 'Misty, Mitzi, Molly,'" he recited.

Suddenly, he thumped the book. "I know which name you picked."

"Which?" she asked, eyes twinkling with mirth.

"'Worthy of admiration,'" he quoted, then said with meaning. "Miranda."

"Do you like it?"

"I love it." He took the baby from her arms, held the tiny bundle tight against him and kissed her soft pink cheek. "Now," he said, drawing his big face close to his daughter's tiny nose. "I'm going to read you your Miranda rights. Number one—you have the right to have a healthy, happy daddy all the days of your childhood—number two—you have the right to the bravest, most loving mommy in the world—number three—you have the right to—"

"Mitch, what are you talking about?"

"I'm talking about my new job. I've been thinking," he announced, "and you're right. I've built up a lot of seniority at the Bureau. I can retire earlier if I hang in there...."

She lifted her chin and smiled.

Lord, I love her grit and determination, he said to himself. She thinks she's in for a lifetime of same-ole, same-ole, but wait till she gets a load of this:

"I talked to the director, not half an hour ago."

"The director? *Of the FBI?*"

"Hey," he said, looking wounded, "don't act so surprised. He takes calls from agents who bring in the big tuna...."

Ciara stroked the baby's head. "Did you hear that, Miranda? Your daddy has the big boss's ear." She wiggled her eyebrows and bobbed her head coquettishly. "Ooh-la-*la*.... So why did you call him?"

"To quit."

Her eyes widened.

"But he begged me to stay. He's putting me in charge of assignments, Miss Smarty Pants...or should I say *Mrs.* Smarty Pants."

She wasn't smiling when she said, "Sounds dangerous."

"Yeah. I guess it does," he said, squinting one eye. "But it isn't. It's the best of both worlds. I don't have to take a boring desk job, but I won't be on the front lines anymore."

Her eyes brightened. "You won't?"

"I'll have to do some minor investigating, so I'll know which agents should work on what cases, but I won't have to go undercover ever again."

She gasped. "Never?"

"Never. Probably won't ever fire my weapon again, except on the gun range."

"Never?"

"Never." Balancing Miranda in the crook of one arm, he slid the other across Ciara's shoulders. "So what do you think of that, pretty Mommy?"

"I think God works in mysterious ways."

"How do you mean?"

"Well, you know the story 'Gift of the Magi' don't you?"

Mitch nodded. "The one where the guy sells his watch to buy combs for his wife's long hair, and she sells her hair to buy a chain for his watch?"

"That's the one. It's a direct parallel to us, don't you see?"

He gave it a moment's thought, then said, "Ahh, because you were willing to live the rest of your life in fear, so I could be happy, and I was willing to give up the job that made me happy, so you wouldn't worry."

"Exactly! Neither of us has to make a sacrifice. God has seen to it we *both* have our heart's desire. It's a miracle, Mitch. He has given us a bona fide *miracle*."

"I can't very well deny that, now can I?" He slid the tray table aside, and laid Miranda in her mother's arms. "But let's make that miracles, *plural*, because I'm lookin' at two more, right this minute."

Ciara smiled sweetly. "There's a present for you...in my bag."

"Another present, you mean," he said, one hand on his daughter's head. He dug in her suitcase, pulled out the needlework project she'd been working on for weeks. "Except for your nightie, this is the only thing in here."

"That's it."

Mitch handed it to her.

"I'm going to have it framed and hang it over our bed."

"Lemme see this thing," he said. To Miranda he added, "It's been a big secret, for weeks." He turned it around, read aloud: ''I am my beloved, and my beloved is mine.''

''From the 'Song of Songs,''' she explained.

''From the bottom of my heart,'' he said, and kissed her.

She saw a wistful look and then a radiant smile come across his face. ''Mitch, what is it?''

He met her eyes. ''It suddenly struck me,'' he said, grinning happily, ''I'm a daddy!''

* * * * *

Dear Reader,

When people ask where I got the idea for the five-book SUDDENLY! series, I say, "It came to me…suddenly!" Seriously, the truth is, I was sitting near the yogurt shop in the mall, eating a low-fat cone, when a handsome young man sat down beside me. He was so totally captivated by the beauty in his arms that he barely noticed anything going on around him.

"First baby?" I asked. And without looking up from his little girl's face, he nodded. His loving, awestruck smile reminded me of the way my uncle looked as he recalled the day, so long ago, when he found out *he* was going to be a daddy….

One of many soldiers returning from World War II, Sam stood at the rail of his aircraft carrier, staring out to sea. "I was thinking of my sweet Margie," he said. Except for a weekend pass, he'd barely seen his bride in two long years. "The last time I saw her," he said, "Margie was slim as a dime." Imagine Sam's surprise when he stepped off that ship and saw that Margie "looked like she'd swallowed a watermelon!"

What must it have been like, I wondered, to find out in such a sudden, surprising way that you're going to be a father?

The answer conceived the idea that gave birth to the SUDDENLY! series. If you enjoyed *Suddenly Daddy*, please drop me a note c/o Steeple Hill Books, 233 Broadway, New York, NY 10279. I love hearing from my readers and always try to answer every letter personally.

All my best,

Loree Lough

P.S. Be sure to look for my upcoming Love Inspired series, ACCIDENTAL BLESSINGS!

HEAVEN KNOWS

BY

JILLIAN HART

John Corey's soul ached for his late wife but he tried to move forward as best he could for their beloved little girl's sake. Like a gift from God, drifter Alexandra Sims wandered into their lives and turned it around. Suddenly, John began to believe in love again, but would Alexandra's painful secret stand in the way of true happiness?

Don't miss

HEAVEN KNOWS

On sale June 2003

Available at your favorite retail outlet.

Visit us at www.steeplehill.com

LIHK

HOME TO
SAFE HARBOR

BY

KATE WELSH

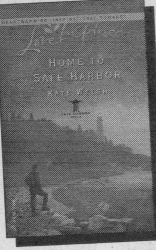

Determined to prove herself, Reverend Justine Clemens returned to the town where she'd spent her troubled youth. Resigned to living her life alone, she poured all her hopes and dreams into her new ministry. But God clearly had other plans for this as He brought her head-to-head with Chief Matthew Trent. Would Justine finally take a chance on love?

Don't miss

HOME TO SAFE HARBOR

the final installment of

SAFE HARBOR

The town where everyone finds shelter from the storm!

On sale June 2003

Available at your favorite retail outlet.